Perfect

Also by Judith McNaught

Almost Heaven
Double Standards
A Kingdom of Dreams
Once and Always
Paradise
Something Wonderful
Tender Triumph
Whitney, My Love

Available from POCKET BOOKS

Judith McNaught

Perfect

POCKET BOOKS
New York   London   Toronto   Sydney   Tokyo   Singapore

This book is a work of fiction. Names, characters, places, and incidents are either products of the author's imagination or are used fictitiously. Any resemblance to actual events or locales or persons, living or dead, is entirely coincidental.

 POCKET BOOKS, a division of Simon & Schuster Inc.
1230 Avenue of the Americas, New York, NY 10020

Library of Congress Catalog Card Number: 93-83306

ISBN: 0-671-79552-X

First Pocket Books hardcover printing May 1993

10 9 8 7 6 5 4 3

POCKET and colophon are registered trademarks of
Simon & Schuster Inc.

Design by A. P. Rosenblatt

Printed in the U.S.A.

Grateful acknowledgment is made for permission to reprint the following:

"Nobody Loves Me Like You Do" by Pamela Phillips and James P. Dunne. Copyright © 1983, 1984 by Ensign Music Corporation. All Rights Reserved. Used by permission of The Famous Music Publishing Companies.

"Long Ago and Far Away" by Ira Gershwin and Jerome Kern. Copyright © 1944 by PolyGram International Publishing, Inc. Copyright Renewed. All Rights Reserved. Used by permission of PolyGram International Publishing, Inc.

"What Are You Doing the Rest of Your Life" by Michel Legrand, Alan Bergman and Marilyn Bergman. Copyright © 1969 by EMI UNART CATALOG INC. All Rights Reserved. International Copyright Secured. Used by permission CCP/Belwin, Inc.

This book is dedicated with love and understanding to those millions of American women who cannot read it or any other book, women whose childhood circumstances have deprived them of the adult pleasure, and the dignity, of being able to read. And it is dedicated to the special, caring people who've given their time and efforts to the "Literacy. Pass It On." program.

Acknowledgments

It is my name that appears on the front of this novel, but behind every scene has been a group of people who've contributed unstintingly of their time and talents, support and friendship. Each of these people have, in one way or another, enriched the novel you're about to read, and enriched my life. My deepest thanks to . . .

Ron Bellisario, and the cast and crew of *Quantum Leap*.

Gerald Schnitzer for sharing his thirty years experience in the film business and acting as "technical advisor" on all the aspects of movie-making in this novel.

Susan Spangler—secretary, researcher, and friend—who brings new meaning to the words *competence, dedication,* and *cooperation.*

Nancy Williams—National Program Manager, Coors "Literacy. Pass It On."—for her unflagging commitment to women's literacy, and the confident optimism that served as a constant reinforcement while I worked on this novel.

Pat and Terry Barcelo, who offered the seclusion of their ranch so I could work in solitude, and a wealth of love and friendship to go with it.

Lloyd Stansberry, for his repeated assistance on the legal technicalities involved in the plot.

William C. McCord, for a decade of favors that have bettered—and will always better—one young man's entire life.

Debby Brown, for the example she is of kindness.

Pauline Marr, whose generosity and selflessness is a gift to her profession . . . and to her friends.

Amnon Benjamini, provider of fabulous jewels and priceless advice.

And last but never least, Linda Marrow—editor, advisor, and friend.

Perfect

Prologue

1976

MARGARET STANHOPE STOOD AT THE DOORS THAT OPENED onto the veranda, her aristocratic features set into an icy mask as she watched her butler pass a tray of drinks to her grandchildren who had just returned for the summer holidays from their various private schools. Beyond the veranda, in the lush valley below, the city of Ridgemont, Pennsylvania, was clearly visible with its winding, tree-lined streets; manicured park; quaint shopping area; and, off to the right, the rolling hills of Ridgemont Country Club. Situated precisely in the center of Ridgemont was a sprawling cluster of red brick buildings that comprised Stanhope Industries, which was responsible, either directly or indirectly, for the economic prosperity of most of Ridgemont's families. Like most small communities, Ridgemont had a well-established social hierarchy, and the Stanhope family was as firmly ensconced at the pinnacle of that social structure as the Stanhope mansion was entrenched upon Ridgemont's highest bluff.

Today, however, Margaret Stanhope's mind was not on the view from her veranda or the lofty social standing she had possessed since birth and improved with her marriage; it was on the staggering blow she was about to deliver to her three loathsome grandchildren. The youngest boy, Alex, who was sixteen, saw her watching him and reluctantly took iced tea instead of champagne from the butler's silver tray. He and his sister were just alike, Margaret thought contemptuously as she studied the pair. They were both spoiled, spineless, promiscuous, and irresponsible; they drank too much, spent too much, and played too much; they were overindulged brats who knew nothing of self-discipline. But all that was about to stop.

Her gaze followed the butler as he offered the tray to Elizabeth, who was wearing a skin-tight yellow sundress with a plunging neckline. When Elizabeth saw her grandmother watching, the seventeen-year-old threw a haughty, challenging look at her and, in a typical gesture of infantile defiance, she helped herself to *two* glasses of champagne. Margaret Stanhope watched her but said nothing. The girl was practically the image of her mother—a shallow, oversexed, frivolous lush who had died eight years ago when the sports car Margaret's son was driving went out of control on an icy patch of highway, killing his wife and himself and orphaning their four young children. The police report indicated that they had both been intoxicated and their car had been traveling in excess of one hundred miles per hour.

Six months ago, heedless of his advancing age and bad weather, Margaret's own husband had died while flying his plane to Cozumel, supposedly to go fishing. The twenty-five-year-old fashion model who was also in that plane must have been along to bait his hook, she thought with uncharacteristic crudity and frigid disinterest. The fatal accidents were eloquent illustrations of the lechery and carelessness that had characterized the lives of all the Stanhope men for generations. Every arrogant, reckless, handsome one of them had lived each day of their lives as if they were indestructible and accountable to no one.

As a result, Margaret had spent a lifetime clinging to her ravaged dignity and self-control while her profligate husband squandered a fortune on his vices and taught his grandsons to live exactly as he lived. Last year, while she slept upstairs, he had brought prostitutes into this very house, and he and the boys had shared them. All of them except Justin. Her beloved Justin . . .

Gentle, intelligent, and industrious, Justin had been the only one of her three grandsons to resemble the men on Margaret's side of the family, and she had loved him with every fiber of her being. And now, Justin was dead, while his brother Zachary was alive and healthy, taunting her with his very vitality. Turning her head, she watched him stride swiftly up the stone steps that led to the veranda in answer to her summons, and the explosion of hatred that raged through her at the sight of the tall, dark-haired eighteen-year-old was almost past bearing. Her fingers tightened on the glass in her hand, and she fought down the wild urge to hurl it at his tanned face, to rake her nails down it.

Zachary Benedict Stanhope III, who had been named after Margaret's husband, looked exactly like his namesake at the same age, but that wasn't why she loathed him. She had a much better reason for that, and Zachary knew *exactly* what that reason was. In a few minutes, however, he was finally going to pay for what he had done—not enough, of course. She couldn't exact full retribution for that, and she despised her helplessness almost as much as she despised him.

She waited until the butler had served him a glass of champagne, then she strolled onto the veranda. "You are probably wondering why I've called this little family meeting today," she said. Zachary watched her in noncommittal silence from his position at the balustrade, but Margaret intercepted a look of impatient boredom between Alex and Elizabeth, who were sitting at the umbrella table. They were both undoubtedly eager to escape the veranda and meet up with their friends, teenagers who were just like themselves—amoral young thrill seekers with weak characters who did as they damned pleased because they knew their family's money would buy them out of any unpleasant consequences. "I can see you're impatient," she said turning to the two at the table, "so I will go directly to the point. I'm sure it has not occurred to either of you to wonder about anything as mundane as your financial status, however, the fact is that your grandfather was too busy with his 'social activities' and too convinced of his immortality to establish proper trusts for you after your parents died. As a result, I am now in complete control of his estate. In case you are wondering what that means, I shall hasten to explain it to you." Smiling with satisfaction, she said, "So long as you both remain in school, improve your grades, and comport yourselves in a manner that I do not deem unacceptable, I will continue to pay your tuition and I'll allow you to keep your fancy sports cars. Period."

Elizabeth's immediate reaction was more puzzled than alarmed. "What about my allowance and my living expenses when I start college next year?"

"You won't have any 'living expenses.' You will live here and attend the junior college! If you prove yourself trustworthy during the next two years, then and only then will I allow you to go away to school."

"The junior college," Elizabeth repeated furiously. "You can't be serious about all this!"

"Try me, Elizabeth. Defy me and watch me cut you off without a cent. Let word reach me of any more of your drunken parties and drugs and promiscuity, and you'll never see another dollar." Glancing at Alexander, she added, "In case you have any doubt, all that goes for you, too. Also, you won't be returning to Exeter next autumn, you'll finish high school right here."

"You can't do this to us!" Alex exploded. "Grandfather would never have let you!"

"You have no right to tell us how to live our lives," Elizabeth wailed.

"If you don't like my offer," Margaret informed her in a steely voice, "then I suggest you get yourself a job as a waitress or find yourself a pimp, because those are the only two careers for which you're fit right now."

She watched their faces pale and nodded with satisfaction, then Alexander said sullenly, "What about Zack? He gets great grades at Yale. You aren't going to make him live here, too, are you?"

The moment she'd been waiting for had arrived. "No," she said, "I'm not."

Turning fully toward Zachary so she could watch his face, she snapped, "Get out! Get out of this house and don't ever come back. I never want to see your face or hear your name again."

Had it not been for the sudden clenching of his jaw, she would have thought her words had no effect. He didn't ask for an explanation because he didn't need one. In fact, he'd undoubtedly been expecting this from the moment she began to give her ultimatum to his sister. Wordlessly, he straightened from the balustrade and stretched his hand toward the car keys he'd tossed on the table, but when his fingers touched them, Margaret's voice lashed out and stilled his hand. "Leave them! You're to take nothing but the clothes on your back." He took his hand away and looked at his sister and brother, as if half-expecting them to say something, but they were either too immersed in their own misery to speak or too afraid of sharing his fate if they alienated her.

Margaret detested the younger two for their cowardice and disloyalty at the same time she endeavored to make absolutely certain neither of them might later show a flare of latent courage. "If either of you ever contacts him or permits him to contact you," she warned them as Zachary turned and headed toward the steps leading from the veranda, "if you so much as attend the same party at someone's house with him, you'll suffer the same fate he has, is that clear?" To her departing grandson, she issued a different warning: "Zachary, if you're thinking of throwing yourself on the mercy of any of your friends, don't bother. Stanhope Industries is the primary source of employment in Ridgemont, and I now own every scrap of it. No one here will want to help you at the risk of incurring my displeasure—and the loss of their jobs."

Her warning made him turn on the bottom step and look up at her with such cold contempt that she belatedly realized he would never have considered taking charity from friends. But what interested her the most about his expression was the emotion she glimpsed in his eyes before he turned his head. Was it anguish she'd seen there? Or was it fury? Or fear? She hoped, very devoutly, that it was all those things.

The moving van slowed to a lumbering stop in front of the solitary male walking along the shoulder of the highway with a sport jacket slung over his shoulder and his head bent as if he were bucking a high wind. "Hey," Charlie Murdock called out, "you need a ride?"

A pair of dazed amber eyes lifted to Charlie's, and for a moment the young man looked completely disoriented, as if he'd been sleepwalking down the highway, then he jerked his head in a nod. As he climbed into the cab, Charlie noted the expensive tan slacks his passenger was wearing, the shiny loafers, matching socks, and stylish haircut and assumed he'd picked up a preppie college student who was, for some reason, hitching a ride. Confident of his intuition and powers of observation, Charlie said conversationally, "What college do you go to?"

The boy swallowed as if his throat were constricted and turned his face toward the side window, but when he spoke his voice was cold and final. "I don't go to college."

"Did your car break down somewhere out here?"

"No."

"You got family that lives around here?"

"I don't have a family."

Despite his passenger's brusque tone, Charlie, who had three grown sons of his own back in New York, had the distinct feeling the boy was exerting every ounce of his control to keep his emotions in check. He waited a few minutes before asking, "You got a name?"

"Zack . . ." he replied, and after a hesitant pause, he added, ". . . Benedict."

"Where you headed?"

"Wherever you're going."

"I'm going all the way to the West Coast. Los Angeles."

"Fine," he said in a tone that discouraged further conversation. "It doesn't matter."

It was hours later when the young man spoke voluntarily for the first time. "Do you need any help unloading this rig when you get to Los Angeles?"

Charlie looked sideways at him, quickly revising his initial conclusions about Zack Benedict. He dressed like a rich kid and he had the diction of a rich kid, but this particular rich kid was evidently out of money, out of his element, and down on his luck. He was also perfectly willing to swallow his pride and do ordinary manual labor, which Charlie thought showed a certain amount of grit, all things considered. "You look like you could handle the heavy lifting easy enough," he said, casting a quick, appraising eye over Benedict's tall, well-muscled body. "You been working out with weights or something?"

"I used to box at—I used to box," he amended shortly.

At college, Charlie finished mentally, and maybe it was because Benedict somehow reminded him of his own boys when they were his age and trying to tough things out or maybe it was because he sensed that Zack Benedict's problems were pretty desperate, but he decided to give him some work. Having reached that decision, Charlie held out his hand. "My name's Murdock, Charlie

Murdock. I can't pay you much, but at least you'll get a chance to see an honest-to-God movie lot when we get to L.A. This truck's loaded with props that belong to Empire Studios. I got a contract to do some of their hauling, and that's where we're going."

Benedict's grim indifference to that information somehow added to Charlie's conviction that his passenger was not only broke but probably had no idea of how to rectify the problem in the near future. "If you do a good job for me, maybe I could put in a word for you at Empire's hiring office—that is, if you don't mind pushing a broom or using your back?"

His passenger turned his face to the side window, staring out into the darkness again. Just when Charlie had reversed his earlier opinion and decided that Benedict actually thought he was too good to do menial labor, the young man spoke in a voice that was hoarse with relief and embarrassed gratitude. "Thanks. I'd appreciate that."

1

1978

"I'M MRS. BOROWSKI FROM THE LASALLE FOSTER CARE facility," the middle-aged woman announced as she marched across the Oriental carpet toward the receptionist, a shopping bag from Woolworth's over her arm. Gesturing toward the petite eleven-year-old who trailed along behind her, she added coldly, "And this is Julie Smith. She's here to see Dr. Theresa Wilmer. I'll come back for her after I finish my shopping."

The receptionist smiled at the youngster. "Dr. Wilmer will be with you in a little while, Julie. In the meantime, you can sit over there and fill out as much of this card as you can. I forgot to give it to you when you were here before."

Self-consciously aware of her shabby jeans and grubby jacket, Julie glanced uneasily at the elegant waiting room where fragile porcelain figurines reposed on an antique coffee table and valuable bronze sculptures were displayed on marble stands. Giving the table with its fragile knickknacks a wide berth, she headed for a chair beside a huge aquarium where exotic goldfish with flowing fins swam leisurely among lacy greenery. Behind her, Mrs. Borowski poked her head back into the room and warned the receptionist, "Julie will steal anything that isn't nailed down. She's sneaky and quick, so you better watch her like a hawk."

Drowning in humiliated anger, Julie slumped down in the chair, then she stretched her legs straight out in front of her in a deliberate attempt to appear utterly bored and unaffected by Mrs. Borowski's horrible remarks, but her effect was spoiled by the bright red flags of embarrassed color that stained her cheeks and the fact that her legs couldn't reach the floor.

After a moment she wriggled up from the uncomfortable position and looked with dread at the card the receptionist had given her to complete. Knowing she'd not be able to figure out the words, she gave it a try anyway. Her tongue clenched between her teeth, she concentrated fiercely on the printing on the card. The first word began with an *N* like the word *NO* on the NO PARKING signs that lined the streets—she knew what those signs said because one of her friends had told her. The next letter on the card was an *a*, like the one in *cat*, but the word wasn't *cat*. Her hand tightened on the yellow pencil as she fought back the familiar feelings of frustration and angry despair that swamped her whenever she was expected to read something. She'd learned the word *cat* in first grade, but nobody ever wrote that word anywhere! Glowering at the incomprehensible words on the card, she wondered furiously why teachers taught kids to read dumb words like *cat* when nobody ever wrote *cat* anywhere except in stupid books for first graders.

But the books weren't stupid, Julie reminded herself, and neither were the teachers. Other kids her age could probably have read this dumb card in a blink! She was the one who couldn't read a word on it, *she* was the one who was stupid.

On the other hand, Julie told herself, she knew a whole lot about things that other kids knew nothing about, because she made a point of *noticing* things. And one of the things she'd noticed was that when people handed you something to fill out, they almost always expected you to write your name on it . . .

With painstaking neatness, she printed J-u-l-i-e-S-m-i-t-h across the top half of the card, then she stopped, unable to fill out any more of the spaces. She felt herself getting angry again and rather than feeling bad about this silly piece of paper, she decided to think of something nice, like the feeling of wind on her face in springtime. She was conjuring a vision of herself stretched out beneath a big leafy tree, watching squirrels scampering in the branches overhead, when the receptionist's pleasant voice made her head snap up in guilty alarm.

"Is something wrong with your pencil, Julie?"

Julie dug the lead point against her jeans and snapped it off. "The lead's broken."

"Here's another—"

"My hand is sore today," she lied, lurching to her feet. "I don't feel like writing. And I have to go to the bathroom. Where is it?"

"Right beside the elevators. Dr. Wilmer will be ready to see you pretty soon. Don't be gone too long."

"I won't," Julie dutifully replied. After closing the office door behind her, she turned to look up at the name on it and carefully studied the first few letters so she'd be able to recognize this particular door when she came back. "*P*," she whispered aloud so she wouldn't forget, "S. Y." Satisfied, she headed down the long, carpeted hall, turned left at the end of it, and made a right by the water fountain, but when she finally came to the elevators, she discovered there were two doors there with words on them. She was almost positive these were the bathrooms because, among the bits of knowledge she'd carefully stored away was the fact that bathroom doors in big buildings usually had a different kind of handle than ordinary office doors. The problem was that neither of these doors said BOYS or GIRLS—two words she could recognize, nor did they have those nice stick figures of a man and woman that told people like her which bathroom to use. Very cautiously, Julie put her hand on one of the doors, eased it open a crack, and peeked inside. She backed up in a hurry when she spotted those funny-looking toilets on the wall because there were two other things she knew that she doubted other girls knew: Men used weird-looking toilets. And they went a little crazy if a girl opened the door while they were doing it. Julie opened the other door and trooped into the right bathroom.

Conscious of time passing, she left the bathroom and hurriedly retraced her steps until she neared the part of the corridor where Dr. Wilmer's office should have been, then she began laboriously studying the names on the doors. Dr. Wilmer's name began with a P-S-Y. She spied a P-E-T on the next door, decided she'd remembered the letters wrong, and quickly shoved it open. An unfamiliar, gray-haired woman looked up from her typewriter. "Yes?"

"Sorry, wrong room," Julie mumbled, flushing. "Do you know where Dr. Wilmer's office is?"

"Dr. Wilmer?"

"Yes, you know—Wilmer—it starts with a P-S-Y!"

"P-S-Y . . . Oh, you must mean Psychological Associates! That's suite twenty-five-sixteen, down the hall."

Normally, Julie would have pretended to understand and continued going into offices until she found the right one, but she was too worried about being late now to pretend. "Would you spell that out for me?"

"I beg your pardon?"

"The numbers!" she said desperately. "Spell them out like this: three—six—nine—four—two. Say it that way."

The woman looked at her like she was an idiot, which Julie knew she was, but she hated it when other people noticed. After an irritated sigh, the woman said, "Dr. Wilmer is in suite two—five—one—six."

"Two—five—one—six," Julie repeated.

"That's the fourth door on the left," she added.

"Well!" Julie cried in frustration. "Why didn't you just say that in the first place!"

Dr. Wilmer's receptionist looked up when Julie walked in. "Did you get lost, Julie?"

"Me? No way!" Julie lied with an emphatic shake of her curly head as she returned to her chair. Unaware that she was being observed through what looked like an ordinary mirror, she turned her attention to the aquarium beside her chair. The first thing she noticed was that one of the beautiful fish had died and that two others were swimming around it as if contemplating eating it. Automatically, she tapped her finger on the glass to scare them away, but a moment later they returned. "There's a dead fish in there," she told the receptionist, trying to sound only slightly concerned. "I could take it out for you."

"The cleaning people will remove it tonight, but thank you for offering."

Julie swallowed an irate protest at what she felt was needless cruelty to the dead fish. It wasn't right for anything so wonderfully beautiful and so helpless to be left in there like that. Picking up a magazine from the coffee table, she pretended to look at it, but from the corner of her eye she kept up her surveillance of the two predatory fish. Each time they returned to prod and poke their deceased comrade, she stole a glance at the receptionist to make sure she wasn't watching, then Julie reached out as casually as possible and tapped the glass to scare them off.

A few feet away, in her office on the other side of the two-way mirror, Dr. Theresa Wilmer watched the entire little scenario, her eyes alight with a knowing smile as she watched Julie's gallant attempt to protect a dead fish while maintaining a facade of indifference for the sake of the receptionist. Glancing at the man beside her, another psychiatrist who'd recently begun donating some of his time to her special project, Dr. Wilmer said wryly, "There she is, 'Julie the terrible,' the adolescent terror who some foster care officials have judged to be not only 'learning-disabled,' but unmanageable, a bad influence on her peers, and also 'a troublemaker bound for juvenile delinquency.' Did you know," she continued, her voice taking on a shade of amused admiration, "that she actually organized a hunger strike at LaSalle? She talked forty-five children, most of whom were older than she, into going along with her to demand better food."

Dr. John Frazier peered through the two-way mirror at the little girl. "I suppose she did that because she had an underlying need to challenge authority?"

"No," Dr. Wilmer replied dryly, "she did it because she had an underlying need for better food. The food at LaSalle is nutritious but tasteless. I sampled some."

Frazier flashed a startled look at his associate. "What about her thefts? You can't ignore that problem so easily."

Leaning her shoulder against the wall, Terry tipped her head to the child in the waiting room and said with a smile, "Have you ever heard of Robin Hood?"

"Of course. Why?"

"Because you're looking at a modern-day adolescent version of Robin Hood out there. Julie can filch the gold right out of your teeth without your knowing it, she's that quick."

"I hardly think *that's* a recommendation for sending her to live with your unsuspecting Texas cousins, which is what I understand you intend to do."

Dr. Wilmer shrugged. "Julie steals food or clothing or playthings, but she doesn't keep anything. She gives her booty to the younger kids at LaSalle."

"You're certain?"

"Positive. I've checked it out."

A reluctant smile tugged at John Frazier's lips as he studied the little girl. "She looks more like a Peter Pan than a Robin Hood. She's not at all what I expected, based on her file."

"She surprised me, too," Dr. Wilmer admitted. According to Julie's file, the director of the LaSalle Foster Care Facility, where she now resided, had deemed her to be "a discipline problem with a predilection for truancy, troublemaking, theft, and hanging around with unsavory male companions." After all the unfavorable comments in Julie's file, Dr. Wilmer had fully expected Julie Smith to be a belligerent, hardened girl whose constant association with young males probably indicated early physical development and even sexual activity. For that reason, she'd nearly gaped at Julie when the child sauntered into her office two months ago, looking like a grubby little pixie in jeans and a tattered sweatshirt, with short-cropped dark, curly hair. Instead of the budding femme fatale Dr. Wilmer had expected, Julie Smith had a beguiling gamin face that was dominated by an enormous pair of thick-lashed eyes the startling color of dark blue pansies. In contrast to that piquant little face and innocently beguiling eyes, there was a boyish bravado in the way she'd stood in front of Dr. Wilmer's desk that first day with her small chin thrust out and her hands jammed into the back pockets of her jeans.

Theresa had been captivated at that first meeting, but her fascination with Julie had begun even before that—almost from the moment she'd opened her file at home one night and began reading her responses to the battery of tests that was part of the evaluating process that Theresa herself had recently developed. By the time she was finished, Theresa had a firm grasp of the workings of the child's facile mind as well as the depth of her pain and the details of her current plight: Abandoned by her birth parents and rejected by two sets of adoptive parents, Julie had been reduced to spending her childhood on the fringes of the Chicago slums in a succession of overcrowded foster homes. As a result, throughout her life, her only source of real human warmth and support came from her companions—grubby, unkempt kids like herself whom she philosophically regarded as "her own kind," kids who taught her to filch goods from stores and, later, to cut school with them. Her quick mind and quicker fingers had made Julie so good at both that no matter how often she was shuffled off to a new foster home, she almost immediately achieved a certain popularity and respect among her peers, so much so that a few months ago, a group of boys had condescended to demonstrate to her the various techniques they used for breaking into cars and hot-wiring them—a demonstration that resulted in the entire group of them being busted by an alert Chicago cop, including Julie, who was merely an observer.

That day had marked Julie's first arrest, and although Julie didn't know it, it also marked Julie's first real "break" because it ultimately brought her to Dr. Wilmer's attention. After being—somewhat unjustly—arrested for attempted auto theft, Julie was put into Dr. Wilmer's new, experimental program that included an intensive battery of psychological tests, intelligence tests, and personal interviews and evaluations conducted by Dr. Wilmer's group of volunteer psychiatrists and psychologists. The program was intended to divert juveniles in the care of the state from a life of delinquency and worse.

In Julie's case, Dr. Wilmer was adamantly committed to doing exactly that, and as everyone who knew her was aware, when Dr. Wilmer set her mind on a goal, she accomplished it. At thirty-five, Terry Wilmer had a pleasant, refined bearing, a kind smile, and a will of iron. In addition to her impressive assortment of medical degrees and a family tree that read like *The Social Register,* she had three other special attributes in great abundance: intuition, compassion, and total dedication. With the tireless fervor of a true evangelist dedicated to saving wayward souls, Theresa Wilmer had abandoned her thriving private practice and was now dedicated to saving those helpless adolescent victims of an over-crowded, underfunded state foster care system. To achieve her goals, Dr. Wilmer was shamelessly willing to exploit every tool at her disposal, including recruiting support from among her colleagues like John Frazier. In Julie's case, she'd even enlisted the aid of distant cousins, who were far from wealthy but who had room in their home, and hopefully in their soft hearts, for one very special little girl.

"I wanted you to have a peek at her," Terry said. She reached out to draw the draperies over the glass, just as Julie suddenly stood up, looked desperately at the fish tank, and plunged both her hands into the water.

"What the hell—" John Frazier began, then he watched in stunned silence as the girl marched toward the preoccupied receptionist with the dead fish cradled in her dripping hands.

Julie knew she shouldn't get water on the carpet, but she couldn't stand to see anything as beautiful as this fish with its long, flowing fins being mangled by the others. Not certain whether the receptionist was unaware of her or simply ignoring her, she walked up close behind her chair. "Excuse me," she blurted in an overloud voice, holding out her hands.

The receptionist, who was thoroughly engrossed in her typing, gave a nervous start, swung around in her chair, and emitted a choked scream at the sight of a shining, dripping fish directly in front of her nose.

Julie took a cautious step backward but persevered. "It's dead," she said boldly, fighting to keep her voice empty of the sentimental pity she felt. "The other fish are going to eat it, and I don't want to watch. It's gross. If you'll give me a piece of paper, I'll wrap it up and you can put it in your trash can."

Recovering from her shock, the receptionist carefully suppressed a smile, opened her desk drawer, and removed several tissues, which she handed to the child. "Would you like to take it with you and bury it at home?"

Julie would have liked to do exactly that, but she thought she heard amusement in the woman's voice, and so she hastily wrapped the fish in its tissue-paper shroud and thrust it at her instead. "I'm not that stupid, you know. This is just a fish, not a rabbit or something special like that."

On the other side of the window, Frazier chuckled softly and shook his head. "She's dying to give that fish a formal burial, but her pride won't let her admit it." Sobering, he added, "What about her learning disabilities? As I recall, she's only at a second-grade level."

Dr. Wilmer gave an indelicate snort at that and reached for a manila folder on her desk containing the results of the battery of tests Julie had recently been given. Holding the open file toward him she said with a smile, "Take a look at her scores when the intelligence tests are administered orally and she's not required to read."

John Frazier complied and gave a low laugh. "The kid's got a higher IQ than I do."

"Julie is a special child in a lot of ways, John. I saw glimpses of it when I reviewed her file, but when I met her face-to-face, I *knew* it was true. She's feisty, brave, sensitive, and very smart. Under all that bravado of hers, there's a rare kind of gentleness, an unquenchable hope, and quixotic optimism that she clings to even though it's being demolished by ugly reality. She can't improve her own lot in life, and so she's unconsciously dedicated herself to protecting the kids in whatever foster care facility she's put into. She steals for them and lies for them and organizes them into hunger strikes, and they follow wherever she leads as if she were the Pied Piper. At eleven years old, she's a born leader, but if she isn't diverted very quickly, some of her methods are going to land her in a juvenile detention center and eventually prison. And that's not even the worst of her problems right now."

"What do you mean?"

"I mean that despite all her wonderful attributes, that little girl's self-esteem is so low, it's almost nonexistent. Because she's been passed over for adoption, she's convinced she's worthless and unlovable. Because she can't read as well as her peers, she's convinced she's completely stupid and can't learn. And the most terrifying part of it is that she's on the verge of giving up. She's a dreamer, but she's clinging to her dreams by a thread." With unintentional force, Terry finished, "I will *not* let all Julie's potential, her hope, her optimism, go to waste."

Dr. Frazier's brows shot up at her tone. "Forgive me for bringing this up, Terry, but aren't you the one who used to preach about not getting too personally involved with a patient?"

With a rueful smile, Dr. Wilmer leaned against her desk, but she didn't deny it. "It was easier to follow that rule when all my patients were kids from wealthy families who think they're 'underprivileged' if they don't get a $50,000 sports car on their sixteenth birthday. Wait until you've done more work with kids like Julie—kids who are dependent on the 'system' that we set up to provide for them and have somehow fallen through the cracks in that same system. You'll lose sleep over them, even if you've never done it before."

"I suppose you're right," he said with a sigh, as he handed back the manila folder. "Out of curiosity, why hasn't she been adopted by someone?"

Teresa shrugged. "Mostly, it's been a combination of bad luck and bad timing. According to her file at the Department of Children and Family Services, she was abandoned in an alley when she was only a few hours old. Hospital records indicate she was born ten weeks prematurely and because of that and because of the poor condition she was in when she was brought to the hospital, there was a long series of health complications until she was seven years old, during which time she was repeatedly hospitalized and very frail.

"The Family Services people found adoptive parents for her when she was two years old, but in the middle of the adoption proceedings, the couple decided to get a divorce, and they dumped her back into the arms of Family Services. A few weeks later, she was placed again with another couple who'd been screened as carefully as humanly possible, but Julie came down with pneumonia, and the new couple—who'd lost their own child at Julie's age—went completely to pieces emotionally and pulled out of the adoption. Afterward, she was placed with a foster family for what was only to be a temporary time, but a few weeks later, Julie's case worker was seriously injured in an accident and never returned to work. From then on it was the proverbial 'comedy of errors.' Julie's file got misplaced—"

"Her what!?" he uttered in disbelief.

"Don't judge the Family Services people too harshly, which I can see you're doing. For the most part, they're extremely dedicated and conscientious, but they're only human. Given how overworked and underfinanced they are, it's amazing they do as well as they do. In any event, to make a long story short, the foster parents had a houseful of kids to look after, and they assumed Family Services couldn't find adoptive parents for Julie because she wasn't very healthy. By the time Family Services realized she'd gotten lost in their shuffle, Julie was five, and she'd passed the age of greatest appeal to adoptive parents. She also had a history of poor health, and when she was removed from the foster home and placed in another, she promptly came down with a series of asthma attacks. She missed large chunks of first and second grade, but she was "such a good little girl" the teachers promoted her from one grade to the next anyway. Her new foster parents already had three physically handicapped children in their care, and they were so busy looking after those children that they didn't notice Julie wasn't keeping up in school, particularly because she was getting passing grades. By fourth grade, though, Julie herself realized she couldn't do the work, and she started pretending to be ill so that she could stay home. When her foster parents caught on, they insisted she go to school, so Julie took the next obvious route to avoid it—she started cutting school and hanging around with kids on the street as often as she could. As I said earlier, she's feisty, daring, and quick—they taught her how to snitch merchandise from stores and avoid being picked up as a truant.

"You know most of the rest: Eventually she did get picked up for truancy and shoplifting and was sent to the LaSalle facility, which is where kids who aren't doing well in the foster care system are sent. A few months ago, she got busted—unfairly, I think—along with a group of older boys who were demonstrating to her their particular prowess with hot-wiring cars." With a muffled laugh, Terry finished, "Julie was merely a fascinated observer, but she knows how to do it. She offered to demonstrate for me. Can you imagine—that tiny girl with those enormous, innocent eyes can actually start your car without a key! She wouldn't try to steal it though. As I said, she only takes things the kids at LaSalle can use."

With a meaningful grin, Frazier tipped his head toward the glass. "I assume they can 'use' one red pencil, a ballpoint, and a fistful of candy."

"What?"

"In the time you've been talking to me, your prize patient has filched all that from the reception room."

"Good God!" said Dr. Wilmer but without any real concern as she stared through the glass.

"She's quick enough to do sleight-of-hand tricks," Frazier added with reluctant admiration. "I'd get her in here before she figures out a way to get that aquarium out the door. I'll bet the kids at LaSalle would love some exotic tropical fish."

Glancing at her watch, Dr. Wilmer said, "The Mathisons are supposed to call me right about now from Texas to tell me exactly when they'll be ready to take her. I want to be able to tell Julie everything when she comes in here." As she spoke, the intercom on her desk buzzed and the receptionist's voice said, "Mrs. Mathison is on the phone, Dr. Wilmer."

"That's the call," Terry told him happily.

John Frazier glanced at his own watch. "I'm having my first session with Cara Peterson in a few minutes." He started toward the connecting door that opened into his office, paused with his hand on the knob, and said with a grin, "It's just occurred to me that the distribution of workload in your program is grossly unjust. I mean," he joked, "you get to work with a girl who filches candy and pencils to give to the poor, while you give me Cara Anderson who tried to kill her foster father. You get Robin Hood and I get Lizzie Borden."

"You love a challenge," Theresa Wilmer replied, laughing, but as she reached for the phone, she added, "I'm going to ask the Family Services people to transfer Mrs. Borowski out of LaSalle and into an area where she'll only be involved with infants and small children. I've worked with her before, and she's excellent with them because they're cuddly and they don't break rules. She shouldn't be dealing with adolescents. She can't distinguish between minor adolescent rebellion and juvenile delinquency."

"You aren't by any chance getting revenge on her because she told your receptionist that Julie will steal anything she can get her hands on?"

"No," Dr. Wilmer said as she picked up the phone. "But that was a good example of what I meant."

When she finished her call, Dr. Wilmer got up and walked to her office door, looking forward to the surprise she was about to deliver to Miss Julie Smith.

2

JULIE," SHE SAID FROM THE DOORWAY, "WOULD YOU COME IN please." As Julie closed the door behind her and walked forward, Terry added cheerfully, "Your time in our testing program is over. All the results are in."

Rather than sitting in a chair, her young patient took up a position in front of Terry's desk, her small feet planted slightly apart, hands jammed into the back pockets of her jeans. She gave a jaunty, dismissive shrug, but she did not ask about the results of the tests, because, Terry knew, she was afraid to hear the answers. "The tests were dumb," she said instead. "This whole program is dumb. You can't tell anything about me from a bunch of tests and talks in your office."

"I've learned a whole lot about you, Julie, in the few months we've known each other. Would you like me to prove it by telling you what I've discovered?"

"No."

"Please, let me tell you what I think."

She sighed, then gave an impish grin and said, "You're going to do that whether I want to hear it or not."

"You're right," Dr. Wilmer agreed, suppressing a smile of her own at the astute remark. The blunt methods she was about to use on Julie were completely different than those she would normally use, but Julie was innately intuitive and too streetwise to be fooled with sugared phrases and half-truths. "Please sit down," she said, and when Julie had slumped into the chair in front of her desk, Dr. Wilmer began with quiet firmness. "I've discovered that despite all your daring deeds and your show of bravado to your companions, the truth is that you are scared to death every moment of every day, Julie. You don't know who you are or what you are or what you're going to be. You can't read or write, so you're convinced you're stupid. You cut school because you can't keep up with the other kids your age, and it hurts you terribly when they laugh at you in class. You feel hopeless and trapped, and you hate those feelings.

"You know you were passed over for adoption when you were younger, and you know your mother abandoned you. A long time ago, you decided that the reason your birth parents didn't keep you and adoptive parents didn't want to adopt you was because they all realized you were going to turn out to be 'no good' and because you weren't smart enough or pretty enough. And so you cut your hair like a boy's, refuse to wear girls' clothes, and steal things, but you still don't feel any happier. Nothing you do seems to matter, and that's the real problem: No matter what you do—unless you get into trouble—it doesn't matter to anyone, and you hate yourself because you want to matter."

Dr. Wilmer paused to let the last part of that sink in and then she thrust harder. "You want to matter to someone, Julie. If you had only one wish, *that* would be your wish."

Julie felt her eyes sting with humiliating tears as Dr. Wilmer's relentless verbal thrusts found their mark, and she blinked to hold them back.

Her rapid blinking and damp eyes weren't lost on Terry Wilmer, who saw Julie's tears as what they were—confirmation that she'd hit raw nerves. Softening her voice, Dr. Wilmer continued, "You hate hoping and dreaming, but you can't seem to stop, so you make up wonderful stories and tell them to the little kids at LaSalle—stories about lonely, ugly children who find families and love and happiness someday."

"You've got everything all wrong!" Julie protested hotly, flushing to the roots of her hair. "You're making me sound like some—some wimpy sissy. I don't need anybody to love me and neither do the kids at LaSalle. I don't need it, and I don't want it! I'm happy—"

"That's not true. We're going to tell each other the complete truth today, and I haven't quite finished." Holding the child's gaze, she stated with quiet force: "The truth is this, Julie: During the time you've spent in this testing program, we've discovered that you're a brave, wonderful, and *very smart* little girl." She smiled at Julie's stunned, dubious expression and continued, "The only reason you haven't learned to read and write yet is because you missed so much school when you were ill that you couldn't catch up later on. That has nothing to do with your ability to learn, which is what you call being 'smart' and we call 'intelligence.' All you need in order to catch up with your school work is for someone to give you a helping hand for awhile. Now, besides being smart," she continued, changing the subject slightly, "you also have a perfectly normal, natural need to be loved for what you are. You're very sensitive, and that's why your feelings get hurt easily. It's also why you don't like to see other children's feelings get hurt and why you try so hard to make them happy by telling them stories and stealing things for them. I know you hate being sensitive, but believe me, it's one of your most precious traits. Now, all we have to do is put you in an environment that will help you become the sort of young woman you can be someday . . ."

Julie paled, thinking the unfamiliar word *environment* sounded like an institution, like, maybe, jail.

"I know just the foster parents for you—James and Mary Mathison. Mrs. Mathison used to be a teacher, and she's eager to help you catch up with your schoolwork. Reverend Mathison is a minister—"

Julie shot out of her chair as if her backside had been scorched. "A preacher!" she burst out, shaking her head, recalling loud lectures about hellfire and damnation she'd heard often enough in church. "No, thanks, I'd rather go to the slammer."

"You've never been in the slammer, so you don't know what you're talking about," Dr. Wilmer stated, then she continued talking about the next foster home as if Julie had no choice in the matter, which of course Julie realized she didn't. "James and Mary Mathison moved to a small Texas town several years ago. They have two sons who are five and three years older than you, and unlike the other foster homes you've been in, there won't be any other foster children there. You'll be part of a *real* family, Julie. You'll even have a room of your very own, and those are both firsts for you, I know. I've talked with James and Mary about you, and they're very anxious to have you with them."

"For how long?" Julie asked, trying not to get excited at what was probably only a temporary thing that wouldn't work out anyway.

"Forever, assuming you like it there and that you're willing to follow one strict rule they have for themselves and their children: honesty. That means no more stealing, no more lying, and no more cutting school. All you have to do is be honest with them. They believe you'll do that, and they're very, very anxious to have you be part of their family. Mrs. Mathison called me a few minutes ago, and she was already on her way to go shopping for some games and things to help you learn to read as quickly as possible. She's waiting for you to go with her and pick out things for your bedroom, so it will be just the way you like it."

Squelching her flare of delight, Julie said, "They don't know that I've been busted, do they? I mean, for truancy?"

"Truancy," Dr. Wilmer said pointedly, stating the horrible truth, "*and* attempted grand theft, auto. Yes, they know everything."

"And they still want me to live with them?" Julie countered with cutting derision. "They must really need the money Family Services pays to foster parents."

"Money has nothing to do with their decision!" Dr. Wilmer shot back, the sternness of her voice offset by a faint smile. "They are a very special family. They aren't rich in money, but they feel that they are rich in other ways—with other kinds of blessings, and they want to share some of those blessings with a deserving child."

"And they think *I'm* deserving?" Julie scoffed. "Nobody wanted me before I had a police record. Why would anybody want me now?"

Ignoring her rhetorical question, Dr. Wilmer stood up and walked around her desk. "Julie," she said gently, waiting until Julie reluctantly raised her eyes, "I think you are the most deserving child I've ever had the privilege of meeting." The unprecedented, glowing compliment was followed by one of the few physical gestures of affection Julie had ever known: Dr. Wilmer laid her hand alongside Julie's cheek as she said, "I don't know how you've stayed as sweet and special as you are, but believe me, you deserve all the help I can give you and all the love that I think you're going to find with the Mathisons."

Julie shrugged, trying to steel herself against inevitable disappointment, but as she stood up, she couldn't quite douse the flare of hope in her heart. "Don't count on that, Dr. Wilmer."

Dr. Wilmer smiled softly. "I'm counting on *you*. You're an extremely intelligent and intuitive girl who'll know a good thing when she finds it."

"You must be really good at your job," Julie said with a sigh that was part hope, part dread of the future. "You almost make me believe all that stuff."

"I am *extremely* good at my job," Dr. Wilmer agreed. "And it was very *intelligent* and *intuitive* of you to realize that." Smiling, she touched Julie's chin and said with gentle solemnity, "Will you write to me once in a while and let me know how you're doing?"

"Sure," Julie said with another shrug.

"The Mathisons don't care what you've done in the past—they trust you to be honest with them from now on. Will you be willing to forget the past, too, and give them a chance to help you become the wonderful person you can be?"

All the unprecedented flattery wrung a self-conscious giggle from Julie who rolled her eyes. "Yep. Sure thing."

Refusing to let Julie dismiss the importance of her new future, Theresa continued somberly, "Think of it, Julie. Mary Mathison has always wanted a daughter, but you're the only little girl she's ever invited to come live with her. As of this moment, you get to start all over with a clean slate and your own family. You're all shiny and brand new, just like you were as a baby. Do you understand?"

Julie opened her mouth to say she did, but she seemed to have a funny lump in her throat, so she nodded instead.

Theresa Wilmer gazed into the huge blue eyes looking back at her from that enchanting gamin face, and she felt a constriction in her own throat as she reached out and brushed her fingers through Julie's tousled brown curls.

"Maybe someday you'll decide to let your hair grow," she murmured, smiling. "It's going to be beautiful and thick."

Julie found her voice at last and her forehead furrowed into a worried frown. "The lady—Mrs. Mathison, I mean—you don't think she'll try to curl it and put ribbons in it or anything dopey like that, do you?"

"Not unless you want to wear it that way."

Theresa's sentimental mood lingered as she watched Julie leave. Noticing that she'd left the office door slightly ajar and knowing her receptionist was at lunch, Theresa straightened and walked over to close it herself. She was reaching for the knob when she saw Julie go out of her way to pass by the coffee table without actually stopping and then step out of her way again in order to pass the receptionist's vacant desk.

Lying on the coffee table after she left was a large fistful of purloined candy. On the receptionist's cleared desk, there was one red pencil and one ballpoint pen.

A feeling of joy, pride, and accomplishment made Theresa's voice husky as she whispered to the departed child, "You didn't want anything to spoil your nice clean slate, did you, sweetheart? That's my girl!"

3

THE SCHOOL BUS PULLED TO A STOP IN FRONT OF THE COZY Victorian house that Julie had let herself think of as her home during the three months she'd lived with the Mathisons. "Here you are, Julie," the kindly bus driver said, but as Julie stepped off the bus, none of her new friends called good-bye to her like they usually did. Their cold, suspicious silence compounded the stark terror that was already making her stomach churn as she trudged up the snow-covered sidewalk. Money that had been collected from Julie's class for the week's lunches at school had been stolen from the teacher's desk. All of the kids in her room had been questioned about the theft, but it was Julie who had stayed in at recess that day to put the finishing touches on her geography project. It was Julie who was the main suspect, not only because she'd had the perfect opportunity to steal the money, but also because she was the newcomer, the outsider, the kid from the big bad city, and since nothing like this had happened in her class before, she was already guilty in everyone's eyes. This afternoon, while waiting outside the principal's office, she'd heard Mr. Duncan tell his secretary that he was going to have to call Reverend and Mrs. Mathison and tell them about the stolen money. Obviously, Mr. Duncan had done so because Reverend Mathison's car was in the driveway, and he was rarely home this early.

When she reached the gate in the white picket fence that surrounded the yard, she stood there, looking at the house, her knees shaking so hard that they banged together at the thought of being banished from this place. The Mathisons had given her a room of her very own, with a canopy bed and a flowered bedspread, but she wasn't going to miss all that nearly so much as she was going to miss the hugs. And the laughter. And their beautiful voices. Oh, they all had such soft, kind, laughing voices. Just thinking of never hearing James Mathison say "Good night, Julie. Don't forget your prayers, honey," made Julie long to fling herself into the snow and weep like a baby. And how would she go on living if she could never again hear Carl and Ted, who she already thought of as her very own big brothers, calling to her to play a game with them or go to the movies with them. Never again would she get to go to church with her new family and sit in the front pew with them and listen to Reverend Mathison talking gently about "the Lord" while the entire congregation listened in respectful silence to everything he said. She hadn't liked that part at first; church services seemed to go on for days, not hours, and the pews were hard as rock, but then she'd started really listening to what Reverend Mathison said. After a couple of weeks, she'd almost started *believing* that there was really a kind, loving God who actually watched out for everybody, even trashy kids like Julie Smith. As she stood in the snow, Julie mumbled, "Please" to Reverend Mathison's God, but she knew it was no use.

She should have known all this was too good to last, Julie realized bitterly, and the tears she'd been fighting not to shed blurred her vision. For a moment, she allowed herself to hope that she'd merely be given a whipping instead of being sent back to Chicago, but she knew better than that. In the first place, her foster parents didn't believe in whippings, but they did believe that lying and stealing were grievous offenses that were totally unacceptable to "the Lord" and to them. Julie had promised not to do either one and they'd trusted her completely.

The strap of her new nylon book bag slipped off her left shoulder and the bag slid to the snow, but Julie was too miserable to care. Dragging it by the remaining strap, she walked with numb dread toward the house and up the porch steps.

Chocolate chip cookies, Julie's favorites, were cooling in trays on the kitchen counter as she closed the back door. Normally the delicious aroma of freshly baked cookies made Julie's mouth water; today it made her feel like throwing up because Mary Mathison would never again make them especially for her. The kitchen was strangely deserted, and a glance into the living room confirmed that it, too, was empty, but she could hear her foster brothers' voices coming from their bedroom down the hall. With shaking hands, Julie looped the strap of her book bag over one of the pegs beside the kitchen door, then she pulled off her quilted winter jacket, hung it there, and headed down the hall in the direction of the boys' bedroom.

Carl, her sixteen-year-old foster brother, saw her standing in their doorway and looped his arm around her shoulders. "Hi, Julie-Bob," he teased, "What do you think of our new poster?" Ordinarily, Carl's nickname for her made her smile; now it made her feel like bawling because she wouldn't hear that again either. Ted, who was two years younger than Carl, grinned at her and pointed toward the poster of their latest movie idol, Zack Benedict. "What do you think, Julie, isn't he great? I'm going to have a motorcycle just like Zack Benedict's someday."

Julie glanced through tear-glazed eyes at the life-sized picture of a tall, broad-shouldered, unsmiling male who was standing beside a motorcycle, his arms crossed against a broad, deeply tanned chest with dark hair on it. "He's the greatest," she agreed numbly. "Where's your mother and father?" she added dully. Although her foster parents had originally invited her to call them Mom and Dad, and she'd eagerly accepted, Julie knew that privilege was about to be revoked. "I need to talk to them." Her voice was already thick with unshed tears, but she was determined to get the inevitable confrontation over with as soon as possible because she honestly couldn't endure the dread another moment.

"They're in their bedroom having some sort of private powwow," Ted said, his admiring gaze fastened on the poster. "Carl and I are going to see Zack Benedict's new movie tomorrow tonight. We wanted to take you with us, but it's rated PG-13 because of violence, and Mom said we couldn't." He tore his eyes from his idol and looked at Julie's woebegone face. "Hey, kiddo, don't look so glum. We'll take you to the first movie that—"

The door across the hall opened and Julie's foster parents walked out of their bedroom, their expressions grim. "I thought I heard your voice, Julie," Mary

Mathison said. "Would you like a snack before we start on your homework?" Reverend Mathison looked at Julie's taut face and said, "I think Julie's too upset to concentrate on homework." To her he said, "Would you like to talk about what's bothering you now or after dinner?"

"Now," she whispered. Carl and Ted exchanged puzzled, worried glances and started to leave their room, but Julie shook her head so they would stay. Better to get it all over with in front of everyone, all at once, she felt. When her foster parents were seated on Carl's bed, she began in a quavering voice, "Some money was stolen at school today."

"We know that," Reverend Mathison said dispassionately. "Your principal has already called us. Mr. Duncan seems to believe, as does your teacher, that you are the guilty party."

Julie had already decided on the way home from school that no matter how painful or unjust the things they said to her might be, she wouldn't beg or plead or humiliate herself in any way. Unfortunately, she hadn't figured on the incredible agony she would feel at this moment when she was losing her new family. She shoved her hands into the back pockets of her jeans in an unconsciously defiant stance, but to her horror, her shoulders started to shake violently and she had to wipe away hated tears from her face with her sleeve.

"Did you steal the money, Julie?"

"No!" The word exploded from her in an anguished cry.

"Then that's that." Reverend Mathison and Mrs. Mathison both stood up as if they'd just decided she was a liar as well as a thief, and Julie started begging and pleading despite her resolve not to do that. "I s-swear I didn't take the lunch money," she wept fiercely, twisting the hem of her sweater in her hands. "I prom-promised you I wouldn't lie or steal again, and I haven't. I *haven't!* Please! Please believe me—"

"We do believe you, Julie."

"I've changed, really, I have, and—" She broke off and gaped at them in blank disbelief. "You . . . what?" she whispered.

"Julie," her foster father said, laying his hand against her cheek, "when you came to live with us, we asked you to give us your word that there would be no more lying or stealing. When you gave *us* your word, we gave *you* our trust, remember?"

Julie nodded, remembering that moment in the living room three months ago with crystal clarity, then she glanced at her foster mother's smile and flung herself into Mary Mathison's arms. They closed around her, wrapping Julie in the scent of carnations and the silent promise of a whole lifetime filled with good-night kisses and shared laughter.

Julie's tears fell in torrents.

"There now, you'll make yourself ill," James Mathison said, smiling over Julie's head into his wife's shimmering eyes. "Let your mother take care of dinner, and trust the good Lord to take care of the matter of the stolen money."

At the mention of "the good Lord," Julie suddenly stiffened, then she dashed from the room, calling over her shoulder that she'd be back to set the table for dinner.

In the stunned silence that followed her abrupt, peculiar departure, Reverend Mathison said worriedly, "She shouldn't be going anywhere right now. She's still very upset, and it'll be dark in a bit. Carl," he added, "follow her and see what on earth she's up to."

"I'll go, too," Ted said, already yanking his jacket from the closet.

Two blocks from the house, Julie grabbed the freezing brass door handles and managed to drag open the heavy doors of the church where her foster father was pastor. Pale winter light shown through the high windows as she walked down the center aisle and stopped at the front. Awkwardly uncertain of exactly how to proceed in these circumstances, she raised her shining eyes to the wooden cross. After a moment, she said in a shy little voice, "Thanks a million for making the Mathisons believe me. I mean, I know You're the One who made them do it, because it's a real-life miracle. You won't be sorry," she promised. "I'm going to be so perfect that I'll make everybody proud." She turned, then turned back again. "Oh, and if You have the time, could you make sure Mr. Duncan finds out who really stole that money? Otherwise, I'm going to take the rap for it anyway, and that's not fair."

That night, after dinner, Julie cleaned her bedroom, which she already kept neat as a pin, from top to bottom; when she took her bath, she washed behind her ears twice. She was so determined to be perfect that when Ted and Carl invited her join them in a game of Scrabble before bedtime—a game they played at her level in order to help her practice her reading skills, she did not even *consider* peeking at the bottom of the tiles so she could choose letters she was most able to use.

On Monday of the following week, Billy Nesbitt, a seventh grader, was caught with a six-pack of beer that he was generously sharing with several friends under the school bleachers during the noon hour. Stuffed in the empty six-pack carton was a distinctive tan envelope with the words "Lunch Money— Miss Abbott's Class" written on it in Julie's teacher's handwriting.

Julie received a formal apology in front of her classmates from her teacher and a more grudging private one from the dour-faced Mr. Duncan.

That afternoon, Julie got off the school bus in front of the church and spent fifteen minutes inside it, then she ran the rest of the way home to share her news. Bursting into the house, red-faced from the icy weather, desperately eager to offer the hard proof that would completely exonerate her from theft, she raced into the kitchen where Mary Mathison was preparing dinner. "I can prove I didn't take the lunch money!" she panted, looking expectantly from her mother to her brothers.

Mary Mathison glanced at her with a puzzled smile, then continued peeling carrots at the sink; Carl scarcely looked up from the floor plan of a house he was drawing for his Future Architects of America project at school; and Ted gave her an absentminded grin and continued reading the movie magazine with Zack Benedict on the cover of it. "We know you didn't take their money, honey," Mrs. Mathison finally replied. "You said you didn't."

"That's right. You told us you didn't," Ted reminded her, turning the page of his magazine.

"Yes, but—but I can make you really believe it. I mean I can *prove* it!" she cried, looking from one bland face to another.

Mrs. Mathison laid the carrots aside and began to unfasten Julie's jacket. With a gentle smile, she said, "You already did prove it—you gave us your word, remember?"

"Yes, but my word isn't like real proof. It isn't good enough."

Mrs. Mathison looked straight into Julie's eyes. "Yes, Julie," she said with gentle firmness, "it is. Absolutely." Unfastening the first button on Julie's quilted jacket, she added, "If you're always as honest with everyone as you are with us, your word will soon be proof enough for the entire world."

"Billy Nesbitt swiped the money to buy beer for his friends," Julie said in obstinate protest to this anticlimax. And then, because she couldn't stop herself, she said, "How do you *know* I'll always tell you the truth and not swipe stuff anymore either?"

"We know that because we know *you*," her foster mother said emphatically. "We know you and we trust you and we love you."

"Yes, brat, we do," Ted put in with a grin.

"Yep, we do," Carl echoed, looking up from his project and nodding.

To her horror, Julie felt tears sting her eyes, and she hastily turned aside, but that day marked an irrevocable turning point in her life. The Mathisons had offered their home and trust and love to *her,* not to some other lucky child. This wondrous, warm family was hers forever, not just awhile. They knew all about her, and they *still* loved her.

Julie basked in that newfound knowledge; she blossomed in its warmth like a tender bloom opening its petals to the sunlight. She threw herself into her schoolwork with even more determination and surprised herself with how easily she was able to learn. When summer came, she asked to go to summer school so she could make up more missed classwork.

The following winter, Julie was summoned into the living room where she opened her very first gift-wrapped birthday presents while her beaming family looked on. When the last package had been opened and the last piece of torn gift wrap picked up, James and Mary Mathison and Ted and Carl gave her the most exquisite gift of all.

It came in a large, inauspicious-looking brown envelope. Inside was a long sheet of paper with elaborate black printing on the top that read, PETITION FOR ADOPTION.

Julie looked at them through eyes swimming with tears, the paper clutched against her chest. "Me?" she breathed.

Ted and Carl misinterpreted the reason for her tears and started talking at the same time, their voices filled with anxiety. "We, all of us, just wanted to make it official, Julie, that's all, so your name could be Mathison like ours," Carl said, and Ted added, "I mean, like, if you aren't sure it's a good idea, you don't have to go along with it—" He stopped as Julie hurtled herself into his arms, nearly knocking him over.

"I'm sure," she squealed in delight. "I'm sure, I'm sure, I'm sure!"

Nothing could dim her pleasure. That night, when her brothers invited her to go to the movies with a group of their friends to see their hero, Zack Benedict, she agreed instantly, even though she couldn't see why her brothers thought he was so neat. Wrapped in joy, she sat in the third row at the Bijou Theater with her brothers on either side of her, their shoulders dwarfing hers, absently watching a movie featuring a tall, dark-haired guy who didn't do much of anything except race motorcycles, get into fistfights, and look bored and kind of . . . cold.

"What did you think of the movie? Isn't Zack Benedict cool?" Ted asked her as they left the theater with a crowd of teenagers who were generally saying the same thing Ted had just said.

Julie's dedication to total honesty won by a very narrow margin over her desire to agree with her wonderful brothers about everything. "He's . . . well . . . he seems sort of *old*," she said, looking for support to the three teenage girls who'd gone to the movies with them.

Ted looked thunderstruck. "Old! He's only twenty-one, but he's really lived! I mean, I read in a movie magazine that he's been on his own since he was six years old, living out West, working on ranches to earn his keep. You know—breaking horses. Later he rode in rodeos. For a while, he belonged to a motorcycle gang . . . riding around the country. Zack Benedict," Ted finished on a wistful note, "is a man's man."

"Yes, but he looks . . . cold," Julie argued. "Cold and sort of mean, too."

The girls laughed out loud at what had seemed a reasonable criticism to Julie. "Julie," Laurie Paulson said, giggling, "Zachary Benedict is absolutely gorgeous and totally sexy. Everyone thinks so."

Julie, who knew that Carl had a secret crush on Laurie Parker, instantly and loyally said, "Well, I don't think so. I don't like his eyes. They're brown and mean-looking."

"His eyes aren't brown, they're *golden*. He has incredible sexy eyes, ask anybody!"

"Julie isn't a good judge of stuff like that," Carl intervened, turning away from his secret love and walking beside Ted as they headed home. "She's too young."

"I'm not too young to know," Julie argued smugly as she tucked her small hands in the crooks of both their elbows, "that Zack Benedict isn't nearly as handsome as you two!"

At that piece of flattery, Carl flashed a superior grin over his shoulder at Laurie Paulsen and amended, "Julie is very *mature* for her age, though."

Ted was still absorbed in the wonderous life of his movie hero. "Imagine being on your own as a kid, working on a ranch, riding horses, roping steers . . ."

4

1988

"MOVE THOSE DAMNED STEERS OUT OF HERE, THE STENCH IS enough to gag a corpse!" Seated on a black canvas chair with the word DIRECTOR stenciled in white above his name, Zachary Benedict snapped the order and glowered at the cattle moving around in a temporary pen near a sprawling, modernistic ranch house, then he continued making notes on his script. Located forty miles from Dallas, the luxurious residence with its tree-lined drive, lavish riding stable, and fields dotted with oil wells had been leased from a Texas billionaire for use in a movie called *Destiny*, a movie that, according to *Variety*, was likely to win Zack another Academy Award for Best Actor as well as one for Best Director—assuming he ever managed to complete the picture that everyone was calling jinxed.

Until last night, Zack had thought things couldn't possibly get worse: Originally budgeted at $45 million with four months allotted for filming it, *Destiny* was now one month behind schedule and $7 million over budget, owing to an extraordinary number of bizarre production problems and accidents that had plagued it almost from the day shooting began.

Now, after months of delays and disasters, there were only two scenes remaining to be filmed, but the elated satisfaction Zack should have felt was completely obliterated by a raging fury that he could hardly contain as he tried ineffectually to concentrate on the changes he wanted to make in the next scene.

Off to his right, near the main road, a camera was being moved into position to capture what promised to be a fiery sunset with the Dallas skyline outlined on the distant horizon. Through the open doors of the stable, Zack could see grips positioning bales of hay and best boys scrambling up in the beams and adjusting lights, while the cameraman called directions to them. Beyond the stable, well out of the camera's range, two stuntmen were moving automobiles bearing Texas State Highway Patrol insignias into place for a chase scene that would be shot tomorrow. At the perimeter of the lawn beneath a stand of oak trees, trailers reserved for the main cast members were drawn into a large semicircle, their blinds closed, their air conditioners laboring in the battle against the relentless July heat. Beside them the caterer's trucks were doing a land-office business dispensing cold drinks to sweating crew members and overheated actors.

The cast and crew were all seasoned pros, accustomed to standing around and waiting for hours in order to be on hand for a few minutes of shooting. Ordinarily, the atmosphere was convivial, and on the day before a final wrap, it was usually downright buoyant. Normally, the same people who were standing in uneasy groups near the catering trucks would have been hanging around Zack, joking about the trials they'd endured together or talking enthusiastically about a wrap party tomorrow night to celebrate the end of shooting. After what had happened last night, however, no one was talking to him if they could avoid it, and no one was expecting a party.

Today, all thirty-eight members of the Dallas cast and crew were giving him a conspicuously wide, watchful berth, and all of them were dreading the next few hours. As a result, instructions that were normally given in reasonable tones were being rapped out with taut impatience by anyone in a position to give them;

directions that were normally carried out with alacrity were being followed with the clumsy inaccuracy that comes when people are nervously eager to finish something.

Zack could almost feel the emotions emanating from everyone around him; the sympathy from those who liked him, the satisfied derision from those who either didn't like him or were friends of his wife, the avid curiosity from those who had no feelings for either of them.

Belatedly realizing that no one had heard his order to move the cattle, he looked around for the assistant director and saw him standing on the lawn, his hands on his hips and his head tipped back, watching one of the helicopters lift off for a routine run to the Dallas lab where each day's film was taken for processing. Beneath the helicopter, a typhoon of dirt and dust swirled and spread out, sending a fresh blast of hot gritty wind laced with the odor of fresh cow manure straight at Zack. "Tommy!" he called in an irritated shout.

Tommy Newton turned and trotted forward, brushing dust off his khaki shorts. Short of stature with thinning brown hair, hazel eyes, and wire-rimmed glasses, the thirty-five-year-old assistant director had a studious appearance that belied an irrepressible sense of humor and indefatigable energy. Today, however, not even Tommy could manage a lighthearted tone. Pulling his clip board from beneath his arm in case he needed to make notes, he said, "Did you call me?"

Without bothering to look up, Zack said curtly, "Have someone move those steers downwind."

"Sure, Zack." Touching the volume control on the transmitter at his waist, Tommy moved the mouthpiece of his headset into place and spoke to Doug Furlough, the key grip, who was supervising his crew while they set up a breakaway corral fence around the stable for tomorrow's final shot. "Doug," Tommy said into the mouthpiece.

"Yeah, Tommy?"

"Ask those ranch hands down by the pen to move the steers into the south pasture."

"I thought Zack wanted them in the next shot."

"He's changed his mind."

"Okay, I'll take care of it. Can we start striking the set in the house, or does he want it left alone?"

Tommy hesitated, looked at Zack, and repeated the question.

"Leave it alone," Zack answered curtly. "Don't touch it until after I've seen the dailies tomorrow. If there's a problem with them, I don't want to spend more than ten minutes setting up for another take."

After relaying the answer to Doug Furlough, Tommy started to turn away, then he hesitated. "Zack," he said somberly, "you probably aren't in the mood to hear this right now, but things are going to be pretty . . . hectic . . . tonight, and I may not have another chance to say it."

Forcing himself to appear interested, Zack looked up as Tommy continued haltingly. "You deserve another pair of Oscars for this picture. Several of the performances you've given in it—and forced out of Rachel and Tony—have raised goose bumps on the whole crew, and that's no exaggeration."

The mere mention of his wife's name, particularly in connection with Tony Austin, sent Zack's temper to the boiling point, and he stood up abruptly, script in hand. "I appreciate the compliment," he lied. "It won't be dark enough to shoot the next scene for another hour. When everything's ready in the stable, give the crew a dinner break, and I'll check it out. In the meantime, I'm going to get something to drink and go someplace where I can concentrate." Nodding toward the cluster of oak trees at the edge of the lawn, he added, "I'll be over there if you need me."

He was heading for the catering trucks when the door of Rachel's trailer opened and she walked out at the same moment Zack passed the steps. Their eyes clashed, conversations ground to a taut halt, heads swiveled, and expectation crackled in the air like heat lightening, but Zack merely moved around his wife and continued on, pausing at the catering truck to talk to Tommy Newton's assistant and to exchange pleasantries with two of the stuntmen. It was an Academy Award performance on his part, requiring a supreme force of will, because he couldn't see Rachel without remembering her as she'd been last night when he returned unexpectedly to their suite at the Crescent Hotel and found her with Tony Austin . . .

Earlier in the day, he'd told her he intended to have a late meeting with the camera crew and assistant directors to go over some new ideas and that he planned to sleep in his trailer on the set afterward. When the crew gathered in his trailer for the meeting, however, Zack realized he'd left his notes at his Dallas hotel, and rather than sending someone for them, he decided to save time by inviting them all back to the Crescent with him. In an unusually lighthearted mood because the end was finally in sight, the six men had walked into the darkened suite, and Zack flipped on the lights.

"Zack!" Rachel cried, rolling off the naked man she was straddling on the sofa and grabbing for her peignoir, her eyes wild with shock. Tony Austin, who was costarring with her and Zack in *Destiny*, jackknifed into a sitting position. "Now, Zack, stay calm—" he pleaded, leaping to his feet and scurrying behind the circular sofa as Zack started forward. "Don't touch my face," he warned in a rising shout just as Zack launched himself over the back of the sofa. "I'm in two more scenes and—" It took all five crew members to pull Zack off him.

"Zack, don't be insane!" the head gaffer cried, trying to restrain him. "He can't finish the goddamned picture if you ruin his face!" Doug Furlough panted, holding Zack's arms.

Zack flung both the smaller men off, and with icy, deliberate calculation, he broke two of Tony's ribs before they could restrain him again. Panting more from rage than exertion, Zack watched them all help the naked, limping Austin out of the suite, forming a circle around him. A half-dozen hotel guests were standing in the hall beyond the open doors, drawn, no doubt, by Rachel's screams at Zack to stop. Stalking forward, Zack slammed the door in their faces.

Rounding on Rachel, who'd wrapped a peach satin peignoir around herself, he started forward, trying to control the urge to do physical violence to her, too. "Get out of my sight!" he warned her as she backed away from him. "Get out or I won't be responsible for what I do to you!"

"Don't you dare threaten me, you arrogant son of a bitch!" she shot back with so much contemptuous triumph that it checked him in midstride. "If you lay one finger on me, my divorce attorneys won't just settle for one-half of everything you have, I'll take it *all!* Do you understand me, Zack? I'm divorcing you. My attorneys are filing the papers in L.A. tomorrow. Tony and I are getting married!"

The realization that his wife and her lover had been screwing each other behind his back while calmly plotting to live on the money Zack had worked so hard to acquire snapped his control. He grabbed her arms and shoved her hard toward the living room door. "I'll kill you before I let you take half of anything! Now get out."

She stumbled to her knees, then stood up, her hand on the doorknob, her face a mask of jubilant loathing as she fired her parting shot: "If you're thinking of keeping either Tony or me off the set tomorrow, don't bother trying. You're just the director. The studio has a fortune wrapped up in this film. They'll force you to finish it, and they'll sue your ass off if you do anything to delay it or sabotage it. Just think," she finished with a malicious smile as she yanked open the door, "either way, you lose. If you don't finish the picture, you'll be ruined. If you do, I'm going to get half of what you make!" The door crashed into its frame behind her.

She was right about finishing *Destiny.* Even in his infuriated state, Zack knew it. There were only two more scenes left to shoot, and Rachel and Tony were in one of them. Zack had no choice except to tolerate his adulterous wife and her lover while he directed their scene. He walked over to the bar and poured himself a stiff Scotch, tossed it down, and poured another. Carrying his glass, he walked over to the windows and stared out at the glittering Dallas skyline while the rage and pain he'd felt began to subside. He'd phone his attorneys in the morning and instruct them to proceed with divorce negotiations on his terms, not hers, he decided. Although he'd amassed a sizable fortune as an actor, he'd multiplied it many times over through astute investments, and those investments were carefully guarded by a series of complicated trusts and legalities that should protect most of his assets from Rachel. Zack's hand relaxed its death grip on the glass he was holding. He was under control now; he would survive this and go on. He knew he could—and would. He knew it, because long ago, at the age of eighteen, he had faced a far more agonizing betrayal than Rachel's, and he had discovered that he possessed the capacity to walk away from anyone who betrayed him and never, ever look back.

Turning from the windows, he went into the bedroom, pulled Rachel's suitcases out of the closet, and stuffed all her clothes into them, then he picked up the telephone beside the bed. "Send a bellman up to the Royal Suite," he told the switchboard operator. When the bellman arrived a few minutes later, Zack thrust the cases with her clothing dangling out the sides at him. "Take these to Mr. Austin's suite."

At that moment, if Rachel had returned and begged him to take her back, if she'd been able to *prove* to him that she'd been drugged out of her mind and hadn't known what she was doing or saying, it would have been too late, even if he believed her.

Because she was already dead to him.

As dead to him as the grandmother he'd once loved and the sister and the brother. It had taken a concentrated effort to eradicate them from his heart and mind, but he'd done it.

5

PULLING HIS MIND FROM RECOLLECTIONS OF LAST NIGHT, ZACK sat down beneath a tree where he could see what was going on without being observed himself. Drawing his knee up, he rested his wrist against it and watched Rachel walking into Tony Austin's trailer. This morning's newscasts were filled with lurid details of the scene in the suite and the fight that followed it, details that were undoubtedly provided by the hotel guests who'd witnessed it. Now the press had descended on the area where they were shooting, and Zack's security people had their hands full trying to keep them at the gate near the main road with promises of a statement later. Rachel and Tony had already given statements, but Zack had no intention of saying a single word to them. He was as icily indifferent to having the press at his "doorstep" as he was to the news he'd gotten this morning that Rachel's attorneys had filed for divorce in Los Angeles. The only thing that was tearing at his control was the knowledge that he had to direct one remaining scene between Tony and Rachel before they could wrap tonight—a steamy, violently sensual scene—and he didn't know how he was going to stomach that, particularly with the entire crew looking on.

Once he got over that hurdle though, putting Rachel out of his life was going to be much easier than he'd thought last night, because, he admitted to himself, whatever he'd felt for her when they were married three years ago had vanished shortly afterward. Since then, they'd been nothing but a sexual and social convenience for each other. Without Rachel, his life was going to seem no emptier, no more meaningless or superficial than it had seemed for most of the past ten years.

Frowning at that thought, Zack watched a tiny insect make its arduous way up a blade of grass near his hip, and he wondered why his own life frequently seemed so frustratingly aimless to him, without important purpose or deep gratification. He hadn't always felt like this, though, Zack remembered . . .

When he arrived in Los Angeles in Charlie Murdock's truck, survival itself had been a challenge, and the job he'd gotten on the loading docks at Empire Studios with Charlie's help had seemed like an enormous triumph. A month later, a director who was shooting a low-budget picture on the back lot about a gang of inner-city thugs that terrorized a suburban high school decided he needed a few more faces in a crowd scene, and he recruited Zack. The part required only that Zack lean against a brick wall, looking aloof and tough. The extra money he'd made that day had seemed like a boon. So had the director's announcement several days later when he sent for him: "Zack, my boy, you have something we call presence. The camera loves you. On film, you come across like a moody, modern-day James Dean, only you're taller and better-looking than he was. You stole that scene you were in just by standing there. If you can act, I'll cast you in a Western we're going to start shooting. Oh—and you'll need to get a waiver from the union."

It wasn't the prospect of being in a movie that really excited Zack, it was the salary he was offered. So he got a waiver from SAG and learned to act.

Actually, acting hadn't been all that difficult for him. For one thing, he'd been "acting" for years before he left his grandmother's house, pretending things didn't matter when they did; for another, he was totally dedicated to a goal: He was determined to prove to his grandmother and everyone else in Ridgemont that he could survive on his own and prosper on a grand scale. To achieve that goal, he was prepared to do almost anything, no matter how much effort it required.

Ridgemont was a little city, and there'd been no doubt in Zack's mind that the details of his ignominious departure were common knowledge within hours after he left his grandmother's house on foot. When his first two movies were released, he went through every piece of fan mail, hoping that someone he used to know would have recognized him. But if they did, they didn't bother to write.

For a while after that, he fantasized about returning to Ridgemont with enough money to buy Stanhope Industries and run it, but by the time he was twenty-five and had amassed enough money to buy the company, he'd also matured enough to realize that buying the whole goddamned city and everything in it wouldn't change a thing. By then he'd already won an Oscar, gotten his degree from USC, been hailed as a prodigy, and called a "Legend in the Making." He had his choice of staring roles, a fortune in the bank, and a future virtually guaranteed to be even more spectacular.

He'd proven to everyone that Zachary Benedict could survive and prosper on the grandest of scales. He had nothing else to strive for, nothing left to prove, and the lack of both left him feeling strangely deflated and empty.

Deprived of his former goals, Zack looked elsewhere for gratification. He built mansions, bought yachts, and drove race cars; he escorted beautiful women to glittering social functions, and then he took them to bed. He enjoyed their bodies and often their company, but he never took them seriously and they rarely expected it. Zack had become a sexual trophy, sought after solely for the prestige of sleeping with him and, in the case of actresses, coveted for the influence and connections he had. Like all the superstars and sex symbols before him, he was also a victim of his own success: He could not step off an elevator or eat in a restaurant without being accosted by adoring fans; women shoved hotel room keys into his hand and bribed clerks to let them into his suite. Producers' wives invited him to their homes for weekend parties and slipped out of their husbands' beds to climb into his.

Although he frequently availed himself of the banquet of sexual and social opportunities spread out before him, there was a part of him—his conscience or some latent streak of conventional Yankee morality—that was revolted by the promiscuity and superficiality, the junkies and sycophants and narcissists, everything that made Hollywood seem like a human sewer, a sewer that had been sanitized and deodorized to protect the public's sensibilities.

He woke up one morning and suddenly couldn't tolerate it any longer. He was tired of meaningless sex, bored with loud parties, sick of neurotic actresses and ambitious starlets, and completely disgusted with the life he'd been living.

He started looking for a different way to fill the void in his days, for a new challenge and a better reason to exist. Acting was no longer much challenge, so he turned his thoughts to directing instead. If he failed as a director, he'd be a very public flop, but even the risk of laying his reputation on the line had a stimulating effect. The idea of directing a film, which had been hovering on the fringes of his consciousness long before that, became his new goal, and Zack pursued it with all the single-minded determination he'd devoted to achieving his others. Empire's president, Irwin Levine, tried to talk him out of it, he pleaded and reasoned and wheedled, but in the end he capitulated, as Zack had known he would.

The movie Levine gave him to direct was a low-budget thriller called *Nightmare* that had two leading roles, one for a nine-year-old child, another for a woman. For the role of the child, Empire insisted on Emily McDaniels, a former child star with Shirley Temple dimples who was almost thirteen but looked nine and was still under contract to them. Emily's career was already on the downslide; so was the career of a glamorous blonde named Rachel Evans, who they cast in the other role. In her prior films, Rachel Evans had only minor parts, and none of them showed much acting ability.

Zack's studio had foisted both females off on him for the patently transparent reason that they wanted to teach him a lesson—that acting was his forte, not directing. The film was virtually guaranteed to barely earn back its investment and, the studio executives hoped, simultaneously put an end to their most famous star's desire to waste his money-making potential behind the cameras.

Zack had known all that, but it hadn't stopped him. Before they went into production, he spent weeks looking at Rachel's and Emily's old films in his screening room at home, and he knew there were moments—brief moments—when Rachel Evans actually showed some genuine talent. Moments when Emily's "cuteness," which had faded with her adolescence, was replaced by a charming sweetness that spoke to the camera because it was genuine.

Zack coaxed and dragged all of that and much more out of his two female leads during the eight weeks they were in production. His own determination to succeed transmitted itself to both of them, his sense of timing and lighting had helped too, but mostly it was his intuitive knack of knowing how to use Emily and Rachel to their best advantage.

Rachel had been furious over his badgering and the endless numbers of takes he made her do for each scene, but when he showed her the first week's rushes, she'd looked at him with awe in her wide green eyes and said softly, "Thank you, Zack. For the first time in my life, it actually looks as if I can really, really act."

"And it also looks as if I can really, really direct," he'd teased, but he was relieved and he let it show.

Rachel was amazed. "You mean you've had doubts about it? I thought you were totally sure of everything we've done!"

"Actually, I haven't had a peaceful night's sleep since we started shooting," Zack confessed. It was the first time in years he'd dared to admit to anyone that he had any misgivings about his work, but that day was special. He'd just seen proof that he had a talent for directing. Furthermore, that newly discovered talent was going to dramatically brighten the future of a winsome child named Emily McDaniels when the critics saw her superb performance in *Nightmare*. Zack was so fond of Emily that working with her had made him long for a child of his own. Watching the closeness and laughter she shared with her father, who stayed on the set to look after her, Zack had suddenly realized he wanted a family. *That* was what was missing from his life—a wife and children to share his successes, to laugh with and strive for.

Rachel and he celebrated that night with a late dinner served by his houseboy. The mood of shared candor that had begun earlier when they'd admitted their private doubts about their individual abilities led to a relaxed intimacy that, on Zack's part, was as unprecedented as it was therapeutic. Seated in his living room in Pacific Palisades in front of the two-story glass wall that looked out over the ocean, they talked for hours, but not about "the business," which came as a welcome change to Zack, who'd despaired of meeting an actress who could concentrate on anything else. They ended up in his bed where they further indulged themselves with a night of highly pleasurable and inventive lovemaking. Rachel's passion seemed genuine rather than a repayment for making her look good on film, and that pleased him, too. In fact, he was thoroughly contented with everything as they lay in his bed—the rushes, Rachel's sensuality, her intelligence, and her wit.

Beside him, she levered herself up on her elbows. "Zack, what do you really want from life? I mean, *really* want?"

For a moment, he stayed silent, and then perhaps because he was weak from hours of intercourse or perhaps because he was sick of pretending that the life he'd carved for himself was exactly what he wanted, he answered with only a touch of derision, "Little House on the Prairie."

"What? You mean, you want to star in a movie sequel to 'Little House on the Prairie'?"

"No, I mean I want to *live* it. The house doesn't have to be on the prairie, though. I've been thinking about a ranch in the mountains somewhere."

She burst out laughing. "A ranch! You hate horses and you despise cattle, everyone knows it. Tommy Newton told me so," she said, referring to *Nightmare*'s fledgling assistant director. "He worked as a grip on the first Western you made when you were a kid—the one where Michelle Pfeiffer played your girlfriend." Smiling, she rubbed her finger across his lips. "What have you got against horses and cattle anyway?"

He gave her finger a playful nip and said, "They don't take direction worth a damn, and they stampede in the wrong direction. That's what happened in that first picture—the steers turned and headed right for us."

"Michelle says you saved her life that day. You picked her up and carried her to safety."

Zack tipped his chin down and grinned. "I *had* to," he joked. "I was running like hell for the rocks, and the steers were right behind me. Michelle was in my path. I picked her up to get her out of my way."

"Don't be so modest. She said she was running for her life and screaming for someone to help her."

"So was I," he teased. Sobering, he added, "We were both kids back then. It seems like a hundred years ago."

She shifted onto her side and stretched out beside him, her finger tracing an enticing path from his shoulder to his navel, then stopping. "Where are you really from? And please do not give me all that studio bullshit about growing up on your own and riding in the rodeo circuit and hanging around with motorcycle gangs."

Zack's candid mood did not extend to discussing his past. He had never done so before, nor would he ever. When he was eighteen and the studio publicity department wanted to know about that, he'd coolly told them to invent one for him, which they had. His real past was dead, and the discussion of it was off limits. His evasive tone made that emphatically clear. "I'm not from anyplace special."

"But you're no vagabond kid who grew up without knowing which fork to use, that much I do know," she persisted. "Tommy Newton told me that even when you were eighteen, you already had a lot of class, a lot of 'social polish,' he called it. That's all he knows about you, and he's worked with you on several films. None of the women who've worked with you know anything either. Glenn Close and Goldie Hawn, Lauren Hutton and Meryl Streep—they all say you're wonderful to work with, but you keep your private life to yourself. I know, because I've asked them."

Zack made no attempt to hide his displeasure. "If you think you're flattering me with all your curiosity, you're wrong."

"I can't help it," she laughed, pressing a kiss to his jaw, "You're every woman's fantasy lover, Mr. Benedict, and you're also Hollywood's mystery man. It's a well-known fact that none of the women who've preceded me in this bed of yours have gotten you to do any talking about anything really personal. Since I happen to be in this bed with you, and since you've talked to me tonight about a lot of things that *are* personal, I figure I'm either catching you at a weak moment, or that . . . just maybe . . . you like me better than the others. Either way, I have to try to discover something about you that no other woman has found out. It's my feminine pride that's at stake here, you understand."

Her jaunty bluntness reduced Zack's annoyance to exasperated amusement. "If you want me to keep liking you better than the others," he said half-seriously, "then stop prying and talk about something more pleasant."

"Pleasant . . ." She draped herself across his chest and smiled teasingly into his eyes as she threaded her fingers through the mat of hair on his chest. Based on her body language, Zack expected her to say something suggestive, but the topic she chose startled a surprised chuckle from him: "Let's see . . . I know you hate horses, but you like motorcycles and fast cars. Why?"

"Because," he teased, threading his fingers through hers, "*they* do not gather into herds with their friends when you leave them parked and then try to run you down when you turn your back. *They* go where you point them."

"Zack," she whispered, lowering her mouth to his, "Motorcycles aren't the only things that go where you point them. I do, too."

Zack knew exactly what she meant. He pointed. She moved lower and bent her head.

The next morning, she cooked him breakfast. "I'd like to make one more picture—a big one—to prove to the world I can really act," she said while she popped English muffins into the oven.

Sated and relaxed, Zack watched her moving around his kitchen in pleated slacks and a shirt knotted at the midriff. Devoid of sexy clothes and extravagant makeup, she was far more appealing and infinitely lovelier to him. As he'd already discovered, she was also intelligent, sensual, and witty. "Then what?" he asked.

"Then I'd like to quit. I'm thirty. Like you, I want a real life, a meaningful life with something more to think about than my figure and whether or not I'm getting a wrinkle. There's more to life than this glossy, superficial fantasyland we inhabit and perpetrate on the rest of the world."

An unprecedented statement like that from an actress made Rachel an unexpected breath of fresh air to him. Moreover, since she was planning to stop working, it seemed as if he'd actually met a woman who was interested in him, not in what he could do for her career. He was thinking of that when Rachel leaned over his kitchen table and softly said, "How do my dreams compare with yours?"

She was making him an offer, Zack realized, and doing it with quiet courage and no games. He studied her in silence for a moment and then made no attempt to hide the emphatic importance he was placing on his next question. "Do you have children in your dreams, Rachel?"

Sweetly and without hesitation, she said, "Your children?"

"My children."

"Can we start now?"

Zack burst out laughing at her unexpected reply, then she plopped onto his lap and his laughter faded, replaced by stirrings of tenderness and a vibrant hope, emotions he thought had died when he was eighteen. His hands slid under her shirt, and tenderness merged with passion.

They were married in the graceful gazebo on the lawn of Zack's Carmel estate four months later, while a thousand invited guests, including several governors and senators, looked on. Also present, although uninvited, were dozens of helicopters that hovered overhead, their blades creating cyclones on the lawn that whipped up women's gowns and dislodged toupees, while the reporters who occupied the choppers aimed cameras at the festivities below. Zack's best man was his neighbor in Carmel, industrialist Matthew Farrell, who came up with a solution to the invasion of the press: Glowering at the helicopters hovering frantically overhead, he said, "They ought to repeal the damned First Amendment."

Zack grinned. It was his wedding day, and he was in a rare mood of utter conviviality and quiet optimism, already envisioning cozy evenings with children on his lap and the sort of family life he'd never known. Rachel had wanted this big wedding, and he had wanted to give it to her, although he'd have preferred flying to Tahoe with just a couple of friends. "I could always send someone to the house for some rifles," he joked.

"Good idea. We'll use the gazebo for a bunker and shoot the bastards down."

The two men laughed, then they fell into a companionable silence. They'd met three years ago when a group of Zack's fans climbed the security fence around his house and set off the security systems at both residences as they fled. That night, Zack and Matt had discovered they shared several things in common, including a liking for rare Scotch, a tendency toward ruthless bluntness, an intolerance of pretension, and, later, a similar philosophy toward financial investments. As a result, they were not only friends, they were also partners in several business ventures.

* * *

When *Nightmare* was released, it didn't receive an Oscar or even a nomination, but it made a healthy profit, received excellent reviews, and completely revived Emily's and Rachel's faltering careers. Emily's gratitude was boundless and so was her father's. Rachel, however, abruptly discovered she was not at all ready to give up her career, nor was she ready to have the baby Zack had wanted so badly. The career she'd claimed she didn't want was, in fact, an obsession that consumed her. She could not bear to miss an "important" party or ignore an opportunity for publicity no matter how minor, and she kept Zack's household staff, his secretary, and his publicist in an uproar as they tried to cope with her social demands and cover up her more outrageous publicity ploys. She was so desperate for fame and acclaim that she despised any actress who was better known than herself and so pathetically insecure about her own ability that she was afraid to work in any picture unless Zack directed it.

The optimism Zack had experienced on his wedding day collapsed under the weight of reality: He'd been gulled into marriage by a clever, ambitious actress who believed that he alone held the key to fame and fortune for her. Zack knew it, but he blamed himself even more than he blamed Rachel. Ambition had caused her to marry him, and Zack could empathize with her motive, even if he didn't admire her methods because he, too, had once felt driven to prove himself. He, on the other hand, had been compelled to commit matrimony out of an uncharacteristic and embarrassingly naive streak that had actually let him believe, albeit briefly, in a cozy picture of devoted spouses and rosy-cheeked, happy children clamoring for bedtime stories. As he should have known from his own youth and experience, such families were a myth perpetrated by poets and movie producers. Faced with that realization, Zack's life seemed to stretch before him like a monotonous plateau.

Among those in Hollywood afflicted with a similar case of ennui, the prescribed solution was a line of coke, a variety of drugs, legal and otherwise, or else a bottle of liquor taken twice daily. Zack, however, possessed his grandmother's contempt for weakness, and he scorned such emotional crutches. He solved his problem in the only way he knew how: Each morning, he immersed himself in his work, and he kept at it until he finally dropped into bed at night. Rather than divorcing Rachel, he rationalized that, although his marriage was not idyllic, it was far better than his grandparents' had been and no worse than many other marriages he'd seen. And so he offered her a choice: She could either get a divorce, or she could curb her ambitions and settle down, and he in turn would grant her wish and direct her in another picture. Rachel wisely and gratefully accepted the latter offer, and Zack increased his hectic schedule in order to keep his part of the bargain. After his success directing *Nightmare,*

Empire was eager to let him star in and direct any film of his choice. Zack found a script he loved for an action thriller called *Winner Take All,* with starring roles for himself and Rachel, and Empire put up the money. Using a combination of patience, cajolery, acid criticism, and an occasional show of icy temper, he manipulated Rachel and the rest of the film's cast until they gave him what he wanted, and then he manipulated the lighting and camera angles so they captured it.

The results were spectacular. Rachel received an Academy Award nomination for her role in *Winner Take All.* Zack won an Oscar for Best Actor and another for Best Director for his work in it. The latter award merely confirmed what Hollywood moguls had already noted: Zack had a genius for directing. He knew instinctively how to turn a suspenseful shot into a hair-raising scene that gave the audience chills, he could coax a belly laugh with what had been written as a mildly amusing remark, and he could steam up the movie screens with a love scene. Moreover, he could do it within the film's budget.

His two Oscars brought Zack tremendous satisfaction but no deep contentment. Zack didn't notice. He no longer expected or sought contentment, and he deliberately kept himself too busy to notice the lack of it. In his quest to stay challenged, he directed and starred in two more films during the next two years—an erotic action/thriller costarring with Glenn Close and an action/adventure movie in which he teamed up with Kim Bassinger.

He was fresh out of challenges and looking for a new one when he flew to Carmel to finalize a joint business venture that Matt Farrell was putting together. Late that night, he went looking for something to read and picked up a novel left there by an unknown houseguest. Long before he finished it at dawn, Zack knew *Destiny* was going to be his next picture.

The following day, he walked into the president's office at Empire Studios and handed the book to him. "Here's my next picture, Irwin."

Irwin Levine read the blurb on the book jacket, leaned back in his tall suede chair, and sighed. "This looks like heavy drama, Zack. I'd like to see you do something lighthearted for a change." Abruptly, he swung his chair around, picked up a script from the glass table behind his glass desk, and handed it to Zack with an eager smile. "Somebody passed me this script under the table. It's already got a buyer, but if you say you'll do it, we could try to negotiate for it. It's a romance. Good stuff. Fun. Nobody's made a film like this in decades, and I think the public's hungry for it. You're perfect for the lead and you could play the part in your sleep, it's so easy. Making it will be cheap and quick, but I've got a hunch the picture's going to be a runaway hit."

The script, which Zack agreed to read that night, turned out to be a fluffy, predictable romance where true love changes the life of a cynical tycoon who then lives happily ever after with his beautiful new wife. Zack hated it, partly because the lead role would require no effort from him at all, but mostly because it reminded him of the foolish fantasies about love and marriage he'd quietly cherished as a youth and acted on as an adult. The next morning, he tossed the script for *Pretty Woman* on Levine's desk and said disdainfully, "I'm not a good enough actor or a good enough director to make this tripe seem believable."

"You've become a cynic," Levine said, shaking his head and looking aggrieved. "I've known you since you were a kid, and I love you like my own son. I'm disappointed to see it happening to you. Very disappointed."

Zack responded to that sentimental crap by lifting his brows and saying absolutely nothing; Levine loved him like his own bank account, and he was disappointed because Zack wouldn't agree to do *Pretty Woman*. Levine didn't try to force the issue, however. The last time he'd done that, Zack had walked out of his office and made a movie for Paramount and another one for Universal.

"You were never a starry-eyed teenager," he said instead. "You were tough and realistic, but you weren't a total skeptic either. Ever since you married Rachel, you've been changing." He saw the flare of annoyance in Zack's face and hastily said, "Okay, enough sentimentality. Let's talk business. When do you want to start shooting *Destiny,* and who do you have in mind for the main roles?"

"I'll play the husband, and I'd like Diana Copeland for the wife if she's available. Rachel would be excellent for the mistress. Emily McDaniels for the daughter."

Levine's brows shot up. "Rachel's going to have one of her raging tantrums over getting the lesser female role."

"I'll deal with Rachel," Zack said. Rachel and Levine detested each other, although neither of them ever gave a reason. Zack suspected they'd had an affair years ago that ended badly.

"If you haven't already made up your mind about the part of the drifter," Levine continued after a hesitant pause, "I have a favor to ask. Would you consider Tony Austin for it?"

"Not a chance," Zack said flatly. Austin's addictions to booze and drugs were as legendary as his other vices, and he was totally unreliable. His last accidental overdose at the beginning of a picture he was making for Empire had landed him in a rehab center for six months, and another actor had to fill his role.

"Tony wants to go to work and prove himself," Levine continued patiently. "His doctors assure me he's kicked his habits and he's a new man. I'm inclined to believe them this time."

Zack shrugged. "What's different about this time?"

"Because this time when they rushed him into Cedars-Sinai, he was DOA. They brought him back, but the experience has finally scared the shit out of him and he's ready to grow up and get to work. I'd like to give him that chance, a new start." Levine's voice took on a pious note. "It's the only decent thing to do, Zack. We're all on this earth together. We have to take care of each other, look out for each other. We have to help Tony get work because he's broke and because—"

"And because he owes you a chunk of money for that picture he never finished," Zack speculated flatly.

"Well, yes, he is into us for a sizable amount of money for that picture," Levine reluctantly admitted. "He came to us though and asked to work off his debt so that he could prove himself. Since you seem to be invulnerable to an emotional appeal, consider the practical reasons to use him: Despite all his bad publicity, the public still adores him. He's their bad, misguided, beautiful boy, the man every woman wants to comfort."

Zack hesitated. If Austin was really a reformed man, he was perfect for the role. At thirty-three, his youthful, blond good looks had been marred by dissipation, which somehow only made him more appealing to women from twelve to ninety. Austin's name on a marquee was a guarantee of fabulous box office sales. So was Zack's; as a combination, they stood a chance of breaking some records. Since Zack intended to have a sizable piece of the profits as part of his price for making *Destiny,* that had a strong bearing on his decision. So did the fact that even when Austin was drunk he was a better actor than most, and he *was* perfect for the part. On the other hand, using Austin in this film would be a favor to Empire, and Zack intended to exact concessions from Empire in return. For that reason, he hid his enthusiasm for the idea and said only, "I'll let him read for the part, but I'm not crazy about being a baby-sitter for a junkie, reformed or otherwise. I'll have Dan Moyes call you in the morning," he added, referring to his agent as he arose to leave, "and the two of you can start working out the contractual details."

"This picture's going to cost a ransom to make, with all the locations it calls for," Irwin reminded him, already dreading the price Zack was bound to ask for starring in it and directing it, not to mention the favors he was likely to extract for using Austin in the film. Carefully hiding his enthusiasm for the project, he stood up and shook hands with Zack. "I'm only going along with this deal because you want to do it so badly. I'm personally going to be praying on my knees that it at least earns back what it costs to make."

Zack suppressed a knowing smile. The opening volley of contractual negotiations had just taken place over a handshake.

Diana Copeland turned down the role of Zack's wife because she had a prior commitment, so Zack gave the role to Rachel, who'd been his second choice. A few weeks later, Diana's plans changed, but by then, Zack had a moral, and legal, obligation to let Rachel keep the better role. To Zack's surprise, Diana asked for the lesser part of his former mistress instead. Emily McDaniels eagerly accepted the part of the teenage daughter and Tony Austin was given the part of the drifter. The minor roles were filled without difficulty, and Zack's favorite, hand-picked film crew was reunited as a team again to work on another of his films.

A month after shooting started on *Destiny*, the word was out that although the filming was plagued with accidents and delays, the rushes—the portions of the film that were sent to the lab for processing each day—were fantastic. The Hollywood gossip mill began to churn out premature predictions of Academy Award nominations.

6

A RUSTLING IN THE GRASS YANKED ZACK FROM HIS REVERIE and he looked over his shoulder to see Tommy Newton walking toward him in the deepening twilight. "The crew is on dinner break and everything's ready in the stable," he said.

Zack rolled to his feet. "Fine. I'll check it out." He'd already done that earlier today, but he didn't believe in leaving anything to chance, and besides, it gave him an excuse to avoid socializing with the others for a while longer. "We're not going to have a rehearsal tonight," he added. "We'll try for a take right from the beginning."

Tommy nodded. "I'll spread the word."

Inside the stable, Zack studied the setting for the last major scene. In the past months the story had come to life in front of the cameras, more vibrant and suspenseful than even he had believed it could be—a tale of a woman caught between her love for her daughter and the preoccupied tycoon she'd married and her passionate involvement with a handsome drifter, whose need for her had become a dangerous obsession. Zack had played the part of the seemingly neglectful husband, a man whose financial empire was collapsing and who considers making a deal with drug runners rather than see his wife and daughter deprived of their lifestyle. Emily McDaniels was the teenage daughter who cared nothing for the luxuries her parents provided and who only wanted more of their interest and attention. The plot was strong, but what really distinguished the story was the depth and richness of the character portrayals, the insight into human nature and needs, its weaknesses and strengths. There were no "bad guys" in *Destiny;* each character was portrayed in a way that Zack knew would have a powerful emotional effect on movie audiences.

Most of the scenes had been shot out of sequence as was the norm, but because of logistics, the last two scenes about to be filmed were actually the last two scenes of the movie itself. In the one they were about to shoot, Rachel meets her lover in the stable, where several of their past trysts have occurred. Forced to see him "just once more" because he has threatened to reveal their affair to her husband and daughter if she doesn't, Rachel hides a gun in the stable, which she intends to use to frighten him away. When he tries to force her to have sex with him, she threatens him with the gun, and, in the struggle that follows, they're both wounded. The scene was meant to be violently sexual and it was Zack's job as the director to make sure it was *very* sexy and *very* violent.

Looking around, he walked slowly down the corridor that divided the dimly lit stable in half lengthwise. Everything was exactly as he wanted it: The horses were in their stalls along the wall on his left, their noses poked inquiringly over half-doors as he strolled past. Bridles and riding crops hung on pegs on the opposite wall; saddles were on wooden racks; paraphernalia for grooming horses and cleaning tack was in its proper place on a table against the far wall outside the tack room.

The real focus of the scene, however, was on that table at the end of the corridor, beside some bales of hay, where the two protagonists would have their final struggle. The bales were in place, and the gun that would be used in the scene was lying on the table, hidden among the liniment bottles and grooming brushes. In the rafters above, a second camera was already aimed at the double doors to catch Emily when she rode into the stable after hearing the gunshot, and all the lights were positioned for maximum effect when turned on.

With his knee, Zack nudged the table an inch to the left, then he shifted a couple of bottles on it and moved the butt of the gun so that a glimpse of it would be in view of the camera, but he did it more out of restlessness than necessity. Sam Hudgins, the director of photography, and Linda Tompkins, the set dresser, had already done their usual impeccable job of translating Zack's ideas for a scene into an actual set that was perfectly arranged and complete in every detail creating exactly the effect Zack envisioned. Suddenly anxious to get started and get the ordeal over with, Zack turned and headed for the door, his footsteps echoing hollow on the gleaming floor tiles.

Huge floodlights illuminated the side yard where the crew was helping themselves from a buffet and eating at picnic tables or sitting on the grass. Tommy spotted Zack as soon as he walked into the lit area, and at Zack's nod, he called out, "All right everybody, ten more minutes, then we get started."

There was a flurry of movement as crew members stood up and headed toward the stable or went to the buffet table to grab another cold drink. In an effort to trim unnecessary expense from the swollen budget, Zack had kept only the essential crew here and sent everyone else back to the West Coast, including a second and third assistant director and several production assistants. Even without the extra help, Tommy Newton was managing to handle everything with little loss of efficiency.

Zack watched him send his only production assistant over to Austin's trailer, and a moment later, he saw Austin and Rachel both emerge from it, followed by their hairdressers and a makeup artist. Austin looked uneasy and slightly ill; Zack hoped his ribs were killing him. Rachel, on the other hand, walked right past the crew and Zack with her head proudly high—a queen who was accountable to no one. Emily McDaniels was pacing back and forth in front of her real-life father, practicing her lines with him. With her Shirley Temple dimples, she was sixteen years old and still looked little more than eleven. She glanced up just as Rachel walked past her, and her face froze with dislike, then she jerked her gaze back to her father and continued practicing her lines. Since Emily had originally liked Rachel very well, Zack attributed the child's sudden change in attitude to her loyalty to him, and he was momentarily touched by that. He was reaching for a roast beef sandwich from the buffet when Diana Copeland's soft, sympathetic voice startled him. "Zack?"

He turned, his brows drawing together in surprise. "What are you doing out here tonight? I thought you were leaving for L.A. this morning."

Clad in white shorts and a red halter top with her auburn hair in a French braid, she looked beautiful and uneasy. "I intended to, but when I heard about what happened last night at the hotel, I decided to stick around today and be on hand tonight."

"Why?" Zack asked bluntly.

"Two reasons," Diana said, trying desperately to make him understand that she was sincere. "One reason is to give you some moral support if you need it."

"I don't," Zack said politely. "What's the other reason?"

Diana looked at him, at the proud chiseled features, the striking amber eyes turning cool beneath thick black lashes, and she realized she'd made it sound as if she pitied him. Unnerved by his unwavering stare and prolonged silence, she finally burst out, "Look, I don't know how to say this . . . but I—I think Rachel is a fool. And if I can do anything to help, please let me. And, Zack," she finished with great feeling, "I—I'd work with you anytime, any place, in any role. I just wanted you to know that, too."

She watched as his unfathomable expression turned to grim amusement and she belatedly realized she'd now made it sound as if ambition was behind her avowals of sympathy.

"Thank you, Diana," he replied with such grave courtesy that she felt even more foolish. "Have your agent call me in a few months when I'm casting for another picture."

She watched him walk away, his strides long and sure, dark blue polo shirt emphasizing wide shoulders, khaki trousers clinging to narrow hips . . . a lithe, powerful body of hard sinew and rippling muscle, but with a lion's grace . . . a lion's eyes . . . a lion's aloof pride. The only thing that spoiled the analogy was his beautiful, thick hair, Diana thought wistfully. It was so dark it was nearly black. Flushed with embarrassment and defeat, she slumped against the tree behind her and looked at Tommy who'd been standing beside Zack during most of her speech. "I really blew it, didn't I, Tommy?"

"I'd say that was the worst performance I've ever seen you give."

"He thinks what I really wanted was a role in one of his movies."

"Well, wasn't it?"

Diana shot him a withering look, but Tommy was watching Tony Austin and Rachel. After a moment, she said, "How can that bitch possibly prefer Tony Austin to Zack? How *can* she?"

"Maybe she likes to feel needed," Tommy replied. "Zack doesn't need anyone, not really. Tony needs everybody."

"He *uses* everybody," Diana corrected contemptuously. "That blond Adonis is actually a vampire—he devours people, drains them dry, then he throws them away when they aren't useful to him anymore."

"You should know," he said, but he slipped a comforting arm around her shoulders then and gave her a light squeeze.

"He used to send me to meet his dope dealer. I got busted for possession one of those times, and when I called him from jail to come and bail me out, he was furious because I got caught and he hung up on me. I was so scared, I called the studio and they bailed me out and covered it up. Then they charged me back for all the legal costs."

"He obviously had redeeming qualities or you wouldn't have fallen for him."

"I was twenty years old and completely starstruck when I fell for him," she countered. "What's your excuse?"

"Middle-age crisis?" he said with a lame attempt at humor.

"It's too damned bad the hospital revived him after his last overdose."

The interior lights were going on in the stable, and he nodded in that direction. "Come along—it's show time."

Diana slid her arm around his waist and they trooped down to the stable. "You know what they say," she announced, "What goes around comes around."

"Yeah, but the trip usually takes too long."

In his own trailer, Zack hastily splashed cold water on his face and chest, pulled on a fresh shirt and left. He stopped when he saw Emily's father pacing back and forth in front of hers. "Is Emily down at the stable?"

"No, not yet, Zack. The heat has been making her sick for days," George McDaniels complained. "She shouldn't have had to spend so much time in the sun either. Couldn't she stay in our trailer where it's air-conditioned, until you're sure you need her down there? I mean, you're bound to want several takes with Rachel and Austin before Emily's cue."

In other circumstances, the suggestion that a director should wait for a cast member because she wished to languish in comfort would have gotten McDaniels a scathing reply. Zack, however, had a soft spot for Emily, as did most of the world, and so he tempered his voice and said, "That's out of the question, and you know it, George. Emily's a trooper. She'll handle the heat while she waits for her cue."

"But—I'll get Emily," he amended when Zack's expression turned ominous.

Normally, Zack had nothing but contempt for the pushy parents of child actors, but Emily's father was different. His wife had run out on both of them when Emily was still a baby. A fluke coincidence brought Emily to the attention of a producer who saw the dimpled child playing in the park with her father. When that same producer offered Emily a part in a movie, her father had given up his day job to chaperon her on the movie set and started working nights instead. McDaniels had felt that she would be less likely to be "corrupted" if left alone with a sitter at night than with a paid chaperon on the set during the day. That alone wouldn't have endeared the man to Zack, but it was also a known fact that he put every cent that Emily made into a trust fund for her. Her interests were all that mattered to him, and his vigilance had paid off: Emily was a good kid, astonishingly so for a Hollywood child star. She didn't fool with booze or drugs, she didn't sleep around, she was polite and decent, and all of that was due, Zack knew, to her father's unstinting devotion to keeping her that way.

Emily came rushing up behind him as he neared the stable, and he called over his shoulder, "Get your pretty self on that horse and let's get this over with!"

She passed him at a run, wearing the jodhpurs and riding jacket that were her costume. "I'm ready if you are, Zack," she called, her eyes filled with unspoken anguish for what he was about to go through, then she disappeared around the corner where two grips were waiting with the horse she was to be riding.

Zack knew he had little chance of getting the scene perfect on the first attempt with or without a rehearsal, but considering everything that had happened last night, he wanted to get it over with in as few tries as possible. Moreover, the charged atmosphere between his wife, her lover, and himself was only going to become worse the more times he had to direct the sexually explosive scene.

A shadow moved out from the shrubs near the doors, and Austin's carefully modulated, conciliatory voice stopped Zack cold. "Look, Zack, this scene is going to be hard enough to shoot without hard feelings between us over Rachel," he said as he moved into the light. "You and I have been around, we're sophisticated adults. Let's act like it." He held out his hand for a handshake.

Zack looked contemptuously at his outstretched hand and then at him. "Go fuck yourself."

7

TENSION, THICK AND HOT, HUNG LIKE A PALL OVER THE STABLE as Zack walked past the onlookers and headed down the aisle toward the darkened set. Sam Hudgins was already positioned at the floor camera, and Zack stopped beside him at a pair of monitors that were connected to the camera lenses, allowing Zack to see exactly what both cameras were seeing. He nodded at Tommy and things began to move in familiar sequence:

"Light it up!" the assistant director called out sharply.

There was the metallic sound of switches being flipped and the giant lights came on, drenching the area in hot white light. Shoving his hands into his pockets, Zack studied the images on both monitors. No one spoke, no one coughed, no one moved, but he was only dimly aware of the unusual stillness. For years, he had compensated for whatever was lacking in his life by totally submerging himself in his work and blocking out everything else, and he did it now without conscious effort. For the moment, this scene they were about to shoot was all that mattered; it was his baby, his mistress, his future, and he scrutinized every detail on both monitors, envisioning it all on a thirty-foot-wide theater screen.

In the rafters above, a best boy and an electrician were waiting for instructions to move a light or change the angle of a deflector if necessary. The head gaffer was positioned behind Sam's floor camera, waiting for directions, and two more electricians were beside a crane, looking up at the second cameraman, who was seated twenty feet above so that he could shoot the scene from that angle. Grips were standing by to move anything Zack wanted rearranged; the sound man had his earphones looped around his neck, ready to put them on, and the script supervisor was holding her script in one hand and a stopwatch in the other. Beside her, a production assistant was writing on the clappers that would be used to mark the scene when Zack gave the order to roll the cameras. Tony and Rachel were standing off to the side, waiting.

Satisfied, Zack nodded and glanced at Sam. "How does it look to you?"

As he'd already done repeatedly during the day, the director of photography put his eye to the camera and took a final look. With his eye still pressed to it, he said hesitantly. "That table bothers me a little, Zack. Let's move it closer to the hay bales."

At his words, two grips sprang into action and rushed forward, grasping the table and moving it an inch at a time, watching Sam as he continued to look through his camera, directing them with his raised hand. "That's good, right there."

Eager now to get going, Zack looked up at the cameraman on the boom up above. "Les? How's it look up there."

"Looks good, Zack."

Zack took a last look around and nodded at Tommy who made the routine call for silence and attention, even though the set was quiet as a tomb: "Quiet please! Places, everyone. This is *not* a rehearsal. We're going for a take on the first try."

Tony and Rachel moved to their respective marks on the floor, and while a makeup artist did a last-minute brush of powder on Tony's sweating brow and a wardrobe mistress tugged the bodice of Rachel's dress down, Zack began rapping out his customary recap of the scene they were about to shoot. "All right," he said, his voice brisk, businesslike, and decisive, "you know the story and you know the ending. We may be able to get it on the first try. If not, we'll use this one as a run-through." His gaze sliced to Rachel, but he addressed her by her character's name as he customarily did: "Johanna, you come into the stable, knowing Rick's lurking in here somewhere. You know what he wants from you. You're afraid of him, and you're afraid of yourself. When he starts trying to seduce you, you weaken, but just for a few moments—and they're *hot* moments," Zack finished, deciding he didn't need to be specific about the sort of passion he expected to see between her and her real-life lover. "Got it?" he asked. "Very hot."

"Got it," she replied and only a flicker of her green eyes betrayed a trace of uneasiness at what she was about to do in front of a roomful of people.

Zack rounded on Tony, who'd assumed his place just inside an empty stall. "You've been waiting here for Johanna over an hour," he reminded him in a clipped voice. "You're afraid she won't come, and you hate yourself for wanting her. You're obsessed with her, you're thinking about going up to the house and telling her daughter and the housekeeper and anyone else who'll listen that she's slept with you. You're humiliated because she's been avoiding you and because you have to meet her in stables while her husband sleeps in her bed. When she comes in here and walks by that stall door without seeing you, all that rage and anguish that's been building inside you for months explodes. You grab her, but the minute you touch her, you want her again, and you're determined to make her want you. You force her to kiss you, and you feel her initial response. When she changes and starts to struggle, you're too far gone to believe she wants you to stop. You don't believe it until she grabs that gun and points it at you, and then you're furious. Out of control. You grab for the gun, and when she shoots you, you're too enraged to realize that it was accidental. All that passion and obsession you felt for her is converted to momentary rage as you wrestle with her for the gun. The gun goes off a second time, Rachel crumples to the floor, and you drop the gun—you're sick with regret and fear when you realize she's badly hurt. You hear Emily—you hesitate, and then you split." Unable to completely hide his loathing, Zack added in an acid voice, "Do you think you can handle that?"

"Yeah," Austin said tightly, sarcastically, "I think I can manage."

"Then do it and we'll end this nauseating charade," Zack snapped before he could stop himself. Turning to Rachel, he added, "You never intended to use that gun on him and when it goes off, I want to see that you're horrified—so horrified that you don't react fast enough when it's pointed at you."

Without waiting for her to acknowledge his instructions, Zack turned to Emily and softened his voice a little. "Emily, you hear the shots and you come riding in here. Your mother is wounded but conscious and you realize she's not fatally hurt. You're panicked. Her lover is running for his truck and you grab that telephone in the groom's office and call for an ambulance, then you call your father. Okay with all that?"

"What about Tony—I mean, Rick? Shouldn't I start to chase him a few steps or pick up the gun like I'm thinking of going after him?"

Normally they'd have covered all this in a rehearsal, and Zack realized he'd been foolish to think they could use the rehearsal for a take, particularly when he'd been toying with a notion since yesterday that Rachel probably shouldn't fire the first shot, even though the script called for that. After a brief hesitation, he shook his head at Emily. "Let's play it the way it's written the first time through. After that, we'll improvise if we need to." He glanced around at the cast and crew, his tone turning brisk. "Questions?"

He gave them a split second to answer before he nodded at Tommy and said, "Let's do it."

"Kill the air-conditioning," Tommy called out, and an instant later the air conditioners went silent. The sound man put on his earphones, both cameramen leaned forward, and Zack took a position between the camera and the monitors where he could both see the monitors and watch the live action in front of him.

"Red light, please," he called, instructing that the red light outside the stable be turned on to warn that filming was underway. "Roll cameras." He waited for verbal confirmation that the cameras and sound equipment were rolling at proper speed.

"Rolling!" the cameraman on the crane called out after a moment.

"Rolling!" Sam Hudgins echoed.

"Speed!" the sound man called.

"Mark it," Zack ordered, and the production assistant quickly stepped in front of Sam's camera holding the black and white clappers that listed the scene number they were shooting and the number of takes they'd had. "This is scene 126," he announced, repeating what was written on the clappers, "take 1." He slapped the clappers together for the benefit of the editors who'd use that later to synchronize the sound with the action, then he quickly stepped out of the way.

"Action!" Zack called.

On cue, Rachel entered the stable from the side, moving nervously, looking around, her face a perfect mirror of terror, excitement, and apprehension. "Rick?" she called in a shaky voice, exactly as the script required, and when her lover's hand shot out from his hiding place in the empty stall, her choked scream was perfect.

Standing beside the camera, his arms crossed against his chest, Zack watched it all through narrowed, impersonal eyes, but when Austin started to kiss and fondle Rachel and drag her down onto the hay bales, everything went wrong. Austin was awkward and clearly embarrassed. "CUT!" Zack shouted, infuriated by the realization that he was probably going to have to watch Austin fondle and kiss his wife repeatedly at this rate. Stalking forward into the pool of light, he raked the actor with a look of glacial scorn. "You weren't kissing her like an inept choirboy in my hotel room, Austin. Let's see a little reenactment of that scene instead of this amateur performance you're giving us now."

Austin's face, which had been likened to Robert Redford's for its boyish charisma, turned a bright red. "Jesus, Zack, why can't you be adult about all this—"

Ignoring him, Zack rounded on Rachel, who was glaring at him, and with unprecedented crudity, he said, "And you—you're supposed to be in heat, not dreaming of giving yourself a manicure while he mauls you."

The next two takes were very good, and the entire crew knew it, but both times, Zack stopped them before Rachel could even reach for the gun, and he made them do it over. He did it partly because he'd suddenly developed a perverse satisfaction in forcing them to publicly perform the same adulterous groping and fondling that had made a public fool out of him but mostly because he felt something was still wrong with the scene. "CUT!" he called, interrupting the fourth take and walking forward.

Austin came up from the hay bale furious and spoiling for a fight, his arm around Rachel, who'd finally developed enough sensitivity to be embarrassed and equally furious. "Now look, you sadistic son of a bitch, there was nothing wrong with the last two takes! They were perfect," Austin ranted, but Zack ignored him and decided to try the scene the way he'd considered doing it yesterday.

"Shut up and listen," he snapped, "we're going to try this a different way. Despite what the author thought when he wrote this scene, the fact is that when Johanna shoots her lover, even accidentally, she loses all our empathy. The man's been obsessed with her, sexually and emotionally, and she's been using him to fill her own needs, but she never had *any* intention of leaving her husband for him. She has to be wounded with that gun before he is, or he becomes the only victim in this film, and the entire point of this picture is that they were *all* victims."

Zack heard a murmur of surprise and approval from people behind the camera, near the doorway of the stable, but he didn't need it to reinforce his judgment. He knew now he was right. He knew it with the same gut instincts that had enabled him to win an Academy Award nomination for a film that had seemed routine and ordinary until he directed it. Turning to Rachel and Tony, who looked reluctantly impressed with the change, he said curtly. "One last time, and I think we'll have it. All you have to do is reverse the outcome of the original struggle over the gun so that Johanna is wounded first.

"Then what?" Tony demanded. "What do I do after I realize I've shot her?"

Zack paused, thinking, then he said decisively, "Let her get control of the gun.

You didn't mean to hurt her, but she doesn't realize it. You step back, but she's got the gun and she's pointing it at you now, crying—for herself and for you. You start backing away. Rachel," he said turning to her, completely absorbed, "I want to see sobs from you, then you close your eyes and pull the trigger."

Zack moved back into position. "Mark it—"

The camera assistant stepped in front of the camera with the clappers. "Scene 126, take 5!"

"Action!"

This was going to be the last take, a perfect take—Zack sensed it as he watched Austin grab Rachel and force her down onto the hay bales, his hands and mouth devouring her. There was no dialogue now, but a background score would be dubbed in later, so when Rachel groped for the gun and got it between the two of them, Zack urged her on, goading her to fight harder. "Struggle!" he barked, and on a stroke of irony, he snapped, "Pretend he's me!" The ploy worked, she squirmed and hammered at Tony's shoulders in furious earnest, she got her hand on the gun.

Later, an actual gunshot would be dubbed in, in place of the soft *pop* of the blank shell in Rachel's gun, and Zack watched Tony wrest the gun from her, waiting for the perfect moment in their struggles before he called, "Gunshot!" so that Tony would pull the trigger, fire the blank, and Rachel would fall back and grab the packet of fake blood concealed near her shoulder. It was now! *"Gunshot!"* he shouted and Rachel's whole body gave a violent jerk as a gunshot exploded like a firecracker in the cavernous barn, echoing off the metal roof.

Everyone froze, momentarily immobilized by the unexpectedly loud sound where there should only have been the *pop* of a blank shell with a light load in it. Rachel slowly slid out of Tony's arms and onto the floor, but there was no fake blood spreading across her arm from a fake shoulder wound.

"What the—" Zack began, already dashing forward. Tony was bending over her, but Zack shoved him away. "Rachel?" he said, rolling her over. There was a small hole in her chest, but only a trace of blood was seeping from it. Zack's first coherent thought, as he shouted for someone to go get the ambulance and the medics while he felt frantically for her nonexistent pulse, was that this wound couldn't be fatal: Rachel was scarcely bleeding, the wound was nearer her collarbone than her heart, and besides, professional medical help was only a few yards away, on hand on the set, as required under law. Pandemonium was erupting everywhere; women were screaming, men were shouting, and the crew was rushing forward in a suffocating crowd. "Stay the hell back!" he yelled, and because he couldn't find a pulse, he started giving her CPR.

*   *   *

An hour passed while Zack stood just outside the stable doors, a few yards away from everyone else, waiting for some word from the hoard of medics and cops inside with Rachel. Squad cars and ambulances were parked all over the lawn and driveway, their eerie red and blue emergency lights whirling frantically in the still, humid night.

Rachel was dead. He sensed it, knew it. He'd seen death once before; he remembered how it looked. Despite that, he could not believe it.

The cops had already questioned Tony and the cameramen. Now they were starting to question everybody who'd been in there when it happened. But they weren't asking Zack what he'd seen. He thought, as much as he was capable of rational thought, that it was very odd of them not to want to talk to him.

Above him a brilliant light began to sweep the area and he heard the loud whine of helicopter blades. He saw the bright red cross on the side of the chopper and relief poured through him; apparently they were going to airlift Rachel to the nearest hospital, which surely must mean the medics had gotten her vital signs stabilized. Just as the comforting thought took hold, he saw something else that made his blood freeze: The cops who'd cordoned off the entire area when they arrived were letting a dark sedan through. In the light from the descending helicopter, he could read the emblem on the side of the driver's door: It said County Coroner.

Everyone else saw it too. Emily began to sob in her father's arms, and Zack heard Austin's savage curse followed by a comforting murmur of words from Tommy. Diana was staring at the coroner's car with a pale, set face, and everyone else was just . . . staring at each other.

But no one was looking at him or attempting to approach him. In his dazed state, that seemed a little strange to Zack even though he preferred it that way.

8

THE ENTIRE CAST AND CREW WERE QUARANTINED AT THEIR hotel the next day for questioning by the police. Zack spent the time in a restless stupor, while the police refused to give him any information and the news media spewed out a steady stream of it for the entire country. According to the NBC program he watched at noon, the gun that killed Rachel had been loaded with a hollow point shell, which was designed to break up and spread out on impact, inflicting total destruction in a wide area of the body rather than merely passing through it, which was why her death had been instantaneous. "CBS Evening News" provided a ballistics expert on their program who stood in front of an easel with a pointer and a diagram of Rachel's body and explained to America exactly what damage the shell had done and precisely where it was located. Zack slammed the off button on the television's remote controller, then he went into the bathroom and threw up. Rachel was dead, but despite the fact that there'd been no real warmth in their marriage, despite the fact that she'd intended to divorce him for Tony, he could not come to grips with her death or the gruesome, evil way it had occurred. The ABC 10 o'clock network news dropped a verbal bomb on him when it was announced that according to the autopsy report, which had just been released, Rachel Evans Benedict had been six weeks' pregnant.

Zack sank back on the sofa and closed his eyes, swallowing bitter bile, feeling as if he was in the middle of a hurricane that was spinning him around. Rachel had been pregnant. But not by him. He hadn't slept with her in months.

Unshaven and unable to eat, he prowled around his hotel suite, occasionally wondering if everyone else was being detained and if so, why none of them had come to his room to talk or commiserate or pass the time. The hotel switchboard was under siege from people in Hollywood trying to reach him, most of them, he knew, more interested in getting the dirt than expressing any real regret at her death. And so he refused to answer phone calls from everyone except Matt Farrell and spent his time wondering who in God's name had hated Rachel enough to want her dead. As the hours passed, he suspected every single person on the set for one absurd reason or another, then he discarded that suspect and groped for another because his reasons for suspecting them were so impossibly flimsy.

In the back of his mind he was aware that the police might believe he had some very strong motives for murdering her, and yet the thought was so ludicrous that he remained steadfastly convinced that the police would realize that.

Two days after her death, Zack answered a knock on the door to his suite and glared at the two tall, grim-faced detectives who'd questioned him yesterday. "Mr. Benedict," one of them began, but Zack's patience and temper had been strained past the breaking point.

"Why in the living hell are you bastards wasting your time with me!" he exploded. "I demand to know what progress you're making finding my wife's killer—"

He was so enraged that he was caught off guard when one of them, who'd walked into the suite and positioned himself at Zack's back, suddenly shoved him into the wall, grabbed his wrists, and jerked his hands up behind his back. Zack felt the cold bite of the handcuffs at the same time the other one said, "Zachary Benedict, you are under arrest for the murder of Rachel Evans. You have the right to remain silent, you have the right to an attorney. If you cannot afford an attorney—"

9

"LADIES AND GENTLEMEN OF THE JURY, YOU'VE HEARD THE shocking testimony and seen the incontrovertible proof . . ." Alton Peterson, the prosecuting attorney, stood perfectly still, his piercing gaze moving slowly over the faces of the twelve Dallas County jurors who were about to decide the outcome of a trial that had generated a holocaust of public attention with its scandalous revelations of adultery and murder among Hollywood's superstars.

Outside the courtroom, the halls were packed with reporters from all over the world who were waiting to discover the latest titillating developments in the trial of Zachary Benedict. Once, the media had fawned over him, now they reported every detail of Zack's fall from prestige with even greater relish, serving up each juicy morsel of conjecture and allegation to fascinated Americans, who digested each tidbit along with their dinners and the evening news.

"You've heard the *proof*," Peterson reminded the jury more emphatically as he continued his final summation, "the unimpeachable testimony from dozens of witnesses, some of whom were actually Zachary Benedict's friends. You know that the night before Rachel Evans was murdered, Zachary Benedict discovered her naked in Anthony Austin's arms. You know that Benedict was enraged, that he attacked Austin and had to be dragged off the man. You've heard testimony from guests in the hotel who were in the hall outside Benedict's suite and who heard the loud argument that ensued. From these witnesses you know that Rachel Evans told Benedict that she was planning to divorce him and marry Anthony Austin and that she intended to gain half of everything Zachary Benedict possessed in that divorce. These same witnesses testified that Benedict warned his wife, and I quote . . ." Peterson paused to glance at his notes, but it was all for effect, because no one in the courtroom could forget that threat. Raising his voice for emphasis, he repeated, *"I'll kill you before I let you and Austin get half of anything!"*

Gripping the railing around the juror's box, he searched each rapt face. "And he *did* kill her, ladies and gentlemen. He killed her in cold blood, along with the innocent, unborn baby she carried! You know he did it and I know he did it. But the *way* he did it makes this crime even more revolting, more heinous, because it shows the kind of cold-blooded monster Zachary Benedict is." Turning, he began to pace, recapping the way the crime had taken place, working up to his conclusion: "Zachary Benedict didn't murder in an unpremeditated rage of passion like your ordinary killer. No indeed, not him. He waited twenty-four hours so that his precious movie could be finished first, and *then* he chose a method of revenge that is so bizarre, so cold-blooded it makes me gag! He put hollow point shells in a gun, and then at the last minute while they were filming the end of that movie, he changed the way the script had been written, so that his wife, not Anthony Austin, would be shot during their fake struggle!"

Alton paused and gripped the railing again. "None of this is conjecture on my part. You've heard the testimony that proves every word: On the afternoon of the murder, while the rest of the film crew was on a break, Zachary Benedict went into that stable alone, ostensibly to rearrange some things on the set. Several people saw him go in there—he admitted it himself—yet no one on the film crew could think of a single thing that looked different when they returned to the set. What was he doing in there? You know what he was doing! He was switching the harmless blank shells, which a production assistant testified he had put in the gun himself, for deadly hollow points. I remind you once again that Benedict's fingerprints were on that gun. His and his alone, left there no doubt by mistake, after he'd wiped the gun clean. And once all his preparations were made, did he finish the gruesome deed and get it over with like an ordinary murderer? No, not him. Instead of that," Alton turned to face the defendant, and he did not have to feign his loathing and revulsion as he said, "Zachary Benedict stood beside a cameraman in that stable, watching his wife and her lover embrace and kiss and fondle each other, and he made them do it *over and over again!* He stopped them each time his wife was ready to reach for the gun. And then, when he'd had enough 'fun,' enough sick vengeance, when he could no longer prolong the moment that the script called for—the moment when his wife was supposed to reach for the gun and shoot Tony Austin—Zachary Benedict *changed the script!*"

Twisting around, Peterson pointed a finger at Zack, his voice ringing with loathing. "Zachary Benedict is a man who is so corrupted by wealth and fame that he actually believed himself above and beyond all the laws that apply to you and to me. He believed you'd let him get away with it! Look at him, ladies and gentlemen of the jury—"

Compelled by Peterson's booming baritone, every single face in the crowded courtroom turned in unison toward Zack, who was seated at the defendant's table. Beside him, Zack's chief defense attorney hissed without actually moving his lips, "Damn it, Zack, look up at the jury!"

Zack raised his head and complied automatically, but he doubted that anything he did was going to make a difference in the jury's collective minds. If Rachel had set out to frame him for her murder, she could never have done a better job at making the "evidence" point to him than he had done on his own.

"Look at him," Alton Peterson commanded with renewed fervor and fury, "and you'll see what he is—a man who is guilty of murder in the first degree! That is the verdict, the *only* verdict, you can return in this case if justice is to be done!"

The following morning, the jury retired to debate their verdict and Zack, who was free on $1 million bail, returned to his suite at the Crescent, where he alternately considered trying to make a run for South America and trying to murder Tony Austin instead. Tony seemed like the most logical suspect to him, yet neither Zack's lawyers nor the private detectives they hired could turn up any damning evidence against him except that he still had an expensive drug habit—a habit that he would have been better able to indulge if Rachel had lived to marry him after divorcing Zack. Furthermore, if Zack hadn't decided at the last minute to change the script, Tony, not Rachel, would have been the one shot. Zack tried to remember if he'd ever mentioned to Tony that he didn't like the ending as written and was thinking of changing it. Sometimes, he thought out loud and bounced ideas off others without remembering he'd done it. He'd written notes about changing the ending in his copy of the script, and he'd left the script lying around, but all of the witnesses denied having known anything about it.

Like a caged tiger, he prowled the length of his suite, cursing fate and Rachel and himself. Over and over again, he went through his own lawyer's closing statement, trying to make himself believe Arthur Handler had been able to sway the jury from convicting him. Handler's only real, only plausible defense had been that Zack would have had to be a complete fool to commit so blatant and bizarre a crime when he knew every scrap of evidence was going to point directly at him. When it came out during the trial that Zack owned a large gun collection and was fully familiar with various types of guns and shells, Handler had tried to point out that since that was true, Zack would have also been able to switch the shells without leaving a clumsy fingerprint on the gun.

The idea of trying to make a run for South America and then vanish revolved around in Zack's mind, but it was a lousy idea, and he knew it. For one thing, if he ran, then the jury would decide he was guilty even if they'd been going to acquit him. Second, his face was so well known, particularly now with all the press coverage of the trial, that he'd be spotted within minutes wherever he went. The only good thing he could count on was that Tony Austin would never work in films again, now that all his vices and perversions had come out in the trial and made headlines.

By the next morning when there was a knock at the door, frustration and suspense had twisted every muscle of his body into knots. He yanked the door open and frowned at the only friend he had ever trusted implicitly. Zack hadn't wanted Matt Farrell at the trial, partly because he was humiliated and partly because he didn't want the taint Zack now carried to rub off on the famous industrialist. Since Matt had been in Europe until yesterday negotiating for a company he was buying, it had been easy for Zack to sound optimistic when his friend phoned. Now, Zack took one look at his friend's grim features and knew that he'd already discovered the dire truth and had obviously flown to Dallas because of it.

"Don't look so happy to see me," Matt said dryly, walking into the suite.

"I told you there was no reason to come here," Zack countered, closing the door. "The jury's out right now. Everything is going to be fine."

"In which case," Matt replied, undeterred by his unenthusiastic greeting, "we can while away the hours playing some poker. O'Hara's putting the car away and arranging for our rooms," he added, referring to his chauffeur/bodyguard. He shrugged out of his suit coat, glanced at Zack's haggard features, and reached for the telephone. "You look like hell," he said as he ordered an enormous breakfast for three sent up to the room.

"This sure is my lucky day," Joe O'Hara said six hours later as he scooped a handful of winnings from the center of the table. A huge man with a prizefighter's battered features and a wrestler's physique, he hid his private worry over Zack's future behind an attitude of boisterous optimism that fooled no one, but somehow made the tense atmosphere in the suite more bearable.

"Remind me to cut your salary," Matt said wryly, looking at the pile of money accumulating at his chauffeur's elbow. "I shouldn't be paying you enough to sit in on a game with these stakes."

"You always say that whenever I beat you and Zack at cards," O'Hara replied cheerfully, shuffling. "This is like the good old days in Carmel when we used to do this a lot. Except it was always nighttime."

And Zack's life wasn't hanging in the balance . . .

The unspoken thought swelled in the heavy silence, broken by the shrill ring of the telephone.

Zack reached for it, listened, and stood up. "The jury's reached a verdict. I have to go."

"I'll go with you," Matt said.

"I'll bring the car around." O'Hara put in, already reaching for the car keys in his jacket pocket.

"It's not necessary," Zack said, fighting down his panic. "My attorneys are picking me up." He waited until O'Hara had shaken his hand and left, then he looked at Matt and walked over to the desk. "I have a favor to ask of you." He took a formal document out of the drawer and handed it to his friend. "I had this prepared just in case something goes wrong. It's a power of attorney granting you the absolute right to act on my behalf on anything that pertains to my finances or assets."

Matt Farrell looked down at it and his color drained at this proof that Zack obviously thought there was at least a fifty–fifty chance he'd be convicted.

"It's just a formality, a contingency plan. I'm sure you'll never need to use it," Zack lied.

"So am I," Matt said just as untruthfully.

The two men looked at each other, nearly identical in their height, build, and coloring and in their matching expressions of proud, false confidence. As Zack reached for his suit coat, Matt cleared his throat and reluctantly said, "If . . . if I were to need to use this, what do you want me to do?"

Looking in the mirror, Zack knotted his tie and said with a shrug and a lame attempt at humor, "Just try not to bankrupt me, that's all."

An hour later, in the courtroom, standing beside his attorneys, Zack watched the bailiff hand the judge the jury's verdict. As if the words were spoken in a faraway tunnel, he heard the judge say,

"—guilty of murder in the first degree . . ."

Then after a brief trial to assess punishment, Zack heard another verdict more excruciating than the last: "Punishment is assessed at forty-five years to be served in the Texas Department of Criminal Justice at Amarillo. . . . Bail pending appeal is denied on the basis of sentence exceeding fifteen years. . . . Prisoner is remanded into custody . . ."

Zack refused to wince; he refused to do anything that might reveal the truth: He was screaming inside.

He stood rigidly straight, even when someone grabbed his wrists, yanked them behind his back, and slapped handcuffs around them.

10

1993

"LOOK OUT, MISS MATHISON!" THE SHRILL WARNING FROM the boy in the wheelchair came too late; Julie was dribbling the basketball down center court, laughing as she whirled to make the shot, then she caught her ankle in a footrest of a wheelchair and went flying backward, landing squarely and ignominiously on her rump.

"Miss Mathison! Miss Mathison!" The gymnasium reverberated with the alarmed shouts of handicapped kids in the gym class Julie supervised after school, when her regular teaching duties were over. Wheelchairs gathered around her along with kids with crutches and leg braces. "You okay, Miss Mathison?" they chorused. "You hurt, Miss Mathison?"

"Of course I'm hurt," Julie teased as she shoved herself up on her elbows and scooped the hair out of her eyes. "My pride is very, very hurt."

Willie Jenkins, the school's nine-year-old macho jock who'd been acting as observer and sideline coach, shoved his hands in his pockets, regarded her with a puzzled grin, and remarked in his deep, bullfrog's voice, "How come your pride hurts when you landed on your bu—"

"It's all in your perspective, Willie," Julie said quickly, laughing. She was rolling to her feet when a pair of wing tip shoes, brown socks, and tan polyester pants legs entered her field of vision.

"Miss Mathison!" the principal barked, scowling ferociously at the scuff marks all over his shiny gymnasium floor. "This hardly looks like a basketball game to me. What sort of game are you playing?"

Even though Julie now taught third grade in the Keaton Elementary School, her relationship with its principal, Mr. Duncan, hadn't improved a whole lot since the time he accused her of stealing the class lunch money fifteen years ago. Although her integrity was no longer an issue with him, her constant bending of the school rules for her students was a permanent thorn in his side. Not only that, but she plagued him to death with innovative ideas and when he nixed them, she rounded up moral support from the rest of the town and, if needed, financial support from private citizens. As a result of one of her notions, Keaton Elementary now had a specially designed educational and athletic program for physically handicapped children, which she'd created and was constantly altering with what Mr. Duncan viewed as typical, frivolous disregard of his preestablished procedures. Miss Mathison had no sooner gotten her handi-capped program under way last year than she'd gone on another—stronger—tangent, and there was no stopping her: She was now waging a private campaign to stamp out illiteracy among the women in Keaton and the surrounding area. All it had taken to set her off on this crusade was the discovery that the janitor's wife couldn't read. Julie Mathison had invited the woman to her own house and started tutoring her there, but it soon evolved that the janitor's wife knew another woman who couldn't read, and that woman knew someone, who knew someone, who knew someone else. Within a short time there were seven women to be taught to read, and Miss Mathison had pleaded with him to let her use a classroom two evenings a week to teach her students.

When Mr. Duncan had protested sensibly about the added cost of utilities to keep a classroom open at night, she'd sweetly mentioned that she'd speak to the principal of the high school then. Rather than look like a heartless ogre when the high school principal yielded to her blue eyes and bright smile, Mr. Duncan had agreed to let her use her own classroom at Keaton Elementary. Soon after he capitulated on that, the irritating crusader decided she needed special learning materials to help speed up the learning process for "her" adults. And as he'd discovered to his everlasting frustration, once Julie Mathison had set her mind on some goal, she didn't stop until she found a way to achieve it. Sure that she was right, that some important principle was at stake, Julie Mathison possessed a stubborn resiliency combined with a boundless, energetic optimism that was as remarkable as it was annoying to him.

She'd been frustratingly single-minded about her handicapped kids, but this literacy program was a private quest of hers, and nothing he said or did was going to deter her. She was determined to get the special materials she needed, and he was certain her need for two days off in order to go to Amarillo had something to do with finding the money to pay for them. He knew for a fact that she'd persuaded the wealthy grandfather of one of her handicapped students—a man who happened to live in Amarillo—to donate funds for some of the equipment they needed for the handicapped program. Now, Mr. Duncan suspected, she intended to try to prevail upon the unsuspecting man to donate funds to support her women's literacy program.

That particular "fund-raising" penchant of hers was what he found most distasteful and most embarrassing. It was completely undignified when she went "begging" for extra funds by appealing to wealthy citizens or their relatives. In the four years she'd been teaching at Keaton Elementary, Julie Mathison had managed to become the proverbial thorn in his side, the blister on his heel. For that reason, he was completely immune to the fetching picture she presented as she got to her feet and waived her students into the locker room, calling instructions to them about the game next week. With her face scrubbed clean of makeup, as it was now, and her shoulder-length chestnut hair pulled off her forehead and held in a ponytail, there was a glowing wholesomeness about her and a youthful vitality that had fooled Mr. Duncan into thinking she was sweet, pretty, and uncomplicated when he hired her. At 5'5" tall, she was fine-boned and long-legged, with an elegant nose, classic cheekbones, and a full, soft mouth. Beneath gracefully winged dark brows, her large eyes were a luminous indigo blue, heavily fringed with curly lashes, eyes that seemed both innocent and gentle. As he'd learned to his misfortune, however, the only feature on that delicate face of hers that gave a real hint of the woman beneath was that stubborn chin of hers with its tiny, unfeminine cleft.

Mentally tapping his foot, he waited until his troublesome young teacher had finished dealing with her "team," smoothed her sweat suit, and raked her fingers through the sides of her hair before he deigned to explain the reason for his unusual afterschool visit to the gym. "Your brother Ted called. I was the only one upstairs to answer the phone," he added irritably. "He said to tell you that your mother wants you to come to dinner at eight o'clock and that he'll give you Carl's car for your trip. He—ah—mentioned you were going to Amarillo. You hadn't said that when you asked for the time off for personal reasons."

"Yes, Amarillo." Julie said with a smile of bright innocence that she hoped would put him off but merely put him on his guard instead.

"You have friends up there?" he said, his brows snapping together over the bridge of his nose.

Julie was going to Amarillo to meet with a wealthy relative of one of her handicapped students in hopes of persuading him to donate money to her literacy program . . . and she had an awful feeling Mr. Duncan already guessed it. "I'm only going to be gone for two school days," she evaded. "I've already arranged for a substitute to take my classes."

"Amarillo is several hundred miles away. You must have important things to do up there."

Instead of responding to that thinly veiled query about her purpose for the trip, Julie shoved up the sleeve of her sweatshirt, glanced at her watch, and said in a rushed voice, "Goodness! It's four-thirty. I'd better hurry if I'm going to go home, shower, and get back here in time for my six o'clock class."

When Julie emerged from the school building, Willie Jenkins was waiting beside her car for her, his small face furrowed in a deep frown. "I heard Mr. Duncan and you talking about you going to Amarillo," he announced in the incredibly gravelly voice that made him sound like a grown man with laryngitis. "And I was wondering, Miss Mathison—I mean, am I going to get to sing or not in the Winter Pageant?" Julie suppressed a smile. Like his older brothers, Willie Jenkins could play any sport and play it well; he was always picked first for every team; he was the most popular kid in the lower grades, and so it rankled him sorely that he was *last* choice when it came to anything that had to do with music. The reason he was never given a singing part was because when Willie opened his mouth to belt out music, he emitted sounds that sent the entire audience into paroxysms of helpless giggles.

"It's not my decision, Willie," Julie said, tossing her briefcase onto the passenger seat of her old Ford compact. "I'm not in charge of the Winter Pageant this year."

He gave her the impish, thoughtful grin of a male who knows instinctively that a female is soft on him—and Julie was. She loved his spunk, his pluck, his spirit, and most especially his innate kindness toward a particular handicapped boy in her class named Johnny Everett. "Well," he croaked, "if you was, I mean *were,* in charge, would you let me sing?"

"Willie," Julie said, smiling as she turned the key in the ignition, "the day that I get to decide who sings, you'll sing."

"Promise?"

Julie nodded. "Try coming to church someday and I'll prove it. I'll let you sing in the children's choir."

"My folks don't hold with too much preachin'."

"Well there you have it—a real dilemma," Julie said as she began to back slowly out of her parking space in the teacher's lot, talking to him through the open window.

"What's a de-lemma?"

She reached out and rumpled his hair. "Look it up in the dictionary."

The route to her house took her through the center of "downtown" Keaton, four blocks of shops and businesses that formed a square around the stately old county courthouse. When she first came to Keaton as a child, the little Texan town without boulevards or skyscrapers—or slums—had seemed very odd and foreign to her, but she'd quickly come to love its quiet streets and friendly atmosphere. It hadn't changed noticeably in the last fifteen years. It was much as it had always been—picturesque and quaint, with its pretty white pavilion in the center of the municipal park and its brick-paved streets surrounded by shops and immaculately kept homes. Although the population of Keaton had grown from 3,000 to 5,000, the town had absorbed its new citizens into its own lifestyle, rather than altering to suit theirs. Most of the citizens still went to church on Sunday, the men still assembled at the Elk's Club on the first Friday of each month, and summer holidays were still celebrated in the time-honored way—in the grassy town square, with the Keaton Municipal Band playing in the bandstand, which was draped in red, white, and blue for those occasions. Original Keaton residents had arrived on horseback and in buggies for those festivities. Now they came in pickup trucks and compact cars, but laughter and music still rang out on the summer breeze, just as it always had. Children still played tag among the ancient oaks or strolled about, holding onto their parents with one hand and an ice cream cone with the other, while their great-grandparents sat on park benches and reminisced. It was a town where people clung tightly to old friendships, old traditions, old memories. It was also a town where everyone knew everything about everybody.

Julie was a part of all that now; she loved the sense of security, of belonging, that it gave her, and from the time she was eleven, she had scrupulously avoided doing anything whatsoever that might bring down the censure of the gossips. As a teenager, she dated only those few boys of whom her parents and the entire town approved, and she only attended school-sanctioned activities and chaste church socials with them. She never broke a deadline or a traffic law or a serious rule; she lived at home while she attended college, and when she finally rented her own little house on the north side of town last year, she kept it immaculately neat and made it a policy not to allow any males who weren't family members into it after dark. Other young women growing up in the 1980s would have chafed under such restrictions, self-imposed or not, but Julie didn't. She had found a real home, a loving family who respected and trusted her, and she was determined that she would always be worthy of it all. So effective were her determined efforts that, as an adult, Julie Mathison had become Keaton's model citizen. Besides teaching at Keaton Elementary and volunteering her time to the handicapped program and her reading program, she also taught Sunday school, sang in the choir, baked cookies for church bake sales, and knitted afghans to help raise money for a new firehouse.

With absolute determination she had eradicated all traces of the reckless, impulsive little street urchin she had been. And yet, every sacrifice she'd made brought her such rewards that she always felt as if she was the one who was blessed. She loved working with children and she got a thrill out of teaching adults. She'd carved a perfect life for herself. Except that sometimes, at night and alone, she couldn't quite banish the feeling that something wasn't quite right about all this. Something was false or missing or out of place. She felt as if she'd created a role for herself and wasn't certain exactly what she was supposed to do next.

A year ago, when the new assistant pastor, Greg Howley, had arrived to help out Julie's father, she realized what she should have considered long before: She needed a husband and family of her own to love now. Greg thought so, too. They'd talked about getting married, but Julie had wanted to wait until she was certain, and now Greg was in Florida with his own congregation, still waiting for her to decide. The town gossips, who thoroughly approved of the handsome young assistant pastor for Julie's husband, had been disappointed when Greg had left last month after Christmas without putting an engagement ring on her finger. Julie approved of him, too, objectively. Except sometimes, late at night, when those vague, inexplicable doubts set in . . .

11

LEANING HER HIP AGAINST HER DESK, JULIE SMILED AT THE seven women between the ages of twenty and sixty who were learning to read. Her heart had already been won over by their determination, their courage, and their intensity, and she was only beginning to learn to know them. She had less than twenty minutes before she was due at her parents' house for dinner, and she hated to end the class. Reluctantly she looked at her watch and said, "Okay, everybody, that about does it for tonight. Are there any questions about the assignment for next week or anything that anyone wants to say?"

Seven earnest faces looked up at her. Rosalie Silmet, twenty-five and a single mother, raised her hand and said shyly, "We—all of us—want to say how much it means to us that you're doing this. I got elected to tell you because I'm the best reader so far. We want you to know what a difference you're making just by believing in us. Some of us," she hesitated and looked at Pauline Perkins, who had recently joined the class at Rosalie's urging, "don't think you can teach us, but we're willing to give you a chance."

Following the direction of her gaze to the dark-haired, solemn woman of about forty, Julie said gently, "Pauline, why do you think you can't learn to read?"

The woman stood up as if she were addressing a person of great importance and admitted to Julie with painful dignity, "My husband says if I weren't stupid, I'd have learned how to read when I was a kid. My kids say the same thing. They say I'm wastin' your time. I only came here because Rosalie said she's learnin' real quick and never thought she could, neither. Either. I said I'd give it a try for a few weeks."

The other women in the room nodded reluctant agreement, and Julie briefly closed her eyes before she admitted to them the truth she'd hidden so long ago and forever. "I *know* you can all learn to read. I know for a fact that not being able to read doesn't have anything to do with being stupid. I can prove it."

"How?" Pauline asked bluntly.

Julie drew a deep breath and then said wryly, "I know it, because when I came to Keaton, I was in the fourth grade and couldn't read as well as Rosalie already does after a few weeks in this class. I know how it feels to think you're too stupid to learn. I know how it feels to grope your way down a hall and not be able to read the names on the bathroom doors. I know the ways you've figured out to hide it from people so they won't laugh at you. *I'm* not laughing at you. I'll never laugh at you. Because I know something else . . . I know how much courage it takes for each one of you to come here twice a week."

The women gaped at her openmouthed, and then Pauline said, "Is that the truth? You couldn't read?"

"It's the truth," Julie said quietly, meeting her gaze. "That's why I'm teaching this class. That's why I'm so determined to get you all the new tools that are available for adults who want to read now. Trust me," she said, straightening. "I'll find a way to get you all those things, that's why I'm going to Amarillo in the morning. All I ask for now is that you have a little faith in me. And in yourselves."

"I got plenty of faith in you," Peggy Listrom joked, standing up and gathering her notebook and pencils. "But I don't know about myself yet."

"I can't believe you said that," Julie teased. "Didn't I hear you bragging at the beginning of class that you were able to sound out some of the street names on the signs in town this week?"

When Peggy grinned and picked up the infant who was napping in the chair in front of her, Julie sobered and decided a little reinforcement was needed to keep them going at this early stage. "Before you all go, maybe you should remind yourselves about why you *wanted* to learn to read? Rosalie, what about you?"

"That's easy. I want to go to the city where there's plenty of jobs and get off welfare, but I can't get a job because I can't fill out an application form. Even if I could figure out a way to get by that, I still couldn't get a decent job unless I could read."

Two other women nodded agreement, and Julie looked at Pauline. "Pauline, why do you want to learn to read?"

She grinned a little sheepishly. "I'd sort of like to show my husband he's wrong. I'd like to be able to stand up to him just once and prove I'm not stupid. And then . . ." she trailed off self-consciously.

"And then?" Julie prodded gently.

"And then," she finished on a winsome sigh, "I'd like to be able to sit down and help my kids with their homework."

Julie looked at Debby Sue Cassidy, a thirty-year-old with straight brown hair, luminous brown eyes, and a quiet demeanor who'd been pulled out of school repeatedly by her itinerant parents before she finally dropped out of school in the fifth grade. She in particular struck Julie as being unusually bright and, from what little she'd said in class, very creative and rather well spoken. She worked as a maid; she had the studious demeanor of a librarian. Hesitantly, she admitted, "If I could do anything after I learn to read, there's just one thing I'd do."

"What's that?" Julie asked, smiling back at her.

"Don't laugh, but I'd like to write a book."

"I'm not laughing," Julie said gently.

"I think I could do it someday. I mean, I have good ideas for stories, and I know how to tell them out loud, only I can't write them down. I—I listen to books on tape—you know, for the blind, even though I'm not blind. I feel like I am sometimes, though. I feel like I'm in this dark tunnel, only there's no way out, except maybe now there is. If I can really learn to read."

Those admissions brought an outpouring of other admissions, and Julie began to get a clearer picture of the life these women were relegated to living. Each of them had no self-esteem; they clearly took a lot of bullying from the men they lived with or were married to, and they thought they deserved nothing better. By the time she closed the classroom door behind her, she was ten minutes late for dinner and more resolved than ever to get the money she needed to buy the sort of classroom aids that would help them the fastest.

12

TED'S SQUAD CAR WAS PARKED IN FRONT OF HER PARENTS' house when Julie pulled up, and Carl was walking up the drive, talking to him. Carl's blue Blazer, which he insisted she take to Amarillo instead of her less reliable car was parked in the driveway, and Julie pulled in beside it. Both men turned to wait for her, and even after all these years, she still felt a glow of pride and astonishment at how tall and handsome her brothers had grown up to be and how warm and loving they had remained to her. "Hi, Sis!" Ted said, wrapping her in a hug.

"Hi," she said, returning it. "How's the law business?" Ted was a Keaton deputy sheriff, but he'd just earned his law degree and was waiting to get the results of his bar exams.

"Thriving," he joked. "I gave Mrs. Herkowitz a citation for jaywalking this afternoon. It made my day." Despite his attempt at humor, there was a thread of cynicism in his voice that had been there for the past three years, since the failure of his brief marriage to the daughter of Keaton's richest citizen. The experience had hurt and then hardened him, and the entire family knew it and hated it.

Carl, on the other hand, had been married for six months and was all smiles and optimism as he gave her a bear hug. "Sara can't come to dinner tonight, she still isn't over her cold," he explained.

The porch light was on and Mary Mathison appeared in the open doorway beneath its glow, an apron around her waist. Except for some gray strands in her dark hair and the fact that she'd slowed a little since her heart attack, she was still as pretty and vital and warm as ever. "Children," she called, "hurry up! Dinner's getting cold."

Reverend Mathison was standing behind her, still tall and straight, but he wore glasses all the time now, and his hair was almost completely gray. "Hurry along," he said, hugging Julie and patting his sons on their shoulders as they shed their jackets.

The only thing that had changed about Mathison family dinners over the years was that Mary Mathison preferred to use the dining room and treat these meals as special occasions, now that all three of her children were grown and had places of their own. The dinners themselves, however, hadn't changed; they were still an occasion for laughter and sharing, a time when problems were occasionally mentioned and solutions offered. Conversation passed around the dinner table along with platters of roast beef, mashed potatoes, and fresh vegetables. "How is construction going on the Addleson house?" Julie's father asked Carl as soon as they'd said grace.

"Not great. In fact, it's driving me crazy. The plumber connected the hot water to the cold water taps, the electrician connected the porch light to the switch above the disposal, so when you turn on the disposal, the porch light goes on—"

Normally, Julie was extremely sympathetic to the trials and tribulations of her brother's construction business, but at the moment, Carl's predicament struck her as more humorous than distressing. "Where did he put the switch for the disposal?" she teased.

"Herman connected that to the oven fan. He was in one of his 'moods' again. I honestly think he's so glad to have work that he deliberately messes it up so that he can make it last longer."

"In that case, you'd better make sure he didn't connect the line for the dryer to something else. I mean, it would be a shame if Mayor Addelson moved in, turned on the dryer, and blew up his built-in microwave ovens."

"This is not completely a joking matter, Julie. Mayor Addelson's attorney insisted on putting a penalty clause in the building contract. If I don't have his place finished by April, it could cost me $150 a day, unless there's an act of God that prevents it."

Julie struggled to keep her face straight, but remnants of laughter lingered in her eyes at the image of Mayor Addelson flipping the switch on his porch light and having his disposal roar to life instead. Besides being mayor, Edward Addelson owned the bank, the Ford dealership, and the hardware store, as well as much of the land that lay to the west of Keaton. Everyone in Keaton knew about Herman Henkleman; he was an electrician by trade, a bachelor by choice, and an eccentric by genetic heritage. Like his father, Herman lived alone in a tiny shack on the edge of town, worked when he pleased, sang when he drank, and expounded on history with a vocabulary and knowledge that would have done credit to a university professor when he was sober. "I don't think you have to worry about Mayor Addelson invoking a penalty clause," Julie said with amusement, "Herman definitely qualifies as an act of God. He's like hurricanes and earthquakes—unpredictable, uncontrollable. Everyone knows that."

Carl laughed then, a deep throaty chuckle. "You're right," he said. "If Mayor Addleson takes me to court, a local jury would rule in my favor."

The moment of silence that followed was filled with shared, if unspoken, understanding, then Carl sighed and said, "I don't know what got into him. When Herman's not in one of his 'moods,' he's the best electrician I've ever seen. I wanted to give him a chance to get back on his feet with some money in his pocket, and I figured he'd be okay."

"Mayor Addelson is not going to take you to court if you're a few days late with his house," Reverend Mathison put in, his lips curved in an appreciative smile as he helped himself to roast beef. "He's a fair man. He knows you're the best builder this side of Dallas and that you're giving him excellent value for his money."

"You're right," Carl agreed. "Let's talk about something more cheerful. Julie, you've been very evasive for weeks. Now come clean: Are you going to marry Greg or not?"

"Oh!" she said. "Well, I . . . we . . ." The whole family watched in amusement as she began to reposition the silverware beside her plate, then she carefully turned the bowl of mashed potatoes so the design was exactly in the center. Ted burst out laughing and she caught herself up short, flushing. Since childhood, whenever she felt uncertain or worried, she had a sudden compulsive need to straighten objects out and put them in perfect order, whether that "object" was her bedroom closet, her kitchen cabinets, or the tableware. She slanted them an embarrassed grin, "I think so. Someday."

She was still thinking so when the three of them were leaving the house and Herman Henkleman came walking up the sidewalk, hat in his hand, looking sheepish and apologetic. At seventy, he was tall and gaunt, but when he straightened his shoulders, as he did now, there was a dignity about him that invariably tugged at Julie's heart. "Evenin', everyone," he said to the group gathered on the front porch, then he turned to Carl and said, "I know I'm off the Addelson job, Carl, but I was hoping you'd just let me fix up the work I botched. That's all I ask. I don't want to be paid or nothing, but I let you down, and I'd like to make up for that, best as I can."

"Herman, I'm sorry, but I can't—"

The older man held up his hand, a long-fingered, surprisingly aristocratic hand. "Carl, ain't nobody but me who can figure out what all I screwed up there. I wasn't feelin' good for a whole week, only I didn't want to say nothing to you, because I was afraid you'd think I'm old and sickly and take me off the job. I'm not serious-sick, it was just the flu. Right now, your new electrician probably thinks he knows what all I did wrong, but if something shows up after you drywall that place, you'll be tearin' down walls a week after Addleson moves in. You know you can't switch electricians in the middle of a job without having trouble later."

Carl hesitated and Julie and Ted delicately gave him a chance to relent in privacy. After saying good-bye, they headed for Carl's Blazer.

"There's a blue norther headed for the Panhandle," Ted said, shivering a little in his light jacket. "If it starts snowing up there, you'll be glad you have four-wheel drive. I wish Carl didn't need his phone in his pickup. I'd feel better if he'd been able to leave it in the Blazer."

"I'll be fine," Julie promised cheerfully, pressing a kiss to his cheek. She watched him in the rearview mirror as she drove away. He stood on the sidewalk with his hands in his pockets, a tall, slender, attractive blond man with a cold, forlorn look on his face. It was the same expression she'd seen often since his divorce from Katherine Cahill. Katherine had been her best friend and still was even though she'd moved to Dallas now. Neither Katherine nor Ted spoke ill of the other to Julie, and she couldn't understand why two people she loved so much couldn't love each other. Shoving that depressing thought aside, Julie turned her mind to her trip to Amarillo tomorrow. She hoped it didn't snow.

"Hey, Zack," the whisper was almost inaudible, "What are you gonna do if it starts snowing the day after tomorrow, like the weather forecast said?" Dominic

Sandini leaned down from the upper bunk and looked at the man who was stretched out on the cot below, staring at the ceiling. "Zack, did you hear me?" he added in a louder whisper.

Pulling his mind from the endless thoughts of his imminent escape and the risks associated with it, Zack slowly turned his head and looked at the wiry, olive-skinned thirty-year-old who shared his cell in the Amarillo State Penitentiary and was privy to his escape plans because he was part of them. Dominic's uncle was a major part of those same plans—a retired bookie, according to information in the prison library, with supposed connections to the Las Vegas Mafia. Zack had paid Enrico Sandini a fortune to pave the way once he made his escape. He had done it on Dominic's assurance that his uncle was "an honorable man," but he had no actual way of knowing for a few more hours if the money he'd instructed Matt Farrell to transfer into Sandini's Swiss bank account was actually buying him a thing. "I'll handle it," he said flatly.

"Well, when you 'handle it,' don't forget you owe me ten bucks. We had that bet on the Bears game last year and you lost. Remember?"

"I'll pay you when I get out of here." In case anyone was listening, Zack added, "Someday."

With a conspiratorial grin, Sandini leaned back, slid his thumb under the flap of the letter he'd received earlier that day, crossed his feet at the ankles, and lapsed into silence as he read.

Ten lousy dollars . . . Zack thought grimly, remembering when he used to hand out ten-dollar tips to messengers and bellmen as casually as if it was play money. In this hellhole where he'd spent the last five years, men killed each other for ten dollars. Ten dollars could buy anything that was available here, like a fistful of marijuana cigarettes, a handful of uppers or downers, and magazines that catered to any perversion. Those were just a few of the little "luxuries" that money could buy in this place. Normally he tried never to think of the way he had once lived; it made this twelve by fifteen-foot cell with a sink, a toilet, and two cots even more unbearable, but now that he was resolved to escape or die trying, he wanted to remember it. The memory would reinforce his resolve to make the break, no matter the cost or the risk. He wanted to remember the rage he felt the first day when the cell door clanged shut and the next day, when a gang of thugs surrounded him in the prison yard, taunting, *"C'mon, mooovie staaaar, show us how you won all them mooovie fights."* It was pure, blind, irrational fury that had sent him plowing into the biggest of the group, fury and an unformed wish to end his life there and then, as quickly as possible, but not until he'd inflicted pain on his tormentor. And he inflicted plenty that day. He'd been in good shape, and all those moves he'd learned for the phoney fights in his "tough guy" roles weren't wasted. By the time the fight was stopped, Zack had three broken ribs and a bruised kidney, but two of his opponents looked a hell of a lot worse.

His triumph landed him in solitary for a week, but no one fooled with him after that. Word spread that he was a maniac, and even the worst of the goons gave him a wide berth. He was, after all, a convicted murderer, not an ordinary petty felon. That also won him a certain amount of respect. It had taken him three years to wise up and realize that the easiest path was to become a trustee, which meant behaving himself and playing the game like a good little soldier. And he had done that, he had even come to like some of the cons, but he had never, in all these years, known peace. Peace could only come with acceptance of his fate, and not once during his long incarceration, not even for a moment, had he been able to do what convicts were advised to do: He could not accept his confinement and simply put in his time here. He'd learned to play the game and pretend that he had "adjusted," but the truth was just the opposite. The truth was that every morning, when his eyes opened, the inner battle began again and it continued to rage until he finally fell asleep. He had to get out of here before it drove him insane. His plan was solid: Every Wednesday, Warden Hadley, who ran the prison like his own personal Stalag 17, attended a community meeting in Amarillo; Zack was his driver, and Sandini, his gofer. Today was Wednesday, and everything Zack needed to make good his escape had been waiting for him in Amarillo, but at the last minute, Hadley, who was the featured speaker this week had told Zack the meeting was rescheduled for Friday. Zack's jaw clenched. If not for that delay, Zack would already be free. Or dead. Now, he had to wait until the day after tomorrow to make his break, and he didn't know how he was going to bear the suspense.

Closing his eyes, he went over the plan again. It was filled with pitfalls, but Dominic Sandini was trustworthy, so he had help on the inside. Everything on the outside was supposedly taken care of by Enrico Sandini—money, transportation, and a new identity. After that, the rest was up to Zack. At this point, what worried him the most were the things he couldn't accurately predict or allow for, like the weather and the location of possible roadblocks. Even with his careful planning, there were a thousand tiny things that could happen and cause a domino effect that could result in the collapse of his entire scheme. The risk was enormous, but it didn't matter. Not really. He only had two choices: to stay in this hellhole and let it destroy what was left of his mind or escape and risk the probability of being shot down when they tried to capture him. As far as he was concerned, being killed was infinitely preferable to rotting in here.

Even if he made good his escape, he knew they'd never stop hunting for him. For the rest of his life—probably his very *short* life—he'd never be able to relax or stop looking over his shoulder, no matter what part of the world he made it to. It was worth it. Anything was worth it.

"Holy shit!" Sandini's exuberant shout jolted Zack from his preoccupation with his escape plans. "Gina's getting married!" He waved the letter he'd been reading, and when Zack merely turned his head and gave him a blank look, he said it louder. "Zack, did you hear what I said? My sister Gina's getting married in two weeks! She's marrying Guido Dorelli."

"That's a good choice," Zack said dryly, "since he's the one who got her pregnant."

"Yeah, but like I told you, Mama wasn't going to let her marry him."

"Because he's a loan shark," Zack assumed after pausing for a moment to recall what he knew of Guido.

"Hell, no. I mean, a guy's got to make a living, Mama understands that. Guido just lends money to people in need, that's all."

"And if they can't pay him back, he breaks their legs."

Zack watched Sandini's face fall and instantly regretted his sarcasm. Despite Sandini's having stolen twenty-six automobiles and having been arrested sixteen times before he was twenty-eight, there was something endearingly childlike about the skinny little Italian. Like Zack, he was a trustee, but his sentence was up in four more weeks. Sandini was cocky as hell, always ready for a fight, and he was intensely loyal to Zack, whose movies he'd loved. He had a huge, colorful family who visited him regularly in the prison yard on visitors' days. When they discovered Zack was his cellmate, they were awed, but when they found out no one ever came to see him, they forgot about who he was and adopted him as if he were a close relative. Zack had thought he wanted to be left alone, and he made it clear to them by making himself scarce and pointedly ignoring their overtures when he absolutely couldn't get away from them. It was a futile effort. The harder he tried to shut them out, the more persistently they surrounded him in their laughing, loving group. Before he realized how it happened, he was being hugged and kissed by rotund Mama Sandini and Dominic's sisters and cousins. Dark-haired toddlers with lollipops and sticky hands and heart-rending smiles were plunked on his lap while their olive-skinned mothers chattered about the affairs of Dominic's enormous family, and Zack tried helplessly to keep track of all their names and simultaneously keep an alert eye on the lollipops that inevitably ended up getting stuck in his hair anyway. Sitting on a bench in a crowded prison yard, he had watched a chubby Sandini baby take its first uncertain steps and stretch its arms out to Zack, not to any of the Sandinis, but to him for help.

They enfolded him in their warmth and when they left, they sent him Italian cookies and smelly salami wrapped in grease-stained brown paper twice a month, like clockwork, just like they sent to Dominic. Even though it gave him indigestion, Zack always ate some of his salami and all of the cookies, and when Sandini's female cousins started sending him notes and asking for autographs, Zack dutifully responded. Sandini's Mama sent Zack birthday cards and admonishments about being too thin. And on those rare occasions when Zack actually felt like laughing, Sandini was invariably the cause. In a bizarre sort of way, he was closer to Sandini and his family than he'd ever been to his own.

Trying to negate his last damning remark about Sandini's future brother-in-law, Zack said with admirable solemnity, "Now that I think about it, banks aren't much better. They throw widows and orphans out on the street when they can't pay."

"Exactly!" Sandini said, nodding emphatically, his good humor restored.

Realizing that it was a relief to set aside his agonizing worry about eventualities in his escape plans that he couldn't control, Zack concentrated on Sandini's news and said, "If your mother didn't object to Guido's profession or his jail record, why wouldn't she let Gina marry him?"

"I told you, Zack," Sandini said gravely, "Guido was married before—in the church—and he's divorced now, so he's excommunicated."

Straightfaced, Zack said, "Right. I forgot about that."

Sandini returned to his letter. "Gina sends you her love. So does Mama. Mama says you don't write to her enough and you don't eat enough."

Zack looked at the plastic watch he was allowed to wear and rolled to his feet. "Haul ass, Sandini. It's time for another prisoner count."

13

JULIE'S ELDERLY NEXT-DOOR NEIGHBORS, THE ELDRIDGE TWINS, were seated upon the swing on their front porch, a favorite vantage point that enabled them to observe most of their neighbors' activities along a four-block stretch of Elm Street. At the moment, the two spinsters were watching Julie toss her overnight bag into the back seat of the Blazer.

"Good morning, Julie," Flossie Eldridge called out, and Julie jerked around, startled to find that the two white-haired ladies were already up and outside at 6 A.M.

"Good morning, Miss Flossie," she called softly, dutifully turning toward them and walking across the damp grass to pay her respects. "Good morning, Miss Ada."

Although they were in their middle seventies, the two ladies still looked remarkably alike, a resemblance that was reinforced by their lifelong habit of wearing identical dresses. However, there the similarities between them ended, for Flossie Eldridge was plump, sweet, docile, and cheerful, whereas her sister was thin, sour, domineering, and nosy. Gossip had it that when Miss Flossie was young, she'd been in love with Herman Henkleman, but that Miss Ada had put a spike in the couple's marital plans by convincing her submissive sister that Herman, who was several years younger than Flossie, was interested only in Flossie's share of their modest inheritance and that he'd squander it all on liquor and make Flossie into the town laughingstock to boot.

"It's a beautiful morning," Miss Flossie added, tugging her shawl around her against the crisp January air. "These mild days that happen now and again certainly make winter seem shorter and easier, don't they, Julie?"

Before Julie could answer, Ada Eldridge got directly to her primary interest: "Are you going away again, Julie? You just got back a few weeks ago."

"I'll only be gone for two days."

"Another business trip or is it pleasure this time?" Ada persisted.

"Business, sort of." Ada lifted her brows, silently demanding additional information and Julie yielded rather than being rude. "I'm going up to Amarillo to talk to a man about donating some money to a school program."

Ada nodded, digesting this information. "I hear your brother is having trouble finishing Mayor Addelson's house. He should know better than to hire Herman Henkleman. That man is a complete ne'er-do-well."

Suppressing the urge to glance at Miss Flossie to see how she reacted to this condemnation of her alleged former sweetheart, Julie said to Ada, "Carl is the best builder this side of Dallas, which is why Mayor Addelson's architect selected him. Everything in that house has to be custom-made. It takes time and patience." Ada opened her mouth to continue her inquisition, but Julie forestalled her by glancing at her watch and saying quickly, "I'd better get on the road. It's a long drive to Amarillo. Bye, Miss Flossie, Miss Ada."

"Be careful," Miss Flossie admonished. "I heard a cold front's coming through here tomorrow or the day after, from up near Amarillo. They get an awful lot of snow up there in the Panhandle. You wouldn't want to get caught in a blizzard now."

Julie smiled affectionately at the plump twin. "Don't worry. I have Carl's Blazer. Besides, the weather forecast says there's only a twenty percent chance of snow up there."

The two elderly ladies watched the Blazer back out of the driveway, then Miss Flossie gave a wistful little sigh. "Julie leads such an adventurous life. She went to Paris, France, with all those teachers last summer, and she went to the Grand Canyon the year before. I declare, she travels all the time."

"So do hobos," said Ada in an acid voice. "If you ask me, she ought to stay home and marry that assistant pastor who's sweet on her while she's still got the chance."

Rather than put herself through the pointless misery of a verbal confrontation with her strong-willed twin, Flossie did what she always did: She simply changed the subject. "Reverend and Mrs. Mathison must be very proud of all their children."

"They won't be if they discover their Ted spends half the night with that girl he's going around with now. Irma Bauder said she didn't hear his car pull away until almost four o'clock in the morning two nights ago!"

Flossie's expression turned dreamy. "Oh, but, Ada, they may have lots to talk about. I'll bet they're already in love!"

"They're in *heat!*" Ada snapped back, "and you're still a romantic fool, just like your mama. Papa always said so."

"She was your mama, too, Ada," Flossie cautiously pointed out.

"But I'm like Papa. I'm nothing like she was."

"She died when we were babies, so you can't be sure."

"I'm sure because Papa always said so. He said you were a fool, like her, and I was strong, like him. That's exactly why he gave me control of his estate, if you recall—because you couldn't be trusted to look out for yourself, so I had to look out for both of us."

Flossie bit her lip, then she cautiously changed the subject again. "Mayor Addelson's house is going to be a showplace. I heard he's going to have an elevator."

Ada put her foot against the porch and gave the swing an angry shove that set it rocking and creaking. "With Herman Henkleman on the premises, the mayor will be lucky if his elevator isn't wired to his commode!" she countered with stinging contempt. "That man is a hopeless good-for-nothing, just like his daddy was, and his daddy's daddy, too. I told you he would be."

Flossie looked down at her plump little hands lying folded in her lap. She said nothing.

14

ZACK WAS STANDING BEFORE A SMALL SHAVING MIRROR ABOVE the sinks in the showers, staring blindly at his reflection, trying to tell himself that Hadley wouldn't change his plans again today, when Sandini hurried in wearing a look of suppressed excitement and threw a cautious look over his shoulder into the hall behind him. Satisfied that no one was lurking within hearing, Sandini moved close and said in an elated whisper, "Hadley sent word he wants to leave for Amarillo at three o'clock! This is it!"

Tension and impatience had been eating Zack alive for so long that he could hardly adjust to the fact that the payoff was actually here: Two long years of pretending to go along with the system, of becoming a model prisoner so they'd make him a trustee with all the attendant freedoms—all the months of planning and scheming—they were finally coming to fruition. In a few hours, if the delay hadn't caused irreparable damage to his arrangements, he'd be on the road in a rented car with a new identity, a minutely planned itinerary, and plane tickets that would lead the authorities on a wild-goose chase.

At the sink beside him, Sandini said, "Jesus, I wish I could go with you. I'd sure like to be at Gina's wedding!"

Zack bent down and splashed water on his face, but he heard the suppressed excitement in Sandini's voice and it scared the hell out of him. "Don't even consider it! You'll be out of here in four weeks," he added, yanking a towel off the rack.

"Yeah," he said. "You're right. Here, take this," he added, holding out his hand.

"What is it?" Zack asked, wiping his face. He tossed the towel down and looked at the piece of paper in Sandini's outstretched hand.

"This is Mama's address and phone number. If things don't work out like they should, you get your ass to Mama, and she'll get you to my uncle. He has connections everywhere," he boasted. "I know you've had your doubts about whether he'll come through for you, but in a few hours, you'll see that everything's waiting in Amarillo, just like you want. He's a great guy," Sandini added proudly.

Zack absently rolled down the sleeves of his rough white cotton prison shirt, trying not to think about anything now except each moment as it happened, but his hands were unsteady when he tried to button his shirt cuffs. He warned himself to calm down and concentrate on the conversation. "There's something I've wanted to ask you for a long time, Dom," Zack said cautiously. "If he's such a 'great guy' and he's got so many 'connections,' why the hell didn't he pull some strings to keep you from doing hard time in here?"

"Oh. That. I made an innocent mistake, and Uncle Enrico thought I needed to learn a lesson."

Sandini sounded so chagrined that Zack glanced up at him. "Why?"

"Because one of the cars I stole the last time belonged to him."

"Then you're lucky you're still alive."

"That's what *he* said."

Tension strangled Zack's laugh.

"He'll be at Gina's wedding. I sure hate to miss that." Changing the subject, he said, "It's a good thing Hadley likes people to recognize you when you drive him around. If you had to keep your hair as short as the rest of the cons, you'd be a lot more conspicuous when you're outside. That little bit of extra hair you've got is gonna—"

Both men started as another trustee walked into the showers and jerked his thumb to the door. "Get a move on, Sandini," he snapped. "You, too, Benedict. The warden wants his car in five minutes."

15

GOOD MORNING, BENEDICT," HADLEY SAID WHEN ZACK knocked on the door of the warden's residence, near the gates of the prison compound. "You're looking as grim and unpleasant as usual, I see. Before we go," he added, "take Hitler for his walk around the yard." As he spoke, he handed Zack a leash that was attached to a large Doberman.

"I'm not your damned butler," Zack snapped, and a slow, gratified grin spread across Hadley's smooth face. "You tired of enjoying my beneficence and the freedom of a trustee? Are you getting an itch to spend some time in my conference room, Benedict?"

Mentally cursing himself for letting his hatred show on a day when he had so much to lose, Zack shrugged and took the leash. "Not particularly." Although Hadley was only 5'6" tall, he had a giant-size ego and an urbane manner that disguised a streak of sadistic, psychopathic viciousness that was known to everyone except, apparently, the State Board of Corrections, who either didn't know or didn't care about the high mortality rate attributed to "prisoner fights" and "attempted escapes" at his facility. The "conference room" was the prison acronym for the soundproof room that adjoined Hadley's office. Prisoners who displeased him were brought there kicking and sweating in real terror; when they left, they were carried out either to solitary, the infirmary, or the morgue. He got a sadistic thrill from making men squirm and grovel; in fact, it wasn't Zack's good behavior that caused Hadley to make him a trustee, it was Hadley's ego. The little warden got a big kick out of having Zachary Benedict at his beck and call, waiting on him. Zack thought it pleasantly ironic that it was Hadley's ego that was finally providing him the means for his escape.

He'd started around the corner of the house when Hadley called, "Benedict, don't forget to clean up after Hitler."

Zack retraced his steps, jerking the snarling dog with him and got the miniature shovel Hadley kept beside the front door. He buttoned his jacket and looked up at the sky; it was cold and the sky looked leaden. It was going to snow.

16

SEATED IN THE BACK SEAT OF THE CAR, WAYNE HADLEY tucked his lecture notes into his briefcase, then he loosened his tie, stretched his legs out, and exhaled a satisfied sigh as he looked at the two trustees in the front seat. Sandini was a petty crook, a skinny wop, a nothing; the only reason he was a trustee was because one of his crooked relatives had clout with somebody in the system, and that somebody sent word down that Dominic Sandini should be a trustee. Sandini provided no amusement, no diversion, no prestige for Hadley at all; there was no pleasure in baiting him. Ah, but Benedict was another story. Benedict the movie star, the sex symbol, the rich tycoon who used to have planes and chauffeur-driven limos. Benedict had been a world-class big shot, and now he waited on Wayne Hadley hand and foot. There was justice in the world, Hadley thought. Real justice. More importantly, even though Benedict tried to hide it, there were times when Hadley could pierce his thick skin and make him squirm and yearn for what he couldn't have, but it wasn't easy. Even when he made Benedict watch the newest movies on videotape and the Academy Awards on television, Hadley couldn't be sure that he'd hit a nerve. With that pleasant goal in mind, Hadley cast around for the right topic and randomly decided on sex. As his car braked to a stop at a traffic light near his destination, he said in a tone of pleasant inquiry, "I'll bet the women begged to get into bed with you when you were rich and famous, didn't they, Benedict? Do you ever think about women, about how they used to feel and smell and taste? You probably didn't like sex that much. If you'd been any good in the sack, that beautiful blond bitch you were married to wouldn't have been getting it on with that guy, Austin, would she?"

In the rearview mirror, he watched with satisfaction as Benedict's jaw tensed slightly and he erroneously assumed it was the sex talk that got to him, not Austin's name. "If you ever get paroled—and I wouldn't count on my recommendation if I were you—you'll have to settle for hookers when you get out. Women are all whores, but even whores have some scruples, and they don't like dirty ex-cons in their beds, did you know that?" Despite his desire to maintain a facade of smooth urbanity at all times around the scum who were his prisoners, Hadley perpetually found it difficult to restrain his temper, and he felt it begin to erupt. "Answer my questions, you son of a bitch, or you'll spend the next month in solitary." Realizing his control had slipped, he said almost pleasantly, "I'll bet you had your own chauffeur in the good old days, didn't you? And now, look at you—you're my chauffeur. There *is* a God." The glass midrise building came into view, and Hadley sat up taller, straightening his tie. "Do you ever wonder what happened to all your money—whatever was left after you paid your lawyers, I mean?"

In answer, Benedict slammed his foot on the brake and brought the car to a teeth-jarring stop in front of the building. Swearing under his breath, Hadley collected the papers that had slid onto the floor and waited in vain for Zack to get out. "You insolent son of a bitch! I don't know what's gotten into you today, but I'll deal with you when we get back. Now get your ass out of the car and open my door!"

Zack got out, oblivious to the biting wind that whipped his thin white jacket off his shoulder but concerned about the snow that was falling in earnest. Five more minutes and he'd be on the run. With a mocking flourish, he jerked open the back door of the car and gestured wide with his arm. "Can you get out on your own, or shall I carry you?"

"You've pushed me for the last time," Hadley warned, getting out and yanking his briefcase off the seat. "You need to learn a few lessons when we get back." Reining in his temper, Hadley glanced at Sandini, who was staring off into space, trying to look docile and deaf. "You have your list of errands, Sandini. Get them done and get back here. You," he ordered Zack, "get your ass over to that grocery store across the street and find me some nice imported cheese and some fresh fruit, then stay in the car. I'll be finished in an hour and a half. Have the car warm and running!"

Without waiting for a reply, Hadley started up sidewalk. Behind him, the two men stood watching his back, waiting for him to enter the building. "What a prick," Sandini said under his breath, then he turned to Zack. "This is it. Good luck." He glanced up at the dark, snow-filled clouds. "This has all the makings of a real blizzard."

Ignoring the weather problem, Zack said quickly, "You know what to do. Don't deviate from the plan and don't, for God's sake, change your story. If you play it exactly the way I told you, you'll come off like a hero instead of an accomplice."

Something about Sandini's lazy grin and preoccupied, restless stance alarmed the hell out of Zack. Clearly and succinctly he repeated the plan that they'd only been able to whisper about before now. "Dom, just do it the way we decided. Leave Hadley's shopping list on the floor of the car. Do your errands for an hour, then tell the clerk in the store that you left your list in the car and can't be sure you got everything. Tell her you have to get it, and come back here. The car will be locked." As he spoke, Zack took the list from Sandini's hand, tossed it on the floor on the passenger side, then he locked and closed the door. With an inner calm he didn't feel, he took Sandini's arm and propelled him firmly toward the corner.

Pickup trucks sped by as they waited for the light to turn green, then they crossed the street unhurriedly—two men who looked like ordinary Texans casually discussing the state of the economy or the next pro football game— except that they wore white pants and white jackets with the initials TDC stenciled in black across the backs. As they neared the curb, Zack continued under his breath, "When you get to the car and discover the door is locked, go across the street to the grocery store, look around a minute, then ask the clerks if they've seen anyone who looks like me. When they tell you they haven't, go to the drugstore and the bookstore and ask if they've seen me. When they tell you no, head straight into that building and start opening doors, asking where the warden's meeting is. Tell everyone you need to report a possible escape. The clerks in all the stores you went to earlier will verify your whole story, and since you're going to alert the warden that I'm missing a half hour before he'd have come out here and discovered it himself, he'll be convinced you're as innocent as a baby. He'll probably let you out early to attend Gina's wedding."

Sandini grinned and gave Zack a jaunty thumbs up instead of a more conspicuous solemn handshake. "Stop worrying about me and get going." Zack nodded, turned, then turned back. "Sandini?" he said solemnly.

"Yeah, Zack?"

"I'm going to miss you."

"Yeah, I know."

"Give Mama my love. Tell your sisters they'll always be my favorite leading ladies," Zack added, then he turned and walked quickly away.

The grocery store was on the corner with a recessed entrance on the street facing the building Hadley was in and another one facing a side street. Forcing himself not to deviate from the plan, Zack walked into the main entrance. In case Hadley should be watching from the building, which he occasionally did, he lingered just inside the doors, unnoticed, and counted slowly to thirty.

Five minutes later, he was several blocks away, his prison jacket tucked under his arm, walking swiftly toward his first destination—the men's room in the Phillips 66 Station on Court Street. His heart beating with suspense and dread, he crossed Court Street on a red light, dashing between a taxi and tow truck that had slowed to make a right turn, then he saw what he was looking for—a nondescript black coupe parked halfway down the block, with Illinois license plates. The car was still there, even though he was two days late getting to it.

With his head bent and his hands in his pockets, he slowed his pace to normal. The snow was beginning to fall in earnest as he strode past the red Corvette pulled up at the gas pumps, heading directly for the men's room at the side of the station. He grasped the door knob and twisted it. It was locked! Resisting the urge to ram his shoulder into the door and try to break it down, he grabbed the knob and rattled it hard. An angry male voice shouted from inside, "Keep your pants on, buster. I'll be out in a minute."

The occupant of the men's room finally emerged several minutes later, yanked open the door, looked around at the empty area outside the building, and then headed for the red Corvette at the pumps. Behind him, Zack moved out from the cover of the dumpster, went into the men's room, and carefully locked the door behind him, all his attention fastened on the overflowing trash can inside it. If anyone had emptied it in the last two days, his luck had just run out.

Grabbing it he turned it over. A few paper towels and beer cans came loose. He shook it again and loosened a deluge of refuse, and then—from the very bottom—two nylon duffel bags tumbled out onto the grimy linoleum floor with a satisfying thud. He yanked open the first bag with one hand and started unbuttoning his prison shirt with his other. That bag yielded up a pair of jeans in his size, a nondescript black sweater, an ordinary denim jacket, boots in his size, and a pair of aviator sunglasses. The other bag contained a map of Colorado with his route highlighted in red, a typewritten list of directions to his ultimate destination—a secluded house deep in the Colorado mountains—two thick, brown envelopes, a .45-calibre automatic pistol, a box of shells, a switchblade, and a set of car keys that he knew would fit into the ignition of the black coupe across the street. The switchblade surprised him. Evidently, Sandini didn't think the well-dressed, escaped convict should be without one.

Mentally ticking off the precious seconds, Zack stripped off his clothes, pulled on the new ones, then he stuffed the old ones into one of the duffel bags and refilled the trash can with the debris from the floor. Vanishing, without leaving a trace or clue about how he'd done it, was vital to his future safety. He opened the thick envelopes and checked the contents: The first contained $25,000 in unmarked twenty-dollar bills and a passport in the name of Alan Aldrich; the second contained an assortment of prepaid airline tickets to various cities, some of them in the name of Alan Aldrich, others in different names that he could use when and if the authorities discovered the alias he was using. Showing his face at an airport was a risk Zack had to avoid taking until things cooled down. Right now, he was pinning most of his hopes on a plan that he had conceived and directed as best he could from a prison cell, using the expensive expertise of some of Sandini's contacts who'd supposedly hired someone who could be mistaken for Zack—a man who was waiting in a Detroit hotel for Zack's phone call. Once he got it, he would rent a car in the name of Benedict Jones and cross the border into Canada at Windsor later tonight.

If the police fell for the scam, then the massive manhunt they were bound to unleash would be centered in Canada, not here, leaving Zack able to head for Mexico and then South America when the search for him lost some of its momentum.

Privately, Zack had grave doubts the diversion would work for long or that he'd ever reach his first destination before he was killed. But none of that mattered right now. At the moment, all that mattered was that he was temporarily free and that he was practically on his way to the Texas–Oklahoma border, ninety miles to the north. If he made it that far without being apprehended, he might be able to make it across the narrow Oklahoma Panhandle, a distance of only thirty-five miles, to the Colorado border. In Colorado, somewhere high in the mountains, was his first destination—a secluded house deep in the woods that, he had long ago been assured, he could use for a "hideaway" whenever he wished.

Between now and then, all he had to worry about was crossing the borders of two states, getting to the safety of that house without being observed by anyone, and, once there, controlling his impatience while he waited until the initial furor over his escape died down so that he could embark on the second stage of his plan.

He picked up the pistol, rammed a full clip into it, checked the safety, and put the gun in his jacket pocket along with a fistful of twenty-dollar bills, then he grabbed the duffel bags and car keys and opened the door. He was going to make it, he was on his way.

He rounded the corner of the building and stepped off the curb, heading toward his car, then he stopped dead, momentarily unable to believe his eyes. The tow truck he'd passed when he crossed the street on his way toward the service station a few minutes ago was pulling away. Hanging from its winch was a black coupe with Illinois plates.

For several seconds, Zack stood there, immobilized, watching it sway through traffic. Behind him, he heard one of the gas station attendants shout to the other, "I told you that car'd been abandoned. It's been sitting there for three days."

Their voices snapped Zack's brain out of its temporary paralysis. He could either go back into the men's room, change into his prison clothes, leave everything behind, and try to reschedule everything for another time or he could improvise now. The choice was really no choice at all. He wasn't going back to prison; he'd rather be dead. Once he remembered that, he did the only thing he could think of — he dashed toward the corner, looking for the only other sure means of getting out of town. A bus was coming down the street. After snatching a discarded newspaper from a trash container, he flagged the bus down and climbed aboard. Holding the newspaper in front of his face as if intent on an article, he made his way down the aisle, past a horde of college students chattering about the next football game, to the back of the bus. For twenty agonizingly slow minutes, the bus lumbered through traffic, belching out fumes and passengers at nearly every corner, then it swung to the right onto a highway that led toward the interstate. By the time the interstate came into view, the passengers had thinned down to a half-dozen rowdy college students, and all of those got up to leave when what seemed to be a favorite beer joint/roadhouse came into view.

Zack had no choice; he left with them via the rear doors and began walking toward the intersection a mile ahead where he knew the interstate on ramp and the access road all joined with the highway. Hitchhiking was his only option, and that option would only be good for a maximum of thirty minutes. Once Hadley realized he was gone, every cop in a fifty-mile radius would be looking for him and focusing their attention on any hitchhiker on the road.

Snow clung to his hair and swirled around his feet as he bent his head into the wind. Several trucks roared past him, the drivers ignoring his upraised thumb, and he fought down a panicky premonition of impending doom. Traffic was heavy on the highway, but everybody was evidently in a hurry to reach their destination before the storm struck, and they weren't stopping for anything. Up ahead at the intersection was an old-fashioned gas station/cafe with two cars in the large parking lot—a blue Blazer and a brown station wagon. Carrying his duffel bags, he walked up the driveway and when he passed the cafe, he glanced carefully through the large front window at the occupants. There was a lone woman in one booth and a mother with two young children in the other. He swore under his breath because both cars belonged to women, and they weren't likely to pick up hitchhikers. Without slowing his pace, Zack continued toward the end of the building, where their two cars were parked, wondering if the keys were in the ignitions. Even if they were, he knew it was insanity to steal one of those cars because he'd have to drive it right past the front window of the cafe in order to get out of the parking lot. If he did that, whoever owned the car would have the cops on the phone, describing him and his vehicle, before he got out of the damned parking lot. What's more, from up here, they could see which way he went on the interstate. Maybe he could try to bribe one of the women in the cafe to give him a ride when she came out.

If money didn't persuade her to agree, he had a gun that could convince her. Christ! There had to be a better way to get out of here than that.

In front of him and below, trucks roared down the interstate making miniblizzards with their wheels. He glanced at his watch. Nearly an hour had passed since Hadley had gone into his meeting. He didn't dare try hitchhiking on that interstate any more. He'd be visible down there from the overpass for a mile. If Sandini had followed instructions, Hadley would be sounding an alert to the local cops in about five minutes. As if his thought had caused it to happen, a local sheriff's car suddenly appeared on the overpass, slowed down, then turned into the cafe's parking lot fifty yards away from Zack's hiding spot, coming toward him.

Instinctively, Zack crouched down, pretending that he was inspecting the tire on the Blazer, and then inspiration struck—too late perhaps, but maybe not. Yanking the switchblade out of the duffel bag, he rammed it into the side of the Blazer's tire, ducking to one side to avoid the explosion of air. From the corner of his eye, he watched the patrol car glide to a stop behind him. Instead of demanding to know what Zack was doing loitering around the cafe with duffle bags, the local sheriff rolled down his car window and drew the obvious conclusion. "Looks like you got a flat there—"

"Sure as hell," Zack agreed, slapping the side of the tire, careful not to look over his shoulder. "My wife tried to warn me this tire had a leak—" The rest of his words were drowned out by the sudden frantic squawking of the police radio, and without another word, the cop wheeled the patrol car into a screeching turn, accelerated sharply, and roared out of the parking lot with its siren wailing. A moment later, Zack heard more sirens coming from every direction, and then he saw the patrol cars racing across the overpass, their warning lights revolving.

The authorities, Zack knew, were now aware that an escaped convict was on the loose. The hunt had begun.

Inside the cafe, Julie finished her coffee and groped in her purse for money to pay the check. Her visit with Mr. Vernon had gotten her more than she'd expected, including an invitation to spend more time with his wife and him that she hadn't been able to refuse. She had a five-hour drive in front of her, longer with all this snow, but she had a fat check in her purse and enough excitement about that to make the miles fly past. She glanced at her watch, picked up the thermos she'd brought in from the car to be filled with coffee, smiled at the children eating with their mother in the adjoining booth, and walked up to the cash register to pay her bill.

As she emerged from the building, she stopped in surprise as a squad car suddenly made a frantic U-turn in front of her, turned on its siren, then shot out of the parking lot onto the highway, its rear end fishtailing in the thin blanket of snow. Distracted by that, she didn't notice the dark haired man squatting beside the rear wheel of her car on the driver's side until she almost stumbled over him. He stood up abruptly, towering over her from a height of about 6'2", and she took a startled, cautious step backward, her voice shaky with alarm and suspicion. "What are you doing there?" she demanded, frowning at her own image as it was reflected back at her from the silvery lenses of his aviator sunglasses.

Zack actually managed a semblance of a smile because his mind had finally started working, and he now knew exactly how he was going to get her to offer him a ride. Imagination and the ability to improvise had been two of his biggest assets as a director. Nodding toward her rear tire, which was very obviously flat, he said, "I'm planning to change your tire for you if you have a jack."

Julie's breath came out in a rush of chagrin. "I'm sorry for being so rude, but you startled me. I was watching that squad car tearing out of here."

"That was Joe Loomis, a local constable," Zack improvised smoothly, deliberately making it sound as if the cop was a friend of his. "Joe got another call and had to leave, or he'd have given me a hand with your tire."

Julie's fears were completely allayed, and she smiled at him. "This is very kind of you," she said, opening the tailgate of the Blazer and looking for a jack. "This is my brother's car. The jack is somewhere in here, but I'm not sure where."

"There," Zack said, quickly locating the jack and taking it out. "This will only take a few minutes," he added. He was in a hurry, but no longer fighting down panic. The woman already thought he was friendly with the local sheriff, so she'd naturally think he was trustworthy, and after he changed her tire, she'd *owe* him a ride. Once they were on the road, the police wouldn't give them a second glance because they'd be looking for a man who was traveling alone. For now, if anyone noticed him, he would appear to be an ordinary husband changing a tire while his wife looked on. "Where are you headed?" he asked her, using the jack.

"East toward Dallas for a long way and then south," Julie said, admiring his easy skill with the heavy vehicle. He had an unusually nice voice, uncommonly deep and smooth, and a strong, square jawline. His hair was dark brown and very thick, but poorly cut, and she wondered idly what he looked like without the concealing barrier of those reflective sunglasses. Very handsome, she decided, but it wasn't his good looks that kept drawing her eyes back to his profile, it was something else, something illusive that she couldn't pinpoint. Julie shrugged the feeling off, and cradling the thermos in her arm, she embarked on polite conversation. "Do you work around here?"

"Not any more. I was supposed to start a new job tomorrow, but I have to be there by seven in the morning or they'll give it to someone else." He finished jacking the car up and began loosening the lug bolts on the tire, then he nodded toward the nylon duffel bags that Julie hadn't seen before because they had somehow gotten shoved under her car. "A friend of mine was supposed to pick me up here two hours ago and give me a ride part of the way," he added, "but I guess something happened and he isn't going to make it."

"You've been waiting out here for two hours?" Julie exclaimed. "You must be frozen."

He kept his face averted, apparently concentrating on his task, and Julie restrained the peculiar urge to try to bend down and get a longer, closer look at him. "Would you like a cup of coffee?"

"I'd love one."

Rather than use up what was in the thermos, Julie headed back into the cafe. "I'll get it for you. How do you drink it?"

"Black," Zack said, fighting to keep his frustration in check. She was heading southeast from Amarillo, whereas his destination was four hundred miles to the northwest. He stole a glance at his watch and began working even faster. Nearly an hour and a half had passed since he walked away from the warden's car, and his risk of capture was increasing every moment he stayed around Amarillo. Regardless of which way the woman was going, he had to go with her. Putting some miles between himself and Amarillo was all that mattered now. He could ride with her for an hour and double back via a different route later.

The waitress needed to brew another pot of coffee, and by the time Julie returned to her car with the steaming paper cup, her rescuer had nearly finished changing the tire. Snow was already two inches deep on the ground and the biting wind was gathering force, whipping the sides of her coat open and making her eyes water. She saw him rub his bare hands together and thought of the new job that was waiting for him tomorrow—if he could get there. She knew jobs in Texas, especially blue-collar jobs, were scarce, and based on his lack of a car, he was probably badly in need of money. His jeans were new, she realized, noticing for the first time the telltale vertical crease down the front of the legs when he stood up. He had probably bought them in order to make a good impression on his future employer, she decided, and the thought of him doing that sent sympathy pouring through her.

Julie had never before offered a hitchhiker a ride; the risks were far too high, but she decided to do it this time, not only because he'd changed her tire or because he seemed nice, but also because of a simple pair of jeans—new jeans. New jeans, stiff and spotless, obviously purchased by a jobless man who was pinning all his hopes on a brighter future that wasn't going to materialize unless someone gave him a ride at least partway to his destination so he could start to work.

"It looks like you're finished," Julie said, walking up to him. She held the cup of coffee out to him and he took it in hands that were red from the cold. There was an aloofness about him that made her hesitate to offer him money, but on the chance he'd prefer that to a ride, she offered anyway. "I'd like to pay you for changing the tire," she began, and when he curtly shook his head, she added, "In that case, can I give you a ride? I'm going to take the interstate east."

"I'd appreciate the ride," Zack said, accepting her offer with a brief smile as he quickly reached down and pulled the nylon duffel bags out from under the car. "I'm heading east, too."

When they got into the car, he told her his name was Alan Aldrich. Julie introduced herself as Julie Mathison, but to make certain he realized she was offering him a ride and nothing more, she carefully addressed him the next time she spoke as Mr. Aldrich. He picked up her cue and thereafter called her Miss Mathison.

Julie relaxed completely after that. The formality of Miss Mathison was completely reassuring, and so was his immediate acceptance of their situation. But when he remained absolutely silent and distant thereafter, she began to wish she hadn't insisted on formality. She knew she wasn't good at hiding her thoughts, therefore he'd probably realized at once that she was putting him in his place—a needless insult, considering that he'd shown her only gallant kindness by changing her tire.

17

THEY'D BEEN ON THE ROAD FOR FULLY TEN MINUTES BEFORE Zack felt the strangling tension in his chest begin to dissolve, and he drew a long, full breath—his first easy breath in hours. No, months. Years. Futility and helplessness had raged in him for so long that he felt almost lightheaded without them. A red car roared past them, cut across their lane to exit the interstate, lost traction, and spun around, missing the Blazer by inches—and then only because the young woman beside him handled the four-wheel-drive vehicle with surprising skill. Unfortunately, she also drove too damned fast, with the daredevil aggressiveness and fearless disregard of danger that was uniquely and typically Texan in his experience.

He was wishing there was some way he could suggest she let him drive, when she said in a quietly amused voice, "You can relax now. I've slowed down. I didn't mean to scare you."

"I wasn't afraid," he said with unintentional curtness.

She glanced sideways at him and smiled, a slow, knowing smile. "You're holding onto the dashboard with both hands. That's usually a dead giveaway."

Two things struck Zack at once: He'd been in prison so long that lighthearted banter between adult members of the opposite sex had become completely awkward and alien to him and Julie Mathison had a breathtaking smile. Her smile glowed in her eyes and lit up her entire face, transforming what was merely a pretty face into one that was captivating. Since wondering about her was infinitely preferable to worrying about things he couldn't yet control, Zack concentrated on her. She wore no makeup except for a little lipstick, and there was a freshness about her, a simplicity in the way she wore her thick, shiny brown hair, all of which had made him think she was in her late teens or very early twenties. On the other hand, she seemed too confident and self-assured for a twenty-year-old. "How old are you?" he asked bluntly, then winced at the brusque tactlessness of the question. Obviously if they didn't catch him and send him back to prison, he was going to have to relearn some things he'd thought were bred into him—like rudimentary courtesy and conversational etiquette with women.

Instead of being irritated by the question, she flashed him another one of those mesmerizing smiles of hers and said in a voice laced with amusement, "I'm twenty-six."

"My God!" Zack heard himself blurt, then he closed his eyes in disgusted disbelief at his gaucheness. "I mean," he explained, "you don't look that old."

She seemed to sense his discomfiture, because she laughed softly and said, "Probably because I've only been twenty-six for a few weeks."

Afraid to trust himself to say anything spontaneous, he watched the windshield wipers carve a steady half-moon in the snow on the windshield while he reviewed his next question for any trace of the tastelessness that had marred his previous words. Feeling this one was safe, he said, "What do you do?"

"I'm a schoolteacher."

"You don't look like one."

Inexplicably, the laughter rekindled in her eyes and he saw her bite back a smile. Feeling completely disoriented and confused by her unpredictable reactions, he said a little curtly, "Did I just say something funny?"

Julie shook her head and said, "Not at all. That's what most older people say."

Zack wasn't certain whether she'd referred to him as being "older" because he actually looked like an antique to her or if it was a joking retaliation for his ill-advised remarks about her age and appearance. He was puzzling over that when she asked what he did for a living, and he answered with the first occupation that seemed to suit what he'd already told her about himself.

"I'm in construction."

"Really? My brother's in construction work, too—a general contractor. What sort of construction work do you do?"

Zack barely knew which end of a hammer to use on a nail, and he sorely wished he'd picked a more obscure job or, better yet, had remained completely silent. "Walls," he replied vaguely. "I do walls."

She took her eyes from the road, which alarmed him, and regarded him intently, which alarmed him even more. "Walls?" she repeated sounding puzzled. Then she explained, "I meant, do you have a specialty?"

"Yes. Walls," Zack said shortly, angry with himself for having begun such a conversation. "That's my specialty. I put up walls."

Julie realized she must have misunderstood him the first time. "Drywall!" she exclaimed ruefully. "Of course. You're a drywall taper?"

"Right."

"In that case, I'm surprised you have any trouble finding work. Good tapers are usually in great demand."

"I'm *not* a *good* one," Zack stated flatly, making it clear he wasn't interested in continuing that conversation.

Julie choked back a startled laugh at his answer and his tone and concentrated on the road. He was a very unusual man. She couldn't decide whether she liked him and was glad of his company . . . or not. And she couldn't get over the uneasy feeling that he reminded her of someone. She wished she could see his face without those sunglasses so she could figure out who it was. The city vanished in the rearview mirror and the sky turned the heavy, ominous gray of an early dusk. Silence hung in the car and fat snow smacked her windshield, slowly gaining an edge on the car's windshield wipers. They'd been on the road for about a half hour when Zack glanced in the outside rearview mirror on his side—and his blood froze. A half mile behind them, and closing fast, was a police car with its red and blue lights rotating furiously.

A second later, he heard the siren begin to wail.

The woman beside him heard it, too; she glanced in the rearview mirror and took her foot off of the gas pedal, slowing the Blazer and angling it onto the shoulder. Zack reached into his jacket pocket, his hand closing on the butt of the automatic, although he had no precise idea at that moment exactly what he meant to do if the cop tried to pull them over. The squad car was so close now, he could see there were not one, but two cops in the front seat. They pulled around the Blazer . . .

And kept going.

"There must be an accident up there," she said as they crested the hill and came to a stop behind what looked like a five-mile traffic jam on the snowy interstate. A moment later two ambulances came tearing around them.

Zack's rush of adrenalin subsided, leaving him shaken and limp. He felt as if he'd suddenly exceeded his capacity to react with violent emotion to anything whatsoever, which was probably due to his having been trying to execute for two days a carefully thought-out escape plan that should have been a guaranteed success by virtue of its sheer simplicity. And would have been if Hadley hadn't postponed his trip to Amarillo. Everything else that had gone wrong was a result of that. He wasn't sure even now if his contact was still in his Detroit hotel, waiting for Zack's call before he rented a car to drive to Windsor. And until Zack was further away from Amarillo, he didn't dare stop to find a telephone. Moreover, although Colorado was only 130 miles from Amarillo, with a tiny piece of Oklahoma's Panhandle in between, he needed to be traveling northwest to get there. Instead, he was now heading southeast. Thinking his Colorado map might also contain a small piece of the Oklahoma and Texas panhandles, he decided to occupy his time productively by looking for a new route from here to there. Twisting around in his seat, he said, "I think I'll have a look at a map."

Julie naturally assumed he was checking his route to whatever Texas town his new job was located in. "Where are you heading?" she asked.

"Ellerton," he replied, sending her a brief smile as he reached past the folded down back seat for his duffel bag near the tailgate. "I interviewed for the job in Amarillo, but I've never been out to the site," he added so she wouldn't ask questions about the place.

"I don't think I've ever heard of Ellerton." Several minutes later, when he neatly refolded the map with its typewritten sheet on the top, Julie said, "Did you find Ellerton?"

"No." To dissuade her from asking any further questions about the location of a nonexistent town, he flashed the typewritten sheet at her as he bent over the seat to put it back into his duffel. "I have detailed instructions right here, so I'll find it."

She nodded, but her gaze was on the exit up ahead. "I think I'll get off the interstate here and take a side road to get past the accident."

"Good idea." The exit turned out to be a rural road that ran roughly parallel with the interstate then began angling off to the right. "This might not have been a good idea after all," she said several minutes later when the narrow blacktop road began to wind steadily further away from the main highway.

Zack didn't immediately reply. At the intersection up ahead, there was a deserted gas station and at the edge of the empty lot near the road was an open phone booth. "I'd like to make a phone call if you wouldn't mind stopping. It won't take more than a couple of minutes."

"I don't mind at all." Julie pulled the Blazer to a stop underneath the street lamp near the phone booth and watched him walk across the headlight's beams. Dusk had descended even earlier than usual, and the storm seemed to be outrunning them, dumping snow with surprising force, even for the blustery Texas Panhandle. Deciding to exchange her bulky coat for a cardigan sweater that would be more comfortable while she drove, she turned on the radio, hoping for a weather forecast, then she got out of the car, walked around to the tailgate, and opened it.

With the tailgate down she could hear the Amarillo announcer extolling the wisdom of buying a new car at Wilson Ford:

"Bob Wilson will meet any price, anywhere, anytime . . ." he enthused.

Listening for a mention of the weather, she took off her coat, pulled her tan mohair sweater out of her suitcase, and glanced at the map that was sticking out of his duffel bag. Since she didn't have a map with her and wasn't entirely sure what route would intersect with the interstate or if she was taking her passenger so far out of his way that he'd prefer to try to hitchhike with someone else, she decided to look at his map. She glanced at him in the phone booth, intending to hold up the map and ask his permission, but his shoulder was turned to her and he seemed to be speaking into the phone. Deciding he couldn't possibly object, Julie folded the typewritten instructions back and opened the map he'd been studying. Spreading it across the tailgate, she held the ends down while the wind tried to whip them out of her hands. It took a full moment before she realized it wasn't a map of Texas, but of Colorado. Puzzled, she glanced at the neatly typed instructions attached to the map: "Exactly 26.4 miles after you've passed the town of Stanton," it said, "you'll come to an unmarked crossroads. After that, begin looking for a narrow dirt road that branches off from the right and disappears into the trees about fifteen yards off the highway. The house is at the end of that road, about five miles from your turnoff, and is not visible from the highway or any side of the mountain."

Julie's lips parted in surprise. He was heading not for a job in some unknown Texas town, but for a house in Colorado?

On the radio, the announcer finished his commercial and said, *"We'll have an update on the storm coming our way, but first, here's some late breaking news from the sheriff's department . . ."*

Julie scarcely heard him, she was staring at the tall man using the phone, and she felt again that strange, slithering unease . . . of shadowy familiarity. He'd kept his shoulder turned to her, but he'd removed his sunglasses and was holding them in his hand now. As if he sensed she was staring at him, he twisted his head toward her. His eyes narrowed on the open map in her hands at the same instant Julie had her first clear, brightly lit view of his face without the concealing sunglasses.

"At approximately four o'clock this afternoon," said the voice on the radio, *"Prison officials discovered that convicted murderer Zachary Benedict escaped while in Amarillo—"*

Momentarily paralyzed, Julie stared at that rugged, harsh face of his.

And she recognized it.

"No!" she cried as he dropped the phone and started running toward her. She bolted around her side of the car, yanking her door open and diving across the front seat, slapping at the lock on the passenger door a split second after he yanked the door open and grabbed for her wrist. With a strength born of pure terror, she managed to wrench her arm free and throw herself sideways through her open door. She hit the ground on her hip, scrambled to her feet, and started running, her feet sliding on the slippery snow, screaming for someone to help, knowing there was no one around to hear her. He caught her before she'd run five yards and yanked her around and back, trapping her against the side of the Blazer. "Hold still and shut up!"

"Take the car!" Julie cried. "Take it and leave me here."

Ignoring her, he looked over his shoulder at the map of Colorado that had blown against a rusty trash container fifteen feet away when she dropped it. As if in slow motion, Julie watched him remove a shiny black object from his pocket and point it at her, while he backed toward the map and picked it up. A gun. God in heaven, he had a gun!

Her entire body began to tremble uncontrollably while she listened in a kind of hysterical disbelief to the newscaster's voice belatedly confirming that fact as the news bulletin came to an end: "*Benedict is believed to be armed and he is dangerous. If seen, his whereabouts should be reported immediately to the Amarillo police. Citizens should not attempt to approach him. A second escaped convict, Dominic Sandini, has been apprehended and taken into custody . . .*"

Her knees threatened to buckle as she watched him coming toward her with a gun in one hand and the map and directions blowing from his other hand. Headlights crested the hill a quarter of a mile away, and he slid the gun back into his pocket to keep it out of sight, but he kept his hand there with it. "Get into the car," he ordered.

Julie flashed a look over her left shoulder at the approaching pickup truck, frantically calculating the impossible odds of outrunning a bullet or even being able to attract the notice of the vehicle's driver before Zachary Benedict shot her down. "Don't try it," he warned in a deadly voice.

Her heart thundering against her ribs, she watched the pickup turn left at the crossroads, but she didn't disobey his order. Not here, not yet. Instinct warned her that this deserted stretch of road was too isolated to succeed in anything but getting killed.

"Get moving!" He took her arm and headed her to the open door on the driver's side. Cloaked in the deepening dusk of a snowy winter evening, Julie Mathison walked unsteadily beside a convicted murderer who was holding a gun on her. She had the chilling sensation they were both living a scene from one of his own movies—the one where the hostage got killed.

18

HER HANDS SHOOK SO VIOLENTLY SHE HAD TO GROPE FOR THE keys in the ignition, and when she tried to start the car she nearly flooded the engine because even her legs were jerking with fright. He watched her unemotionally from the passenger seat. "Drive," he snapped when the engine was started. Julie managed to turn the car around and guide it to the end of the parking lot, but she stopped at the main road, her mind so paralyzed with terror that she couldn't think of the words to ask the obvious question.

"I said drive!"

"Which *way?*" she cried, hating the timid, pleading sound of her voice and loathing the animal beside her for making her experience this uncontrollable terror.

"Back the way we came."

"B-back?"

"You heard me."

Rush hour traffic on the snowbound interstate near the city limits was moving at a crawl. Inside the car, the tension and silence were suffocating. Trying desperately to calm her rampaging nerves while she watched for some chance to escape, Julie lifted her shaking hand to change the radio station, fully expecting him to order her not to do it. When he said nothing, she turned the dial and heard a disk jockey's voice exuberantly introducing the next country/western song. A moment later the car was filled with the cheerful sounds of "All My Ex's Live in Texas."

While George Strait sang, Julie looked around at the occupants of the other cars, homeward bound after a long day. The man in the Explorer beside her was listening to the same radio station, his fingers tapping on the steering wheel, keeping time with the melody. He glanced her way, saw her looking at him, and nodded sociably, then he returned his gaze to the front. She knew he hadn't seen anything abnormal. Everything looked perfectly normal to him, and if he were sitting where she was in the Blazer, it would have seemed perfectly normal. George Strait was singing, just like normal, and the expressway was crowded with motorists who were eager to get home, just like normal, and the snow was beautiful, just like normal. Everything was normal.

Except for one thing.

An escaped murderer was sitting in the seat beside her, holding a gun on her. It was the cozy normalcy of appearances juxtaposed against the demented reality of her situation that suddenly shoved Julie from paralysis to action. Traffic began to move, and her desperation gave birth to inspiration: They'd already passed several cars in ditches on both sides of the road. If she could fake a skid toward the ditch on the right and if she could throw the steering wheel to the left just as they went into the ditch, her door should remain usable while his might very well be trapped. It would work in her own car, but she wasn't sure how the Blazer's four-wheel drive would respond.

Beside her, Zack saw her gaze flick repeatedly to the side of the road. He sensed her mounting panic and knew that fear was going to drive her to try something desperate at any moment. "Relax!" he ordered.

Julie's capacity for fear suddenly reached its limits and her emotions veered crazily from terror to fury. "Relax!" she exploded in a shaking voice, whipping her head around and glaring at him. "How in God's name do you expect me to relax when you're sitting there with a gun aimed at me? You tell me that!"

She had a point, Zack thought, and before she attempted something else that might actually get him captured, he decided that helping her to relax was in both of their best interests. "Just stay calm," he instructed.

Julie stared straight ahead. Traffic was thinning out slightly, picking up some speed, and she began to calculate the feasibility of ramming the Blazer into the cars around her in an attempt to cause a major pileup. Such an action would cause the police to be summoned. That would be very good.

But she and the other innocent motorists involved in the collision would likely end up being shot by Zachary Benedict.

That would be very bad.

She was wondering if his gun had a full clip of nine shells in it and whether he would actually massacre helpless people, when he said in a calm, condescending voice that adults use on hysterical children, "Nothing is going to happen to you, Julie. If you do as you're told, you'll be fine. I need transportation to the state line, and you have a car, it's as simple as that. Unless this car is so important to you that you want to risk your life to get me out of it, all you have to do is drive and not attract anyone's attention. If a cop spots us, there's going to be shooting, and you'll be in the middle of it. So just be a good girl and relax."

"If you want me to relax," she retorted, goaded past all endurance by his patronizing tone and her strained nerves, "then you let *me* hold that gun, and I'll show you relaxed!" She saw his brows snap together, but when he didn't make a retaliatory move, she almost believed that he truly didn't intend to harm her—so long as she didn't jeopardize his escape. That possibility had the perverse effect of subduing her fears and simultaneously unleashing her frustrated fury at the torment he'd already put her through. "Furthermore," she continued wrathfully, "don't speak to me like I'm a child and don't call me Julie! I was *Ms. Mathison* to you when I thought you were a nice, decent man who needed a job and who'd bought those d-damned jeans to impress your em-employer. If it hadn't been for those damned j-jeans, I wouldn't be in this mess—" To Julie's horror, she felt the sudden sting of tears, so she shot him what she hoped was a disdainful look and then glared fixedly out the windshield.

Zack lifted his brows and regarded her in impassive silence, but inwardly he was stunned and reluctantly impressed by her unexpected show of courage. Turning his head, he looked at the traffic opening up ahead of them and at the thick, falling snow that had seemed like a curse a few hours ago but had actually diverted the attention of the police who had to deal with stranded motorists before they could begin to search for him. Last, he considered the stroke of luck that had put him not in the small rented car that had been towed away while he watched, but in a heavy four-wheel-drive vehicle that could easily navigate in the snow without getting bogged down on the less traveled route he intended to take up into the Colorado mountains. All of the delays and complications that had infuriated him for the last two days had turned out to be bonuses, he realized. He was going to make it to Colorado—thanks to Julie Mathison. *Ms.* Mathison, he corrected himself with an inner grin as he relaxed back in his seat. His flash of amusement vanished as quickly as it had come, because there was something about that newscast he'd heard earlier that was belatedly beginning to worry him: Dominic Sandini had been referred to as "another escaped convict" who "was apprehended and taken into custody." If Sandini had stuck to the plan, then Warden Hadley should have been crowing to the press about the loyalty of one of his trustees rather than referring to Sandini as an apprehended convict.

Zack told himself that the information on the newscast had simply been jumbled, which accounted for the mistake about Sandini, and he forced himself to concentrate on the irate young teacher beside him instead. Although he desperately needed her and her car right now, she was also a serious complication to his plans. She probably knew he was heading for Colorado; moreover, she might have seen enough of that map and the directions with it to be able to tell the police the vicinity of Zack's hideaway. If he left her at the Texas–Oklahoma border or a little further north at the Oklahoma–Colorado border, she'd be able to tell the authorities where he was going and exactly what kind of car he was driving as well. By now, his face was already plastered all over every television screen in the country, so he couldn't possibly hope to rent or buy another car without being recognized. Furthermore, he wanted the police to believe he'd managed to fly to Detroit and cross into Canada.

Julie Mathison seemed to be both a godsend and a disastrous kink in his plans. Rather than curse fate for saddling him with her and the deadly threat to his freedom that she represented, he decided to give fate an opportunity to work out this problem and to try to help them both relax. Reaching behind him for the thermos of coffee, he thought back to her last remarks and came up with what seemed like a good conversational opening. In a carefully offhand, nonthreatening tone, he inquired sociably, "What's wrong with my jeans?"

She gaped at him in blank confusion. "What?"

"You said something about my 'damned jeans' being the only reason you offered me a ride," he explained, filling the top of the thermos with coffee. "What's wrong with my jeans?"

Julie swallowed an hysterical surge of angry laughter. She was concerned about her life, and he was concerned about making a fashion statement!

"What," he repeated determinedly, "did you mean?"

She was on the verge of an angry retort when two things occurred to her at once—that it was insane to deliberately antagonize an armed man and that if she could make him relax his guard by indulging in small talk with him, her chances to either escape or get out of this alive would be vastly improved. Trying to inject a polite, neutral tone into her voice, she drew a long breath and said without taking her eyes from the road, "I noticed your jeans were new."

"What did that have to do with your deciding to offer me a ride?"

Bitterness at her own gullibility filled Julie's voice. "Since you didn't have a car and you implied you didn't have a job, I assumed you must be having a hard time financially. Then you said you were hoping to get a new job, and I noticed the crease in your jeans . . ." Her voice trailed off when she realized with a disgusted jolt that instead of the nearly destitute man she'd thought him to be he was actually a megamillionaire movie star.

"Go on," he prodded, his voice tinged with puzzlement.

"I leapt to the obvious conclusion, for heaven's sake! I figured you'd bought new jeans so you could make a good impression on your employer, and I imagined how important that must have been to you while you were buying them in the store and how much hope you must have been feeling when you bought them, and I-I couldn't bear the thought that your hope was going to be trashed if I didn't offer you a ride. So even though I've never picked up a hitchhiker in my life, I couldn't stand to see you miss having your chance."

Zack was not only stunned, he was unwillingly touched. Kindness like hers, a kindness that also required some kind of personal risk or sacrifice, had been absent from his existence for all the years he'd spent in prison. And even before that, he realized. Shoving the unsettling thought aside, he said, "You envisioned all that from a crease in a pair of jeans? You've got one hell of an imagination," he added with a sardonic shake of his head.

"I'm obviously a bad judge of character, too," Julie said bitterly. From the corner of her eye, she saw his left arm swing toward her and she jumped, muffling a scream before she realized he was only holding out a cup of coffee from the thermos. In a quiet tone that almost seemed to carry an apology for adding to her fright, he said, "I thought this might help."

"I'm not in the slightest danger of falling asleep at the wheel, thanks to you."

"Drink some anyway," Zack ordered, determined to ease her terror even while he knew his presence was the source of it. "It will—" he hesitated, feeling at a loss for words, and added, "It will make things seem more normal."

Julie turned her head and gaped at him, her expression making it eloquently clear she found his "concern" for her not only completely revolting, but insane. She was on the verge of telling him that, but she remembered the gun in his pocket, so she took the coffee in a shaking hand and turned away from him, sipping it and staring at the road ahead.

Beside her, Zack watched the telltale trembling of the coffee cup as she raised it to her lips, and he felt a ridiculous urge to apologize for terrifying her like this. She had a lovely profile he thought, studying her face in the light of the dashboard, with a small nose and stubborn chin and high cheekbones. She also had magnificent eyes, he decided, thinking of the way they'd shot sparks at him a few minutes ago. Spectacular eyes. He felt a sharp stab of guilty shame for using and frightening this innocent girl who'd been trying to be a good samaritan— and because he had every intention of continuing to use her, he felt like the animal everybody believed he was. To silence his conscience, he resolved to make things as easy on her as he possibly could, which led him to decide to engage her in further conversation.

He'd noticed she wore no wedding ring, which meant she wasn't married. He tried to remember what people—civilized people on the "outside"—talked about for idle conversation, and he finally said, "Do you like teaching?"

She turned again, her incredible eyes wide with suppressed antagonism. "Do you expect me," she uttered in disbelief, "to engage in polite *small talk* with you?"

"Yes!" he snapped, irrationally angry at her reluctance to let him make amends. "I do. Start talking!"

"I love teaching," Julie shot back shakily, hating how easily he could intimidate her. "How far do you intend for me to drive you?" she demanded as they passed a sign that said the Oklahoma border was twenty miles away.

"Oklahoma," Zack said, half-truthfully.

19

"WE'RE IN OKLAHOMA," JULIE POINTED OUT THE INSTANT they drove past the sign announcing they were there.

He shot her a look of grim amusement. "I see that."

"Well? Where do you want to get out?"

"Keep driving."

"Keep driving?" she cried in nervous fury. "Now look, you miserable—I'm not driving you all the way to Colorado!"

Zack had his answer; she knew where he was going.

"I won't do it!" Julie warned shakily, unaware that she had just sealed her fate. "I can't."

With an inner sigh at the battle she was bound to wage, he said, "Yes, Ms. Mathison, you can. And you will."

His unflappable calm was the last straw. "Go to hell!" Julie cried, swinging the steering wheel hard to the right before he could stop her and sending the vehicle careening onto the shoulder as she slammed on the brakes and brought it to a lurching stop. "Take the car!" she pleaded. "Take it and leave me here. I won't tell anyone I've seen you or where you're going. I swear I won't tell anyone."

Zack reined in his temper and tried to soothe her with an attempt at levity. "In the movies, people always promise that same thing," he remarked conversationally, glancing over his shoulder at the cars flying past. "I've always thought it sounded asinine."

"This isn't the movies!"

"But you do agree that it *is* an absurd promise," he argued with a slight smile. "You know it is. Admit it, Julie."

Shocked that he was apparently trying to *tease* her as if they were friends, Julie stared at him in furious silence, knowing he was right about the promise being ridiculous, but refusing to admit it.

"You can't really expect me to believe," he continued, his voice softening a little, "that you'd let me get away with kidnapping you and stealing your car and then be so grateful to me for doing both that you'd keep a promise to me you made under extreme duress? Doesn't that sound a little insane to you?"

"Do you expect me to debate psychology with you when my whole life is at stake!" she burst out.

"I realize you're afraid, but your life isn't at stake unless you put it there. You aren't in any danger unless you create it."

Perhaps it was exhaustion or the low timbre of his voice or the steadiness of his gaze, but as Julie looked at his solemn features, she found herself almost believing him.

"I don't want you to get hurt," he continued, "and you won't, as long as you don't do anything that attracts attention to me and alerts the law—"

"In which case," Julie interrupted bitterly, snapping out of her trance, "you will blow my brains out with your gun. That's very comforting, Mr. Benedict. Thank you."

Zack held his temper in check and explained, "If the cops catch up with me, they'll have to kill me, because I'm not going to surrender. Given the vigilante mentality of most cops, there's a good chance you'll be hurt or killed in the fray. I don't want that to happen. Can you understand that?"

Furious with herself for being subdued by empty gentle words from a ruthless murderer, Julie jerked her gaze from his and stared out the front window. "Do you actually think you can convince me you're Sir Galahad and not a depraved monster?"

"Evidently not," he said irritably.

When she refused to look at him again, Zack gave an impatient sign and said curtly, "Stop sulking and start driving. I need to find a roadside telephone at one of these exits."

The moment his voice chilled, Julie realized how foolish she'd been to ignore his "friendly" overture and antagonize him. What she probably ought to be doing, she belatedly decided as she pulled back out onto the highway, was fooling him into believing she was resigned to going along with him. As the snowflakes danced in front of her headlights, her mind began to calm and she thought carefully about possible ways out of her predicament, because it now seemed horribly likely that he was going to force her to drive him through Colorado as well as Oklahoma. Finding a means to foil his plan and get away became not only a necessity, but a downright challenge. To do that, she knew she had to be objective and to keep all traces of fright and fury from clouding her thoughts. She should be able to do that, Julie reminded herself bracingly. After all, she was no sheltered, unworldly, pampered hothouse flower. She'd spent the first eleven years of her life on the streets of Chicago and done just fine! Chewing on her lower lip, she decided to try to think of her ordeal as if it were merely a plot in one of the mystery novels she loved to read. She'd always felt some of the heroines in those novels behaved with sublime stupidity, which was what she'd been doing by antagonizing her captor, she decided. A clever heroine would do the opposite, she'd be devious and find ways to make Benedict relax his guard completely. If he did that, her chances to escape—and get him returned to prison where he belonged—would be dramatically increased. To accomplish that goal, she could try to pretend she was coming to think of this nightmare as an adventure, maybe she could even pretend to be on the side of her captor, which would require a stellar performance, but she was willing to try.

Despite her grave misgivings about her ability to succeed, Julie suddenly felt a welcome calm and determination sweep through her, banishing her fear and leaving her head clearer. She waited several moments before speaking, so that her capitulation wouldn't seem too sudden and suspicious to him, then she drew a steadying breath and tried to inject a rueful note into her voice: "Mr. Benedict," she said, actually managing to cast him a slight, sideways smile, "I appreciate what you said about not intending to hurt me. I didn't mean to be sarcastic. I was afraid, that's all."

"And now you aren't afraid?" he countered, his voice laced with skepticism.

"Well, yes," Julie hastened to assure him. "But not nearly so much. That's what I meant."

"May I inquire what brought about this sudden transformation? What were you thinking about while you were so quiet?"

"A book," she said because it seemed safe. "A mystery."

"One you've read? Or one you're thinking about writing?"

Her mouth opened, but no words came out, and then she realized he'd inadvertently handed her the perfect means to his own defeat. "I've always wanted to write a mystery someday," she improvised madly, "and it occurred to me that this could be, well, first-hand research."

"I see."

She darted another glance at him and was startled by the warmth of his smile.

This devil could charm a snake, she realized, recalling that same smile from the days when it had flashed across movie screens and raised the temperature of the entire female audience.

"You are a remarkably brave young woman, Julie."

She choked her irate demand to be called Ms. Mathison. "Actually, I'm the world's greatest coward, Mr.—"

"My name is Zack," he interrupted, and in his impassive tone she sensed a return of his suspicion.

"Zack," she hastily agreed. "You're quite right. We ought to use first names, since we're apparently going to be together for—?"

"A while," he provided, and Julie made a Herculean effort to conceal her frustrated fury at his oblique reply.

"A while," she agreed, careful to keep her tone neutral. "Well, that's probably long enough for you to help me with some preliminary research," she hesitated, thinking of what to ask him. "Would you, well, consider giving me some insight into what prison is really like. That would be helpful for my story."

"Would it?"

He was scaring the hell out of her with the subtle, ever-changing nuances in his voice. Never before had she known a man or woman who could convey so much with imperceptible changes in his voice, nor had she heard a voice like his in her life. It had a rich baritone timbre that could switch instantly and unaccountably from polite to amused to icy and ominous. In answer to his question, Julie nodded vigorously, trying to counteract his skeptical tone by injecting energy and conviction in her own. "Absolutely." In a flash of inspiration, she realized that if he thought she might be on his side, he'd be even more likely to lower his guard. "I've heard that a lot of innocent people get sent to prison. Were you innocent?"

"Every convict claims he's innocent."

"Yes, but are you?" she persisted, dying for him to say he was so she could pretend to believe him.

"The jury said I was guilty."

"Juries have been wrong before."

"Twelve honest, upstanding citizens," he replied in a voice suddenly iced with loathing, "decided I was."

"I'm sure they tried to be objective."

"Bullshit!" he said so furiously that Julie's hands tightened on the steering wheel under a fresh onslaught of fear and dread. "They convicted me of being rich and famous!" he snapped. "I watched their faces during the trial, and the more the district attorney raved about my privileged life and the amoral standards of Hollywood, the more that jury wanted my blood! The whole damned, sanctimonious, God-fearing bunch of them knew there was a 'reasonable doubt' I didn't commit that murder and that's why they didn't recommend the death penalty. They'd all watched too much Perry Mason—they figured if I didn't do it, I should be able to prove who did."

Julie felt the perspiration break out on her palms at the rage in his voice. Now, more than ever before, she realized how imperative it was to make him believe she sympathized with him. "But you weren't guilty, were you? You just couldn't prove who really murdered your wife, is that it?" she persevered in a trembling voice.

"What difference does it make?" he snapped.

"It m-makes a difference to me."

For a moment he studied her in frozen silence and then his voice made one of its abrupt, compellingly soft turns. "If it truly makes a difference to you, then no, I didn't kill her."

He was lying, of course. He had to be. "I believe you." Trying to heap more reassurances on him, she added, "And if you are innocent, then you have every right to try to escape from prison."

His answer was an uncomfortably long silence during which she felt his piercing gaze examining every feature on her face, then he said abruptly, "The sign said there's a phone up ahead. Pull over when you see it."

"All right."

The telephone was beside the road and Julie pulled off into the drive. She was watching the outside rearview mirror in hopes of seeing a trucker or some other driver she could flag down but there was little traffic on the snowy road. His voice made her snap her head around just as he pulled her car keys from the ignition. "I hope," he said in a sardonic voice, "you won't think I doubt your word about believing I'm innocent and wanting to see me escape. I'm simply taking the car keys because I happen to be a very cautious man."

Julie amazed herself by managing to shake her head and say convincingly, "I don't blame you." With a brief smile, he got out of the car, but he kept his hand in his pocket with the gun as a deliberate menacing reminder to her, and he left the passenger door open, undoubtedly so he could see what she was doing while he made his call. Short of trying to outrun him and a possible bullet, Julie had no hope of escaping right now, but she could start preparing for the future. As he stepped into the snow, she said with all the meekness she could muster, "Would you mind if I get a pen and paper out of my purse so that I can make some notes while you're on the phone—you know, jot down feelings and things so that I can use them in my book?" Before he could refuse, which he looked about to do, she reached cautiously for her purse on the back seat while pointing out reasons he shouldn't deny her request. "Writing always calms my nerves," she said, "and you can search my purse, if you like. You'll see I don't have another set of keys or any weapons." To prove it she opened the purse and handed it to him. He gave her an impatient, preoccupied look that made her feel as if he didn't believe her story about writing a novel for a moment and was simply going along with it to keep her docile.

"Go ahead," he said, handing the purse to her.

As he turned away, Julie pulled out a small note pad and her pen. Keeping an eye on his back, she watched him pick up the telephone and put coins in it, then she quickly wrote the same message on three different slips of paper: *CALL POLICE. I'VE BEEN KIDNAPPED.* From the corner of her eye, she saw him watching her and she waited until he turned away to talk to whoever he was calling, then she tore off the first three sheets, folded them in half and tucked them into the outside pocket of her purse where she could easily reach them. She opened the notebook again and stared at it, her mind frantically searching for ways to pass the notes to people who could aid her. Struck with a plausible idea, she stole a glance at him to be sure he wasn't looking, then she quickly took one of the notes from her purse and folded it into a ten-dollar bill from her wallet.

She had a plan, she was executing it, and the knowledge that she was now taking some control of her future banished much of her lingering fear and panic. The rest of her newfound calm owed itself to something besides having a plan in mind. The feeling came from an instinctive but unshakable conviction that one thing Zachary Benedict had said was true: He did not want to harm her. Therefore, he wasn't going to shoot her in cold blood. In fact, if she tried to escape now, she was certain he would chase her, but he wouldn't shoot her unless it looked as if she were going to flag down a passing car. Since there were no cars coming, Julie saw no point in flinging open her door and making a break for it right now—not when he could outrun her, and all she would gain was to put him permanently on his guard. Better by far to appear to cooperate and lull him into relaxing as much as possible. Zachary Benedict might be an ex-con, but she wasn't the gullible, easily intimidated coward she'd been acting like until now. Once, she'd had to live by her wits, she reminded herself bracingly. While he was a pampered teenage movie idol, Julie was lying and stealing and surviving on the streets! If she concentrated on that now, she'd be able to hold her own with him, she was absolutely positive! Well, *almost* positive. So long as she kept her head, she had an excellent chance of winning this contest of wits. Taking her notebook out, she began jotting down saccharine comments about her kidnapper in case he asked to see what she'd written. Finished, she reread her absurd commentary:

Zachary Benedict is fleeing from unjust imprisonment caused by a biased jury. He seems to be an intelligent, kind, warm man—a victim of circumstances. I believe in him.

The commentary was, she decided with an inner grimace, the worst piece of pure fiction ever written. So engrossed was she that she experienced only a momentary jolt of dread when she realized he'd finished his call and was climbing into the car. Quickly closing the notebook and shoving it into her purse, she asked politely, "Did you talk to whoever it is you're trying to call?"

His eyes narrowed sharply on her smile and she had an uneasy feeling she was overdoing her "comradely" performance. "No. He's still there, but he isn't in his room. I'll try again in a half hour or so." Julie was digesting that tidbit of useless information when he reached for her purse and took out her notebook. "Just a precaution," he said in a sardonic voice as he flipped open the notebook. "You understand, I'm sure?"

"I understand," Julie averred, caught between nervous hilarity and chagrin as she watched his jaw slacken when he read what she'd written.

"Well?" she said, widening her eyes with sham innocence. "What do you think?"

He closed the notebook and slid it back into her purse. "I think you're too gullible to be turned loose in the world if you actually believe all that."

"I'm very gullible," she eagerly assured him, turning on the ignition and pulling out onto the highway. If he thought her stupid and naive, that was great, terrific.

20

FOR THE NEXT HALF HOUR, THEY DROVE IN SILENCE WITH only an occasional desultory comment about the bad weather and worsening driving conditions, but Julie was watching the side of the road for a billboard that would enable her to put her plan into action. Any billboard that advertised a fast food restaurant at an approaching exit would do. When she finally saw one, her heart doubled its beat. "I know you probably don't want to stop and go into a restaurant, but I'm starving," she said carefully, pleasantly. "That sign says there's a McDonald's up ahead. We could get some food at the drive-through window."

He glanced at the clock and started to shake his head, so she hastily added, "I have to eat something every couple of hours because I have . . ." she hesitated a split second, thinking frantically for the right medical term for a problem she didn't have ". . . hypoglycemia! I'm sorry, but if I don't eat something, I get very ill and faint and . . ."

"Fine, we'll stop there."

Julie almost shouted with nervous triumph when she pulled off on the exit ramp and the McDonald's golden arches came into view. The restaurant was between two open lots with a kiddy playground on the side of it. "We're stopping just in time," she added, "because I'm feeling so dizzy that I won't be able to drive much longer."

Ignoring his narrowed look, Julie flipped on the turn indicator and pulled into the McDonald's entrance. Despite the storm, there were several cars in the parking lot, though not nearly so many as Julie wished there were, and she could see a few families seated at the tables inside the restaurant. Following the directions on the sign, she drove around behind the restaurant to the drive-through window and stopped at the speaker. "What would you like?" she asked.

Before his imprisonment, Zack wouldn't have stopped at a fast-food restaurant like this if he had to go all day without eating. Now he discovered his mouth was watering at the thought of a simple hamburger and french fries. Freedom did that, he decided after telling Julie what he wanted to eat. Freedom made the air smell fresher and food sound better. It also made a man more tense and suspicious, because there was something about his captive's overbright smile that was making him extremely wary. She looked so fresh and ingenuous with those big blue eyes and soft smile, but she'd switched much too quickly from terrified captive to furious hostage to her current attitude of friendly ally.

Julie repeated their order into the microphone—two cheeseburgers, two french fries, two Cokes.

"That'll be $5.09," the voice said over the microphone. "Please drive around to the first window."

As she pulled up alongside the first window, she saw him dig into his pocket for money, but she shook her head adamantly, already reaching into her purse. "I'll buy," she said, managing to look straight into his eyes. "It's my treat. I insist."

After a moment's hesitation, he took his hand out of his pocket, but his dark brows drew together into a baffled frown. "That's very sporting of you."

"That's me. I'm a good sport. Everyone always says so," she babbled mindlessly, removing the folded ten-dollar bill with her handwritten note saying that she was being kidnapped folded inside of it. Unable to meet his unnerving gaze any longer, Julie hastily looked away and focused all her attention on the teenage girl in the drive-through window, who was regarding her with bored impatience. The girl's name tag said her name was Tiffany.

"That'll be $5.09," Tiffany said.

Julie held out the ten dollar bill and stared hard at the girl, her face beseeching. Her life depended on this bored-looking teenager with a frizzy ponytail. As if in slow motion, Julie saw her unfold the ten-dollar bill . . . The small notepaper floated to the ground . . . Tiffany bent and picked it up, popping her gum . . . She straightened . . . She glanced at Julie . . . "This yours?" she asked, holding it up, peering into the car without reading what it said.

"I don't know," Julie said, trying to force the girl to read the words. "It might be. What does it say—" she began, then stifled a scream as Zachary Benedict's hand clamped on her arm and the barrel of the pistol dug into her side. "Never mind, Tiffany," he said smoothly, leaning around Julie and holding out his hand. "That's my note. It's part of a joke." The cashier glanced at the note, but it was impossible to tell if she'd actually read it in the instant before she held it in her outstretched hand toward the car. "Here you are, sir," she said, leaning forward past Julie and handing it to him. Julie ground her teeth as Zachary Benedict gave the girl a phoney, appreciative smile that made Tiffany blush with pleasure as she counted out the change due them from Julie's ten-dollar bill. "Here's your order," she said. Julie automatically reached for the white bags of food and Cokes, her frightened face silently pleading with the girl to call the police or the manager or someone! She passed the bags to Benedict without daring to meet his gaze, her hands trembling so violently she nearly dropped the Cokes. As she drove away from the window, she expected some sort of repercussions from him, but since her plan had failed miserably, Julie was not prepared for the eruption of raw rage she heard: "You stupid little bitch, are you *trying* to get yourself killed? Pull over in the parking lot, right there where she can see us, she's watching."

Julie obeyed automatically, her chest rising and falling in sharp, shallow little breaths. "Eat this," he commanded, shoving the cheeseburger in her face. "And smile with every bite, or so help me God . . ."

Again, Julie obeyed. She chewed without tasting, every fiber of her being concentrated on calming her shattered nerves so that she could think again. The tension in the car grew into a taut, living thing that added to her strained nerves. She spoke simply to break the silence. "C-could I have m-my Coke," she said, reaching for the white sack of drinks on the floor near his feet. His hand clamped on her wrist in a vice that threatened to break the fragile bones. "You're hurting me!" Julie cried, assailed by a fresh onslaught of panic. His hand tightened more painfully before he flung her wrist away. She reared back in her seat, leaned her head back, and closed her eyes, swallowing and rubbing her throbbing arm. Until a few moments ago, he hadn't actually tried to inflict pain on her, and she'd lulled herself with the misconception that he wasn't a depraved indiscriminate killer but rather a man who'd taken revenge on his unfaithful wife in an act of jealous insanity. Why, she wondered desperately, had she allowed herself to think that he wouldn't be just as likely to murder a woman whom he'd taken captive or a teenager who could sound an alarm and get him captured. The answer was that she'd been fooled and deluded by her memories—memories of all those glamorous stories about him in magazines, memories of countless hours spent in theaters with her brothers and, later, with her dates admiring him and even fantasizing about him. At eleven years old, she hadn't understood why her brothers and all their friends thought Zack Benedict was so special, but within a few years, she'd understood it perfectly. Ruggedly handsome, unattainable, sexy and cynical, witty and tough. And since Julie had been away on a summer scholarship in Europe during his famous trial, she had no knowledge of any of the sordid details, nothing concrete to offset all those lovely on-screen images that had seemed so real to her in theaters. The shameful truth was that when he'd told her he was innocent, she'd believed it might be possible he was telling the truth because it then made sense for him to try to escape so he could prove it. For some incomprehensible reason, a tiny part of her still clung to that possibility, probably because it helped her control her fear, but it didn't lessen her desperation to get away from him. Even if he was innocent of the crime for which he was sent to prison, that didn't mean he wouldn't kill to prevent being sent back there, and that was *if* he was innocent—a very big, highly unlikely *if*.

Her whole body jerked in alarm when the bag on the floor crackled. "Here," he snapped, shoving a Coke toward her.

Refusing to look at him, Julie stretched her hand out and took it, her gaze fastened on the view through the front windshield. She now realized her only hope of escaping without getting anyone hurt or killed was to make it easier for him to take off in her car and leave her behind than it was to stick around and try to shoot his way out of his predicament. Which meant she had to be out of the car and in full view of onlookers. She'd blown her first attempt to escape; he knew now she was desperate enough to try again. He'd be waiting. Watching. When she tried again, everything would have to be exactly right. She knew instinctively she wasn't likely to live to have a third chance. At least there was no further need to carry on any nauseating charade that she was on his side.

"Let's get going," he snapped.

Wordlessly, Julie turned on the ignition and pulled out of the parking lot.

A quarter of an hour later, he ordered her to pull over at a roadside phone again, and he made another phone call. He had not spoken a word except to tell her to pull over, and Julie suspected he knew that silence wreaked more havoc on her nerves than anything else he could do to intimidate her. This time when he made his phone call, he never took his eyes off her. When he got back into the car, Julie looked at his impassive features and couldn't endure the silence another moment. Giving him a haughty stare, she nodded at the phone booth and said, "Bad news, I hope?"

Zack bit back a grin at her rigid, unremitting rebellion. Her pretty face belied a stubborn courage and acid wit that continually caught him off guard. Instead of replying that the news was very good, he shrugged. Silence ate at her, he'd noticed. "Drive," he said, leaning back in his seat and stretching out his legs, idly watching her graceful fingers on the steering wheel.

In a few short hours, a man who looked very much like Zack would drive from Detroit through the Windsor Tunnel into Canada. At the border, he would make enough of a nervous spectacle of himself to cause the customs officials there to remember him. When Zack remained at large for a day or two, those customs officials should remember him and notify U.S. authorities that their escaped convict had probably crossed into Canada. Within a week, the hunt for Zack Benedict should be mostly centered in Canada, leaving Zack much more free to continue with the rest of his plan. For now, for the next week, it rather looked as if he had nothing whatsoever to do except relax and revel in his freedom. It seemed like a delightful notion and it would have put him rather in charity with the world if it weren't for his troublesome hostage. She was the only kink in his relaxation. A very big kink, since she apparently wasn't half so easily subdued as he'd thought she would be. At the moment, she was driving unnecessarily slow and casting angry looks at him. "What's the problem?" he clipped.

"The problem is that I need to use a bathroom."

"Later!"

"But—" He looked at her then and Julie realized it was useless to argue.

An hour later, they crossed the Colorado state line and he spoke for the first time. "There's a truck stop up ahead. Get off at the exit and if it looks all right, we'll stop there."

That truck stop turned out to be too busy to suit him, and it was another half hour before he found a service station that was relatively empty and laid out to please him with an attendant positioned in the island between the pumps so he could pay for gas without going inside and with rest rooms on the outside of the building. "Let's go," he said. "Take it slow," he warned as she got out of the car and started toward the rest room door. He grasped her elbow as if to help her walk through the snow, his feet crunching the crusty powder in perfect rhythm with hers as he matched her stride for stride. When they reached the rest room, instead of letting go of her arm, he reached out and opened the door, and Julie's temper exploded. "Do you intend to come in here with me and watch?" she burst out in furious disbelief.

Ignoring her, he looked around the tiny tiled room, checking for windows, she supposed, and finding none, he let go of her arm. "Make it quick. And, Julie, don't do anything stupid."

"Like what?" she demanded. "Hang myself with toilet paper? Go away, damn you." Yanking her arm free, she marched inside, and it was as she was closing the door, that the obvious solution of locking the door and staying inside hit her. With an inner cry of triumph, she turned the lock with her fingertips and slammed the door at the same time, throwing her shoulder against it. The door slammed into the jam with a satisfying metallic thud, but the lock didn't seem to catch, and she had a sickening feeling he was holding the doorknob on the other side to prevent it from happening.

From the other side of the door, he twisted the knob and it turned in her hand at the same time his tone of amused resignation told her she was right. "You have a minute and a half before I open this door, Julie."

Great. He was undoubtedly a pervert too, she thought as she hastily finished what she'd gone in there to do. She was washing her hands in freezing water in the sink when he opened the door and said, "Time's up."

Instead of getting into the Blazer, he hung back, his hand in his pocket with the gun. "Put gas in the car," he instructed, lounging against the side of the car and watching her while she obeyed. "Pay for it," he ordered when she was done, keeping his face turned away from the man in the booth.

Julie's outraged sense of thrift momentarily overrode her frustration and fear, and she started to object when she realized he was holding two twenty-dollar bills in his outstretched hand. Her resentment was compounded a dozen times by the realization that he was biting back a half-smile. "I think you're starting to enjoy this!" she snapped bitterly, yanking the money out of his hand.

Zack watched her rigid shoulders as she turned away and reminded himself that it would be far wiser and far more beneficial if he could neutralize some of her hostility as he'd intended to do earlier. If he could put her in a decent humor, that would be even better. And so he said with a low chuckle, "You're absolutely right. I think I am beginning to enjoy this."

"Bastard," she replied.

Dawn was edging the gray sky with pink when Julie decided he might have fallen asleep. He'd made her stick to the back roads, avoiding the interstates, which made traveling in the deep snow so treacherous that she'd only averaged thirty miles per hour for long stretches. Three times they'd been held up for hours because of accidents on the highway, and still he made her go on. All night long, the radio had been filled with news bulletins about his escape, but the further into Colorado they traveled, the less was being made of his disappearance, no doubt because no one expected him to be traveling north, away from major airports, trains, and buses. The sign she'd passed a mile back said there was a picnic-rest area five miles ahead, and Julie was praying that this one, like the last one they'd passed, would have at least a few trucks pulled off into it, their drivers asleep in the cab. The most feasible idea she'd been able to come up with during the endless, exhausting drive was the only one that fulfilled the dual criteria of forcing him to take the car while leaving her behind. It seemed as foolproof as anything under the circumstances: She was going to pull into the rest area and when she was alongside the parked trucks, she would slam on the Blazer's brakes and jump out of the car, screaming for help in a voice loud enough to wake up the trucks' occupants. Then, if her entire fantasy came true, several burly truck drivers—preferably gigantic men holding guns and wearing brass knuckles—would lurch awake and jump out of the trucks, racing to her rescue. They would wrestle Zachary Benedict to the ground, with Julie pitching in to help, then they'd disarm him and call the police on their CB radios.

That was the best possible scenario, Julie knew, but even if only a fraction of that happened—if only one driver woke up and got out to investigate the cause of her screams—she was still relatively certain she'd be free of Zachary Benedict. Because from the moment she raised an alarm and attracted notice, his only sensible choice would be to take off in the Blazer. He'd have nothing to gain by hanging around to shoot her and then walking from truck to truck to shoot the drivers, not when the first gunshot would only alert all the other drivers. Any attempt on his part to reenact the final scene from *The Gunfight at OK Corral* would be just plain stupid, and stupid was one thing Benedict was not.

Julie was so certain of that, that she was going to bet her life on it.

She slanted another searching look at him to make certain he was sleeping; His arms were crossed over his chest, his long legs were stretched out in front of him, his head rested against the side window. His breathing was steady and relaxed.

He was asleep.

Elated, Julie gently eased her foot off the accelerator slowly, imperceptibly, watching the speedometer drop from forty-five miles per hour to forty-two, then very slowly to forty. In order to pull into the rest area without a sudden change in speed that would alert her passenger, she needed to be traveling at no more than thirty miles an hour when she reached the exit. She held the speed at forty for a full minute, then she eased up on the accelerator again, her leg trembling with the effort to make each change undetectable. The car slowed to thirty-five miles an hour, and Julie reached out and turned the radio a little louder to compensate for what seemed like a quieter atmosphere inside the car.

The rest area was still a quarter mile away, shielded from view of the highway by a stand of pine trees, when Julie reduced her speed to thirty and turned the steering wheel a fraction of an inch at a time to begin angling off the highway. Uttering a disjointed prayer that she'd find trucks there, she held her breath as she drove around the trees, then expelled it in a silent rush of gratitude and relief. Up ahead, three trucks were parked across from the small building that housed the rest rooms, and although there was no one moving about in the early dawn, she thought she could hear one of the diesel engines running. Her heart racing like a trip hammer, she ignored the temptation to make her move now. To maximize her chances, she needed to be directly beside the trucks, so that she could reach the door of one before Benedict could catch her.

Fifteen yards behind the first truck, Julie was absolutely certain she heard the engine, and her toe angled stealthily toward the brake, all her other senses so focused on the cab of the truck that she yelped in shock when Zachary Benedict suddenly sat up. "Where the hell—" he began, but Julie didn't give him a chance to finish. Slamming on the brake, she grabbed the door handle and flung open the door, throwing herself out of the moving car, landing on her side in the snowy ruts. In a blur of pain and terror she saw the Blazer's rear tire roll past, missing her hand by inches before the car lurched to a jarring stop. "HELP ME!" she screamed, scrambling to her knees, her feet sliding as they fought for traction in the slush and snow. "HELP ME!"

She was on her feet, running toward the cab of the closest truck when Zachary Benedict exploded from the Blazer, cutting around the rear of it and running straight toward her, blocking her path to help. Julie changed direction to avoid him, "PLEASE SOMEONE," she screamed, cutting across the snow in an effort to make it into the rest room and lock the door. Off to her left, she saw a truck door being flung open and a driver stepping down, frowning at the commotion; close behind her she heard Benedict's feet pounding into the snow. "HELP ME!" she yelled at the driver, and she glanced over her shoulder just in time to see Zachary Benedict scoop up a handful of snow.

A snowball hit her hard in the shoulder and she screamed as she ran, "STOP HIM! He's—"

Zachary Benedict's laughing shout a few feet behind her drowned out her words: "CUT IT OUT, Julie," he yelled at the same time he launched himself at her in a running tackle. "YOU'RE WAKING EVERYONE UP!"

Trying to drag in enough air to scream again, Julie twisted, landing underneath his sprawled body in the snow, the breath knocked out of her, her terrified blue eyes only inches from his enraged ones, his teeth clenched into a fake smile designed to fool the truck driver. Panting, Julie jerked her head aside to scream, just as he smashed a handful of wet snow onto her face. Choking and blinded, she heard his savage whisper as he caught her wrists and yanked them above her head. "I'll kill him if he comes any closer," he bit out, tightening his grip on her hands. "Damn you, is that what you want! Does someone have to die for you?"

Julie whimpered, unable to speak, and shook her head, her eyes clenched shut, unable to bear the sight of her captor, unable to endure knowing she'd come within a few feet of freedom, and all for nothing, for this—to end up on her back in the snow with his body crushing her, her hip throbbing from her deliberate fall from the Blazer. She heard his swift intake of breath, the furious urgency. "He's walking over here. Kiss me and make it look good, or he's dead!"

Before she could react, his mouth crushed down on hers. Julie's eyes flew open, her gaze riveting on the truck driver who was cautiously walking toward them, frowning as he tried to peer at their faces. "Goddammit, put your arms around me!"

His mouth was imprisoning hers, the gun in his pocket was jabbing into her stomach, but her wrists were free now. She could struggle, and very possibly, the truck driver with the jovial face beneath a black cap that said PETE on it would see that something was very wrong and come to her rescue.

And he would die.

Benedict had ordered her to put her arms around him and "make it look good." Like a puppet, Julie moved her leaden wrists from the snow and let them drop limply onto his shoulders, but she could not make herself do more than that.

* * *

Zack tasted her stiff lips beneath his; he felt her body, rigid as stone beneath his weight, and he assumed that she was trying to gather her strength for the next moment when she, with the help of three truck drivers, would put an end to his brief freedom and his life. From the corner of his eye, he saw the driver slow down, but he was still coming toward them, and his expression was growing increasingly cautious and skeptical. All this and more raced through Zack's mind in the space of the three seconds they laid there, pretending— unconvincingly—to kiss.

In a last helpless effort to stop the inevitable from happening to him, Zack dragged his mouth to her ear and whispered a single word he hadn't let himself use in years: *"Please!"* Tightening his arms around the rigid woman, he said it again with a groaning urgency he couldn't suppress. *"Please,* Julie . . ."

Feeling as if the world had suddenly gone insane, Julie heard the plea wrench from her captor as if it were torn from his chest a moment before his lips seized hers and he said in a tormented whisper, "I didn't kill anyone, I swear it." The pleading and desperation she'd heard in his voice were eloquently alive in this kiss, and it accomplished what his threats and anger could not: It made Julie hesitate and waiver; it made her believe that what she heard in his voice was truth.

Dazed by the confusing messages racing through her brain, she sacrificed her immediate future for the safety of a truck driver. Driven by the need to spare the man's life and by something less sensible and completely inexplicable, Julie blinked back tears of futility, slid her hands tentatively over Zachary Benedict's shoulders, and yielded to his kiss. The moment she did, he sensed her capitulation; a shudder ran through him and his lips gentled. Unaware of the footsteps crunching to a stop in the snow, Julie let him part her lips and of their own volition, her fingers curved around his neck, sliding into the soft, thick hair at his nape. She felt his swift, indrawn breath when she tentatively returned the kiss, and suddenly everything began to change. He was kissing her in earnest now, his hands shifting, sliding over her shoulders, and then burying in her wet hair, lifting her face closer to his hungry, searching mouth.

Somewhere far above her, a man's bewildered Texas drawl called out, "Lady, you need help or not?"

Julie heard him, and she tried to shake her head, but the mouth that was slanting fiercely over hers now had robbed her of the ability to speak. Somewhere in the back of her mind, she knew this was only a performance for the driver's benefit; she knew it as clearly as she knew she had no choice but to participate in the performance. But if that was true, then why couldn't she at least shake her head or open her eyes.

"I guess you don't," the Texas drawl said on a lewd chuckle. "How 'bout you, mister? You need any help with what you're doin'? I could spell you for a bit down there . . ."

Zack's head lifted just enough to break contact with her mouth, his words husky and soft. "Find your own woman," he joked with the driver. "This one is mine." The last word was breathed against Julie's lips before his mouth touched hers, his arms sweeping around her, his tongue sliding tentatively across her lips, urging them to part, his hips hard and demanding against hers. With a silent moan of surrender, Julie gave herself up to what became the hottest, sexiest, most insistent kiss she'd ever tasted.

Fifty yards away, a truck door opened and a new male voice called, "Hey, Pete, what's goin' on over yonder in the snow?"

"Hell, man, what does it look like? A couple of grown ups is playin' at bein' kids, having snowball fights and neckin' in the snow."

"Looks to me like they're goin' to be *makin'* a kid if they don't slow down."

Perhaps it was the new male voice or the sudden realization that her captor was becoming physically aroused that snapped Julie into reality or perhaps it was the slamming of the truck door followed by the roar of an engine as the big semi began to pull away from the rest area. Whatever the cause, she put her hands against his shoulders and exerted pressure, but it took an unnatural effort for her to move, and her shove was puny at best. Panicked by her inexplicable lethargy, Julie shoved harder. "Stop it!" she cried softly. "Stop it. He's gone!"

Stunned by the sound of tears in her voice, Zack lifted his head, staring at her dewy skin and soft mouth with a hunger that he was finding difficult to control. The exquisite sweetness of her surrender, the way she felt in his arms, and the gentleness of her touch almost made the notion of making love in the snow at dawn seem plausible. Slowly, he looked around at where they were and reluctantly levered himself up off her. He didn't completely understand why she'd decided not to warn the truck driver, but whatever her reasons, he owed her more than an attempted rape in the snow as repayment. Silently, he held his hand out to her, suppressing a smile when the same woman who'd melted in his arms a moment ago rallied her defenses, pointedly ignored his gesture, and shoved herself up and out of the snow. "I'm soaking wet," she complained, scrupulously avoiding his gaze and swatting at her hair, "and covered with snow."

Automatically, Zack reached out to brush the snow off her, but she jumped out of his reach, avoiding his touch as she brushed off her arms and the back of her jeans.

"Don't think you can touch me just because of what happened just now!" she warned him, but Zack was preoccupied with admiration for the results of their kiss: Her huge, dark-lashed eyes were lustrous, her porcelain skin tinted with roses at the high cheekbones. When flustered and a little aroused, as she was now, Julie Mathison was absolutely breathtaking. She was also courageous and very kind, for although he'd not been able to subdue her with threats or cruelty, she'd somehow responded to the desperation in his plea.

"The only reason I let you kiss me was because I realized you were right—there's no need for anyone to get killed just because I'm scared. Now, let's get going and get this ordeal over with."

Zack sighed. "I gather from that sour tone of yours that we're adversaries again, Ms. Mathison?"

"Of course we are," she replied. "I'll take you wherever you're going without any more tricks, but let's get one thing straight: As soon as I get you there, I'll be free to leave, right?"

"Right," Zack lied.

"Then let's get moving."

Brushing snow off the sleeves of his jacket, Zack followed along behind her, watching her hair tossing in the wind and the graceful sway of her slim hips as she stalked toward their car. Judging from her words and the rigid set of her shoulders, there was no doubt she was determined to avoid any further romantic confrontations between them.

In that, as in everything else, Zack was now firmly committed to accomplishing a goal that was in diametric opposition to her own: He had tasted her lips and felt their response to him. His starved senses wanted to feast on the entire banquet.

One part of his mind warned that any sexual involvement with his captive was insane. It would complicate everything, and he didn't need any more complications.

The other part of his mind listened to the clamor of his aroused body and argued—very compellingly and very conveniently—that it was clever. After all, contented captives became almost like accomplices. They were also much more delightful company.

Zack decided to try to seduce her, but not because she had endearing qualities that intrigued and appealed to him or because he was very attracted to her or because he harbored any sort of budding tenderness for her.

Instead, he told himself, he was going to seduce Julie Mathison because it was practical. And, of course, extremely pleasurable.

With a gallantry that had been absent before their kiss and which Julie felt was entirely ludicrous—and even alarming in their present, altered circumstances—he escorted her around to the driver's seat, but he didn't have to open the door for her; it was still open from her aborted attempt to escape. He closed the car door and walked around the front of the vehicle, but as he slid into the seat beside her, he noticed that she winced and gasped when she shifted her position. "What's wrong?"

"I hurt my hip and leg when I jumped out of the car and when you tackled me," Julie retorted bitterly, angry with herself for having actually enjoyed that kiss. "Does that fill you with concern and remorse."

He said quietly, "Yes, it does."

She jerked her eyes from his somber smile, unable and adamantly unwilling to be charmed into believing such an implausible lie. He was a convicted murderer, and she must not, dared not, forget that ever again. "I'm hungry," she announced, because it was the first thing she could think of to say. She knew it was the wrong thing the moment his gaze fastened on her lips. "So am I."

She stuck her nose in the air and turned on the ignition.

His answer was a soft chuckle.

21

"WHERE IN HELL CAN SHE BE?" CARL MATHISON PACED ACROSS the small cubicle that his brother occupied in the Keaton Sheriff's Office, then he stopped and glowered at the silver shield on Ted's gray uniform shirt. "You're a cop and she's a missing person, so do something, damn it."

"She's not officially missing until she's been gone for at least twenty-four hours," Ted replied, but his blue eyes were troubled as he added, "I can't do anything through official channels until then, you know that."

"And *you* know," Carl countered angrily, "that it's not like Julie to suddenly change her plans; you know how methodical she is. And if she absolutely had to change her plans, she'd telephone one of us. Besides, she knew I needed my car back this morning."

"You're right." Ted walked over to the windows. With his hand resting on the butt of the 9-millimeter semiautomatic he wore at his side, he stared absently at the cars parked in the town square while their owners browsed in the local stores or hunted for bargains in what had become a haven for antique hunters. When he spoke again, his voice was hesitant as if he feared to voice his thoughts aloud. "Zachary Benedict escaped from Amarillo yesterday. He'd been made a trustee and he skipped out after driving the warden into Amarillo."

"I heard it on the news. So what?"

"Benedict, or at least a man answering Benedict's general description, was last seen at a restaurant near the Interstate."

Very slowly, very carefully, Carl laid down the paperweight he'd been rolling between his hands and stared hard at his younger brother. "What are you getting at?"

"Benedict was seen near a vehicle that sounds like your Blazer. The cashier in the restaurant thinks she saw him get into the Blazer with a woman who'd stopped there for a sandwich and coffee." Ted turned away from the window and reluctantly raised his gaze to his brother's face. "I talked to the cashier— unofficially, of course—five minutes ago. The description she gave me of the woman who drove away with Benedict in the Blazer sounds exactly like Julie."

"Oh, my God!"

The clerk at the desk, a middle-aged woman with wiry gray hair and the face of an irate bulldog had been listening to the Mathisons' conversation about Julie while simultaneously filling out an arrest warrant and watching for an assistant deputy to arrive in a black and white patrol car. Now, she glanced up and her gaze riveted on a shiny red BMW convertible that pulled up beside Ted's patrol car across the street. When a beautiful blond woman of about twenty-five stepped out of the car, Rita's eyes narrowed to slits and she swung around on her chair to the two men in the office. "It never rains, but it pours," she warned Ted, and when both men glanced at her, she tipped her head toward the window and explained. "Look who's back in town—Miss Rich Bitch herself."

Despite his effort to feel and show no reaction to the sight of his ex-wife, Ted Mathison's face tightened. "Europe must be boring this time of year," he said as his gaze ran insolently over the blonde's perfect curves and long, graceful legs. She disappeared into the seamstress shop across the square as Rita added, "I hear that Flossie and Ada Eldridge are going to make her wedding dress. The silk and lace and all the geegaws are coming in from Paris, France, on a plane, but Miss High and Mighty wanted the dress made by the Eldridge twins because nobody's handwork is as fine as theirs." Belatedly realizing that Ted Mathison might not want to hear the details of his former wife's extravagant wedding plans involving another man, the loyal woman swung back to the paperwork on her desk and said, "I'm sorry. That was dumb of me."

"Don't apologize. It doesn't matter a damn to me what she does," Ted said, and he meant it. The knowledge that Katherine Cahill was planning to remarry, this time to a fifty-year-old Dallas socialite named Spencer Hayward, was of no interest to Ted, nor did it come as a surprise. He'd read about it in the newspapers, including the glowing account of Hayward's jet planes, twenty-two-room mansion, and alleged friendship with the president, but none of that evoked any feelings of jealousy or envy in Ted. "Let's go talk to Mother and Dad," he said, shrugging into his jacket and holding the door open for Carl to proceed him. "They know Julie didn't get back last night and they're worried sick. Maybe they've thought of some detail about her plans that I don't know."

They had just crossed the street when the door to the Eldridge sisters' shop swung open and Katherine stepped forward. She halted in midstep when she found herself a sidewalk's width from her former husband, but Ted merely nodded at her with the sort of distant courtesy one bestows on a total stranger of no importance whatsoever, then he opened the driver's door on his black and white. Katherine, however, apparently had other—more socially correct—notions about how divorced couples ought to behave when meeting each other in public for the first time since their divorce. Refusing to be ignored, she stepped forward and her cultured voice reached Ted, forcing him to pause. "Ted?" she said. Pausing to smile briefly and with impeccable courtesy at Carl, who'd stopped with one foot already in the car, she turned back to her ex-husband and added, "Were you really going to drive off without saying hello to me?"

"I intended to do exactly that," he replied, his face impassive, even as he registered a new softer and more somber quality to her voice.

She walked forward in a cherry red wool suit that hugged her narrow waist, her long blond hair spilling over her shoulders, her hand held out. "You look . . . well," she finished a little lamely when Ted ignored her hand. When he refused to respond, she sent a look of appeal at Carl. "You look well, too, Carl. I hear you married Sara Wakefield?"

In the shop behind her, Ada Eldridge's eyeball appeared in the crack between the shutters, and in the beauty shop next door, two of the town's biggest gossips were standing in the window with rollers in their hair, blatantly spying. Ted's patience snapped. "Are you finished with what you learned in Social Interaction 201?" he asked sarcastically. "You're causing a scene."

Katherine glanced at the window of the beauty shop, but she persevered despite the flush of humiliation staining her cheeks at his contemptuous attitude. "Julie wrote me that you finished law school."

He turned his back on her and opened the car door.

Her chin came up. "I'm getting married—to Spencer Hayward. Miss Flossie and Miss Ada are making my gown."

"I'm sure they're glad of any business, even yours," Ted said, climbing into the car. She put her hand on the door to stop him from closing it.

"You've changed," she said.

"You haven't."

"Yes, I have."

"Katherine," he said with deadly finality, "I don't give a damn whether you've changed or not."

He closed the door in her face, started the engine, and drove away, watching in the rearview mirror as her shoulders straightened with the haughty dignity that wealthy, privileged people seemed to be born with, then she turned and glowered at the faces in the beauty shop window. If he didn't despise her so thoroughly, Ted would have admired her spunk in the face of such public humiliation, but he felt no admiration nor any jealousy at the thought of her marrying again. All he felt was a vague sort of pity for the man who was about to get himself a wife who was nothing but an ornament—beautiful, hollow, and brittle. As Ted had already learned to his agonized disappointment, Katherine Cahill Mathison was spoiled, immature, selfish, and vain.

Katherine's father owned oil wells and a cattle ranch, but he preferred to spend much of his time in Keaton where he'd been born and where he enjoyed a position of unquestioned prominence. Although Katherine had grown up there, she'd been away at fancy boarding schools since she was twelve years old. Ted and she had never really met until she was nineteen years old, when she came home after her sophomore year at a ritzy eastern college to spend the summer in Keaton. Her parents, who were spending two months in Europe, had insisted she remain in Keaton as a punishment, she'd later told Ted, for her having cut so many of her college classes that she'd nearly flunked out of school. In a typically childish tantrum of the sort that Ted was later to become accustomed to, Katherine had retaliated against her parents by inviting twenty friends from her college to spend a month, partying at her family's mansion. It was during one of those parties that gunshots were fired and the police were called.

Ted had arrived with another local sheriff to check on the disturbance, and Katherine herself had answered the doorbell, her eyes wide with fear, her body scantily clad in a revealing string bikini that showed off nearly every tanned centimeter of her beautiful, curvaceous young form. "I called you," she burst out, gesturing toward the back of the house where French doors opened onto a swimming pool and terraces that overlooked the town of Keaton. "My friends are out there, but the party's getting a little wild, and they won't put my father's guns away. I'm afraid someone will get hurt!"

Trying to keep his lustful gaze off her rounded derriere, Ted had followed her through the mansion with its Persian carpets and magnificent French antiques. Outdoors, he and his partner found twenty young adults, several of them nude, all of them drunk or stoned on pot, frolicking in the swimming pool and shooting skeet off the back terrace. Calming the party down was easy: The moment one of the swimmers yelled, "Oh God, the cops are here!" the revelry screeched to an abrupt halt. Swimmers emerged from the pool and the skeet shooters laid down their shotguns—with one alarming exception: a twenty-three-year-old, high on marijuana, who decided to reenact a scene from *Rambo* with Ted as his adversary. When he turned the shotgun on Ted, Katherine had screamed and Ted's partner had drawn his service revolver, but Ted had motioned him to put it away. "There's not going to be any trouble here," he told the youth. Improvising quickly, he added, "My partner and I came to enjoy the party. Katherine invited us." He glanced at her and smiled winningly. "Tell him you invited me, Kathy."

The nickname he'd invented on the spur of the moment may well have saved a life, because it either startled the boy enough to tip down his weapon or it convinced him Ted was actually a family friend. Katherine, who had never been called by any nickname whatsoever, had collaborated by hurrying to Ted's side and draping her body against his side, her arm around Ted's back. "Of course I did, Brandon!" she told the young man with only a tiny betraying tremor in her voice, her eyes fixed on the loaded shotgun he still held.

Intending only to play along, Ted put his arm around her, his hand curving around her incredibly narrow waist as he bent his head to say something to her. Whether by accident or design, Katherine misunderstood her cue, and she leaned up on her toes and kissed him full on the mouth. Ted's lips parted in surprise but his arm tightened automatically, and suddenly she turned fully into his arms, kissing him deeply. And just as automatically, he responded to her unexpected ardor; his arms tightened and his body hardened with desire. His tongue slipped between her eager lips and he kissed her back while a bunch of cheering, drunken, stoned rich kids looked on and another kid named Brandon held a loaded gun on him.

"Okay, okay, he's one of the 'good guys'" Brandon shouted. "So, let's shoot some skeet!"

Ted let go of Katherine and sauntered toward the young man, his gait slow, relaxed, a fake smile pinned to his face. "What'd you say yer name was?" Brandon demanded as Ted neared him.

"Officer Mathison," Ted snapped as he jerked the shotgun out of the young man's hand and spun him around, shoving his face into the fence and slapping handcuffs on his wrists. "What's yours?"

"Brandon Barrister III," came the outraged reply. "My father is Senator Barrister. His voice shifted to an ugly, wheedling whine. "I'll make you a deal, Mathison. You get these cuffs off of me and get the hell out of here and I won't tell my father about the way you treated us tonight. We'll forget this misunderstanding ever happened."

"No, I'll make *you* a deal," Ted countered, spinning him around and shoving him toward the house. "You tell me where your stash is, and I'll let you spend a nice quiet evening in our jail without booking you on the dozen charges I can think of right now—all of which would deeply embarrass your father the senator."

"Brandon," one of the girls pleaded when the boy balked, "he's being really decent about this. Do what he tells you."

Slightly mollified by their reactions, Ted said, "That goes for all of you. Get in the house, collect all the pot and anything else you've got here and bring it to the living room. He turned to Katherine, who was watching him with a strange, absorbed little smile. "That goes for you, too, Miss Cahill."

Her smile warmed and yet her voice seemed almost shy. "I liked Kathy better than Miss Cahill."

She looked so delicious standing there with the moonlight gilding her hair, wearing a sexy bikini and a Madonna's smile, that Ted had to remind himself that she was too young for him as well as too rich and too spoiled. Remembering all that became even more difficult in the days that followed, because Katherine Cahill possessed all the determination of her pioneering ancestors who'd trekked across half a continent to stake their claim in Texas's oil fields. Wherever Ted went and no matter how coolly he treated her, she seemed to continually reappear. She fell into step beside him when he left the office to go home at night, asking him about police work; she invited him for dinner; she came to the sheriff's office to ask his advice about what car to buy; when he went to lunch, she slid into the booth across from him and pretended it was a chance meeting. After three weeks of such fruitless antics, she tried a final, desperate ploy: She put in a fake burglary call to the police station at ten o'clock one night after making certain Ted was on duty.

When he arrived to check the house, she was standing in the doorway wearing a seductive black silk lounging robe, holding a plate of what she called canapés in one hand and a drink she'd made for him in the other. The realization that the burglary call had been nothing but a childish trick to bring him to her snapped Ted's strained nerves. Since he couldn't let himself take advantage of what she was offering, no matter how badly he wanted to, or how much he'd enjoyed her company, he let himself lose his temper instead. "What the hell do you want from me, Katherine?"

"I want you to come in and sit down and enjoy the lovely dinner I made for you." She stepped aside and gestured with her arm to the candlelit dining room table, which had been set with sparkling crystal and gleaming silver.

To his horror, Ted actually considered staying. He wanted to slide into a chair at that table, to see her face in the candlelight while he savored the wine in the silver cooler; he wanted to eat slowly, enjoying each bite, knowing that she was going to be his dessert. He wanted to taste her so badly he could hardly bear to stand there without dragging her into his arms. Instead he spoke as harshly as he could, attacking her in the one place he knew instinctively she'd be the most vulnerable—her youth. "Stop acting like a childish, spoiled brat!" he said, ignoring the tug he felt when she stepped back as if he'd slapped her. "I don't know what the hell you want from me or what you think you're going to accomplish with all this, but you're wasting your time and mine."

She looked visibly shaken, but her eyes were level and direct, and he found himself admiring her courage in the face of such ruthless opposition. "I fell in love with you the night you came to break up our party," she told him.

"That's crap! People don't fall in love in five minutes."

She managed a wavering smile at his vulgarity and persevered. "When you kissed me that first night, you felt something for me, too—something strong and special and—"

"What I felt was common, ordinary indiscriminate lust," Ted snapped, "so knock off the infantile fantasies about love and stop pestering me. Do I need to make it any clearer than that?"

She gave up the fight with a slight shake of her head. "No," she whispered shakily, "you've made it perfectly clear."

Ted jerked his head in a nod and started to turn, but she stopped him. "If you really want me to forget about you, about us, then I guess this is good-bye."

"It's good-bye," he said shortly.

"Kiss me good-bye, then, and I'll believe you. That's my bargain."

"Oh, for God's sake!" he exploded, but he yielded to her "bargaining." Or more correctly to his own desire. Pulling her into his arms, he kissed her with deliberate roughness, crushing her soft lips, then he pushed her away while something deep inside him howled in protest at what he'd done—and what he'd deprived himself of by doing it.

She pressed the back of her fingers to her bruised lips, her eyes filled with accusation and bitterness. "Liar," she said. And then she closed the door.

For the next two weeks, Ted found himself watching for her wherever he went, whether he was off duty or patrolling or doing paperwork in the office, and when he failed to see a glimpse of her or her white Corvette, he felt . . . let down. Empty. He decided she must have left Keaton and gone off to wherever rich girls go when they get bored in the summer time. Not until the following week, when a burglar was sighted two miles from her house, did he realize how obsessed with her he truly was. Telling himself that it was in the line of duty for him to drive up a winding hill that no burglar in his right mind would climb on foot, Ted drove up to her house—to make certain it was secure. There was a light on in a window at the back of the house, and he got out of the car . . . slowly, reluctantly, as if his legs understood what his mind was denying—that his being here could have long-lasting and probably disastrous results.

He raised his hand to ring the doorbell then dropped it. This was insane, he decided, turning away, then he jerked around as the front door opened and she was standing there. Even in a simple pink tank top and white shorts, Katherine Cahill was so beautiful she drugged his mind. She was different tonight, though—her expression was sober, her voice softly frank rather than flirtatious. "What do you want, Officer Mathison?"

Confronted with her calm, direct maturity, Ted felt like a complete fool. "There was a burglary," he dissembled, "not far from here. I came up here to check—"

To his disbelief, she started to close the door in his face, and he heard himself say her name. It tore out of him before he could stop it: "Katherine! Don't—"

The door opened, and she was smiling just a little, her head tipped to the side as she waited. "What do you want?" she repeated, her eyes searching his.

"Christ! I don't know—"

"Yes, you do. Furthermore," she said with a funny teasing catch in her voice, "I don't think the son of Keaton's very own Reverend Mathison should go around lying about his feelings or using words like *crap* or taking God's name in vain."

"Is that what this is all about?" Ted snapped, completely off balance, a drowning man, grasping at straws to save himself from a fate he's about to embrace. "You think it would be a sexual kick to sleep with a minister's son? To find out how we make love?"

"Was anyone talking about sex, Officer?"

"Now I get it," he said scornfully, seizing on her use of his title. "You've got a hang-up about cops, haven't you. You've got me mixed up with Bruce Willis and you think having sex with—"

"There you go again, talking about sex. Is that all you can think about?"

Nonplussed and furious with himself, he shoved his hands into his pockets and glared. "If it isn't sex with me that you have on your mind, then what the hell is it?"

She stepped forward onto the porch, looking gutsier and more worldly than he felt, but his hands reached for her arms drawing her closer to his hungry body. Softly she said, "Marriage is what I have on my mind. And don't swear."

"Marriage!" Ted exploded.

"You sound shocked, darling."

"You're crazy."

"About you," she agreed. Leaning up on her toes, she slid her hands up his chest and around his neck, and Ted's body ignited as if hers was a torch held against it. "You get one chance to make up for hurting me the last time you kissed me. I didn't like it."

Helplessly, Ted bent his head, touching his lips to her soft ones, and his tongue slid across them. She moaned and the sound snapped his control. He seized her mouth, his hands shifting over her, pulling her hips tightly against his, but he gentled the kiss, and then he deepened it. She tasted like heaven and felt like it; her breasts swelled to fill his hands, and her body fit his as if they'd been sculpted exclusively for each other. Many minutes later, he finally managed to lift his head and speak, but his voice was hoarse with desire and he couldn't pull his hands from her waist. "We're both crazy."

"About each other," she agreed. "I think September is a lovely month for weddings, don't you?"

"No."

She tipped her head back and looked at him, and Ted heard himself say, "I like August better."

"We could get married in August on my twentieth birthday, but August is hot."

"Not nearly as hot as I am."

She tried to look censorious at his sexual remark and ended up giggling instead as she teasingly admonished, "I'm shocked to hear such talk from a minister's son."

"I'm an ordinary man, Katherine," he warned her, but he didn't want her to believe it. Not really. He wanted her to believe he was all the extraordinary things she made him feel—powerful, soft, strong, wise. Still, he felt she should have more time to find out exactly who and what he was. "September is fine with me."

"I don't think it's fine with me, though," she said as she studied his face with a teasing smile. "I mean, your father is a minister, and that probably means you'll insist on waiting until *after* we're married."

Ted managed to look innocent and confused. "To do what?"

"Make love."

"I'm *not* a minister, my father is."

"Make love to me then."

"Not so fast!" Suddenly Ted found himself in the awkward position of taking a stand about the kind of marriage he expected when he hadn't expected, one hour ago, to get married at all. "I won't take a cent of your father's money. If we get married, you'll be a cop's wife until I get my law degree."

"Okay."

"Your parents aren't going to like the idea of you marrying me one damned bit."

"Daddy will adjust."

She was right, Ted discovered. When it came to wheedling her way around people, Katherine was a genius. Everyone, including her parents, just automatically adapted to her willful little whim. Everyone except Ted. After six months of marriage, he couldn't adjust to living in a house that was never cleaned and eating meals that came from cans. Most of all, he couldn't adjust to her sulky moods or irrational demands.

She'd never wanted to be a wife to Ted in any real sense, and she certainly didn't want to be a mother. She'd been furious when she realized she was pregnant two years after they were married and pleased when she managed to miscarry. Her reactions to being pregnant had been the last straw for Ted, the final motivating factor in his decision to give her the divorce she'd threatened him with every time he refused to give in to whatever she wanted.

Carl's voice broke into his reverie, and Ted glanced up at his older brother as he said, "There's no point in mentioning Benedict's name to Mother and Dad. If Julie's in danger, let's keep it from them as long as possible."

"I agree."

22

WE'RE LOST, I KNOW IT! WHERE IN GOD'S NAME ARE WE going? What could possibly be up here except a deserted logging camp?" Julie's voice shook with nervous tension as she peered through snow hurtling at her windshield. They'd left the highway and turned onto a steep road that climbed the mountain in an endless series of hairpin turns, turns that would have made her nervous in the summer; now, with slippery snow and poor visibility to complicate things, the climb was hair-raising. And just when she thought the drive couldn't get worse, they'd turned onto a twisting road so narrow that the branches of the thick black pines on either side of it reached out and brushed against the sides of the car.

"I know you're tired," her passenger said. "If I'd thought there was a chance you wouldn't try to jump out of the car, I'd have done the driving and let you get some rest."

Ever since their kiss nearly twelve hours ago, he'd been treating her with a warm courtesy that was far more alarming to Julie than his anger had been, because she couldn't shake the feeling that he'd altered his plans—and his intended uses—for her. As a result, she'd responded to all his pleasant conversational efforts with sharp, barbed remarks that made her seem and feel like a shrew. She blamed him completely for that, too.

Ignoring his statement, she gave him a frosty shrug. "According to the map and the directions, we're going the right way, but there wasn't any indication about a road that goes straight up! This is a car, not a plane or a snow plow!"

He handed her a soft drink they'd bought at a gas station/convenience store, where they'd also gotten fuel and he'd escorted her once again to the rest room. As before, he'd prevented her from locking the door, and then he'd inspected the rest room to see if she'd tried to leave some sort of note there. When he handed her the soft drink without replying to her complaint about the treacherous conditions, Julie fell silent. Under any other circumstances, she'd have been enthralled with the breathtaking views of majestic snow-covered mountains and soaring pine trees, but it was impossible to enjoy the view when it required all her concentration and effort just to keep the car moving in the right direction. At long last, they were nearing their destination, Julie assumed, because they'd turned off the last decent road over twenty minutes ago. Now they were wending their way up a mountain in a full-fledged blizzard on a road that seemed only inches wider than the car. "I hope whoever gave you that map and the directions knew what he was doing," she said.

"Really?" he teased. "I'd expect you to hope we were lost."

She ignored the good-natured amusement in his voice. "I'd love it if *you* were lost, but I have no desire to be lost with you! The point is, I've been driving in terrible weather on rotten roads for over twenty-four hours and I'm ex- hausted—" She broke off in alarm at the sight of the narrow wooden bridge ahead of them. Until two days ago, the weather had been unseasonably warm in Colorado and melting snow had caused little creeks, like this one, to become swollen, rushing minirivers that flowed out of their banks. "That bridge doesn't look safe. The water's too high—"

"We don't have much choice." She heard the concern in his voice and fright sent her foot to the brake pedal. "I am not driving across that damned bridge."

Zack had come too far to turn back, and besides, turning back on the narrow snow-rutted lane was impossible. So was backing down the mountain on those hairpin turns. The road had been plowed recently—probably this morning—as if Matt Farrell had learned of Zack's escape and guessed why Zack had asked him to phone someone weeks ago with detailed directions to the mountain house. Evidently Matt had also had a caretaker plow the road to make certain Zack could get in if he tried. Still, the bridge didn't look safe. The swollen creek had taken large tree limbs with it, and it was moving fast enough to have put intolerable stress on the structure. "Get out," he said after a moment.

"Get out?! I'll freeze to death in an hour! Is that what you intended all along—for me to drive you this far and then leave me to die in the snow?" None of her barbed remarks had pierced his good humor all day, but her agitated words did just that—his jaw tightened, and icy anger edged his voice. "Get out of the car," he snapped. "I'll drive it across the bridge. If it holds, you can walk across it and get into the car on the other side."

Julie needed no further urging. Clutching her sweater around her, she opened the door and got out, but her relief at being safe turned to something else, something utterly absurd under the circumstances: As she watched him move under the steering wheel, she felt guilty for leaving the car, ashamed of her cowardice and worried about his safety. And that was before he reached in the back seat and took out her coat and two of Carl's blankets that he passed to her through the open door and said, "If the bridge doesn't hold, wrap yourself up in these and find a narrow place where you can cross on foot. At the top of the hill, there's a house with a telephone and plenty of food. You can call for help and wait the storm out up there until it arrives."

He'd said "if the bridge doesn't hold" without betraying an iota of emotion in his voice or face and Julie shivered at the realization that Zachary Benedict could risk his own life without the slightest apparent concern. If the bridge didn't hold, then he and the heavy car would both end up plunging into that swollen, icy creek. She clutched the door to prevent him from closing it. "If it doesn't hold," she said, "I'll throw you a rope or a branch or something so that you can get to the bank."

He closed the door on her last words, and shivering, Julie clutched the coat and blankets to her. The car's tires spun in the snow then caught, and the automobile began inching forward. She held her breath, mumbling disjointed prayers as she stumbled through the snow to the bridge. There, she looked down into the rushing water, trying to gauge its depth. Logs raced past, swirling and bobbing, while she dragged a dead limb about eight feet long to the edge and stuck it in. When it didn't touch the bottom, her fear escalated to panic. "Wait!" she yelled, trying to make him hear her over the howling wind. "We can leave the car here and we can both walk!" If he heard her at all, he ignored her. The motor revved harder as the tires slipped in the snow and grabbed, then the car rocked and bumped forward gathering enough speed to plow through the snow across the bridge. Suddenly Julie heard the timbers of the bridge begin to groan and she screamed, "Don't try it! The bridge won't hold you! Get out! Get out of the car—"

It was too late. The Blazer was moving steadily across the creaking timbers, plowing snow with its bumper, tires spinning and grabbing and spinning again as the four-wheel-drive gear did its work.

Blankets clutched to her chest, snow swirling all around her, Julie stood in a state of helpless paralysis, forced to watch what she could not prevent.

Not until the car, along with its insane driver, reached safety did she breathe again, and then she felt a perverse rush of fury at him for putting her through yet another new terror. Ungracious and ungraceful, she trudged across the bridge, opened the passenger door, and climbed in.

"We made it," he said.

Julie gave him a killing look. "Made it to what?"

The answer to that came minutes later when they made one last hairpin turn at the top of the mountain. There in the middle of a secluded clearing in the dense pines was a magnificent house made of native stone and cedar and surrounded by wooden decks, with huge expanses of glass. "To this," he said.

"Who in God's name built this place up here, a hermit?"

"Someone who obviously likes privacy and solitude."

"Does it belong to a relative?" she asked, suddenly suspicious.

"No."

"Does the owner know you're going to use his place for a hideout while the police are looking for you?"

"You ask too damned many questions," he said, pulling the car to a stop beside the house and climbing out. "But the answer is no." He came around to her side of the car and opened the door. "Let's go."

"Go?" Julie burst out, pressing into the back of the seat. "You said I could leave when I got you here."

"I lied."

"You—you bastard, I believed you!" she cried, but she was lying, too. All day long she'd been trying desperately to ignore what her common sense had warned her: He'd kept her with him this long to prevent her from telling the authorities where he was; if he released her now, there was absolutely nothing to prevent her from doing exactly that.

"Julie," he said with strained patience, "don't make this any harder on yourself than it needs to be. You're stuck here for a few days, and it's not that bad a place to spend some time." With that he reached across her, snatched the keys out of the ignition, and stalked off toward the house. For a split second she was too furious and too miserable to move, then she blinked back the tears of futility stinging her eyes and got out of the car. Shivering uncontrollably in the freezing blasts of wind, she trudged in his wake, carefully placing her feet in the knee-high craters his feet made in the snow drifts surrounding the house. Wrapping her arms around herself, she watched him try the doorknob. It was locked. He rattled it hard. It was locked tight. He let go of the door handle and stood there, his hands on his hips, looking about him, momentarily lost in thought. Julie's teeth began to chatter. "N-n-now wh-what?" she demanded. "H-h-how do you in-intend to g-get in?"

He gave her an ironic glance. "How do you think I do?" Without waiting for a reply, he turned and headed toward the deck that wrapped around the front and opposite side of the house. Julie trotted doggedly at his heels, freezing and angry. "You're going to break a window, aren't you," she speculated with revulsion, then she looked up at the giant panes of glass that soared to the peak of the roof at least twenty-five feet above and added, "If you break one of those, it'll fall down and cut you to pieces."

"Don't sound so hopeful," he said, his gaze switching to several large mounds of snow that had obviously accumulated over something beneath them. He began digging in one of the mounds and unearthed a large flowerpot, which he picked up and carried toward the back door.

"Now what are you doing?"

"Guess."

"How should I know?" Julie snapped. "You're the criminal, not me."

"True, but I was sent up for murder, not breaking and entering."

In disbelief, she watched him trying to dig in the frozen soil in the clay pot, then he slammed the pot against the side of the house and broke it, dumping the soil onto the snow beside the door. Wordlessly, he crouched down and began hammering his bare fist on the soil while Julie watched in incredulous amazement. "Are you having a temper tantrum?" she demanded.

"No, Miss Mathison," he said with exaggerated patience, as he plucked up a piece of dirt and brushed at it with his finger. "I am looking for a key."

"No one who can afford a house like this and pay to put a road up an entire mountain in order to get to it is going to be naive enough to hide a key in a flowerpot! You're wasting your time."

"Have you always been such a shrew?" he said with an irritated shake of his dark head.

"A shrew!" Julie said, her voice strangled with frustration. "You steal my car and take me hostage, threaten my life, lie to me, and now you have the—the gall to criticize my manners?" Her tirade was interrupted as he held up a dirt-encrusted silver object that Julie realized was a key, which he then inserted in the door. With an exaggerated flourish he swung open the door and gestured her inside with a sweep of his arm. "We've already agreed that I've broken all of Emily Post's rules of etiquette where you're concerned. Now, I suggest you go inside and look around while I get our things out of the car. Why don't you try to relax," he added. "Get some rest. Enjoy the view. Think of this as a vacation."

Julie glared at him open-mouthed, then snapped her jaws together and said irately, "I'm not on a vacation! I'm a hostage, and don't expect me to forget it!"

In answer, he gave her a long-suffering look, as if she were being impossibly difficult, so she jerked her gaze from his and marched into the house. Inside, the mountain retreat was both rustic and startlingly luxurious, built around a gigantic center room shaped like a hexagon, with three doors opening off of it into bedroom suites. Soaring wood ceilings were supported by gigantic crossbeams of rough-hewn cedar, and a winding staircase led up to a loft that was lined with handsome bookcases. Four of the six walls were made entirely of glass, offering a view of the mountains that Julie knew would be breathtaking on a clear day. The fifth wall was built of native stone with an enormous fireplace carved into the center above a raised hearth. Facing the fireplace was a long L-shaped sofa upholstered in a butter soft silvery leather. Opposite the sofa and facing the windows were two overstuffed chairs and ottomans upholstered in silver and green stripes that blended with the fat throw pillows on the sofa and raised hearth. A thick carpet with the same design as the throw pillows sculpted into the border covered part of the gleaming wooden floor in front of the fireplace. Two more pairs of chairs were positioned invitingly near two of the windows and a desk was tucked into an angle created by the glass walls. At any other time, Julie would have been awed and intrigued by what was the most unique and beautiful place she'd ever seen, but she was too upset and too hungry to give it more than passing notice.

Turning, she wandered into the kitchen area, an efficient, modernistic galley-type affair that stretched across the back wall of the house and was divided from the living room by a high counter with six leather stools in front of it. Her stomach growled as she looked at the oak cabinets and oak-fronted built-in refrigerator, but her appetite was already losing the battle with exhaustion. Feeling like a sneak thief, she opened a cabinet that contained dishes and glassware, then another that contained—luckily—a wide variety of canned goods. Deciding to make a sandwich and then go to bed, she was reaching timidly for a can of albacore tuna fish when Zack opened the back door and saw her. "Dare I hope," he said, kicking snow off his boots, "that this means you're domestically inclined?"

"Do you mean, can I cook?"

"Yes."

"Not for you." Julie put the can of tuna back and closed the cabinet door just as her stomach let out an audible growl of protest.

"Jesus, you are stubborn!" Chafing his hands against the cold, he walked over to the thermostat on the wall and turned up the heat, then he headed for the refrigerator and opened the freezer door. Julie peeked around him and spied dozens of thick steaks and pork chops, huge roasts, some packages wrapped in white freezer paper, and boxes and boxes of vegetables, some raw and others prepared. It was a display that would do justice to any gourmet market. Her mouth began to water as he reached for a steak that was an inch and a half thick, but exhaustion was already overwhelming her. Her relief at being in a warm house instead of the car and at having arrived at a destination after an endless, nerve-wracking drive was suddenly making her feel limp, and she realized she wanted a hot shower and long nap a great deal more than food. "I have to get some sleep," she said, scarcely able to muster the strength to sound cool and authoritative any more. "Please. Where?"

Something in her pale face and heavy eyes made him respond without argument. "The bedroom is this way," he said, already turning on his heel and heading for a doorway that opened off the living room. When he flipped on the light switch, Julie found herself in an enormous bedroom suite with a fireplace and an adjoining bathroom of black marble with mirrored walls. She spotted the telephone on the nightstand beside the king-size bed at the same moment he did. "It has its own bath," he told her unnecessarily as he walked over to the nightstand and briskly unplugged the telephone, tucking it under his arm.

"But no telephone, I see," she added with bitter resignation as she headed back into the living room to get her suitcase.

Behind her, he checked the doors to the bathroom and bedroom, then he caught her arm as she bent over in the living room to pick up her suitcase. "Look," he said, "we might as well get the rules established. Here's the situation: There are no other houses on this mountain. I have the car keys, so the only way you can leave here would be on foot, in which case you'll freeze to death long before you ever get near the highway. The bedroom door and the bathroom door both have those useless little locks in the door handle that anyone can open from the other side with a hairpin, so I don't recommend that you try to barricade yourself in there, because it would be a waste of time, not to mention unnecessarily confining for you. Are you following me, so far?"

Julie tried unsuccessfully to jerk her arm free. "I'm not a moron."

"Good. Then you should already have realized you can have the run of the house—"

"The run of the house? Just like a trained beagle, is that it?"

"Not exactly," Zack said, his mouth quirking in a smile as he let his admiring glance rove over her thick, wavy chestnut hair and slim, restless figure. "More like a skittish Irish Setter," he corrected.

Julie opened her mouth to give him the biting retort he deserved, but she couldn't get words out before she yawned again.

23

THE MOUTH-WATERING AROMA OF STEAK SIZZLING ON A GRILL lured her from a deep sleep. Dimly aware that the huge bed on which she slept was too big to be her own bed, she rolled onto her back, completely disoriented. Blinking in the inky darkness of an unfamiliar room, she turned her face the opposite direction, searching for the pale source of illumination spilling through what turned out to be a narrow parting of the draperies on the wall. Moonlight. For a few blissful moments, she imagined she was in a luxuriously large hotel room somewhere on vacation.

She glanced at the digital clock on the nightstand. Wherever she was, the local time was 8:20 P.M. And it was chilly in the room—the kind of deep chill that made her sleepily rule out California or Florida as her possible whereabouts. It hit her then that hotel rooms were never redolent with the aroma of cooking food. She was in a house somewhere, not a hotel, and there were footsteps in the next room.

Heavy, masculine footsteps . . .

Awareness hit her like a punch in the stomach and she sat bolt upright in bed, already throwing the covers off and standing up, adrenalin pumping. She took a quick step toward the window, her mind's escape mechanism working before her logic caught up. Goose bumps lifted on her bare legs, and she looked down in shivering disbelief at what she was wearing—a man's Tee-shirt she'd removed from a dresser drawer after her shower. Her captor's warning came back to her: *"I have the car keys and there are no other houses on this mountain . . . You'll freeze to death if you try to escape on foot . . . The door locks can be opened easily . . . You have the run of the house."*

"Just relax," Julie told herself aloud, but she was rested now and fully alert, and her mind was tumbling over itself with possible escape solutions, none of which were even remotely feasible. On top of that she was famished. Food first, she decided, then she'd try to think of a way out of here.

From her suitcase, she pulled out the jeans she'd worn to Amarillo. She'd washed out her underwear after her shower, but it was still soaking wet. Pulling on her jeans, she went into the large closet and looked at the heavy men's sweaters neatly folded on the shelves, longing for something clean to wear. She took out a bulky cream fisherman's knit and held it up to herself. It hung down to her knees. Deciding with a shrug that she didn't care how she looked, and the thick sweater would hide the fact that she wasn't wearing a bra, she put it on. She'd washed her hair and blown it dry before she went to bed, so there was nothing to do but brush it. Automatically, she bent over, brushing the shoulder-length tresses from underneath as she always did, finding an odd comfort in following this one small, familiar routine. Finished, she straightened, gave her hair a few more brush strokes, then brushed it back off her forehead, letting it fall into natural waves at the sides. She reached for her purse to put on lipstick then she changed her mind. Looking nice for an escaped convict was not only completely unnecessary but probably a major mistake, considering that kiss in the snow she'd participated in at dawn this morning.

That kiss . . .

It seemed like weeks, not merely hours since he'd kissed her, and now that she was rested and alert, Julie felt reasonably sure his only interest in her was merely to ensure his safety. Not sexual.

Definitely not sexual.

Please, God. Not sexual.

She glanced at the mirrors on the bathroom walls and felt reassured. She'd always been too busy and preoccupied to worry much about her appearance. When she had taken time to study it, she always felt she had a rather odd face filled with startling features that were too prominent, like her eyes and cheekbones and that absurd cleft in her chin that had deepened to real visibility when she was thirteen. Now, however, she was thrilled with her looks. In jeans and an oversized sweater, with her hair like this and no makeup on, she wouldn't appeal sexually to any man, particularly one who'd been to bed with hundreds of gorgeous, glamorous, famous women. His interest in her would definitely not be sexual, Julie decided with absolute confidence.

Drawing in a long, steadying breath, she reached for the door handle and turned it, reluctant but ready to face her captor—and hopefully a delicious meal. The bedroom door wasn't locked. She distinctly remembered locking that door, on principal, when she went to bed.

Silently, she opened the door and stepped into the main room of the house. For a split second, the inviting beauty of the scene made her feel completely disoriented. A fire was roaring in the fireplace, the lights on the beams high above were dimmed, and candles were lit on the coffee table, flickering on the crystal wine glasses he'd set out beside linen place mats. It might have been the wine glasses and candles that suddenly made Julie feel as if she was walking into a seduction scene, or perhaps it was the dimmed lights or the soft music playing on the stereo. Trying to inject a brisk, businesslike tone into her voice, she headed toward Zachary Benedict, who was standing in the kitchen, his back to her, taking something out of the broiler. "Are we expecting company?"

He turned and looked at her, an inexplicable, lazy smile sweeping over his face as he surveyed her from head to foot. Julie had the staggering, and impossible, impression that he actually liked what he saw, an impression that was reinforced by the way he lifted his wine glass to her in the gesture of a toast and said, "Somehow, you look adorable in that oversize sweater."

Belatedly realizing that after five years in prison, any woman would probably appeal to him, Julie took a cautious step backward. "The last thing I want to do is look nice for you. In fact, I'd rather wear my own clothes, even if they're not fresh," she said, turning on her heel.

"Julie!" he snapped, all goodwill gone from his voice.

She lurched around, amazed and alarmed by the dangerous swiftness of his mood swings. She took another cautious step backward as he stalked toward her, a wine glass in each hand. "Have something to drink," he ordered, thrusting a long-stemmed glass toward her. "Drink it, damn it!" He made a visible effort to soften his tone. "It'll help you relax."

"Why should I relax?" she countered obstinately.

Despite the stubborn lift of her chin and her rebellious tone, there was a tiny quaver of fear in her voice, and when Zack heard it, his annoyance with her evaporated. She'd shown so much courage, such indefatigable spirit during the last twenty-four hours; she'd fought him so relentlessly that he'd actually believed she wasn't very frightened most of the time. Now, however, as he looked at her upturned face, he saw that the ordeal he'd put her through had left faint blue smudges beneath her glorious eyes, and her smooth skin was decidedly pale. She was amazing, he thought—courageous, kind, and plucky as hell. Perhaps if he didn't like her—genuinely like her—it wouldn't have mattered that she was watching him as if he were a dangerous animal. Wisely suppressing the urge to put his hand against her cheek and try to reassure her, which would undoubtedly panic her, or to offer an apology for kidnapping her, which she'd definitely find hypocritical, he did something he'd promised himself he'd never bother to do again: He tried to convince her of his innocence. "A moment ago, I asked you to relax, and—" he began, but she interrupted him.

"You ordered me to relax, you didn't ask."

Her prim reprimand brought a reluctant smile to his lips. "Now I am asking."

Thrown completely off balance by what sounded like gentleness in his voice, Julie took a sip of her wine, stalling for time, steadying her confused senses, while he stood only two feet away, towering over her, his broad shoulders blocking out her view of anything but him. It hit her suddenly that he'd evidently showered, shaved, and changed clothes while she slept . . . and that, in a pair of charcoal trousers and a black sweater, Zachary Benedict was far more handsome than he'd ever looked on screen. He lifted his hand and braced it against the wall beside her shoulder, and when he spoke again, his deep voice had that same strange, compellingly gentle quality. "On the way here, you asked me if I was innocent of the crime I was sent to prison for, and I gave you a flippant answer the first time and a grudging answer the next. Now I'm going to tell you the truth simply and voluntarily . . ."

Julie tore her gaze from his and stared into the ruby wine in her glass, suddenly afraid that in her state of weak weariness, she might actually believe the lie she sensed he was about to tell her.

"Look at me, Julie."

With a mixture of dread and helpless anticipation, she lifted her eyes and met his steady amber gaze.

"I didn't kill or plot to kill my wife or anyone else. I was sent to prison for a crime I didn't commit. I'd like you to at least believe there's a *possibility* I'm telling you the truth."

Noncommittally, she stared into his eyes, but in her mind she suddenly saw the scene at the rickety bridge: Instead of insisting she drive across the bridge with him, he had let her get out of the car and then he had given her blankets to keep warm in case the bridge collapsed, in case he drowned when the car plunged into that deep, icy creek. She remembered the harsh desperation in his voice when he kissed her in the snow, pleading with her to go along with the ploy, so the truck driver wouldn't be hurt. He'd had a gun in his pocket, but he'd not attempted to use it. And then she remembered his kiss—that urgent, hard kiss that had gentled suddenly and then become soft and insistent and sensual.

Since dawn that morning, she'd been forcibly trying to forget the memory of that kiss, but now it came back—vibrant and alive and dangerously exciting. Those recollections combined seductively with the rich timbre of his deep voice as he added, "This is the first normal night I've had in over five years. If the authorities are close behind on my trail, it will be my last one. I'd like to enjoy it if you'll cooperate."

Julie was suddenly inclined to cooperate: For one thing, despite her nap, she was mentally exhausted and not up to sparring with him; she was also starving and heartily sick of being afraid. But the memory of that kiss had nothing to do with her capitulation. Nothing whatsoever! she told herself. Nor did it have anything to do with the sudden, impossible conviction she had that he *was* telling her the truth!

"I'm innocent of that crime," he repeated more forcefully, his gaze never leaving hers.

The words hit her with a jolt, yet still she resisted, trying not to let her foolish emotions overrule her intellect.

"If you can't actually believe that," he said with a harsh sigh, "could you at least pretend you believe it and cooperate with me tonight?"

Stifling the urge to nod, Julie said cautiously, "What sort of 'cooperation' do you have in mind?"

"Conversation," he said. "Lighthearted conversation with an intelligent woman is a forgotten pleasure to me. So is decent food, a fireplace, moonlight in the windows, good music, doors instead of bars, and the sight of a pretty woman." A definite note of cajolery lightened his voice as he added, "I'll do all the cooking if you'll agree to a truce."

Julie hesitated, stunned by his reference to her as a pretty woman, then she decided he'd meant nothing by it except a little empty flattery. A night without tension and fear was being offered to her and her battered nerves cried out for relief. What harm was there in what he asked. Particularly if he were truly innocent. "You'll do all the cooking?" she bargained.

He nodded, a lazy grin sweeping over his rugged face as he realized she was about to agree, and the unexpected glamour of that white smile did treacherous things to her heart rate. "Okay," she agreed, smiling a little despite her desire to remain at least partially aloof, "but only if you'll do the cleaning up as well as the cooking."

He chuckled at that. "You drive a hard bargain, but I accept. Sit down while I finish dinner."

Julie obeyed and sat down on one of the stools at the counter that divided the kitchen from the living room.

"Tell me about yourself," he said, taking a baked potato out of the oven.

She took another swallow of the wine for courage. "What do you want to know?"

"General things, for a start," Zack said casually. "You said you aren't married. Are you divorced?"

She shook her head. "I've never been married."

"Engaged?"

"Greg and I are talking about it."

"What is there to discuss?"

Julie choked on her wine. Stifling an embarrassed laugh, she said, "I don't actually think that question falls in the category of general information."

"Probably not," he agreed with a grin. "So, what's holding up the engagement?"

To her disgust, Julie felt herself blush beneath his amused gaze, but she answered with admirable calm. "We want to be certain we're completely compatible—that our goals and philosophies match."

"Sounds like to me you're stalling. Do you live with this Greg?"

"Absolutely not," Julie said in a censorious voice, and he lifted his brows as if he found her quaintly amusing.

"Any roommates?"

"I live alone."

"No husband and no roommates," he said, as he poured more wine in her glass. "So no one is looking for you now, wondering where you are?"

"I'm sure a lot of people are."

"Who, for instance?"

"My parents, for a start. By now they're undoubtedly frantic and calling people to see if anyone's heard from me. The first person they'll call is my brother, Ted. Carl will be looking for me, too. It's his car I'm driving, and by now my brothers are organizing a manhunt, believe me."

"Is Ted the brother who's a builder?"

"No," Julie stated with amused satisfaction, "He's the brother who's a Keaton sheriff."

His reaction was gratifyingly sharp. "He's a sheriff!" As if to wash away the unpleasant information, he took a long swallow of his wine and said with heavy irony, "And I suppose your father is a judge?"

"No. He's a minister."

"My God!"

"You got it. That's his employer. God."

"Of all the women in Texas," he said with a grim shake of his head, "I managed to kidnap the sister of a sheriff and the daughter of a minister. The media will have a field day when they get ahold of who you are."

The brief feeling of power Julie felt at seeing him alarmed was even headier than the wine she was drinking. Nodding happily, she promised, "Loyal lawmen everywhere will be hunting you down with dogs and guns, and Godfearing Americans will be praying they find you right away."

Turning slightly aside, he poured the last of the bottle of wine into his glass and tossed it down. "Great."

The mood of conviviality had been such a relief that Julie soon regretted its loss, and she searched for something to say that might restore it. "What are we having for dinner?" she said finally.

The question shook him from his reverie, and he turned to the stove. "Something simple," he said, "I'm not much of a cook." With his body blocking her view of the preparations, she had little to occupy her, and so Julie idly watched the way his sweater stretched across his wide shoulders. He was amazingly muscular, as if he'd been working out in the prison gym. Prison. She'd read somewhere that many people who are sent to prison are actually innocent, and she found herself suddenly clinging to the comforting hope that Zachary Benedict might actually have been one of them. Without turning, he said, "Sit down on the sofa. I'll bring the food over there."

Julie nodded and got off the stool, noting that the second glass of wine was definitely affecting her, making her feel a little too relaxed. With Zack following her, carrying plates, she went over to the sofa and sat down at one of the linen place mats he'd laid on the coffee table in front of the fire. He put down two plates, one of which contained a juicy steak and baked potato.

In front of her, he plopped down a plate on which he had upended a can of tuna fish. That was all. No vegetable, no garnish, no nothing.

After having her mouth water for so long in anticipation of a thick, juicy sizzling steak, Julie's reaction to that cold, round mound of unadorned, unappetizing tuna fish was swift and unguarded. Her irate gaze snapped to his face, her mouth open in angry dismay.

"Isn't that what you wanted?" he asked innocently. "Or would you prefer a nice steak like the one I left in the kitchen?"

There was something about the boyish prank, something about his engaging grin and smiling eyes that caused an unexpected, uncontrollable, and, under the circumstances, bizarre reaction from Julie: She started to giggle. And then she started to laugh. Her shoulders were still shaking when he walked back to the sofa carrying another plate with a steak on it and put it in front of her.

"Like that a little better?"

"Well," she said, trying to sound severe despite the laughter still shimmering in her eyes, "I can forgive you for kidnapping and terrifying me, but it's a hanging offense to give me tuna while you eat steak." Julie would have been content to eat in peaceful silence, but as she cut the first bite of steak he noticed the bruise on her wrist and asked her how she'd gotten it. "That's a football injury," she explained.

"A what?"

"I was playing touch football last week and I got tackled."

"By some big halfback?"

"No, by a small boy and a big wheelchair."

"What?"

It was obvious that he craved conversation as much as he'd claimed, and Julie managed to give him an abbreviated version of the game while she ate. "It was my own fault," she finished, smiling at the memory. "I love basketball, but I've never understood football. It's a game that makes no sense."

"Why do you say that?"

She waved her fork dismissively. "Consider the players, for a start. You have a fullback and a halfback and a quarterback. But there's no three-quarters back. You have a tight end but no loose end." His burst of laughter collided with her last sentence as she finished, "It's definitely not my game, but it doesn't matter, because my kids love it. One of my boys is probably going to go to the Wheelchair Olympics."

Zack noted the softness that crept into her voice and the glow that lit her eyes as she spoke of "my boys," and he continued to smile at her, marveling at her capacity for compassion and her sheer sweetness. Unwilling to let her stop talking, he cast about for another subject and asked, "What were you doing in Amarillo the day we met?"

"I'd gone there to see the grandfather of one of my handicapped students. He's quite wealthy, and I hoped to convince him to donate money to an adult literacy program I'm involved in at school."

"Did you succeed?"

"Yes. His check is in my purse."

"What made you decide to become a teacher?" he said, strangely unwilling to let her stop talking. He'd chosen the right topic, Zack realized when she gave him a heart-stopping smile and warmed to her subject with gratifying immediacy. "I love children, and teaching is an old and respectable profession."

"Respectable?" he repeated, startled by the subtle quaintness of the notion. "I didn't think being 'respectable' was of much concern to anyone these days. Why is it so important to you?"

Julie evaded the all-to-perceptive comment with a lift of her shoulders. "I'm a minister's daughter, and Keaton is a small town."

"I see," he said, but he didn't completely see at all. "There are other professions that are just as respectable."

"Yes, but I wouldn't get to work with people like Johnny Everett and Debby Sue Cassidy."

Her face glowed at the mere mention of Johnny's name, and Zack was instantly curious about the male who seemed to mean more to her than her almost-fiancé. "Who is Johnny Everett?"

"He's one of my students—one of my favorite students, actually. He's paralyzed from the waist down. When I first started teaching at Keaton, he never spoke and he was such a discipline problem that Mr. Duncan wanted to send him away for special education with mentally handicapped kids. His mother swore he could talk, but no one ever heard him, and since she never let him out of the house to play with the other kids, no one could be sure she wasn't trying to make her son seem . . . more normal. In class, Johnny would do disruptive things, like knocking books onto the floor or blocking the doorway during recess—small things—but they were constant and so Mr. Duncan decided to send him off to a special school."

"Who is Mr. Duncan?"

She wrinkled her small nose with such distaste that Zack grinned. "He's our principal."

"You don't like him very well, I take it?"

"He's not a bad man, he's just too rigid. He would have been right at home a hundred years ago when a student who spoke out in class was disciplined with a hickory stick."

"And Johnny was terrified of him, is that it?"

She giggled merrily and shook her head. "Actually, it was just the opposite. Quite by accident, I discovered that Johnny hated being treated with kid gloves. He *wanted* to be disciplined."

"How did you discover that?"

"One night, after school, I was in Mr. Duncan's office being chewed out, as usual."

"You get into trouble with the principal?"

"Constantly," she averred, her smile bursting like sunshine. "Anyway, on that particular day, Johnny was waiting for his mother to pick him up, and he overheard what was happening. When I came out of the principal's office, there he was—grinning at me from his wheelchair like I was some sort of hero. Then he said, 'You gonna get a detention, Miss Mathison?'

"I was so startled to hear him talk that I nearly dropped the armload of books I was carrying. But when I assured him I wasn't going to get a detention, he looked disappointed in me. He said he guessed girls never got detention, just boys. Normal boys. That's when I knew!" When he looked baffled, Julie hastened to explain, "You see, he'd been so sheltered by his mother that he'd been dreaming of going to school like ordinary children, but the thing was, neither the other students nor the teachers were treating him as if he was ordinary."

"What did you do?"

She leaned back against the sofa, her leg curled beneath her and said, "I did the only kind and decent thing I could do: I waited and watched him all the next day, and the moment he tossed a pencil at the little girl in front of him, I pounced on him like it was a federal crime. I told him he'd deserved a detention for weeks, and from now on he was getting one just like everyone else. Then I gave him not one, but two days' detention!"

Laying her head against the back of the sofa, she slanted him a soft smile and said, "Then I hung around school to watch him and make sure I was right about what he was up to. He looked happy enough, sitting in the detention room with all the other little rabble rousers, but I couldn't be sure. That night, his mother called me on the phone and tore into me for what I'd done. She said I'd made him ill and that I was heartless and vicious. I tried to explain, but she hung up on me. She was frantic. He wasn't at school the next day."

When she fell silent, Zack prodded gently, "What did you do?"

"After school, I went over to his house to see him and talk to his mother. I did something else on a hunch; I took another student with me—Willie Jenkins. Willie is a totally macho kid, the class cutup, and the hero of the third grade. He's good at everything, from football to baseball to cursing—at everything except," she clarified with a sideways grin, "singing. When Willie talks, he sounds exactly like a bullfrog, and when he sings, he makes this loud, croaking noise that makes everybody start to laugh. Anyway, on a hunch, I took Willie with me, and when I got to Johnny's house, he was in the backyard in a wheelchair. Willie had brought along his football—I think he sleeps with it—and he stayed outside. As I went into the house, Willie was trying to get Johnny to catch the football and he wouldn't even try. He looked at his mother and then he just sat there. I spent a half hour talking to Mrs. Everett. I told her I honestly thought we were ruining Johnny's chances to be happy by treating him as if he were too delicate to do anything but sit in a wheelchair. I'd finished talking and still hadn't convinced her, when all of a sudden, there were shouts and a crash from outside and we both ran out into the backyard. There was Willie," Julie said, her eyes shining at the memory, "flat on his backside in a heap of overturned trash cans, clutching the football with a grin on his face a mile wide. It seems that Johnny couldn't *catch* the football very well but—according to Willie—Johnny has a right arm as good as John Elway's! Johnny was beaming and Willie told him that he wanted Johnny on his team, but they'd need to practice, so Johnny could learn to catch as well as pass."

When she fell silent, Zack asked softly, "And do they practice?"

She nodded, her expressive features glowing with delight. "They practice football, along with the rest of Willie's team, every day. Then they go to Johnny's house where *Johnny* coaches *Willie* with his schoolwork. It turned out that although Johnny didn't participate in school, he was absorbing everything like a sponge. He's extremely bright and now that he has things to strive for, he never quits trying. I've never seen so much courage—so much determination." A little embarrassed by her emotional enthusiasm, Julie lapsed into silence again, and concentrated on her meal.

24

WHEN HE WAS FINISHED EATING, ZACK SETTLED BACK AGAINST the sofa and propped his ankle on the opposite knee, watching the flames leaping and dancing on the hearth, as he gave his dinner companion a chance to finish her meal without further interruptions from him. He tried to concentrate on the next stage of his journey, but in his state of sated relaxation he was more inclined to dwell on the amazing—and perverse—quirk of fate that had caused Julie Mathison to be sitting across from him. Throughout all the long weeks of working out every detail of his escape—throughout the endless nights he'd lain in his cell, dreaming of his first night in this house—not once had he ever imagined that he'd be other than alone. For a thousand reasons, it would have been far better if he *were* alone, but now that she was here, he couldn't just lock her in a room, bring her food, and pretend she wasn't. After the last hour in her company, however, he was sorely tempted to do exactly that, because she was forcing him to recognize and reflect on all the things he had missed in his life and the things that were going to be lacking in it for all time. At the end of a week, he'd be on the run again, and where he was going, there'd be no luxurious mountain cabins with cozy fires; there'd be no more poignant conversations about handicapped little boys with prim third-grade teachers who happened to have eyes like an angel and a smile that could melt stone. He couldn't remember ever seeing a woman's entire face light up the way hers had when she talked about those children! He'd seen ambitious women light up at the possibility of getting an acting role or a piece of jewelry from him; he'd seen the world's finest actresses—on stage and off, in bed and out of it—give thoroughly convincing performances of passionate tenderness and caring, but until tonight, he had never, *ever* witnessed the real thing.

When he was eighteen years old, sitting in the cab of a semitruck, bound for Los Angeles and almost strangling on tears he refused to shed, he'd vowed never, ever to look back, to wonder how his life might have been "if only things had been different." Yet, now, at the age of thirty-five, when he was hardened beyond recall by the things he'd done and been and seen, he looked at Julie Mathison and succumbed to the temptation to wonder. As he lifted the brandy snifter to his lips, he watched a log tumble off the grate in a shower of sparks and wondered what would have happened if he'd met someone like her when he was young. Would she have been able to save him from himself, to teach him to forgive, to soften his heart, to fill up the empty spaces in his life? Would she have been able to give him goals greater and more rewarding than the acquisition of money and power and recognition that had shaped his life? With someone like Julie in his bed, would he have experienced something better, deeper, more profound, more lasting, than the mindless pleasure of an orgasm?

Belatedly, the sheer unlikelihood of his musings hit him, and he marveled at his own folly. Where in the hell would he have ever met someone like Julie Mathison? Until he was eighteen, he'd been surrounded by servants and relatives, whose very presence were daily reminders of his social superiority. Back then, the daughter of a small-town minister, such as Julie, would never have entered his sphere.

No, he wouldn't have met her then, and he damned sure wouldn't have met someone like her in Hollywood. But what if he had, by some quirk of fate, met Julie there? Zack wondered, frowning with concentration. If she'd somehow survived unscathed in that sea of social depravity, unbridled self-indulgence, and raging ambition that was Hollywood, would he have really *noticed* her, or would she have been completely eclipsed in his eyes by more glamorous, showy, worldly women? If she'd walked into his office on Beverly Drive and asked him for a screen test, would he have noticed that lovely fine-boned face of hers, those incredible eyes, that lithesome figure? Or would he have overlooked all that because she wasn't spectacularly beautiful and built like an overfilled hourglass? If she spent an hour in his office talking to him there as she had done tonight, would he have truly appreciated her wit, her intelligence, her unaffected candor? Or would he have hustled her out because she wasn't talking about "the business" nor giving any indication that she'd like to go to bed with him, which would have been his two primary interests.

Zack rolled his glass between his hands as he contemplated his answers to those rhetorical questions, trying to be brutally honest with himself. After several moments, he decided that he *would* have noticed Julie Mathison's delicate features, glowing skin, and striking eyes. After all, he was an expert judge of beauty, conventional or otherwise, so he would not have overlooked hers. And, yes, he *would* have appreciated her straightforward candor, and he *would* have been as touched by her compassion and gentleness, her sheer sweetness as he had been tonight. He would *not*, however, have given her a screen test.

Nor would he have recommended she put herself in the hands of a good photographer who, Zack was absolutely certain right now, could capture that all-American girl freshness of hers and turn it into a million-dollar magazine cover, even though she was well past the age for starting out as a model.

Instead of that, Zack honestly believed he would have ushered her straight out of his office and told her to go home and marry her almost-fiancé, have his children, and live a life with meaning. Because, even at his most calloused, most jaded moments, Zack would never have wanted to see anything that was as fine and unspoiled as Julie Mathison become handled and used and corrupted, not by Hollywood or by him.

But what if she had insisted on staying in Hollywood anyway, despite his advice, would he have then taken her to bed later, if and when she seemed to be willing?

No.

Would he have wanted to?

No!

Would he have even wanted to keep her around, perhaps see her for lunch, evenings, or invite her to parties?

Christ, no!

Why not?

Zack already knew exactly why not, but he glanced over at her anyway as if to confirm what he felt: She was sitting with her feet curled beneath her on the sofa, the firelight gleaming on her shiny hair as she looked up at a beautiful landscape portrait hanging above the fireplace—her entire profile was as serene and as innocent as a choirgirl's at Christmas Mass. And *that* was why he would never have wanted to be around her before he went to prison and why he didn't really want to be around her now.

Although he was only nine years older than she in actual years, he was centuries older than she in experience, and most of that experience had not been the sort she would admire or even approve of—and that was true even before he went to prison. Beside her youthful idealism, Zack felt terribly old and jaded.

The fact that he found her incredibly sexy and desirable right now, even engulfed in that shapeless, bulky sweater, and the fact that he had an erection at this very moment only made him feel like a dirty, old, disgusting letch.

On the other hand, she'd also made him laugh tonight, and he appreciated that, he decided as he tossed down a swallow of brandy. Leaning forward, he propped his arms on his knees, smiling absently at the empty glass as he rolled it in his hands. He wondered if he'd ever listen to another football game without remembering her laughing protest at the idea of having a fullback, a halfback, a quarterback, *but not* a "three-quarters" back. And would he ever hear a football player referred to as a "tight end" without smiling because Julie Mathison had felt, very seriously, that simple common sense required a "loose end" as well.

It suddenly occurred to him that she had not asked him a single question about his old life in the film business. He couldn't remember meeting a single woman, or a man, who hadn't gushingly—if dishonestly—proclaimed that Zack was their favorite movie star and then plied him with personal questions about himself and the other stars they particularly admired. Even some of the toughest, most bloodthirsty cons in prison had been absurdly dazzled by his past and anxious to tell him which of his movies they liked most. Normally, all that fawning inquisitiveness had annoyed and disgusted him. Now he was just a little irked that Julie Mathison seemed not to have ever heard of him. Maybe they didn't have a theater in that obscure little town she lived in, he decided. Maybe she'd never seen a movie in her entire, sheltered little life in Mayberry RFD.

Maybe . . . God, maybe . . . she only went to pristine movies rated G! His own movies had been either PG or R—for profanity, violence, or sexual content or all three. To his extreme annoyance, Zack suddenly felt vaguely ashamed of that, which was another good reason that he'd never have willingly chosen to be around a woman like her.

He was so lost in his thoughts that he jumped when she said with a hesitant smile, "You don't look like you're enjoying your evening very much."

"I was thinking about watching the news," he said vaguely.

Julie, who'd been uneasily aware of his frowning silence, leapt at the opportunity to occupy herself with something other than wondering if he was truly innocent of murder . . . and if he was going to try to kiss her again before the evening was over. "That's a good idea," she said, getting up and reaching for her dish on the table. "Why don't you find the channel on the television set and I'll clear off the dishes?"

"And have you accuse me of welching on our deal? No way. *I'll* clear the dishes."

Julie watched him gather up plates and flatware and head for the kitchen.

For the last hour, when she wasn't answering his questions, doubts about his guilt had continued to plague her. She remembered the furious way he'd spoken of the jury that sent him to prison. She remembered the terrible despair in his voice when he'd pleaded with her in the snow to kiss him in order to mislead the truck driver *"Please! I didn't kill anyone, I swear it!"*

At that moment, he'd planted a treacherous seed of doubt in her mind about his guilt; now, seventeen hours later, that seed was taking root deep within her, nourished by her horror at the possibility that an innocent man had spent five long years in a penitentiary. Other things that were equally beyond her control were combining to make her feel helplessly drawn to him, things like the memory of his hungry kiss, the shudder that had run through his body when she'd finally yielded, the restraint he'd shown when she did yield. In fact, he had treated her with restraint and even courtesy during most of the time they'd been together.

For the dozenth time in the last hour, she decided a true murderer surely wouldn't bother to be gentle when he kissed a woman nor would he treat her with the kindness and humor that Zack had generally shown her.

Her mind argued that she was being a fool to decide a jury was wrong; but tonight, whenever she looked at him, every instinct she possessed shouted that he was innocent. And if he was, then she could hardly bear the thought of what he had been put through.

He walked back into the living room, turned on the television set, and sat down across from her, stretching his long legs out and crossing them at the ankles. "We'll watch whatever you'd like after the news," he said, his attention already on the television's giant-size screen.

"Fine," Julie said, studying him surreptitiously across the width of the coffee table. There was indomitable pride chiseled into his handsome face, determination in the jut of his chin, arrogance in his jaw, intelligence and hard-bitten strength etched into every feature of his face. Long ago, she'd read dozens of articles about him written by gushing reporters as well as reputable movie critics. Often, they tried to define him in terms of other megastars who'd preceded him. One critic Julie particularly remembered watching on television had tried to turn him into a human conglomerate by saying that Zachary Benedict had the animal magnetism of a young Sean Connery, the talent of a Newman, the charisma of Costner, the raw machismo of a young Eastwood, the smooth sophistication of Warren Beatty, the versatility of Michael Douglas, and the rugged appeal of Harrison Ford.

Now, after spending almost two days with the man himself in very close quarters, Julie decided that none of the articles she'd read had actually described him nor had any movie camera ever really done him justice, and she vaguely understood why: In real life, there was an aloof strength, a powerful charisma about him that had nothing whatsoever to do with his tall, broad-shouldered physique or that famous mocking smile of his. There was something else . . . a feeling Julie got whenever she looked at him that, discounting his imprisonment, Zachary Benedict had already done and seen everything there was to do and see and that all those experiences were permanently locked away behind an unbreachable wall of polite urbanity, lazy charm, and piercing golden eyes. Beyond any woman's reach.

And therein lay his real appeal, Julie realized: the challenge. Despite everything he'd done to her in the last two days, Zachary Benedict made her—and probably every other woman who'd known him or seen his movies—want to get past that barricade. To discover what was underneath, to soften it, to find the boy he must have been, to make the man he had become shout with laughter and grow tender with love.

Julie gave herself a stern mental shake. None of that mattered! All that mattered was whether he was guilty of murder or innocent. She stole another look at his profile and felt her heart turn over.

He was innocent. She knew it. She could feel it. And the thought of all that male beauty and intelligence being caged up for five long years made her throat constrict. A vision of a prison cellblock flashed through her mind . . . the sound of cell doors clanging shut, of prison guards shouting, of men working in laundries and prison yards, deprived of all their freedom and privacy. All their dignity.

The newscaster's voice snapped her wandering attention to the television set: *"We'll have news on the state and local scene, including information on the blizzard heading our way, tonight, after we switch to the network and Tom Brokaw for news of special import."* Julie stood up, suddenly too nervous to sit there doing nothing. "I'm going to get a glass of water," she said, already heading for the kitchen, but Tom Brokaw's voice stopped her in her tracks:

"Good evening, ladies and gentlemen. Two days ago, Zachary Benedict, who was once regarded as one of Hollywood's greatest leading men and a gifted director, escaped from the State Penitentiary at Amarillo, where he was serving a forty-five-year prison term for the Machiavellian slaying of his wife, actress Rachel Evans, in 1988."

Julie swung around in time to see a picture of Zack wearing a prison uniform with numbers across his chest filling up the screen, and she walked into the living room as if mesmerized by the ugliness of what she saw and heard and felt while Brokaw continued, *"Benedict is believed to be traveling with this woman . . ."*

A gasp escaped Julie as her own picture, which was taken last year with her third-grade class, flashed on the screen. She'd been wearing a shirtwaist dress with a demure bow at the collar.

"Authorities in Texas report that the woman, Julie Mathison, twenty-six, was last seen in Amarillo two days ago where a man fitting Benedict's description was observed getting into a blue Chevrolet Blazer with her. At first, authorities believed that Ms. Mathison had been taken as a hostage against her will . . ."

"At first?" Julie burst out, looking at Zack who was slowly standing up. "What does he mean *at first?*"

The answer to that was immediate and horrifying as Brokaw said, *"The hostage theory was exploded late this afternoon when Pete Golash, a truck driver, reported that he saw a couple matching Benedict's and Mathison's descriptions at a Colorado rest stop near dawn this morning . . ."*

Pete Golash's cheerful face filled the screen next, only it was on videotape and what he was saying made Julie feel sick with fury and shame: *"The pair of them were havin' a snowball fight like a couple of kids. Then the woman—Julie Mathison—I'm sure as hell, I mean heck, the woman was her! Anyway, she tripped and fell, and Benedict landed on top of her and the next thing I knew they was nochin'. Kissin'. If she's a hostage, she sure wasn't actin' like one."*

"Oh my God!" Julie said, wrapping her arms around her stomach, swallowing the bile rising in her throat. In a few moments, ugly reality had invaded the falsely cozy atmosphere of the mountain cabin, and she rounded on the man who had taken her there, seeing him as he'd been on television and what he truly was: a convict wearing a prison uniform with numbers across his chest. Before she could recover, another more tormenting scene lit up the screen and Brokaw said, *"Our reporter Phil Morrow is in Keaton, Texas, where Mathison has been living and teaching third grade in the local elementary school. He was able to get a brief interview with her parents, Reverend and Mrs. James Mathison—"*

A scream of denial escaped Julie's lips as her father's solemn, dignified face looked out at her, his voice emphatic, trusting, trying to convince the world of her innocence. *"If Julie is with Benedict, then she's with him against her will. That truck driver who says differently is either mistaken about who he saw or what he saw happening,"* he finished with a stern, disapproving look at the reporters who started shouting questions at him. *"That is all I have to say."*

With shame streaking through her in sick waves, Julie snapped her face from the screen and stared at Zachary Benedict through a blur of hot tears as he walked swiftly toward her. "You bastard!" she choked, backing away as he neared her.

"Julie," Zack said, reaching for her shoulders in a helpless attempt to comfort her.

"Don't touch me!" she cried, trying to fling his hands away, writhing and shoving against his chest while a torrent of sobs erupted from her. "My father is a minister!" she wept. "He's a respected man and you've made his daughter into a public slut! I'm a teacher!" she cried hysterically, "I teach little children! Do you think they'll let me teach children now that I'm a national scandal who wallows in the snow with escaped murderers?"

The realization that she was probably right slashed through Zack like a jagged razor, and he tightened his grip on her arms. "Julie—"

"I've spent the last fifteen years of my life," she sobbed brokenly, struggling harder against his grasp, "trying to be perfect. I've been so perfect!" she wept, and the sound of her pain transmitted itself to Zack even though he didn't fully understand its source. "And it—it was all for nothing!"

As if she'd finally exhausted herself physically, she stopped struggling and her head fell forward, but her shoulders continued to jerk with sobs. "I tried so hard," she choked. "I became a teacher so they'd be proud. I—I go to church and I teach Sunday school. They won't let me teach any more after this—"

Suddenly Zack couldn't bear the weight of her sorrow or his own culpability any more. "Stop it, please," he whispered achingly, wrapping her in his arms, cupping his hand around her head and holding her face pressed to his chest. "I understand and I'm sorry. When this is all over, I'll make them see the truth."

"You understand!" she repeated with bitter scorn, lifting her tear-streaked, accusing face to his. "How can someone like *you* understand how I feel!" Someone like him. An animal like him. "Oh, I understand!" he bit out, holding her away, shaking her until she looked up at him. "I understand *exactly* what it feels like to be despised for something you didn't do!"

Julie choked back her protest at his rough handling as she registered the fury on his face and the agony in his eyes. His fingers bit into her arms, and his voice was raw with emotion. "I didn't kill anyone! Do you hear me? Lie to me and say you believe me! Just say it! I want to hear someone say it!"

Having just experienced herself a tiny part of what he would feel if he was truly innocent, Julie cringed inwardly at the thought of what he could be feeling.

If he was truly innocent . . . She swallowed, her blurry eyes searching his haggard, handsome face, and she spoke her thought aloud: "I believe you!" she whispered, fresh tears starting to spill over her lashes and down her cheeks. "I do."

Zack heard the sincerity in her tearful voice; in her blue eyes he saw the dawning of true compassion, and deep within him the wall of ice he'd kept around his heart for years began to thaw and crack. Lifting his hand, he laid it against her soft cheek, his thumb helplessly rubbing away her hot tears. "Don't cry for me," he murmured, his voice hoarse.

"*I believe you!*" she repeated, and the tender fierceness of her reply demolished what was left of his reserve. Zack's throat constricted around an unfamiliar knot of emotion, and for a moment he stood there, immobilized by what he saw and heard and felt. Her tears were streaming down her cheeks, clinging to her sooty lashes, wetting his hand; her eyes looked like damp blue pansies, and she was biting down on her lower lip, trying to stop it from trembling.

"Please, don't cry," he whispered achingly as he lowered his mouth to hers to stop her lips from trembling. "Please, please don't . . ." At the first touch of his mouth, she went rigidly still, her breath indrawn, though Zack hadn't any idea if it was fear or surprise that paralyzed her. He didn't know and didn't care at that moment. His only desire was to hold her, to savor the sweet feelings swelling inside him—the first sweetness he'd felt in years—to share it all with her.

Telling himself to go slowly, to be content with whatever she was willing to permit, Zack slid his lips back and forth over the contours of hers, tasting the saltiness of her tears. He told himself not to push her, not to force her, and even while he did, he began to do both. "Kiss me back," he urged, and the helpless tenderness he heard in his voice was as alien to him as the other feelings coursing through him. "Kiss me back," he repeated, sliding his tongue over the seam of her lips. "Open your mouth," he coaxed. When she obeyed and leaned into him, crushing her parted lips to his, Zack almost groaned aloud with the pleasure of it. Desire, primitive and potent, poured through his veins, and suddenly he was acting on pure instinct. His arm tightened, angling across her back, holding her hips pressed to his while his lips forced hers to part wider, and his tongue plunged into the wine-flavored softness of her mouth. He backed her against the wall, kissing her with all the persuasive force at his disposal, his mouth slanting over hers, his tongue teasing and provoking, his hands sliding down her spine and then up, under her sweater. Her soft, bare skin felt like liquid satin beneath his hands as he caressed her narrow waist, stroked her back, and spread his fingers over her midriff, and then he finally let himself seek her breasts. She pressed closer to him and moaned into his mouth when he touched her breasts, and the sweet sound was almost his undoing; it made his entire body throb while his fingers explored every inch of breast and nipple, his lips locked to hers, his tongue exploring with rampant hunger.

To Julie, what he was doing to her was like being imprisoned in a cocoon of dangerous, terrifying sensuality where she had no control over anything. Particularly herself. Beneath the exploration of his long fingers her breasts were beginning to ache with need; against her will, her heated body was molding itself to the hardened contours of his; and her parted lips were welcoming the continued invasion of his tongue.

Zack felt her fingers sliding into the soft hairs at his nape, and he dragged his mouth across her cheek to her ear.

"God, you are sweet!" he whispered while he took her nipples between his fingers, forcing them to harden into tight, hard buds, wanting to lavish her with pleasure. "Little one," he murmured hoarsely, "you are so damned beautiful . . ."

It might have been the endearment he'd used—one she was sure she remembered hearing him use in a movie—or perhaps it was his ridiculous use of the word *beautiful* that finally broke the sensual spell she was under, but Julie slowly realized that she'd watched him play this same kind of scene dozens of times with dozens of truly beautiful actresses in the movies. Only *this* time, it was *her* bare flesh that his hands were exploring with such practiced certainty. "Stop it!" she warned sharply, pulling free of his arms, shoving him away and yanking down her sweater. For a moment, Zack simply stood there, breathing deeply, arms at his sides, feeling completely disoriented. Her face was flushed with desire, and her glorious eyes were still glazed with it, but she looked as if she wanted to bolt for the door. Softly, as if speaking to a skittish colt, he said, "What's wrong, little—?"

"Just stop it right now!" she burst out. I am not your 'little one'—that was another woman in some other scene like this with you. I do not want to hear you call me that. I don't want to hear that I am beautiful either."

Zack gave his head a shake to clear it. Belatedly realizing that she was breathing in quick, shallow pants, watching him as if she half-expected him to pounce on her, tear off her clothes, and rape her, he said very quietly and very carefully, "Are you afraid of me, Julie?"

"Of course not," Julie said shortly, but she realized as soon as she said it that it was a lie. When the kiss had begun, she'd understood instinctively that, somehow, kissing her had represented a kind of cleansing for him, and she'd wanted to give him that. But now that her heart had taken that kiss as an urgent demand to give him much, much more, she was terrified. Because she wanted to do exactly that. She wanted to feel his hands rushing over her naked skin and his body driving into hers. In the moments she'd been silent, he'd evidently replaced passion with anger, because his voice was no longer gentle or kind, it was cool, clipped, and hard. "If you aren't afraid, then what's bothering you? Or is it that you can give an escaped convict a little empty sympathy, but you don't want him too close. Is that it?"

Julie nearly stamped her foot in frustration at his narrow logic and her own stupidity for letting things go this far. "It's nothing like revulsion if that's what you mean."

His voice became a bored drawl. "Then what is it, or shouldn't I ask?"

"You shouldn't need to ask!" she said, raking her hair off her forehead as she looked around a little wildly for something to do, some way to restore order to a world that had suddenly become alarmingly out of her control. "I'm not an animal," she began. Her eyes fell on a picture on the wall beside her that was a fraction of an inch crooked and she turned around to fix it.

"And you think I am? An animal? Is that it?"

Trapped by his questions and his nearness, she glanced over her shoulder and spied a cushion on the floor. "I think," she told him flatly as she walked over to the cushion, "that you're a man who has been locked away from women for five long years."

"That's right, I am. So what?"

She placed the cushion at a vertical angle against the arm of the sofa and began to feel more in control, now that there was distance between them. "So," she explained and actually managed an impersonal little smile at him across the width of the sofa, "I can understand that, to you, any woman would be like a . . ."

His dark brows snapped together over ominous eyes, and she trailed off uneasily, then she hastily bent and began rearranging the other throw pillows into a more artistic display, but she persevered with her explanation. "To you, after being in prison for so long, any woman would be like a—a banquet to a starving man. Any woman," she emphasized. "I mean, I didn't mind letting you kiss me if that made you feel, well, better."

Zack was humiliated and furious at the discovery she regarded him as some animal to whom she'd been tossing a crumb of human feeling, a sex-starved beggar to whom she was reluctantly willing to give a little kiss. "How noble you are, Miss Mathison," he jeered, ignoring the way the color drained out of her cheeks as he continued with deliberate brutality, "You've sacrificed your precious self twice to me. But contrary to your opinion, even an animal like myself is capable of some sort of restraint and discrimination. In short, Julie, you may think you're a 'banquet,' but you're completely resistible to this particular man, sex-starved though I may be."

His volatile anger was tangible, terrifying, and completely incomprehensible to Julie in her agitated state. She stepped back, wrapping her arms around herself as if to fend off the hurt he was deliberately inflicting on her raw emotions.

Zack read her every reaction in her expressive eyes, and satisfied that he'd done the utmost possible damage, he turned on his heel and walked over to the cabinet beside the television, where he began looking over the various titles of the videotaped movies on the shelves.

Julie knew she'd just been discarded like a used piece of tissue and summarily dismissed, but her ravaged pride rebelled at the thought of creeping into her bedroom like a wounded rabbit. Adamantly refusing to shed even one tear or show any fluster, she walked over to the table and began straightening the magazines on it. His frigid command made her lurch upright. "Go to bed! What are you anyway, some sort of compulsive housewife?"

The magazines slid out of her hand and she glared at him, but she did as he told her.

From the corner of his eye, Zack watched her retreat, noticing the haughty lift of her chin and the proud grace of her walk, and with the skill he'd perfected when he was eighteen, he turned away and coldly dismissed Julie Mathison completely from his mind. He concentrated, instead, on the Tom Brokaw newscast that Julie had interrupted with her angry outburst. He could have sworn that while he was trying to comfort her, Brokaw had said something about Dominic Sandini. Sitting down on the sofa, he frowned at the television set. He wished to God he could have heard exactly what it was. In two hours or so, there should be a late-night news update or at least a recap before the station went off the air. Propping his feet on the coffee table, Zack leaned back, prepared to wait for that. Sandini's face with its daredevil grin took shape in his mind, and a faint smile touched his lips as he thought of the wiry, irrepressible Italian. In all these years, there were only two men who he had come to regard as true friends: One of them was Matt Farrell and the other was Dominic Sandini. Zack's smile deepened as he considered the total dissimilarities between the two men he regarded as a "friend." Matt Farrell was a world-class tycoon; Zack and he had forged their friendship out of dozens of common interests and a deep mutual respect.

Dominic Sandini was a world-class petty thief; he didn't have one single thing in common with Zack, and Zack had done absolutely nothing to earn Sandini's respect or his loyalty. Yet, Sandini had given him both, freely and without reservation. He had broken through Zack's isolation with dumb jokes and funny stories about his large, unconventional family. Then, without Zack realizing it, Sandini had intentionally drawn him into that family. They came to the prison and they behaved as if the prison yard was a perfectly normal place for festive family reunions. They thrust their babies into his inexpert arms to hold, and they treated him with the same confusing, boisterous combination of warm affection and stern familial concern that they showed to Dom. Looking back, Zack realized how much their letters and cookies—and even Mama Sandini's garlic salami—had really meant to him. He was going to miss them all much more than he'd have imagined. Leaning his head back against the sofa, he closed his eyes, his mood considerably lightened by his memories of them. He would find a way to send Gina a wedding present, he decided. A silver tea service. And he'd send a gift to Dom, too. Something special. But what could he possibly buy for Dominic Sandini that Dom would need and like? The most logical gift that came to mind made Zack chuckle at his own absurdity: a used car sales lot!

Just before midnight, as he'd hoped, they reran the Brokaw story along with a brief video that Zack had already seen earlier in the day. The video showed Dom, with his hands behind his head, being frisked, handcuffed, and shoved into the back of an Amarillo sheriff's car an hour after Zack's escape, but it was the newscaster's words that made Zack frown: "*The second escaped convict, Dominic Sandini, aged thirty, was recaptured and taken into custody after a brief skirmish with authorities. He has been transferred for questioning to Amarillo State Penitentiary where he had shared a cell with Benedict, who is still at large. Warden Wayne Hadley described Sandini as extremely dangerous.*" Leaning forward, Zack stared hard at the television and was relieved to see that Dom didn't look as if he'd been roughed up by the Amarillo cops. And yet, the things that were being said about him didn't make sense. The media and Hadley should have been treating Dom as a hero—a reformed convict trustee who'd sounded the alarm on a fellow inmate who'd made a break for it. Yesterday, when the newscasters kept describing Dom as "the second escaped convict," Zack had assumed they simply hadn't had time to interview Hadley yet and get the facts straight. Now they'd had plenty of time, and they'd obviously interviewed the warden. Hadley, however, was describing Sandini as dangerous. Why the hell would he do that, Zack wondered, when he should be taking public bows for the fact that at least *one* of his trustees was such an honest, upstanding citizen.

The answer that came immediately to Zack's mind was unthinkable, unbearable: Hadley hadn't bought Dom's story. No, that couldn't be true, Zack decided, because he'd made certain Dom's alibi was airtight. Which left only one other possibility: Hadley *had* bought Dom's alibi, but he was too infuriated by Zack's escape to hold Dom blameless. Zack hadn't counted on that; he'd assumed Hadley's gigantic ego would prompt him to praise Dom, particularly with so much media attention focused on the incident. He'd never imagined Hadley's viciousness might override either his ego or his common sense, but if it had, then the methods Hadley might use to avenge himself on Dom were chillingly brutal. The prison was rampant with lurid stories of the beatings, some of them fatal, that had taken place in Hadley's infamous conference room, with the assistance of several of Hadley's favorite prison guards. Hadley's routine excuse for the battered bodies that later arrived in the prison infirmary or the prison morgue was always "injuries resulting from convict being subdued during attempted escape."

Zack's alarm escalated to panic at the end of the newscast when the local Colorado newscaster added, "*We have a late-breaking development in the Benedict–Sandini prison break. According to a statement issued by the Warden's Office at Amarillo State Prison an hour ago, Dominic Sandini attempted a second prison break while being questioned about his duplicity in Benedict's escape. Three guards were assaulted before Sandini was finally recaptured and subdued. He has been taken to the prison infirmary, where he is listed in critical condition. No additional details as to the nature and extent of his injuries are available as yet.*"

Zack's whole body turned cold with shock and rage, his stomach heaved, and he leaned his head back, fighting down the urge to vomit. He stared at the ceiling high above, swallowing convulsively as memories of Dominic's grinning, optimistic face and foolish jokes paraded across his mind.

The newscaster's words continued, but they scarcely registered:

"*Rumors of a convict uprising at the Amarillo State Penitentiary have been confirmed, and Texas Governor Ann Richards is reportedly considering sending in National Guard troops if necessary. Prisoners at Amarillo, apparently taking advantage of the media coverage of the Zachary Benedict–Dominic Sandini escape, are protesting what they call unjustified cruelty on the part of certain prison officials and employees, overcrowded living conditions, and bad food.*"

Long after the television station had gone off the air, Zack remained where he was, so filled with torment and despair that he couldn't summon the energy to get up. The determination to escape and survive that had kept him sane for the last five years was slowly draining away. It seemed as if death had been at his side or stalking him from behind forever, and he was suddenly tired of running from it. First his parents had died, then his brother, his grandfather, and then his wife. If Sandini died, there was no way to blame anyone except himself for it. Sitting there, Zack actually felt as if there were some sort of macabre curse attached to him that sent anyone he cared about to an early death. Even through his despair, Zack realized thoughts like that were dangerous, unbalanced, insane. But then he felt as if his hold on sanity was becoming very, very fragile.

25

CARRYING THE SMALL BUNDLE OF CLOTHES SHE'D JUST TAKEN out of the dryer, Julie padded barefoot and wet-haired through the silent living room and into the room where she'd spent a nearly sleepless night. It was eleven o'clock in the morning, and judging from the sound of rushing water, she assumed Zack had also slept late and was now in the shower.

Squinting against a dull, throbbing headache, she went listlessly through the ritual of blowing her hair dry, then she brushed it and pulled on the jeans and sweater she'd worn three days ago when she drove to Amarillo. That morning seemed like weeks ago, because it was the last time everything had been normal. Now nothing was normal anymore, least of all her feelings about herself. She'd been taken hostage by an escaped convict—an event that would have made an ordinary, decent, upstanding woman hate her captor and despise everything he represented. Any other moral, respectable twenty-six-year-old woman would have fought Zachary Benedict at every turn while simultaneously trying to foil his plans, escape from his clutches, and get him recaptured and sent to prison, where he belonged! That's what a good, decent, God-fearing young woman would do.

But that wasn't what Julie Mathison had done, Julie thought with bitter self-revulsion. No indeed. Instead, she'd allowed her captor to kiss and touch her; worse, she'd reveled in it. Last night, she'd pretended to herself she only meant to comfort an unfortunate man, that she was merely being kind as she'd been taught to be, but in the harsh light of day, she knew that was a complete lie. If Zachary Benedict had been some ugly old man, she wouldn't have flung herself into his arms and tried to *kiss* away his unhappiness. Nor would she have been so damned eager to believe he was innocent! The truth was that she'd believed Zachary Benedict's ridiculous assertions of innocence because she *wanted* to believe him, and then she'd "comforted" him because she was disgustingly attracted to him. Instead of escaping and getting him recaptured at that rest stop yesterday morning, she'd lain in the snow and kissed him, ignoring the very viable possibility that the truck driver named Pete wouldn't have been hurt if a struggle ensued.

In Keaton, she'd scrupulously evaded the sexual advances of good, decent men while hypocritically congratulating herself on the high moral standards she'd acquired from her adoptive father and mother. Now, however, the truth was glaringly and painfully obvious: She'd never been sexually attracted to any one of those fine, upstanding men, and now she understood why: It was because she could only be attracted to her own kind—social outcasts like Zack Benedict. Decency and respectability didn't turn her on; violence and danger and illicit passion obviously did.

The nauseating reality was that on the outside Julie Mathison might appear to be a righteous, dignified, upstanding citizen, but in her heart, she was still Julie Smith, the street urchin of unknown parentage. The ethics of society hadn't meant anything to her then; obviously, they didn't now. Mrs. Borowski, the head of LaSalle Foster Care Facility, had been right all along. Julie gave the brush a vicious tug while in her mind she heard the woman's acid voice and saw her face, twisted with contempt and knowledge: "A leopard can't change its spots, and neither can you, Julie Smith. You might be able to fool that hoity-toity psychiatrist, but you can't fool me. You're a bad seed just like that movie we saw on television. . . . You'll come to no good, you mark my words. . . . You can't make a silk purse out of sow's ear, and that's what you are—a sow's ear: Birds of a feather flock together, that's why you hang around with trashy street kids. They're just like you—no good. . . . *NO GOOD.*"

Julie squeezed her eyes closed, trying to shut out the painful memories and to concentrate on the gentle man who'd adopted her. "You're a good girl, Julie," he whispered in her mind, just as he'd whispered to her often after she'd come to live with his family. "A fine, good, loving little girl. You're going to grow up to be a fine young woman, too. You'll choose a good, church-going man someday and you'll be a wonderful wife and mother, just as you are a wonderful daughter now."

Ravaged by the memory of his misplaced faith in her, Julie braced her hands on the dresser and bent her head. "You were wrong . . ." she whispered brokenly. She realized the ugly truth now: She wasn't *attracted* to good, church-going men, not even handsome ones like Greg Howley. Instead, she was attracted to men like Zack Benedict, who'd fascinated her from the moment she saw him in the restaurant parking lot. The revolting truth was that she'd wanted to go to bed with him last night, and he'd known it then. Like birds of a feather, he'd recognized her as his own kind. That, Julie knew, was the real reason why he'd been angry and disgusted with her when she called a halt to the lovemaking—he'd been contemptuous of her cowardice. She'd wanted to go to bed with him as soon as he began kissing and touching.

A leopard can't change it's spots. Mrs. Borowski had been right.

But Reverend Mathison had specifically disagreed with that, Julie suddenly remembered. When she'd repeated that proverb to him, he'd given her a little shake and said, "Animals can't change, but people can, Julie! That's why the Lord gave us minds and wills. If you want to be a good girl, all you have to do is *be* one. Just make up your mind and do it!"

Make up your mind, Julie . . .

Slowly, Julie lifted her face and gazed at her reflection in the mirror while a new strength, a new force, built inside of her. She hadn't yet done anything that was completely inexcusable. Not yet.

And before she did do something to inexorably betray herself and her upbringing, she was going to get the hell out of Zachary Benedict's clutches! No, she corrected herself grimly, she was going to get the *heck* out of his clutches. Today. She had to get away today, before her weak will and fragile moral fiber crumbled in the face of his dangerous appeal. If she stayed, she would become his accomplice in fact, and when she did, she would sink beyond social and moral redemption. With an almost hysterical fervor, Julie vowed to get away from him today.

Walking over to the bedroom window, she pulled back the draperies and peered out at the gray, ominous-looking morning. Overhead, heavy snow clouds were piled high and the wind was howling through the pines, rattling the window panes. As she stood there, mentally retracing the route they'd taken up here, the first snowflakes blew past and she grimaced. In the past two days, she'd seen enough snow to last her a lifetime! Twenty yards away, beyond the wooden deck that surrounded the house, someone had nailed a big round outdoor thermometer onto a tree at the perimeter of the woods; it showed the temperature at twenty-eight degrees, but that didn't take into account the wind-chill factor, which Julie assumed would surely reduce the temperature to near zero.

She lifted her head, startled by the sudden sound of a radio. The man who had caused her all this misery was obviously dressed now and in the living room, probably waiting for the news to be broadcast.

For a minute she considered trying to barricade herself in this nice warm room until he finally left for wherever he was going, but that was implausible and impractical. She'd still have to eat, and even if she barricaded the door, she couldn't do anything about the window. Moreover, the longer she stayed with him, the less chance she had of convincing the authorities and the citizens of Keaton that she hadn't been a willing accomplice nor the bedmate of a convicted murderer.

With a nervous sigh, Julie faced the fact that the only route to "freedom"— and respectability—was outdoors, across an unfamiliar snow-covered mountain, in the Blazer, if she could figure out how to hot-wire it, or else on foot. If it was going to be on foot, which seemed likely, the first requirement was warmth.

Turning away from the window, Julie headed for the large walk-in closet, hoping to "borrow" some warmer clothes. A few moments later she uttered a little cry of glee: Near the back of it were what seemed to be one-piece snowsuits for adults. They were both navy blue with red and white trim, but one was much smaller, and when she held it up to herself, she knew she could get into it. Tossing it over her arm, she returned to the bedroom and began searching through the contents of the drawers in the chest. A moment later, she suppressed another shout of delight as she withdrew a long-sleeved, long-legged set of insulated underwear.

It was a struggle to zip her jeans over the bulky underwear she'd put on, and once she did get the zipper up, the jeans were so tight she couldn't bend her knees, but Julie scarcely noticed the inconvenience. Her mind was on the best way to deceive Zachary Benedict into relaxing his guard long enough for her to escape and, if she had to leave on foot, to trick him somehow into not coming after her until she had an excellent head start. For that reason, she delayed putting on the snowsuit for the time being. At present, it seemed far wiser to make him think she was simply going outdoors for a few minutes to get some air.

Fixing a polite, impersonal expression on her face, Julie tugged the bottom of her own sweater and jacket over her hips, hoping he wouldn't notice that her legs looked—and moved—liked a pair of stiff, overstuffed sausages, then she opened the door and stepped into the living room.

Her eyes went automatically to the sofa by the fire where she expected to see him. Instead he was across the room, staring out the windows at the falling snow, his back turned to her, his hands shoved deep into his pants pockets. Delaying the moment when she would have to face him for the first time since last night, she watched him lift his hand. As he absently rubbed the muscles at the back of his neck, her treacherous mind suddenly recalled how skillfully those long fingers had caressed her breasts and the exquisite pleasure he had made her feel. It occurred to her at that moment that he actually deserved some credit for showing a certain amount of restraint and decency last night. He had been as physically aroused as she, she remembered, feeling her face grow warm at the vivid memory of his rigid erection pressing against her.

She had aroused him and then inadvertently insulted and angered him, and yet he hadn't tried to resort to rape . . .

He turned his head slightly and she saw the stern pride stamped on that rough-hewn profile, the mobile mouth that had kissed her with such soul-destroying passion. Surely a man who was capable of so much tenderness and restraint even in the throes of passion, and when he hadn't been near a woman in five years, couldn't really be a murderer . . .

Julie gave herself an angry mental shake! She was being an utter fool again—standing there, feeling sorry for the villain, romanticizing him, simply because he was tall, handsome, and incredibly sexy and because she was an idiot—a spineless idiot who was disgustingly and helplessly attracted to him! "Excuse me," she said briskly, raising her voice to be heard above the radio.

He twisted around, his gaze narrowing on her outdoor clothing. "Where do you think you're going?"

"You said," Julie replied, matching his clipped tone perfectly, "that I could have the run of the house and grounds. I'm going crazy being stuck indoors. I intend to go outside for some fresh air."

"It's freezing out there."

Realizing he was on the verge of refusing, she switched quickly to a calm, logical approach. "As you pointed out, I'd die of exposure if I tried to escape on foot. I just need some exercise and fresh air. All I want to do is explore the yard a little and—" she faltered, then inspiration struck and she tried to inject a childlike eagerness in her voice as she finished, "I want to build a snowman! Please don't say I can't," she cajoled, "I haven't seen this much snow since I moved to Texas as a little girl."

He wasn't impressed and he wasn't friendly. "Suit yourself, but stay where I can see you from these windows."

"Yes, warden!" Julie snapped back, instantly angered by his high-handedness. "But may I be allowed to vanish from view now and then—just to gather up branches and things I need?"

Instead of answering, he lifted his brows and regarded her in cold silence.

Julie decided to take his silence for assent, even though she knew it wasn't intended as anything of the sort. She had made up her mind to get away from him, and to accomplish that urgent goal, she was prepared to stoop to almost anything, including pandering and placating. "I used to give my snowmen carrot noses," she told him, and with an ability at acting and subterfuge heretofore unnoticed, she smiled a little as she added, "I'll look in the refrigerator to see what we have."

The refrigerator was beside a drawer that she'd noticed last night contained some oddly shaped keys to unknown locks. With her left hand, Julie opened the refrigerator, and with her right, she silently pulled the drawer open, her fingers groping for the flat metal keys she'd seen. "No carrots," she said over her shoulder, glancing up at him with another artificial smile, then she snuck a quick look in the drawer. She saw one of the keys and picked it up, but she knew there had been more than just this one. She saw it then—three other keys peeking out from under some spatulas and mixing spoons. With her eyes on the contents of the refrigerator, she managed to pick up another one of them, but her shaking hand and long fingernails made it impossibly awkward to pick up the other two, particularly without looking. Just when she nearly had one of them, she heard him move, and when she looked up, he was stalking straight toward her. She yanked her hand out of the drawer and closed it, two keys pressed in her palm, her voice shaking with nerves. "Wh-what do you want?"

"Something to eat, why?"

"I just wondered, that's all." She scooted past him as he rounded the counter. "Help yourself."

He paused, his gaze following her as she walked stiffly over to the closet. "What's wrong with your legs?"

Julie's mouth went dry. "Nothing. I mean—I found a pair of long johns in a drawer and put them on under my jeans, so I could stay warmer when I'm outside."

"Stay close to the house," he warned. "Don't make me come looking for you."

"I will," she lied, already opening the door of the hall closet where she'd seen some ski hats and gloves belonging to the owner of house. "What do you think I should use for his eyes and nose?" she asked, prattling about the details of her project in hopes of boring him into letting his guard down.

"I don't know and, to be perfectly honest, I don't give a damn."

Affecting a look of guileless enthusiasm, she looked over her shoulder as she pawed through the boots in the closet. "Snowmen are very important artistic projects in some cultures," she informed him, unconsciously affecting the same tone she used when she addressed her third-grade students. "Did you know that?"

"No."

"They take a great deal of forethought," she added ingenuously.

Instead of replying, he studied her in speculative silence for a moment then he rudely turned his back on her and returned to the kitchen.

Julie would have dropped all further attempts at conversation, but she'd just thought of an excuse to disappear more often from his view and she instantly put it to use, shamelessly inventing her own facts as she went along: "I mean, in those cultures where snow and ice figures are considered meritorious art forms, there's much more to a snowman than just three big balls of snow. You build an entire little scene around the snowman using branches and berries and rocks," she said, pulling on a pair of waterproof ski gloves she'd found at the bottom of the closet. Glancing over her shoulder with a bright smile as she stood up and closed the closet door, she added, "Isn't that interesting?"

He took a knife out of the cutlery drawer and opened a cabinet. "Fascinating," he mocked.

"You don't *sound* very fascinated," Julie complained, determined to goad him into telling her to go outside and leave him alone, which was exactly what she wanted to do. "I mean, the least you could do is try to concentrate on the project. You could have some input. Think of how much fun and satisfaction you would get when the snowman scene is—"

He slammed the cabinet door with a crash that made Julie lurch around, and her gaze riveted on the knife in his fist. "Julie," he warned, "shut the hell up!"

His sudden mood swing would have been enough to remind her that Zachary Benedict was a dangerously unpredictable foe, but with a knife blade flashing in his hand and his eyes glittering with menace, he looked fully capable of committing cold-blooded murder.

Zack saw the color drain from her face, he saw the way she was staring at the knife, and he knew exactly what she was thinking about him. His simmering anger built to a fury. "That's right," he taunted. "I'm a convicted murderer."

"B-but you said you didn't do it," she reminded him, trying very unsuccessfully to sound calm and convinced.

"I said that," he jeered in a silken voice that sent chills up her spine, "but you know better, don't you, Julie?"

She swallowed convulsively and started backing down the short hallway. "Can I go outside?" Without waiting for him to answer, she grabbed blindly for the door and opened it.

Behind her, Zack stood perfectly still, fighting to calm himself and to block out the horror he'd seen in her face. He told himself it didn't matter what she thought or that she'd looked adorable chattering about snowmen or that she was sweet and good and clean and that, compared to her, he felt inhuman and filthy.

A few minutes later, the news came on the radio and his mood lifted considerably: According to the newscaster, Sandini was no better, but he was no worse either. He was holding his own. Zack changed radio stations and finally found one that was all news and no music. He'd just started into the living room when the commentator announced that a man whom Canadian officials now believed to be Zachary Benedict had crossed the border into Canada at Windsor two nights ago driving a rented black sedan.

26

"DAMN," JULIE SAID SOFTLY AS SHE SLID OUT OF THE BLAZER, which was still parked at the back of the house, out of sight of the picture windows at the front and sides. In the fifteen years since she'd had her first and only lesson on hot-wiring a car, the wiring systems in them had obviously changed or else she hadn't been a very adept student, because she hadn't the slightest idea which of the fistful of wires she'd pulled from beneath the dashboard were the right ones.

Shivering convulsively, she bent down and gathered up the armload of pine boughs she'd collected and raced through the wind and snow to the side of the house. For the entire fifteen minutes that she'd been outside, he'd remained at the windows, watching her like an expressionless stone statue. The alleged need for "props" for the imaginary snowman scene enabled her to vanish from view for a few minutes at a time without rousing his suspicions, exactly as she'd hoped it would, but she was afraid to be gone too long. So far, she'd made three short trips of increasing duration, returning each time with pine boughs after trying to hot-wire the Blazer. She was counting on the hope that he'd soon decide she was actually idiotic enough to spend her time building a snowman in freezing weather, and he'd grow bored with sentry duty.

Raising her arms, Julie pulled the knitted ski cap she'd taken from the closet down over her frozen ears, then she began to roll the bottom ball of the snowman's body, while she reviewed her remaining alternatives for escape: To try to escape on foot would be suicidal insanity in this weather, and she knew it. Even if she didn't get lost trying to go cross-country down the mountain, she'd likely freeze to death long before she reached the main road. If by some chance, she did make it, she'd surely die of exposure before a motorist came along. On the way here, they hadn't passed another car for the last two hours. The possibility of finding out where he'd hidden the keys to the Blazer seemed equally remote, and she couldn't start the car without them.

"There has to be a way to get out of here!" Julie said aloud as she pushed and shoved the ball of snow closer to the pile of pine boughs. There was a padlocked garage at the back of the house, which Zachary Benedict had told her was used for storage and thus couldn't accommodate the Blazer. Maybe he was lying. Maybe he didn't know for certain. One of the keys in her pocket looked like it was meant to fit a padlock, and the only padlock she'd seen anywhere was on the side door of that garage. The possibility that the homeowner had left a car in there did little to elevate her spirits right now. Assuming she could find the car's keys and get it started, the Blazer was blocking the garage door.

That left her with only one likely option: Even without seeing the interior of the garage, she had a hunch what she was going to find inside of it:

Skis.

There were ski boots in the bedroom closet, but no skis in the house, which meant they were probably in the garage.

She'd never skied in her life.

She was prepared to try. Besides, it didn't look very hard whenever she saw people skiing on television and in the movies. How hard could it possibly be? Children could ski. Surely she could, too.

And so could Zachary Benedict, she remembered with a thrill of raw fear. She'd seen him skiing in one of his movies, a mystery set in Switzerland. He'd looked as if he were an expert skier in that film, but probably a stuntman had done the hard stuff.

Grunting as she rolled the heavy ball through the snow, making it fatter and fatter, Julie finally maneuvered it into position ten minutes later—no mean feat, given that she could scarcely bend her knees in her tight jeans. Finished with the first one-third of the snowman, she quickly scattered the pine boughs around it in a half circle as if she had some plan in mind, then she stopped and pretended to contemplate her handiwork. From the corner of her eye, she stole a sidelong glance at the windows, and saw that he was still there, immobile as a stone sentry.

It was time, she decided with a nervous tremor, for a foray into that locked garage.

Her gloved hands clumsy from suspense and cold, Julie tried unsuccessfully to fit the first key she'd found into the bottom of the heavy padlock. Holding her breath, she slid the second key into it, and the lock separated into two parts in her hand. Glancing over her shoulder at the back door of the house, she made certain he hadn't suddenly decided to come outdoors, then she stepped over the snowdrift blocking her way and went into the garage, closing the door behind her.

Inside, it was dark as pitch, but after stumbling over a shovel and bumping into an unknown object with enormous tires, she finally found a light switch on the wall and flipped it on. A bank of large overhead spotlights exploded with light. Momentarily blinded, Julie blinked and then glanced around the crowded area, her heart beginning to hammer with anticipation and foreboding. Skis. There were several pairs of skis and ski poles secured in racks on the far wall. On her left was an enormous tractor equipped with a huge contraption for blowing snow. Julie tried to envision herself sitting in the cab of the tractor, plowing her way along the treacherous road that wound down the mountain, then she discarded the possibility. Even if she were foolhardy enough to try to push the Blazer out of the way and drive the tractor down the mountain, the machine would make enough noise to alert the man in the house. Moreover, it would move so slowly that he'd be able drag her out of it without breaking into a run.

The other half of the two-car garage was filled with tractor equipment, snow tires, boxes, and some other equipment that was covered with a large black tarpaulin.

Skis. She was going to have to try to ski her way down the mountain; if she didn't die of exposure, she'd probably die of a broken neck. Equally as depressing, she'd have to wait until tomorrow or the day after to try it, because the wind was picking up outside and the snow was beginning to fall as if it were a real blizzard. More out of curiosity than hope, Julie lifted the corner of the tarpaulin and peered underneath it, then she threw it aside with a cry of joyous disbelief.

Beneath the tarp were two shiny, dark blue snowmobiles with helmets perched on the seats.

Fingers trembling, she tried the second key in the nearest snowmobile's ignition. It slid in and turned. It fit! It worked! Elation and anticipation soared through her as she raced out of the garage and carefully closed the side door behind her. The weather that had seemed so forbidding a few minutes ago was now only a minor annoyance. In a half hour or less—as soon as she could change into that snowmobile suit in her closet and sneak out of the house— she'd be on her way to freedom. She'd never used a snowmobile before, but there was no doubt in her mind that she could manage somehow, and much better than she could have handled those skis and poles. Intent on keeping up the ploy that was working so well for her, Julie paused long enough to grab some more pine branches, then she dashed to the site of the snowman and dumped the branches there, as if she'd been gathering them all this time. Zachary Benedict was still standing at the windows, watching her, and Julie forced herself to pause and look about her as if searching the yard for more "props" to use for her snowman, while she gave a last few seconds' thought to the details of her forthcoming bolt for freedom. All she truly had to do was change clothes and put on dry gloves and take the key to the other snowmobile so he couldn't follow her when he realized how she'd escaped.

She was ready to go. Neither snow nor wind nor an escaped convict with a gun could foil her now. She was as good as on her way.

From within the house, Zack watched her clamp her hat down over her ears and trudge off out of sight to look for whatever it was she needed to create whatever unidentifiable "scene" she was making out there. The anger he'd felt earlier was gone now, greatly alleviated by the news that Sandini's condition hadn't worsened and, to a lesser extent, by the unwilling amusement he felt as he watched Julie wrestle with that enormous ball of snow, pushing and shoving at it, even though she could scarcely bend over in those tight jeans she was wearing. His lips quirked in a half-smile as he recalled watching her solve the problem: When the snowball was large enough, she'd stopped pushing it with her hands and arms, and instead, she'd turned around, braced her back against the snowy boulder, and shoved it using her feet and legs. Zack had been sorely tempted to go outside and help her, an offer that he knew she'd angrily reject and would have simultaneously deprived him of the pleasure of watching her from his vantage point. Until that moment, he had never imagined there could be such pleasure in simply watching a woman build a snowman. On the other hand, he'd never known a grown woman who would consider doing such a mundane, innocently wholesome thing as play in the snow.

She was a complete enigma, he thought as he waited for her to reappear at the window. Intelligent and ingenuous, compassionate and fiery, passionate and skittish—she was a mass of contrasts, and they were all vastly appealing. But if there was one thing about Julie Mathison that intrigued him the most, it was her unaffected wholesomeness. At first, he'd been half-convinced he was imagining that aura of prim innocence, but last night he'd discovered that she barely knew how to kiss! It made him wonder what sort of wimpy males lived in Keaton, Texas. And what sort of inconsiderate jerk was her almost-fiancé that *he* hadn't introduced her to foreplay? She'd jumped like a startled rabbit when Zack touched her breasts. If he didn't know it were impossible in this day and age, he'd almost think she was still a virgin.

He realized where his thoughts had ventured and he uttered a silent curse, then he turned in surprise at the sound of Julie coming in the back door.

"I—I need some clothes to put on the snowman," she said with a brilliant smile.

"Why don't you wait until tomorrow to finish," he said, and her smile died.

"But I—I'm having fun!" she protested, sounding desperate. "What pleasure can you possibly get in denying me something to do to occupy my time!"

"I'm not an ogre!" Zack snapped, hating the fear and mistrust in her eyes.

"Then let me finish my—my project!"

"All right," he said with an annoyed sigh. "Fine."

Another of her smiles appeared, lighting up her entire face. "Thank you."

Zack melted beneath the radiant heat of that smile. "You're welcome," he said and was exasperated by the gentleness he heard in his voice. On the radio in the kitchen, the announcer said they had another development in the Benedict–Sandini escape that would follow the next commercial break. Trying to hide his reaction to her behind a curt nod of dismissal, he watched her race into the bedroom, then he walked into the kitchen and turned up the volume on the radio.

He was pouring himself a cup of coffee when the news commentator said, *"Ten minutes ago, an unnamed source at Amarillo State Penitentiary infirmary phoned NBC News with the information that Dominic Carlo Sandini, who attempted to escape two days ago with his cellmate, Zachary Benedict, died this morning at 11:15 while being transferred by ambulance to St. Mark's Hospital. Sandini, who was a nephew of reputed underworld figure, Enrico Sandini, died as a result of injuries he sustained when he attacked two guards during his second escape attempt yesterday . . ."*

Julie was walking out of the bedroom, the ski clothes hidden behind her back when she heard the announcer's words followed by a bellow of rage from her captor and an explosion of shattering glass as he hurtled his coffee mug against the glazed tile floor of the kitchen.

Out of his direct line of vision, she stood, momentarily paralyzed with terror, while Zachary Benedict hurtled everything he could pick up against the walls and floor, shouting vivid obscenities and violent threats. The toaster crashed against the floor, followed by a blender and the coffee pot, then he swept his arm along the counter sending dishes, cups, and glass canisters crashing into shattered heaps atop mangled appliances. He was still cursing when the counters were clear, and then, as quickly as it had erupted, the explosion of maddened wrath seemed to come to an abrupt end. As if he'd exhausted both his rage and his strength, he braced his flattened hands against the counter top. His head fell forward and he closed his eyes.

Snapping out of her mesmerized horror, Julie wisely abandoned all hope of getting the snowmobile key out of the drawer beside his hip and sidled down the hall, her back pressed to the wall. As she opened the door, the eerie silence in the kitchen was split by his tortured groan: "Dom . . . I'm sorry, Dom. I'm sorry!"

27

THE FRIGHTENING SCENE SHE'D WITNESSED ROLLED AROUND and around in Julie's head as she raced through the swirling snow to the garage and stumbled through the doorway at the side. Her fingers fumbling in their haste, she changed into the snowmobile suit, yanked on the gloves and helmet, then she began dragging the snowmobile toward the door, afraid to turn the motor on for fear of whatever noise it was going to make. Outside, she swung her leg over the seat, fumbled with the chin strap on the helmet, and turned the ignition key. The motor sprang to life with much less noise than she expected it to make, and moments later, she was flying over the snow toward the woods at the far edge of the yard, struggling to keep her balance, praying that the snowmobile wasn't loud enough to be heard inside the house.

Shaking with a combination of exhilaration and fear, Julie careened through the trees, fighting for control of the machine beneath her, sideswiping pine branches and skirting boulders beneath the snow. When she was well out of sight of the house and certain he wasn't following her, she'd turn the snowmobile toward the winding road and follow that down to the highway, but for now, she was glad of the need to keep in the woods. Beyond their shelter, the wind had risen to a howl and the snowstorm was working itself into a full-fledged blizzard.

Five minutes became ten, and a sense of success and freedom gave her courage, but its joy was unexpectedly diminished by the memory of the grief she'd witnessed in the man she'd left behind. The thought occurred to her that it seemed incongruous, in fact, almost impossible, that a cold-blooded murderer would feel such anguish at the death of his cellmate.

She glanced over her shoulder to make certain she wasn't being followed, then cried out in alarm as she nearly hit a tree, swung wildly to avoid it and almost overturned the snowmobile.

Shoving himself upright, Zack looked listlessly about him at the mangled appliances and broken glass on the kitchen floor. "Shit," he said dully and reached for the brandy decanter. He poured some of the fiery liquid into a glass and tossed it down, trying to numb the ache in his chest. He kept hearing Dom's cheerful voice as he read that last letter from his mother, *"Hey Zack, Gina's getting married! I sure hate to miss that wedding."* He remembered other things too, like Sandini's unorthodox advice and knowledge. *"You want a fake passport, Zack, you don't go to some guy named Rubin Schwartz that no one's ever heard of. You come to me and I put you in touch with Wally the Weasel. He's the best picture book man in the country. You gotta start letting me help you Zack . . ."*

Zack had let him help, and now Dom was dead because of it.

"Hey Zack, you want some more of Mama's salami? I got plenty of Rolaids."

Standing at the windows, drinking the brandy and staring blindly at the snowman Julie had been building, Zack could almost feel Dom's cheerful presence beside him. Dom had found such delight in stupid little things. He'd probably have been out there with Julie, building the snowman . . .

Zack froze, the brandy glass suspended partway to his mouth, his gaze searching the yard. Julie!

"Julie!" he shouted, stalking toward the back door and jerking it open. A blast of snow hit him in the face and he had to put his shoulder to the door to force it open in the rising wind. "Julie, get in here before you freeze your—" The wind hurtled his voice back in his face, but Zack didn't notice. His gaze had riveted on the deep footprints already filling up with snow and he was running beside them toward the garage at the back of the house.

"Julie!" he thundered as he slammed the side door of the garage open. "What the hell do you think you're doing in here—"

Zack drew up short, momentarily unable to believe the answer he saw with his own eyes as his gaze ricocheted from the snowmobile sticking out from beneath a tarpaulin to the doorway. There, a set of snowmobile tracks began and led straight into the woods.

A few minutes ago, he would have sworn that he was incapable of feeling any angrier or more desolate than he had at the news of Dom's death, but the explosion of fury and foreboding he felt at that moment eclipsed even that.

Cold. Minutes after she left the protection of the forest and pointed the snowmobile down the steep, tree-lined lane they'd taken in the Blazer, Julie felt a deep, bone-freezing cold that was nearly unbearable. Droplets of ice were clinging to the corners of her eyes; snow was driving into her face, blinding her; her lips and arms and legs were stiff. The snowmobile flew over a rut and slid sideways, but when she tried to slow the vehicle down, her limbs were so numb that it took precious moments before her body could obey her brain's frantic command to react.

The only thing that wasn't numb from cold was her sense of fear, fear that Zack would catch her and prevent her from escaping and a new, debilitating fear that if he didn't, she would likely die out here, lost in a blizzard, buried beneath the snow. In her mind, she conjured up a vision of a search party in the spring locating her perfectly preserved remains beneath a mound of thawing snow, her body and head still clad in this chic navy blue little snowmobile suit and matching helmet, which also coordinated—not by chance, she was sure—with the snowmobile she rode. A "perfect" ending, she thought with grim misery, for a girl from the Chicago slums who wanted to be perfect.

Far below, through the branches of trees sliding by her, she caught a glimpse of the state road that snaked around the mountain, but it was a straight dropoff from here to there, a nearly vertical descent made even more treacherous by the trees and giant snow-covered boulders that rose up from the mountain. If she took that route, she might make better time for a few seconds down the mountain, but there was no chance she'd ever reach the highway in one piece. Besides, before she could seriously consider going down the face of the mountain, she first had to use the bridge to get across that swollen stream. She tried to remember where the bridge was. It seemed to her that it should be around the next sharp bend in the road, but it was hard to gauge anything when the "road" had been reduced to a narrow path between snow drifts.

It occurred to her that what she probably ought to do was get off the snowmobile and do something to generate some body heat, like running in place or something like that. On the other hand, she was afraid to take the time to do that. If the snow had already filled in her tracks from the garage to the woods by the time he realized she was gone, he'd automatically assume she was using the road and he'd overtake her much sooner and more easily than if he tried to follow her circuitous trail through the woods. Julie had deliberately been avoiding looking over her shoulder because she was afraid to take her eyes off the path and risk losing control of the unfamiliar vehicle again, but now that she realized everything hinged on how fast the snow was filling in her tracks, she couldn't resist. She stole a swift look over her shoulder and choked back a scream. Above and still well behind her, a snowmobile was flying out of the woods and angling down toward the road, its rider crouched low over the front—an ominous specter of doom, swerving around boulders and trees with what appeared to be effortless skill.

Terror and rage overrode everything, even the numbing cold, and sent adrenalin pumping wildly through her veins. Praying he hadn't yet spotted her through the dense trees that lined both sides of the narrow road, she looked around for a place to veer off and try to hide so that he would overshoot her. Up ahead, around the next switchback, she glimpsed a narrow plateau, but the road there was edged with boulders to stop cars from plunging over the side. Somehow, she had to angle between the boulders and slow the snowmobile down before it reached the edge of the plateau, then find a hiding place down there among the trees, whose tops rose above the left side of the road. With no time to think of another plan, Julie aimed the snowmobile for a spot between two shoulder-high boulders, then she clamped down on the brakes as she shot over the edge of the mountain.

The plateau was much narrower than it had seemed, and for terrifying seconds, she was airborne, soaring toward the tops of a thick stand of pine trees, then the nose of the snowmobile dived to earth like an out-of-control rocket, heading straight for a clump of trees and, a few feet beyond them, the creek. Screaming, Julie felt gravity tearing the snowmobile out from under her just as the middle branches of a pine tree rose up in front of her, opening their arms to her. The snowmobile plunged down the embankment, rolling over itself, sliding across the ice that had formed near the bank, and finally coming to a stop on its side, its handlebars hanging over the rushing water, its skis snagged in the branches of a partially submerged aspen.

Dazed with relief and a little disoriented, Julie lay beside the pine that had broken her fall and she watched a snowmobile shoot over the edge of the embankment. In pursuit of her . . . Forcing her body to react, she rolled over, staggered to her knees, and scrambled under the tree. The skis on his snowmobile were air-bound when they flashed past her hiding place, and Julie crawled further back beneath the branches, but she needn't have bothered, because he never even glanced in her direction. He'd spotted her snowmobile overturned on the ice and beginning to be tugged into the stream's rushing water, and all of his attention was focused on that.

Unable to completely assimilate what was happening or accept her own good fortune, she watched him leap off his snowmobile before it came to a stop and run toward the stream. "JULIE!" he shouted over and over again into the howling wind, and to her utter disbelief, he started walking out across the thin ice. Obviously, he thought she'd fallen through it, and just as obviously, he should have been glad that she was no longer a complication with which he had to contend.

Julie assumed he merely intended to try to recover her snowmobile, and her gaze flew to the snowmobile he'd abandoned. It was now much closer to her than to him; she could get to it long before he could and, unless he could drag her snowmobile to safety, she could still make good her getaway. Keeping her gaze glued to his back, she crawled out from under the tree, straightened, and took a stealthy step away from her hiding place and then another and another, intending to sidle from tree to tree.

"JULIE, ANSWER ME, FOR GOD'S SAKE!" he shouted, stripping off his jacket. The ice around him began to crack and the rear end of her snowmobile rose in the air as the machine tumbled into the creek and vanished. Instead of trying to reach safety, he grabbed ahold of the branches of the fallen aspen and to her utter disbelief, he deliberately lowered himself into the icy water.

His shoulders disappeared and then his head, and Julie darted to the shelter of the next tree. He broke the surface for air, shouting her name again, then he dove beneath the water, and Julie raced to the last tree. Less than three yards away from his snowmobile and absolute freedom, she stopped, her gaze riveted helplessly on the stream where he had disappeared. Her mind shouted that Zachary Benedict was an escaped convict who had compounded his crimes by taking a hostage, and she had to leave now while she had the chance. Her conscience screamed that if she left him now and took his snowmobile, he would freeze to death because he'd tried to save her.

Suddenly his dark head and shoulders broke the surface beside the submerged tree trunk, and a sob of relief rose in her throat as she saw him haul himself up onto the ledge of ice. Dimly amazed by his sheer strength of will and body, Julie watched him brace his hands on the ice, shove himself upright, and stagger over to the jacket he'd flung off. Instead of putting it on, he sank down beside it near a snow-covered boulder next to the stream.

The internal war between Julie's mind and her heart escalated to tumultuous proportions: He hadn't drowned; he was safe for the moment; if she was going to leave him, it had to be now, before he looked up and saw her.

Paralyzed with indecision, she watched him lift the jacket in his hand. The moment of foolish relief she felt at the thought that he was going to put it on became horror as he did something that was the macabre opposite: He flung the jacket aside, reached up, and began slowly unbuttoning his shirt, then he leaned his head against the boulder and closed his eyes. Snow swirled around him, clinging to his wet hair and face and body while it slowly dawned on her that he wasn't even going to *try* to make it home! He obviously thought she had drowned trying to get away from him, and he had assigned himself the death sentence as his own punishment.

"Tell me you believe I'm innocent," he'd ordered her last night, and at that moment, Julie knew beyond all doubt that the man who wanted to die because he'd caused her own "death" had to be exactly that—innocent.

Unaware that she was crying or that she'd started running, Julie plunged silently down the slope to where he sat. When she was close enough to see his face, remorse and tenderness almost sent her to her knees. With his head thrown back and his eyes shut, his handsome face was a mask of ravaged regret.

The cold forgotten, she scooped up his jacket and held it out to him. Swallowing past the awful lump of contrition in her throat, she said in an aching whisper, "You win. Let's go home now."

When he didn't respond, Julie dropped to her knees and started trying to force his limp arm into the jacket.

"Zack, wake up!" she cried. Her shoulders shaking with suppressed sobs, she pulled him into her arms, cradling his head against her chest, trying to infuse some of her warmth into him, rocking him back and forth. "Please!" she babbled, on the edge of hysteria. "Please get up. I can't lift you. You have to help me. Zack, please. Remember when you said you wanted someone to believe you're innocent? I didn't completely believe you then, but I do now. I swear it. I *know* you didn't kill anyone. I believe everything you've said. Get up! Please, please get up!"

His weight seemed to be getting heavier, as if he was completely losing consciousness, and Julie panicked. "Zack, don't go to sleep," she said in a near scream. Grabbing his wrist, she began shoving his limp arm into his jacket while resorting to mindless bribery in an effort to jar him into alertness. "We'll go home. We'll go to bed together. I wanted to last night, but I was afraid. Help me get you home, Zack," she pleaded as she forced his other arm into the jacket and struggled with the zipper. "We'll make love in front of the fire. You'd like that wouldn't you!"

When she'd gotten his jacket on him, she stood up, grabbed his wrists, and pulled with all her might, but instead of moving him, her feet lost traction and she slid down beside him. Scrambling to her feet again, Julie raced to his snowmobile and brought it over to where he was lying. Bending over him, she shook him and when she couldn't wake him, she closed her eyes for courage, then she swung her arm in a wide arc and slapped him hard across the face. His eyes opened, then closed. Ignoring the scream of pain that shot up her arm from her frozen fingers, she grabbed his wrists and tugged, trying to tell him something different that might make him try to get up. "I can't find the way home without you," she lied, yanking on his wrists. "If you won't help me get home, I'll die out here with you. Is that what you want? Zack, please help me," she cried. "Don't let me die!"

It was a second before she realized that he wasn't completely the dead weight he'd been and that he was reacting to something she'd said and using what feeble strength he had left to try to stand. "That's right!" Julie panted, "Stand up. Help me get home so I'll be warm."

His movements were terrifyingly sluggish and when his eyes opened, his gaze was unfocused, but he was instinctively trying to help her now. It took several attempts, but Julie managed to get him to his feet, loop his arm over her shoulders, and get him onto the snowmobile, where he slumped over the handle bars.

"Try to help me balance," she said, steadying him with her arms and quickly getting on behind him. She glanced up at the path he'd taken down here, realized it would be impossible to make the steep climb back there now, and decided to follow the creek around the bend in hopes there would be a way to get up to the bridge and onto the road from there. Her former fear of the unfamiliar machine's power forgotten, Julie crouched low over him to shield him from the wind with her body and sent the machine flying over the snow. "Zack," she said near his ear, scanning the path and talking to him in a desperate effort to keep him conscious and hold her own terror at bay, "you're still shivering a little. Shivering is good. It means your body temperature hasn't dropped to the bottom danger point. I read that somewhere." They rounded the bend, and Julie aimed the snowmobile at the only path she thought they might be able to climb.

28

HE COLLAPSED TWICE IN THE HALL BEFORE JULIE GOT HIM TO her bedroom where she knew for certain the fireplace was filled with wood and ready to be lit. Breathless from exertion, she staggered to the bed and let his weight carry him onto it. His outer clothes were stiff and crusted with ice, as she started pulling them off of him. It was while she was yanking off his pants that he spoke the only words he'd said since she'd run to his rescue. "Shower," he mumbled feebly. "Hot shower."

"No," she retorted, trying to sound businesslike and impersonal as she began to yank off his icy underwear. "Not yet. People suffering from hypothermia need to be warmed slowly but not with direct heat, I learned that in a first aid class in college. And don't give a thought to me undressing you. I'm a teacher and you're just another little boy to me," she lied. "A teacher's almost like a nurse, did you know that?" she added. "Stay awake! Listen to my voice!" She eased the shorts down his muscled legs, glanced down to see how she was doing, and felt a fiery blush heat her cheeks. The magnificent male body that was sprawled out before her eyes looked like a Playgirl centerfold she'd seen in college. Except that this real-life body was blue with cold and vibrating with deep shivering chills.

Grabbing the blankets, she tucked them around him, chafing them on his skin as she worked, then she went to the closet and got out four more blankets and spread them over him. Satisfied with his covering, she hurried over to the fireplace in the corner and lit the kindling. Not until the logs were blazing on the hearth did Julie stop long enough to take off her own outdoor clothes. Afraid to leave him, she stood at the foot of his bed, watching his slow, shallow breaths as she stripped off her snowmobile suit. "Zack, can you hear me?" she asked, and although he didn't answer, Julie began talking to him in a mindless string of disjointed comments intended to both encourage him to recover and boost her flagging confidence that he would. "You're very strong, Zack. I noticed that when I watched you changing my tire and when you crawled out of the creek.

And you're brave, too. There's a little boy in my class—his name is Johnny Everett—he wants to be strong more than anything in the world. He's crippled, so he has to stay in a wheelchair, and it breaks my heart to watch him, but he *never* gives up. Remember, I told you about him last night?" Unaware of the tenderness in her voice, she added, "He's very brave, just like you are. My brothers used to have pictures of you in their room. Did I ever tell you that? There's so much I'd like to tell you, Zack," she said brokenly. "And I will, if you'll just stay alive and give me a chance. I'll tell you anything you'd like to know."

Panic set in. Maybe she should be doing more to warm him or keep him awake. What if he died because of her ignorance? Grabbing a thick terry cloth robe from the closet, she pulled it on, then she sat down on the bed beside his hip and pressed her fingertips to the pulse in his neck, her gaze riveted to the clock on the dresser. His pulse seemed alarmingly slow. Her hands and voice shook as she smoothed the blankets around his wide shoulders and said, "About last night—I'd like you to know that I loved it when you kissed me. I didn't want you to stop there, and that's what scared me. It didn't have anything to do with the fact that you'd been in jail, it was because I . . . because I was losing control, and I've never had that happen before." She knew he probably wasn't hearing a word she said, and she fell silent as another spasm of deep chills racked his body. "Shivering is good," she said aloud, but she was thinking frantically for something else to do for him. A sudden vision of St. Bernard dogs with miniature kegs around their necks for people stranded by avalanches made her snap her fingers and jump to her feet. A few minutes later, she returned to his bedside holding a glass filled with brandy and brimming with excitement over what she'd heard on the kitchen radio. "Zack," she said eagerly, sitting down beside him and shoving her arm beneath his head so she could lift it to the glass, "drink some of this, and try to understand what I'm telling you: I just heard on the radio that your friend—Dominic Sandini—is in the hospital in Amarillo. He's doing better! Do you understand? He *didn't* die. He's conscious now. They think the inmate in the prison infirmary who gave out the false information was either mistaken or trying to turn the prisoners' protest into a full-fledged riot, and that's exactly what happened . . . Zack?"

After several minutes she'd managed to get only a tablespoon of brandy into him, and Julie gave up. She knew she could find the telephone he'd hidden and call for a doctor, but the doctor would recognize him and immediately call the police. They'd take him out of here and haul him back to prison, and he'd said he'd rather be dead than go back.

Tears of uncertainty and exhaustion slid from the corner of Julie's eyes as the minutes slipped past and she sat with hands folded in her lap, trying to think what to do until she finally resorted to a whispered prayer. "Please help me," she prayed. "I don't know what to do. I don't know why You brought the two of us together. I don't understand why You're making me feel this way about him or why You want me to stay with him, but somehow I think this is all Your doing. I know it because . . . because I haven't felt as if You were standing with Your hand on my shoulder like this since I was a little girl—when you gave the Mathisons to me."

Julie drew a long, shaky breath and brushed away a tear from the corner of her eye, but as she said the last of her prayer, she was already feeling steadier: "Please take care of us."

After a moment she looked up at Zack and watched his body tremble with more chills, then he moved lower into the covers. Realizing that he was deeply asleep, not unconscious as she'd feared, she leaned forward and pressed a light kiss to his forehead. "Keep shivering," she whispered tenderly. "Shivering is very good."

Unaware that a pair of amber eyes flickered open and then drifted closed again as she stood up, Julie went into the bathroom to take a hot shower.

29

SHE WAS WRAPPING HERSELF IN THE ROBE AGAIN WHEN IT occurred to her that she could at least find the telephone he'd hidden and call her parents to let them know she was safe. Stopping beside her bed, she laid her hand on Zack's forehead, watching him breathe. His temperature felt closer to normal, and his breathing was deeper now, in the steady rhythm of exhausted slumber. The rush of relief she felt made her knees weak as she turned to stoke up the roaring fire she'd built. Satisfied that he was warm enough, she left him to sleep and went to look for the telephone, closing the door behind her. Deciding the bedroom he'd slept in was a logical place to begin looking, she opened his bedroom door and stopped short, staring in wonder at the incredible luxury spread out before her. She'd thought her room with its stone fireplace, mirrored doors, and spacious tiled bath was the absolute height of plushness, but this room was four times as large and ten times as lavish. Mirrors lined the entire wall on her left, reflecting an enormous bed with hugh skylights above it and a gorgeous white marble fireplace opposite the bed. Long windows covered the back wall then fanned out in a semicircle on the end wall to create a wide alcove for a white marble hot tub on a raised dias. A pair of curving silk sofas upholstered in an ivory-, mauve-, and seafoam-green–striped fabric were positioned by the fireplace. On the dias, on either side of the hot tub were two more overstuffed chairs and ottomans upholstered in the same colors but in a quilted flowered fabric that matched the bedspread.

Julie walked slowly forward, her feet sinking into the deep wool pile of the pale green carpeting. On her left she saw brass handles on two of the mirrored panels and she gingerly pushed them open then drew in a startled breath at the sight of a vast marble-floored sky-lit bath that was divided precisely down the center by two long marble vanities with double sinks and a mirrored half wall above them. Each half of the bathroom had its own enormous shower stall enclosed in clear glass and its own marble tub with gold fittings.

Although the rest of the house could have been furnished to suit a man or a woman, there was no mistaking the feminine touches that had given this suite an aura of inviting opulence that would surely make a man feel as if he'd been invited into a woman's private boudoir. Julie had read in some home furnishing magazine that married men who were confident of their own masculinity rarely objected to their wives' desires for feminine bedrooms and, in fact, rather enjoyed the implied illicitness of invading a formerly "forbidden" domain. Until that moment, she'd thought the notion odd, but as she noted the subtle touches designed for a man like the huge bed and comfortable, overstuffed chairs by the hot tub, she decided the theory had definite merit.

She headed for the door to the walk-in closet that opened off the right half of the bathroom and went inside to look for the telephone. After a thorough and fruitless search of both closets and all the drawers in the bedroom, Julie yielded to temptation and borrowed a red silk Japanese kimono embroidered in gold threads from the woman's closet. She chose that partly because it was sure to fit and partly because she had a helpless urge to look nice if Zack woke up before morning. She was tying the belt around her waist wondering where on earth he'd hidden the phone when she remembered the small closet in the hall, the one with a deadlock on it. She went straight to it and tried the knob, and when it proved to be locked tight, she tiptoed into her own bedroom. She found the key where she expected it to be—in the pocket of his soaked trousers.

The locked closet contained an enormous stock of wine and liquor and four telephones, which she found on the floor behind a case of Dom Perignon champagne, where Zack had hidden them.

Stifling an unexpected attack of nervousness, Julie took one of the phones into the living room, plugged it in, and sat down on the sofa, her legs curled beneath her, the phone in her lap. She'd already dialed half the long distance number when she realized the enormous mistake she was probably making, and she hastily slapped the receiver onto its cradle to disconnect the call. Since kidnapping was a federal offense—and Zack was an escaped murderer—it stood to reason that the FBI would probably be at her parents' house, waiting for her to phone, so they could trace the call. At least, that's what always happened in the movies. She'd already made her decision to stay here with Zack and to let God handle whatever came along, but she absolutely had to talk to her family and reassure them. Idly tracing the flamboyant gold peacock embroidered on the lap of her red kimono, she concentrated on how to accomplish her goal. Since she didn't dare call family members, she had to reach someone else first, someone she could trust implicitly, someone who wouldn't be flustered by the errand she was going to give them.

Julie ruled out the other teachers. They were terrific women, but they were more timid than daring, and they didn't have the kind of panache required for the task. Suddenly she burst into a beaming smile and went for the little address book she carried in her purse. Opening it to C, she pulled the phone onto her lap and checked the home number she'd had for Katherine Cahill before Katherine had become Mrs. Ted Mathison. Earlier that month, Katherine had sent her a note asking if they could get together when she was in Keaton this week. With a satisfied chuckle, Julie decided Ted was going to be furious at her for sending Katherine back into the Mathison family's midst, where he couldn't avoid or ignore her . . . and Katherine was going to thank her for doing just that. "Katherine?" Julie said quickly as soon as the other woman answered the phone at her family's house, "This is Julie. Don't say anything unless you're alone."

"Julie! My God! Yes, I'm alone. My-my parents are in the Bahamas. Where are you? Are you okay?"

"I'm fine. I swear I'm completely safe." She paused to steady her nerves and then said, "Do you know if there are people—police or FBI agents, I mean—at my parents' house?"

"They're at your parents' and asking questions all over town, too."

"Look, I need to ask you a very important favor. You won't be breaking the law, but you'll have to agree to keep this call a secret from them."

Katherine's voice dropped to a teary whisper. "Julie, I'd do *anything* for you. I'm—I'm honored you called me—that you're giving me a chance to repay you for all the things you did to try to stop Ted from divorcing me, for the way you've always stood by—" She brought herself up short just as Julie was about to interrupt her. "What do you want me to do?"

"I'd like you to get word to my parents and my brothers right away that I'm going to call you back in an hour so I can talk to them. Katherine, make absolutely certain you don't do or say anything to alert the FBI. Act natural, get my family off alone, give them my message. You aren't going to be intimidated by meeting FBI agents, are you?"

Katherine gave a sad little laugh. "As Ted used to very correctly point out—I was a spoiled little princess whose daddy made her believe she could do as she damned well pleased. Now, there is no way," she finished with more humor, "that a few lowly FBI agents could possibly fluster a former princess like me. If they try," she joked, "I'll have Daddy call Senator Wilkins."

"All right, great," Julie said, smiling at the tone of reckless daring in Katherine's voice, then she sobered, trying to phrase a warning that would deter Katherine as well as Julie's family from possibly deciding it might be in Julie's best interests to alert the FBI about Julie's next call, regardless. "There's one more thing: Make certain my family understands that I'm completely safe right now, but that if anyone traces this call, I'll be in terrible danger. I—I can't explain exactly what I mean—I don't have time, and even if I did—"

"You don't have to explain anything to me. I can tell from your voice that you're all right, and that's all that matters to me. As far as where you are . . . and who you're with . . . I know that whatever you're doing, you're doing what you believe is the right thing. You are the best person I've ever known, Julie. I'd better get going. Call back in an hour."

Julie lit the fire in the living room fireplace, then she paced back and forth in front of it, checking her watch, waiting impatiently for one hour to pass. Because of Katherine's calm, unquestioning acceptance of everything Julie said, Julie wasn't at all prepared for what happened when she made her second phone call. Her normally stoic father snatched up the Cahills' phone on the first ring. "Yes? Who is this?"

"This is Julie, Dad," she said, squeezing the telephone hard, "I'm okay. I'm fine—"

"Thank God!" he said, his voice hoarse and gruff with emotion, then he called out, "Mary, it's Julie, and she's okay. Ted, Carl—Julie's on the phone, and she's fine. Julie, we did what you said, we didn't tell the FBI about this."

Over a thousand miles away, Julie could hear several extension telephones being snatched off their cradles and a jumble of relieved, panicked voices, but over them all was Ted's voice—calming, authoritative. "Quiet, everyone," he ordered. "Julie, are you alone? Can you talk?" Before she could answer, he added, "That student of yours with the deep voice—Joe Bob Artis—he's worried sick about you."

For a split second Julie gaped in confusion at his opening topic and his use of a name she'd never heard of, then she muffled a nervous laugh as she understood that he'd used the wrong name intentionally. "You mean *Willie*," she corrected. "And I really am alone, at least for the moment."

"Thank God! Where are you, honey?"

Julie's mouth opened, but no sound came out. For the first time since she'd come to live with the Mathisons, she was going to lie to them, and despite the importance of her reason, she still dreaded it and felt ashamed. "I'm not certain exactly," she evaded with a telltale awkwardness they had to have heard. "It's—it's cold here, though," she provided lamely.

"What state are you in? Or are you in Canada?"

"I—I can't say."

"Benedict's there, isn't he!" Ted said, and the anger he was suppressing came bursting through. "That's why you can't say where you are. Put the bastard on the phone right now, Julie!"

"I can't! Listen to me, everyone, I can't stay on the phone, but I want you to believe me when I tell you that I'm not being mistreated in any way. Ted," she said, trying somehow to communicate with the one person who would understand the law and, hopefully, that judicial mistakes could happen, "he didn't kill anyone, I know he didn't. The jury made a mistake, and so you can't—*we* can't—blame him for trying to escape."

"A mistake!" Ted exploded. "Julie, don't fall for that crap! He's a convicted murderer and he is a *kidnapper!*"

"No! He didn't intend to kidnap me. All he wanted was a car, you see, to get him away from Amarillo, and he'd fixed a flat tire on the Blazer, so naturally I offered him a ride. He would have let me go, but he couldn't because I saw his map—"

"What map did you see, Julie? A map of what? Of where?"

"I have to go now," she said miserably.

"Julie!" Reverend Mathison's voice interrupted, "when are you coming back?"

"As soon as he'll let me, no—as soon as I can. I—I have to go. Promise me you won't tell anyone about this call."

"We promise, and we love you, Julie," Reverend Mathison said with touching, unconditional trust. "The whole town is praying for your safety."

"Dad," she said, because she couldn't stop herself, "could you ask them to pray for his safety, too?"

"Have you lost your mind!" Ted burst out. "The man's a convicted—" Julie didn't hear the rest of what he said. She was already putting the receiver back in its cradle and blinking back tears of sorrow. By asking them to pray for her captor, she had inadvertently forced her family to assume that she was either Zachary Benedict's dupe or his accomplice. Either one was a betrayal of everything they stood for and believed in, a betrayal of everything they'd believed of her, too. Shaking off the depression settling over her, Julie reminded herself that Zachary Benedict was innocent and *that* was what really mattered right now. Helping an innocent man to stay out of prison was not immoral or illegal, and it was *not* a betrayal of her family's trust.

Getting up, she added wood to both fireplaces, put the phone back in the closet, then went into the kitchen and spent the next hour cleaning it up and then making homemade stew to warm her patient when he awoke. She was cutting up potatoes when she realized that if he knew she'd made a phone call, she'd have a difficult, if not impossible, time convincing him that her family and her former sister-in-law were trustworthy and wouldn't tell the authorities she'd called. Since he already had enough to worry about, she decided not to tell him.

Finished, she wandered into the living room and sat down on the sofa, the radio still on in the kitchen so that she could hear if there was more news that would interest Zack.

It was funny, in an awful ironic sort of way, she thought with a rueful smile as she stretched out on the sofa, staring up at the ceiling, all the years she'd spent behaving like Mary Poppins and never, ever straying from the straight and narrow path, only to come to this.

In high school, she'd had lots of friends who were boys, but she never let them become more than friends, and they'd seemed willing to accept that. They picked her up for football games, offered her rides to school, and included her in their raucous, laughing groups. In her senior year, Rob Kiefer, the school's undisputed "hunk," had thrown her into a quandary of longing and frustration by asking her to the prom. Julie'd had a secret crush on Rob for years, but she refused his coveted invitation anyway, because everyone said that Rob Kiefer could get a girl's underwear off quicker than Mary Kostler could undress the mannequins in the window at Kostler's Dress Shop.

Julie didn't believe Rob would try anything with her because they were friends. She was also Reverend Mathison's daughter, which gave her a certain "immunity" from unwanted passes, but she couldn't go to the prom with Rob. Even though she was dying to say yes and even though he promised solemnly that he'd behave on prom night, she knew the whole school, and eventually the whole town, would assume that Reverend Mathison's daughter had become another on the long list of Rob's sexual conquests. Instead, Julie went to the prom with nice Bill Swensen, whose father was the school's bandleader, and Rob escorted Denise Potter, one of the cheerleaders. That night, she'd watched in sublime misery as Rob, who was crowned king of the prom, leaned over and kissed his queen, Denise Potter.

Denise got pregnant that night. When the couple got married three months later and rented a dingy one-room apartment instead of going off to college as they'd planned, the entire town of Keaton knew why. Some of Keaton's citizens pitied Denise, but most of them acted as if she'd invited it on herself by going near Rob Kiefer.

Julie felt irrationally responsible for the entire nightmare. The experience also caused her to reinforce her resolve to avoid trouble and scandal at all costs. In college, she steadfastly refused dates with Steve Baxter, even though she had a crush on him, because the handsome football player was a notorious flirt with a reputation for scoring in the bedroom even more often than he did on the football field. Steve, for reasons she never understood, spent almost two years pursuing her, appearing alone at social functions if he knew she was going to be there, staying at her side, and doing his sincere and charming best to convince her that she really was special to him. They laughed together, they talked for hours, but only in groups, because Julie adamantly refused to start dating him.

Now, as Julie compared her staid past to her chaotic present and uncertain future, she didn't know whether to laugh or cry: In all these years, she hadn't stepped out of line once because she didn't want her family and the people in Keaton to think badly of her. Now that she was about to stray from the "straight and narrow path," however, she wasn't going to settle for some minor infraction of moral and social rules that would stir up a little gossip in Keaton. No indeed, not her, Julie thought wryly. What she was going to do was violate not only moral precepts, but probably the laws of the United States of America, and while she was doing that, the entire news media would be providing gossip about it for the entire world—just as they were already doing!

The moment of humor vanished and Julie looked somberly at her hands. From the time she went to live with the Mathisons, she'd chosen to make certain "sacrifices," up to and including her decision to become a teacher, rather than pursuing another career that would have paid much more. And yet, each sacrifice invariably brought her such rich rewards that she always felt as if she received much more than she gave.

Now, she had the distinct feeling that fate was calling in her debts for a lifetime of unearned rewards. Zachary Benedict was as innocent of cold-blooded murder as she was, and she couldn't shake the feeling that she was expected to do something about it.

Rolling over onto her side, she tucked her arm beneath the throw pillows, watching the flames leaping in the grate. Until the real murderer was discovered, no one in the world, including her parents, was going to condone anything she did from now on. Of course, once her family realized that Zack was innocent, they'd approve completely of everything she'd done and might yet have to do. Well, probably not everything, Julie thought. They wouldn't approve of her falling in love with him so quickly, if what she felt for him was actually love, and they definitely wouldn't approve of her sleeping with him. With a mixture of quiet acceptance and nervous anticipation, Julie realized that loving him was actually out of her hands; sleeping with him was virtually a foregone conclusion unless he'd drastically changed his wishes since last night. Although, she rather hoped he'd give her a few days to know him better.

Beyond that, all she could do was try to guard her heart from needless pain and to refrain from doing or saying anything that would make her even more vulnerable to being hurt by him than she already was. She wasn't an utter fool, after all. Long before Zachary Benedict had gone to prison, he'd lived in an elite world of luxury populated by glamorous, sophisticated people with notoriously loose morals and no code of personal conduct or ethics. She'd read enough about him in magazines before he went to prison to know that the man she was with in this secluded mountain retreat had once possessed fabulous homes and villas of his own, where he gave lavish parties attended not only by famous movie stars, but by international business tycoons, European royalty, and even the president of the United States.

He was *not* a comfortable, genial assistant pastor of a small town church.

Compared to him, Julie knew she was as naive and unsophisticated as the proverbial newborn babe.

30

IT WAS AFTER 10 P.M. WHEN SHE WOKE UP WITH A CONFUSED start, a sofa pillow clutched to her chest. A slight movement off to her left caught her attention, and Julie quickly turned her head at the same time an amused male voice remarked, "A nurse who abandons her patient and falls asleep while on duty does not get paid her full rate."

Julie's "patient" was standing with his shoulder propped casually against the fireplace mantle and his arms crossed over his chest, watching her with a lazy smile. With his hair still damp from a shower and a cream chamois shirt that was open at the throat and tucked into fawn-colored trousers, he looked incredibly handsome, completely recovered . . . and very amused about something.

Trying to ignore the treacherous leap her heart gave at the sight of that enthralling, intimate smile, Julie hastily sat up. "Your friend—Dominic Sandini —he didn't die," she told him, wanting to put his mind at ease about that immediately. "They think he's going to be all right."

"I heard that."

"You did?" Julie said cautiously. It occurred to her that he might have heard it on the radio while he was dressing. If not—if he remembered her telling him that—then it was mortifyingly possible he might remember the other things she'd said in those unguarded minutes when she thought he was beyond hearing. She waited, hoping he'd refer to the radio, but he continued watching her with that smile tugging at his lips, and Julie felt her entire body grow warm with embarrassment. "How do you feel?" she asked, hastily standing up.

"Better now. When I woke up, I felt like a potato being baked in its own skin."

"What? Oh, you mean the bedroom got too hot?"

He nodded. "I kept dreaming I'd died and gone to hell. When I opened my eyes, I saw the fire leaping around me, and I was pretty sure of it."

"I'm sorry," Julie said, anxiously searching his face for any sign of lingering ill effects from his exposure to the elements.

"Don't be sorry. I realized very quickly that I couldn't really be in hell."

His light-hearted mood was so infectious and so utterly disarming that she reached up to lay the back of her hand against his forehead to test his body temperature without realizing what she was doing. "How did you know you weren't in hell?"

"Because," he said quietly, "part of the time, an angel was hovering over me."

"You were obviously hallucinating," she joked.

"Was I?"

This time, there was no mistaking the husky timbre in his voice, and she pulled her hand away from his head, but she couldn't quite free her gaze from his. "Definitely."

From the corner of her eye, Julie suddenly noticed that a porcelain duck was turned the wrong way on the mantle beside his shoulder, and she reached out to straighten it, then she rearranged the two smaller ducks beside that one.

"Julie," he said in a deep, velvety voice that had a dangerous effect on her heart rate, "look at me." When she turned to look at him, he said with quiet gravity, "Thank you for saving my life."

Mesmerized by his tone and the expression in his eyes, she had to clear her throat to stop her voice from shaking. "Thank you for trying to save mine."

Something stirred in the fathomless depths of his eyes, something hot and inviting, and Julie's pulse tripled even though he didn't attempt to touch her. Trying to switch the mood to one of safe practicality, she said, "Are you hungry?"

"Why didn't you leave?" he persisted.

His tone warned her that he wouldn't allow a change of subject until he'd gotten answers, and she sank down onto the sofa, but she looked at the centerpiece on the table because she couldn't quite meet his searching gaze. "I couldn't leave you out there to die, not when you'd risked your life thinking I'd drowned." She noticed that two of the white silk magnolias in the centerpiece were bent at awkward angles and she obeyed the automatic impulse to lean forward and fix them.

"Then why didn't you leave after you got me back here and into bed?"

Julie felt as if she were wandering through a field filled with land mines. Even if she had the courage to look at him and blurt out exactly how she felt about him, she couldn't be certain the announcement wouldn't blow up in her face. "For one thing, I honestly didn't think of it, and besides," she added on a note of relieved inspiration, "I didn't know where the car keys were!"

"They were in my pants pocket—the pants you took off me."

"Actually, I . . . I didn't think of looking for the car keys. I suppose I was simply too worried about you to think clearly."

"Don't you find that a little odd given the circumstances that brought you here?"

Julie leaned forward and picked up a magazine that was lying half off the table and laid it fanlike atop the other two, then she moved the crystal bowl of silk flowers two inches to the left, to the precise center of the table. "Everything has seemed pretty odd for three days," she hedged cautiously. "I can't begin to guess what would be normal behavior in these circumstances." Standing up, she began straightening the throw pillows she'd disarranged during her nap. She was bending down to pick one up from the carpet when he said in a laughter-tinged voice, "That's a habit you have, isn't it—straightening things out when you feel uneasy?"

"I wouldn't say that. I'm just a very tidy person." She stood up and looked at him, and her composure slipped a notch toward laughter. His brows were raised in mocking challenge and his eyes were gleaming with amused fascination. "All right," she said with a helpless laugh, "I admit it. It *is* a nervous habit." As she finished putting the pillow where it belonged, she added with a rueful smile, "Once, when I was nervous about failing an exam in college, I reorganized everything in the attic, then I alphabetized all my brothers' stereo records and my mother's recipes."

His eyes laughed at her story, but his voice was puzzled and solemn. "Am I doing something that makes you nervous?"

Julie gaped at him in stunned laughter, then she said with a lame attempt at severity, "You've been doing things that make me *extremely* nervous for three solid days!"

Despite her censorious tone, the way she was looking at him filled Zack with poignant tenderness: There was no trace of fear or suspicion or revulsion or hatred anywhere on her lovely, expressive face, and it seemed like a lifetime since anyone had looked at him like this. His own lawyers hadn't really believed he was innocent. Julie did. He'd have known it just by looking at her, but the memory of her words at the stream, the way her voice had broken when she said them, made it a thousand times more meaningful: *"Remember when you said you wanted someone to believe that you're innocent? I didn't completely believe you then, but I do now. I swear it! I know you didn't kill anyone."*

She could have left him to die at the stream, or if that was unthinkable to a minister's daughter, she could have gotten him back here, then taken the car and called the police from the nearest phone. But she hadn't. Because she really believed he was innocent. Zack wanted to pull her into his arms and tell her how much that meant to him; he wanted to bask in the warmth of her smile and hear her infectious peal of laughter again. Most of all, he wanted to feel her mouth on his, to kiss her and caress her until they were both wild, and then to thank her for the gift of her trust with his body. Because that was the only thing he had to give her.

He knew she sensed a change in their relationship and for some incomprehensible reason, it was making her more nervous than she'd been when he was holding a gun on her. He knew that just as surely as he knew they were going to make love tonight and that she wanted to almost as much as he did.

Julie waited for him to say something or to laugh at her last jibe, and when he didn't, she stepped back and gestured toward the kitchen. "Are you hungry?" she asked for the second time.

He nodded slowly, and her hand stilled at the husky intimacy she thought she heard in his voice. "Starved."

Julie told herself very firmly that he had *not* deliberately chosen that particular word because it had been used during their quarrel last night in a sexual context. Trying to look innocent of all such thoughts, she said very politely, "What would you like?"

"What are you offering?" he countered, playing verbal chess with her with such ease that Julie wasn't at all certain if all the double meanings to their exchange existed only in her fevered imagination.

"I was offering food, of course."

"Of course," he solemnly agreed, but his eyes were glinting with amusement.

"Stew, to be specific."

"It's important to be specific."

Julie elected to make a strategic retreat from the strangely charged conversation and began backing away toward the counter that separated the kitchen from the living room. "I'll put out the dinner things and serve the stew over there."

"Let's eat here by the fire instead," he said, his voice like a soft caress. "It's cozier."

Cozier . . . Julie's mouth went dry. In the kitchen, she worked with outward efficiency, but her hands were trembling so hard she could hardly ladle the thick stew into bowls. From the corner of her eye, she saw him walk over to the stereo and flip through the stacks of CDs, loading them into the revolving tray; a moment later, Barbra Streisand's lilting voice filled the room. Of all the CDs in the cabinet that ranged from Elton John to jazz, he'd picked Streisand.

Cozier.

The word swirled around in her brain; she reached for two napkins, put them on the tray, and then, with her back to the living room, Julie braced her palms on the counter top and drew a long, steadying breath. Cozier. By his definition, she knew perfectly well that meant "more conducive to intimacy." "Romantic." She knew it, just as clearly as she knew that the situation between them had altered irreversibly from the moment she chose to stay here with him rather than leaving him at the creek or bringing him here and calling the police. He knew it, too. She could see the evidence: There was a new softness in his eyes when he looked at her and a smiling tenderness in his voice, and they were both utterly shattering to her self-control. Julie straightened and shook her head at her foolish, futile attempt to deceive herself. There was nothing left of her self-control, no more arguments that mattered, nowhere she could go to hide from the truth.

The truth was that she wanted him. And he wanted her. They both knew it.

She put silverware on the tray, slanted another glance at him over her shoulder, and hastily looked away. He was sitting on the sofa, his arms spread out across the back of it, his foot propped casually atop the opposite knee, and he was watching her—relaxed, indulgent, and sexy. He wasn't going to rush her, and he wasn't a bit nervous either, but then he'd undoubtedly made love thousands of times with hundreds of women—all of whom were much prettier and unquestionably more experienced than she was.

Julie stifled a compulsive urge to start reorganizing the kitchen drawers.

Zack watched her return to the sofa and, bending down, place the tray on the table, her movements graceful and uncertain, like a frightened gazelle. Firelight gleamed on her heavy chestnut hair as it spilled forward over her shoulders from a single side part; it glowed on her soft skin as she arranged the place mats and bowls. Her long, sooty lashes cast fan-shaped shadows on her smooth cheeks, and he noticed for the first time that she had beautiful hands, the fingers slender, nails long and tapered. He had a sudden poignant memory of those hands clasping his face to her at the stream as she rocked him in her arms and pleaded with him to get up. At the time, it had seemed like a dream in which he had merely been an uninvolved spectator, but later, after he staggered into bed, his recollections were clearer. He remembered her hands smoothing blankets over him, the frantic worry in her lovely voice . . . As he looked at her now, he marveled anew at the strange aura of innocence about her, then he suppressed a puzzled smile at the realization that, for some reason, Julie was assiduously avoiding his eyes. For the last three days she had opposed, defied, and challenged him; today, she had outwitted him and then saved his life. And yet, for all her dauntless courage and her spunk, she was amazingly shy, now that the hostilities between them were over. "I'll get some wine," he said, and before she could decline he got up and returned with a bottle and two stemmed glasses.

"I didn't poison it," he remarked a few minutes later when he saw her reach automatically for the glass then yank her hand away.

"I didn't think you did," she said with a self-conscious laugh. She picked up the glass and drank some, and Zack noticed that her hand was shaking. She was uneasy about going to bed with him, he decided; she knew he hadn't been near a woman in five years. She was probably worried that he was going to jump on her the moment they were done with their meal or that once they started making love, he'd lose control and finish in two minutes. Zack didn't know why she should be concerned about all that; if anyone should be worried about his ability to pleasurably prolong the act and perform well after five years abstinence, it was him.

And he was.

He decided to try to reassure her by engaging her in some sort of pleasant, casual conversation. Mentally, he rifled through those topics of immediate interest to him and reluctantly discarded the subject of her beautiful body, her gorgeous eyes, and—most reluctantly of all—her whispered statement at the stream that she wanted to go to bed with him. The last reminded him of the other things she'd said to him in the bedroom this afternoon, when he hadn't been able to shake off his numb paralysis and respond. Now, he was almost certain he hadn't been meant to hear most of them. Or else he'd only imagined some of them. He wished she'd talk about her students; he loved her stories. He was about to try to get her to talk about them, when he realized she was giving him an odd, curious look. "What?" he asked.

"I was wondering," she said, "that day—at the restaurant—did I *really* have a flat tire?"

Zack struggled to suppress his guilty smile. "You saw it with your own eyes."

"Are you saying that I ran over a nail or something and didn't realize my tire was going flat?"

"I wouldn't say it happened exactly like that." He was pretty certain she suspected him now, but her face was so marvelously bland that he had no idea if she was playing cat and mouse with him or not.

"How *would* you say it happened?"

"I'd say that the side of your tire probably came into sudden contact with a sharp, pointed object."

Finished with her stew, she leaned back and fixed him with a level look that would have shamed an instant confession and apology out of any recalcitrant eight-year-old male. He could almost see her, standing outside her classroom with a wrongdoer, looking at him with exactly that same expression. "A sharp, pointed object?" she speculated, lifting her brows. "Like a knife?"

"Like a knife," Zack confirmed, trying desperately to keep his face straight.

"Your knife?"

"Mine." With an impenitent grin, he added in a boyish chant, "I'm sorry, Miss Mathison."

She didn't miss a beat. Raising her brows, she said drolly, "I'll expect you to fix that tire, Zack."

The only thing that quelled his shout of laughter was the sweet shock of hearing her finally say his name. "Yes, ma'am," he said. It was unbelievable, Zack thought, his entire life was in dire chaos, and all he wanted to do was burst out laughing and drag her into his arms. "I don't have to write a three-page essay on why I shouldn't have done it, do I?" he asked, watching her huge indigo eyes shimmer with answering amusement as she looked pointedly at the bowl he'd just pushed aside. "No," she said, "but you're on KP tonight."

"Aw, gee!" he replied, but he stood up obediently and picked up his bowl. As he reached for hers, he added, "You're mean, Miss Mathison!"

To which she firmly replied, "No whining, please."

Zack couldn't help it. He burst out laughing, turned his head, and surprised her with a quick kiss on her forehead. "Thank you," he whispered, choking back a chuckle at her flustered expression.

"For what?"

He sobered, holding her gaze. "For making me laugh. For staying here and not turning me in. For being brave and funny and incredibly lovely in that red kimono. And for making me a wonderful meal." He chucked her under the chin to lighten the mood a split second before he realized the expression in her shining eyes wasn't embarrassment.

"I'll help you," she said, starting to stand.

Zack put his hand on her shoulder. "Stay there and enjoy the fire and the rest of your wine."

Too tense to sit still, waiting to see what would happen next, no, *when* it was going to happen, Julie got up and walked over to the windows. Leaning her shoulder against the pane, she gazed out at the spectacular panorama of snowcovered mountaintops gleaming in the moonlight. In the kitchen, Zack touched the rheostat on the wall, dimming the lights on the beams above the living room to a mellow glow. "You'll be able to see outside better that way," he explained when she threw a questioning look over her shoulder at him. And, Julie thought, it was also much cozier with only the dimmed lights and the glow from the fireplace to illuminate the room. Very cozy and very romantic, especially with the music playing on the stereo.

31

ZACK SAW HER SHOULDERS STIFFEN IMPERCEPTIBLY WHEN HE came up behind her at the windows, and her unpredictable reactions to him began to genuinely unnerve him. Rather than turning her into his arms and kissing her, which was what he would have done if she were any other woman he'd known, he hit on a more subtle method of getting her where he wanted her to be. Shoving his hands into his pockets, he met her gaze in the window, tipped his head toward the stereo, and said with teasing formality, "May I have the next dance, Miss Mathison?"

She turned, her enchanting smile aglow with surprise, and Zack's spirits soared crazily simply because she was pleased. He shoved his hands deeper into his pockets to keep from touching her and said with a wry grin, "The last time I asked a teacher to dance, I was more properly dressed for the occasion in a white shirt, maroon tie, and my favorite navy blue suit. She turned me down though."

"Really? Why?"

"She probably thought I was too short for her."

Julie smiled because he was easily 6'2" tall, and she thought he was either joking or else the woman had been a giant. "Were you really shorter than she was?"

He nodded. "By about three feet. I, however, didn't regard that as a serious obstacle at the time because I had a wild crush on her."

She caught on then and her smile faded. "How old were you?"

"Seven."

She looked at him as if she knew the slight had hurt him, which, now that he thought about it, it had. "I would never have turned you down, Zack."

The little catch in her voice and the soft look in her eyes were almost Zack's undoing. Mesmerized by the feelings unfolding inside him, he pulled his hands out of his pockets and silently held his left palm out to her, his gaze locked to hers. She laid her hand in his, and he slid his arm around her narrow waist, drawing her close against him, while Streisand's incredible voice slid effortlessly into the first bars of "People."

A jolt shook him when he felt her legs and thighs coming into intimate contact with his own as she matched his steps with effortless grace, and when she laid her cheek lightly against his chest, his heart began to beat much too fast. He hadn't even kissed her yet, and desire was already pounding through every nerve ending in his body. To distract himself, he tried to think of an appropriate topic of conversation that would further his ultimate goal without immediately stimulating him more than he already was. Recalling that it had felt good to joke about the tire he'd slashed, he decided that it would benefit both of them if they could laugh about other events that hadn't been one bit funny at the time. Linking his fingers through hers, he brought her hand against his chest and said lightly against her hair, "By the way, Miss Mathison, about your unscheduled flight on that snowmobile today—"

She caught his wry tone immediately, tipped her head back, and affected an expression of such exaggerated, wide-eyed innocence that Zack had to fight not to laugh. "Yes?" she said.

"Where the hell did you go when you shot over the edge of the mountain like a rocket and vanished?"

Her shoulders shook with laughter. "I landed in the embrace of a large pine tree."

"That was very clever planning," he teased. "*You* stayed nice and dry and tricked *me* into acting like a demented salmon in that freezing stream."

"That part wasn't funny. What you did today was the bravest thing I've ever seen anyone do."

It wasn't the words she said that melted him, it was the way she was looking at him—the admiration in her eyes, the awed wonder in her voice. After the humiliation of his trial and the dehumanizing effects of prison, it was heady merely to be looked at like a man, not an animal. But to have her look at him as if he were brave and fine and decent was a gift more precious to him than anything he'd ever been given. He wanted to crush her in his arms, to lose himself in her sweetness, to wrap her around him like a blanket and bury himself in her; he wanted to be the best lover she'd ever had and to make this night as memorable for her as it was going to be for him.

Julie watched his gaze drop to her lips, and in a state of anticipation that had mounted to dizzying heights in the last hour, she waited for him to kiss her. When it became obvious he wasn't going to do it, she covered her disappointment with her best, brightest smile and tried to be amusing. "If you ever come to Keaton and meet Tim Martin, please don't tell him I danced with you tonight."

"Why not?"

"Because he picked a fight with the last person I danced with."

Despite the absurdity of it, Zack felt the first sharp twinge of jealousy in his adult life. "Is Martin a boyfriend?"

She chuckled at his dark scowl. "No, he's one of my students. He's the jealous type—"

"Witch!" he chided her, pulling her tightly against his length while John Denver began to sing "Annie's Song" on the stereo. "I know exactly how the poor kid must have felt."

She rolled her eyes. "You don't really expect me to believe that you were jealous just now, do you?"

Zack's eyes fixed greedily on her lips. "Five minutes ago," he murmured, "I would have said I was incapable of such a lowering emotion."

"Oh. Right," she said with amused derision, and then she added with laughing severity, "You are overacting, Mr. Movie Star."

Zack went cold all over. If he had to make a choice between having Julie Mathison imagine him as an escaped convict when he took her to bed tonight or as a movie star, he'd have chosen the former without hesitation. At least the former was real, not illusionary, sickening, and phoney. He'd spent more than a decade of his life living with an image that made him into a sexual trophy. Like football players and hockey stars, he'd had his privacy and his life invaded by female groupies who wanted to sleep with Zachary Benedict. Not the man. The image. In fact, this evening had been the first time he'd ever been absolutely certain a woman wanted him simply for himself, and it made him angry to think he'd been wrong.

"Why," she said cautiously, "are you looking at me like that?"

"Suppose *you* tell *me* why," he countered, "you brought up the expression 'movie star' at this particular moment."

"You aren't going to like the answer."

"Try me," he clipped.

Her eyes narrowed at his tone. "All right. I said it because I have an aversion to insincerity."

Zack's brows snapped together. "Do you think you could possibly be a little more specific?"

"Certainly," Julie replied, repaying his sarcasm with uncharacteristic bluntness: "I said it because you pretended that you were jealous, and then you made it worse by pretending you hadn't ever, in your entire life, felt that way before. I thought it was not only corny but insincere, particularly because I know, and *you* know, that I have to be the least attractive woman you've bothered to flirt with in your entire adult life! Furthermore, since I'm not treating you like an escaped murderer any more, I'd appreciate it if you wouldn't start treating *me* like . . . like some witless fan of yours who you can charm into fainting at your feet with a few words of empty flattery."

Belatedly registering the thunderous expression on his face, Julie jerked her gaze from his and stared at his shoulder, embarrassed and ashamed for letting her hurt feelings drive her to such an outburst. She braced herself for a verbal blasting, but after a moment of ominous silence she said in a small, contrite voice, "I suppose I probably didn't *need* to be *that* specific. I'm sorry. Now it's your turn."

"To do what?" he retorted.

"I imagine to tell me that I was rude and obnoxious just now."

"Fine. You were."

He'd stopped dancing, and Julie drew a long fortifying breath before she raised her gaze to his impassive face. "You're angry, aren't you?"

"I'm not certain."

"What do you mean, you aren't certain?"

"I mean that, where you're concerned, I haven't been certain of anything since about noon today, and the uncertainty is getting worse by the moment."

He sounded so strange, so . . . off balance . . . that Julie felt a wayward smile touch her lips. She doubted very much if any other woman, no matter how beautiful, could have put him in exactly this state. She didn't know how it had happened, but she felt rather proud. "I think," she said, "I like that."

He wasn't amused. "Unfortunately, I don't."

"Oh."

"In fact, I think we'd better reach some sort of clear understanding about what is going on between us and what we *want* to go on between us." In the back of his mind, Zack knew he was being completely irrational, but five years of imprisonment along with the harrowing emotional and physical events of the day and the roller-coaster ride she'd had him on for the last twenty-four hours were all combining to play havoc with his temper, his emotions, and his judgment. "Well, do you agree?"

"I—guess so."

"Fine, do you want to go first, or shall I?"

She swallowed, torn between dread and amusement. "You go first."

"Half the time I have the craziest feeling that you're not real . . . that you're too naive to be twenty-six years old . . . that you're a thirteen-year-old girl pretending to be a woman."

She smiled with relief that he hadn't said anything worse. "And the other half of the time?"

"You make me feel like *I'm* thirteen." He could tell she liked that from the quick amused sparkle in her eyes, and suddenly Zack felt perversely compelled to shatter whatever remaining illusions she might conceivably have about him personally as well as his intentions for the evening. "Despite how you perceive what happened at the stream today, I am *not* a knight in shining armor. I am *not* a movie star, and I am a *long* way from being a naive, idealistic teenager! Whatever innocence and idealism I was born with, I lost long before I lost my virginity. I'm not a child and neither are you. We're adults. We both know what's happening between us right now, and we know exactly what all of this is leading up to." The laughter left her eyes replaced by something that was not quite fear and not quite anger either. "Do you want me to spell it out, so there's no mistaking my motives?" he persisted, watching a heated blush stain her smooth cheeks. Stung because the knowledge that he wanted to go to bed with her had doused her smile, he deliberately pushed his point. "My motives aren't noble; they're adult and they're natural. We aren't thirteen years old, this isn't a school dance, and my mind isn't on whether or not I'll be able to kiss you good night.

It's already a foregone conclusion that I'm going to kiss you good night. The fact is that I want you, and I think you want me almost as much. Before this night is over, I intend to make sure you do, and when I've done that, I intend to take you to bed and undress you and make love to you as thoroughly and leisurely as I can. For now, I want to dance with you, so that I can feel your body against mine. While we're dancing, I'll be thinking of all the things I'm going to do to you—and with you—when we're in bed together. Now, have I made everything clear? If none of that suits you, then you tell me what you want to do, and we'll do that. Well?" he snapped impatiently when she remained silent with her head bent. "What do *you* want to do?"

Julie bit her trembling lip and raised eyes glowing with laughter and desire to his. "How would you like to help me rearrange the hall closet?"

"Do you have a *second* choice?" he demanded, so irritated that he didn't realize she was joking.

"Actually," she said, furrowing her brow and lowering her gaze to the vee at the throat of his open shirt collar. "That *was* my second choice."

"Well then, what the hell is your *first* choice? And don't pretend I'm making you so nervous you want to clean out closets, because I couldn't make you nervous at gunpoint!"

Julie added irascibility and obtuseness to the things she loved about him and drew a shaky breath, ready to call an end to the game, but she couldn't quite meet his gaze as she said softly, "You're right, you couldn't possibly make me nervous at gunpoint after today, because I know you wouldn't hurt me for the world. In fact, the only way you could make me nervous is by doing exactly what you've been doing since I woke up tonight and saw you standing by the fireplace."

"Which is?" he clipped.

"Which is making me wonder if you're *ever* going to kiss me the way you did last night . . . Which is acting like you very much want to do it one minute, and then, like you don't the next min—"

Zack caught her face between his hands, turned it up, and abruptly captured the rest of her words in his mouth, shoving his fingers through the sides of her hair as he kissed her. And when she proved she meant it, when she slid her hands up his chest and around his neck, holding him close and kissing him back, he felt a burgeoning pleasure and astonished joy that was almost past bearing.

Trying to atone for his earlier roughness, he dragged his lips from hers and brushed a kiss along her jaw and cheek and temple, then he sought her mouth again, rubbing his lips over their soft contours. He traced the trembling line between her lips with his tongue, urging them to part, insisting, and when they did, he drove fully into her mouth—a starving man helplessly trying to satisfy a hunger by teaching her to intensify it. And the woman in his arms was a willing and gifted student. Melting against him, she crushed her mouth to his, welcoming his tongue and giving him hers with only the merest hint from him that he wanted it.

Long minutes later, Zack finally forced himself to lift his head, and he gazed down into her eyes, unconsciously memorizing the way she looked, all flushed and fresh and alluring. Trying to smile, he slid his hand around her nape and slowly rubbed his thumb over her soft bottom lip, but the deep indigo pools of her eyes were pulling him inexorably into their depths again. His thumb stopped moving, he pressed it down to force her lips apart and hungrily captured her mouth. Trembling in his arms, she leaned up on her toes and the slight increase in pressure against his rigid erection made his heart thunder and his fingers clench convulsively against her back. He crushed her pliant body into his, his hands rushing over the sides of her breasts and back, then angling across her buttocks, holding her tightly against his straining body. He was losing control, and he knew it.

Zack told himself to slow down, ordered himself to stop before he forced her to the floor and followed her down, before he behaved like the sex-starved convict he was instead of the leisurely lover he'd promised to be in his angry tirade. It was the distant, nagging memory of his promise that finally made him try to prolong the prelude, to heed the warning of his pounding arousal that the culmination was going to happen much too quickly for her, once it began.

He forced his hands away from her breasts and settled them on the curve of her waist instead; but it was harder by far to stop the driving movements of his tongue when she was clinging to him and answering and digging her nails into his back. When he finally pulled his mouth an inch from hers, Zack wasn't certain if it was she or he who moaned with the loss before she leaned her forehead weakly against his chest. Eyes closed, his heart pumping fast, he dragged air into his lungs and slid his arms around her back to steady her against him. But it was no use—he had to have her, all of her, now. Drawing a ragged breath, he put his hand under her chin and tipped her face up. Her eyes were closed, long lashes lying on her creamy cheeks, as she instinctively lifted her lips to his.

Zack's control snapped. His mouth seized hers with fierce desperation, forcing her lips to part as his hands pulled the silk tie of her robe open, then shoved it apart, pushing the material down her arms and sending it to the floor in front of the fireplace so that he could feast on the sight and touch of her skin.

Wrapped in his arms, Julie felt him lowering her to the floor, but she didn't surface from her state of mindless pleasure until he took his mouth and hands from her. She opened her eyes and saw him hurriedly unbutton his shirt and yank it out of his pants, tossing it aside, but not until he looked up at her did she feel the first stirrings of panic. In the firelight, his eyes had a fierce glitter as they moved restlessly over her body; passion had turned his face hard and intense, and when she lifted her arm self-consciously to cover her breasts, his voice was harsh: "Don't!"

She shivered convulsively at that stranger's voice, that stranger's face, and when he pulled her hand away and covered her with his upper body, she realized instinctively that the preliminaries were abruptly over and he was going to be driving into her in a matter of moments unless she slowed him down. "Zack," she whispered, trying to make him listen without just blurting out the situation. "Wait!"

The word didn't register with Zack, but the panic in it struck a mildly discordant note, and so did the fact that she was shoving on his shoulders and squirming against his thigh in a way that was wildly provocative.

"Zack!"

Zack knew he was going too fast, cheating on the foreplay, and he thought she was objecting to that.

"There's something I need to tell you!"

With an effort that nearly sapped his strength, he made himself move onto his side, but when he bent his head to her breast to oblige her, she caught his face in her hands to stop him and forced it up.

"*Please!*" Julie said, looking into his smoldering eyes. She spread her fingers over his rigid jaw, softening it, and when he turned his face into her palm and kissed it, her heart swelled with relief and tenderness. "We have to talk first."

"You talk," he said gruffly, pulling her tighter to him, kissing the side of her mouth and her neck, sliding his hand over her breast, "I'll listen," he lied, his fingers stroking down, past her flat belly, sliding into the triangle of curls. She jerked beneath him, grabbing his hand, and the topic she chose to discuss was, in his opinion, the most inanely inopportune one ever brought up by any woman in history at a time like this: "How old were you the first time you made love?"

He closed his eyes and swallowed an understandably impatient retort. "Twelve."

"Don't you want to know how old I was?"

"No," he said tightly, moving up to kiss her breast since for some reason, known only to her, she didn't want to be touched more intimately. His entire body was straining with need and he was trying his damndest to touch her in the places that he remembered very clearly gave women the quickest and greatest pleasure.

"I was twenty-six," she provided in a panicky voice when his mouth closed tightly on her nipple.

His blood was roaring in his ears; he heard the words but not the import. She tasted so good; she felt even better. Her breasts weren't large or heavy, but they were pretty and exquisitely feminine, just like she was, and if she'd only be as receptive to him as she'd been when they were standing up, he'd give her a climax now, before he came inside her, and then afterward he'd make love to her properly. He had five years of pent-up desire to expend; he'd be able to make love to her all damned night without stopping if she'd just let him do this and stop clamping her legs together, and stop talking about how old she was the . . . first time . . . she had . . . sex . . .

Julie knew the moment it registered on him, because he lifted his mouth a fraction of an inch from her skin, and his body went so still she had the feeling he'd stopped breathing. "This is the first time for me," she said shakily.

He dropped his forehead on her breast, shut his eyes, and swore. "Christ!"

The explosive whisper made it eloquently clear to Julie that he was not pleased by her revelation—a conviction that was reinforced when he finally raised his head and stared hard at her face, his eyes minutely inspecting each feature as if he were hoping to find some proof she was lying. He was either angry or disgusted, Julie realized with a sinking heart. She hadn't wanted him to stop, only to slow down and not handle her like . . . like a body that was *used* to being handled.

Zack was not disgusted, he was dumbstruck. He was disoriented. Within his personal frame of reference, he had never heard of a twenty-six-year-old virgin, let alone a beautiful, witty, intelligent, desirable one.

But as he gazed at her lovely, apprehensive face, suddenly everything about her that had puzzled him last night and tonight began to make some sense. He remembered her heartbroken outburst after the news program last night: *"My father is a minister!"* she'd wept. *"He's a respected man. I've spent the last fifteen years of my life trying to be perfect."* He remembered her answer when he asked her if she was engaged: *"We're talking about it."* Evidently they'd been doing a lot of talking and no lovemaking. And last night, Zack himself had likened her to a choirgirl.

Now that he understood the past, he was more confused than ever by the present. Apparently, she had withheld her virginity from her own boyfriend, who obviously loved her and wanted to offer her respectability and a future. Tonight, however, she was willing to surrender it to an escaped convict who was incapable of loving anyone and who had nothing whatsoever to offer her. Zack's conscience chose that moment to reassert itself for the first time in years by reminding him that Julie's almost-fiancé hadn't coerced her into surrendering her virginity; if Zack had any scruples, any decency whatsoever, he'd keep his hands off of her. He'd already kidnapped her, verbally abused her, and subjected her to public embarrassment and censure. Compounding all of that by robbing her of her virginity was inexcusable.

But the feeble protest of his conscience wasn't enough to deter him. He wanted her. He had to have her. He was going to have her. Fate had deprived him of his dignity, his freedom, and his future, but it had for some reason given her to him during these brief days of what was likely to be the end of his life. Neither his conscience nor anything else was going to deprive him of having her. Unaware of the passage of time, he stared at her until her shaky voice snapped him from his thoughts, and her words were poignant testimony to her lack of experience with men. "I didn't expect you to be angry," she said, completely misinterpreting the reason for his silence.

With a harsh sigh, he said, "I'm angry with myself, not you."

Julie searched his face. "Why?"

"Because," he said gruffly, "it isn't going to stop me. Because it isn't going to matter a damn to me that you've never done this before, not even with someone who loved you or who could stay with you if he got you pregnant. Nothing matters to me right now . . ." he whispered, lowering his mouth to hers, "but this . . ."

But her inexperience did matter. It mattered enough to Zack to make him break off the kiss and try to get his lust under control, so that he could start over with her. "Come here," he whispered, gathering her into his arms and rolling onto his side so that she was facing him, her head pillowed against his shoulder. Breathing deeply, he waited for his pulse to return to normal, slowly running his hand down her trim back in a soothing caress, while he resolved to make this good for her, even if he died of unassuaged lust in the process. Somehow, he was going to have to arouse her thoroughly without arousing himself more than he already was.

Julie lay in his arms, bewildered by the sudden change in his mood and terrified that, despite his words to the contrary, she'd apparently turned him off on the idea of making love altogether. Unable to stand it any longer, she kept her eyes on his throat and said shakily, "I didn't mean to make such a—a big deal out of this being my first time. I was only trying to slow you down a little—not stop you."

Zack knew how hard it must have been for her to say a thing like that, and he felt another unfamiliar surge of tenderness toward her as he tipped her chin up and said with quiet gravity. "Don't spoil this for either of us by belittling its importance. The truth is, I've never had the responsibility—or the privilege—of being a woman's first lover, so it's a first time for me, too." Lifting his hand, he brushed her tousled hair off her cheek, slowly combing his fingers through it, watching it spill over her left shoulder as he mused aloud, "You must have been driving the boys in Keaton crazy all these years, wondering what you'd be like."

"What do you mean?"

He pulled his gaze from her hair and smiled wryly into her eyes. "I mean that I've been fantasizing about running my fingers through this gorgeous mane of yours since yesterday, and I'd only been looking at it for two days."

Julie felt a warmth begin to seep through her entire body at his stirring words, and Zack instantly sensed the change in her expression and the way her body relaxed against his. Belatedly remembering that words could arouse a woman almost as well and as quickly as the most skillful sexual stimulation, Zack realized that was also the best way to accomplish his goal without driving himself to the dangerous extremes of lust that came with touching and kissing her. Softly and truthfully, he confessed, "Do you know what I was thinking last night during dinner?"

She shook her head.

"I was wondering how your mouth would taste on mine, and if your skin could possibly feel as soft as it looks."

Julie felt herself sinking into a deep, delicious sensual spell as he spread his fingers over her cheek and said, "Your skin is even softer than it looks." His thumb moved over her lips and his eyes watched the movement. "And your mouth . . . God, you taste like heaven." His hand slid inexorably down her throat, over her shoulder, then slowly covered her breast, and she dropped her gaze to the mat of dark, curly hair on his chest.

"Don't look away," he whispered, and she forced her gaze back to his. "You have beautiful breasts."

That, Julie felt, was so far from true that it made her doubt the other things he'd just said. He saw the skeptical look on her face, and his mouth quirked in a somber smile. "If that wasn't the truth," he said, his thumb moving back and forth over her nipple, "then you tell me why I'm dying to touch them and look at them and have my mouth on them right now." Her nipple tightened into a taut little bud against his thumb, and Zack felt lust begin to rage through him again. "You know it's true, Julie. You can see on my face how badly I want you."

She did see it—it was there in his smoldering, heavy-lidded gaze.

Dying to kiss her, Zack drew a long, steadying breath and bent his head, fighting to hold himself in check as he touched his tongue to her lips. "You are so sweet," he whispered. "You are so damned sweet."

Julie's restraint broke before his did. With a silent moan, she slid her hand around his nape and kissed him with all the passion building inside of her, pressing herself against his rigid length, glorying in the shudder that racked his body as his mouth opened over hers in a rough, tender kiss. With an instinct she didn't know she possessed, she sensed his desperate struggle to prevent the kiss from becoming too erotic, and the tenderness she felt was almost past bearing. Brushing her parted lips over his, she coaxed him to deepen the kiss, and when that failed, she started kissing him the way he'd done earlier. She touched her tongue to his lips and felt the gasp of his indrawn breath; encouraged by that, she let her tongue make a brief, sensuous foray in his mouth, probing lightly . . .

And she accomplished her goal.

Zack's restraint broke with a low groan as he rolled her onto her back, kissing her with a raw, urgent hunger that made her feel at once powerful and helpless. His hands and mouth claimed her body, sliding over her breasts and waist and back, and when his mouth returned to hers again, he shoved his fingers into her hair, holding her a willing prisoner. When he finally lifted his mouth from hers, Julie's whole body was on fire with desire.

"Open your eyes, little one," he whispered.

Julie obeyed and found herself staring at a muscular male chest covered with curly dark hairs. The mere sight of that chest made her pulse pound. Hesitantly, she raised her gaze from his chest and beheld the changes that passion had made in him. A muscle was moving spasmodically in his throat, his face was hard and dark, and his eyes were burning. She watched his sensual lips form two words and heard the rasp in his voice as he enunciated them: "Touch me." It was an invitation, an order, and a plea.

Julie responded equally to all three. Raising her hand she laid it on his cheek. Without taking his eyes from hers, he turned his face into her hand and slid his lips back and forth against her sensitive palm. "Touch me."

Her heart beginning to pound ferociously, she trailed her fingertips down his hard cheek, over the thick cords of his neck, to his shoulder, then lower along the rigid planes of his chest. His skin felt like satin over granite, and when she leaned forward and kissed his chest, his muscles contracted reflexively. Heady with her newfound power, she kissed his small nipples, then trailed a long kiss downward toward his waist. A half-laugh, half-groan escaped him, and he abruptly rolled her onto her back, pinning her hands beside her head, his body half covering hers. His tongue plunged into her mouth, tangling with hers, plunging and retreating in blatant imitation of what he wanted to do to her with his body, and the fire that had been building inside Julie exploded into flames. She pulled her wrists from his hands, wound her arms around him, and turned into his arms, returning his drugging kisses, stroking his shoulders and back, moaning with joy as his mouth touched her breasts. So lost was she in the desire he was skillfully building in her that she scarcely noticed when his hand reached down between her thighs until his fingers began to explore her intimately.

Clenching her eyes closed, she fought back waves of embarrassment and let herself yield to the exquisite pleasure his knowledgeable fingers were giving her.

Fighting back his rampaging desire, Zack watched the reactions flicker across her lovely face as her body submitted to the unfamiliar, intimate stroking of his fingers. Each sound she made, each restless movement of her head, each time she quivered at his touch, filled him with poignant tenderness. Each second became crystallized in his mind, as bright as a diamond. Beneath his fingers, she was opening for him, wet and warm, and he was desperate to bury himself in her. Instead he held back, and bending his head, he kissed her long and thoroughly while he slid his finger deeply into her. She wrapped her arms around his shoulders and shivered, and the convulsive movement reminded him poignantly of her earlier words to him. "Shivering is good," he whispered, increasing the depth of his exploration. "Shivering is very, very good." Around his fingers, she seemed unusually narrow and extremely tight, and he had an awful feeling that he was built too large for her, that she wouldn't be able to take his erection without being torn or hurt.

Her hands were moving over him, gaining courage, and his breath caught when she finally brushed her fingers over his rigid arousal and then took him in her hand. The moment her fingers wrapped around him, her eyes flew open in shock, riveting on his face. If the situation weren't so dire and so urgent, Zack would have chuckled at the expression in her eyes. But he was in no mood to laugh or feel flattered that he'd obviously "impressed" her with his size. In the firelight, she looked at him as if she were waiting for something—a decision from him, a movement, and all the while her fingers were driving him crazy, until he was on the verge of exploding in her hand. Her other hand lifted to his jaw, soothing away the tension, and the words she whispered to him made him melt. "You were worth waiting twenty-six years for, Mr. Benedict."

Zack lost control of his breathing. With his palms on either side of her flushed face, he bent his head to kiss her, only this time the word he whispered was hoarse with awed reverence. "Christ . . ."

With blood pounding in his ears and foreboding weighing him down, Zack eased himself on top of her and between her legs, probing at the entrance of her body, easing his way slowly into her tight, wet passage, expelling his breath at the exquisite sensation as her body expanded to take him in, her wet warmth clasping him. When he encountered the fragile barrier, he lifted her slim hips, held his breath, and lunged. Her body stiffened with the brief pain, but before he could react, her arms were around him and she was opening for him like a flower . . . welcoming him, sheathing him. Fighting to control the orgasm that was threatening to erupt, Zack moved slowly within her, but when she began moving with him, clutching him to her, his restraint broke along with his desire to prolong the act. Seizing her mouth in a plundering kiss, he drove into her, forcing her faster and faster to the peak, driving her toward it, reveling in her muffled cry as she dug her nails into his back and began to shudder convulsively beneath him. Lifting her hips higher and tighter to him, he plunged harder, driven by some uncontrollable need to be as deep within her as possible when he came. He exploded inside her with a force that tore a low groan from him, and still he kept moving, as if she could somehow empty him of the bitterness of his past and the bleakness of his future. The second climax erupted in a jolt of sensation that screamed down his nerve endings, shook his entire body, and left him weak. Spent.

In a state of boneless exhaustion, he collapsed on top of her and shifted onto his side, still joined with her. Breathless from exertion, Zack held her in his arms, stroking her spine, trying not to think, clinging to the fading euphoria as he fought to hold reality at bay, but after a few minutes, it was no use. Now that his passion was finally spent, there was no barrier between his brain and his conscience, and as he stared into the fire, he began to see all his actions and motives of the past three days in the light of glaring truth: The truth was that he had taken a defenseless woman as a hostage at gunpoint; he had blackmailed her into believing he would let her go if she took him to Colorado; he had threatened her with physical violence if she tried to escape, and when she defied him anyway, he forced her to kiss him in front of a witness, so that now the national press was crucifying her by intimating she was an accomplice. The truth was that he'd begun thinking about having sex with her the same day he'd taken her captive, and he'd been campaigning for it using every means he had at hand from intimidation to kindness to flirtation. The sickening truth was that he'd just managed to achieve his final, loathsome goal: He'd seduced the virginal daughter of a minister, a lovely, spirited, innocent human being who'd repaid all his cruelties and injustices by saving his life today. *Seduced* was much too polite a word for what he'd just done, Zack decided with sick disgust as his gaze shifted to the carpet. He'd taken her right here on the damned floor, not even in a bed! His conscience clawed at him with renewed vengeance for using her too roughly, for forcing her to take two climaxes from him, for burying himself all the way inside of her instead of using a little decent restraint. The fact that she hadn't cried out or struggled or given any sign of being either hurt or humiliated did nothing to assuage his guilt. She didn't know she was entitled to more that what she'd gotten, but he did. He'd been promiscuous as hell as a teenager; as an adult he'd had more sexual flings than he could begin to count. The entire responsibility for the mess he'd made of Julie's entire life and now, her first encounter with sex, was solely and exclusively his. And that was looking at the matter optimistically—without considering the possibility of pregnancy! It didn't take a genius to figure out that the daughter of a minister probably wouldn't consider having an abortion, so she'd either have to bear the public shame of having a baby out of wedlock, moving to another city and doing it there, or foisting his child off on her almost-fiancé to father.

Zack fully expected to be shot to death within days, or even hours, after he left the safety of this house. Now, he wished to God he'd have been caught before he ever got into the car with her. Until he went to prison, he'd never have considered involving an innocent human being in his problems, let alone pointing a gun at her or getting her pregnant. In prison, he'd obviously become a sick sociopath without conscience, scruples, or morals.

Shooting, he now realized, was too good for the monster he had become.

He was so involved with his own thoughts that it took all that time before it finally penetrated his brain that the woman he was holding in his arms was crying, and the dampness on his chest wasn't his sweat, but her tears. Speechless with remorse, Zack loosened his hold on her and let her lay back on the carpet, but she kept her hand curved round his shoulder in a death grip and her wet face pressed against his chest.

Leaning up on his elbow, helplessly trying to soothe her by brushing wayward strands of shiny hair off her wet cheek, he swallowed to clear the knot of remorse in his throat. "Julie," he whispered gruffly, "if I could undo all the things I've done to you, I would. Until tonight, the things I've done were at least done out of desperate necessity . . . But this—" He paused to swallow again and awkwardly brushed a curl off her temple. With her face still turned into his chest, he couldn't judge her reaction, other than the fact that she seemed to have gone perfectly still from the moment he began to speak. "But what I just did to you," he continued, "was completely inexcusable. There are explanations for it, but not excuses. You can't be so naive that you don't realize that five years is a long time for a man to go without . . ." Zack broke off abruptly, belatedly realizing that he was adding insult to injury by making it seem as if any woman would have suited him in his state of sexual deprivation. "That's not why I did this tonight. It was part of the reason. The main part of the reason was that I've wanted you ever since . . ." Self-disgust welled up like bile in his throat and he couldn't continue.

After a prolonged moment of silence, the woman in his arms finally spoke. "Go on," she said softly.

He tipped his chin down, trying to see her shadowy features, his brows drawing together in a puzzled frown. "Go on?" he repeated.

She nodded, her soft face brushing against his skin. "Yes. You were just getting to the good part."

"The good part?" he repeated blankly.

She looked up at him and, although her eyes were still damp with tears, there was a winsome smile on her face that made Zack's heart slam against his ribs. "You got off to a very bad start," she whispered, "by saying you were sorry we did this. And you made it much worse by saying that I'm naive and then making it sound as if any woman would have suited you just fine after five years' abstinence—"

He gazed at her while relief began to pour through his body like a balm. He knew that he was getting off much too easily, but he seized his unexpected reprieve with the grateful desperation of a drowning man grabbing at a life preserver. "Did I say that?"

"Pretty much."

He grinned helplessly at her infectious smile. "How ungallant of me."

"Very," she agreed with sham indignation.

A minute ago, she'd had him in the grip of black despair, five minutes ago she'd sent him into sexual paradise, now she made him feel like laughing. Somewhere in the back of his mind, Zack was aware that no woman had ever had this effect on him before, but he didn't want to examine the explanation for it. For now, he was content to bask in the present and ignore what little future he had left. "Under the circumstances," he whispered, smiling as he brushed his knuckles over her cheek, "what should I have done and said?"

"Well, as you know, I haven't much experience in moments like these—"

"No experience whatsoever, in fact," he reminded her, suddenly and crazily pleased by that.

"But I have read hundreds of love scenes in novels."

"This isn't a novel."

"True, but there are distinct similarities."

"Name one," he teased, distracted by the sheer joy of her.

To his astonishment, she sobered, but there was a look of wonder in her eyes as they gazed deeply into his. "For one thing," she whispered, "the woman often feels the way I felt when you were inside of me."

"And how did you feel?" he asked because he couldn't stop himself.

"I felt wanted," she said with a tiny break in her voice. "And needed. Desperately needed. And very, very special. I felt—complete."

Zack's heart constricted with an emotion so intense that it made him ache. "Then why were you crying?"

"Because," she whispered, "sometimes beauty does that to me."

Zack gazed into her glowing eyes, and he saw the kind of gentle beauty and unquenchable spirit that could almost make a man feel like crying. "Has anyone ever told you," he whispered, "that you have the smile of Michelangelo's Madonna?"

Julie opened her mouth to protest, but he forestalled her answer by giving her a hard, swift kiss. "Don't you think," she belatedly and breathlessly replied as he rolled her onto her back, "that remark is a little sacrilegious, when you consider what we just did a few minutes ago?"

He muffled a laugh against her throat. "No, but it probably is when you consider what we're about to do now."

She tipped her head down. "What's that?"

His shoulders began to shake with helpless mirth at the sheer joy of her, even while his mouth began its slow descent. "I'll show you."

Julie caught her breath and arched her hips beneath the sensual onslaught of his seeking hands and mouth.

The laughter faded from Zack's mind, replaced by something much deeper.

32

PROPPED UP AGAINST A MOUND OF FEATHER PILLOWS IN THE master bedroom's huge bed, Julie gazed at the dishes on the low table in front of the fireplace across the room. They'd eaten a late breakfast there, and then Zack had taken her back to bed and made love to her. He'd kept her awake most of the night, making love to her with a mixture of demanding urgency and exquisite tenderness that Julie found wildly exciting and tormentingly sweet. Each time he finished, he pulled her into his arms and held her close while they dozed. Now it was past noon, and she was sitting beside him, curved against his body, his arm around her shoulders, his hand lazily caressing her arm. Unfortunately, in daylight, she was finding it far more difficult to cling to the illusion that this was a little cottage where she was safe and warm in bed beside a wonderfully ordinary man who also happened to be her devoted lover. In broad daylight, she was unhappily aware that the man who made love to her with such violent tenderness and need, who groaned with passion in her arms and made her cry out and feel as if she were the only woman who'd ever done this with him, had also made love to countless movie stars and sexy socialites. That had been his world—a luxurious, frenetic world populated by rich, beautiful, talented people with the right connections.

That had been his old life, and even though he'd lost everything, she had no doubt that he would prove his innocence, now that he was free to search out the real killer—with her inexpert but willing help, if possible. Once he did that, he'd be free to return to his former life, to resume his brilliant career in Hollywood. His need of her would cease to exist then. And when that happened, when she was reduced to the status of an "old friend" of his, she knew the pain was going to be terrible.

He wasn't going to fall in love with her and make undying declarations of love. He simply needed her now, and for some reason God had meant for her to be here for him. All she could do was live each moment as it came, savor it, and memorize it for the years ahead. That meant never asking him for more than he could give, never burdening him with her feelings, and keeping as much of her heart intact as she possibly could. That meant finding a way to keep things as light and frivolous as possible. She wished she were sophisticated and experienced with men; that would have been a tremendous help to her now in accomplishing those things and a lot of others.

"What are you thinking about?" Zack asked.

She turned her head and found him studying her with a concerned frown. "Nothing too profound," she hedged with a bright, artificial smile. "Life in general."

"Tell me about it."

Trying to avoid both his searching gaze and the entire discussion, Julie moved out from under his arm and drew her knees up, wrapping her arms around them. "It really wasn't worth discussing."

"Why don't you let me decide that."

She shot him a dark look. "Have you always been so persistent?"

"It's one of my most unattractive qualities," he replied smoothly and impenitently. "What were you thinking about—specifically?"

She rolled her eyes at him in laughing exasperation, but when he continued to regard her in waiting silence, she gave in and told him a part of the truth. Perching her chin on her knees to avoid his gaze, she said, "I was thinking how strange life is. Everything can seem completely predictable, and then in one short minute—in the time it takes to decide to pull off the interstate for some coffee—everything can change."

Zack leaned his head back against the pillows, closed his eyes, and swallowed with relief. He'd thought she was reflecting on the more logical and accurate fact that he was ruining her life.

From the corner of her eye, Julie stole a quick look at his tense face and her heart sank. Laughter and lightness and sensuality were what he wanted and needed, not philosophy or anything with emotional intensity, and she resolved not to let him corner her into a discussion like this again.

He gave a deep sigh and without opening his eyes, he asked in a flat voice, "Do you want to stay here with me, Julie?"

"Are you giving me a choice?" she teased, adhering to her decision to keep things light. As soon as she said it, she saw the imperceptible tightening of his jaw, and she had the strange feeling that she hadn't given him the sort of answer he wanted this time either.

"No," he said, after a long pause, "I'm afraid not."

"Do you think I'd tell the authorities where you are if you let me go? Is that it?"

"No. If you gave me your word not to do that, I'd accept it."

"Then why?"

"Because I don't think you could stand up to the kind of relentless interrogation they'd put you through. Even if you told them I blindfolded you until we got here, they'd keep badgering you, trying to 'help' you remember something significant, and sooner or later, you'd slip without meaning to or even realizing you did."

Julie struggled to strike a balance between sincerity and humor this time. "Okay. Then I guess I'll just have to stay here in this drab little cottage and spend a few days with this exasperating, dictatorial, moody man I met who has an insatiable sexual appetite. I'll probably leave here unable to walk or stand unaided."

His eyes remained closed, but his lips quirked in a half-smile. "I am not moody."

"Exasperating, dictatorial, and insatiable though," she countered, chuckling, feeling much better and more in control of the situation and herself. "I know, let's go outside."

The grooves beside his mouth deepened into a full smile that was lazy, complacent, and smug. "Not a chance. You'll freeze your ass off out there."

"I intended to put clothes on it first," Julie primly informed him, then was dumbstruck by how easily she'd heard and responded to the lewd remark. "Fresh air and physical activity," she hastily added as his shoulders rocked with laughter at her obvious discomfiture, "cure almost everything."

"Except frostbite."

She smacked him with a pillow, laughing because she'd caught him with his eyes closed, and started to disentangle her limbs from the bedding. "Do you always have to have the last word?"

"Apparently."

"Then you'll have to carry on both sides of the conversation, because I'm going to go outdoors," she told him, pulling her robe on. "Despite the sybaritic delights of staying in here with you, I need to get some sunlight and fresh air. If I were home, I'd be outdoors with my class now for noon recess."

"Sybaritic delights," he repeated, chuckling. "A very nice turn of phrase. I like that."

"You would," she flipped back with a smile, heading for the bathroom in her room to shower and dress. Behind her he said, "Use this bathroom, it's much nicer."

33

JULIE STOOD ON ONE SIDE OF THE HUGE DRESSING ROOM mirror, beneath the twinkling brass lights that framed it, blowing her hair dry, while Zack shaved on his side of the mirror. Instead of using her smaller bathroom, which was what she thought he'd intended to do, he'd used this one, too. There was a strange sort of intimacy involved in sharing a bathroom with a man, Julie decided, even a bathroom that was the size of half her house and afforded complete privacy so long as one stayed on one's side of the mirrors. Still, the sounds were there—the sound of his shower being turned on while she was in hers, and now the sound of water running in the sink while he shaved. When she'd gotten into the shower, she'd carefully draped one of the huge fluffy towels over the clear glass door so that she wouldn't be on display if he passed by, a precaution that had proved to be wise.

Wrapped in another of the green towels, she was heading for her bedroom to get her jeans when Zack called out behind her, "Wear something from the closet in here."

Startled because they hadn't spoken since their joint occupancy of the bathroom, she turned around and saw him standing at the sink, a towel like hers knotted around his slim hips, half of his face covered with shaving cream. "No," she said, "I did that last night, and it didn't feel right." Helplessly enthralled, she watched him tip his head back and stroke the razor up his neck and jaw as he said, "Somehow, I knew you were going to argue about that."

Julie gave him a smug smile. "It's nice to win a debate with you for a change."

She walked into the bedroom and over to the chair where she'd put her clothes yesterday. They were gone. For a split second she gaped stupidly at the printed fabric on the chair as if her clothes were going to materialize, then she caught herself up short, rounded on her heel, and marched back into the bathroom, a militant look in her eye. "I am not going to wear any of the clothes in that closet!"

He slanted her an amused look before he continued stroking the razor over his cheek. "Now there's a thought to titillate an insatiable male such as myself—having you around here all day wearing absolutely nothing."

She used her teacher's voice—the cool, warning one that said, "You are pushing me too far young man." "Zack, I am trying very hard not to lose my temper—"

Zack swallowed a shout of laughter because he thought she was utterly adorable and refused to reply.

"Zack!" she said darkly, her tone growing more firmly authoritarian as she advanced on him. "I expect you to get my clothes from wherever you've hidden them this very minute."

His shoulders starting to shake with laughter, Zack leaned down and splashed water on his face, then he pulled the towel from around his neck and dried it. "And if I don't, Miss Mathison?" he said behind the towel, "Then what—do I get a detention?"

Julie had dealt with enough adolescent rebellion to know better than to show her frustration and lose valuable ground. With lofty, emphatic firm, she stated very clearly to his face towel, "I am not *negotiable* on this issue."

He tossed down the towel and turned, a glamorous white smile sweeping across his rugged face. "You have a wonderful vocabulary," he said with sincere admiration. "Why don't you have a Texas drawl, by the way?"

Julie hardly heard him. She was staring in blank shock at the living, breathing image of the sexy, charismatic male she'd watched for years on giant movie screens and television sets. Until that moment, Zachary Benedict the man had never quite looked to her like Zachary Benedict the movie star, so it had been easy to ignore who and what he had been. Five years inside a prison had hardened his face and etched lines of strain at his eyes and mouth, making him look older and harsher, but all that had changed in one night. Now that he was well rested, sexually satisfied, and freshly shaven, the resemblance was so striking that she stepped back in nervous surprise, as if from a stranger. "Why are you looking at me like I have hair sprouting out of my ears?"

The voice was familiar. She knew the voice. That was reassuring. With a mental shake, Julie forced herself to stop these ridiculous fantasies and return to the discussion under way. More determined than ever to win, she crossed her arms over her chest and said stubbornly, "I want my clothes."

He perched a hip on the edge of the long marble vanity and, mimicking her posture, he crossed his own arms over his chest, but he was grinning, not glowering. "Not a chance, sweetheart. Pick something out of the closet."

The endearment coming on the heels of his sudden change in persona from convict to movie star sounded casual and meaningless to Julie. She was so frustrated and off balance that she felt like stamping her foot. "Damn it, I want my—"

"Please," he interrupted quietly. "Wear something from the closet." When she opened her mouth to argue, he said flatly, "I tossed your clothes in the fireplace."

Julie knew she was outmaneuvered, but the thoughtless way he'd gone about it hurt and angered her. "They may have seemed like dispensable rags to a former movie star," she fired back, "but they were my clothes. I worked to pay for them, I bought them, and I liked them!"

She spun on her heel and headed for the closet, unaware that her parting shot had hit its mark with more deadly accuracy than she could ever have hoped. She marched into the closet, ignoring the dresses and skirts hanging on twenty-foot racks on both sides of her and headed for the back where she snatched down the first pair of slacks and sweater she came across. Holding them up to her waist to see if they'd possibly fit, she decided they would and unceremoniously pulled them on. The slacks were soft emerald green cashmere and the matching turtleneck sweater had delicate violets with dark green leaves woven into the full sleeves. Leaving the sweater on the outside of the slacks, she grabbed a green leather belt on her way out of the closet, paused to put it on, turned around, and almost collided with Zack's chest.

He was standing in the doorway, his hand braced high on the door frame, blocking the exit.

"Excuse me," she said, trying to walk around him without giving him the courtesy of looking up.

His voice was as implacable as his stance. "It's my fault you've had to wear the same clothes for the past three days. I just wanted you to have something else to wear so I wouldn't feel guilty every time I looked at your jeans." Wisely leaving out the fact that he'd also been longing to see her in something beautiful and fine that was worthy of her face and figure, he said, "Would you please look at me and let me explain."

Julie had more than enough stubborn courage to withstand the force of his persuasive tone, but she wasn't so angry that she couldn't understand his logic, nor was she unmindful of the idiocy of spoiling what little time they had with a pointless argument.

"I hate it when you ignore me and stare at the floor like that," he said. "It makes me feel like you think my voice is coming from some cockroach down there, and you're wondering where it is so you can step on it."

Julie had intended to graciously look up at him in her own good time, but she was no match for such humor, and she ended up collapsing against the clothes behind her and shaking with laughter. "You are completely incorrigible," she said, giggling and raising eyes swimming with mirth to his.

"And you are completely wonderful."

Julie's heart missed a beat at his solemn expression, but he was an actor, as she'd just been forcefully reminded, and it would only hurt her more later if she started treating what were only casual pleasantries to him as if they were avowals of deep affection.

When she didn't respond, Zack smiled and headed for the bedroom. Over his shoulder, he said, "Let's put on jackets and go outside if that's what you still want to do."

She gaped at him in utter disbelief, followed him, and spread her arms out wide, looking down at her clothes and making him look too as she said, "In these clothes?! Are you crazy? These cashmere slacks must have cost . . . at least two hundred dollars!"

Recalling some of Rachel's charge account bills, Zack gauged the price at more like six hundred dollars, but he didn't say that. In fact, he was so intent on getting her to go outside, which he knew she'd very much wanted to do, that he put his hands on her shoulders, gave her a little shake, and said much more than he'd meant to tell her. "Julie, these clothes belong to a woman who has department stores full of beautiful clothes. She wouldn't care in the least if you wore some of them—" Before he finished the sentence, he couldn't believe he'd been foolish enough to reveal so much. Julie's eyes were wide with shock, and he could see her mind working even before she said, "You mean you know the people who own this house? They're letting you use it? Isn't that a terrible risk for them to take, I mean knowingly harboring an escaped—"

"Stop it!" he ordered more roughly than he intended. "I didn't mean anything of the sort!"

"But I'm only trying to understand—"

"Damn it, I don't *want* you to understand." Reminding himself of the injustice of taking his anger at himself out on her, he raked a hand through the side of his hair and said with only slightly more patience, "I'll try to explain this as clearly and succinctly as I can, and then I want the subject dropped." She gave him a look that made it plain she thought his attitude and his tone were unreasonable and objectionable, but she kept silent. Shoving her hands into her pants pockets, she leaned her shoulders against the bedroom wall, crossed her ankles, and watched him with unnerving absorption.

"When you go back home," Zack began, "the police are going to question you about everything I said and did while we were together, so that they can try to figure out how much help I had escaping and where I'm going next. They'll make you go over it and over it and over it until you're exhausted and can't think clearly any more. They'll do it in the hope you'll remember something you forgot that's significant to them even if it wasn't to you at the time. As long as you can tell them the truth, the whole truth—which is exactly what I'm going to advise you to do when you leave here—you won't have anything to worry about. But if you try to protect me by hiding something from them or if you lie, you'll eventually contradict yourself, and when you do, they'll catch it and they'll tear you apart. They'll start thinking you were my accomplice from the very beginning, and they'll treat you as if you were.

"I'm going to ask you to tell one small, uncomplicated lie that should help us both without tripping you up during questioning. Beyond that, I don't want you to lie or conceal anything from the police. Tell them everything. At this point you don't know one thing that could harm me or anyone involved with me. I intend to keep it that way," he finished emphatically, "for my sake and for your own. Is that clear? You understand why I don't want you to ask any more questions?" His brows snapped together when she asked a question instead of acquiescing, but when he heard it, he relaxed: "What lie are you going to ask me to tell?"

"I'm going to ask you to tell the police that you don't know exactly where this house is. Tell them I blindfolded you after you nearly got away from me at that rest stop and that I made you lie down in the back seat for most of the rest of the trip, so that you couldn't try to get away from me again. It's believable and logical and they'll buy it. It will also help to neutralize that damned truck driver's version of what he saw; he is the only reason the police would ever suspect you of aiding and abetting my escape. I'd do anything in the world to avoid asking you to lie for me like this, but it's the best way."

"And if I refuse?"

His entire face instantly became hard, shuttered, and aloof. "That's up to you, of course," he said in a chillingly courteous voice. Until that moment, as she witnessed the change in him when he thought his trust in her was misplaced, Julie hadn't fully realized how much he'd truly softened toward her since yesterday. His teasing nonchalance and tender lovemaking weren't merely a convenient and pleasant way to while away their time together—at least some part of that was actually real. The discovery was so sweet that she almost missed what he was saying: "If you choose to tell the police where this house is, I would appreciate your remembering to also tell them that I did not have a key and intended to break into it if I couldn't find one. If you don't emphasize that, then the people who own this house, who are as innocent as you of collaborating in my original escape plans, will be subject to the same unjust suspicions that you're being subjected to because of what the truck driver said."

He wasn't trying to protect himself at all, she realized. He was trying desperately to protect whoever owned the house. Which meant he knew them. They were, or had been, friends . . .

"Would you care to tell me which choice you intend to make?" he said in that same coolly detached voice that she hated. "Or would you prefer to think about it?"

When she was eleven years old, Julie had vowed never to lie again, and she'd not broken that vow in fifteen years. Now she looked at the man she loved and said softly, "I intend to tell them I was blindfolded. How could you think I'd decide anything else?"

Relief flowed through her as she watched the tension drain from his face, but instead of saying something sweet, he gave her a scathing glare and announced, "You have the distinction, Julie, of being the only woman alive who has *ever* managed to make me feel like an emotional yo-yo dancing on a damned string from the end of your finger."

Julie bit down on her lower lip to stop her smile because it seemed wonderfully significant to be able to affect him in a way no other woman ever had. Even if he didn't like the way she did it at all. "I'm . . . sorry," she finished lamely and dishonestly.

"The hell you are," he retorted, but the edge was gone from his voice and there was a tinge of reluctant amusement in it. "You're doing your damnedest not to laugh."

Swallowing a giggle at his discomfiture, she lifted her forefinger and inspected it closely, turning it left to right. "It looks like a pretty ordinary finger to me," she teased.

"There's nothing ordinary about you, Miss Mathison," he said with that same combination of irritated amusement. "God help whoever marries you because the poor bastard's going to grow old and gray long before his time!"

His obvious and unconcerned conviction that she was going to end up with someone besides him—someone who he pitied, to boot—doused Julie's spurt of happiness and jerked her back to earth. Vowing to keep things light from this moment on and never again to read more into his words and actions than there really was, she smiled, nodded, shoved away from the wall, and switched to jaunty tennis jargon: "I think that last point you scored gives you the game, set, and match. I concede this verbal victory to you along with all our others."

Despite her casual attitude, Zack had the uneasy feeling he'd somehow hurt her feelings. A few moments later, he walked out of the bedroom and joined her at the hall closet where she was putting on the snowmobile suit she'd worn yesterday. "I'd forgotten about this outfit," she explained. "It will protect what I'm wearing. I got the other one out of my closet for you," she added, nodding toward the larger snowmobile suit hanging on the door.

Reaching for it and starting to pull it on, Zack decided their conversation in the bedroom still needed some clarification. "Look," he said with quiet sincerity, "I don't want to quarrel or spar with you, that's the last thing in the world I want to do. And I most definitely do not want to discuss my future plans or present concerns with you. I'm trying my damnedest not to worry about them myself and to simply enjoy the surprise gift of having you here. Try to understand that these next few days, here in this house with you, are going to be the last "normal" days of my life. Not that I have the slightest idea of what normal really is," he added bluntly. "But the point is, even though we both know all of this is a fantasy that's going to come to an abrupt end, I'd still like to have it—an idyllic few days up here with you to remember and look back on. I don't want to spoil it with thoughts of the future. Do you understand what I'm trying to say?"

Julie hid the sympathy and sorrow his words evoked behind a warm smile and nodded. "Am I allowed to know how long we're going to be here together?"

"I—haven't decided. No more than a week."

She tried very hard not to think of how little time that was and resolved to do exactly as he asked, but she voiced the question that had been unnerving her since she left the bedroom: "Before we can drop the entire discussion about the police and everything, there's something I have to ask you. I mean, clarify."

Zack watched a gorgeous blush creep up her cheeks, and she hastily bent her head, concentrating fiercely on shoving her heavy hair into a blue knitted cap. "You said you wanted me to tell the police everything. You can't honestly mean you expect me to tell them that we—you—I—"

"You've given me all the pronouns," Zack teased, guessing exactly what she was getting at, "could you toss me a verb to go with them?"

She pulled on her gloves, plunked her hands on her slim hips, and gave him a look of comic disapproval. "You're entirely too glib, Mr. Benedict."

"I have to be to keep up with you."

She shook her head in mock disgust and turned toward the back door at the end of the short hall. Regretting his timing, if not his reply, Zack caught up with her just as she stepped outdoors. The sky was a bright, blinding blue overhead, it was cold but not bitterly so, and the world outside looked like an arctic wonderland, with high snow drifts and low craters created by the wind. "I didn't mean to treat your last question with indifference," he explained, closing the door behind him, pulling on his gloves, and stepping carefully onto a wind-created path with a five-foot-high drift next to it. She turned and waited for him to walk the few paces to her and he lost his train of thought at the sunlit wonder of her face. With all her hair tucked severely under that cap and no makeup on except lipstick, she was a breathtaking marvel of clear porcelain skin and huge, jewel-bright sapphire eyes framed with dark lashes and graceful brows. "Of course I didn't mean you should volunteer the information that we've been intimate; that's no one's business but our own. On the other hand," Zack added, recovering his composure, "considering the fact that I was convicted of murder, they're going to assume I wouldn't hesitate to coerce or force you to have sex with me. Given the gutter mentality of most cops, when you deny I forced you, they're going to ponder and pry and try to get you to reveal that maybe you wanted me to screw you, and so I did."

"Don't say it that way!" she said, looking like a prim, outraged virgin, which, Zack realized with an inner smile, she was.

"I'm saying it the way they'll think of it," he explained. "They'll come at the subject from a dozen different, seemingly unrelated ways, like asking you to describe the house I used for a hideout, ostensibly so they can locate and identify it and search it for clues. Then they'll ask about the bedrooms and then the decor of all the bedrooms. Who knows how they'll get at you, but the minute you reveal too much knowledge—or too much feeling—about something that concerns me personally, they'll assume the worst and pounce. When I brought you here, I never imagined they'd have such good reason to think you might have become an ally. And they wouldn't have if that damned truck driver hadn't—" He broke off and shook his head, "When you nearly got away at that rest stop, I didn't think about anything beyond the immediate need to stop you. I didn't think the truck driver got a good enough look at us to recognize us later. Anyway, the harm is done and there's no point dwelling on what I can't fix.

When the cops ask you about that episode, just tell them exactly what happened. They'll think you were heroic. And you were." Putting his hands on her arms for emphasis, he said, "Listen closely to me and then I want to drop the subject once and for all: When the police are questioning you about our relationship here, if you do happen to slip in some way that reveals we were intimate, I want you to promise me something."

"What?" Julie said, desperate now to end the discussion before their mood was beyond salvaging.

"I want you to promise me that you'll tell them I raped you."

She gaped at him, open-mouthed.

"I've already been convicted of murder," he emphasized, "believe me, my reputation isn't going to be besmirched one bit by the added charge of rape. But your reputation can be saved by it, and that's all that matters. You understand, don't you?" he said studying the extremely odd look she was giving him.

Her voice was soft and very, very sweet. "Yes, Zack," she said with uncharacteristic meekness. "I understand. I understand that you are *out of . . . your . . . mind!*" Her hands hit him squarely on the shoulders, catching him by surprise and sending him flying backward, landing spread-eagle in a five foot snowdrift.

"What the hell was that for!?" he demanded, as he struggled to get out of the deep hole he'd made in the drift.

"That," she told him smiling her most angelic smile, her hands on her hips, her legs braced slightly apart, "was for daring to suggest that I would even *consider* telling anyone that you raped me!"

34

ZACK GOT TO HIS FEET AND CONCENTRATED ON BRUSHING snow off his hair and jacket and legs, but he wasn't immune to the sudden exhilaration that came from being outdoors beneath a bright blue sky, surrounded by a winter wonderland of snow-covered pine trees and in the company of a young woman who had suddenly turned playful. Grinning, he finished brushing himself off, then advanced on her slowly and purposefully. "That was extremely childish," he chided.

She watched him, backing away, step for step. "Don't try it," she said, choking on a laugh, "I'm warning you—"

Zack lunged, she twisted suddenly, tangling her leg around the back of his knee, jerking hard and up, and the next thing he knew, he was toppling backward in slow motion again, flapping his arms like a wounded goose, trying to regain his balance. He landed flat on his back with an audible thud at her feet while her laughter pealed like bells through the pines.

"That," Julie informed him, enjoying herself hugely, "was partial payment for smashing snow in my face at that rest stop." She stood over him, waiting for him to get up, but he continued to lie there, his face strangely thoughtful, his eyes focused on the bright blue sky above her head. "Aren—aren't you going to get up?" she chortled after a minute.

He turned his head toward her. "What's the point?"

"I didn't hurt you, did I?" she said cautiously.

"My pride is in tatters, Julie."

A sudden memory of all his tough-guy movies flashed through her mind, and she suddenly understood why he was embarrassed. She could tell he wasn't faking it either by the way he was lying there and the strained tone in his voice. Evidently a double who looked like him had done all his fighting for him on film, she realized, overcome with contrition for adding to his burdens with such petty revenge. "That was stupid of me. Please get up."

He squinted against the sun and said quietly, "Are you going to knock me down again?"

"No, I promise I won't. You're absolutely right, I was being childish." She reached out a hand to help him, bracing herself on the slim off chance that this was a trick and he was going to try to jerk her off her feet, but he took her assistance gratefully.

"I'm too old for this," he complained, rubbing the back of his knee and brushing off snow.

"Look at that—" Julie said, anxious to make him forget his embarrassment, pointing to the snowman she'd started yesterday. Giving him a sunny smile, she explained, "The wind made a crater over there and the snow isn't nearly as deep. How would you feel about helping me rebuild a snowman?"

"That's fine," he said and to her delighted shock, he reached for her hand and held it—two lovers walking through the snow, holding hands. "What was that you did to me back there?" he asked admiringly. "Was it some sort of karate move, or was it judo? I always mix up the two."

"Judo," she said uneasily.

"Why in hell didn't you pull that on me at that rest stop instead of running?"

She gave him an embarrassed look. "My brother Ted gives self-defense classes, but I thought the idea was silly in a place like Keaton and I refused to go. So he taught that particular move to me at home a long time ago. When you were chasing me that day, I panicked and ran. I never even remembered I knew how to do that. Today, I planned to do it beforehand, which is why I was able to pull it off so easi—" she stopped in midword, trying desperately, if belatedly, to spare his pride.

They'd reached the snowman and he let go of her hand, looking down at her with an admiring smile. "Do you know any other fancy moves like that?"

Julie knew several more. "No, actually, I don't."

Still smiling down at her, he said very softly and very gently, "Then please permit me teach you another one—" He moved so swiftly that Julie let out a startled screech at the same time she left the ground, propelled backward into a pile of snow with exactly the right of amount of controlled momentum to land her, sitting up, legs sprawled straight out in front of her, unhurt.

She gaped at him, laughing helplessly at her ignominious flight through the air, then she got to her feet. "You are really awful," she chided, pretending to concentrate on brushing the snow off while she tried to think how to get even. She turned away from him for a second, then she turned back and gave him an innocent smile as she walked toward him.

"Had enough?" he countered, grinning, his hands loosely at his sides.

"Yep, you win. I give up."

This time, however, Zack saw the sparkle in those bewitching blue eyes. "Liar," he laughed when she began slowly circling him, looking for a place to aim her body. He turned with her, both of them laughing now—Zack determined not to give her an opening when she charged, Julie knowing exactly how she intended to force him to give her one.

"Time out," she laughed, stopping and pretending to fiddle with the zipper she'd pulled down herself a minute ago. "No wonder I'm freezing. This zipper keeps sliding down."

"Here," Zack said with swift courtesy, exactly as Julie had hoped. "Let me try." He pulled off his right glove and looked down at the zipper. The moment his fingers touched the tab, Julie twisted sharply, aimed her shoulder at his chest with all her might and plowed at him like a football halfback. He moved aside, and Julie's shoulder rammed thin air with so much might that she went plowing right past him, head down. Propelled by her own force, she charged straight into the snow bank behind him, burying her head in it all the way up to her shoulders.

Trying to breath, laugh, and dig the snow off her face at the same time, she backed out of the snow bank, turned around, and leaned against it, while his laughing voice remarked, "I've never seen anyone turn their own head into a snow drill before. Interesting demonstration. Do you think we could sell the idea to a manufacturer?"

That did it. With a shriek of laughter, Julie slid down, collapsing at his feet, convulsed with laughter. Trying to catch her breath, she looked up at his grinning face. He was looming over her, his hands on his hips, a picture of vastly amused male superiority. "When you're ready to get down to serious snowman business," he smugly informed her with his chin thrust in the air as he walked off, "you—"

Julie stuck out her foot. He tripped, twisted, and went down like a felled tree. Howling with laughter, she rolled hastily aside, scrambled to her feet, and backed out of his reach. "Pride cometh before a fall—" she reminded him, giggling, backing further away as he got up.

He was smiling, but there was a dangerous gleam in his eyes as he slowly, purposefully advanced on her. "That does it!" he said softly. "That does it."

"Don't—don't do anything you'll regret—" she chortled helplessly, holding her hand out as if to fend him off as she backed away faster. He increased his pace dramatically. "Now, Zack—" she laughed shakily. "Don't you dare!" she cried, whirling to bolt for the woods as he lunged. He brought her down with a tackle around her waist before she took the first step, shoving her into the snow beneath his body, then rolling her over onto her back, straddling her at the waist. Grinning at her futile struggles, he pinned her wrists above her head with one hand. "Brat," he said cheerfully and softly, while Julie laughed harder and squirmed and struggled to catch her breath. "Give up?"

"Yes, yes, yes!" she managed brokenly.

"Say 'Uncle'."

"Uncle!" she chortled. "Uncle!"

"Now close your eyes and give me a kiss."

Her shoulders shaking with mirth, she closed her eyes and deliberately gave him a childish pucker. Cold, wet snow kissed her back—a face full of it. He smashed it all over her cheeks while she sputtered and laughed harder, then he got up. "Now," he said, grinning like a satisfied sultan as he held a hand out to help her up, "you're *sure* you've had enough?"

"Enough," Julie laughed, belatedly noticing how boyishly happy and relaxed he looked after what had been nothing more meaningful than frolicking in the snow. The last traces of tension were gone from his handsome face, and she felt a mixture of tenderness and amazement that something as ordinary as a snow fight evidently gave him so much pleasure. Of course, it didn't snow in Los Angeles, so maybe this was new to him. Either way, she realized one thing: He'd been exactly right when he said to concentrate only on enjoying the present and creating memories for the future. It was clearly what he needed.

Zack stepped through the deep snow holding her arm for support, his mind on the project ahead of him. "I assume we can get down to serious snowman business," he announced, standing in front of the formless lump of snow that had been her original snowman and studying it with his hands on his waist and his back to her, "now that you understand the supreme folly of provoking someone so much larger, stronger, and wiser than yourself. Since I've finally gotten your proper respect, I have some very specific ideas about this proj—"

A huge snowball hit him disrespectfully on the back of his head.

High on a secluded Colorado mountaintop, laughter rang out often during a long winter afternoon, startling the squirrels who watched from the trees while two humans shattered the peace, cavorting like children in the snow, chasing each other around trees, flinging a barrage of snowballs, and then got down to the business of completing a snowman that, when finished, resembled no other snowman in the annals of recorded history.

35

SEATED TOGETHER ON THE SOFA, WITH THEIR LEGS STRETCHED out, their feet propped side by side on the coffee table and a cream knitted afghan stretched over them, Julie gazed out the glass wall across the room. She was deliciously exhausted from their day outdoors, a hearty meal, and Zack's thorough lovemaking on the sofa. Even now, when the lovemaking was long over and he was lost in thought, gazing into the fireplace, she noticed he kept his arm around her, holding her close to his side, her head on his shoulder, as if he very much enjoyed having her close and touching her. She liked that, but at the moment her mind was on his "snowman" just beyond the glass wall. With the living room lights dimmed to a mellow glow and the fire in the fireplace reduced to orange cinders, she could just make out the looming, shadowy form of it. He was incredibly creative and imaginative, she thought with a smile, which shouldn't have been surprising, given his film career. But even so, a snowman ought to *look* like a snowman, not a leering mutant dinosaur.

"What are you thinking about?" he asked, his lips brushing a soft kiss on the top of her hair.

She tipped her chin up to see his face and grinned. "Your snowman. Didn't anyone ever tell you a snowman is supposed to be jolly?"

"That," he corrected looking proud and boyish as he studied it through the window, "is a snow *monster.*"

"It looks like something Stephen King would dream up. What kind of depraved childhood did you have, anyway?" she teased.

"Depraved," Zack confirmed, smiling and tightening his arm around her. He could not seem to get enough of her, in bed or out of it, and that was an unprecedented experience for him. She fit the curve of his arm as if she were made for him; in bed, she was a temptress, an angel, and a courtesan. She could drive him to unparalleled heights of passion with a sound, a look, a touch. Out of bed, she was funny, fascinating, stubborn, witty, and intelligent. She could anger him with a word and then disarm him with a smile. She was artlessly sophisticated, devoid of pretension, and filled with so much life and love that she mesmerized him at times, like when she talked about her students. He had kidnapped her, and in return, she had saved his life. He was supposed to be the wily, hardened convict, and yet she had been clever enough and brave enough to escape right out from under his nose. Then she had turned around and willingly surrendered her virginity to him with a poignant sweetness that made him ache whenever he thought about it. He was humbled in the face of her courage, gentleness, and generosity.

He was nine years older and a thousand times harder than she, and yet something about her softened him and made him *like* being soft, both of which were new experiences for him. Before he went to prison, he'd been accused by women of being everything from distant and unapproachable to cold and ruthless. Several women had told him he was like a machine, and one of them had carried the analogy to a definition: She said he turned on for sex and then turned off for everything else except his work. During one of their frequent arguments, Rachel had told him he could charm a snake and he was just as cold as one.

On the other hand, he'd never known a woman in his adult life, including Rachel, whose primary interest wasn't in her own career and what he could do for it. When you added that to all the other phonies and sycophants he'd had to endure from the time he arrived in Hollywood, it wasn't particularly surprising that he'd become cynical, disillusioned, and callous. No, Zack thought, that wasn't true. The truth was he'd already been that way before he got to Los Angeles—callous and cold enough to be able to turn his back on his old life, his family, and even his own name when he was only eighteen. Enough to banish it all from his mind and never, ever look back or discuss it with anyone—not the studio publicity office who complained at having to "invent" a whole background for him when he made his first film, not his lovers, and not his wife. His former name, his family, and his past were dead facts that he'd buried permanently and irrevocably seventeen years ago.

"Zack?"

The simple sound of her voice saying his name had a magical effect on him; his name sounded special, different. "Hmm?"

"Do you realize I don't know very much about you, even though we're . . . er, we've been . . ." Julie stopped, not certain if it was assuming too much to use the word *lovers*.

Zack heard the embarrassed uncertainty in her voice and smiled because he assumed she was probably searching for some prim and proper—ergo, wholly inappropriate—word to use to describe the unbridled passion they'd shared or else a word to use for what they were to each other, now that they'd shared it.

He smiled into her hair and said, "Which would you prefer, one word or a phrase?"

"Don't be so smug. I happen to be qualified to teach sex education all the way up to the junior high school level."

"Then what's the problem?" Zack chuckled.

Her answer banished his laughter, stopped his breath, and melted him completely. "Somehow," she said, studiously studying her hands in her lap, "the clinical term *sexual intercourse* seems all wrong to describe something that is so . . . so sweet when we do it. And so deep. And so profound."

Zack leaned his head against the back of the sofa and closed his eyes, steadying himself, wondering why she had this insane effect on him. A moment later, he managed to say in a seminormal voice, "How does the term *lovers* sound?"

"Lovers," she agreed, nodding her head several times. "What I was trying to explain is that even though we've been lovers, I don't really know anything about you."

"What would you like to know?"

"Well, for a start, is Zachary Benedict your real name, or did you change it when you started making movies?"

"My first name was Zachary. Benedict was my middle name, not my last, until I had it legally changed when I was eighteen."

"Really?" She turned her head, her soft cheek rubbing against his arm as she looked up at him. Even with his eyes closed, he could feel her watching him, see her curious smile, and while he waited for the inevitable question he knew was coming next, he remembered other things . . .

"I would never have turned you down, Zack."

"How dare you suggest I would even consider telling anyone you raped me!"

"'Sexual intercourse' seems all wrong to describe something that is so . . . so sweet when we do it. And so deep. And so profound."

Her voice intruded on the memories: "What was your last name before you changed it to Benedict?"

It was exactly the question he'd expected, the one he'd never answered for anyone. "Stanhope."

"What a beautiful name! Why did you change it?" Julie saw the tension in his jaw, and when he opened his eyes, she was stunned by the harsh expression in them.

"It's a long story," he said shortly.

"Oh," she said, and decided that it was an unpleasant enough story that it was best left completely alone for the time being. Instead, she said the first thing that came to mind to distract him: "I already know a lot of things about your youth, because my older brothers were avid fans of yours back then."

Zack looked down at her, well aware that she'd set aside her natural curiosity about his "long story," and it warmed the chill that had come over him when he'd said the name Stanhope. "They were, were they?" he teased.

Julie nodded, pleased and relieved that her change of topic had worked so quickly. "Because they were, I already know you grew up on your own, traveling around with rodeos and roping steers, living on ranches and breaking horses—did I just say something funny?"

"At the risk of ruining all your illusions, princess," Zack said, chuckling, "those stories were all products of the studio publicity department's overactive imagination. The truth is that I would rather spend two days on a Greyhound bus than two hours on the back of a horse. And if there is anything in this world that I dislike more than horses, it's cows. Steers, I mean."

"Cows!" she sputtered, and her infectious laughter rang out like music, lightening his heart as she shifted on the sofa to face him, pulling her knees up against her chest. Wrapping her arms around them, she studied him in fascinated absorption.

"What about you?" he teased, reaching for his brandy glass on the table, trying to distract her from asking the next inevitable question. "Is Mathison the name you were born with or did you change it?"

"I wasn't born with a name."

Zack stopped in the act of swallowing his drink. "What?"

"I was actually found in a cardboard box on top of a trash can in an alley, wrapped in a towel. The janitor who found me took me inside to his wife until I was warm enough to be taken outdoors again to the hospital. He felt I should be named after his wife who'd looked after me that day, and so they called me Julie."

"My God," Zack said, trying not to look as horrified as he felt.

"I was lucky! It could have been much, much worse."

Zack was so appalled, he missed the laughter in her entrancing eyes. "How?"

"His wife's name could have been Mathilda. Or Gertrude. Or Wilhimena. I used to have nightmares about being named Wilhimena."

He felt it happening again, that peculiar sharp tug on his heart, the funny ache in his chest when she smiled like that. "The story has a happy ending at any rate," he said, trying to reassure himself, which seemed ridiculous at this late date, even to him. "You were adopted by the Mathisons, right?" When she nodded, he concluded, "And they got themselves a beautiful baby girl to love."

"Not quite."

"What?" he said again, feeling stupid and dazed.

"What the Mathisons actually got was an eleven-year-old girl who'd already tried to embark on a life of crime on the Chicago streets—aided and abetted by some boys a little older than me who showed me certain . . . ah . . . tricks. Actually," she added gaily, "I probably would have had quite an illustrious career." She held up her hand and wiggled her long fingers at him, explaining, "I had very quick fingers. Sticky ones."

"You stole?"

"Yes, and I got busted when I was eleven."

"For stealing?" Zack uttered in disbelief.

"Certainly not," she said, looking stung. "I was much too quick to get caught. I got hauled in on a bum rap."

Zack gaped at her. Just hearing her use the street cant made him feel like shaking his head to clear it. And yet, the finely honed imagination that had made him a successful director was already at work, visualizing her as she'd probably been as a little girl: small and thin, he decided, from poor nourishment . . . a gamin face dominated by those huge Dondi eyes of hers . . . small, stubborn chin . . . dark hair, short and shaggy from inattention . . . feisty.

Ready to square off and take on the hard, cruel world . . .

Ready to take on an ex-convict. . . .

Ready to change her mind and stay with him in defiance of everything she had become, because she believed in him now . . .

Caught between laughter, tenderness, and amazement, he sent her an apologetic look. "My imagination just ran away with me."

"I'll bet it did," she said with a whimsical, knowing smile.

"What were you doing when you got busted?"

She gave him a long, amused look. "Some older boys were very kindly demonstrating a technique to me that would have been extremely useful in dealing with you. Except when I tried it on the Blazer yesterday, I couldn't remember exactly what went where."

"Excuse me?" Zack said blankly.

"I tried to hot-wire the Blazer yesterday."

Zack's shout of laughter rebounded off the ceiling and before Julie could react, he wrapped his arms around her, hauled her next to him, and buried his laughing face in her hair. "God help me," he whispered. "No one but I could manage to kidnap a minister's daughter who also knows how to hot-wire a car."

"I'm sure I could have done it yesterday if I hadn't had to stop every couple minutes and appear in front of your window," she informed him, and he laughed harder.

"Good Lord!" she burst out, dumbstruck. "I should have tried to pick your pocket instead!" His second shout of laughter nearly drowned out her next sentence. "I'd have done it in a second, if I'd guessed the keys were in your pocket." Inordinately pleased that she could make him laugh like this, Julie leaned her head against his chest, but as soon as he stopped laughing she said, "Now it's your turn. Where did you really grow up if it wasn't on ranches, and things?"

Zack slowly lifted his face from her fragrant hair and tipped her chin up. "Ridgemont, Pennsylvania."

"And?" Julie prompted, confused by her odd impression that he felt a special significance in answering that question.

"And," he said, looking into her puzzled eyes, "the Stanhopes own a large manufacturing company there that has been the economic backbone of Ridgemont and several surrounding communities for nearly a century."

She shook her head in disgust. "You were rich! All those stories about you growing up on your own, no family, living on the rodeo circuit—that's completely dishonest. My brothers believed that stuff!"

"I apologize for misleading your brothers," he said, chuckling at her indignant look. "The truth is, I didn't know what the publicity department had invented about me until I read it in the magazines myself, and then it was too late to raise hell—not that it would have done me any good in those days, anyway. At any rate, I did leave Ridgemont before I was nineteen, and I was on my own after that."

Julie wanted to ask why he'd left home, but she stuck to basics for the moment. "Do you have brothers and sisters?"

"I had two brothers and a sister."

"What do you mean 'had'?"

"I mean a lot of things, I suppose," he said with a sigh, leaning his head back against the sofa again, feeling her shift and return to their former position with their legs stretched out on the table.

"If you would rather not talk about this for some reason," she said, sensitive to his changing mood, "there's no need to do it."

Zack knew he was going to tell her all of it, but he didn't want to examine the myriad feelings that were compelling him to do it. He'd never felt the need or desire to answer these same questions from Rachel. But then he'd never trusted her or anyone else with anything that might bring him pain. Perhaps because Julie had already given him so much, he felt he owed her answers. He tightened his arm around her and she moved closer, her face partially on his chest. "I've never talked about any of this with anyone before, although God knows I've been asked about it thousands of times. It isn't that long or interesting a story, but if I sound strange, it's because it's very unpleasant for me and because I feel a little odd discussing it for the first time in seventeen years."

Julie kept silent, stunned and flattered that he was going to tell her.

"My parents died in a car wreck when I was ten," he began, "and my two brothers, my sister, and I were raised by our grandparents—when we weren't away at boarding schools, that is. We were all a year apart in age; Justin was oldest, I was next, then Elizabeth, then Alex. Justin was—" Zack paused, trying to think of the right words and couldn't. "He was a great sailor, and unlike most older brothers, he was always willing to let me tag along with him wherever he went. He was—kind. Gentle. He committed suicide when he was eighteen."

Julie couldn't stop her horrified intake of breath. "My God, but why?"

Zack's chest lifted beneath her cheek as he drew in his breath and slowly expelled it. "He was gay. No one knew it. Except me. He told me less than an hour before he blew his brains out."

When he fell silent, Julie said, "Couldn't he have talked to someone—gotten some support from his family?"

Zack gave a short, grim laugh. "My grandmother was a Harrison and came from a long line of rigidly upright people with impossibly high standards for themselves and everyone else. They'd have regarded Justin as a pervert, a freak, and turned their backs on him publicly if he didn't recant at once. The Stanhopes, on the other hand, have always been the complete opposite— reckless, irresponsible, charming, fun-loving, and weak. But their most out- standing trait, one that has bred truest throughout the male line, is that Stanhope men are womanizers. Always. Their lechery is legendary in that part of Pennsylvania, and it is a trait of which they have all been extremely proud. Including, and especially, my grandfather. I'm not sure the Kennedy men had anything on the Stanhope men when it came to wanting women. To give you a nonoffensive example, when my brothers and I each turned twelve, my grandfather gave us a hooker for a birthday present. He had a little private birthday party at the house, and the hooker he'd selected was brought there to attend the party and then go upstairs with the birthday boy."

"What did your grandmother think of that?" Julie said in disgust. "Where was she?"

"My grandmother was somewhere in the house, but she knew she couldn't change it or stop it, so she held her head up as best she could and pretended she didn't know what was going on. She handled my grandfather's philandering the same way." Zack grew quiet, and Julie thought he wasn't going to say anything else, and then he added, "My grandfather died a year after Justin, and he still managed to leave her a legacy of humiliation: He was flying his own plane to Mexico, and there was a beautiful young model with him when it crashed. The Harrisons own the Ridgemont newspaper, so my grandmother was able to keep that fact out of it, but it was an exercise in futility because the wire services picked it up and it was all over the big city newspapers, not to mention radio and television newscasts."

"Why didn't your grandfather simply get a divorce if he didn't care about her?"

"I asked my grandfather that same question the summer before I went away to Yale. He and I were celebrating my forthcoming college career by getting drunk together in his study. Instead of telling me to mind my own damned business, he'd had just enough to drink to tell me the truth and not so much that he wasn't lucid." He reached for his brandy and tossed down the rest of it as if he were trying to wash away the taste of his words, then he stared absently into the empty glass.

"What did he tell you?" she asked finally.

He glanced at her as if he'd almost forgotten she was there. "He told me that my grandmother was the only woman in the world he'd ever loved. Everyone thought he'd married her to merge the Harrison fortune with what was left of his own, particularly because my grandmother was a long way from being beautiful, but my grandfather said that wasn't true, and I believe him. Actually, when my grandmother grew older, she became what is sometimes called a handsome woman—very aristocratic looking."

He stopped again and Julie said in disgust, "Why did you believe him? I mean, if he loved her, it seems to me he wouldn't have cheated on her like that."

A sardonic smile tugged at his lips. "You had to know my grandmother. No one could meet her high standards, least of all my devil-may-care grandfather, and he knew it. He told me he just gave up and quit trying to do it soon after they were married. The only one of us my grandmother ever actually approved of was Justin. She adored Justin. You see," he explained with something closer to genuine amusement, "Justin was the only male in the entire family who looked anything like her people. He was fair like she was, medium height instead of tall—in fact he had a striking resemblance to her own father. The rest of us, including my father, all had the Stanhope height and features—me, in particular. I happened to have been a dead ringer for my grandfather, which, as you can imagine, did *not* endear me to my grandmother in the least."

Julie thought that was the most ridiculously biased thing she'd ever heard, but she kept her feelings to herself and said, "If your grandmother loved Justin so much, I'm sure she would have stood by him if he'd told her he was gay."

"Not on your life! She despised weakness, any and all weakness. His announcement would have revolted and shattered her." He slanted her a wry look and added, "Considering all that, she certainly married into the wrong family. As I mentioned earlier, the Stanhopes were rife with every kind of weakness. They drank too much, drove too fast, squandered their own money, then married people who had enough to revive their flagging fortunes. Having fun was their one and only avocation. They never worried about tomorrow or gave a damn about anyone but themselves, not even my own parents, who died on their way home from a drunken party, driving over a hundred miles an hour on a snowy road. They had four children who needed them, but it didn't slow them down."

"Are Alex and Elizabeth like your parents?"

He answered in a matter-of-fact, nonjudgmental voice, "Alex and Elizabeth possessed the usual Stanhope weaknesses and excesses. By the time they were sixteen, they were both heavily into drugs and booze. Elizabeth had already had an abortion. Alex had been busted twice—and of course released with nothing on the record—for drugs and gambling. In fairness to them, there wasn't anyone to try to take them in hand. My grandmother would have, but my grandfather wouldn't hear of it. We were, after all, created in his own mold. Even if she'd tried, it wouldn't have done any good because we were only at home for a couple months during summers. At my grandfather's insistence, we spent the rest of the year in exclusive private schools. Nobody really gives a damn in those schools what you do so long as you don't get caught and cause them trouble."

"So your grandmother probably didn't approve of your sister and brother, is that it?"

"That's it. They didn't like her either, believe me. Although my grandmother believed they had possibilities if they could have been gotten under control in time."

Julie had absorbed every word he'd said so far; more than that, she'd absorbed every subtle nuance of his tone and expression. Even though he'd invariably included himself when he discussed the Stanhope "weaknesses," she'd caught the disdain lacing his voice when he spoke of them. She was also drawing some very interesting conclusions from what he had not said. "And what about you?" she asked cautiously. "How did you feel about her?"

He quirked a challenging brow at her. "What makes you think I felt any differently about her than Alex and Elizabeth?"

She didn't hedge. "I sense you did."

He nodded silent approval at her acuity. "Actually, I admired her. As I said, she had impossibly high standards for us, but at least she *had* standards. She made you want to try to be something better than you were. Not that you could ever satisfy her. Only Justin was able to do that."

"You told me how she felt about your brothers and sisters. How did she feel about you."

"She felt I was the image of my grandfather."

"In *looks*," Julie corrected.

"What's the difference?" he said shortly.

Julie had a feeling she was treading into forbidden territory, but she took the leap anyway. With quiet firmness, she said, "I think you must know the difference, even if she didn't recognize it. You may have *looked* like your grandfather, but you weren't like him at all. You were like her. Justin resembled her physically, but he wasn't like her. *You* were."

When he couldn't intimidate her into retracting her opinion with a revolted scowl, he said dryly, "You're awfully confident of your opinions for a child of twenty-six."

"Nice tactic," she replied, looking impressed and matching his tone perfectly. "If you can't fool me, ridicule me."

"Touché," he whispered softly, bending his head to kiss her.

"And," she continued, turning her head so that his only available target was her cheek, not her mouth, "if ridiculing me fails, try to distract me."

His chuckle was rich and deep as he took her chin between his thumb and forefinger and firmly tipped her mouth up to his. "You know," he said with a slow smile, "you could become a real pain in the ass."

"Oh, please, no—don't resort to flattery now," she laughed, effectively preventing him from kissing her. "You know I go all to pieces when you say sweet things to me. What happened to make you leave home?"

He covered her laughing lips with his. "A *first-class* pain in the ass."

Julie went down in defeat. Sliding her hands up his shoulders, she yielded to the demanding persuasion of his kiss, putting her heart and soul into it, feeling that no matter how much she gave, he gave back more.

When he finally let her go, she expected him to suggest they go to bed. Instead he said, "Since I can't outwit you, I suppose I owe you an answer about why I left home. After that, I'd like to drop the subject of my background entirely, assuming your curiosity is satisfied?"

Julie didn't think she could ever learn enough about him to be satisfied, but she understood his feelings about this particular subject. When she nodded, he explained: "My grandfather died during my first year at college, leaving my grandmother in absolute control of his estate. She summoned Alex, who was sixteen then, Elizabeth, who was seventeen, and myself home during summer vacation and had a little gathering for the four of us on the terrace. To put it simply, she told Alex and Elizabeth that she was pulling them out of their private schools, sending them to local schools, and putting them on a strict allowance for living expenses. And she said if they so much as broke one rule of hers about drugs, drinking, promiscuity, and so forth, that she would throw them out of the house and cut them off without a cent. To fully appreciate the impact of that, you have to realize that we were accustomed to having an endless supply of money at our disposal. We all drove sports cars, bought any clothes we wanted—the works." He shook his head smiling a little. "I'll never forget the look on Alex's and Elizabeth's faces that day."

"They agreed to her decree then?"

"Of course they did. What earthly choice did they have? Besides being very fond of having and spending money, they weren't fit to do anything to earn a cent on their own and they knew it."

"But you wouldn't accept her deal, so you left home," Julie guessed, smiling a little.

His face took on that masklike look—carefully blank, deliberately expressionless, and it made her extremely uneasy whenever he did that. "That wasn't the deal she offered me." After a prolonged moment of silence, he added, "She told me to get out of the house and never come back. She told my brother and sister that if they ever attempted to contact me or if they let me contact them, they were out, too. I was permanently disowned as of that moment. So I handed over my car keys—at her demand—and walked down the driveway and down the hill to the highway. I had around fifty dollars in my checking account in Connecticut and the clothes I was wearing that day. A few hours later, I hitched a ride with a truck that happened to be loaded with props bound for Empire Studios and I ended up in Los Angeles. The driver was a nice guy and he put in a good word for me at Empire. They offered me a job on their loading dock, where I worked until some idiot director belatedly realized he needed some extras for a scene he was shooting on the back lot. I made my film debut that day, went back to college at USC and got my degree, and continued making pictures. End of story."

"But why did your grandmother do that to you and not your brother or sister?" Julie said, trying not to look as stricken as she felt.

"I'm sure she thought she had her reasons," he said with a shrug. "As I said, I reminded her of my grandfather and everything he'd done to her."

"And you never—you never heard from your brother and sister after that? You never tried to contact them in secret or they you?"

She had the feeling that of everything he'd said, the subject of his brother and sister was the one he found most painful. "I sent them each a letter with my return address when my first film was going to be released. I thought they might . . ."

Be proud, Julie thought when he fell silent. *Be happy for you. Write back to you.*

She knew from the cold, blank look on his face that none of that had happened, but she had to know for sure. She was understanding more about him with every passing moment. "Did they answer?"

"No. And I never tried to contact them again."

"But what if your grandmother intercepted their mail and they never got your letters?"

"They got them. They were both sharing an apartment and going to a local college by then."

"Oh, but, Zack, they were so young and, you said yourself, they were weak. You were older and wiser by far than they. Couldn't you have waited until they'd grown up a little and given them a second chance?"

That suggestion somehow put her instantly beyond all limits of his tolerance, and his voice took on a chilling, deadly finality. "Nobody," he said, "gets a second chance from me, Julie. Ever."

"But—"

"They are dead to me."

"That's ridiculous! You're losing as much as they are. You can't go through life burning bridges instead of mending them. It's self-defeating and, in this case, completely unfair."

"It is also the end of this discussion!"

His voice had a dangerous edge, but Julie refused to back down. "I think you're much more like your grandmother than you know."

"You're pushing your luck, lady."

She actually flinched at the bite in his voice. Wordlessly, she got up and gathered their empty glasses and took them into the kitchen, alarmed by this new side of him, the streak of ruthless finality that enabled him to cut people out of his life without a backward glance. It wasn't so much what he'd said, it was the way he'd said it and the look on his face! When he'd first taken her hostage, all his actions and words had been motivated by necessity and desperation, never unwarranted harshness, and she'd understood that. But until these last few minutes—when she'd heard the menace in his voice and seen it on his face—she'd never been able to understand how anyone could possibly think Zachary Benedict was cold-blooded enough to commit murder, but if other people had seen him this way, she could well imagine. More clearly than ever before, Julie realized that although they were intimate in bed, they were still virtual strangers. She walked into her room to get something to sleep in, turned on the overhead light, and changed in her bathroom. She was so preoccupied that instead of immediately going to his room, she sat down on her bed, lost in thought.

Several minutes later, she jumped and jerked her head around as he issued a warning: "This is a very unwise decision on your part, Julie. I suggest you reconsider it carefully."

He was standing in the doorway, his shoulder propped against the frame, arms crossed over his chest, his face impassive. Julie had no idea what decision he was referring to, and although he still looked distant, he did not look or sound like the sinister specter he'd seemed in the dimly lit living room. She almost wondered if much of what had alarmed her had been a combined trick of imagination and firelight.

She stood up and started slowly toward him, uncertain, searching his face. "Is that supposed to be your idea of an apology?"

"I wasn't aware I have anything to apologize for."

The arrogance of that was so typical of him that she almost laughed. "Try out the word *rude* and see if that touches a nerve."

"Was I rude? I didn't mean to be. I warned you that the discussion was going to be extremely unpleasant for me, but you wanted to have it anyway."

He looked as if he honestly felt that he was being unjustly vilified, but she persevered anyway. "I see," she said, stopping in front of him. "Then this is actually all my fault?"

"It must be. Whatever 'this' is referring to."

"You don't know, is that it? You are completely unaware of the fact that your tone of voice to me in there was . . ." she searched for the right words and settled for something that didn't quite fit, ". . . cold and callous and needlessly harsh."

He shrugged with an indifference that Julie suspected was partially feigned: "You aren't the first woman to accuse me of being all those things and a lot more. I'll defer to your judgment. I am cold, callous, and—"

"Harsh," Julie provided, bending her head, trying not to laugh at how ridiculous the whole debate sounded now. Zack had risked his life to save her and he had wanted to die when he thought he'd failed. He was anything but cold and callous. Those other women had been wrong. Her laughter faded abruptly, and she felt an aching remorse for what she had said and what they had all said.

Zack could not decide whether she'd actually intended to retaliate against him for some imagined slight by sleeping in here alone, which was what had originally angered him, or if she were innocent of that nauseating female ploy. "Harsh," he agreed bluntly and belatedly, wishing she'd look up so he could get a good look at her face.

"Zack?" she said to his chin. "The next time a woman tells you you're any of those things, tell her to look much closer." She raised her eyes to his and said softly, "If she does, I think she'll see a rare kind of nobility and an extraordinary gentleness."

Zack slowly uncrossed his arms, completely taken aback, feeling his heart turn over exactly the way it always did when she looked at him that way.

"I don't mean to imply that you aren't also autocratic, dictatorial, and arrogant, you understand—" she added with a choked laugh.

"But you like me anyway," he teased, brushing his knuckles over her cheek, disarmed, defused, and absurdly relieved. "Despite all that."

"Add vain to my list," she quipped, and he pulled her tightly into his arms. "Julie," he whispered, bending his head to kiss her, "shut up."

"And peremptory, too!" she stated against his lips.

Zack started to laugh. She was the only woman who'd ever made him feel like laughing while he was kissing her. "Remind me never again," he said, deciding to kiss her ear instead because it couldn't move out from under his lips, "to go near another woman with a vocabulary like yours!" He traced the curve of her ear with his tongue and she shivered, holding him close as she whispered another breathless summation of his character:

"And incredibly sensual . . . and very, very sexy . . ."

"On the other hand," he smilingly amended, kissing her nape, "there is just no substitute for an intelligent and discerning woman."

36

CARRYING A BOWL OF POPCORN, JULIE HEADED INTO THE living room, where they'd been watching a videotaped movie. They'd spent the morning and afternoon talking about everything *except* the one thing Julie was desperately interested in: His plans to find out who murdered his wife and clear himself. The first time she brought the subject up, he repeated what he'd said yesterday about not wanting to spoil their present with worries about the future. When she explained she wanted to help him however she could, he'd teased her about being a frustrated Nancy Drew. Rather than ruining their day by pressing the issue, she'd let the subject drop for the time being and agreed with his suggestion that they watch one of the movies in the large cabinet of videotapes. Zack had insisted she pick the movie out, and Julie had her first moment of unease when she realized there were several of his movies on the cabinet shelves. Unable to bear the thought of watching him making love to some other woman in one of those steamy love scenes for which he was justifiably famous, she'd chosen a movie she was almost certain he'd like and which he hadn't seen.

He seemed perfectly satisfied with her choice before the movie began, but as she discovered moments afterward, the seemingly simple pastime of movie watching was something quite different to Zachary Benedict, former actor-director. To her complete discomfiture, Zack seemed to regard a movie as some sort of art form to be minutely scrutinized, analyzed, dissected, and evaluated. In fact, he'd been so critical of it, that she'd finally invented the excuse of making popcorn just to escape his derogatory comments.

She glanced at the television set's giant-sized screen as she placed the popcorn bowl on the table and heaved a silent sigh of relief that the climactic ending was nearly over. Zack evidently didn't think it was very climactic because he looked up at her in the middle of it and said with a grin, "I love popcorn. Did you put salt on it?"

"Yep," Julie said.

"Butter, too, I hope?"

One look at his boyish grin and Julie forgot how exasperated she'd been with him a moment before. "It's swimming in it," she joked. "I'll be right back with turkish towels and something to drink."

Chuckling at her quip, Zack watched her going toward the kitchen, admiring the easy, natural grace of her walk and the subtle élan with which she wore clothes. At his insistence, she'd chosen another outfit from the closet that afternoon—a simple white silk shirt with wide, blousy sleeves and a pair of black wool crepe slacks with a pleated cummerbund waistband. When he'd first seen the clothes lying on the bed, he'd been rather disappointed that she hadn't chosen something more special for herself. When he saw her in the outfit, however, with a narrow, hammered gold belt around her slender waist, a borrowed gold bracelet at her wrist, and the collar on her shirt turned up, he'd instantly changed his mind. With her luxuriant mane of shiny hair tumbling in waves and curls about her shoulders, Julie dressed with a casual chic that suited her perfectly. He was trying to decide what sort of evening gown would most compliment that artless sophistication of hers when he realized that he'd never have an occasion to take her to the sort of social functions that required evening gowns. His days of attending Hollywood premiers, charity balls, Broadway openings, and Academy Award dinners were long past, and he couldn't imagine how he'd forgotten that. He wasn't going to be able to take Julie to any of those affairs. He wasn't going to be able to take her anywhere, ever.

The realization was so amazingly depressing that he had to struggle not to let it spoil what had been another completely memorable day with her. With a supreme force of will, he made himself think only of the evening that stretched before him, and he smiled as she sat down beside him on the sofa. "Don't you want to pick out another movie?"

The last thing Julie felt like doing was enduring another critique of a movie she selected. Since he obviously wanted to watch another one, she was willing to be present, but not accountable. Giving him a look of exaggerated horror she said, "*Pleeeease* don't make me do that. Ask me to iron your socks, ask me to starch your handkerchiefs, but do not ask me to choose another movie for you to watch."

"Why not?" he asked, looking innocent and bewildered.

"Why!" Julie sputtered, laughing. "Because you're worse than the worst critic! You tore my movie to pieces."

"I merely pointed out a few flaws in it. I did not tear it to pieces."

"You did, too! You laughed so hard during that death scene that I couldn't hear what they were saying."

"Because it was funny," he loftily replied. "The writing and acting were so bad, they were hilarious. Tell you what," he compromised good-naturedly, standing up and holding out his hand to her. "We'll collaborate. Let's pick out the next one together."

Reluctantly, Julie got up and went over to the built-in cabinet that contained more than a hundred movies, from old classics to new ones.

"Do you have any preferences?" he said.

Julie scanned the titles, her gaze riveting uneasily on Zack's own movies in the cabinet. She knew that out of politeness, if nothing else, she should suggest watching one of his, but she just couldn't do it, especially not on a television set with a five-foot screen where she'd be able to see every sexy detail of his love scene. "I—can't decide," she said after a long minute. "You pick several out and I'll choose one from those."

"All right. Give me an idea of what actors you like."

"In older movies," she said, "Paul Newman, Robert Redford, and Steve McQueen."

Zack kept his eyes on the cabinet. He was surprised that courtesy alone hadn't prompted her to include his name. Surprised and a little hurt. Although, as he reconsidered it, his movies didn't really fall into the category of "older." Completely ignoring the presence of movies by all three of those actors, he said, "These movies are mostly within the last ten years. What newer actors do you like?" He waited for her to mention his name.

"Um . . . Kevin Costner, Michael Douglas, Tom Cruise, Richard Gere, Harrison Ford, Patrick Swayze, Mel Gibson," Julie said, rattling off the names of every actor she could think of, "—and Sylvester Stallone!"

"Swayze, Gibson, Stallone, and McQueen . . ." Zack said disdainfully, piqued now beyond all rational sense, because she hadn't included his own name in her list of favorites. "How long have you had this peculiar obsession with short men, anyway?"

"Short?" Julie looked at him in surprise. "Are they short?"

"Petite," Zack unfairly and inaccurately replied.

"Steve McQueen was little?" she said, rather enchanted with his inside knowledge. "I never would have guessed—I thought he was terribly macho when I was young."

"He was macho in real life," Zack replied brusquely, turning back to the video cabinet and feigning complete absorption in its contents. "Unfortunately, he could not act."

Still bothered that Zack had not given any sign that he was determined to find the real killer of his wife so that he could resume his old life, it suddenly occurred to Julie that gently reminding him of the benefits of his former life might bolster his resolve. She tipped her head to the side and smiled. "I'll bet you knew Robert Redford, didn't you?"

"Yes."

"What was he like?"

"Short."

"He is not!"

"I didn't say he was a dwarf, I meant he isn't particularly tall."

Despite his unencouraging attitude, she continued, "I'll bet all sorts of famous actors were intimate friends of yours. . . . people like Paul Newman and Kevin Costner and Harrison Ford and Michael Douglas?"

No answer.

"Were they?"

"Were they what?"

"Intimate friends."

"We didn't make love, if that's what you mean."

Julie choked on her laughter. "I can't believe you said that! You know it isn't what I meant at all."

Zack pulled out movies staring Costner, Swayze, Ford, and Douglas. "Here, take your pick."

"The top one, *Dirty Dancing*," Julie said, smiling her approval, though she truly hated to waste any of their time watching movies.

"I can't believe you actually want to see this," he said disdainfully, shoving Swayze's movie into the videotape player.

"You picked it out."

"You wanted to see it," Zack retorted, trying unsuccessfully to sound completely indifferent. For twelve years, women had annoyed and revolted him when they hung all over him, oozing admiration and gushing that he was their favorite actor. They'd hunted him down at parties, interrupted him in restaurants, stopped him on the street, chased his car, and slipped hotel keys into his pocket. Now, for the first time in his life, he actually wanted a woman to admire his work, and she seemed to prefer every actor in the world to him. He pushed the start button on the remote controller and in silence watched the credits begin to roll.

"Want some popcorn?"

"No, thanks."

Julie studied him surreptitiously, trying to figure out what was wrong with him. Was he yearning for his old life now? If so, that wasn't all bad. Although she hated to cause him any misery, she couldn't banish the uneasy feeling that he should at least be talking about wanting to prove he didn't kill his wife, even if he didn't want to discuss with her how he planned to do it. The movie began in earnest. Zack stretched his legs out in front of him, crossed his feet at the ankles, folded his arms over his chest, and looked like a man who was *waiting* to be displeased.

"We don't have to watch this," she said.

"I wouldn't miss it for the world."

A few minutes later he let out a snort of disgust.

Julie paused with her hand in the bowl of popcorn. "Is something wrong?"

"The *lighting* is wrong."

"What lighting?"

"Look at the shadow on Swayze's face."

She looked up at the television. "I think it's supposed to be shadowy. It's nighttime."

He gave her a disgusted look that mocked her assumption and said nothing.

Dirty Dancing had always been a favorite of Julie's. She loved the music and the dancing and the refreshing simplicity of the love story; she was just starting to enjoy all that when Zack drawled, "I think they used axle grease on Swayze's hair."

"Zack—" she said in a warning tone, "if you are going to start ripping this movie apart, I'm turning it off."

"I won't say another word. I'll just sit here."

"Good."

"And watch bad editing, bad directing, and bad dialogue."

"That does it—"

"Sit still," Zack said when she moved to get up. Thoroughly disgusted with himself for behaving like a jealous adolescent and denigrating actors who'd been his friends as well as criticizing a movie that was very good in its category, he laid his hand on her arm and promised, "I won't say another thing unless it's complimentary." In keeping with that promise, Zack did not utter another word until Swayze was dancing with the girl who played his dancing partner in the movie, and then he said, "At least *she* can dance. Nice casting there."

The blonde on the screen was beautiful and talented with a gorgeous figure. Julie would have cut off a limb to look exactly like her, and she felt an absurd stab of jealousy that was harder to hide when confronted with Zack's unprecedented moodiness. Added to that, she thought his deliberate omission of Patrick Swayze's dancing talent was unjust. She was on the verge of remarking on the fact that the *women* in the films all seemed to please him when it hit her that he might have been feeling the same way when she raved about his competition. Gaping at his stony profile, she blurted, "Are you *jealous* of him?"

He slanted her a look of withering scorn. "How could I possibly be jealous of Patrick Swayze!"

Obviously he did like watching beautiful women, Julie thought, and it hurt her even though she knew she had absolutely no right to feel that way. He also hated this movie and it was obvious. Keeping her face scrupulously polite, she reached for the stack of videotapes on the table and said quietly, "Let's watch *Dances with Wolves* instead. Kevin Costner was wonderful in that, and it's a story that would appeal to a man."

"I saw it in prison."

He'd seen most of the others there too he'd said earlier today, so she didn't see what that had to do with anything. "Did you like it?"

"I thought it dragged in the middle."

"Really," she shot back, realizing now that none of the movies except his own was going to meet his approval and that she was going to have to suffer through it or else endure his mood. "How did you like the end?"

"Kevin changed it from the book. He should have left it alone." Without a word, Zack got up and headed for the kitchen to make some coffee, trying to get control of himself. He was so furious with his irrational and unjust remarks over both films that he mismeasured the amount of ground coffee twice and had to start over. Patrick Swayze had done a very nice job in the first film; Kevin had not only been a friend, but *Dances with Wolves* had earned him the acclaim he richly deserved, and Zack had been glad to see it happen.

He was so lost in his own thoughts that he didn't realize that Julie had switched movies until he was halfway across the living room with two cups of coffee. His steps faltered, and for a moment he stared in blank shock, then uneasiness at what she'd done. She'd not only switched movies and put in one of Zack's, she'd fast-forwarded it to a love scene in the middle of it and was watching it without sound. Of all the love scenes he'd ever played, this one in *Intimate Strangers,* released over seven years ago, was the most blatantly sexual. And in the moments he stood there, adjusting to the unreality of watching himself in bed with Glenn Close, in a movie he hadn't seen since it was released, Zack felt uncomfortable for the first time in his life over something he'd done in a picture. No, not *what* he'd done, he realized, but that Julie was watching him do it and with a stony blank look on her face that did not escape him. Nor did the fact that although she'd pretended not to be familiar with any of his films in the cabinet, she actually knew them well enough to know exactly where to find certain scenes in them. All in all, when he considered that cool look on her face along with the scene she'd deliberately chosen to watch, he had the distinct sensation of having been better off ten minutes ago when all he had to cope with was his own nonsensical jealousy. He put the coffee cups on the table and straightened, not certain exactly why she was suddenly so angry. "What's the idea, Julie?"

"What do you mean?" she asked with sham innocence, turning up the volume on the remote controller, her gaze riveted on the television screen.

"Why are you watching that?"

"Watching what?" Julie asked with an indifference that completely belied the twisting ache in her stomach at the sight of Zack's hands on Glenn Close's body, his mouth on hers in a torrid kiss like the ones he gave Julie, his tanned torso gleaming against the stark white of a sheet that barely covered his hip.

"You know exactly what I mean. First you acted like you'd never seen a movie of mine in that cabinet and didn't care to, and when you do decide to watch one, you go directly to a scene like this."

"I've seen all your movies," she informed him, watching the television set and refusing to look at him when he sat down beside her. "I have most of them, including this one, on videotape. I've watched this particular one at least a half-dozen times." She nodded toward the picture. "How's the lighting there?"

Zack pulled his gaze from her rigid features and flicked a glance at the television screen. "Not bad,"

"What about the acting?"

"Not bad."

"Yes, but do you think you did a good enough job with that kiss? I mean, could you have kissed her deeper or harder just then? Probably not," she answered herself bitterly. "Your tongue was in her mouth already."

She was making her point eloquently, and now that he understood what was eating her, he regretted everything he'd said that had ultimately caused her to do this. He'd never imagined it would upset her to watch him do anything in what was, to him, simply a movie, a performance given in the presence of dozens of people on a sound stage.

"How did you *feel* when she was kissing you back like that?"

"Hot," he said. When she flinched at the word he used, he clarified quickly, "The lights were hot—too bright—I could tell they were, and I was worried about it."

"Oh, but I'm sure you weren't thinking about lights right now," she nodded toward the set as if mesmerized by it. "Not with your hands all over her breasts."

"As I recall, I was thinking how much I wanted to strangle the director for making us do another take of that same scene."

She ignored that truth completely and said with a hurt that was poorly concealed beneath sarcasm, "I wonder what Glenn Close was thinking just then—when you kissed her breasts."

"She was fantasizing about murdering the director, too, for the same reason."

"Really?" she said sarcastically. "What do you suppose she was thinking about when you rolled on top of her like that?"

Zack reached out and caught Julie's chin, gently forcing her face toward his. "I *know* what she was thinking about. She was praying I'd get my elbow out of her stomach before she got the giggles again and spoiled another take."

In the face of his calm sincerity and matter-of-fact attitude, Julie suddenly felt foolish and completely unsophisticated. With an exasperated sigh, she said, "I'm sorry for behaving like an idiot. The reason I pretended I wasn't interested in watching your movies was because I dreaded seeing a scene like this with you in it. I know it's stupid, but it makes me feel—" she broke off, refusing to say jealous because she knew she had no right to be that.

"Jealous?" he suggested, and the word sounded even more revolting when spoken aloud.

"Jealousy is a destructive and immature emotion," she hedged.

"One that makes a person irrational and impossible to get along with," he agreed.

Julie said a silent prayer of thanks that she hadn't used that word and nodded. "Yes, well, watching you in those scenes simply makes me wish . . . we could watch a different movie."

"Fine, whose movie would you like to watch? Name any actor you choose." She opened her mouth to reply, but before she could, he added flatly, "So long as it isn't Swayze, Costner, Cruise, Redford, Newman, McQueen, Ford, Douglas, or Gere."

Julie gaped at him. "Who's left?"

Curving his arm around her shoulders, he drew her close and whispered his answer against her hair. "Mickey Mouse."

Julie didn't know whether to laugh or demand an explanation. "Mickey Mouse! But why?"

"Because," he murmured, sliding his lips to her temple, "I think I could listen to you rave about Mickey without getting 'irrational' again and 'impossible to get along with.'"

Trying to hide the poignant pleasure she felt at what he'd just admitted, Julie lifted her face to his and teasingly said, "There's always Sean Connery. He was wonderful in *The Hunt for Red October*."

Zack raised his brows in mocking challenge. "There's always the other six of my movies in that cabinet, too."

Now that she'd made a joke of his admission and safely avoided admitting her own jealousy, Julie instantly regretted her cowardice and the fact that she'd belittled a special moment. Sobering, she looked into his eyes and said shakily, "I *hated* watching you making love to Glenn Close."

The reward for her courage was a brush of his long fingers against her jaw and a roughtender kiss that stole her breath.

37

JULIE GLANCED OUT THE KITCHEN WINDOW AT THE SETTING sun, put down her paring knife, and went into the living room to turn on the television set. A satellite dish somewhere on the mountain enabled them to bring in CNN, and she hadn't heard the news since this morning.

Zack had spent the day clearing the drive all the way down to the bridge, using the huge tractor in the garage that spewed snow in a seventy-foot arc from a blower attached to it, and now he was taking a shower. This morning, when he first told her what he planned to do, she'd thought he intended for them to leave today or tomorrow, and she'd been seized with a panic that nearly strangled her. As if he read her thoughts, he said, "I'll tell you the day before it's time to leave." When she tried to get him to say if he already knew what day that was going to be, he replied vaguely that he wasn't certain, which gave Julie the impression he was waiting for something to happen . . . or for someone to contact him.

He was right, of course, that the less she knew, the better off they both were. He was equally right to insist they simply enjoy each moment of the time they had together and not think beyond that moment. He was right about everything, but it was impossible not to wonder and worry what was going to happen to him next. She couldn't imagine how he could hope to find out who killed his wife when his face was so well known that he'd be recognized immediately wherever he went.

Still, he'd been an actor, so makeup and disguises would be easy for him. She was counting on that to keep him safe. And she was terrified it wouldn't.

The television screen lit up, and she listened absently to some psychologist who was evidently the guest on CNN as she headed back to the kitchen. She was nearly there when she realized the psychologist was talking about *her,* and she whirled around. Eyes wide with disbelief, she walked toward the television set, staring at the subtitle on the screen that identified the speaker as William Everhardt, Ph.D. With absolute confidence, Dr. Everhardt was expounding on what Julie Mathison was going through emotionally as a result of being taken hostage:

"*A great deal of research has been done with hostages like Miss Mathison,*" he was saying. "*I myself coauthored a book on this subject, and I can tell you with all certainty, that the young lady is living through a highly stressful, but very predictable sequence of emotions.*"

Julie tipped her head to the side, fascinated to learn what was going on in her mind from this unknown expert on the subject.

"*During the first and second day, fear is the primary emotion—and a very paralyzing one, I might add. The hostage feels helpless, too terrified to think or act, but they hold out hope that they'll be rescued. Later, usually on the third day, rage sets in. Rage at the injustice being done them and at the victim role they're forced to endure.*"

With amused derision, Julie held up her fingers and counted off the days, comparing her reality with his "expert knowledge." On the first day, she had gone from fear to fury within hours and tried to slip a note to the clerk in the fast-food restaurant. On the second day, she had tried to escape from him at the rest stop—and nearly succeeded. On the third day, she'd succeeded in escaping. She'd been a little afraid and extremely nervous, but certainly not paralyzed. Shaking her head in disgust, she concentrated on Dr. Everhardt's next remarks:

"*By now, Miss Mathison has reached the stage that I like to call the gratitude-dependent syndrome. She sees her captor as her protector, almost an ally, because he hasn't killed her yet. Er—we're assuming that Benedict has no reason to do that to her. In any case, she is now furious with the legal authorities for not being able to rescue her. She is beginning to think of them as impotent, while her captor, who is clearly outwitting them, becomes an object of reluctant admiration. Added to that admiration is a profound feeling of gratitude that he hasn't harmed her. Benedict is an intelligent man with some degree of questionable charm, I understand, which means that she is very much at his mercy, both physically and emotionally."*

Julie gaped at the bearded face on the screen, caught between disbelief and hilarity at the pompous generalities being used in discussing her. Plunking her hands on her hips she advised Dr. Everhardt aloud, "You're lucky you aren't on Larry King's show! He'd never let you get away with such sweeping assumptions!" The only thing Everhardt had gotten right so far was that Zack was intelligent and charming. She couldn't believe Everhardt hadn't stopped to consider that, since she hadn't been taken hostage by crazed terrorists in a foreign country, she probably wouldn't be going through that "predictable sequence."

"She is going to need intensive psychological counseling in order to fully recover from this ordeal, and it will take considerable time, but the prognosis is good if she will seek help."

Julie could not believe the nerve of the man—now he was telling the world she was going to be a mental case! She ought to have Ted sue him!

"Of course," the moderator interjected smoothly, *"this is all presupposing that Julie Mathison was actually taken hostage rather than being Benedict's accomplice, as some people believe she is."*

Dr. Everhardt pondered that, stroking his beard. *"In my opinion, based on what I've been able to learn about the young woman, I do not subscribe to that theory."*

"Thank you," Julie told him aloud. "That remark just saved you from my megalawsuit."

She was so engrossed that she didn't register the unmistakable sound of helicopter blades until they were hovering directly overhead. Even when she heard the sound, it was so out of place in this quiet, mountain wilderness that she looked out of the window with surprise, not fear, and then it hit her. "Zack!" she screamed, turning and running. "There's a helicopter out there! It's low—" she cried, nearly mowing him down as he ran from the bedroom. "It's hovering!" She stopped cold at the sight of the gun in his hand.

"Get outside and stay in the woods!" he commanded, shoving her down the hall toward the back door, yanking a jacket out of the closet as he passed it and thrusting it at her. "Don't come near this house until I tell you to or until they take me out of here!" He racked a shell into the gun's chamber, moving down the hall with her, holding the weapon high, muzzle up, with the deadly skill of someone who knew how to handle it and was prepared to use it. When she started to open the door, he shoved her out of the way, stepped into the doorway alone, looked up, listening, then he pulled her forward. "Run!"

"For the love of God!" Julie cried stopping just outside the door. "You can't mean to shoot that thing down! There must be—"

"MOVE!" he thundered.

Julie obeyed, her heart hammering with terror as she raced around the side of the house, stumbling in the deep snow, stopping beneath the trees, then moving through them, working her way around the house until she could see Zack inside the front windows. The helicopter had circled and banked to the left, then it flew over again, and for one terror-filled moment, she thought he was raising his gun, intending to shoot through the window. And then she saw he was holding binoculars, watching the helicopter fly overhead and slowly disappear. Her knees gave out and she slid to the ground in relief, the vision of Zack holding that gun as he shoved her down the hall indelibly imprinted on her mind. It was right out of a violent movie, except this was real. She felt her stomach heave and leaned back against the tree, swallowing, trying to keep her lunch—and her fear—down.

"It's all right," Zack said, walking toward her, but she noticed the butt of the gun sticking out from the waist of his pants. "They were skiers swigging wine and circling too low."

She looked up at him but couldn't seem to move.

"Here," he said quietly. "Give me your hand."

Julie shook her head, trying to shake off her paralyzed terror with the movement and reassure him. "That's okay, I don't need any help. I'm fine."

"You're not fine!" he said savagely and leaned down grabbing her by the arms and starting to pick her up. "You're one second from fainting."

The sickness and dizziness receded and she managed a shaky smile as she stopped him from swinging her into her arms. "My brother's a cop, remember? I've seen guns before. I just wasn't . . . prepared."

By the time they got back into the house, she was so relieved that the helicopter had been harmless that she was almost giddy. "Ted used to practice stakeouts in our backyard when he was going through police academy," she tried to joke, hanging up her jacket. "It was very funny to see. I mean, how can you practice something like that?"

"Drink this," he said, walking out of the kitchen and shoving a glass of brandy into her hand. "All of it," he instructed when she took a sip and tried to hand it

PERFECT

back to him. She took another swallow and put the glass down on the counter. "I don't want anymore."

"Fine," Zack said curtly. "Now get in there and take a long, hot bath."

"But—"

"Do it. Don't argue with me. The next time I—" He started to order her to do exactly as he said the next time something like this happened, but he knew there could never be a next time. This had been a false alarm, but it had forced him to see the risk he was taking with her life and the terror he was subjecting her to. God, the terror. He'd never seen anyone look like she had when he found her out there, huddled in the snow.

It was dark when Julie walked into the living room, bathed and dressed again in a sweater and slacks. Zack was standing in front of the fire, staring into it, his jaw as rigid as granite.

Judging from his expression and his actions earlier, she correctly assumed that much of what was bothering him was probably guilt for what he'd just put her through, but the experience had affected her in a much different way, now that it was over. She was furious that people were forcing him to live like this and determined to find out what he intended to do to put an end to it. Whatever he intended, she was adamantly resolved to convince him to let her help in any way she could.

Rather than broaching the subject immediately, she decided to wait until after they'd eaten dinner. Given Zack's amazing ability to shove his worries into the background, she assumed an hour or two would be plenty of time for him to get over what appeared to be an extremely black mood. Walking forward, she said lightly, "Are you going to cook the steaks tonight on that fancy stove-top grill, or do you intend for me to do all the cooking?"

He turned and looked at her for several seconds, his face preoccupied and stony. "I'm sorry. What did you say?"

"I was discussing the cooking chores around here." Shoving her hands into the back waistband of her pants, she teased, "You are in violation of the hostage bill of rights."

"What are you talking about?" Zack said, trying fiercely to believe she'd be safe if she stayed here . . . trying to forget the way she'd looked, crouched under that tree, shaking all over, clutching a jacket to her chest . . . trying to convince himself it had been an isolated incident that wouldn't be repeated.

She gave him one of her breathtaking smiles. "I am talking about cooking chores, Mr. Benedict! Under the laws of the Geneva Convention, a prisoner is not to be subjected to cruel or unjust treatment, and making me do all the cooking for two consecutive days constitutes just that. Don't you agree?"

Zack managed an unconvincing imitation of a smile and nodded. All he wanted to do at that moment was take her to bed and lose himself in her, to forget for a blissful hour what had happened and what he now knew had to happen next, and much sooner than he'd planned.

38

JULIE'S HOPE THAT HE'D BOUNCE BACK FROM HIS SOMBER MOOD proved to be a little too optimistic this time. He was polite but preoccupied through most of their meal and now that she'd cleared the dishes away, she was resorting to the underhanded but hopefully effective trick of trying to loosen him up with wine. She had questions to ask, and she felt she had a better chance to get forthright, complete answers if he were relaxed and his guard was down.

Leaning forward, she picked up the bottle and carefully refilled his glass for the fourth time, then she handed it to him, congratulating herself on her subtlety.

Zack looked from the wine glass to her face. "I hope you aren't trying to get me drunk," he stated drily, "because if you are, wine isn't the way to go about it."

"Shall I get the Scotch instead?" Julie said, stifling a nervous laugh.

Zack stopped with the glass halfway to his lips, belatedly realizing that she *had* been deliberately trying to pour wine down him as fast as he could drink it as well as watching him with a strange look throughout most of the meal. "Am I going to need it?"

"I don't know."

With a feeling of vague foreboding, he watched her shift positions so that her back was against the arm of the sofa and she was facing him. Her opening question seemed like a joking and innocuous one: "Zack, wouldn't you say I've been a model hostage?"

"Exemplary," he agreed, smiling a little at her contagious humor and trying to match her mood.

"Wouldn't you also say I've been obedient, cooperative, pleasant, orderly and—and that I've even done more than my share of the cooking?"

"Yes to all but the 'obedient' part."

She smiled at that. "And as an exemplary prisoner, don't you agree that I'm entitled to certain . . . well . . . extra privileges."

"What do you have in mind?"

"Answers to some questions."

Julie watched his expression turn guarded. "Possibly. It depends on the questions."

A little unnerved by his unencouraging response, she nevertheless forged ahead: "You do intend to try to find out who really killed your wife, don't you?"

"Ask another question," he said flatly.

"Okay. Do you have any ideas about who the murderer really is?"

"Try a different topic."

His unnecessary curtness grated on her, not only because loving him made her extremely sensitive to his attitudes, but because Julie honestly felt she was *entitled* to answers. Keeping her voice sincere and level, she said, "Please don't brush me off like this."

"Then please pick another topic."

"Will you stop being flippant and listen to me? Try to understand—I was away on a foreign-exchange college program when your trial took place. I don't even know exactly what happened, and I want to very much."

"You'll find it all in your local library in old newspapers. Look it up when you get home."

Sarcasm was always guaranteed to rile Julie. "I don't want to read the media's version, damn it! I want to hear yours. I need to know what happened—from you."

"You're out of luck." He stood up, put his glass down, and held out his hand to her.

Julie stood up, too, so that he didn't dwarf her and automatically started to put her hand in his, thinking it was a conciliating gesture.

"Let's go to bed."

She snatched her hand back, hurt and insulted by the injustice of his attitude. "I will not. What I'm asking of you is very little compared to what you've demanded of me since we met and you know it!"

"I am not going to go through a blow-by-blow description of that day again for you or for anybody else," he snapped. "I did it a hundred times before the trial for cops and lawyers. It's over. Closed."

"But I want to help. It's been five years. Your viewpoint and memories may be different. I thought we could start by making out a list of everyone who was there the day it happened, and you could tell me about each of them. I'm completely unbiased, so I'll have a fresh perspective. Maybe I can help you think of something you overlooked—"

His scornful laugh cut her to the quick. "How could you possibly help me?"

"I could try!"

"You're being ridiculous. I spent over $2 million on lawyers and investigators and nobody could turn up a logical suspect other than me."

"But—"

"Drop it, Julie!"

"I won't drop it! I have a right to an explanation!"

"You have no rights to anything," Zack snapped. "And I don't need or want your help."

Julie stiffened as if he'd hit her, but she managed to keep her fury and humiliation out of her voice. "I see." And she did—she saw now that he had no use for her at all except her body. She wasn't supposed to think; she wasn't supposed to feel; she was just supposed to amuse him while he was bored and spread her legs for him whenever he was in the mood.

Reaching out, he put his hands on her arms to draw her forward, "Let's go to bed."

"Take your hands off of me!" Julie hissed, jerking away out of his reach. Shaking with fury and anguish at her own gullibility, she wrapped her arms around her stomach, backing around the sofa and coffee table until she had a free path to her own bedroom.

"What the hell are you trying to pull?"

"I'm not pulling anything, I've just realized what a heartless bastard you really are!" The freezing look on his face as he watched her moving away from him was nothing compared to her own fury. "You're running away when you leave here, aren't you! You have no intention of trying to find the real killer, do you?"

"No!" he snapped.

"You must be the biggest coward on earth!" Julie taunted, too furious to quail before the murderous look tightening his face. "Either that or else you killed her yourself!" She opened the door to her room, turned back, and added scathingly, "I'm leaving here in the morning, and if you intend to stop me, you'd better be prepared to use that gun!"

He raked her with a contemptuous glance. "Stop you?" he jeered. "I'll carry your bag out to the car!"

Julie slammed the bedroom door on his last words. Fighting back tears, she heard him go into his room as she stepped out of her slacks and pulled on a T-shirt from a dresser drawer. Not until she'd turned off the lamp and gotten into bed, did she let herself lose control. Dragging the thick down comforter up to her chin, she rolled over onto her stomach, and buried her face in the pillow. She cried with shame and anger at her stupidity, her gullibility, and her humiliation. She cried until her tears were spent and she was exhausted, then she rolled onto her side, staring blindly out the window at the moonlit winter landscape.

In his own bedroom, Zack pulled off his sweater, trying to calm down and forget the scene in the living room, but the effort was futile. Her words hammered in his mind, more agonizing each time he remembered the contemptuous look on her face when she called him a coward and a murderer. During his trial and imprisonment, he'd inured himself against feeling anything, but somehow she'd gotten under his guard. He hated her for that and himself for letting it happen.

Flinging the sweater onto the bed, he stripped off his pants. It hit him then—the only plausible explanation for her ridiculously volatile reaction to what he'd said in the living room—and he stopped cold in the act of dropping his trousers on the bed.

Julie thought she was in love with him. That's why she thought she had "rights" where he was concerned.

She probably thought he was in love with her. And that he needed her.

"Son of a bitch!" he swore and flung the trousers onto the bed. He didn't need Julie Mathison, and he sure as hell didn't need the added guilt and responsibility for a naive small-town schoolteacher who didn't know the difference between sexual desire and that nebulous emotion called love. She'd be better off if she hated him. He'd be better off, too. Much better off. There was nothing between them except sex, which they both wanted and she was denying them out of some infantile urge to retaliate.

With some half-formed notion of proving all that to her and himself, he stalked toward his bedroom door and pulled it open.

Julie was dismally contemplating what to do tomorrow if he reneged on his remark about letting her go when the bedroom door abruptly opened and Zack strode in, naked. "What do you want?" she demanded.

"That question," he mocked, sweeping the comforter off of her, "is almost as asinine as your decision to sleep in this bed because I won't come to heel."

Infuriated by his obvious intention to sleep with her, Julie flung herself to the opposite side of the bed and scrambled out of it, trying to bolt diagonally for the door. He caught her as she rounded the foot of the bed and pulled her against his bare chest.

"Let go of me, damn you!"

"What I want," he informed her, belatedly answering her original question, "is the same thing you want every time we look at each other!"

Flinging her head back, Julie stopped struggling, gathering her strength for her next move. "You bastard! If you even think of raping me, I'll murder you with your own gun!"

"Rape you?" he repeated with icy scorn. "I wouldn't dream of it. You'll beg me to make love to you in three minutes."

Julie struck just as his mouth seized hers: bringing her knee up hard, she aimed for his groin and then screamed as she missed and landed on her back beneath his heavy body.

Instead of retaliating for her missed blow to his groin by ramming himself into her, which she half expected him to do, she felt his fingers slide into the hair at the juncture of her thighs, probing very lightly, starting to massage and caress with familiar, unerring skill. He wasn't going to force her, Julie realized; he wanted her full cooperation, and if she gave it to him, it would be far more damaging to her pride than being a helpless victim. Her body was already responding against her will, and she was so furious with herself and with him that she actually tried to force him to finish the act before she capitulated completely. "Get it over with, damn you!"

His answer was a whisper as cold as his heart: "Why? So you can call me a rapist as well as a murderer and a coward?" His fingers searched deeper, moving. "Not a chance." His mouth closed over her nipple, tongue circling, lips tugging, and Julie swallowed a scream of furious protest. She bucked her hips beneath his hand, and he laughed softly, sliding his finger deeper inside of her so that she rode it. She stopped abruptly, tensing every muscle in her body to resist what he was doing to her, and in silence, he forced her treacherous body to betray her, his eyes watching her face every moment of the time.

"You're soaking wet," he said, and not even the calculating heartlessness of what he was doing to her could quell the quick, piercing, stabs of desire already beginning to jolt her. "Do you want me, Julie?"

She wanted him inside her, she wanted the climax she knew he could give her so badly she felt like she was going to die. "Go to hell!" she gasped.

"I am in hell," he whispered, moving his body up along hers, and for the first time he kissed her, forcing her lips to part. Abruptly, he gentled the kiss, his lips moving on hers with melting hunger as he slowly moved his hips, forcing her into vibrant awareness of his rigid erection. "Tell me you want me," he coaxed.

Trapped beneath the exquisite promise of his aroused body and the driving persistence of his mouth, her own body began to shake with uncontrollable need, and the words tore out of her in a tormented sob. "I want you—"

The moment she capitulated, he drove into her instantly, circling his hips hard, driving her to a shattering climax within moments—He pulled out while her body was still racked with shudders and lifted off of her, shrugging free of her embrace. "Three minutes was all it took," he told her.

The door slammed behind him with the finality of a death knell.

Julie laid there, physically exposed and freezing with shock, unable to absorb the proof that he was actually vile enough to prove his point this way. Emotionally spent, she crawled slowly to the head of the bed, pulled the comforter off the floor, and closed her eyes, but she did not cry, would not shed one more tear because of him. Ever.

Sitting in the dark in a lounge chair beside the fireplace in his bedroom, Zack leaned forward and put his head in his hands, trying not to think or feel. He had done what he set out to do and more; he had proved to himself and to her that he didn't need her, not even sexually. And he had proved to her that he wasn't worth caring about or worrying about after she left here in the morning.

He had accomplished his goals brilliantly, eloquently, indelibly.

He had never felt more desolate or more ashamed.

She wouldn't imagine she was in love with him after tonight, he knew. She'd hate him completely. But not nearly as much as he hated himself. He despised himself for what he'd done to her and for the unprecedented weakness that made him yearn to go to her and beg her forgiveness. Straightening in the chair, he looked across the room at the bed they'd shared, but he knew he wouldn't be able to sleep in it, not when she was lying in the next room, hating him.

39

THE KEYS TO THE BLAZER WERE ON THE DRESSER WHEN JULIE got out of bed at dawn the next morning, and the house was eerily still. The agony of last night had receded to a dull numbness, and she pulled on clothes without any particular awareness of what she was doing. All she wanted to do was get out of here and never look back, never think back. Forget everything. All her attention was focused on that, on forgetting that she had ever met him and been foolish enough to love him. She never wanted to love anyone again if it meant being this vulnerable. She got her empty nylon duffel bag out of the closet, dumped her toiletries into it, zipped it closed, and picked it up.

At the bedroom door, she paused, looking around the room to make sure she'd left nothing behind her, then she turned off the lights. Quietly, she twisted the doorknob and stepped out into the darkened living room, then she stopped short, her heart slamming in shock and dread. In the watery gray light of early dawn, she could see Zack silhouetted at the windows across the room, his back to her, his left hand shoved into his pants pocket. Jerking her gaze away, Julie turned and started silently down the hall, but before she took the second step, he said without turning: "The list of everyone who was on the set the day of the murder is on the coffee table."

Ignoring the sudden knot in her chest at the realization he'd conceded after all, she forced herself to keep walking down the hall, past the closet.

"Don't go," he called hoarsely. "Please."

Her heart twisted at the harsh desperation in his voice, but her ravaged pride screamed that only a fool without pride or sense would let him near her after last night, and she kept walking. She reached for the knob on the back door and his voice came from somewhere closer behind her, raw with emotion. "Julie—please don't!"

Her hand refused to turn the knob, her shoulders began to shake with silent sobs, and Julie leaned her forehead against the door, tears streaking down her face, the duffel bag sliding from her hand. She wept with shame for her lack of will and with fear for a love that she couldn't control. And even as she wept for herself, she let him turn her into his arms and pull her against his chest.

"I'm sorry," Zack whispered fiercely, helplessly trying to comfort her, his hands rushing over her shoulders and back, clenching her to him. "Please forgive me. Please."

"How could you do that to me last night!" she sobbed. "How *could* you!"

Swallowing, he turned her wet face up to his because it seemed to him that he didn't deserve the protection of anonymity when he admitted, "I did it because you called me a murderer and a coward and I couldn't stand it—not from you. And I did it because I'm a heartless bastard, exactly as you said."

"You're right, you are!" she choked, "and the horrible part of it is that I *love* you anyway!"

Zack pulled her back into his arms and fought down the words he knew she wanted to hear, the words he felt. Instead, he crushed her to him, kissing her forehead and her cheek, then he rested his jaw against her fragrant hair, letting her words bathe him in their sweetness. At thirty-five, he had finally discovered how it felt to be loved for no reason except for himself . . . to be loved when he had neither wealth nor fame nor even respectability to offer as an attraction . . . to be loved unconditionally by a woman of extraordinary courage and loyalty. He knew it now, just as surely as he knew that if he told her how he felt about her, those same qualities would make her wait for him for years after he disappeared. Even so, he couldn't let her sweet avowal pass without comment, and so he rubbed his cheek against her hair and tenderly spoke another truth: "I don't deserve it, sweetheart."

"I know you don't," Julie joked tearily, refusing to be crushed that he hadn't said he loved her, too. She'd heard the aching emotion in his voice just now and the torment when he thought she was leaving. She'd felt the reflexive tightening of his arms and the increased pounding of his heart against her face when she'd told him. It was enough for her. It had to be. She closed her eyes as his hand slid under the hair at her nape, his long fingers stroking sensually, but when he spoke, he sounded incredibly weary. "Would you consider going back to bed with me for a few hours and postponing our discussion about the murder until I've had some sleep? I've been awake all night."

Julie nodded and walked with him into a room she'd never expected to see again.

He fell asleep with his arms wrapped around her and his cheek against her chest.

Unable to sleep herself, Julie watched his face, her fingers toying with the soft hair at his temple. Sleep didn't soften his rugged features, she noticed, probably because he found no real peace, even then. His brows were dark and thick, and so were his eyelashes, she suddenly noticed—spiky lashes so dark they looked black. She shifted a little to make him more comfortable, but his arms tightened instantly—to prevent her from leaving, no doubt. The unconsciously possessive gesture made her smile because it was so unnecessary. She had no intention of slipping away.

Years before, she'd come across a quotation from Shakespeare that life was a stage on which each man must play his part. Ever since she graduated from college, she'd felt as if she was standing just off the stage where her own life was supposed to take place, waiting in the wings, waiting for someone to give her a cue that it was time to step on that stage and do whatever she was meant to do. Julie drew in a shaky breath, smiling a little tearily, because she'd finally gotten her cue. *Now* she knew what she had been waiting for all these years, why she had been created, and who she had been meant for. Despite all her diligent efforts to remake herself into a model of propriety, when it came to falling in love, she'd reverted to form and fallen in love with a man who was a renegade, a black sheep; a daring, cynical, tough social outcast who in some ways reminded her of the boys she'd known on the Chicago streets. She loved him with a fierce protectiveness that made her feel strong and wise and maternal; she loved him with a desperation that made her feel helpless and fragile and under his control.

And she loved all those feelings, every single nerve-racking one.

The future was an uncharted path filled with danger and censure. Julie felt utterly at peace and in perfect harmony with the entire universe.

Laying her hand against his face, she cradled him protectively close to her heart and touched her lips to his dark hair. "I love you," she whispered.

40

SEATED ON THE FLOOR BESIDE THE COFFEE TABLE WITH HER legs curled beneath her, a pencil in her hand, and a small stack of index cards she'd found in a desk at her elbow, Julie studied the list Zack had made out of everyone who'd been on the set of *Destiny* the day his wife was murdered. Beside each person's name, he'd put their job on the film crew, and she was copying each name and the person's job title onto a separate index card so she'd be able to jot notes about the individual when Zack began talking.

Zack sat on the sofa beside her, watching her and carefully suppressing his smile at the absurd notion of Julie being able to succeed where his team of expensive criminal attorneys and professional investigators had failed. Clad in cherry wool slacks and a matching bulky knit sweater, with her long hair gathered at the nape and bound with a jaunty red and yellow scarf, she looked more like an enchanting high school girl than a teacher, and she bore absolutely no resemblance whatsoever to any detective, real or imaginary. Sunlight streamed in from the windows behind her, gilding her shiny hair with russet and gold, highlighting her glowing skin and vivid coloring. She interrupted his pleasurable contemplation of her profile by turning her sapphire eyes up to his and saying in a puzzled voice, "I saw *Destiny,* although they had reshot the ending with stand-ins. Somehow, I thought there would have been lots more people involved in making a movie like that."

"There were dozens more, but they weren't in Dallas," Zack said, reluctantly turning his attention to the business at hand. "When a big picture is going to be shot on several different locations, it's more efficient to divide a large film crew into several units and assign each to a particular location. That way, they've already made whatever preparations are necessary before the cast and primary crew arrives. The people listed on that sheet were part of the Dallas unit. There were others who'd been in Dallas for an earlier segment of the filming. They aren't on that list because I'd already sent them home."

"Why did you do that?"

"Because the picture was millions of dollars over budget, and I was trying to cut corners. We were nearly finished shooting, I wasn't anticipating any need for extra hands, so I kept only the primary crew with me."

She was listening to him with an expression of such rapt fascination that a smile tugged at his lips. "Any other general questions before I tell you what happened that day?"

"Several questions," Julie said with great feeling, glancing at the titles beside the names on his list. "What is a best boy anyway? I've wondered about that every time I watch movie credits."

"A best boy is a gaffer's first assistant."

She rolled her eyes at him, trying to tease him and ease him into the discussion about the murder, which she knew he was dreading. She also thought it wise to learn all the details she could even if they seemed unimportant at the moment. "That's very informative, Mr. Benedict. Now, what's a gaffer?"

Her ploy worked, because he chuckled at her expression. "The head gaffer is both the creative and physical right-hand man of the director of photography. He's in charge of all the electricians on the set and their placement of lights for color intensity, overall values—all that."

"What's a grip?"

"Grips handle props and anything else that needs moving. A key grip also has a best boy."

"Don't, please, tell me a key grip is in charge of moving keys?" she joked.

Zack smiled at the way her romantic mouth tilted up at the corners and at the successful effort she was making to keep the discussion on a lighthearted level. "A key grip is in charge of the other grips."

"What's a production assistant?"

"A gofer, basically, who runs errands and reports to the assistant directors."

Julie nodded. "What's a producer?"

"A pain in the ass."

Her laughter sounded like bells to him, and he found himself grinning at her as she said, "Is the director of photography also a cameraman, or is he a supervisor?"

"He can be both. A good one is involved in all the elements of set design. He and the set dressers translate a director's ideas for a scene into reality and frequently improve on the original ideas."

Julie glanced at her list, found the man he'd named as the director of photography on *Destiny* and reluctantly embarked on specifics: "Was Sam Hudgins a good one?"

"One of the best. We'd worked together on several films, and I specifically asked for him on *Destiny*. In fact, I'd specified all the key crew members because we'd worked well together as a team before, and I knew I could count on them." Her smooth forehead furrowed into a frown, and he said, "What's wrong?"

"I was just wondering why anyone you'd worked with in the past would suddenly decide to frame you for murder."

"It doesn't sound very likely," Zack agreed, a little astonished—and impressed—that she'd arrived at the same conclusion his attorneys and professional investigators had and with such quick ease.

"Could you have done or said anything just before the murder to make one of them hate you so much they wanted revenge?"

"What exactly does someone do to warrant a revenge like that?" Zack countered dryly.

"You're right," she said with a quick nod of her head.

"Also keep in mind that the target wasn't really me, it was either Austin or Rachel. I was simply the patsy who went to prison for it."

Julie drew a long breath and said quietly, "Tell me exactly what happened that day. No, start with the day you found . . ." She hesitated and rephrased the question, trying to be delicate: "As I said, I was in Europe when the murder happened, but I remember seeing magazine headlines at a newsstand that said . . ."

When she trailed off into awkward silence, Zack bluntly finished the sentence for her: "Headlines that said my wife was screwing our costar and I walked in on them in the middle of it."

Julie winced at the thought of that, but she didn't look away. "Tell me everything you can remember, and go slowly so I can make notes."

Based on former experience, Zack expected the discussion that followed to be difficult and demeaning at best and infuriating at worst, but in the past he'd always been questioned by people who interrogated him either out of doubt or curiosity. Recounting the details of Rachel's murder to Julie, who believed utterly in him and in what he said, was a new and even cathartic experience, and by the time he was finished, he felt strangely unburdened.

"Could it possibly have been a freak accident—a mistake?" Julie said when he'd finally told her everything. "I mean, what if the man who was supposed to put blanks in the gun—Andy Stemple—put the hollow-point shells in it by mistake and was too much of a coward to admit it?"

Zack propped his elbows on his knees and shook his head. "Stemple didn't make a mistake, he was a firearms specialist. After a disaster during the filming of a *Twilight Zone* episode, the Directors Guild started requiring that specially trained pyrotechnics people, like Stemple, be put in charge of any firearms being used in a picture. Stemple was qualified and in charge of the gun, but because it was the only weapon being used, and because we were short-handed, he was also filling in as a grip. He'd checked the gun and loaded the clip with blanks himself that morning. Besides, those hollow-point shells didn't get in there by accident. The gun had been wiped clean of all fingerprints before it was put on the table," he reminded her. That little detail is one of the things that sent me to prison."

"But if you'd wiped the gun clean you wouldn't have been stupid enough to leave a fingerprint on it."

"It wasn't a full print, it was a smudge of my forefinger on the very bottom of the gun's butt. The prosecutor convinced the jury I'd overlooked that part of the gun when I wiped it clean."

"But," she mused, "the fingerprint actually got there when you shoved the gun a little forward on the table so it wouldn't be so visible to the camera."

It wasn't a question, she was merely restating what he'd told her as if it was gospel fact, and Zack adored her for her trust. "It wouldn't have mattered if the gun hadn't been wiped clean or if my prints weren't found on it. They'd have said I wore gloves. If I hadn't changed my mind during that last scene and Austin had been shot instead of Rachel, they'd have still said I did it. Because the fact was, and is, that *I* was the only one with a strong enough motive to murder Austin or Rachel." Zack watched her struggle to keep her expressive features from showing her sympathy and ire, and he tried to smile reassuringly at her as he said, "Have you had enough frustration for one day? Can we stop now and enjoy what's left of it? It's after five o'clock."

"I know," Julie said in a preoccupied voice. She'd spread all the index cards out across the coffee table, but it was the four cards in the bottom row, closest to her, that identified the people she was still interested in—or suspicious of. "Just a few minutes more?" she asked, and when he opened his mouth to object, she said desperately, "Zack, one of the cards on this table identifies whoever committed murder and then stood by while you went to prison for it!"

Zack was well aware of that fact, but he didn't have the heart to deny her, so he squelched his frustration and waited patiently for her to finish.

"I don't feel right about Diana Copeland," Julie began, gazing past him, lost in thought. "I think she was in love with you."

"What in God's name would give you that idea?" he replied, caught between amusement and exasperation.

"It's fairly obvious." Propping her elbow on the table and her chin on her hand, she explained, "You said she was supposed to have left for Los Angeles on the morning of the murder, but she stayed in Dallas and came out to the set instead. She told you herself that she stayed because she'd heard about what happened in the hotel room the night before and she wanted to be there in case you needed moral support. I think she was in love with you, so she decided to kill Rachel."

"And let the man she supposedly loved take the rap for it? I don't think so," he mocked. "Besides, there's virtually no chance Diana knew I intended to have Tony fire that shot instead of Rachel. Furthermore," he said, "you have an absurdly naive view of love and Hollywood relationships. The reality is that actresses are desperately in need of constant reinforcement that they're loved by *everybody*. They don't fall in love and give up everything for some man, let alone commit murder for him. They're interested in what a relationship can give *them*. They're emotionally needy, wildly ambitious, and thoroughly egocentric."

"There must be exceptions."

"I wouldn't know from personal experience," he said curtly.

"That was some great world you lived in," she countered, "if it turned you into such a cynic about people and especially women."

"I'm not cynical," Zack retorted, irrationally stung by her obvious disapproval. "I'm realistic! You, on the other hand, are absurdly naive about relationships between the sexes."

Instead of flaring at him, she studied him with eyes like deep blue crystals. "Am I really, Zack?" she asked softly.

Whenever she said his name, his heart seemed to lunge for his ribs, and to compound his discomfiture, he was discovering that the "absurdly naive" girl seated at his feet could make him repent and recant merely by looking up at him through her lashes, as she was now. "One of us is," he said irritably, and when she continued to look at him, he relented even further. "I was probably a cynic before I made my first picture." With an exasperated grin at his inability to withstand the sweet, silent pressure she was putting on him, he added, "Now, stop looking at me like you expect me to admit that I was talking like an ass before, and ask your next question. Who's your next suspect?"

Her infectious smile was his reward, then she obediently complied with his order to continue:

"Tommy Newton," she said, after glancing at one of the cards.

"Why in hell would Tommy want to kill Rachel or Austin?"

"Maybe he wanted to get rid of you permanently, and that was just a means to an end. You said yourself he'd worked with you as an assistant director on several films. Maybe he was tired of playing second fiddle and always being overshadowed by the great Zachary Benedict."

"Julie," Zack said patiently, "in the first place, Tommy had a brilliant career as a director ahead of him and he knew it then. So did I. He was eager to work with me on *Destiny*."

"But—"

"In the second place," Zack finished dryly, "he was also in love with the potential victim of that gunshot, so he wouldn't have switched the shells in the gun."

"But that could make a difference! You didn't tell me he was in love with Rachel—"

"He wasn't."

"But you just said—"

"He was in love with Austin."

"Excuse me?"

"Tommy's gay."

She gaped at him for a moment and then pointedly picked up the card belonging to her third suspect without commenting. "Emily McDaniels. You said she felt deeply indebted to you for reviving her career and, later, for giving her the role in *Destiny*. She'd known you for years, and you said the two of you spent a lot of time together whenever you were working on a film. Children— especially teenage girls—can be fiercely devoted to a male authority figure. It's possible she even imagined she was in love with you. Maybe she thought that if she could get rid of Rachel, you'd reciprocate her feelings."

Zack gave a derisive snort, but his voice softened as he talked about the girl. "Emily was sixteen years old and a sweetheart. Next to you, she was the nicest, most wholesome member of your sex I've ever known. There's no way on earth that child would have done anything to cause me trouble. But let's say you're right—she had a crush on me and was jealous of Rachel. If so, then she didn't need to bother killing Rachel, because it was common knowledge on the set that Rachel had filed for divorce and was going to marry Austin."

"But suppose she hated Rachel so much for humiliating you the night before with Tony Austin that she felt compelled to get even with Rachel on your behalf."

"The theory doesn't work. For all Emily knew, Rachel was going to fire that gun first, the way the script was written."

"Then why don't we assume that *Tony Austin* was the intended victim of the killer and work from there?"

"You can't assume that because, as I mentioned earlier, I'd made notes in my script about changing the sequence of the gun shots, and any number of people might have seen my script lying open and read what I'd written. My attorneys took depositions from the entire cast and crew before the trial, though, and everyone denied knowing I planned to change that scene."

"But let's suppose Tony Austin was really the intended victim. If so, then it's still possible that Emily is the killer. I mean, what if she was so obsessed with you that she despised Tony Austin for having an affair with your wife and humiliating you—"

"Emily McDaniels," Zack interrupted with absolute finality, "did not kill anyone. Period. She couldn't have. Any more than you could." Belatedly realizing that the cards on the bottom row were her chief suspects, Zack tipped his head toward the last card and smiled with relief that the discussion was nearly over. "Whose name is on that last card in the bottom row?"

Julie shot him a long-suffering look and reluctantly said, "Tony Austin."

The amusement vanished from Zack's expression and he rubbed his hands over his face as if he could some how rub away the violent hatred that exploded inside of him whenever he let himself think of Austin as the murderer. "I think Austin did it." He looked up at her, immersed in his own thoughts. "No, I *know* the bastard did it and then deliberately let me hang for it. Someday, if I live long enough—"

Julie recoiled from the savage sound of his voice. "But you said Austin didn't have a cent," she interrupted quickly. "By killing Rachel, who stood to get a lot of money from you in the divorce, he would have lost his chance to get his hands on your money when he married her."

"He was a junkie. Who knows what's going on in a junkie's mind."

"You said he had a very expensive drug habit. Wouldn't getting his hands on your money to pay for his habit have been his first concern?"

"I've had all I can take of this," Zack bit out. "I mean it!" He saw her face pale and immediately regretted his outburst. Softening his tone, he stood up and held his hand out to help her up, "Let's put all this away and decide what to do with the rest of our evening."

Julie fought down her instinctive reaction to his angry outburst and forcibly reminded herself that what had happened last night would never, ever happen again.

41

TEN MINUTES LATER, SHE WAS SEATED ON A STOOL BY THE kitchen counter, completely relaxed, laughing because they couldn't decide what to do with their evening. "I'll make out a list," she teased, pulling a scratch pad and pencil closer to her. "So far, you've suggested making love." She wrote that down while he leaned over her and watched with a grin, his hand resting on her shoulder. "And making love. And making love."

"Did I only bring it up three times?" Zack joked when she finished writing.

"Yes, and I agreed all three times, but we were supposed to be thinking of ideas for the early part of the evening."

It hit him then what he'd noticed earlier when she was writing on the index cards, and he complimented her on it: "Your handwriting is so precise, it looks as if the words have been typeset."

"Which isn't surprising," she replied with a smile over her shoulder, "since I spent years working on it. While other thirteen-year-old girls were starting to drool over you in your early movies, I was staying home, perfecting my handwriting."

He sounded dumbstruck at such a waste of effort. "Why?"

Turning slowly on the stool, Julie looked up at him. "Because," she said, "I was completely illiterate until I was almost twelve. I couldn't read more than a few words and I couldn't write anything other than my name and that not legibly."

"Were you dyslexic or something?"

"No, just illiterate from lack of schooling. When I told you about my youth, I left that part out."

"Purposely?" Zack asked, as she got up and walked around the counter to get a glass of water.

"It might have been deliberate, although I didn't consciously decide to hide it from you. Funny, isn't it, that I could easily admit to being a petty thief, but my mind recoiled from saying I'd been illiterate?"

"I don't understand how that could happen, not to someone as bright as you."

She gave him a look of jaunty superiority that made him long to snatch her into his arms and kiss it off her soft lips as she said loftily, "For your information, it can happen to anyone, Mr. Benedict, and being bright doesn't have a thing to do with it. One out of every five women in this country is functionally illiterate. They missed school when they were little because they were needed at home to help with siblings or because their families were itinerant or a dozen other reasons. When they can't catch up, they decide they're stupid and they just quit trying. Whatever the reason, the results are always the same: They're condemned to a life of menial jobs and welfare; they'll stick with men who abuse them because they feel helpless and unworthy of anything better. You can't imagine what it's like to live in a world filled with information that's beyond your understanding, but I remember how it was. The simplest things, like finding your way to the right office in a building, is completely beyond you. You live in a state of fear and shame. The shame is unbearable, and that's why women hide it."

"Were you ashamed, as young as you were?" Zack asked, reeling from this new insight into her childhood.

She nodded, swallowing some water, then she put the glass aside. "I used to try to sit in the front row when I did go to school, so I wouldn't have to see the other kids' faces when they laughed at me. I convinced the teachers that my eyes were bad."

Zack hardly knew how to cope with the emotions raging inside him at the thought of her as a little child, trying to bluff her way through life in a sprawling, dirty city where no one cared. Clearing his throat, he said, "You said lack of schooling was the initial cause of the problem. Why weren't you sent to school?"

"I was a sickly child, so I missed a lot of first and second grade, but the teachers liked me, so they passed me to the next grade anyway. It's an idiotic, counterproductive thing for a teacher to do, but it happens all the time, especially to 'good little girls.' By third grade, *I* knew I couldn't keep up, so I started cutting school and hanging out with kids on the streets. The foster parents I stayed with had their hands full with other kids, and they didn't catch on until I got picked up for truancy. By then, I was in fourth grade and hopelessly behind."

"So you decided to specialize in hot-wiring cars and picking pockets until the Mathisons straightened you out?"

She gave him an abashed smile and nodded as she started back toward the stool she'd vacated. "A few months ago, by accident, I discovered the janitor's wife couldn't read. I started tutoring her, and pretty soon she brought me another woman, and that woman brought another, and now there are seven, and we've had to move into a regular classroom. When they first come to class, they don't really believe I can help them. They're humiliated, defeated, and completely convinced they're hopelessly stupid. In fact my hardest task is convincing them otherwise." With a soft giggle, she added, "I had to bet Peggy Listrom that I'd babysit for her for an entire month if she couldn't read all the street signs and shop signs in Keaton by springtime."

Zack waited until she was standing beside him, then he hid his burgeoning tenderness behind a joke. "That sounds risky."

"Not as risky as letting her go through life the way she is. Besides, I've practically won the bet already."

"She's reading street signs?"

Julie nodded, and Zack watched her eyes light with excitement. "Oh, Zack, you just can't *imagine* how it feels to watch them start to learn! They go right on believing they're stupid, until suddenly—one day—they sound out all the words in a short sentence, and they look up at me with such . . . such *wonder* in their eyes!" She held out her hand, palm up. "Being able to teach them—it's like holding a *miracle* in your own hand."

Zack swallowed against the unfamiliar constriction in his throat and forced a lighthearted note in his voice. "You're a miracle, Miss Mathison."

She laughed. "No, I'm not, but I have a hunch that Debby Sue Cassidy is going to be one." Since he looked interested, Julie added, "She's thirty, and she looks like the quintessential librarian—straight brown hair, studious features, but she has worked as a house maid for Mrs. Neilson since she was sixteen. She's smart as a whip, very sensitive, very imaginative. She wants to write a book someday." Misinterpreting the reason for Zack's grin, Julie said, "Don't laugh. She just might do it. She's already amazingly articulate for someone who's illiterate. She listens to books on tape from the library all the time. I know because Mrs. Neilson mentioned it to my father. She also mentioned that when the Neilson children were little, Debby Sue used to tell them stories that kept them still for hours. That's why I was in Amarillo the day we met," Julie finished, perching on the stool and turning her attention to her scratchpad. "I was raising money to buy special teaching materials. They're actually quite cheap, but things add up."

"Did you raise the money?"

She nodded, picking up her pencil and smiling over her shoulder at him.

Helpless to keep from touching her, Zack put his hand on her shoulder and playfully nipped her ear. She laughed, then she tipped her head sideways and lightly rubbed her soft cheek against the top of his hand.

The simple, loving gesture made Zack's spirits plummet abruptly, because it forcibly reminded him that after tonight there'd be no more gestures of any kind. He should have let her go this morning, but he couldn't, not when she would have hated him forever, and the longer he kept her with him, the harder it was going to be to let her go at all. Sending her away tomorrow, when there was a chance she'd crack under interrogation, meant that he would have to step up his departure from the United States by over a week, but it was worth the added risk to know she'd be safe from any further helicopter invasions that might not be false next time.

Trying to banish the bleak mood settling over him, he said, "Whatever we do tonight, let's make it special. Festive." It took every ounce of acting ability he possessed to keep the smile on his face so she wouldn't realize he was sending her away in the morning.

Julie thought for a moment and smiled suddenly. "How about dinner by candlelight, followed by dancing—a pretend date, except we'll have it here? I'll get dressed up," she threw in for persuasion before she realized that he didn't need any persuasion at all: He was nodding with a relieved pleasure that Julie thought was surprisingly excessive for her modest idea.

"Great," he agreed at once. He glanced at his watch. "I'll use the bathroom in your room and 'pick you up' in an hour and a half. Will that give you enough time?"

Julie laughed. "I think an hour is plenty of time for whatever transformation I can make."

42

HAVING SUGGESTED THE IDEA, JULIE WAS SUDDENLY DETER-
mined to dazzle him with as much glamour as she could, and she spent more
than an hour getting ready. Hair was one asset she possessed in abundance, and
since Zack evidently gave it special notice, she washed it and blew it dry, then
she styled the heavy mass so that it framed her face, falling into casual waves and
curls from a side part and spilling over her back. Satisfied that she'd done the
best she could with that, she pulled off her robe and stepped into a soft knit
dress in a vibrant shade of cobalt blue that, on the hanger, had looked rather like
a floor-length sweater with a loosely fitted skirt, blousy bodice, and full sleeves
with white satin cuffs and sparkling blue crystal buttons. Not until Julie reached
behind her back to fasten it did she realize there was no zipper. Although the
dress had a wide cowl collar at the front, the collar draped over the shoulders
and left a deep oval of bare skin exposed at the back. The deceptive simplicity of
the design, combined with the modest front and dramatic back, was irresistibly
beautiful, and it made her *feel* beautiful, but Julie stepped back from the mirror,
hesitant to wear so fine—and undoubtedly costly—a dress that also happened
to belong to someone else.

On the other hand, she knew she didn't have many alternatives. She needed
something long to wear because she didn't have any stockings, and she drew the
line at borrowing another woman's lingerie. With the exception of this lounging
dress, everything else in the closet that was ankle length was either very fancy or
else it was pants. Moreover, the owner of these clothes was definitely taller than
she which vastly limited her choices among those things. Biting her lip, she
decided to wear the wonderful blue dress, and she uttered a silent apology to the
unknown woman with the gorgeous wardrobe.

A second foray into the closet yielded a pair of matching blue ballet slippers
that were a half size too large, but perfectly comfortable. Satisfied that she'd

done the absolute best she could with what she had to work with, she fluffed her hair and took a last glance in the mirror. She'd spent more time getting ready for her "date" tonight than she had for her role as a bridesmaid in Carl and Sara's wedding, but it was time well spent, she decided. The cosmetics with the foreign names that she'd used tonight were much different than the inexpensive ones she'd bought in the drug store in Keaton and then discarded—these were far softer and more subtle. The muted eye shadow and mascara flattered her eyes, even though it looked strange to her, and the touch of blush at her cheeks made her cheekbones seem higher and more prominent, but it was the prospect of seeing Zack and spending a lighthearted evening with him that made her eyes sparkle and her skin glow. All in all, she decided, she'd never looked nearly as nice as this. Leaning forward, she applied some of her own lipstick, then she stepped back, smiled at her reflection, and headed for the bedroom door. She'd find out the address here, she decided, and send a check to cover the cosmetics she'd used and the cost of dry cleaning the clothes she'd borrowed.

The candles were already lit on the coffee table when she walked into the living room, the fire was burning brightly on the grate, and Zack was standing at the counter, opening a bottle of champagne. She caught her breath at how handsome he looked in his borrowed dark blue suit that clung to his wide shoulders and contrasted beautifully with his snowy white shirt and patterned tie. She was about to say something when she suddenly remembered that she'd seen him dressed up once before—only in his own clothes—and she felt a sharp pang of sorrow for what he'd lost. That other time, she'd seen him on television during the Academy Awards ceremony, once when he presented an Oscar and then again when he strode up onto the stage to accept his own Oscar for Best Actor. He'd been wearing a black tuxedo that night with a white pleated shirt and black bow tie, and she remembered thinking how gorgeously, elegantly male he was, so tall and sophisticated. She couldn't recall what he'd said in his acceptance speech, but she remembered that it had been brief and very witty, because the entire audience had exploded with laughter and kept on laughing while he walked off stage.

The fact that he was now relegated to hiding like a hunted animal and wearing borrowed clothes made her feel like crying.

Even while she thought it, she realized that he never complained and he wouldn't welcome either her sympathy or her pity. Since this was supposed to be a festive, lighthearted evening, Julie resolved to make certain it was. Feeling a little shy and self-conscious, she shoved her hands into the pockets concealed in the side seams of her dress and stepped forward. "Hi," she said with a bright smile.

Zack looked up, his eyes riveting on her, and the champagne he was pouring began to spill over the side of the glass. "My God," he said in an awed, husky whisper, his gaze moving slowly down her face and hair and body. "How could you possibly be jealous of Glenn Close?"

Not until that moment did Julie realize that was *exactly* why she'd wanted to dress up and put on makeup and fix her hair: She'd been trying to compete with the glamorous women he'd known on more even ground. "You're spilling the champagne," she said softly, so pleased she hardly knew how to behave.

He swore under his breath, jerked the bottle upright, and reached for a dish towel to mop it up.

"Zack?"

"What?" he said ruefully over his shoulder, picking up the glasses.

"How could you possibly have been jealous of Patrick Swayze?"

The glamour of his sudden white smile made it clear he was as pleased by her compliment as she was by his. "I honestly don't know," he joked.

"Which singers did you choose?" Julie teased after their candlelit dinner as he slid CDs into the player. "Because if you picked out Mickey Mouse, I'm not going to dance with you."

"Yes, you will."

"What makes you so sure?"

"You like dancing with me."

Despite the playful exchange, Julie was well aware that his mood had been disintegrating during their meal. Although he'd specifically asked her to treat the evening as a festive occasion, there was an indefinable tension and a grimness in his features that were becoming more pronounced as the evening wore on. She told herself it was their discussion of the murder that had caused his strange mood, because the only other explanation that came to her mind was that he was thinking about sending her away, and that she could not bear to consider. Despite her desire to stay with him, she knew perfectly well that the final decision was not going to be hers to make. And even though she was in love with him, she had no idea how he really felt about her, except that he very much liked having her around. Here.

Behind her on the stereo, Barbra Streisand's voice lifted effortlessly into the first bars of an intensely romantic song, and Julie tried again to shake off her foreboding as Zack opened his arms to her. "That's definitely not Mickey Mouse's voice," he pointed out. "Will she do?"

Julie nodded, smiling with pleasure. "Streisand is my absolute favorite singer."

"Mine, too." Zack slid his arm around her waist, moving her closer to him.

"If I had a voice like hers," Julie said, talking to keep her worries at bay, "I'd sing just to hear myself. I'd sing when I answered the door and used the telephone."

"She's phenomenal," Zack agreed. "Operatic sopranos are a dime a dozen, but Barbra is . . . unique, incomparable."

Julie suddenly realized his hand was roving slowly up her bare back; she saw the banked fires in his eyes kindling slowly into flame, and deep within her, she felt the answering stirrings of longing begin again—a longing for the tormenting sweetness of his touch, for the stormy insistence of his kiss, and the shattering joy of his body possessing hers. How thrilling it was to know she was going to have all that before the night ended and to be able to savor and prolong the moment, just as she sensed Zack also wanted to do. But was she going to have all this tomorrow night and the night after, she wondered, struggling to hold down her panic over what her intuition was telling her was behind his somber mood. "Did you know her?" she asked.

"Barbra?"

Julie nodded.

"Yes, I used to know her."

"What is she like? I read somewhere that she isn't very nice to people who work with her."

Zack thought for a moment, trying to explain. "She has a gift unlike anyone else's in the world," he said after a moment. "She knows how she wants to use it, and she doesn't like other people treating her as if they know better than she how to do that. In short, she doesn't suffer fools easily."

"You liked her, didn't you?"

"I liked her very much."

Julie listened to the poignant words of the song, wondering if he was noticing them, too, or if he, like most men, merely listened to the music and ignored lyrics. "Pretty song," she said because she desperately wanted him to hear the words as if they came from her.

"Beautiful lyrics," Zack agreed, trying to steady himself, to tell himself that what he was feeling would soon fade when he was away from her. He gazed at her face, and the words of Streisand's song seem to pierce his heart:

> *Those tomorrows waiting deep in your eyes—*
> *In the world of love you keep in your eyes—*
> *I'll awaken what's asleep in your eyes.*
> *It may take a kiss or two.*

Through all of my life . . .
Summer, winter, spring, and fall of my life . . .
All I ever will recall of my life, is all of my life.
With you.

He was actually relieved when Streisand's voice faded and a Whitney Houston/Jermaine Jackson duet began to play. But Julie chose that moment to lift her cheek from his chest and look up at him, and as he looked into her eyes and heard the lyrics of the song, he felt his chest tighten.

Like a candle burning bright—
Love is glowing in your eyes.
A flame to light our way
that burns brighter every day.

I was words without a tune,
I was a song still unsung.
A poem with no rhyme, a dancer out of time . . .
But now there's you.
And nobody loves me like you do.

When the song came to an end, she drew a shaky breath, and he realized she was trying to pull out of the music's spell by picking up their conversation about their mutual favorites. "What's your favorite sport, Zack?"

Zack tipped her chin up. "My favorite sport," he said in an aching, husky voice he scarcely recognized as his own, "is making love to you."

Her eyes darkened with a love she wasn't trying to conceal from him any more. "What's your favorite food?" she asked shakily.

In answer, Zack bent his head and touched her lips in a soft kiss. "You are." And in that moment, he realized that sending her out of his life tomorrow was going to be harder than it had been to hear the prison gates clanging shut behind him five years ago. Without realizing what he was doing, he tightened his arms around her, buried his face in her hair, and squeezed his eyes closed.

Her hand touched his face, her fingers spreading over his rigid jaw, and her voice was shattered. "You're planning to send me home tomorrow, aren't you?"

"Yes."

Julie heard the absolute finality in the word, and she was so attuned to him that she knew it was going to be futile to argue, but she did it anyway. "I don't want to go!"

He lifted his head, and even though his voice was still soft, it was steadier and more resolute. "Don't make it harder than it already is."

Julie wondered desolately how it could possibly be any harder, but she swallowed back that futile protest and did as he asked for the time being. She went to bed with him when he asked and tried to smile when he asked. After he'd brought them both to a shattering climax, she turned in his arms and whispered, "I love you. I love—"

His fingertips covered her lips, silencing the words when she tried to say them again. "Don't."

Julie dragged her gaze from his and bent her head, staring at his chest. She wished he would say it back to her even though he didn't mean it. She wanted to hear the words from him, but she didn't ask because she knew he would refuse.

43

THE BLAZER'S MOTOR WAS IDLING, EXHAUST CURLING THICKLY from its tailpipe into the frosty air of dawn as they stood beside the car. "There's no snow in the weather forecast," Zack said, glancing up at the faint pink sunrise streaking the sky as he reached around the steering wheel and put a thermos full of coffee on the passenger seat beside it. He looked down at her, his expression composed. "You should have clear roads all the way back to Texas."

Julie understood the rules for this departure because he'd made them clear this morning—no tears, no regrets—and she was trying desperately to seem composed. "I'll be careful."

"Don't speed," he said. As he spoke, he reached out and pulled the zipper of her jacket up higher and then smoothed the collar up closer to her chin. The simple gesture almost made her cry. "You drive too damned fast."

"I won't speed."

"Try to get as far from here as possible without being recognized," he reminded her again, taking her sunglasses from her hand and sliding them onto her nose. "Once you make it across the Oklahoma line, pull into the first rest stop you pass and leave the car in front of it. Stay out of sight for fifteen minutes, then go straight to the pay phones and call your family. The Feds will be listening in on the conversation, so sound as nervous and confused as you can. Tell them I left you at the rest stop on the floor of the back seat, blindfolded, and that I vanished and you've gotten free. Tell them you're coming home. Once you get home, stick strictly with the truth."

He'd already taken a neck scarf from the house, knotted it as if it had been tied around her head and tossed it in the car this morning. Julie swallowed and nodded because there was nothing left to do or to say—at least, nothing that he wanted to hear.

"Any questions?" he asked.

Julie shook her head.

"Good. Now, kiss me good-bye."

Julie leaned up on her toes to kiss him and was surprised when his arms closed around her with stunning force, but his kiss was brief, then he set her away from him. "It's time," he said flatly.

She nodded but couldn't seem to move, and her resolve not to make any sort of uncomfortable scene cracked a little. "You'll write to me, won't you?"

"No."

"But you could let me know how you are," she said desperately, "even if you can't tell me where you are. I have to know you're safe! You said yourself they won't watch my mail for very long, if at all."

"If I'm caught, you'll hear about it on the news within hours. If you don't, you'll know I'm safe."

"But *why* can't you write to me?" she burst out and instantly regretted it when his face became stiff and aloof.

"No letters, Julie! It's over when you leave here today. *We're* over." The words lashed her like whips even though there was no unkindness in his tone. "Tomorrow morning, you are to pick up your old life where you left it. Pretend none of this ever happened, and you'll forget it within weeks."

"Maybe you'll be able to do that, but I won't," she said, hating the sound of pleading and tears in her voice. She shook her head as if to negate her words and turned toward the car, angrily brushing her shoulder against her wet eye. "I'm leaving before I make an even bigger fool of myself," she choked.

"Don't," he whispered harshly, catching her arm and stopping her from leaving. "Not like this." She looked up into his fathomless eyes, and for the first time, Julie wasn't so certain he was handling this morning's leave-taking as easily as she thought. Putting his hand against the side of her face, he smoothed her hair back and said solemnly, "The only foolish thing you've done in the last week is caring too much about me. Everything else you said and did was . . . right. It was perfect."

Closing her eyes, fighting back tears, Julie turned her face into his hand and kissed his palm as he'd kissed hers once before and she whispered against it, "I love you so much."

He jerked his hand away, and his voice turned condescendingly amused. "You don't love me, Julie. You're naive and inexperienced, and you don't know the difference between good sex and real love. Now be a good girl, go home where you belong, and forget about me. That's exactly what I want you to do."

She felt as if he'd slapped her, but her wounded pride forced her chin up. "You're right," she said with quiet dignity, getting into the car. "It's time to return to reality."

Zack watched her car disappear around the first curve and vanish from view between the towering snowdrifts. He remained there long after she was gone, until the freezing wind finally forced him to remember that he was standing outside in a light jacket. He'd hurt her because he *had* to do it, he reminded himself again as he turned to the house. He couldn't let her waste one extra moment of her precious life loving him or missing him or waiting for him. He'd done the right thing, the noble thing, by ridiculing her love.

He went into the kitchen, listlessly picked up the coffee pot, and reached for a mug from the cabinet, then he saw the mug Julie had used that morning, sitting on the counter top. He reached out slowly and picked it up, then he pressed the rim to his cheek.

44

TWO HOURS AFTER SHE LEFT THE MOUNTAIN HOUSE, JULIE pulled the car off onto the shoulder of a deserted stretch of highway and reached for the thermos on the seat beside her. Her throat and eyes hurt from the tears she adamantly refused to shed, and her mind was dazed from her futile effort to block out the painful memory of his parting words:

"You don't love me, Julie. You're naive and inexperienced, and you don't know the difference between good sex and real love. Now be a good girl, go home where you belong, and forget about me. That's exactly what I want you to do."

Her hand shook with misery as she poured coffee into the top of the thermos. How pointlessly cruel of him to ridicule her that way, particularly when he knew she had to face the police and the press as soon as she got back. Why couldn't he have either ignored her words or lied and said he loved her, too, just so she'd have something to cling to during the ordeal ahead. It would have been so much easier for her to face that if he'd only said he loved her.

"You don't love me, Julie. . . . Now be a good girl, go home where you belong, and forget about me . . . ."

Julie tried to swallow the coffee, but it stuck in her constricted throat as another painful realization hit her, leaving her more desolate and bewildered than before: Despite his having mocked her feelings, Zack had to have known damned well she really did love him. In fact, he was so sure of it, that he'd assumed he could treat her that way, and she'd *still* go home and not betray him to the authorities. She knew he was right, too. As hurt as she was by his callousness, she could never attempt to strike back at him. She loved him too much to want to hurt him, and her belief in his innocence and her desire to protect him were, strangely enough, every bit as strong now as they'd been yesterday.

A pickup truck shot by her, spewing slush against the side of the car, and she remembered his warning to get as far away as possible without attracting notice. Wearily, she sat up and put the car into gear, looking over her shoulder to make certain it was safe to pull out, but she set the Blazer's cruise control at sixty-five miles an hour. Because he'd told her not to speed. And because getting stopped for a speeding violation fell under the category of "attracting attention."

Julie made it to the Colorado–Oklahoma border in much less time than it had taken her to drive the same distance in blizzard conditions. Following Zack's instructions, she pulled over at the first rest stop on the Oklahoma side and made her phone call.

Her father answered on the first ring. "Dad," she said, "it's Julie. I'm free. I'm on my way home."

"Thank God!" he exploded, "Oh, thank God!"

In all these years, she'd never known her father to sound so upset, and she felt sick with remorse for what she'd put him through. Before either of them could speak again, however, an unfamiliar voice broke in, "This is Agent Ingram of the FBI, Miss Mathison, where are you?"

"I'm in Oklahoma at a rest stop. I'm free. He—left me in the car, with the keys, blindfolded. But he's gone. I'm sure he's gone. I don't know where."

"Listen carefully," the voice said. "Get back into your car and lock the doors and leave there at once. Do not stay in the vicinity where you last saw him. Drive to the nearest populated area and call us back from there. We'll notify the local authorities and they'll come to you. Now get out of there, Miss Mathison!"

"I want to come home!" Julie warned with genuine desperation. "I want to see my family. I don't want to stay in Oklahoma and wait. I can't! I just wanted someone to know I'm on my way." She hung up the phone and headed for her car, and she did not call from the next populated area at all.

Two hours later, a helicopter that had obviously been searching for the distraught hostage who was on her way home somehow spotted her on the dark Texas interstate and hovered overhead. Minutes after she noticed it, patrol cars with revolving red and blue lights began racing onto the interstate from the entrance ramps, positioning themselves in front and behind her, forming a motorcade to escort her home. Or more likely, Julie thought nervously, to prevent Zack Benedict's alleged accomplice from changing her mind and trying to escape before she was questioned.

It was horrifying to realize the true scope of the hunt that had evidently been under way for both of them, and Julie thoroughly resented her official escort—until she pulled into Keaton and neared her parents' house. Although it was two o'clock in the morning, reporters were swarming all over the yard and street, and camera lights blazed at her as she got out of the car. It took three Texas troopers and both her brothers to get her through the throngs of reporters shouting questions at her and onto the front porch.

Two FBI agents were waiting inside the house, but her parents rushed past them, enfolding her in the protective warmth of their arms and love. "Julie," her mother kept saying, hugging her and crying and smiling, "My Julie, my little Julie." Her father wrapped her in a bear hug and said, "Thank God, thank God," over and over, and Julie felt tears blur her eyes because she'd never truly realized how much they loved her. Ted and Carl hugged her and tried to joke about her "adventure," but they both looked positively haggard, and the tears she'd fought for over twenty-four hours slid down her cheeks. In the last ten years, she hadn't shed more than a few tears—and those were over sad movies—but in the last week she felt like she'd cried an ocean. That, she decided fiercely, had to stop immediately and permanently. The family reunion was interrupted by the blond-haired FBI agent who stepped forward and said in a calm, authoritative voice, "I'm sorry to intrude, Miss Mathison, but time is of the essence right now, and we have questions that need answers. I'm David Ingram, we spoke on the phone." He gestured toward the tall, dark-haired agent beside him and said, "This is Agent Paul Richardson, who's in charge of the Benedict case."

Mrs. Mathison spoke up. "Let's go into the dining room—there's space for all of us at the table." She tossed in her old cure-all for any of Julie's childhood woes: "I'll get some milk and cookies and some coffee, too," she added.

"No, I'm sorry, Mrs. Mathison," Paul Richardson said firmly. "I think this interview is best conducted in private. Your daughter can bring you up to date in the morning."

Julie had started into the dining room between Ted and Carl, but she stopped and turned at that. Reminding herself that these men were not really enemies and were only trying to do their job, she said with quiet firmness, "Mr. Richardson, I realize how anxious you are to ask your questions, but my family is just as eager to hear my answers, and they have even more right to do that than you do. I'd like them to be present tonight if you don't mind."

"And if I do mind?" His height and coloring reminded her poignantly of Zack, and after the grueling drive, all her defenses were down. As a result, the weary smile she gave him was unintentionally personal. "Please try not to mind. I'm exhausted and I truly don't want to argue with you."

"I suppose your family can be present," he relented, then he shot his frowning associate a peculiar, quelling look. Julie missed the exchange completely, but Ted saw it and so did Carl.

"Very well, Miss Mathison," Agent Ingram said abruptly, taking over as soon as they were seated. "Let's begin at the beginning." Julie felt a tiny tremor of fear when Richardson reached into his pocket, removed a tape recorder, and put it on the table in front of her, but she reminded herself of what Zack had told her to expect.

"Where do you want me to start?" she asked, smiling gratefully at her mother when she handed Julie a glass of milk.

"We already know you supposedly went to Amarillo to meet with the grandfather of one of your students," Richardson began.

Julie's head snapped around. "What do you mean *supposedly?*"

"There's no need to feel defensive," Ingram quickly interposed in a soothing voice. "You tell us what happened. Let's start with when you first encountered Zachary Benedict."

Julie crossed her arms on the table and tried not to feel any emotion at all. "I'd stopped for coffee in a restaurant on the interstate. I don't remember the name of the place, but I'd recognize it if I saw it. When I came outside, it was snowing, and a tall, dark-haired man was crouched near my tire. It was flat. He volunteered to fix it . . ."

"Did you notice if he was armed at that point?"

"If I'd noticed he had a gun, I certainly wouldn't have offered him a ride."

"What was he wearing?" The questions came at her in rapid-fire succession after that, on and on, hour after hour . . .

"Miss Mathison, you must be able to remember something more about the location of the house he used for a hideout!" That was Paul Richardson who'd been watching her as if she was an insect under his microscope and using an authoritative tone of voice on her that reminded her a little of Zack when he was annoyed. In her exhausted state, she found that more endearing than annoying.

"I told you, I was blindfolded. And please, call me Julie—it's shorter and takes less time than Miss Mathison."

"At any time during your stay with Benedict, were you able to discover his destination?"

Julie shook her head. They'd already been over all this once already. "He told me that the less I knew the safer he would be."

"Did you ever *try* to discover his destination?"

She shook her head. That was a new question.

"Please answer aloud for the tape recorder."

"All right!" she said, abruptly deciding he wasn't like Zack at all—he was younger and smoother and actually better looking, but he didn't have Zack's warmth. "I did not ask him where he was going because he'd already told me that the less I knew the safer he'd be."

"And you want him to be safe, don't you?" he said, pouncing on her answer. "You don't want to see him apprehended, do you?"

The moment of reckoning was here. Richardson waited, tapping the end of his ballpoint pen on the table, and Julie glanced out the dining room window at the reporters swarming in the yard and lining the street while weariness crashed over her in waves. "I've already told you, he tried to save my life."

"I fail to see why that should negate the fact that he is a convicted murderer and he'd taken you hostage."

Leaning back in her chair, she gazed at him with a mixture of disdain and frustration. "I don't believe for one minute that he killed anyone. Now, let me ask you something, Mr. Richardson." Ignoring Ted's warning squeeze on her knee at her combative tone, she said, "Put yourself in my place and assume for the sake of rhetoric that I took you as a hostage and you managed to escape from me. You hide from me, but I think you've fallen into a deep, icy creek. From your hiding place, you watch me run down to the creek and dive into that frigid water. I dive again and again, calling your name, and when I can't find you, you watch me stagger out of the creek and collapse in the snow. But I don't get back on my snowmobile and go home. Instead of that, I give up. I open my soaking shirt so the cold will kill me faster, and I lean my head back and close my eyes and stay there, letting the falling snow cover my head and face . . ."

When Julie went silent, Richardson raised his brows. "What's your point?"

"My point is," she said tersely, "would you, after seeing that, believe I actually murdered someone in cold blood? Would you try to wheedle information out of me that could only get me shot down before I could prove I didn't kill anyone?"

"Is that what Benedict intends to do?" he demanded, leaning forward.

"It's what I would do," she evaded, "and you didn't answer my question: Would you—after you knew I tried to save your life and wanted to die when I thought I failed—try to wheedle information out of me so you could get me captured and probably killed in the process?"

"I would feel compelled," Richardson retorted, "to do my duty and help see that justice was done to a convicted murderer who also happens to be a kidnapper now."

She looked at him for a long moment and said quietly, "In that case, I can only hope that you find a donor heart because you obviously don't have one of your own."

"I think that's enough for today," Agent Ingram intervened, his voice as pleasant as his smile. "We've all been up since last night when you called."

The Mathison family shoved to their feet in various stages of sleepless stupor. "Julie," Mrs. Mathison said stifling an embarrassed yawn, "you'll sleep here in your old room. You, too, Carl—Ted," she added. "There's no point trying to get through all those reporters again, and besides, Julie may need you with her later today."

Agents Ingram and Richardson lived in the same condominium complex in Dallas; they were friends as well as co-workers. Locked in thought, they rode in silence to the motel on the outside of town where they'd been staying for a full week. Not until David Ingram pulled their sedan to a stop in front of their rooms, did he finally venture an opinion. He gave it in the same disarmingly pleasant tone that had fooled Julie into thinking he believed everything she said. "She's covering up something, Paul."

Paul Richardson frowned at the peeling white numbers on the door of his room, then he shook his head, "Nope. She's on the level. I don't think she's hiding a thing."

"Then maybe," Ingram said sarcastically, "you'd better start thinking with your brain instead of the organ that took over as soon as she looked at you with those great big blue eyes of hers."

His head jerked around. "What the hell is that supposed to mean?"

"It means," Ingram said in disgust, "that you've been developing an obsession with that woman ever since we got here and you started checking her out with the local citizens. Every time you learned of some new good work of hers, you got softer; every time you talked to another one of those handicapped kids she teaches, and whose parents adore her, you got in deeper. Shit, when you found out she also tutors illiterate women and sings in the church choir, you were ready to nominate her for sainthood. Tonight, every time she looked disapproving of your voice or your question, you lost your momentum. You were already biased in her favor when you only had her picture, but when you saw her in the flesh tonight, your objectivity went straight to hell."

"That's bullshit."

"Really? Then suppose you tell me why you were so damned desperate to find out if she slept with Benedict. She told you twice that he didn't rape her or force her in any way to have sex with him, but that wasn't enough for you. Why the hell didn't you just come out and ask her if she *let* him screw her. Jesus," he said in disgust, "I couldn't believe it when you asked her if she could describe the bed linens on his bed for us, so we could try to trace the manufacturer and locate the owner of his hideout that way!"

Richardson shot him an uncomfortable look. "Was it that obvious?" he asked, opening his car door and getting out. "I mean, do you think the family noticed?"

Ingram got out, too. "Of course they noticed!" he snorted. "Nice little Mrs. Mathison was fantasizing about smothering you with some of her cookies. Paul, use your head. Julie Mathison is no angel, she's got a juvenile arrest record—"

"That we wouldn't have known about if a copy hadn't been left in the files from the Illinois foster care authorities instead of being destroyed years ago, like it should have been," Paul interrupted. "Furthermore, if you want to hear the truth behind Julie's petty rap sheet, then call Dr. Theresa Wilmer in Chicago like I did, and let that shrink chew your ass off. She thought—and still thinks—that Julie is as straight and as fine as they come and always was. Be honest, Dave," he said as they walked side by side up the path to their adjoining rooms. "Have you ever in your life seen a pair of eyes like Julie Mathison's in your life?"

"Yeah," he said with a derisive snort, "Bambi had 'em."

"Bambi was a deer. And his eyes were brown. Hers are blue—like translucent dark blue crystals. My kid sister had a doll with eyes like that once."

"I do not *believe* this conversation!" Ingram exploded in a low voice. "Listen to you for God's sake!"

"Relax," Paul sighed, raking his fingers through his hair. "If you're right—if she helped Benedict in his original escape or if she gives us any reason to believe she's concealing information about him now—I'll be the first one to read her Miranda, and you know it."

"I know," Ingram said, shoving his key into the lock and opening his door while Richardson did likewise. "But Paul?"

Paul leaned back from his own doorway. "Yeah?"

"What are you going to do if the only thing she's guilty of is sleeping with Benedict?"

"Find the bastard and shoot him myself for seducing her."

"And if she's innocent of that as well as collusion with him, then what?"

A slow smile tugged at Paul's mouth. "In that case, I'd better find myself a heart she'll approve of and get myself a transplant. Did you see the way she looked at me earlier tonight Dave? It was almost as if she knew me somehow, as if we knew each other. And liked each other."

"There are women all over Dallas who know you in the biblical sense of the word, and they all like your great big—"

"You're just jealous because that gorgeous blonde who used to be married to her brother won't give you a second look when she comes over to the house," Richardson interrupted with a grin.

"For a dinky little town," Ingram reluctantly agreed, "there are some highly unusual women here. Too bad they don't have a decent motel."

45

"I DON'T BELIEVE WE HAVE TO GO THROUGH THIS JUST TO HAVE some peace and privacy!" Julie cried in helpless exasperation late that afternoon as Ted flipped on the revolving lights and siren on his patrol car and floored it, racing away from her parents' house beneath the banner stretched across Main Street that read WELCOME HOME, JULIE, with the press in hot pursuit. "How am I ever going to teach my classes when I go back to work on Monday? When I went home today, I got mobbed by reporters before I could get inside the house. While I was in there, the phone never stopped ringing. Flossie and Ada Eldridge are in seventh heaven with all the excitement to watch and gossip about next door," she added tiredly.

"You've been back for over twelve hours without making a statement," Ted said, watching the cars that were tailing them in his rearview mirror.

Twelve hours, Julie thought. Twelve hours without a moment to spare to think of Zack, to review the bittersweet memories, to recover her strength, to try to put her mind into some semblance of order. She'd slept badly and when she got out of bed, the FBI agents were already waiting in the living room to question her, and they hadn't finished until two hours ago. Katherine had phoned to suggest Julie come there, and they were on their way now, but she had an uneasy feeling Ted and Carl both intended to ask her questions at Katherine's that they hadn't wanted to ask in front of their parents. "Can't you get rid of those reporters," she said crossly. "There must be a hundred of them, and they're surely violating some sort of city ordinance."

"Mayor Addelson said they're arriving at the courthouse in droves now that word is out that you've returned, and they're demanding a statement from you. They're taking full advantage of their liberties under the first amendment, but they aren't breaking any city ordinances that I know of."

Julie twisted around in her seat and saw that most of the cars tailing them were staying even with Ted. "Pull over and give the whole bunch of them speeding tickets. We're going ninety miles an hour and so are they. Ted," she added, feeling suddenly limp with weariness, "I don't know how I'm going to stay sane if people don't leave me alone for a while so I can think and rest."

"If you're going to spend the night at Katherine's," he said, glancing in the rearview mirror, "you'll have plenty of time to sleep there after Carl and I hear what you have to say."

"If what you and Carl have in mind is another interrogation," Julie said shakily, recoiling from this indication that both brothers wanted more answers than the ones they'd heard at the dining room table last night, "I'm warning you, I'm not up to it."

"You're up to your ears in it, lady!" he said in a sharp tone he'd never used on her before. "I know it and so does Carl. So probably do Ingram and Richardson. I decided to have our talk at Katherine's today because she happens to live in the only house in Keaton with electric gates and a high fence to keep out our friends back there." As he spoke, they rounded a bend in the road, and he hit the brake, swung the steering wheel, and sent the squad car jolting and bumping up the Cahills' private drive, racing between the trees for the gates that were already opening up ahead, controlled from the house where there was a remote camera.

Behind them, the cars loaded with reporters sailed passed the turnoff, but Julie was too unnerved by Ted's attitude to feel relieved. Carl's Blazer was already parked in the circular drive in front of the Cahills' sprawling brick mansion, but when Julie started to get out, Ted stopped her with his hand on her arm. "I think we'd better have part of our conversation now, in private." He turned toward her and stretched his arm across the back of the seat. "As your attorney, I cannot be forced to repeat anything you tell me. Carl doesn't have that immunity and Katherine certainly doesn't."

"Attorney? Did you pass your bar exams?"

"I haven't heard yet," he said curtly. "Let's just assume I did and consider lack of notification as a technicality for now."

Julie felt a chill that had nothing to do with the fact that he'd turned off the car's engine. "I don't need an attorney."

"I think you're going to."

"Why?"

"Because you didn't tell the whole truth last night. You're a lousy liar, Julie, owing no doubt to your inexperience with it. Stop glaring at me. I'm trying to help."

Julie shoved her bare hands inside the sleeves of her fleece-lined jacket to warm them and studied a speck of lint in her lap.

"Let's hear it," he ordered, "the part you *didn't* tell the FBI."

She'd loved him so well and for so long that she dreaded to see disapproval on his face for the first time in all these years, but she lifted her chin and met his gaze. "Will you give me your solemn word never to tell anyone what I'm going to tell you?"

Her insistence on that made him lean his head back and swear under his breath: "You're in even deeper than I thought, aren't you?"

"I don't know what you thought, Ted. Do I have your word or not."

"Of course you have my word!" he said savagely. "I'd walk through hell for you, Julie, and you know it! So would Carl."

Trying to control the poignant tug on her heart from his words, Julie reminded herself of her vow not to shed any more tears and drew a ragged breath, "Thank you."

"Don't thank me, just talk to me! What lies did you tell to the FBI last night?"

"I wasn't blindfolded. I know how to find the house in Colorado."

She saw the effort it took him to stop his face from betraying any reaction to that. "What else?"

"That's all."

"It's what?"

"That's the only thing I actually lied about."

"Then what did you lie about by omission? What did you leave out?"

"Nothing that's anyone's business but my own."

"Don't play games with your lawyer! What did you leave out? I have to know so that I can either protect you or find an experienced lawyer to do it if it's over my head."

"Are you trying to find out if I slept with him?" Julie snapped back as her exhaustion and tension suddenly erupted in anger. "Because if you are, then don't play the same coy games that Richardson plays with me. Just ask me!"

"Don't knock Richardson," Ted shot back. "He is the only reason that Ingram hasn't read you your Miranda rights already. Ingram knows you're hiding something—maybe a lot of somethings—but Richardson is so dazzled by you that he's letting you wrap him around your finger."

"Richardson is rude!"

"And you're oblivious to the effect you have on men. Richardson is *frustrated*," Ted emphasized with absolute finality, "and infatuated as hell. Poor bastard."

"Thanks," she said ungratefully.

"Are we going to continue this adolescent sparring, or are you going to tell me what else you're keeping from the FBI?"

"Has it occurred to you that I might be entitled to some privacy and dignity—"

"If you want dignity, don't shack up with escaped convicts."

Julie felt as if he'd hit her in the stomach. Without a word, she got out of the car and slammed the door. She was reaching for the doorbell when Ted jerked her arm away. "What the hell do you think you're doing?"

"I've already told you the only thing I lied about that could get me into legal trouble if it were known," Julie said, jabbing at the doorbell. "Now I'm going to tell Carl and you at the same time what you're obviously *dying* to know. After that, there's nothing to tell."

Carl answered the doorbell and Julie marched passed him into the slate foyer and spun around. Oblivious to Katherine who was already halfway down the winding staircase, she glared at a stunned Carl and said bitterly, "Ted tells me the two of you have figured out that I'm lying about everything. He tells me if I want dignity and privacy, I shouldn't 'shack up' with escaped convicts, and I'm sure he's right! So here it is, the whole truth: I told the FBI that Zack did not physically abuse me in any way, and he didn't! He risked his life trying to save mine, and not even you two, who obviously despise him no matter what I say, can twist that into 'physical abuse.' He did not hurt me. He did not rape me. I *slept* with him. I slept with him and I would have gone on sleeping with him for the rest of my life if he'd have wanted me to! Are you satisfied now? Is that enough for you? I hope it is, because that's all I have left to tell you! I don't know where Zack is! I don't know where he's going! I wish to God I did—"

Carl pulled her into his arms and glared at Ted. "What the hell is the matter with you, anyway, upsetting her like this?"

Ted was so stunned that he actually looked to his ex-wife for support, but Katherine only shook her head and said, "Ted is very good at making women who love him cry. He doesn't mean to, he just can't forgive us when we break his rules. That's why he's a cop and that's why he's going to be a lawyer. He likes rules. He loves rules! Julie," she said, taking her arm, "come into the library with me. You're exhausted, which neither of your brothers seem to realize."

Following behind them, Ted glared at Carl and said, "I did not intend to upset her, I simply told her not to hide anything from me!"

"You could have tried using a little tact instead of demanding answers and making her feel like a tramp!" Carl bit out as he strode into the library with Ted beside him.

Julie sank into a chair and gaped in guilty surprise as an unprecedented family feud suddenly erupted in full force with Katherine in the lead: "You both have a lot of nerve prying into Julie's personal life and sitting in judgment on her," she informed them angrily as she marched over to a mahogany liquor cabinet and poured wine into four glasses. "Of all the monumental hypocrisy! She may think you're both saints because you've always made sure she thinks that, but I know better." She picked up Julie's glass and her own and left the other two sitting on the cabinet. "Ted, you took my clothes off in this very room before we had our first official date, and I was only nineteen years old!"

Julie automatically accepted the wine as Katherine pointed at a burgundy leather chesterfield and indignantly reminded him, "You took off my clothes and you made love to me on that same sofa! As I recall, you were very pleased and surprised when you realized I was still a virgin. An hour later, you made love to me again in the swimming pool and again in—"

"I remember!" Ted snapped, stalking over to the liquor cabinet and picking up the other two glasses of wine. He thrust one of them into Carl's hand and said, "Unless I miss my guess, you're going to need this in about ten seconds," just as Katherine confirmed his prediction and rounded on his hapless elder brother:

"And you, Carl, you're a *long* way from being any saint! Before you were married you slept with—"

"Leave my wife out of this," he warned tightly.

"I wasn't going to mention Sara," Katherine said with cool derision. "I was thinking about Ellen Richter and Lisa Bartlesman, when you were in your senior year of high school, and then there was Kaye Sommerfeld, when you were nineteen, and—"

Julie's horrified, laughing plea caused them all to turn toward her. "Stop it! Please," she said caught somewhere between amusement and limp exhaustion, "just stop it. We've all ruined enough illusions about each other tonight."

Ted turned to Katherine and raised his glass in a mocking toast. "As usual, Katherine, you've managed to criticize and embarrass the hell out of everyone else while leaving yourself above reproach."

The antagonism seemed to drain from her. "Actually, I have the most to be ashamed of."

"Because you stooped to sleeping with me, I presume?" he said with bored indifference.

"No," she said quietly.

"Then why?" he demanded.

"You know the answer to that."

"Surely not because our marriage failed?" he scoffed.

"No, because I *made* that marriage fail."

His jaw clenched as he angrily rejected the softly spoken—and astonishing— admission. "Why the hell are you hanging around in Keaton anyway?" he snapped instead.

Katherine turned back to the tray of drinks and inserted a corkscrew into a second bottle of chardonnay. "Spencer says that I have a subconscious need to come back here before I marry him in order to confront all the local censure that I ran away from when our marriage went on the rocks. He says that's the only way I'll regain my self-respect."

"Spencer," Ted pronounced with a disdainful glance, "sounds like an asshole."

To his amazement, his fiery ex-wife gave an infectious laugh as she turned and toasted him with her glass.

"What's so funny?" he demanded.

"Spencer," Katherine explained unsteadily, "has always reminded me of you . . ."

Julie put her untouched glass of wine aside and stood up. "You'll have to argue without me here to referee. I'm going to bed. I *have* to get some sleep."

46

PULLING ON A ROBE THAT KATHERINE HAD LENT HER, JULIE walked quietly downstairs and found Katherine in the library, watching the 10 P.M. news.

"I didn't expect to see you down here until morning," Katherine said with a surprised smile as she stood up. "I made up a dinner tray for you though, just in case. I'll get it."

"Was there anything important on the news?" Julie asked, unable to keep the apprehension from her voice.

"Nothing about Zachary Benedict," Katherine assured her. "You were a main topic of the state and national news, however—your return home from captivity, apparently safe and unharmed, I mean."

When Julie dismissed that with a shrug, Katherine put her hands on her hips and teased, "Do you have any idea how famous you've become?"

"Notorious, you mean," Julie joked, falling into their habitual friendly banter and feeling vastly better than she had in the last two days.

Nodding toward a stack of newspapers and magazines on the lamp table beside Julie's chair, Katherine said, "I saved those for you in case you wanted them for a scrapbook or something. Look through them while I get your tray, or have you seen them already?"

"I haven't seen a newspaper or a magazine in a week," Julie said, reaching for the magazine on top and turning it over to the cover. "Oh good God!" she exploded, torn between anger and laughter as she gazed at her own face on the cover of *Newsweek* magazine beneath a lurid headline that read, "Julie Mathison—Partner or Pawn?" She tossed that aside and flipped through the rest of the stack, astonished to see pictures of herself plastered across the front pages of dozens of national magazines and newspapers.

Katherine came back in carrying a tray and put it on the table in front of her.

"The whole town has rallied around you," Katherine said with a brief glance at the *Newsweek* cover. "Mayor Addleson wrote an editorial for the *Keaton Crier* reminding everyone that no matter what the big-city press says about you, we know you here, and we know you'd never 'take up with' a criminal like Zachary Benedict. I think those were his exact words."

Julie's smile wobbled a little and she laid the paper aside. "But you know better. As you heard me tell Carl and Ted, I did 'take up' with him."

"At the time, Addleson was rebutting that truck driver's statement that you seemed to be collaborating willingly in Benedict's escape—frolicking in the snow and all that. Julie," she said hesitantly, "do you want to talk to me about it—about him?"

Looking at her friend, Julie remembered the confidences they'd exchanged over the years. They were the same age and had become fast friends almost from the moment Ted introduced them to each other. When Ted and Katherine's marriage fell apart, Katherine had gone back to college and then moved to Dallas. Until now, she'd adamantly refused to return to Keaton, but Julie had visited her often in Dallas at Katherine's insistence. The special friendship that had sprang up instantaneously had somehow survived time and separation, and it was as vital and natural as it had always been. "I think I *need* to talk about him," Julie admitted after a pause. "Maybe then I'll get him out of my system and be able to start thinking of the future again." Having said that much, she lifted her hands palm up and said helplessly, "I don't even know how to begin."

Katherine curled up on the sofa as if she had all the time in the world and suggested a starting point: "What's Zachary Benedict like in real life?"

"What's he like?" Julie mused, drawing a knitted afghan over her lap. For a moment she stared past Katherine's shoulder, trying to think of how to describe Zack, then she said, "He's hard, Katherine. Very hard. But he's gentle, too. Sometimes, I actually ached inside from the sweetness of the things he did and said." She trailed off and then tried again, with examples. "During the first two days I actually thought he might kill me if I defied him. On the third day, I managed to escape from him on a snowmobile I found in the garage . . ."

Three hours later, Julie finished, having told Katherine almost everything with the exception of intimate moments, which Julie didn't attempt to hide, but didn't describe in specifics either.

Katherine had listened in complete absorption, interrupting only for clarification, laughing at things that were funny like their snowball fight, gaping in disbelief at Zack's jealousy of Patrick Swayze, frowning at other times—sometimes with sympathy, sometimes with disapproval. "What a story!" she said when Julie finished. "If it was anyone but you telling me this, I wouldn't believe a word of it. Did I ever tell you I used to have a big crush on Zachary Benedict? Later I simply thought of him as a murderer. But now . . ." She broke off as if unable to put her thoughts into words, and then she finished, "No wonder you can't stop thinking of him. I mean, the story doesn't have an ending, it just sort of hangs there, unfinished. If he's innocent, then the story is supposed to have a happy ending with the real murderer going to jail. The good guy isn't supposed to spend the rest of his life living like a hunted animal."

"Unfortunately," Julie said grimly, "this is real life, not the movies, and that's the way the story is going to end."

"It's still a lousy ending," Katherine insisted. "And that's all there is to it?" Repeating the last thing that Julie had told her, Katherine summarized, "Yesterday at dawn, you both got up, he walked you out to the car, and then you drove away? Just like that?"

"I wish it had been 'just like that'!" Julie admitted unhappily. "That's how Zack wanted it to be, and I knew it. Unfortunately," she added, trying to keep her voice steady, "I couldn't seem to do it that way. Not only did I start to cry, I made everything even worse by telling him I loved him. I knew he didn't want to hear it because I'd blurted it out the night before, and he pretended he didn't hear me. Yesterday, it was worse. Not only did I humiliate myself by telling him I loved him, but he—he—" Julie trailed off in shame.

"What did he do?" Katherine asked gently.

Forcing herself to look at her friend and to keep her voice emotionless, she said, "He smiled like an adult does to a foolish child and informed me that I did not love him, that I only thought I did because I don't know the difference between love and sex. Then he told me to go home where I belong and forget all about him. Which is exactly what I intend to do."

Astonishment and bewilderment furrowed Katherine's forehead into a frown. "What an odd, ugly way for him to behave," she said sharply, "given the sort of man you portrayed him to be until then."

"I thought it was, too," Julie said miserably, "particularly when I was almost certain that he cared about me. Sometimes, there was a look in his eyes, as if he—" She broke off in disgust at her gullibility and said angrily, "If I could go back to yesterday morning and do it over again, I'd pretend I was perfectly happy to be going. I'd thank him for a great adventure, then I'd drive away and leave him standing there! That's what I should have—" She trailed off, imagining the scene in her mind, then very slowly she shook her head, negating the whole idea, struck by a realization that made her feel much better. "That would have been an incredibly stupid, wrong thing to do," she said aloud.

"Why? You'd have your pride," Katherine pointed out.

"Yes, but I would have spent the rest of my life thinking he might have loved me, too, and that if we'd admitted how we really felt about each other, then maybe I could have talked him into taking me with him and, later, searching for the real killer. In the end," Julie concluded quietly, "I'd have *hated* myself for not telling him again that I loved him, for never trying to change the way our story ended. Knowing that Zack didn't love me even a little is hard, and it hurts, but the other way would have hurt much more and for much, much longer."

Katherine stared at her, dumbstruck. "Julie, you amaze me. You're right about everything you just said, but if I were in your place, it would take me years to be as objective as you are now. I mean, consider what the man did—he kidnapped you, seduced you after you saved his life, took your virginity, then when you told him you loved him, he gave you a cavalier, flippant answer and sent you home to face the FBI and the world media on your own. Of all the heartless, rude—"

"Please don't go into all that," Julie said with a half-laugh as she held up her hand, "or I'll get angry all over again and forget how 'objective' I am. Besides," she added, "he didn't seduce me."

"From the story you just told, it's obvious to me he seduced you with twenty-four-karat charm."

Julie shifted her gaze to the empty fireplace and shook her head, "I wanted to be seduced. I wanted him so *much*."

After a moment, Katherine said, "If he had told you that he loved you, would you truly have turned your back on your family and your job and everything you believe in and gone into hiding with him if he'd asked you to do that?"

In answer, Julie lifted her gaze to Katherine's. "Yes."

"But you'd become an accessory, or whatever it is they call someone who joins in with a criminal."

"I don't think a wife can be prosecuted for standing by her husband."

"My God!" Katherine gasped, "you're completely serious! You'd have *married* him!"

"You of all people shouldn't find that so difficult to believe," Julie said pointedly.

"What do you mean?"

Julie watched her with a sad, knowing smile. "You know what I mean, Katherine. Now it's your turn to confess."

"About what?"

"About Ted," Julie clarified. "You've been telling me for a year that you want to make Ted listen to you because you have things you need to make him understand. Yet tonight, you meekly accepted every nasty, unjust remark he made to you without a word of argument. Why?"

47

KATHERINE SHIFTED UNEASILY BENEATH JULIE'S STEADY GAZE, then she reached nervously for the teapot on the tray in front of her and poured tepid tea into her cup. When she lifted the teacup to her lips, there was a slight tremor in her hand and Julie saw it. "I accepted the way he treated me because it's no more than I deserve after the way I behaved while we were married."

"That's not the way you felt three years ago, when you filed for divorce," Julie reminded her. "You told me then that you were divorcing him because he was selfish, heartless, demanding, overbearing, and a whole lot of other things."

"Three years ago," Katherine stated sadly, "I was a spoiled brat married to a man whose only real crime was that he expected me to be a wife, not an unreasonable child. Everyone in Keaton, except you, knew that I was a ridiculous excuse for a real wife. You were too loyal to your best friend to see what was before your eyes, and I didn't have the maturity or courage to face the truth. Ted knew the truth, but he was too gallant to destroy your friendship and faith in me by telling you what I was really like as a wife. In fact, one of the few things we ever agreed on was that you shouldn't know we were having problems."

"Katherine," Julie interrupted softly, "you're still in love with him, aren't you?"

Katherine's whole body tensed at the words, then she looked down at the huge pear-shaped diamond sparkling on her left hand and twisted it in her fingers, keeping her gaze averted. With a choked laugh, she said, "A week ago, before your disappearance forced Ted to start talking to me, I would have answered no to that question."

"How would you answer it now?"

Katherine drew a long breath and looked up at her. "As you so eloquently phrased it about Zachary Benedict tonight," she said, "I would sleep with your brother for the rest of my life—if he'd only ask me to again."

"If you feel that way," Julie asked quietly, her gaze searching Katherine's face, "how can you justify the fact that you're still wearing another man's engagement ring?"

"Actually, the ring is now on loan to me."

"What?"

"I broke our engagement yesterday, but Spencer asked me not to make it official for a few weeks. He thinks I'm simply overreacting to old, sentimental memories that came back when I saw Ted again."

Restraining the urge to cheer at the news of the broken engagement, Julie smiled and said, "How do you intend to get Ted back?" Her smile faded a little as she added, "It's not going to be easy. He's changed since the divorce, he's still devoted to his family, but he rarely laughs, and he's become distant . . . as if there's a wall around him and he won't let anyone past it, not even Carl or me. The only thing he really seems to care about now is passing his bar exams and opening up his own practice. She paused trying to think of a kind way to phrase it and then opted for the simple truth: "He doesn't like you, Katherine. Sometimes, it's almost as if he actually hates you."

"Did you notice that, too?" Katherine tried to joke, but her voice shook a little. Sobering, she said, "He has good reason to hate me."

"I don't believe that. Sometimes two wonderful people simply can't make a go of being married, and it's no one's fault. It happens all the time."

"Don't whitewash me when I'm finally getting up the courage to tell you the ugly truth," she said shakily. "The truth is that the divorce was entirely my fault. I loved Ted when I married him, but I was so spoiled and so immature that I couldn't understand that loving someone means you make some sacrifices for him. It sounds bizarre, but I actually thought I was entitled to bind Ted to me with matrimony and then to spend the next couple of years being independent and carefree—until *I* was ready to settle down with him. To give you an example," she persevered, her voice ringing with self-disgust, "one month after our wedding, I realized that all my friends were going back to college for the fall semester, and I wasn't. Suddenly, I felt martyred because I was only twenty, and I was already tied down and missing out on college life. Ted had saved enough money by working as a deputy sheriff to go to school and pay my tuition, and he came up with the perfect suggestion: We could schedule our classes on the same days and drive to Dallas together. But that wasn't good enough for me. You see, I wanted to go back East and live in my sorority house like a coed, then spend summers and holidays with my husband."

Julie struggled to keep her face from betraying her surprise at such a hopelessly unfair marital arrangement, but Katherine was so busy condemning herself that she wouldn't have noticed anything. "Ted pointed out the obvious impracticality of such a marriage and added that even if he were willing to live like that, he couldn't possibly afford to send me to Brookline. So I went running home to Daddy to ask for the money, even though Ted had made it plain to me that if I married him, he would never take a penny of Daddy's money. Daddy, of course, told Ted that he would be happy to pay for all my expenses at Brookline, but Ted refused, which made me furious. I retaliated from that day forward by refusing to lift a finger at home. I didn't cook another meal for him or do his laundry. So he did the cooking and grocery shopping, and he took our laundry over to Kealing's Cleaners, all of which made everybody in town start talking about what a lousy wife I was. Despite that," Katherine said, "he never gave up hope that I'd grow up soon and behave like a woman instead of a brat. He felt guilty, you see," Katherine added, looking directly at Julie, "for marrying me when I was so young and hadn't had a chance to really live. Anyway, the only wifely duty I performed during the rest of our first year of marriage was lovemaking, which," she added with a soft smile, "was definitely not an awful chore with your brother."

Katherine fell silent for so long that Julie wasn't certain she intended to go on, then she drew a shaky breath and continued, "After a while, Daddy, who knew how miserable I was because I was forever complaining to him, hit upon the idea that if I had a fabulous house to live in, I'd be a happier wife. I was childish enough to love the idea of playing hostess in a wonderful house of my own with a swimming pool and tennis court, but Daddy was worried that Ted was really inflexible about not accepting any financial support from him. I, on the other hand, foolishly believed that if we presented Ted with a fait accompli, he'd have no choice except to go along with it. So Daddy bought the land over on Wilson's Ridge, and he and I met secretly with an architect and had the plans drawn up for my house. I loved every inch of that house, I planned every detail, every closet, every cabinet," Katherine said, looking up at Julie. "I even started cooking meals for Ted and doing our laundry, and he thought I'd decided to be a wife after all. He was so pleased because I was happy, even though he didn't understand the reason. He thought my parents were building the house on Wilson's Ridge for themselves because they wanted a smaller place, because that's what I let him believe. In fact, that's what everyone in Keaton believed."

This time, Julie was unable to hide her shock, because there was a huge house on Wilson's Ridge, and it was gorgeous—complete with swimming pool and tennis court. "That's right," Katherine said, watching her face. "The house that Dr. and Mrs. Delorik live in was supposed to be my house."

"What happened?" Julie asked because she didn't know what else to say.

"What happened was that when the house was almost finished, Daddy and I took Ted up there, and Daddy handed Ted the key." With a slight shudder,

Katherine said, "As you can imagine, Ted was furious. He was furious at the secrecy, the deceit, and my having gone back on my word before we were married that I'd live on whatever income he could provide. He told my father politely to find someone who could afford to live there and keep the place up, and he left us standing in the house."

Since that would have happened only months before their divorce was filed, Julie naturally assumed that Ted's refusal to accept the house caused the final death blow to their marriage. "And that led to more fights that ended up breaking up your marriage," Julie concluded.

"No. That led to my banishing Ted from our bed, but it was already too late."

"What do you mean?"

Katherine bit her lip and looked down. Her voice shook a little as she said, "A few days later—just before Ted and I split up—I took a bad fall off one of my father's horses, remember?"

"Of course I do," Julie said. "You broke your arm."

"I also broke up my marriage that day along with my husband's heart." She drew a long breath, lifted her gaze to Julie's, and there was a sheen of tears in her eyes. "I was pregnant, Julie. I found out after Ted refused the key to the house on Wilson's Ridge. I was two months' pregnant and I was furious because Ted had refused the house, which had a lovely nursery, but I was even angrier because *he* was getting something he wanted badly—a baby. I went riding the next day, even though Ted specifically told me not to, and I didn't take that horse for a gentle canter. I was racing him along the creek and jumping him over hedges when he threw me."

When she couldn't seem to go on, Julie finished softly for her, "And you lost the baby."

Katherine nodded. "Ted was not only heartbroken, he was . . . infuriated. He thought I deliberately tried to miscarry, which isn't surprising considering the way I acted when I found out I was pregnant. And the funny thing is," she said, her voice filled with tears she was trying to blink away, "that was the only rotten thing in our marriage that I wasn't actually guilty of doing, at least not intentionally. I always rode like a fury when something was bothering me, and I always felt better afterward. The day I took Thunder out, I didn't believe for a moment I was risking a miscarriage. I'd been jumping him over those same obstacles for years and hadn't ever had the slightest problem with him. The only difference that day was that, unknown to me, the vet had been treating him for a sprain and it wasn't healed yet. You see," she added shakily, "Thunder would have jumped off a mountain for me, and he never gave a sign that his foreleg was bothering him until he actually took the last hedge and went down on his knees. I ended up partially pinned beneath him. My father and I both tried to explain all that to Ted, but he didn't believe us, and given our deceit about the house, who could expect him to? Besides, what sensible woman who was worthy of the title wife, would have taken such a risk with her husband's baby?" Her voice filled with shame and tears as she finished, "I didn't decide to divorce Ted, Julie. When I came home from the hospital, he'd already packed his bags. But," she added with a teary smile, "he was gallant to the very end, even when he was heartbroken, furious, and completely disillusioned: He let *me* divorce *him*. And he never told anyone about the baby he still believes I deliberately lost. I grew up the day I saw his suitcases in the hall and realized what I was losing, but it was too late then. You know the rest of the story—I went back East to college and got my degree, then I went to work in Dallas at the museum."

Julie got up, walked quickly across the hall, and returned with a handful of tissues from the powder room.

"I thought," Katherine said chokily, reaching for a tissue and dabbing at her streaming eyes, "that you'd gone upstairs to pack your bag so you could leave my revolting presence."

Wrapping her in a fierce hug, Julie whispered, "You're still my best friend." Then she let her go and moved to the opposite end of the sofa, blowing her own nose.

After a few minutes, the two girls faced each other, wearing sheepish smiles and dabbing at the last of the tears lingering in their eyes. "What a mess!" Julie said.

Katherine blew her nose. "What an understatement!" With a wobbly smile, she added, "I think what we both need is two weeks at my parents' house in St. Barts. Can you plead exhaustion from your ordeal and get Duncan to give you a short leave of absence? We'll forget all about men and toast ourselves in the sun. What do you say?"

Drawing her knees up against her chest, Julie wrapped her arms around them and perched her chin on her knees. "I say," she decreed, "that you'd better stay right here if you intend to win Ted back before it's too late. He's seeing a lot of Grace Halvers, did you know that?"

Katherine nodded at the mention of the beautiful redhead. "I found out from Mr. Kealing when I took some laundry there last week because my parents' washing machine was broken. Can you guess what he said when he saw me?" When Julie shook her head, Katherine provided miserably, "He looked at me like I was a useless child and said, 'How many husbands are you going to have before you finally figure out how to use a washing machine?' And then," Katherine added, "he said, 'I'll bet Grace Halvers won't make Ted Mathison do the laundry and shopping and cooking if she's lucky enough to get him. Nor will Sue Ellen Jury if she beats Gracie out of the running.'"

Julie frowned in thought, then shook her head. "Despite what I said about Ted and Grace a minute ago, I don't think Ted *ever* intends to remarry."

Instead of being reassured, Katherine seemed to wilt with guilt. "Ted should be married to someone, even if it isn't me. He was the sort of sexy, tender husband that most women only dream of having for their own. It would be a crime if he never remarried. He was impossible to dominate or manipulate, which drove me crazy when I was young, but he was incredibly gentle, and on those occasions when I had enough sense to simply ask for what I wanted, instead of trying to demand or wheedle, he was amazingly willing to bend or yield." A note of wonder crept into her voice as she lifted her gaze to Julie's and finished, "We may have been terribly mismatched in a lot of ways, but we were in love with each other within hours of when we met. It was like—like spontaneous combustion."

"The two of you still have that," Julie teased, trying to cheer up her friend. "After watching both of you tonight, I think it's safe to say that you are still a highly volatile combination. Poor Carl," she chuckled, "he looked like he wanted to leap for cover when you two started sparring with each other. And you know what?" she finished seriously. "For Ted to react so strongly to you, even in a negative way, he must still feel something for you."

"He does. It's contempt," Katherine provided. Sadly, she added, "If Ted won't give me anything else before I give up and go back to Dallas, I have to find a way to earn his forgiveness. I don't know how I'm going to do that. For one thing, he avoids me like the plague."

Julie flashed her a smile as she got up and began to stack their dishes onto the trays. "I think I can be of assistance there. How about helping me out after school with our handicapped sports program? I need volunteers who are willing to get mowed down by wheelchairs and tripped by flailing crutches on the football field and gymnasium floor."

"It's not exactly in line with my art degree, but it sounds wonderful," Katherine joked, picking up one of the trays and walking with Julie toward the kitchen, "and I accept the offer. Now, what idea did you have to prevent Ted from avoiding me?"

"That was it. Ted works with the kids two days a week—sometimes more often. And I could really use your help teaching my ladies to read. You won't *believe* the satisfaction you'll get from that."

In the enormous kitchen, Julie put down the tray on the stainless-steel countertop then she turned to look around at the commercial cooktops and ovens that were used for the senior Cahills' famous parties. Preoccupied, she didn't realize that Katherine was standing close behind her until the other girl said softly, "Julie?" When she turned, she found herself wrapped in a tight hug. "I've missed you so much!" Katherine whispered fiercely, hugging her tighter. "Thank you for keeping our friendship alive with your letters and phone calls and the visits you made to see me in Dallas. I wanted so badly to tell you the truth about my marriage to Ted, but I was always afraid you'd hate me if you knew."

"I could never hate you," Julie said, hugging her.

"You're the kindest, sweetest person I've ever known."

Julie pulled back and rolled her eyes. "Right," she teased.

"You are," Katherine persisted. "I used to want to be just like you."

"You're lucky you didn't succeed," Julie said, her face sobering as she thought of Zack. "If you were just like me, you'd have gushed all over Ted tonight about how much you love him, and then he'd have walked all over your heart and sent you home." Katherine started to say something sympathetic, but Julie who was suddenly and perilously close to tears, shook her head to stop her. "I'll be okay in a few days. I'm tired now and my defenses are down, but I'll forget all about him and be just fine, you'll see. Let's call it a night."

48

⁓ KATHERINE SLID A PAN OF SOURDOUGH BISCUITS INTO THE oven and glanced up in surprise as the intercom at the front gates began to buzz insistently on the kitchen wall. Wiping her hands on a dish towel, she pressed the button. "Yes?"

"Is this Miss Cahill?"

Pointedly ignoring that, she said, "Who is this?"

"Paul Richardson," the voice replied impatiently. "Is Julie Mathison with you?"

"Mr. Richardson," Katherine said darkly, "it is seven-thirty in the morning! Julie and I are still in our robes. Go away and come back at a civilized hour, say eleven. I should think the FBI would teach its agents better manners," she added, then she gaped at the intercom speaker because she thought he actually chuckled at her reprimand.

"Uncivilized or not, I have to insist on seeing Jul—Miss Mathison."

"And if I refuse to open the gates?" Katherine persisted stubbornly.

"In that case," he said drolly, "I'm afraid I'll have to blow the lock off of them with my trusty service revolver."

"If you do," Katherine said, irritably pressing the switch to open them, "you'd better keep that trusty revolver loaded, because two of my father's shotguns will be pointed right at you when you get here."

Cutting off any possible reply, she released the intercom button and walked quickly down the hall to the library where she found Julie huddled in a chair watching the morning news. A picture of Zack Benedict was on the screen and the expression of naked tenderness and longing on Julie's face as she smiled at him made Katherine's heart ache. "Is he okay?" she asked.

"They do not have the slightest idea where he is," Julie announced with unhidden pleasure. Wryly she added, "They also do not have the slightest idea whether or not I'm still a suspected accomplice. They make it seem like my silence and the FBI's silence on the subject is practically an admission of guilt. Are you ready for me to give you a hand with the omelets?"

"Yep," Katherine said cheerfully, "however, we have an uninvited guest, who'll probably be joining us for breakfast. Such rudeness as his does not warrant our combing our hair or changing into street clothes," she said when Julie looked askance at her long yellow bathrobe.

"Who is it?"

"Paul Richardson. He thinks of you as 'Julie' by the way. He let that slip on the intercom and tried to cover it up."

The long talk they'd had the night before, combined with all the sleep she'd gotten, had greatly restored Julie's strength and spirits. "Just so he doesn't think of me with numbers across my chest," she joked as the doorbell began to peal. "I'll answer that," she said, tightening the belt on her robe.

Unceremoniously, Julie yanked open the front door, then stepped back in shock as Paul Richardson held his arms up and pleaded in a comic voice, "Don't shoot. Please."

"What a delightful idea," Julie replied, but she was biting back a smile at his humor. "May I borrow your gun?"

He grinned, his gaze roving over the shining chestnut hair tumbling over her shoulders, then shifting to her bright eyes and soft smile. "A night's peace and quiet seems to have done you a world of good," he remarked, then his brows snapped together and he said sternly, "Don't pull another disappearing act like this one again though. I told you before that I want to know where you are at all times!"

Buoyed up by the television news that Zack was still safe, Julie accepted his reprimand without protest. "Have you come to lecture me or arrest me?" she asked cheerfully, knowing instinctively it was the former, as she turned and walked with him down the hall.

"Have you broken any laws?" he countered as they entered the kitchen.

"Are you planning to stay for breakfast?" she evaded, heading for the chopping block in the center of the kitchen.

Paul Richardson looked from Katherine who was breaking eggs into a bowl to Julie who was picking up a knife and getting ready to slice into a green pepper. Both women were devoid of makeup, clad in robes and pajamas, with their hair still rumpled from sleep. They looked lovely, innocent, and utterly charming. "Am I invited?" he asked Julie, grinning.

She looked up at him, her dark blue eyes searching his face as if she were trying to see beyond his skin and into his soul, and he suddenly wished there was more kindness and goodness there for her to see. "Do you want to be invited?"

"Yes."

She smiled then, the first genuine, unstrained smile she'd given him, and it had a radiance that made his heart quicken. "In that case," she said, "sit down at the table while we fix you one of our special omelets. We haven't made these as a team in a year, so don't expect too much."

Paul pulled off his jacket and tie, loosened the top button of his shirt collar and settled down at the table while Julie brought him a cup of coffee and then returned to her tasks at the chopping block. He watched them in silence, listening to their smiling banter, feeling like he'd somehow been admitted to a peaceful kingdom ruled by beautiful fairies with tousled hair and long, pastel robes who joked about past events that enthralled him. Katherine Cahill was drop-dead gorgeous, he decided, while Julie Mathison was merely pretty, but it was Julie who drew his gaze and held it like a magnet. He watched the sun shining through the window, glinting on her hair, studied the infectious glamour of her smile, the softness of her skin, the astonishing lushness of her curly lashes. "Mr. Richardson?" she said quietly without looking up from the small white object she was chopping into tiny bits.

"Call me Paul," he said.

"Paul," she corrected.

He definitely liked the sound of his name on her lips. "Yes?"

"Why are you staring at me?"

Paul lurched guiltily and said the first thing that came to mind. "I was wondering what that stuff is you're chopping up." He watched one long, tapered finger point to what he now realized was an ordinary garlic clove. "You mean this?" she asked, but she lifted her head and leveled an amused stare on him that made him feel like an awkward schoolboy caught cold in a transparent lie. "Yes," he bluffed. "That. What is it?"

He watched her lips form the smiling words and heard her say it ever so sweetly: "It's hemlock."

"Thank God. I was afraid it was garlic."

Her startled laughter rang out like music and when it ended, they were both smiling at each other. "You have a beautiful smile," he said quietly as she returned to her task.

She glanced at him from beneath her lashes and quipped, "Just the thing to set me apart in the FBI's mug book, don't you think."

Paul's smile faded abruptly. "Has Benedict contacted you? Is that why you took off yesterday without a word to me and came up here? Is that why you've referred twice this morning to being arrested?"

She rolled her eyes at him and laughed, "You have an overactive imagination."

"Damn it!" he said, standing up and starting toward her before he realized what he was doing. "Don't play games with me, Julie! When I ask you a question, I want a straight answer." He glanced over her shoulder at Katherine. "Would you mind leaving us alone?" he snapped at her.

"Yes, actually, I would. Do you honestly believe that Julie collaborated in that man's escape from prison?" she demanded indignantly.

"No," he bit out, "not unless she gives me a reason to change my mind. However, I'm not completely certain that she wouldn't protect Benedict from us if she could."

"You can't arrest her for something she hasn't done yet," Katherine pointed out logically.

"I have no intention of arresting her! In fact, I've done my damnedest to make certain that no one else decides to do that either."

Julie's startled voice brought his head around. "Have you really done that?" she asked him, her voice filled with gratitude and surprise.

Paul hesitated, feeling his anger being disarmed and defused by the expression in those eyes, then he nodded. "Yes."

For a moment her smile stayed on him and he basked in its warmth, then she transferred her smile to Katherine and quipped, "Cancel the hemlock!" which made him laugh.

Breakfast was a thoroughly delightful experience, Paul thought contentedly as he got up and filled his coffee cup while Julie and Katherine loaded dishes into the dishwasher. An extraordinarily pleasant time—and he knew exactly why that was so. As he'd just discovered to his complete enchantment, when Julie

Mathison finally decided she liked someone, she liked them wholeheartedly and without reservation. From the moment he'd told her that he'd tried to ensure she wasn't arrested, she'd treated him with unaffected warmth, smiling when he spoke, teasing him if he stiffened up and behaved like an FBI agent. He was thinking about all that when he realized she was asking his advice, which he also found profoundly gratifying: "Yesterday," she explained, as she dried the omelet pan, "I talked to Mr. Duncan, our school principal, and he agreed that I could go back to work tomorrow, but only if the press doesn't disrupt classes trying to get to me. Katherine thinks the only way to stop them from doing that and to get rid of them completely is to call them all together and give them a detailed formal statement about what happened and then answer any other questions they have. What do you think?"

"I think she's absolutely right. In fact, that was one of the things I intended to suggest to you when I came over here this morning."

Frustrated at the necessity to defend herself, Julie yanked open a cupboard and put the omelet pan away. "I can't tell you how much I resent the idea that a world full of strangers thinks they're entitled to an explanation of something that has nothing whatsoever to do with them."

"I can understand that, but you only have two choices: deal with the press now, on your own terms, or let them keep printing damaging conjecture and chasing you everywhere you go."

Julie hesitated and then sighed, "All right, I'll do it, but I would rather face a firing squad."

"Would you like for me to be there to back you up?"

"Would you really do that for me?"

Would he really do that for her, Paul thought wryly. For her, he would not only do that, but he'd probably slay a dragon . . . beard a lion . . . move a mountain. By God . . . he'd even dry a frying pan! "Inasmuch as the FBI's presence here is part of the reason the press is hounding you," he said as he walked over to the sink and picked up the dish towel Katherine had laid aside when she went to answer the phone, "it's the least I can do."

"I—I don't know how to thank you," she said simply, trying not to notice how much more he reminded her of Zack when he was being charming.

"How about thanking me by having dinner with me on Wednesday?"

"Wednesday?" she exclaimed, appalled. "Are you still going to be here on Wednesday?"

The dragon he'd intended to slay for her reared up and sank its teeth into Paul's ass, the lion roared with laughter at his folly, and the mountain rose up before him, gigantic and immovable. "Try not to sound so enthusiastic," he said.

"I didn't mean it that way," she said, laying her hand on his sleeve and looking abjectly apologetic. "Truly I didn't. It's just that I—I hate being spied on and questioned, even by you."

"Has it occurred to you that Benedict could decide to come after you here or that your life could be in danger?" he said, slightly mollified by the sincerity of her apology and much more so by her unconscious gesture. "Benedict is a murderer and by your own admission, you didn't give him any trouble after he tried to save your life. Suppose he decides he misses the pleasure of your company? Or the pleasant security you provided him when you were a hostage? Suppose he suddenly decides you aren't loyal to him any more and decides to get his revenge the same way he got it on his wife?"

"Suppose that frying pan you're polishing decides to become a mirror and hangs itself on the living room wall," she countered, shaking her head at what she obviously viewed as his absurdity.

And at that moment Paul wished, very devoutly, that Benedict would hurry up and make some sort of move against her so that he could save her from the bastard and simultaneously prove to her he was right. For reasons he couldn't explain or understand, every instinct Paul possessed shouted at him that Benedict was going to come for her. Or try to contact her. Unfortunately, Dave Ingram completely disagreed, and he had a derisive explanation for Paul's "instincts" that was embarrassing as hell: Dave said Paul was so damned besotted with her that he couldn't *believe* Benedict wouldn't have fallen for her, too.

"What about dinner Wednesday night?" he said, reaching for the spatulas and drying them, too.

"I can't," Julie said. "I teach an adult reading class on Wednesday and Friday nights."

"Alright, how about Thursday night instead?"

"That sounds nice," Julie said, suppressing her dismay that the FBI intended to keep her under surveillance for so long. "Would you like me to invite Katherine to join us?"

"Why in hell would I want you to do that?"

"I am beginning to feel," Katherine laughingly remarked from the doorway, "quite horribly unwanted around here."

At the sound of her voice, Paul tipped his head back, closed his eyes, and hastily invented an excuse for his tactlessness: "I am not usually so obnoxious or so clumsy. I know Dave Ingram will insist on making it a foursome if you come along, Katherine, and I didn't particularly want to spend another evening with him, which was why I said what I did about inviting you." He opened his eyes and found himself the object of amused pity from both women who were visibly enjoying his plight.

"I think we should forgive him," Katherine said.

"So do I," Julie replied.

Paul was muttering a brief prayer of gratitude for their mutual gullibility, when Katherine added blandly, "He's lying of course."

Julie gave him a knowing smile. "Of course," she agreed.

"About the press conference," Katherine said, turning serious and looking at Paul for advice, "where is it going to be, what time do you want to have it, and who should we notify?"

"What building around here can hold the biggest crowd?" Paul asked, his mind turning to the business at hand.

"The high school auditorium," Julie put in.

After a brief discussion it was decided the press conference should take place at three o'clock. Katherine volunteered to phone the high school principal, who would open up the school, and to call the mayor, who would then handle the press and any other arrangements. "Call Julie's brother Ted," Paul added as he put on his jacket. "Ask him to notify the rest of the sheriff's office so they can be there to keep the press from mobbing Julie if I can't hold them off alone." To Julie, he said, "Why don't you get dressed, then I'll drive you home so you'll have plenty of time to make whatever notes you'll need before you face the world via satellite and newsprint."

"What a terrifying way to put it," Katherine chided.

"It isn't terrifying at all," Julie astonished everyone, including herself, by saying. "It is maddening, and it is also absurd, but it isn't terrifying. I refuse to let them terrify me or intimidate me."

Paul's smile was filled with approval, but all he said was, "I'll go warm up the car while you get dressed. Katherine," he added with a lazy grin, "thank you for a lovely morning and a wonderful breakfast. I'll see you at the press conference."

When the front door closed behind him, Katherine turned to Julie and said bluntly, "In case you haven't noticed, that is one very special man. And he is crazy about you, Julie. That's obvious to anyone who looks closely." She winked then and added, "He also happens to be tall, dark, handsome, and extremely sexy—"

"Don't," Julie interrupted. "I don't want to hear all that."

"Why not?"

"Because he reminds me of Zack," she said simply. "He always has." She pulled off her apron and headed for the foyer.

"There are a few major differences between the two men," Katherine pointed out, following her up the staircase. "Paul Richardson isn't a criminal, he isn't an escaped convict, and instead of trying to break your heart, he's doing everything he can to shield and help you."

"I know," Julie sighed. "You're right about everything you said, except one thing: Zack is *not* a criminal. And before I put him completely out of my mind tomorrow, I intend to take care of something via 'satellite and newsprint' today."

"What's that?" Katherine said worriedly, following Julie partway into the guest bedroom she'd slept in last night.

"I intend to make absolutely certain the rest of the world knows that I don't think he killed anyone. Maybe if I do a good enough job at the press conference, public opinion might force the authorities to reopen the case!"

Katherine watched her peel off her robe. "You would still do that for him, even though he misused and hurt you as badly as he did?"

Julie gave her a winsome smile and nodded emphatically.

Turning, Katherine started to leave, then she turned back and said with a sigh, "If you're determined to make yourself into Zachary Benedict's spokesperson today, my advice is that you look your most beautiful. It's grossly unjust, but a lot of people are more swayed by a woman's looks than what she says."

"Thanks," Julie said, so filled with purpose now that she was completely devoid of nervousness and already mentally reviewing her wardrobe for the best thing to wear. "Any other advice?"

Katherine shook her head. "You'll be wonderful because you're sincere and you care, and that will show through everything you say and do today. It always does."

Julie scarcely heard her, she was searching for some strategy to accomplish her goal. She hit upon the idea of treating the incident—and the media—in a lighthearted way and paused, the clothing in her hand momentarily forgotten. A serious, formal accounting of the incident during which she would try to soften their attitude toward Zack would be best, she decided, followed by a relaxed, smiling attitude when the questions started coming at her.

Smiling. Lighthearted. Relaxed.

Zack was the actor, not she, and she didn't know how she was going to pull that off, but she was going to manage it somehow.

49

IN A CHICAGO PENTHOUSE OVERLOOKING LAKE SHORE DRIVE, Zack's former neighbor and best man, Matthew Farrell, looked up as his young daughter raced into the room, followed by her mother, and plunked herself on his lap. With her silky blond hair and blue eyes, Marissa's resemblance to her mother, Meredith, was already so striking that Matt grinned as he looked at both of his girls. "I thought it was nap time," he said to his daughter.

She looked at the glossy stock prospectus he'd been reading and obviously mistook it for one of her story books. "Story, Daddy. First. Please."

Before answering, he looked inquiringly at Meredith, who was president of Bancroft & Company, a large chain of exclusive department stores founded by her ancestors, and she gave him a helpless smile. "It's Sunday," she said. "Sundays are pretty special. I guess naps can wait a few minutes."

"Mommy says okay," he said, settling his daughter onto his lap as he thought of a story. Meredith saw amusement spark his eyes as she curled up in a chair across from the pair, and she realized the cause of it the moment Matt began his story:

"Once upon a time," he said in a very serious voice, "there was a beautiful princess who sat on a throne at Bancroft & Company."

"Mommy?" Marissa chirped.

"Mommy," he averred. "Now besides being beautiful and wonderful, this princess was very smart. But one day," he said in a tone of dire gravity, "she let a wicked, *wicked* banker talk her into investing some money into a company that—"

"Uncle Parker?" Marissa asked, grinning.

Meredith smothered a laugh at Matt's description of her former fiancé and said hastily, "Daddy's joking. Uncle Parker is not wicked."

"This is my story," Matt argued with a grin, then he continued. "Now it so happened that the princess's husband, who happens to know a *lot* about investing money, warned the princess not to listen to the wicked banker, but she did it anyway. In fact," he added in a deep, emphatic voice, "the princess was so *sure* she was right that she made a bet with her husband that the stock would go up, but it didn't. It closed down two points on Friday. And do you know what happens now that the princess lost the bet to her husband?"

She shook her head, smiling because he was smiling.

Sending a speaking look at his wife, Matt finished meaningfully, "She has to pay up. That means the princess has to take a long, long nap with her husband today."

"Mommy has to take a nap!" Marissa chortled, clapping her hands.

"That's exactly how I feel about it," Matt said.

Standing up, Meredith reached for Marissa's hand, but her warm smile was for Matt. "A wise mommy," she told her daughter, "only makes bets that are nice to lose." The cozy atmosphere was interrupted by the arrival of Joe O'Hara, the family bodyguard/chauffeur, who regarded himself—and was treated like—a member of the family.

"Matt," he said, looking anxious, "I just saw on the television in my room that Julie Mathison, the woman Zack took as hostage, is going to give a press conference. It's starting right now."

Meredith had never met Zachary Benedict, he'd already been sent to prison by the time Matt and she got together, but she knew the two men had been fast friends. Now she took one look at Matt's grim expression as he turned the television on and said quickly, "Joe, would you take Marissa to her room for her nap?"

"Sure thing. C'mon, sweetheart," he said, and the pair walked off hand in hand, a giant of a man and a little girl who regarded him as her personal teddy bear.

Too tense to sit down, Matt shoved his hands into his pants pockets and watched in taut silence as a pretty young woman stepped up to the bank of microphones, wearing a simple white wool dress with gold buttons at the collar and cuffs, her long dark hair caught at the nape in a pleated bow. "God help him," Matt said, referring to Zack. "She looks like Snow White, which is going to make the whole damned world scream for his blood for kidnapping her."

But when the mayor of Keaton finished warning the press about the courtesy he expected them to show her and Julie Mathison began to explain what had happened to her at the hands of her captor, Matt's frown began to fade and then, slowly, it gave way to an astonished smile. Contrary to his expectations, Zack's captive was somehow managing to describe her week with him as if it had been an adventure she'd had, courtesy of a man she carefully described to the world as "extremely kind," instead of a terrifying ordeal at the hands of an escaped murderer.

When she related the truth behind her attempted escape at the rest stop and told of Zack's quick-witted method of thwarting her, she did it in a way that evoked a ripple of reluctant, admiring laughter from several members of the press. And when she solemnly described her second attempted escape on a snowmobile and Zack's effort to "rescue" her from the creek, she made him sound like the compassionate hero she clearly believed he was.

At the end of her statement, the room exploded with shouted questions from the press, and Matt tensed at the sharp edge they all had:

"Miss Mathison," a CBS reporter called out, "did Zachary Benedict at any time threaten you at gunpoint?"

"I knew he had a gun because I saw it," she replied with smiling poise, "and that was enough to convince me—at least in the beginning—that I probably shouldn't pick a fight with him or criticize his old movies."

Laughter erupted in the room punctuated by more shouted questions. "Miss Mathison! When Benedict is recaptured, will you press kidnapping charges against him?"

With a teasing smile, she shook her head and replied, "I don't think I could get a conviction. I mean, if there were women on the jury, they'd acquit him in a minute, as soon as they heard he did half the cooking and cleaning up."

"Did he rape you?"

She rolled her eyes in amused disbelief. "Now really, I've just given you a detailed account of what happened during the entire week, and I specifically said that he did not physically abuse me at any time. I certainly couldn't have said that if he'd even attempted to commit such a despicable act."

"Did he verbally abuse you?"

She nodded solemnly, but her eyes sparkled with laughter as she said, "Yes, actually, he did—"

"Would you describe the occasion?"

"Certainly," she said. "He took grave offense one evening when I deliberately left his name out of my list of favorite movie stars."

Guffaws erupted in the auditorium, but the reporter who'd asked the question didn't seem to realize she was joking. "Did he threaten you at that time?" he demanded. "What exactly did he say and how did he say it?"

"Well, he spoke to me in a very disgusted voice, and he accused me of having a peculiar obsession for short men."

"Were you afraid of him at any time, Miss Mathison?"

"I was afraid of his gun during the first day," she said carefully, "but when he didn't shoot me after my attempt to pass a note to a clerk in a fast-food restaurant nor after my next two escape attempts, I realized that he wasn't going to hurt me, no matter how much I provoked him."

Again and again, Matt watched her deflect their questions and manage to begin swaying them from animosity to empathy toward her captor.

After about thirty minutes of relentless questions, the pace began to slow. A CNN reporter called out, "*Miss Mathison, do you want to see Zachary Benedict captured?*"

She turned her face in the direction of the reporter and said, "How could anyone possibly want to see a man who was unjustly imprisoned sent back to prison? I don't know how a jury ever convicted him of murder, but I do know that he's no more capable of that than I am. If he were capable of it, I would not be standing here now, because as I explained to all of you a few minutes ago, I repeatedly tried to jeopardize his escape. I'd also like you to remember that when he thought we'd been found by a helicopter, his first concern was for my safety, not his own. What I'd like to see happen is for this manhunt to be stopped while someone reviews his case." In a firm, courteous tone, she concluded, "If you have no more questions, ladies and gentlemen, we can end this interview and you can all go back to your homes. As Mayor Addelson explained, the town of Keaton wants to return to normal, and so do I, therefore I will not give any further interviews or answer any other questions. Our town has been delighted to have your 'tourist' money pouring into our cash registers, but if you choose to stay here, I have to warn you that you'll be wasting your time—"

"*I have one more question!*" a reporter from the *Los Angeles Times* shouted imperiously. "*Are you in love with Zachary Benedict?*"

She looked at him, lifted her graceful brows, and disdainfully replied, "I'd expect a question like that from the *National Enquirer,* but not the *Los Angeles Times.*" Her attempt to sidestep that got her laughter, but no success this time, because a reporter from the *Enquirer* shouted, "*Okay, Miss Mathison, we'll ask the question:* Are *you in love with Zachary Benedict?*"

It was the only time Matt saw her falter, and sympathy swelled in his heart as he watched her struggle to keep her smile in place, and her expression noncommittal, but her eyes betrayed her—those huge long-lashed sapphire eyes turned dark and solemn with an emotion that distinctly resembled tenderness. And just when Matt's sympathy for her plight was at its peak, just when he realized the reporters had finally trapped her, she changed tactics and walked willingly into their trap in a way that made him draw in a sharp breath at her courage:

"At one time or another," she said, "most of the female population of this country has probably imagined themselves in love with Zachary Benedict. Now that I've known him," she added with a tiny break in her voice, "I think they showed excellent judgment. He—" she hesitated, visibly searching for the right words, and then she said simply, "he is a very easy man for any woman to love."

Without another word she turned away from the bank of microphones and was quickly surrounded by two men Matt presumed were probably FBI agents and several uniformed deputy sheriffs who ushered her safely off the stage.

He pressed the off button on the remote controller as the CNN reporter began to recap the interview, then he looked at his wife. "What do you think of that?"

"I think," Meredith said quietly, "that she was incredible."

"But did she change your opinion of Zack at all? I'm biased in his favor, but you never knew him, so you'd probably react to her interview pretty much like everyone else did."

"I doubt that I'm as unbiased as you think. You're a very tough judge of character, darling, and you've made it clear that you believe he's innocent. If you believe that, then I'm inclined to believe it, too."

"Thank you for the tribute to my judgment," he said tenderly, pressing a kiss on her forehead.

"Now, I have a question for you," she added, and Matt sensed instinctively what she was going to ask. "Julie Mathison said she was taken to an isolated house somewhere in the Colorado mountains. Was it our house?"

"I don't know," he said truthfully, grinning when she gave him a skeptical look. "But I imagine it was," he added for the sake of honesty. "Zack has been there before, although he always flew in, and over the years, I've repeatedly offered him the use of the place. He would naturally feel free to use it now, so long as he didn't directly involve me—"

"But you are involved!" Meredith burst out a little desperately. "You—"

"I am not involved with Zack in any way that could jeopardize you or me." When she still looked unconvinced, he reiterated calmly, "When he went to prison, Zack gave me his power of attorney so that I could manage his investments and handle his finances, which I continue to do. That is not illegal nor is it a secret from the legal authorities. Until he escaped from prison, he was in regular communication with me."

"But what about now that he's escaped, Matt?" she asked, her eyes searching his face. "What if he tries to communicate with you now?"

"In that case," he said with a casual shrug that worried her more, not less, "I will do what any law-abiding citizen must do and what Zack would expect me to do: I'll notify the authorities."

"How quickly?"

He laughed at her perceptiveness and put his arm around her shoulders as he steered her toward the bedroom. "Quickly enough to stop the authorities from charging me with collusion," he promised. And not one bit quicker than that, he added silently.

"What about his having used our house? Will you tell the authorities what you suspect?"

"I think," he decided after a moment's consideration, "that's an excellent idea! They'll see that as further proof of my innocence and a gesture of extreme good faith on my part."

"A gesture," his wife provided wryly, "that can't possibly harm your friend because, according to Julie Mathison, he left Colorado several days ago."

"Very clever of you, darling," he agreed with a grin. "Now, why don't you climb into bed for our little 'nap' and wait for me while I telephone the local office of the FBI."

She nodded but put her hand on his sleeve. "If I asked you not to have anything more to do with anything that concerns Zachary Benedict—" she began, but he shook his head to silence her.

"I'd do anything in the world for you, and you know it," he said in a voice that was gruff with emotion. "But please don't ask this of me, Meredith. I have to live with myself, and I'd find it very difficult to do if I did that to Zack."

Meredith hesitated, astonished again by the loyalty Matt felt for that one man. Generally regarded as a brilliant, but tough businessman, Matt had hundreds of acquaintances, but he neither trusted them nor gave them his friendship. In fact, to the best of her knowledge, Zachary Benedict was the only one he'd ever truly regarded as a close, trusted friend. "He must be a remarkable man for you to be this loyal to him."

"You'd like him," he promised, chucking her under the chin.

"What makes you so certain?" she teased, trying to match his lighthearted attitude.

"I'm certain," he said with a deliberately smug look, "because you happen to be crazy about *me*."

"You can't mean the two of you are alike?"

"A lot of people probably thought so and not necessarily in a flattering way. However," he added sobering, "the fact is that I'm all Zack has. I'm the only one he trusts. When he was arrested, the sycophants and competitors who'd fawned all over him for years dropped him like he had the bubonic plague and reveled in his downfall. There were other people who stayed loyal to him even after he went to prison, but he cut them off and refused even to answer their letters."

"He was probably ashamed."

"I'm sure he was."

"You're wrong about one thing," she said softly. "He has one other ally besides you."

"Who?"

"Julie Mathison. She's in love with him. Do you think he saw her or heard what she said tonight?"

Matt shook his head. "I doubt it. Wherever he is, it's somewhere very remote and it's not in this country. He'd be a fool to stay in the U.S., and Zack is no fool."

"I wish he could have heard her," Meredith said, her heart going out to him despite her fear for her husband's safety. "Maybe he got lucky and he knows what she's trying to do."

"Zack has never been lucky in his personal life."

"Do you think he fell in love with Julie Mathison while they were together?"

"No," he said with absolute finality. "Besides the fact that he'd have had much more pressing things on his mind at the time, Zack is . . . almost immune to women. He enjoys them sexually, but he doesn't have much respect for them, which isn't surprising given the sort of women he's known. When his acting career was going strong, they stuck to him like flypaper, but when he became a director—with juicy movie roles to dispense to lucky actresses—they swarmed around him like beautiful, sleek piranhas. He was completely inured to them. In fact, the only real tenderness I've ever seen him show is to children, which is the main reason he married Rachel. She promised him children, and she obviously reneged on that as well as her vows." Shaking his head for emphasis, he finished, "Zack wouldn't fall in love with a pretty young schoolteacher from a small town—not in a few days, not even in a few months."

50

SILHOUETTED AGAINST THE SETTING SUN, THE TALL MAN walked down the dusty road that led from the village to the busy docks, a newspaper and several magazines in his hand. As he headed down the pier, he spoke to none of the fishermen who were unloading the day's catch or mending their nets, and none of them spoke to him, but several pairs of curious eyes followed the stranger toward his boat, a forty-one-foot Hatteras with the name *Julie* stenciled on the stern in fresh blue paint. Other than the boat's name, which was required by marine law to be displayed on the stern, there was nothing to note about the craft. From a distance, it looked much like the thousands of boats that glided through the waters off the coast of South America, some of them chartered out to sports fishermen, most of them used strictly as fishing boats, all of them returning each night to unload their catch, then leaving each morning when the stars were still twinkling in the predawn sky.

Like the boat, there was little that stood out about its owner as he strode down the dock. Instead of the shorts and knit shirts preferred by the charter captains, he wore plain fisherman's garb—a white, loose-sleeved shirt of rough cotton, khaki pants, soft-soled shoes, and a dark cap pulled low over his brow. His face was tanned beneath a four-day growth of dark beard, though if anyone had looked closely, they'd have noticed that his skin was not nearly as weathered as the other fishermen's and his boat was actually better equipped for cruising than fishing. But this was a busy, competitive island port, and the *Julie* was merely one of thousands of boats that put in here—boats that often carried cargo that wasn't edible or legal.

Across the pier, two fishermen aboard the *Diablo* looked up as the *Julie's* owner went aboard. Moments later, the boat's generator purred to life and the cabin lights went on below. "He wastes fuel running that generator half the night," one fisherman observed. "What does he do that he needs that engine?"

"Sometimes I see his shadow at a table through the curtains. I think he sits and reads."

The other fisherman looked meaningfully at the five antennas that spiked high above the *Julie's* upper helm. "He has every kind of equipment, including radar, aboard that boat," he observed meaningfully, "yet he never fishes and he seeks no charter customers. I saw him anchored out near Calvary Island yesterday, and he didn't even have his lines in the water."

The first fisherman snorted in disgust. "Because he is no fisherman and no charter captain either."

"He is another drug runner then?"

"What else?" his companion agreed with a disinterested shrug.

Unaware that his presence was causing any comment along the busy docks, Zack studied the maps he'd spread out on the table, carefully charting various courses he could take next week. It was 3 A.M. when he finally rolled the maps up, but he knew he wouldn't be able to sleep even though he was exhausted. Sleep was something that had eluded him almost completely for the last seven days, even though his escape from the United States had gone off without a hitch—thanks to Enrico Sandini's connections and a half million dollars of Zack's money. In Colorado, the small chartered helicopter had appeared, as expected, to pick him up in a clearing 200 yards away from the house, a clearing that existed for precisely that purpose, except that it had been intended for use by the house's owners and their invited guests. Carrying skis and dressed like a skier, complete with large, tinted goggles that covered most of his face, Zack had climbed aboard and been flown to a small ski lodge an hour away. The pilot had asked no questions nor shown any surprise at what was, Zack knew, a fairly ordinary means of transportation used by wealthy skiers who preferred to own their own mountains and ski on someone else's.

A rented car had been waiting for him in the parking lot of the ski lodge, and from there he had driven south to a small landing strip where a private plane was waiting, as scheduled, on a cleared landing strip. Unlike the helicopter pilot, who'd been perfectly innocent and legitimate, the pilot of the four-engine propeller plane was not. The flight plan he filed each time they landed to refuel was not the one they followed as the little plane headed on a course south by southeast.

Soon after they left U.S. air space, Zack had fallen asleep, waking only when they landed to refuel along the way, but from the time they landed until now, he'd only been able to doze for a couple of hours at a time.

Standing up, he went down to the galley and poured brandy into a glass, hoping it would help him sleep, knowing it wouldn't, then he carried it up to the small salon that served as living room and dining room in his sea-going "home." He turned off the cabin's main lights, but he left the small brass lamp lit on the table beside the sofa because it illuminated the picture of Julie that he'd torn from the front page of a week-old newspaper and put into a small frame taken from the wall of a forward berth. Originally, he'd assumed it was probably her college graduation picture, but tonight as he studied it and sipped his brandy, he decided the picture had more likely been taken when she was dressed for a party or perhaps a wedding. She was wearing pearls at her throat and a peach-colored dress with a modest neckline, but what he most liked about the picture was that she was wearing her hair much as she'd worn it the night they'd dressed up for their "date."

Knowing he was torturing himself and yet unable to stop, he reached out and picked up the picture frame, then he propped his ankle on the opposite knee and laid the picture against his leg. Slowly, he ran his thumb over her smiling lips, wondering if she was smiling again now that she was back home. He hoped to God she was smiling, but as he gazed at her picture, what he saw was the last image he had of her—the wrenching look on her face when he'd ridiculed her for saying she loved him. The memory of that haunted him. It tore at him along with other worries about her, like whether or not she was pregnant. He tortured himself constantly wondering if she'd have to endure an abortion or endure the shame of unwed motherhood in a small town.

There were so many things he wanted to tell her, so many things he needed desperately to say to her. He swallowed the rest of his brandy, fighting the urge to write her another letter. Every day, he wrote her letters even though he knew damned well he couldn't send them. He had to stop writing those letters, Zack warned himself.

He had to put her out of his mind before he went insane . . .

He had to get some sleep . . .

And even while he was thinking that, he was reaching for a pen and tablet.

Sometimes he told her where he was and what he was doing, sometimes he described in great detail things he thought would interest her, like the islands on the horizon or the habits of the local fishermen, but tonight he was in a much different mood. Tonight exhaustion and brandy sent his rampaging regrets and worries soaring to new heights. According to the outdated American newspaper he'd bought in the village this morning, Julie was definitely suspected of aiding and abetting his escape. It suddenly occurred to him that she was going to need to hire a lawyer to keep the police and FBI from badgering her or, worse, from charging her with collusion just to terrify her into admitting things that weren't true. If that happened, she'd need a top-notch attorney, not some country bumpkin. She'd need money to hire an attorney like that. A new sense of urgency banished the defeated despair that had clouded his thinking since she left him and his mind began to work furiously, coming up with new problems and sudden solutions.

It was dawn when he leaned back in his chair, incredibly weary and completely beaten. Beaten, because he knew he was going to send her *this* letter. He had to send it to her, partly because of the solutions he'd come up with, but also because he desperately wanted her to know the truth about how he felt. He was now certain that the truth couldn't hurt her nearly as much as he'd hurt her with a lie. This would be their last communication, but at least it would correct the ugly ending to the most exquisitely beautiful days and nights of his life.

Sunlight was peeping through the curtains in the salon and he glanced at his watch. Mail on this island was only picked up once a week, early in the morning on Mondays, which meant he couldn't take the time to rewrite his rambling, incoherent letter, not when he still had to write a letter to Matt and explain what he wanted done.

51

"THAT'S KEATON DOWN THERE, OFF THE STARBOARD WING, Mr. Farrell," the pilot said as the sleek Leer jet slid gracefully out of the cloud cover and began its final approach. "I'm going to make a pass over the airstrip before I set her down, just to make sure it's in as good a shape as it's supposed to be."

Matt reached up and pressed the intercom button. "Fine, Steve," he said absently, studying his wife's worried features. "What's wrong?" he asked Meredith quietly. "I thought I reassured you completely that there's nothing illegal about delivering a letter that was addressed to Julie Mathison in care of me. The authorities are well aware that I have Zack's power of attorney to handle his financial affairs. I've already turned over the envelope his instructions came in so they can try to trace it. Not that it will help them," he added with a chuckle. "It's postmarked from Dallas, where he's obviously paying someone to receive mail intended for me, remove it from its original envelope, and then forward it on to me."

Knowing how strongly he felt about what he was doing, Meredith made a better effort to hide her worry and asked, "Why is he doing that if he trusts you so implicitly?"

"He's doing it so I can freely hand over to the authorities whatever envelopes I receive from him, without giving away his whereabouts. He's protecting both of us. So you see, I've adhered to the strictest letter of the law so far."

Meredith leaned her head back against the curved white leather sofa that dominated the plane's cabin and said with a laughing sigh, "No, you haven't.

You did not tell the FBI that he enclosed a letter to Julie Mathison along with his letter to you, and you didn't tell them you're delivering it."

"The letter to her is in a blank, sealed envelope," he countered lightly. "I have no way of knowing if Zack wrote what's in it. For all I know it contains recipes. I hope," he said with mock horror, "you aren't suggesting that I should open the letter to find out what's in it. It happens to be a federal offense to do things like that. Furthermore, my love, there is no law that specifically requires me to tip off the authorities every time Zack contacts me."

Alarmed and unwillingly amused by his bold nonchalance, Meredith tipped her chin down and looked at the handsome man she'd fallen in love with and lost when she was an innocent eighteen-year-old debutante and he was a twenty-five-year-old steel worker. In one short decade, he'd left the mills behind him and built his own financial empire on a foundation of daring, brilliance, and guts. And then he'd reclaimed her. Despite his veneer of smooth sophistication, tailor-made clothes, yachts, and private planes, however, Matt was, and would always be, a street fighter at heart. And she loved him for it. She loved that reckless, forceful streak in him, even though she knew it was the reason he was now ignoring the possible legal consequences of his actions. He believed in Zachary Benedict's innocence, and that was the only justification he needed for what he chose to do. Period. Even though she knew it was futile and probably unnecessary, she'd insisted on coming along this afternoon, just to make certain he didn't stick his neck out too far.

"Why are you smiling like that?" he asked her.

"Because I love you," she admitted wryly. "Now, why are *you* smiling?"

"Because you love me," he whispered tenderly, putting his arm around her and nuzzling her neck. "And," he admitted, "because of this." From his breast pocket, he took out the letter Zack had written him.

"You said that's just a list of instructions about Julie Mathison. What's funny about a list of instructions?"

"That's what's funny—a *list* of instructions. When Zack went to prison he had a fortune in investments spread out all over the world. Do you know how many instructions he gave me when he gave me power of attorney to handle them all?"

"No. How many?"

"One instruction," he said with a grin, holding up his forefinger. "He said, 'Try not to bankrupt me.'"

Meredith laughed, and Matt glanced out the window as the plane swooped down, racing for the runway, the setting sun glinting off its wings. "Joe's here with the car," he said, referring to their chauffeur, who'd flown into Dallas on a commercial flight that morning, rented a nondescript car, and driven it here to meet them. Matt wanted to arrive and depart without anyone knowing they'd been here, which meant they couldn't call a taxi from the airfield, even if there was a taxi service in Keaton.

"Any problems, Joe?" he asked as they slid into the back seat of the car.

"Nope," he replied cheerfully as he slammed down on the accelerator and sent the car barreling down the runway in his habitual race-car driver fashion. "I got here an hour ago and located Julie Mathison's house. There were a bunch of kids' bicycles in the front yard."

Meredith clutched Matt's arm for balance and rolled her eyes in amused resignation at Joe's daredevil driving. To distract herself from the gravel flying from beneath the car's spinning tires as they shot out onto the highway, she picked up their earlier conversation in the plane: "What sort of instructions did Zack give you about Julie Mathison?"

Removing the folded missive from his coat pocket, Matt glanced at the first few lines and said dryly, "Among other things, I am to take careful notice of how she looks and ascertain whether she seems to have lost weight or lost sleep."

Zack Benedict's unusual concern for his former hostage registered instantly on Meredith and softened her attitude toward him. "How can you know that by looking at her? You don't know how she looked before she spent a week with him."

"I can only assume the stress that Zack has been under has finally worn him down." Forcing himself not to show how badly he felt about that, Matt continued lightly. "You're going to love the next item on this list. I am also supposed to discover whether or not she is pregnant."

"By *looking* at her?" Meredith exclaimed as Joe slowed and turned onto a tree-lined residential street.

"No, I think I'm supposed to ask her, which is why I'm so delighted you volunteered to come with me. If she denies she's pregnant, I am to let Zack know whether or not I believe her."

"Unless she's used some sort of early pregnancy test, she may not know that herself. It's only been three weeks since she left him in Colorado." Meredith pulled on her gloves as Joe O'Hara brought the car to a teeth-jarring stop in front of a neat one-story ranch-style house where little boys were getting on their bicycles and pedaling away. "To be this concerned, he must feel very deeply about her, Matt."

"What he feels is guilt," Matt predicted flatly, getting out of the car, "and responsibility. Zack always took his responsibilities very seriously." As they started up the sidewalk, two little boys in wheelchairs came shooting out the side door and down a ramp onto the driveway, howling with laughter, with a pretty young woman in hot pursuit. "Johnny!" she called, laughing too as she raced after the child, "give that back!" The boy called Johnny executed a nifty wheelie on the driveway, waving a spiral-bound notebook in the air, keeping it just out of her reach, while his companion neatly used his own wheelchair to run interference for him. Matt and Meredith stopped, watching the exuberant interplay as a laughing Julie Mathison tried unsuccessfully to outmaneuver the boys' joint defense.

"All right," Julie called, plunking her fists on her hips, unaware of her adult visitors, "you win, you monsters! No quiz tomorrow. Now give back my grade book." With a triumphant shout, Johnny handed over the book. "Thank you," Julie said, taking it and affectionately yanking his knit cap down over his ears and eyes while he laughed and shoved it up. She bent down in front of the other grinning boy and zipped his jacket up under his chin, then she rumpled his red hair. "You're getting awfully good with those blocking maneuvers, Tim. Don't forget them in the game next Saturday, okay?"

"Okay, Miss Mathison."

Julie turned to watch them wheel off down the driveway, and that was when she saw the well-dressed couple standing near the curb in front of her house. They started forward, and Julie wrapped her arms around herself in the chilly wind, smiling politely as she waited for them, thinking that they both looked vaguely familiar in the deepening twilight.

"Miss Mathison," the man said, returning her smile with one of his own, "I'm Matthew Farrell, and this is my wife, Meredith." At close range, Meredith Farrell was as beautiful as her husband was handsome, as blond as he was dark, and her smile was just as warm as his.

"Are you alone?" he asked, glancing toward the house.

Julie stiffened with alarmed suspicion. "Are you reporters? Because if you are, I've—"

"I'm a friend of Zack's," he interrupted quietly.

Julie's heart slammed into her ribs. "Please," she said quickly, reeling with shock and excitement, "come inside."

She took them in the back door, through her kitchen where copper pots and pans hung from pegs on the wall and into the living room.

"This is very pretty," Meredith Farrell said, relinquishing her coat and looking around at the airy room with its white wicker furniture, bright green and blue plaid pillows, and potted trees and plants thriving in the corners.

Julie tried to smile, but as she took Matt's coat, she blurted desperately, "Is Zack alright?"

"As far as I know, he's fine."

She relaxed a little, but it was hard to be a polite hostess when all she wanted to know was why they'd come, and at the same time she wanted desperately to prolong their visit because Matt Farrell was his friend, and in a way, that brought Zack right here, into her house. "Would you like a glass of wine or some coffee?" she asked over her shoulder as she hung their coats in her front closet and they sat down on the sofa.

"Coffee would be lovely," the woman said, and her husband nodded.

Julie made coffee in record time, put cups and saucers on a tray, and returned to the living room so quickly that both her guests smiled at her, as if they understood and appreciated her dilemma. "I'm awfully nervous for some reason," she admitted with a choked laugh, putting the tray on the table in front of them and rubbing her palms against her thighs. "But I'm . . . I'm *very* glad you've come. I'll get the coffee as soon as it's ready."

"You weren't a bit nervous," Matt Farrell remarked admiringly, "when you confronted the world on television and tried, very successfully, I think, to sway them into Zack's corner."

The warmth in his eyes and voice made her feel as if she'd done something wonderful and courageous. "I hope all Zack's friends feel that way."

"Zack doesn't have many friends anymore," he said flatly. "On the other hand," he added with a slight smile, "with a champion like you behind him, he doesn't *need* many friends."

"How long have you known him?" Julie asked as she sat down in a chair at right angles to the sofa.

"Meredith has never met him, but I've known him for eight years. We were neighbors in California, in Carmel." Matt watched her lean slightly forward, her attention riveted on him, and sensing her wish to learn everything she possibly could from him, he added, "We were also limited partners in several business ventures. When he went to prison, Zack entrusted me with his power of attorney, which gave me the right and responsibility to handle all his financial affairs."

"It's wonderful of you to take all that on," she said graciously, and Matt caught his first glimpse of the rare, unaffected warmth she must have shown to Zack when he most needed it in Colorado. "He must like and respect you very much to trust you so completely."

"We feel the same way about each other," he replied awkwardly, wishing there were some way to ease into the purpose for his visit.

"And that's why you came here from California—" she suggested helpfully, "because as Zack's friend, you wanted me to know you approved of what I said during the press conference?"

Matt shook his head, stalling by digressing to minor details, "We only vacation in Carmel now," he explained. "Our permanent residence is Chicago."

"I think I'd prefer Carmel, although I've never been there," she responded, following his lead and switching to polite small talk.

"We live in Chicago because Meredith is president of Bancroft & Company, which is headquartered there."

"Bancroft's!" Julie exclaimed, impressed by the mention of the elite department store chain and smiling at Meredith. "I've been to your Dallas store and it's wonderful," she said, refraining from saying it was also much too expensive for her. Standing up, she said, "I'll get the coffee, it should be ready by now."

When she left, Meredith touched her husband's sleeve and said softly, "She's already sensed that you've come here for a purpose, and the longer you delay, the more nervous you'll make her."

"I'm not exactly eager to get down to business," Matt admitted. "I've come a thousand miles at Zack's request to ask her bluntly if she's pregnant and pay her off with his check. You tell me a subtle way to say, 'Miss Mathison, I've brought you a check for a quarter of a million dollars because Zack is afraid you're pregnant and because he feels guilty about it and because he wants you to pay a lawyer to hold off the press and the legal authorities.'"

She started to suggest a more obvious and more tactful way to go about it, but before she could speak, Julie returned with a china coffeepot and began filling their cups.

Matt cleared his throat and began in a blunt, awkward voice, "Miss Mathison—"

"Please call me Julie," she interrupted straightening, automatically tensing at his tone.

"Julie," he agreed with a slight, grim smile, "I haven't actually come here because of your press conference. I'm here because Zack asked me to come and see you."

Her face lit up like sunshine bursting out of the clouds. "He—he did? Did he tell you why?"

"He wants me to find out if you're pregnant."

Julie knew she wasn't, and she was so startled and embarrassed by the unexpected topic that she started to shake her head in denial before Meredith came to her rescue. "Matt has a letter to give you that will probably do a much better job of explaining all this than my flustered husband is doing," she said gently.

Julie watched him reach into an inside pocket of his sport jacket and extract an envelope. Feeling as if the world was beginning to spin and tilt around her, she took it from his outstretched hand and said shakily, "Would you mind if I read this letter now—in private?"

"Not at all. We'll enjoy our coffee while you do."

Julie nodded and turned. Quickly opening the envelope with her thumb, she started out of the living room, intending to go to her room, but the dining room was closer so she went there instead, neither caring nor realizing she was still partially in view of her guests. She braced herself for another condescending lecture from Zack about the infantile absurdity of giving any importance to their relationship in Colorado, but when she unfolded the pages and began to read, the tenderness and joy that exploded in her heart healed all her wounds. The world fell away and all that existed for her was the unbelievable words she was reading and the incredible man who had written them to her without ever intending for her to see them. . . .

My darling Julie, I know you'll never see this letter, but it helps to write to you every day. It keeps you close to me. God, I miss you so. You haunt every hour of my life. I wish I'd never met you. No—I don't mean that! What good would my life be without my memories of you to make me smile.

I keep wondering if you're happy. I want you to be. I want you to have a glorious life. That's why I couldn't say the things I knew you wanted to hear when we were together. I was afraid if I did, you'd wait for me for years. I knew you wanted me to say I loved you. Not saying that to you was the only unselfish thing I did in Colorado, and now I regret even that.

I love you, Julie. Christ, I love you so much.

I'd give up all my life to have one year with you. Six months. Three. Anything.

You stole my heart in just a few days, darling, but you gave me your heart, too. I know you did—I could see it in your eyes every time you looked at me.

I don't regret the loss of my freedom any more or rage at the injustice of the years I spent in prison. Now, my only regret is that I can't have you. You're young, and I know you'll forget about me quickly and go on with your own life. That's exactly what you should do. It's what you must do. I want you to do that, Julie.

That's such a lousy lie. What I really want is to see you again, to hold you in my arms, to make love to you over and over again until I've filled you so completely that there's no room left inside of you for anyone but me, ever. I never thought of sexual intercourse as 'making love' until you. You never knew that.

Sometimes I break out in a cold sweat because I'm afraid I got you pregnant. I know I should have told you to abort my baby if I did get you pregnant. I knew it in Colorado, but God, I didn't want you to, Julie.

Wait—I just thought of a solution that never occurred to me before. I know I have no right to ask you to have my baby, but there's a way to work it out, if you're only willing: You could take a leave of absence and go away—I'll see that you have plenty of money to compensate for what you lose from your job and to pay all your expenses. Then when the baby is born, I'd like you to take it to my grandmother. If you're pregnant and you're willing to do this for me, I'll write to her in advance and explain about everything. For all her shortcomings, the woman has never turned away from a responsibility in her life, and she'll see that our baby is properly raised. She has control of what would have been a very large inheritance of mine; a tiny part of that inheritance will be more than enough to pay for all the baby's expenses and education.

You were right when you said I shouldn't have closed the door on my family and burned my bridges. There were things I could have told my grandmother, even after I left home, that would have neutralized her hatred. You were right when you said that I loved and admired her when I was growing up. You were right about everything, and if I could change things now, I would.

I've decided to send this letter to you after all. It's a mistake. I know it is, but I can't stop myself. I have to tell you what to do if you're pregnant. I can't bear the thought that you won't realize there's an alternative to an abortion.

They may be watching your mail, so I'm going to have this letter brought to you instead of using the post office. The man who gives this to you is a friend. He's putting himself in jeopardy for me, just as you did. Trust Matt as completely as you'd trust me. Tell him if you're pregnant and what you want to do so he can relay it to me. One more thing, before I hurry to get this to the village in time for the weekly pickup—I want you to have some money for whatever you need or want. The money Matt will give you is mine, so there's no point in arguing with him about taking it. He'll be acting on my instructions, and he'll follow them to the letter, so don't give the man a hard time, sweetheart. I have plenty of money for my own needs.

I wish I had time to write you a better letter or that I'd kept one of the others I've written so I could send that instead. They were all much more coherent than this one. I won't send another letter to you, so don't watch for one. Letters will make us both hope and dream, and if I don't stop doing that, I will die of wanting you.

Before I go—I see from the newspapers that Costner has a new movie coming out in the States. If you dare to start fantasizing over Kevin after you see it, I will haunt you for the rest of your life.

I love you, Julie. I loved you in Colorado. I love you here, where I am. I will always love you. Everywhere. Always.

Julie would have read the letter again, but she couldn't focus through the torrent of tears racing from her eyes, and the pages slid from her fingers. Covering her face with her hands, she turned against the wall and wept. She wept with joy and bittersweet longing and raging futility; she wept at the injustice that made him a fugitive and at her own stupidity for leaving him in Colorado.

In the living room, Meredith asked Matt a quiet question while reaching for the china coffeepot, but her gaze strayed toward the dining room doorway, and her eyes riveted in alarm on the back of a weeping woman. "Matt, look!" she said quickly, already standing up and rushing forward ahead of him. "Julie—" she said softly when she reached the dining room. Wincing at the heartbroken sobs wrenching from the other woman, she put her hands on Julie's shaking shoulders and whispered, "Can I do anything to help?"

"Yes!" Julie said brokenly. "You can read that letter and tell me how *anyone* could *ever* believe that man murdered anyone!"

Uncertainly, Meredith reached for the pages lying on the floor and glanced at her husband who'd stopped in the doorway, "Matt, why don't you pour us all some of the wine Julie offered us earlier."

It took Matt several minutes to find the wine, locate a corkscrew, and open a bottle. He was taking glasses out of a cupboard when he heard Meredith walk into the kitchen. He looked over his shoulder, intending to thank her again for coming here, but the stricken look on her face made him turn around, the glasses forgotten. "What's wrong?" he asked anxiously, searching her wan, beautiful features.

"His letter—" she whispered, her eyes glazed with tears. "God! Matt—you can't believe this letter!"

Irrationally angry with Zack for upsetting his wife, Matt slid his arm around her, pulling her close while he took the letter from her hand and began to read with narrowed eyes. Slowly, his annoyance gave way to shock, then disbelief, and then to sorrow. He'd just finished reading the last line when Julie appeared in the doorway. Meredith heard her and hastily turned around to face her, taking the handkerchief Matt handed her, while Julie tried to smile and wipe away her own tears with her fingertips.

"This," Matt said, his voice heavy with regret and sympathy, "has turned out to be one hell of an evening. I'm . . . sorry, Julie" he finished lamely, studying the strange look in her wet eyes. "I know Zack didn't mean to make you unhappy."

For one last time, Julie swiftly considered all she'd be leaving behind if she executed her hastily made scheme, but her decision had already been made in the dining room. Fighting to keep her voice steady, she said, "When Zack contacts you, will you kindly remind him that I was abandoned by my own mother and inform him that I will *not* bring a baby into this world and have it know I did the same thing to it." With a teary smile, she added, "Please also tell him that, if he truly wants me to have his baby, which I would *very much* like to do, then all he has to do is let me join him in his exile."

That last sentence dropped like a bomb into the room, and in the silent aftershocks, Julie watched Matt Farrell's expression go from amazement to admiration, but his words were carefully designed to dampen her enthusiasm: "I have no idea when, or if, Zack will contact me again."

Julie laughed a little hysterically. "Oh, yes, he will—and very soon!" she said with absolute certainty, knowing now that her own instincts about Zack had always been right and that if she'd only listened to them she'd probably have been able to talk him into letting her leave Colorado with him. "He'll contact you right away because he won't be able to bear not knowing what I said."

Matt realized she was probably right and stifled a grin, "Is there anything else you want me to tell him when he contacts me?"

Julie nodded emphatically. "Yes. Tell him he has a maximum of . . . four weeks to get me there before I take other action. And, tell him that . . .," she hesitated in embarrassment at the thought of telling Zack something like this through a third party, and then she decided it didn't matter, so long as Zack heard the words. In an aching voice, she said, "Tell him that I am *dying* without him, too. And—and tell him that if he doesn't let me come to him, I will squander all his money on twenty-five thousand videotapes of Kevin Costner's new movie and then I will *drool* over that man for the rest of my life!"

"I think," Meredith said with a choked laugh, "that should make him agree at once." To Matt, she added, "Can you remember all that verbatim, or should I make notes?"

Matt shot a startled glance at his wife, who now looked as determined to involve him in Zack's tangled life as she'd been to keep him out of it two hours ago, then he turned and poured wine into the glasses, "I suppose this calls for some sort of toast," he announced, passing out the wine glasses. "Unfortunately, I find myself a little speechless right now."

"I'm not," Meredith said. Holding up her glass, she looked at Julie and said with a soft smile, "To every woman who loves as deeply as we do," then she lifted her face to her husband and added quietly, "and to the two men we love."

Julie watched him smile at her with tenderness and unembarrassed pride, and she fell in love with both of them at that moment. They were like Zack and herself, she decided; they were love and commitment and unity. "Please say you'll stay for dinner. I'm not much of a cook, but we may never meet again, and I'm dying to know more about . . . about everything."

They both nodded at once, and Matt said straightfaced, "Everything? Well, then, I guess I could start with a detailed analysis of the world financial markets. I have some fascinating insights into the probable causes of the declining world markets." He laughed at her appalled expression and said, "Or, I guess we could talk about Zack."

"What a great idea," his wife teased. "You can tell us both about your days as neighbors."

"Let me start dinner," Julie said, thinking madly of what to make that wouldn't take much of her time from the conversation.

"No," Meredith said, "let's send Joe for a pizza instead."

"Who's Joe?" Julie asked, already reaching for the telephone to order a pizza.

"Officially, he's our chauffeur. Unofficially, he's a member of the family."

A half hour later, the threesome was cozily ensconced in the living room and Matt was doing his best to satisfy both women's curiosity with a carefully censored version of his bachelor days as Zack's neighbor, when the doorbell rang.

Expecting to see a distinguished, lofty, uniformed chauffeur, Julie opened the door and found herself looking instead at a giant of man with an ominously ugly face, a beguiling grin, and a pizza box atop each of his outstretched hands. "Come in and join us," she said delightedly, taking one pizza and drawing him inside. "You didn't need to stay out in the car in the first place."

"That's what I thought, too," Joe joked, but he glanced at Matt to see if he wanted him present. When Matt nodded, Joe stepped inside and took off his coat.

"Let's eat in here where there's more room," Julie called to them over her shoulder as she put plates on the dining room table.

"I'll get the wine," Meredith said, standing up.

Joe O'Hara sauntered into the dining room and shoved his hands into his pockets, studying the courageous young woman who'd spoken up in Zack's behalf on television. She looked more like a pretty coed than a teacher, he thought, with her shiny dark hair tied at the nape with a bow and her soft skin aglow. She didn't look one bit like the overblown sexpots who'd hung onto Zack, and Joe liked that. He sent a questioning look at Matt, who was standing beside him, watching her with an affectionate half-smile. In answer to the unspoken question, his employer slowly nodded and Joe drew the obvious gratifying conclusion. "So," Joe said aloud, "you're Zack's lady."

She stopped in the act of putting napkins next to plates and raised eyes the color and softness of blue violets to his. "That," she told him, "is the *nicest* compliment I've ever gotten." To Julie's amazement, the big man reddened around his collar. "Do you know Zack, too?" she asked to put him at ease and because she was eager to know everything she could.

"You bet I do," he said with a grin as he and the Farrells sat down. "I could tell you stories about him that no one knows, not even Matt."

"Tell me one," Julie said enthusiastically.

O'Hara helped himself to a slice of pizza, thought for a moment, and then said, "Okay, I've got one. One night, Matt had an unexpected guest and he sent me next door to Zack's house because we were out of Stoli—vodka," he explained. Julie nodded her understanding, and he took another bite of pizza before continuing enthusiastically, "It was about midnight, and the lights were on in Zack's house, but no one answered the door. I could hear his voice though, and women's voices, coming from around in back, so I walked around the house, and there was Zack, standing by his swimming pool, still wearing the tuxedo he'd worn to some party he'd been at."

Julie perched her chin on her hand, fascinated. "What was he doing?" she asked when O'Hara took another bite of pizza.

"Swearing," Joe said succinctly.

"Who was he swearing at?"

"The three naked women in his pool. They were fans of his who'd found out his address somehow and figured he'd join them for a little orgy once he saw them nude in his pool."

"O'Hara!" Matt warned.

"No, this story's okay, Matt, honest. Julie won't get jealous or anything. Will you?" he asked her uncertainly.

Laughing, Julie shook her head. Zack loved her, she knew that now. She had nothing whatsoever to be jealous about. "I won't be jealous."

"I knew you wouldn't," he said with a satisfied glance at his employers. "Anyway, Julie," he continued to her, "Zack was boiling mad, and I'll tell you somethin' you may not know—underneath that cool, calm surface of Zack's, that man has got a temper you would not believe! When the women wouldn't get out of his pool like he ordered 'em to, he told me to catch them as he threw them out, and that's exactly what he did. He waded into his pool with all his clothes on, and the next thing I knew some broad about twenty years old rolled out of the pool and landed at my feet, stark naked. Then Zack came wading out of his pool with a girl under each arm."

Julie tried not to look the least bit shocked by the story. "What did you do with them?"

"Just what Zack said to do. He was so damned mad, he wouldn't let 'em get dressed. We carted 'em, howling and protesting and begging for their clothes, down the driveway to where they'd left their car, then Zack stuffed his two in the back seat, while I unloaded mine into the front seat. Then he yanked open the front door, turned on the ignition key, and jerked the car into gear. "Drive it or crash it," he told them, "but get the f—ing hell out of here and don't ever come back!"

The women exchanged gratified looks, obviously in complete accord over Zack's upright morality.

"You never told me about that," Matt said with a puzzled frown.

"Hell, I tried to tell you, but the woman you were entertainin' that night was tryin' to get your clothes off, so I left the Stoli on the bar and went to bed."

Julie delicately focused her laughing gaze on her pizza, Meredith propped her chin on her folded hands and gazed at her husband with amused eyes, and Matt sent a chilling glance to his errant chauffeur, who held up his hands and said defensively, "Meredith's smiling, Matt. She realizes you had no idea you were married to *her* at the time!"

Julie choked on her wine.

"You may as well explain that remark," Matt said irritably after exchanging a glance with his wife, "before Julie decides Zack has entrusted his future to a complete imbecile."

"I thought everybody already knew the story—it was all over the newspapers and everything," Joe said, but when Julie looked blank, he said, "Y'see, Matt and Meredith had gotten married and divorced when Meredith was still eighteen, only no one knew it, not even me. Then, twelve years later, Meredith finds out they'd had a bogus divorce lawyer and they weren't actually divorced, so she invites him to lunch and they talk for the first time in all those years, and she lays the news on him. Jesus, was Matt mad! Meredith was already engaged to somebody else, and the three of them had to give a news conference and try to look friendly, and Matt tried to make it seem like a funny joke—"

"I *do* know the story," Julie uttered as everything suddenly snapped into place. "That's why you both seemed familiar when I first saw you tonight! I *saw* that news conference." She shifted her startled gaze to Matt Farrell and added, "I remember that you and Meredith's fiancé joked about the whole mess and seemed rather like friends. And then . . . just a few days later, you—you hit him! Didn't you? There was a picture of the fight in the newspapers."

"We are all very good friends now, however," Matt said, grinning slightly at her thoughtful expression.

It was after eleven o'clock when the party reluctantly broke up. Julie excused herself to get something from her bedroom. By the time she returned with the green sweater and slacks she'd worn home from Colorado, Joe O'Hara had already gone outside to warm the car up, and Matt and Meredith were waiting near the door.

In accordance with his wife's whispered request to speak to Julie in private, Matt smiled at Julie, said good-bye, and added, "I'll wait in the car with Joe while you and Meredith say your farewells."

She leaned up on her toes to kiss him, and Matt hugged her tightly, surprised by the raw fear he felt for her and for Zack. "If it will make you feel any better," he told her against his better judgment, "my corporation owns an international investigation agency, and for the last three weeks, I've had their people running cross-checks on everyone who'd been to Dallas to work on Zack's film."

Instead of cheering, Julie said, "But why didn't you do that sooner?" Belatedly realizing what she'd said, she apologized, "I'm sorry—that was incredibly rude and ungrateful."

Matt smiled at her and shook his head, admiring her devotion to Zack. "It sounded desperate and concerned, not rude. And the answer is that Zack paid an agency with a reputation as good as ours to do the same thing before his trial began, and they couldn't turn up anything that was meaningful. Also, he told me then that he didn't want or need my help beyond what I was doing for him. Since his pride was already in shreds because of the pretrial publicity, I acceded to his request and let him handle his own case."

"Your investigators—" Julie said anxiously, seizing on some indefinable thread of encouragement she thought she heard in his voice, "they've discovered something new, haven't they?"

After a reluctant hesitation, Matt decided telling her probably couldn't do any harm, not when she'd already decided to share Zack's exile. "Part of it concerns Tony Austin," he began, but Julie interrupted.

"Tony Austin killed her?"

"I didn't say that," Matt warned firmly. "If there was any proof of that, I wouldn't be here, I'd be blasting it all over the media so the legal authorities would have to take action."

"Then what did you find out?"

"We found out that Austin apparently lied on the witness stand. During the trial, he stated that his affair with Rachel Evans had been going on for months and that they were 'wildly in love with each other.' The truth is that he was also involved with another woman."

"Who was she?" Julie demanded breathlessly. "She may have put the real bullets in the gun because she was jealous of Tony and Rachel."

"We don't know who she was. All we know is that two weeks before the murder, a bellboy heard a woman's voice in Austin's suite late at night when he brought up some champagne. That same bellboy had just delivered a late dinner to Zack's suite, and Rachel had answered the door, so whoever was in Austin's bedroom, it wasn't her. In any case, I don't think any woman switched those bullets, I think it was Austin."

"But why do you think so?"

"Possibly because Zack has always insisted Austin was involved, and now it's rubbing off on me," Matt admitted with a harsh sigh. "The thing is, Rachel couldn't have supported herself and Austin in style unless she kept working *and* got a fat divorce settlement from Zack through the California courts. However, she was never a big favorite with the public unless Zack directed her, and from the moment the press got ahold of the fact that she'd been caught cheating on him, her popularity in films—and her earning power—were going to plunge.

"Now that we know Austin was having an affair with someone else at the same time he was having one with Rachel, it pretty much negates his testimony that he was insane about her. That leaves us with the possibility that his main interest in her was financial and that when she blew her financial future by getting caught with him in Zack's suite, he decided to get rid of her. It's also possible he never wanted to marry her in the first place, and he killed her because she was pressuring him. Who knows. Furthermore, Austin was the only one who had physical control of that gun during the scene they were filming.

Even if Zack hadn't changed the script so that Austin, not Rachel, fired the first shot, Austin was strong enough to make certain the gun was pointed at her, not him, when it went off."

Julie shivered at the macabre conversation and its real implications. "Does Zack know this?"

"Yes."

"What did he say. I mean, is he excited or happy about it?"

"Happy?" he repeated with a bitter laugh. "If you'd been convicted of a crime someone else committed and you were completely helpless to alter the situation, would you be happy to finally discover the person you most despise in the world is probably the person who caused it all to happen to you? There's another complication," he added. "We also uncovered some minor information about other people who were on the set in Dallas that could point to *them* instead of Austin."

"What sort of information?"

"For one thing, Diana Copeland had a fling with Austin years before, which was supposedly over. However, she was still jealous enough of Rachel to tell people, after the furor of the trial died down, that she was glad Rachel was dead. Maybe she was jealous enough to have made it happen. Then there's Emily McDaniels, who had to be put on all sorts of medication for a year after the murder, which seems rather an excessive reaction for someone who was supposedly an innocent bystander. Tommy Newton, the assistant director on the film, couldn't get his act together for a long time after the murder either, although it's no secret how he felt about Austin. So there you are," he finished grimly, "new evidence that points simultaneously at everyone and is completely useless because it does."

"Oh, but it doesn't have to be like that. I mean, the police or the district attorney or whoever is in charge could be made to check out the new evidence."

"The legal authorities," he contradicted scornfully, "decided Zack was guilty and they arrested and prosecuted him. I hate to shatter your illusions, but they are the *last* people who'd want to reopen the case and make themselves look like fools by revealing that they were wrong. If we uncovered incontrovertible proof that Austin or someone else was guilty, I'd take it to Zack's lawyers and the media before I'd hand it over to the authorities so they could try to bury it. The problem is that we don't have much chance of finding out more than we have. We've already exhausted every avenue trying to find out who the woman with Austin was. Austin denied there was such a woman. He said the bellboy was mistaken, and whatever voice he'd heard must have been a television program." Matt softened his tone as if by doing that, he could somehow soften the blow he was about to deal her: "Zack understands all that. He knows the chances are ninety-nine percent now that Austin is the murderer, and he also knows the legal system isn't going to do a damned thing about it, unless he or I can give them one-hundred percent of the proof, and I'm afraid that's impossible. It's important you understand that, too, Julie. I only told you what we've learned because you're determined to go to him, and I thought it might help you, in case you ever begin to doubt his innocence."

Julie rejected his fatalistic logic with all her heart. "I'll never stop hoping. I'll pray and hope and badger God until your investigation turns up the proof you need."

She looked ready to take on the entire world for Zack, and Matt impulsively pulled her against him for a brief hug. "Zack finally got lucky when he met you," he said tenderly. "You go right ahead and pray," he added, releasing her. "We can use all the help we can get." Reaching into his pocket, he took out a pen and a business card, then he wrote two phone numbers on the back of it and an address. "These are our private phone numbers in Chicago and Carmel. If you can't reach us either place, call my secretary at the number on the front of the card, and I'll give her instructions to tell you where we are and how to reach us, no matter where that may be. The address on the back of the card is our home in Chicago. I was also supposed to give you this check from Zack."

Julie shook her head. "He told me what the check was for in the letter. I won't need it."

"I'm sorry," Matt said gently, "that there isn't anything more I can do. Truly sorry for you and for Zack."

Julie shook her head. "You've been wonderful. Thank you for telling me what you did."

When he left to wait in the car with Joe O'Hara, Julie held out the clothes she'd worn home from Colorado to Meredith. "I noticed Matt is the same height and build as Zack, and I'm about two inches shorter than you. Because of that and some other things I learned tonight, I have a feeling you might recognize these." When Meredith nodded, Julie held them further out and said, "I had to wear these home, but I've had them dry-cleaned. I intended to mail them back to the house, but I never found out the address."

"Keep them," Meredith said softly, "for the memories they hold."

Julie unconsciously cradled them protectively to her chest. "Thank you."

Swallowing over the lump of emotion in her throat she felt at the revealing gesture, Meredith said, "I agree with you that Zack will contact Matt very soon, but are you absolutely certain you should go through with this? You'll surely be breaking some law, and they'll hunt for you both. If you're lucky, you'll live the rest of your life in hiding."

"Tell me something," Julie said, meeting her gaze unflinchingly. "If it were

Matt somewhere out there, all alone, loving you—if it were Matt who wrote you the letter you read tonight, what would you do? Honestly," she added, sensing that her new friend might try to dissemble.

Meredith breathed a ragged sigh. "I would get on the first plane, boat, car, or truck that would take me to him." Wrapping Julie in a tight hug, she whispered, "I would even lie and tell him I was pregnant so he'd let me come to him."

Julie stiffened in alarm. "What makes you think I'm not pregnant?"

"The expression on your face when Matt first asked you if you were and the fact that you started to shake your head no before you stopped yourself."

"You won't tell Matt will you?"

"I can't tell him," she said with a sigh. "I haven't kept a secret from him during our marriage, but if I tell him this one, he'll tell Zack. He'll do it to protect both of you, because even though he hides it, he's desperately afraid of what you want to do and what it may cause. So am I."

"Then why are you helping me do it?"

"Because," Meredith said simply, "I don't think either of you are going to have any life at all without each other. And because," she added, managing a real smile, "I think you would do the same thing for me if our positions were reversed."

Julie waved good-bye to them from the front porch, then she went back into the house and got Zack's letter. Sitting down in a chair, she read it again, letting the words warm and thrill her and reinforce her courage.

I love you, Julie. Christ, I love you so much. I'd give up all my life to have one year with you. Six months. Three. Anything . . . I never thought of sexual intercourse as 'making love' until you . . . I won't send another letter to you, so don't look for one. Letters will make us both hope and dream, and if I don't stop doing that, I will die of wanting you.

She thought again of his last words to her in Colorado, his condescending amusement when she told him she loved him: "*You don't love me, Julie. You don't know the difference between good sex and real love. Now be a good girl and go home where you belong.*" And then she compared that with the real truth in his letter: *I love you, Julie. I loved you in Colorado. I love you here, where I am. I will always love you. Everywhere. Always.*

The sharp contrast between the two made her shake her head in awed amazement. "No wonder," she whispered tenderly to him, "you won an Academy Award!"

Julie got up and turned off the living room lights, but she took his letter with her to her bedroom so she could read it again. "Call me, Zack," she ordered him in her heart, "and put us both out of this misery. Call me quickly, darling."

Next door, the Eldridge twins were up unusually late, too. "He said to call him," Ada Eldridge pointed out to her balky twin sister. "Mr. Richardson said to call him in Dallas, no matter what time it is, if we noticed any strangers or anything unusual around Julie Mathison's house. Now give me the license number of that car that was parked out there half the night, so I can read it to him."

"Oh, but, Ada," Flossie protested, holding the slip of paper with the license number written on it behind her back. "I don't think we should spy on Julie, not even for the FBI."

"We aren't spying!" Ada said, marching around her and pulling the slip of paper out of Flossie's hand. "We're helping him protect Julie from that—that heathen monster who kidnapped her. Him and his disgusting dirty movies!" she added, picking up the phone.

"They aren't dirty! They're good movies, and I think Zachary Benedict is innocent. So does Julie. She told me so last week, and she said so on television. She also said he didn't do one thing to hurt her, so I can't see why he would try now. I think," Flossie confided, "that Julie is in love with him."

Ada paused in the act of punching out the numbers for a collect call to Dallas. "Well if she is," Ada declared with disgust, "she is as big a romantic fool as you are, and she'll end up pining away for that good-for-nothing movie star, just like you've pined away for that useless Herman Henkleman, who isn't worth an hour of your time and never was!"

52

THE PHONE CALL JULIE HAD BEEN WAITING AND PRAYING FOR came four days later at the last place she expected to receive it. "Oh, Julie," the principal's secretary called out when Julie walked into the office to turn in her attendance report at the end of the day. "A Mr. Stanhope called you this afternoon." Julie glanced up a split second before the name hit her, and when it did, she froze. "What did he say?" she asked, alarmed by the breathless desperation in her own voice.

"He said something about wanting to enroll his son in your handicapped physical ed classes. I told him we're full."

"Why in heaven's name did you tell him that?"

"Because I heard Mr. Duncan say something about us being overcrowded. Anyway, Mr. Stanhope said it was something of an emergency and that he'd call you back at seven tonight. I told him it was no use because our teachers don't work here that late."

In a flash, Julie realized Zack was wary of calling her at home in case her phone was tapped, that he hadn't gotten through to her when he tried here, and that he might not try again, and it was all she could do to keep her frustration and temper from lashing out at the principal's lazy, nosy secretary. "If he said it was an emergency," Julie shot back with unprecedented fury, "why didn't you page me in my classroom?"

"Teachers are not supposed to take personal calls during school hours. That is Mr. Duncan's rule. His very specific rule."

"It was clearly not a personal call," Julie said, her nails biting into her palms. "Did he say whether he intended to call me here or at home tonight?"

"No."

At six forty-five, Julie was sitting alone in the school's administration office, staring at the telephone on the desk where the main line would light up if a call came through. If she'd guessed wrong, if Zack was going to phone her at home tonight instead of here, she was terrified he might think she'd changed her mind about joining him and then he wouldn't call back. Beyond the glass walls that surrounded the administration office, the halls were dark and eerie, and when the janitor poked his head in the door, she jumped guiltily. "You're workin' awful late tonight," Henry Rueheart said with a grin that displayed a missing front tooth.

"Yes," Julie said, hastily pulling a blank tablet in front of her and picking up a pen. "I have some . . . some special reports to write. Sometimes it's easier to think here than it is at home."

"You ain't doin' much writing, gazin' off into space like you've been," he said. "I thought mebbee you was waiting for a phone call or somethin'."

"No, not at all—"

The phone rang shrilly at her elbow, and she grabbed for it, jabbing the button that lit up. "Hello?"

"Hi, sis," Carl said. "I kept calling you at home and decided to take a shot you were still at school when I couldn't reach you anywhere else. Have you had dinner yet?"

Julie raked her hand through her hair, trying to remember if Zack would get a busy signal or if the lines transferred automatically. "I have a lot of work to finish," she said, tossing a harassed look at Henry, who'd decided to shuffle into the office and empty trash cans instead of finishing sweeping the halls. "I'm trying to write some reports, and I'm not making much progress."

"Is everything okay?" he persisted. "I saw Katherine in town a few minutes ago, and she said you've wanted to stay home alone every night this week."

"Everything is great! Terrific! I'm throwing myself into my work just like you advised me to, remember?"

"No, I don't."

"Oh, well it must have been someone else then. I thought it was you. I have to hang up now. Thanks for calling. Love you," she said and hung up the phone. "Henry," she burst out in distraction, "can't you leave cleaning the office for last? I can't think straight if you're going to bang trash cans around," she added somewhat unfairly describing the minor noise he was making.

His face fell. "I'm sorry, Miss Julie. I'll just finish sweeping the hall then. Is that okay?"

"Yes it is. I'm sorry, Henry. I'm a little . . . tired," she finished with an overbright smile that looked anything but sleepy. She watched him shuffle off down the hall and saw the lights at the far end of it come on. She had to stay calm, she warned herself fiercely, and not do or say things that were unusual for her and that might evoke suspicion.

At exactly seven o'clock the phone rang again, and she snatched it out of the cradle and answered it.

Zack's voice sounded even deeper on the telephone, but it was cold, curt, and clipped: "Are you alone, Julie?"

"Yes."

"Is there anything in this world I can say to dissuade you from your insane idea of joining me?"

It wasn't what she wanted to hear, it wasn't the way she wanted him to talk to her, but she concentrated on the words he'd written in his letter, refusing to let him trick or intimidate her with his voice. "Yes, there is," she replied softly. "You can tell me that the things you wrote in your letter were lies."

"Fine," he said. "They were all lies."

Julie squeezed the phone in her hand and closed her eyes. "Now, tell me that you don't love me, darling."

She heard him draw a ragged breath, and his voice dropped to a tortured plea. "Don't make me say that. Please."

"I love you so much," Julie whispered fiercely.

"Don't do this to me, Julie—"

Her fingers loosened on the phone and she smiled because she suddenly sensed that she was going to win. "I can't stop," she said tenderly. "I can't stop loving you. There's only one solution I'm willing to accept, and I gave it to you."

"Christ, that's not—"

"Save your prayers for later, darling," she whispered teasingly. "You're going to wear your knees out when I get there as it is, praying I learn how to cook better, praying I let you get some sleep at night for a change, praying I stop giving you babies . . ."

"Oh, Julie . . . don't. God, don't."

"Don't what?"

He drew in a long, labored breath and was quiet for so long that she thought he wasn't going to reply, and when he finally answered, the words sounded as if they were being wrenched from his chest. "Don't . . . *ever* stop loving me."

"I'll promise not to in front of a priest, a preacher, or a Buddhist monk."

That wrung a reluctant laugh from him, and the memory of his dazzling smile made her heart soar as he said, "Are we talking about marriage here?"

"I am."

"I should have expected you'd insist on that, too."

His attempt to sound disgruntled failed completely, but Julie went along with the game, eager to lighten his mood. "Don't you want to marry me?"

He declared the game over with one solemn word: "Desperately."

"In that case, tell me how to get to you and what ring size you wear."

There was another torturous pause that strung her nerves to the breaking point, and then he began speaking, and she forget everything but his words and the incredible feeling of elation sweeping through her as he spoke. "All right. I'll meet you in Mexico City at the airport eight days from now, on Tuesday night. Early Tuesday morning, get into your car and drive to Dallas. In Dallas, rent a car in your own name and drive it to San Antonio, but don't turn it in. Leave it in the rental car lot at the airport, they'll find it eventually. With luck, the authorities will think you're driving somewhere to meet me instead of flying and they won't alert the airports as quickly. Altogether, the highway traveling should only take you a few hours. A plane ticket for the four o'clock flight to Mexico City will be waiting for you at the Aero-Mexico ticket counter in the name of Susan Arland. Any questions so far?"

Julie smiled at the realization that he'd expected the call to end like this when he made it, because he'd obviously researched all the logistics already. "One question. Why can't I meet you sooner?"

"Because I have some details to finalize first." Julie accepted that, and he continued, "When you leave your house Tuesday morning, don't take anything with you. Don't pack a suitcase, don't do anything to give anyone the idea that you're leaving. Keep your eye in the rearview mirror and make sure you aren't followed. If you're being followed, do some errand or other, then go back home and wait to hear from me again. Between now and then, watch your mailbox closely. Open everything, even advertisements. If there are any changes in the arrangements, someone will contact you either that way or in person. We can't use your phone at home, because I'd bet my life there's a tap on it."

"Who will contact me?"

"I don't have the vaguest idea, and when he does, don't ask for identification."

"Okay," Julie said as she finished writing down his instructions. "I don't think I'm being watched. Paul Richardson and David Ingram—the two FBI agents who were here—gave up and went back to Dallas last week."

"How are you feeling?"

"Wonderful."

"No morning sickness or anything?"

Her conscience jabbed at her, but she tried to soothe it by not actually lying to him. "I'm a very healthy female. I think my body was made for motherhood. And it was definitely made for you."

He swallowed audibly at the sexual reference. "Tease me now, and you'll pay later."

"Promise?"

He laughed then, a throaty laugh that warmed her, but not as much as his husky words. "I miss you. God, I miss you." As if he were afraid to let either of them relax too much, he said, "You realize that you won't be able to say good-bye to your family? You can leave them a letter somewhere where they won't find it until several days after you've gone. After that, you'll never be able to contact them again."

She squeezed her eyes closed. "I know."

"And you're prepared to do that?"

"Yes."

"That's a hell of a way to start a life together," he said tautly, "tearing your family apart and severing all their connections to you. It's like inviting a curse."

"Don't say things like that!" Julie said, suppressing a shiver. "I'll make them understand in my letter when I tell them good-bye. Besides, leaving them to go with you is practically—biblical!" To distract both of them from the grim mood stealing over the conversation, she said, "What are you doing now? Are you standing or sitting?"

"I'm in a hotel room, sitting on a bed, talking to you."

"Are you staying in the hotel?"

"No. I got the room so I could use the phone in privacy and get a decent connection to the States."

"I want to go to sleep tonight, seeing what you'll be seeing when you lie in bed. Describe your bedroom to me and I'll tell you what mine looks like, so you'll know."

"Julie," he said gruffly, "are you trying to drive me to new heights of frustrated sexual desire?"

She hadn't any such intention, but the notion was gratifying. "Can I do that?"

"You know you can."

"Just by talking to you about bedrooms?"

"Just by talking to me about anything."

She laughed then, as easily and as naturally as she'd been able to laugh with him from the beginning.

"What size is it?" he asked with a smile in his voice.

"My bedroom?"

"Your ring finger."

She drew in a shaky breath. "Five and a half, I think. What size is yours?"

"I don't know. Large, I guess."

"And what color is it?"

"My finger?"

"No," she said with a chuckle, "your *bedroom*."

"Smart ass!" he chided, but he answered and his voice got deep. "It's on a boat right now—teak walls, a brass lamp, a small dresser, and a picture of you I cut out from a newspaper hanging on the wall."

"Is that what you see when you fall asleep?"

"I don't sleep, Julie. I just think of you. Do you like boats?"

Julie drew in another shattered breath, trying to memorize each tender thing he said. "I love boats."

"What's your bedroom like?"

"Frilly. White ruffles on the bedspread and canopy and dressing table across the room. A picture of you on my night stand."

"Where did you get it?"

"From an old magazine at the library."

"You swiped a magazine from the library and cut a picture of me out of it?" he said, trying to sound shocked.

"Certainly not. I have scruples, you know. I explained I'd damaged it beyond repair and I paid the fine. Zack—" she said, trying to keep the panic out of her voice, "the janitor is hanging around outside the glass wall. I don't think he can hear me, but he doesn't normally just loiter around like this."

"I'm going to hang up. Keep talking into the phone after I do. Try to mislead him with an innocuous conversation if you can."

"All right. Wait, he's walking away. He must have needed something from the cart."

"We'd better hang up anyway. If there's anything you need to take care of before you leave, do it in the next week."

She nodded, speechless with regret at the thought of letting him go.

"There's one more thing I need to say to you," he added quietly.

"What is it?"

"I meant every word I wrote in that letter."

"I know you did." She sensed he wanted to hang up, and she added quickly, "Before you go, what do you think of what Matt found out about Tony Austin? Even though Matt doesn't think there's anything we can do legally, there has to be some—"

"Stay out of that," Zack warned her, his voice turning icy. "And leave Austin to me. There are other ways to handle him without involving Matt."

"What sort of ways?"

"Don't ask. If you have problems with any of the arrangements I'm making for you, don't look to Matt for help. What we're doing is illegal and I can't let him get involved beyond what he's already done."

Julie suppressed a shiver at his ominous tone. "Say something sweet before you hang up."

"Something sweet," he repeated, his voice softening. "What did you have in mind?"

She was a little hurt when he seemed unable to think of something, and then he said with a smile in his husky voice, "I am going to bed in exactly three hours. Be there with me. And when you close your eyes, my arms will be around you."

Her voice dropped to a shaky whisper. "I love that."

"They've been around you every night since we parted. Good night, sweetheart."

"Good night."

He hung up and at the last minute, Julie remembered his instructions about carrying on an animated conversation. Rather than fake one, which she didn't think would be as convincing, she called Katherine and managed to talk to her for thirty minutes about anything and everything. She hung up and tore off the sheet of paper with Zack's instructions written on it, then she remembered seeing a mystery on television where the case was solved by the imprint of the handwriting on a tablet, so she took the tablet, too.

"Good night, Henry," she called cheerfully.

"Good night, Miss Julie," he said shuffling off down the hall.

Julie left by the side door. Henry left by the same door three hours later, after he made a collect call to a phone number in Dallas.

53

JULIE TOSSED AN OVERNIGHT CASE IN THE BACK OF HER CAR, glanced at her watch to make certain she still had more than enough time to make her noon flight, and went back into the house. As she was loading her breakfast dishes into the dishwasher, the phone on the wall rang and she picked it up. "Hi, beautiful," Paul Richardson's voice was warm and crisp, an odd combination, Julie thought. "I know it's short notice, but I'd love to see you this weekend. I could fly in from Dallas and take you to dinner tomorrow night for Valentine's Day. Better yet, why don't I fly you here, and I'll cook?"

Julie had already decided that if she were actually being watched, an "innocent" trip like the one this weekend might actually fool her spies into letting down their guard. "I can't, Paul, I'm leaving for the airport in a half hour."

"Where are you going?"

"Is that an official question?" Julie asked, cradling the phone between her shoulder and chin and rinsing out a glass.

"If it was official, wouldn't I be asking it in person?"

Her instinctive liking and trust of him warred with the wariness Zack made her feel, but until she actually got into her car to leave Keaton for the last time, it seemed wisest and easiest to stick completely to the truth. "I don't know whether you would or not," she admitted.

"Julie, what can I do to make you trust me?"

"Quit your job?"

"There has to be an easier way."

"I still have some things to do before I leave. Let's talk about this when I get back."

"From where and when?"

"I'm going to visit a friend's grandmother in a little town in Pennsylvania—Ridgemont, to be exact. I'll be home late tomorrow."

He sighed. "Okay, then. I'll call you next week and we'll make a date?"

"Mmm. Fine," she said absently, pouring detergent into the dishwasher and shutting the door.

Paul Richardson hung up the phone in his office, placed a second call, and waited for the answer, drumming his fingers on his desk. He snatched the phone on the first ring, and a woman's voice said, "Mr. Richardson, Julie Mathison has reservations on a flight out of Dallas connecting through Philadelphia to Ridgemont, Pennsylvania, on a commuter flight. Will you need any further information?"

"No," he said with a relieved sigh. He got up, walked over to the windows, and frowned at the scanty weekend traffic moving down the Dallas boulevard. "Well?" Dave Ingram said, coming in from the adjoining office. "What did she tell you about the suitcase she put in her car?"

"The truth, damn it! She told me the truth, because she has nothing to hide."

"Bullshit. You're conveniently forgetting that phone call from South America she waited for at school the other night."

Paul swung around. "South America? Have you gotten a trace then?"

"Yep, five minutes ago. The call she got came through a hotel switchboard in San Lucia Del Mar."

"Benedict!" Paul said, his jaw tightening. "What name did he register under?"

"José Feliciano," Ingram said. "That arrogant son of a bitch actually registered as José Feliciano!"

Paul stared in disbelief. "He's using a passport with that name?"

"The clerk at the desk didn't ask for a passport. She thought he was a native. Why not, he's dark, he had a Spanish name, and he speaks Spanish—helpful when one lives in California, no doubt. He has a beard now, by the way."

"I take it he's already checked out?"

"Naturally. He paid in advance for one night and was gone the next morning. The bed in his room wasn't used."

"He may go there again to use the phone. Put the hotel under surveillance."

"That's taken care of."

Paul walked back behind his desk and sank into his chair.

"She talked to him for ten minutes," Ingram added. "That's long enough to make plans."

"That's also long enough to talk to someone she feels sorry for and to reassure herself that he's all right. She has a soft heart and she believes the bastard is a victim of cruel circumstances. Don't forget that. If she wanted to join him, she'd have left Colorado with him."

"Maybe he wouldn't agree to take her along."

"Right," Paul said sarcastically. "But now, after weeks without seeing her, he's suddenly so crazy about her, he's going to come out from under cover and come after her."

"Shit," Ingram bit out, "you'd do it. Your ass is already on the line with the man upstairs over your continued defense of that woman, and you still fight for her. She lied through her teeth about what went on in Colorado. We should have read her rights and hauled her in . . ."

Paul forcibly reminded himself that Ingram was his friend and that most of the other man's anger stemmed from worry for Paul. "There's a little matter of reasonable grounds for suspicion," he reminded Dave tightly. "We didn't have that, let alone any proof."

"We do as of five minutes ago when we got the report on that phone call!"

"If you're right about everything, she'll lead us straight to Benedict. If you're wrong, we haven't lost anything."

"I ordered her put under constant surveillance before I came in here, Paul."

Clamping his jaws together, Paul bit back a senseless and wrongful protest at Dave's action, but he said through his teeth, "May I remind you that *I'm* in charge of this case until I'm taken off it. Before you do another damned thing, you clear it with me. Got it?" he snapped.

"Got it!" Dave shot back, just as angrily. "Did you find out anything else about the car that was parked out in front of her house last week?"

Shoving a report across the desk at him, Paul said, "It was rented in Dallas from Hertz by Joseph A. O'Hara. Chicago address. No record. He's clean as a whistle. Employed as a chauffeur/bodyguard by the Collier Trust."

"Is that a bank?"

"There's a Collier Bank and Trust in Houston with branches scattered around the country."

"When you called her just now, did you happen to ask Little Miss Muffet about her visitors from Chicago?"

"And alert her that she's being watched, so you can accuse me of favoritism again?"

Ingram breathed a heavy sigh and tossed the report on O'Hara back onto Paul's desk. "Look, I'm sorry, Paul. I just don't want to see you destroy your career over some broad with big blue eyes and great legs."

Relaxing back in his chair, Paul eyed him with a grim smile. "You're going to have to beg her forgiveness on your knees someday, or we won't let you be godfather to our first baby."

With a harsh sigh, Ingram said, "I hope the day comes when I have to do that, Paul. Honest to God, I do."

"Good. Then keep your damned eyes off her legs."

Julie finished tidying the kitchen, got her coat from the closet, and was ready to leave for the trip to Pennsylvania when there was a knock at her front door. With her coat over her arm, she answered the knock and stared in surprise at the sight of Ted and Katherine standing side by side. "It's been a long time," she said with a delighted grin, "since I saw you two standing together on anyone's front porch."

"Katherine tells me you're leaving for Pennsylvania to play goodwill ambassador or some damned thing for Zack Benedict. What's the idea, Julie?" he demanded, walking past her into the house with a guilty-looking Katherine trailing behind him.

Julie shoved her coat aside and looked at her watch. "I have less than five minutes to explain it, although I thought I already explained it to Katherine last night." Ordinarily Julie would have taken serious exception to their interference in her life, but the knowledge that she'd be leaving them both forever in a few days banished whatever resentment she felt. Without rancor, she said, "Although I love seeing the two of you together again, I wish you'd find some common cause for it other than ganging up on me."

"It's my fault," Katherine said quickly. "I saw Ted in town this morning, and he asked about you. You didn't tell me your trip was a secret . . ." she trailed off.

"It's not a secret."

"Then explain to me why you're going," Ted insisted, his face taut with worry and frustration.

Closing the door, Julie absently shoved her heavy hair off her forehead, trying to think what to tell them. She couldn't explain that she was superstitiously troubled by Zack's remark about their marriage being cursed from the beginning because of the heartache it would cause. On the other hand, she wanted to tell them enough of the truth so that they'd remember this and it would help them understand everything and forgive her more quickly later. She looked from Katherine's worried face to Ted's annoyed one and said haltingly,

"Do you believe in the saying that things go on as they begin?" Katherine and Ted exchanged blank looks, and Julie explained, "Do you believe in the idea that when things begin badly, they tend to *end* badly?"

"Yes," Katherine said. "I think I do."

"I don't," Ted said flatly, and what he said made Julie suspect he was thinking about his marriage to Katherine. "Some things that begin beautifully have rotten endings."

"Since you're determined to meddle in my life," Julie said, amused, "then I think I have the right to point out that, if you're referring to your own marriage, the real problem is that it has never ended. Katherine knows that, even if you refuse to face it, Ted. Now, to finish answering your question about my trip to Pennsylvania in the minute I have left before I leave: Zack was raised by his grandmother, and he parted with her under very ugly circumstances. Nothing else in his personal life has gone well since then. He's in danger now, and he's alone, but he's starting a whole new part of his life. I'd like him to have luck and peace in that new life, and I have a feeling—call it a superstition, if you prefer—that, maybe, if I mend the bridges he burned a long time ago, he'll have that at last." In the blank silence that followed her announcement, she watched both of them struggle to find an argument and fail, so she reached for the door. "Remember that, will you both?" she added, fighting to keep the emotion from her voice and disguise the import of her next request. "In order to be truly happy, it helps so much to know your family wishes you well . . . even if you don't do the things they'd like you to do. When your own family hates you, it's almost like a curse."

When the door closed behind her, Ted looked irritably at Katherine. "What the hell did she mean by that?"

"I thought the logic sounded pretty clear," Katherine said, but she was frowning at the odd tension she'd heard in Julie's voice. "My dad's a little superstitious, and so am I. Although the word *curse* seemed a little strong."

"I'm not talking about that. What did she mean when she said our marriage isn't over and you know that?"

During the last weeks, Katherine had watched Julie courageously confront the FBI and the rest of the world, openly expressing her faith in Zack Benedict's innocence, even though he'd rejected her love and hurt her terribly in Colorado. During that same time, Katherine had managed to put herself in Ted's presence a dozen times while they both coached Julie's students' athletic games, but in dealing with him, she'd carefully hidden her deeper feelings and tried only to overcome his hostility. Originally, she'd convinced herself that the best way to handle Ted and accomplish her goal was with a slow, cautious, step-by-step strategy, not an open admission of feelings. Now as she looked at the man she loved, she faced the fact that it was fear of being hurt, of being made to feel like a fool, and of having her hopes shattered once and for all that had been dictating all her actions. She knew he was seeing another woman regularly and that he'd been seeing even more of her since Katherine had returned to Keaton, and it was belatedly obvious to her now that all she'd really accomplished with him was a sort of armed truce; his feelings toward her hadn't changed, she'd simply forced him with her constant presence to mask his contempt behind a coolly polite facade.

She was afraid she was running out of time, afraid she'd lose her nerve if she didn't tell him now, and afraid she was going to make a fatal blunder because she was so desperate and so nervous that she was going to unload everything on him at once.

"Are you thinking about your answer or studying the shape of my nose," he demanded irritably.

To her horror, Katherine felt her knees begin to shake and her palms perspire, but she lifted her eyes to his cool blue ones and said bravely, "Julie thinks our marriage isn't over because I'm still in love with you."

"Where would she get an asinine idea like that."

"From me," Katherine said shakily. "I told her that."

Ted's brows snapped together and he raked her with a contemptuous glance that made her flinch. "You told her you're still in love with me?"

"Yes. I told her everything, including what a pitiful excuse for a wife I was and about how—how I lost our baby."

Even now, years later, the mention of the baby she'd deliberately destroyed made Ted so furious that he had to fight the urge to slap her, and his own pentup fury staggered him. "Don't ever mention the baby to me or anyone else again, or so help me God, I'll—"

"You'll what?" Katherine cried brokenly. "You'll hate me? You can't hate me more than I hate myself for what happened. You'll divorce me? You already did that to me. You'll refuse to believe it was an accident?" she continued hysterically. "Well, it *was* an accident! The horse I was riding went lame—"

"Damn you, shut up!" Ted said, grabbing her arms in a bruising grip and starting to shove her aside to leave, but Katherine ignored the pain of his grip and flattened herself against the door so he couldn't. "I can't!" she cried. "I have to make you understand. I've spent three years trying to forget what I did to us, three years looking for some way to atone for all the things I was and don't want to be."

"I don't want to hear any more of this!" He tried to yank her forward and out of his way, but she pressed against the door, ignoring the bite of his fingers into her flesh.

"What the hell do you want from me?" he demanded, unable to budge her without resorting to serious brute force.

"I want you to believe me when I tell you it was an *accident,*" she wept.

Ted fought to ignore the impact of her words and the effect of her beautiful, tear-streaked face, but in all the time he'd known her, he'd never seen her reduced to tears. She'd been spoiled, proud, and willful, but never, ever had she shed a single tear. Even so, he might have been able to resist her if she hadn't lifted her wet eyes to his at that moment and whispered achingly, "We've both been crying inside over the way our marriage ended for all these years, at least hold me and let's finish it now."

Against his will, his hands loosened their grip on her arms, she pressed her face against his chest, and suddenly his arms were going around her, holding her to him as she cried, and the sweet ache he felt at having her body pressed to his again was almost his undoing. Struggling to keep his voice flat and emotionless, he warned her, "It's over, Katherine. *We're* over."

"Then let me say the things I came back to Keaton to say to you, so we can end it as friends, not enemies." His hand stopped moving down her back and Katherine held her breath, half expecting him to refuse, but when he remained silent, she lifted her gaze to his and began, "Can you possibly find it in your heart to believe there's at least a fifty/fifty chance I didn't deliberately try to lose our baby?" Before he could refuse, she said with painful honestly, "If you think back, you'll realize I never would have had the *courage* to risk my own life for anything. I was such a coward, I was afraid of blood, spiders, snakes—"

Ted was older now and wiser, too; he suddenly recognized the compelling logic in her statement, but more than that, he saw truth in her eyes, and the fury and disgust he'd nurtured all these years began to disintegrate, leaving him feeling incredibly relieved. "You were even afraid of moths."

Katherine nodded, watching the animosity finally fade from his face for the first time in years. "I'm sorrier than I can ever say for the reckless, selfish stupidity that lost us our baby. I'm sorry for the mess I made out of our marriage, for the nightmare I made out of your life the entire time we lived together—"

"It wasn't quite as bad as that," he said reluctantly, "at least not the *entire* time."

"Don't pretend for my sake. I'm all grown up now, I've learned to face the truth and deal with it. And the truth is I was a pitiful excuse for a wife. Besides acting like a spoiled, irrational, demanding child bride, I was completely useless. I didn't cook, I didn't clean, and when you wouldn't give me my own way, I didn't sleep with you. For years, I've needed to admit that to you and to tell you the truth—our marriage didn't fail, you didn't fail—I failed."

To her amazement, he shook his head and sighed. "You were always so damned hard on yourself. That hasn't changed."

"Hard on myself?" Katherine repeated with a choked laugh. "You must be joking, or else you've had two child brides! In case you're confused, *I'm* the one who nearly poisoned you on the rare occasions I bothered to cook. I'm the one who scorched an imprint of an iron into three of your uniform shirts the first week we were married. I'm the one who ironed creases in all the side seams of your pants, instead of the fronts, so the legs all stuck out at the sides."

"You did not nearly poison me."

"Ted, don't patronize me! All the guys on the sheriff's office used to tease you about being the Rolaid King after we got married. I heard them."

"Damn it, I was swallowing antacids like candy because I was married to someone who I couldn't make happy, and it was tearing me up inside."

Katherine had waited all this time to confess her failures and ask his forgiveness and she refused to be held off by some misplaced notion of gallantry on Ted's part. "That's not true, and you know it! My God, your mother even gave me her recipe for your favorite meal, and you could barely eat the goulash when I cooked it! Don't deny it," she said fiercely when he started to shake his head. "I *saw* you throw that goulash down the disposal when I left the kitchen. You must have been getting rid of everything else I cooked the same way, and I don't blame you."

"Damn it, I ate everything you ever cooked for me," he insisted angrily. "Except for the goulash. I'm sorry you saw me get rid of it, but I can't stomach that stuff."

Katherine's expression turned ominous at his continued prevarication. "Ted, your mother specifically told me it was your favorite."

"No, it was *Carl's* favorite. She always got that mixed up."

The absurdity of the heated debate hit them both at the same time; it made Katherine giggle and slump back against the door. "Why didn't you tell me that then?"

"You wouldn't have believed me," Ted said with a harsh sigh as he braced his hand beside her shoulder and tried to explain to her one more time what he hadn't been able to make her understand when she was a twenty-year-old. "Sometime in your young life as Dillon Cahill's beautiful, intelligent daughter, you got the crazy idea that you had to do everything exactly by the book and do it better than anyone else. When you couldn't excel at something, you got so angry and ashamed there was no reasoning with you. To you, life was like one of those paint-by-number canvases, where everything had to be done in exactly the right order and right between the lines or else it was no good. Kathy," he said quietly, and the sound of the nickname that he alone had ever dared to use was almost as devasting to her as the way he absently brushed her hair off her shoulder with his wrist, "you wanted to go to college right after we got married, not because you were shallow or spoiled, but because you had some crazy notion that you'd screwed up the rightful order of things by marrying me first instead of after you got your education at that fancy eastern school. And when you wanted that damned mansion your father built for us, it wasn't because you wanted to lord it over everyone in town, it was because in some part of you, you truly believed we'd be happy there because . . . because it fell into your notion of the natural order of things for Katherine Cahill."

Closing her eyes, Katherine leaned her head against the door and sighed with a mixture of frustration and amusement. "When I went back to college, after our divorce, I spent an entire year seeing a therapist once a week, trying to understand why I was such a mess."

"What did you find out?"

"Not nearly as much as what you just told me in two minutes. And then do you know what I did next?"

A smile tugged at his lips and he shook his head. "I couldn't begin to imagine. What did you do next?"

"I went to Paris and took a Cordon Bleu cooking course!"

"How did you do?"

"Not well, actually," she told him with a rueful smile. "It's the only time in my life I didn't shine in a course I *wanted* to take." He lifted his brows to emphasize the importance of her revealing remark, and she accepted his silent comment with a nod of understanding.

"Did you pass the course?"

"I passed beef," she teased, and his chuckle made her heart sing, "but I failed veal."

For a long moment they smiled at each other, in accord for the first time in years, and then Katherine said softly, "Will you please kiss me?"

He straightened abruptly, shoving away from the door. "Not a chance."

"Are you afraid?"

"Knock it off, damn it! You already ran this seduction number on me years ago, and it's old stuff now. It won't work."

Ignoring the blow to her pride, she crossed her arms over her chest and smiled at him. "For a minister's son, you swear an awful lot."

"So you told me years ago. And as I told you, I'm no minister, my father is. Furthermore," he added with a deliberate attempt to alienate her, "while you were undeniably appealing to me when I was younger, I prefer to do my own seducing these days."

Katherine's wounded pride came out in a soft, ominous whisper as she shoved away from the door and reached for the coat she tossed over a chair. "*Do you now?*"

"You're damned right I do. And now, if you'll take some good advice, you'll go running back to Dallas to Hayward Spencer or Spencer Hayward or whatever his name is and let him soothe your wounded sensibilities with a fifty-carat diamond necklace to match that incredibly vulgar ring you're wearing."

Instead of tearing into him as she would have years ago, she gave him an indecipherable look and said, "I don't need your advice any more. It may surprise you to hear this, but people, including Spencer, actually ask me for advice these days."

"On what?" he jeered. "Making a fashion statement in the society pages?"

"That does it!" Katherine exploded, throwing her coat back on the chair. "I'll let you hurt me when I deserve it, but I'll be damned if I'll let you hide your sexual uncertainties behind an attack on me."

"My WHAT?" he exploded.

"You were perfectly nice, perfectly at ease, until I asked you to kiss me and then you started this absurd personal attack. Now, either apologize or kiss me or admit you're afraid."

"I apologize," he snapped, so quickly and so completely unrepentantly that Katherine started to laugh.

"Thank you," she said sweetly, reaching for her coat. "I accept your apology."

In the past such an exchange would have ended in a royal battle, and Ted was completely taken aback by her new serenity, so much so that he realized that she really had changed. "Katherine," he said shortly, "I apologize for attacking you. I mean it. I'm sorry."

She nodded but carefully kept her eyes from his so they wouldn't give her away. "I know. You probably misunderstood the sort of kiss I was asking you for. I only thought of it as a way to seal our truce and make it lasting."

She raised her eyes to his and could have sworn there was amusement and knowledge in his gaze, but to her shock, he complied. Tipping her chin up he murmured, "All right. Kiss me, but make it quick." Which was why Katherine was laughing and his mouth was smiling when their lips touched for the first time in three years. "Stop laughing," he warned in a muffled chuckle.

"Stop smiling," she countered, but their breaths were mingling and it took only that to ignite the passion they'd shared years before. Ted's hands slid to her waist, moving her closer, then tightened suddenly as she flattened herself against his body, sweeping around her back back and yanking her tightly to him.

54

FOLLOWING THE DIRECTIONS SHE'D BEEN GIVEN BY THE MAN AT the rental car office at Ridgemont's small airport, Julie had no trouble finding Zack's boyhood home. Perched high on a hill overlooking the picturesque little valley, the Tudor mansion where Margaret Stanhope still lived was, according to the man at the rental car office, "practically a landmark hereabouts." Watching for the fancy brick pillars that she'd been told would mark the driveway, Julie saw them on her left and turned off the highway. As she wended her way up the long wide drive that climbed through the trees to the top of the hill, she remembered what Zack had told her about the day he'd left this place. *"I was permanently disowned as of that moment. I handed over my car keys and walked down the driveway and down the hill to the highway."* He'd had a very long walk, she realized with a pang of sad nostalgia, looking around her, trying to imagine what he had felt and seen that day.

At the top of the hill as she made the last turn, the drive widened and swept in a wide arc through manicured lawns and giant trees, barren now in winter. There was a harsh austerity about the sprawling stone house that made her oddly uneasy as she pulled to a stop on the brick-paved entry in front of the steps. She hadn't called in advance because she hadn't wanted to explain the purpose for her visit on a telephone, nor had she wanted to give Zack's grandmother an easy opportunity to refuse to see her. In Julie's experience, delicate personal matters were always better handled in person. Gathering up her purse and gloves, she got out of the car and stopped, looking around at the house and its setting, delaying the moment of reckoning. Zack had grown up here, and it seemed to her this place had left its mark on his personality; it was like him in a way—formidable, proud, solid, impressive.

That made her feel better, braver, as she walked up the steps toward the wide arched door. Firmly suppressing the inexplicable premonition of doom that was trying to steal over her, she reminded herself that she had come on a long-overdue "peace mission" and she lifted the heavy brass door knocker.

An ancient butler with stooped shoulders answered the door wearing a dark suit and bow tie. "I'm Julie Mathison," she told him. "I'd like to see Mrs. Stanhope if she's at home." His shaggy white brows shot up over widened brown eyes when Julie gave her name, but he recovered his composure and stepped back into a cavernous, gloomy foyer with a green slate floor. "I will see if Mrs. Stanhope will see you. You may wait there," he added, gesturing to a straightbacked, uncomfortable-looking antique chair positioned beside a drum table at the left end of the foyer. Julie sat down, her purse on her knees, feeling a little like a supplicant in the stifling, unwelcoming formality of the foyer, and she had a hunch that unexpected guests were intended to feel this way. Concentrating on what she needed to say, she gazed at a German landscape hanging in an ornate dark frame on the opposite wall, then she turned nervously when the butler shuffled into the foyer. "Madam will spare you exactly five minutes," he announced.

Refusing to be daunted by that unpromising beginning, Julie followed him down a wide hall and then passed in front of him as he opened a door and gestured her into a large room with a fire burning in a massive stone fireplace and an Oriental carpet spread across a polished dark wood floor. A pair of highbacked chairs upholstered in a faded tapestry were positioned facing the fireplace, and since no one was sitting on the sofa or any of the other furniture in the room, Julie erroneously assumed she was alone. She wandered over to a table covered with silver-framed photographs, intending to study the faces of what she presumed were Zack's relatives and ancestors, then she saw that the wall on the left was covered with large portraits. With a fascinated smile, she started toward them, realizing that Zack hadn't exaggerated—there was a startling resemblance between himself and many of the Stanhope men. Behind her a sharp voice snapped, "You've just wasted one of your five minutes, Miss Mathison."

Whirling around in surprise, Julie looked for the source of the ominous voice and walked around to the front of the chairs. There she had her second jolt because the woman who was rising to her feet, leaning on a silver-handled ebony cane, was not the diminutive old woman who Julie had rather expected to resemble the butler in stature and demeanor. Instead, she was taller than Julie by several inches, and once she gained her feet, her posture was as rigidly erect as the expression on her unlined face was stony and forbidding. "Miss Mathison!" the woman snapped, "Either sit down or remain standing, but start talking. Why have you come here?"

"I'm very sorry," Julie said hastily, backing quickly into the high-backed chair opposite Zack's grandmother's. She sat down so the woman wouldn't feel obliged to remain on her feet. "Mrs. Stanhope, I'm a friend of—"

"I know who you are, I've seen you on television," the woman interrupted coldly as she sat down. "He took you hostage and then converted you to his media spokesperson."

"Not exactly," Julie said, noting that the woman refrained from even using Zack's name. As always, when Julie was prepared in advance to face a difficult confrontation, she was able to maintain an outward serenity that she didn't always feel, but this situation was even more tense and awkward than she'd expected.

"I asked you why you've come here!"

Instead of letting the older woman rile or intimidate her with her tone, Julie smiled and said quietly, "I'm here, Mrs. Stanhope, because when I was with your grandson in Colorado—"

"I have only one grandson," the other woman bit out, "and he lives here in Ridgemont."

"Mrs. Stanhope," Julie said calmly, "you've only allotted me five minutes. Please don't make me waste them caviling over technicalities because I'm afraid I'll end up leaving here without having explained what I came here to tell you—and I think you're going to want to hear it." The woman's white brows snapped together at Julie's tone, and her mouth thinned, but Julie forged bravely ahead. "I'm aware that you do not acknowledge Zack as your grandson, just as I'm aware that you also had another grandson who died tragically. I'm also aware that the breach between you and Zack has remained during all these years because of his stubbornness."

Her face twisted with derision. "He told you that?"

Julie nodded, trying to ignore the older woman's unexpected sarcasm. "He told me a lot of things in Colorado, Mrs. Stanhope, things he's never told anyone before." She waited, hoping for some sign of curiosity, but when Mrs. Stanhope continued to regard her stonily, Julie had no choice except to continue without encouragement. "Among other things, he told me that if he had his life to live over again, he would have reconciled with you long ago. He admired you very much and he loved you—"

"Get out!"

Julie stood up automatically, but her temper was rapidly igniting and she fought it down with all her strength. "Zack admitted you and he were very much alike, and when it comes to stubbornness, he was clearly telling the truth. I am trying to tell you that your grandson regrets the breach between the two of you and that he loves you."

"I said get out! You should never have come here!"

"Apparently not," Julie agreed tautly, reaching for the purse she'd left beside the chair. "I had no idea a grown woman, facing the end of her life, could still harbor some absurd grudge against her own flesh and blood for something he did when he was still a boy. How bad could it possibly have been that you can't forgive him?"

Mrs. Stanhope's laugh was bitter. "You poor fool! He duped you, too, didn't he?"

"What?"

"Did he actually ask you to come here?" she demanded. "He didn't, did he? He would never have dared!"

Sensing that a negative reply would somehow play right into the woman's hands and harden her even further against Zack, Julie threw all her pride away and gambled everything on this last chance to reach the woman's heart. "He did not ask me to come here and tell you how he felt about you, Mrs. Stanhope. He did something that is even more revealing about the respect and love he still has for you." Drawing a fortifying breath, Julie ignored the woman's freezing expression and said, "I hadn't heard from him until I received his letter a week and a half ago. He wrote to me because he was afraid I was pregnant, and in his letter, he implored me not to have an abortion if I was. He asked me instead to bring his baby to you to raise, because he said you had never shirked a responsibility in your life, and you wouldn't shirk that one. He said he would write you a letter first to explain—"

"If you are pregnant by him and you have any comprehension of genetics," his grandmother interrupted furiously, "you'll have an abortion! Regardless of what you do, I wouldn't have his misbegotten brat in my house."

Julie stepped back from the evil of those remarks. "What kind of monster are you anyway?"

"He is the monster, Miss Mathison, and you are his dupe. Two people who loved him have already died violent deaths at his hand. You're lucky you weren't the third!"

"He did not kill his wife, and I don't know what you're talking about when you say two people—"

"I'm talking about his brother! As surely as Cain killed Abel, that demented monster killed Justin. He shot him in the head after a quarrel!"

Confronted with such vicious lies, Julie lost her control. Shaking with fury and shock, she said, "You're lying! I know exactly how Justin died and why! If you're saying these things about Zack because you're trying to justify turning away his baby, you're wasting your breath! I'm not pregnant, and if I was, I wouldn't leave you alone in the same house with my baby! No wonder your own husband couldn't keep loving you and took up with other women. Oh, yes, I know all about that!" she burst out when shock momentarily cracked Mrs. Stanhope's contemptuous glower. "Zack told me everything. He told me that his grandfather said you were the only woman in the world he'd ever loved, even though everyone thought he'd married you for your money. Your husband told Zack he just couldn't meet your high standards, and he finally quit trying to do it soon after you were married. What I can't understand," Julie finished with contempt, "is why your husband loved you or why Zack admired you! You don't have standards—what you have is ice instead of a heart! No wonder poor Justin couldn't tell you he was gay! Zack isn't the monster, you are!"

"And you," Mrs. Stanhope countered, "are the monster's pawn!" As if Julie's loss of control was contagious, the rigidity drained from the older woman's face and her autocratic voice was suddenly edged with weariness. "Sit down, Miss Mathison!"

"No, I'm leaving."

"If you do," she challenged, "then you're afraid of the truth. I agreed to see you because I watched you plead for him on television, and I wanted to hear what could possibly have brought you here. I thought you must be some sort of opportunist, desperate to remain in the limelight and that you'd come here to dredge up something that might do that for you. Now, it is obvious to me that you are a young woman of considerable courage and strong convictions and that it is your misguided sense of justice that sent you here. I respect courage, Miss Mathison, especially in my own sex. I respect yours enough to discuss things with you that are still intensely painful to me. For your own sake, I suggest you listen to me."

Stunned by the drastic change in the tone of conversation, Julie hesitated beside her chair but remained stubbornly standing.

"I gather from your expression that you've decided not to take my word for anything," Mrs. Stanhope said, watching her. "Very well. Were I as deluded and loyal as you clearly are, I wouldn't listen to me either." She picked up the bell on the table beside her chair and rang it, and a moment later the butler appeared in the doorway. "Come in here, Foster," she ordered, and when he complied, she turned to Julie and said, "How do you think Justin died?"

"I *know* how he died," Julie corrected fiercely.

"What do you think you know?" Mrs. Stanhope retorted, brows raised.

Julie opened her mouth to tell her, and then hesitated, belatedly remembering that this was an old woman and that Julie actually had no right to destroy her memories of Justin merely so that she'd cease to hate Zack. On the other hand, Justin was already dead, but Zack was still alive. "Look, Mrs. Stanhope, I don't want to hurt you any more than I probably have, and the truth is going to do that."

"The truth can't hurt me," she scoffed.

That mocking tone of Mrs. Stanhope's scraped against Julie's raw nerves and broke her slender thread of control. "Justin killed himself," she said flatly. "He shot himself in the head because he was a homosexual and he couldn't face that. He admitted it to Zack an hour before he killed himself."

The other woman's cold gray eyes never flinched; she simply stared at Julie with a mixture of pity and disdain, then she reached for a framed photograph on the table beside her and held it out. "Look at this," she said. Left with no choice, Julie took the photograph and looked at the fair-haired, smiling youth who was standing at the helm of a sailboat. "That is Justin," Mrs. Stanhope said in a carefully expressionless voice. "Does he look like a homosexual to you?"

"That's a ridiculous question to ask. What a male looks like is no indication of his sexual orientation—"

Julie broke off as Mrs. Stanhope turned on her heel and walked over to a large antique cabinet on the far wall of the room. With one hand on her cane, she bent and opened the door, revealing shelves containing crystal glasses, then she pulled hard on the top shelf and the whole panel swung out in an arc. Behind it, Julie saw the door of a concealed safe, and she watched in a state of inexplicable uneasiness as Mrs. Stanhope turned the dial, opened the safe, and extracted a large brown expandable file tied with an elastic cord. Her face wiped clean of expression, Mrs. Stanhope untied the elastic cord and dropped the file onto the sofa in front of Julie. "Since you won't take my word about what happened, there is the record of the coroner's inquiry into Justin's death and the newspaper reports."

Unwillingly, Julie's eyes dropped toward the papers that had spilled partially out of the folder, and her gaze riveted on the front-page newspaper clipping with a picture of an eighteen-year-old Zack, another of Justin, and a headline that read:

ZACHARY STANHOPE ADMITS SHOOTING BROTHER, JUSTIN

Her hand beginning to tremble uncontrollably, Julie reached down and picked up those clippings that had slid from the folder. According to the newspaper story, Zack had supposedly been in Justin's bedroom, talking to his brother, while examining a gun from Justin's collection, a Remington automatic handgun that Zack thought was unloaded. During the conversation, the gun had fired accidentally, striking Justin in the head and killing him instantly. Julie registered the words she read, but her heart rejected them. Tearing her gaze from the clippings, she glared at Mrs. Stanhope and said, "I don't believe any of this! Newspapers print things that aren't true all the time."

Mrs. Stanhope stared at her, her face coldly impassive as she reached down and extracted a bound transcript from the folder on the sofa and thrust it at Julie. "Then read the truth in his own words."

Julie tore her gaze from the woman's expressionless face and looked at the manuscript cover, but she didn't touch it. She was afraid to. "What is that?"

"The file from the coroner's inquest." Unwillingly, Julie stretched her hands out, took it, and opened the cover. It was all there: Zack's verbatim explanation of the event, taken down and transcribed by a stenographer at the inquest. Zack had said exactly what the newspaper clipping had indicated. When her knees threatened to give out, Julie sank down on the sofa and continued to read; she read until she'd finished the report, then she read newspaper clippings, looking for something, *anything*, that would explain away the discrepancy between what Zack had told her and what he'd told everyone else.

When she finally dragged her eyes from the file in her lap to Mrs. Stanhope's face, she understood that Zack had either lied to her about the event . . . or else he'd lied to everyone else under oath. Even so, she struggled to find a way to avoid condemning him for it. Dragging her voice through the knot of emotions in her chest, she said with as much force as she could muster, "I don't know why Zack told me Justin shot himself, but either way it wasn't Zack's fault. According to this file, it was an accident. An *accident!* He said so—"

"It was no accident!" Mrs. Stanhope bit out, her knuckles turning white as she leaned harder on her cane. "You can't ignore the truth when it's staring you in the face: He lied to you and he lied to everyone else during the inquest!"

"Stop it!" Julie lurched to her feet and threw the file onto the sofa as if it were contaminated. "There's an explanation for it. I know there is. Zack didn't lie to me in Colorado, I'd have known if he was lying, I tell you!" She thought desperately for explanations and came up with a logical one. "Justin did kill himself," she said shakily. "He was gay and he—he admitted it to Zack just before he shot himself, then Zack—Zack took the blame for some reason— maybe so that no one would start looking for motives—"

"You idiot!" Mrs. Stanhope said, but her voice was filled with as much pity as anger. "Justin and Zack had quarreled just before that gun went off. His brother Alex heard the quarrel and so did Foster." Twisting her head toward the butler, she said shortly, "Tell this poor deluded young woman what they were quarreling about."

"They were quarreling over a girl, Miss Mathison!" Foster said unhesitatingly. "Justin had asked Miss Amy Price to the Christmas dance at the country club and Zack had wanted to take her himself. Justin wanted to withdraw the invitation for Zack's sake, but Zack wouldn't have it. He was furious."

Bile rose up in Julie's stomach and she reached for her purse, but she still tried to defend Zack. "I don't believe either of you."

"You prefer to believe a man who you know for a fact either lied to you or to the coroner and the newspapers, is that it?"

"Yes!" Julie snapped, desperate to get out of there. "Good-bye, Mrs. Stanhope." She was walking so quickly that Foster had to trot ahead of her to get to the front door ahead of her to open it.

Her heels clicking sharply on the slate floor of the foyer, Julie was almost to the door, when Mrs. Stanhope's voice called her name. She halted in dread and turned, trying to keep her face blank as she looked at Zack's grandmother, who seemed to have aged two decades in the minute it took to follow her in to the foyer.

"If you know where Zachary is," Mrs. Stanhope said, "and if you have any conscience at all, you will notify the police at once. Despite what you may think, it was loyalty to Zachary that prompted me to conceal the facts about his quarrel with Justin from the authorities, instead of repeating it as I should have done."

Julie put her chin up, but her voice was shaking. "Why should you have done that?"

"Because they would have arrested him, and then he would have gotten psychiatric help! Zachary killed his own brother, and he killed his wife. If he had gotten psychiatric help, then perhaps Rachel Evans would not be lying in her grave. The guilt for her death is on my shoulders, and I cannot tell you how crushing a burden it is. If it had not been obvious from the beginning that Zachary was going to be convicted of killing her, I would have had no choice but to come forward with the truth about Justin's death." She stopped, her face twisting as she visibly tried to get control. "For your own sake, turn him in. Otherwise, there will be another victim someday, and you will live the rest of your life carrying the same burden of guilt that I must bear."

"He is not a murderer!" Julie cried.

"Isn't he?"

"No!"

"But you can't deny he's a liar," Mrs. Stanhope put in irrefutably. "Either he lied to you or he lied to the authorities about Justin's death, didn't he?"

Julie refused to answer. She refused because she couldn't bear to admit it aloud.

"He is a liar," Mrs. Stanhope stated emphatically. "And he is such a good liar that he found the perfect career for himself—acting." She started to turn away, then she stopped and looked over her shoulder. "Perhaps," she added in a weary, defeated tone that was somehow more alarming and more effective than her earlier wrath had been, "Zachary truly believes his own lies and that is why he is so convincing. Perhaps he believed he was those men he played in movies, and that is why he was such a 'gifted' actor. In his movies, he played men who murdered needlessly and then escaped the consequences because they were 'heroes.' Perhaps he thought he could murder his wife and also escape the consequences because he was a film 'hero.' Perhaps," she finished emphatically, "he can no longer separate reality from fantasy."

Fighting her reeling senses, Julie clutched her purse to her chest so tightly that it collapsed in her grip. "Are you suggesting he's insane?" she demanded.

Mrs. Stanhope's shoulders drooped and her voice sunk to a whisper, as if the act of speaking suddenly took a supreme effort. "Yes, Miss Mathison. That is *exactly* what I am suggesting. Zachary is insane."

Julie didn't know whether the older woman lingered in the foyer or not. Without a word, she turned and left, walking swiftly out to the car, suppressing the urge to run, to flee from the evil of this house and its secrets and the seed of terrifying doubt it had planted in her heart. She'd intended to stay overnight in a motel and explore Zack's birthplace; instead she drove straight to the airport, returned the rental car, and took the first commuter flight leaving Ridgemont's tiny airport.

55

TOMMY NEWTON GLANCED UP FROM THE SCRIPT HE WAS marking on as his sister walked into the living room of his Los Angeles home, where she was spending the weekend. "What's wrong?" he asked her.

"You just got a crank call," she told him with a nervous laugh. "At least, I hope it was."

"Los Angeles is full of weirdos who make obscene calls," Tommy reassured her. Jokingly, he added, "In southern California that's an ordinary means of communication. Everybody here feels alienated, haven't you heard? That's why this town is a haven for shrinks."

"This wasn't an obscene call, Tommy."

"What was it then?"

She spoke slowly and shook her head, her brow furrowed in doubt. "The man said he was Zack Benedict."

"Zack?" Tommy repeated with a short, derisive laugh. "That's ridiculous. What else did he say?"

"He said . . . to tell you he's going to kill you. He said you know who killed Rachel and he's going to kill you for not testifying."

"That's crazy!"

"He didn't sound crazy, Tommy. He sounded dead serious." She shivered at her unintentional pun. "I think you ought to call the police."

Tommy hesitated then shook his head. "Whoever it was, he was a crank."

"How did a crank get your unlisted phone number?"

"Evidently," he tried to joke, "I'm personally acquainted with a crank."

His sister picked up the telephone from the table beside the sofa and held the receiver toward him. "Call the police. If you won't do it for your own safety, do it because it's your duty."

"All right," he said with a sigh, "but they'll laugh in my face."

In her house in Beverly Hills, Diana Copeland pulled out of her lover's arms and reached for the phone beside the sofa.

"Diana!" he groaned. "Let your maid answer it."

"This is my private line," she explained to the man whose face was as familiar as her own to moviegoers. "It might be a change in shooting schedule tomorrow. Hello?" she said.

"This is Zack, Dee Dee," the deep voice said. "You know who killed Rachel. You let me go to jail for it. Now you're as good as dead."

"Zack, wait—!" she burst out, but the line went silent in her hand.

"Who was that?"

Diana stood up, staring blindly at him, her body stiff with shock. "It was Zack Benedict—"

"What? Are you sure?"

"He—he called me Dee Dee. Zack is the only one who ever called me that."

Turning on her heel, she left him there and went into her bedroom, then she picked up the telephone and dialed a phone number. "Tony?" she said shakily. "I just got a call from—from Zack Benedict."

"So did I. It's some crank. It wasn't Zack."

"He called me Dee Dee! Only Zack ever did that. He said I know who killed Rachel and I let him go to jail for it. He said he's going to kill me now."

"Calm down! It's bullshit! It's some crank, maybe even some tabloid reporter, stirring up a new slant on a dying story."

"I'm calling the cops."

"Make a fool of yourself if that's what you want to do, but leave me out of it. That guy wasn't Zack."

"I tell you it was!"

Emily McDaniels sank down on a chaise lounge beside the swimming pool at the sprawling Benedict Canyon house owned by her husband, Dr. Richard Grover. Life had been one long honeymoon for the six months they'd been married, and she watched him swimming laps in the pool, admiring the way his body effortlessly cleaved the water. He cut the last lap short and surfaced at the edge of the pool, right beside her. "Who was on the phone?" he asked, shoving his hair out of his eyes with the long-fingered hands that performed delicate neurosurgery at Cedars–Sinai Medical Center. "Tell me it wasn't my answering service," he pleaded half-seriously, crossing his arms on the edge of the pool, studying her crestfallen expression.

"It wasn't."

"Good," he said. Reaching out, he grabbed her slender ankles and gave her a comical leer. "Since none of my patients are doing us the discourtesy of interrupting our Saturday night by stroking out, get your sweet body into this pool and show me you still love me."

"Dick," she said in a strained voice, "it was my father who called just now."

"What's wrong?" he said, sobering at once and shoving up and out of the pool.

"He said Zack Benedict just called him."

"Benedict?" Dick repeated scornfully, grabbing a towel and drying his arms. "If that creep is actually hanging around Los Angeles, he's not only a murderer, he's a nut. The cops will grab him in no time. What did he want?"

"Me. Zack told my father," she explained, her voice trembling, "that he thinks I know who really killed Rachel. He said he wants me to tell the newspapers who it was, so he doesn't have to kill everyone who was there that day." She shook her head as if to clear it and when she spoke again, the fear was gone. "It had to be a crank. Zack would never threaten me, let alone hurt me. Regardless of what you seem to think, Zack wasn't a creep. He was the finest man I ever met, next to you."

"You're sure in the minority if that's what you believe."

"It's what I *know*. Regardless of what you heard and saw during the trial, the truth is that Rachel Evans was a vicious, scheming bitch who deserved to die! The only thing that was wrong was that Zack went to jail for it." With a grim laugh, she said, "No one thought Rachel was much of an actress, but the truth is she was a brilliant actress—she was so damned good that hardly anyone ever guessed what she was really like behind that smile of hers. She came off as elegant and sort of reserved and very nice. She was nothing like that. Nothing! She was an alley cat."

"What do you mean? A slut?"

"That too, but it isn't what I meant," Emily said, reaching out and folding a wet towel he'd left near an umbrella table. "I mean that she was like a cat who prowls through alleys, looking through other people's trash cans, feeding on them without them ever realizing it."

"Very colorful," her husband teased, "but not very explanatory."

Emily flopped back on the lounge chair and tried to be more specific. "If Rachel knew someone wanted something—a part in a film, a man, a particular chair on the set—she went out of her way to make sure they didn't get it, even if she didn't want it. I mean, poor Diana Copeland was in love with Zack—really in love with him—but she kept it completely to herself and never made an overture toward him. I was the only one who knew it, and I found out completely by accident."

When she fell silent, staring at the lights in the pool, Dick said, "You've never wanted to talk about Benedict or the trial, but since you're doing it now, I'll admit to having an avid curiosity about the stuff that never made the newspapers. It never came out that Diana Copeland was in love with Benedict."

Emily nodded, accepting his request for more information. "I made it a policy never to talk about any of that because I couldn't trust anyone, even men I dated, not to go blabbing to some reporter who'd misquote the whole thing and stir everything up again." She smiled at him and wrinkled her small nose, "I guess I can make an exception now, though, since you've vowed to honor and cherish me."

"I guess you can," he said with an answering grin.

"I didn't find out how Diana felt until a few months after the trial, when Zack was already in prison. I'd written him one letter and sent it to him there, but it came back unopened with 'Return to sender' scrawled across it in Zack's handwriting. A few days later, Diana came to see me. Of all things, she wanted me to send Zack a letter she'd written to him, but in an envelope from me. He'd returned her letter the same way he'd returned mine. I knew he'd also returned letters from Harrison Ford and Pat Swayze, and I told her all that. The next thing I knew, Diana was crying her heart out."

"Why?"

"Because she'd just come back from Texas, where she'd tried to surprise Zack with a visit. When he saw her on the other side of the screen, he turned his back on her without a word and told the guards to get her out of there. I told her I was certain it was because he was ashamed and didn't want any of his old friends to see him, and that's when she started to cry. She said the prison he was in was like a giant nightmare, that it was dirty and squalid, and that they made Zack wear a prison uniform."

"What did she expect him to be wearing, a Brooks Brothers suit?"

Emily gave a sad little laugh and explained, "Seeing him dressed like that was what hurt her so much. Anyway, she started to cry, and she told me she'd been in love with him and that's why she'd changed her schedule and took a lesser part in *Destiny*—to be near him. Rachel guessed how Diana felt somehow, because she teased her about having a crush on Zack one day, and when Diana didn't deny it, Rachel made a point of climbing all over Zack whenever Diana was around. Keep in mind that Rachel was already having an affair with Tony Austin and intended to file for divorce within days. Then, the following week—the same week Rachel died—several people heard her warn Zack not to use Diana in his next movie.

"Yes, but he never made another movie, so Diana didn't lose anything."

"That's not the point," Emily said. "The point is that Rachel was like a beautiful witch. She couldn't bear to see anyone happy. If she could figure out what you wanted, what would make you happy, no matter how small it was, she'd find a way to stop you from having it or to steal it from you."

Her husband studied her in silence for a long moment, then he said quietly, "What did she steal from you, Emily?"

Emily's head jerked up, and then she said, "Tony Austin."

"You're joking!"

"I wish I was," she said somberly. "There's just no accounting for the blind stupidity of youth. I was completely crazy about him."

"He's a junkie and a drunk! His career was already on the skids—"

"I know all that," Emily said, standing up. "But, you see, I thought I could save him from all that and himself, too. Years later, I figured out that was actually Tony's big appeal to women: He was so sexy and cool on the surface that you felt as if he could protect you from the world, then you discovered that part of him was actually a vulnerable little boy, and suddenly you wanted to protect him, too. That's probably why poor Tommy Newton was in love with him. Now, Zack was just the opposite of Tony—he didn't need anyone, and you *felt* it."

Her husband ignored the last sentence. "Tommy Newton," he repeated in disgust, "the guy who directed your last movie, was in love with Tony Austin?" When Emily nodded, he shook his head and said, "That business you've been in since you were a child reminds me of a human cesspool."

"Sometimes it is," Emily said with a laugh, "but most of the time it isn't—it's just business—just a lot of hard-working people living and working together for four or five months, then going their own way, meeting again someday on another film."

"It can't be all bad," he relented, "because you've lived in it for years, and you're straighter and sweeter than any woman I've ever known." Reverting to their earlier topic, he said thoughtfully, "It's amazing all that stuff with you and Tony and Diana and Rachel didn't come out during the trial."

Emily shrugged. "The police didn't look very far for other suspects or other motives. You see, they knew Zack put the bullets that killed Rachel into that gun. We all knew it. Besides the fact that he'd threatened to kill her the night before and that he had enormous emotional and financial reasons to kill her, he was also the only one of us with enough *guts* to do it."

"He may have had guts, but he had to have been arrogant as hell to think he could actually get away with it."

"He was definitely that," Emily agreed, but her smile was sentimental and her voice was threaded with admiration. "Zack was like . . . like an irresistible force, like the wind coming from so many directions, with so many sides, you never knew which one he was going to show to you. He could be incredibly witty or warm, gallant and sweet, or completely suave and sophisticated."

"He sounds like a damned paragon."

"He could also be brutal, cold, and heartless."

"On second thought," Dick said half-seriously, "he sounds like a multiple personality."

"He was complex," Emily admitted. "And private. He did as he pleased when he pleased, and he didn't give a damn what anybody thought of him. He made a lot of enemies because of that, but even the people who detested him were in awe of him. He didn't care about being hated, and he didn't care about being admired either. As near as anyone could tell, the only thing he cared about was his work. He didn't seem to need people . . . I mean, he didn't like anyone to get too close, except me. I was probably closer to him than almost anyone."

"Don't tell me he was in love with you. I couldn't stand another triangle."

Emily gave a shout of laughter. "I was a mere child to him, which is why he let me get as close as he did. He used to talk to me about things I doubt he talked to Rachel about."

"What sort of things."

"I don't know—little things, like the fact that he loved astronomy. One night, when we were shooting on location on a ranch near Dallas, he sat outside pointing out the stars to me and naming them and telling me stories about how the constellations got their names. Rachel came out and asked what we were doing, and when I told her, she was dumbfounded that Zack was interested in astronomy or that he knew anything about it."

"Given all that, how do you explain the fact that he made a threatening call to your father tonight?"

She swung her legs over the side of the chaise. "I think it was a crank and my father was mistaken," she said. "My father also said he thought he saw someone who looked like Zack hanging around across the street from his apartment last night."

Her husband's concerned frown faded to a look of irritated comprehension. "By any chance was your father drunk when he called you?"

"I . . . I couldn't tell. Maybe. Don't be too hard on him," she said, putting her hand on his arm, "he's lonely with me gone. I was his whole life, and then I deserted him to marry you."

"You didn't 'desert' him! You're his daughter, not his wife."

She put her arm around his waist and laid her head on his shoulder. "I know that, and so does he." As they headed inside, she added, "A few minutes ago, you congratulated me on staying so sweet and straight after all my years in the business. Try to remember that the only reason I managed to become what I am is because of his vigilance. He sacrificed his own life for me."

Her husband kissed her forehead. "I know."

56

BY THE TIME JULIE PULLED INTO HER DRIVEWAY, IT WAS midnight, and she'd spent all seven of the hours since leaving Zack's grandmother fighting a mental battle against the insidious doubt and confusion that had haunted her at that house. She'd won her battle and now that she was home, she felt much better. She opened the front door, turned on the living room lights, and looked at the cheerful, cozy room. Here, the idea that Zack was insane seemed so ludicrous that she was angry with herself for ever entertaining the notion. In this very room, she remembered as she hung her coat in the front closet, Matt and Meredith Farrell had spent a wonderful evening with her and bade her good luck and good-bye. Matthew Farrell, she realized, would have laughed in Mrs. Stanhope's face for suggesting Zack was insane, and that was exactly what she herself should have done!

Shaking her head in self-disgust, she walked into her bedroom, sat down on the bed, and took Zack's letter from the nightstand drawer. She reread every beautiful, loving word, and her shame for ever doubting him was as great as her sudden need to scrub away the traces of her journey to his home. Putting his letter aside, she pulled off her sweater, stepped out of her skirt, then she went into the bathroom and turned on the shower.

She washed her body and her hair as if they'd been contaminated by the malevolent atmosphere of that gloomy pile of rocks that Zack had once called home. There was no warmth there, not in the house nor the people who lived in it, she thought as she blew her hair dry and brushed it. If anyone was suffering from vicious delusions, it was his grandmother! And her butler! And Zack's brother, Alex!

Except, her mind argued, that his grandmother had actually seemed more despondent than vicious, at least toward the very end. And the butler had looked a little forlorn but absolutely certain of what he said. Why would they both lie about Zack's fight with Justin, Julie wondered. Shoving the question aside, Julie yanked the blow dryer's plug out of the wall, tightened the belt of her bathrobe, and walked into the living room. Maybe they only thought Justin and Zack had quarreled, she decided as she turned on the television set and turned it to CNN so she could watch the latest news.

But there was one fact she couldn't avoid, justify, or dispute: Zack had lied about the way Justin died.

Either he'd lied to her or he'd lied to the police, the newspapers, and the coroner.

Her mind skated away from that unsolvable dilemma, and she looked around the living room for something that was out of place, something to physically straighten and put to rights, except there wasn't anything. Her normally neat home was now antiseptically clean because she'd spent all her free time during the last five days making it ready to be examined by police and reporters when she vanished. The plant near her left had a yellow leaf on it, so she reached over and plucked it off, then she stopped, warmed by the sudden memory of Zack in Colorado when he'd watched her doing something like this. "*Is that a nervous habit you have—straightening things out when you feel uneasy?*" Just thinking of that lazy smile of his and the way his eyes had gleamed with amusement made her feel all right somehow. She needed to concentrate on those memories, she realized, because they were real. He was real. And he was waiting for her in Mexico.

He'd lied to everyone else about Justin's death, Julie decided at that moment, he had not lied to her. He couldn't have done that. Wouldn't have. She knew that in her heart. And when she saw him in Mexico, he'd explain why he'd lied to the others. The television program was a special broadcast about China, and since Julie was too keyed up to sleep, she decided to work on the letter she was leaving for her family while she waited for a late-night news update to be certain there wasn't anything about Zack on it. He'd told her to take care of everything within a week and be ready to leave on the eighth day. Five days had already elapsed.

Getting up, Julie went into her room to get her partially written letter, then she sat back down in the rocking chair and reached up to turn on the floor lamp beside her. With the television program droning on in the background about the economic future of China, she reread what she'd written:

Dear Mom and Dad, and dear Carl and Ted,

By the time you read this letter, you'll know that I've left to join Zack. I don't expect you to condone what I'm doing or to forgive me, but I want to explain it to you so that maybe you'll at least be able to understand someday.

I love him.

I want so much to give you more and better reasons that just that one, and I've tried to think of them, but there don't seem to be any. Maybe it's because that's all that really matters.

Dad, Mother, Carl, Ted—all four of you know what love is, you've <u>felt</u> it, I know you have. Dad, I remember so many times when you stayed up late and sat on the sofa with your arm around Mom. I remember all the years of your laughter and hugs. I also remember the day Mom came home from the doctor and told us he'd found a lump in her breast. That night, you went out in the backyard and you cried. I know you did, Dad, because I followed you. These are the things I want to share with Zack—all of them—the good things, the quiet things, the happy things, and the sad ones. Think of them, please, and know that just as Mom and you were meant to be together through them all, I was meant to be with Zack. I believe that. I know it with every breath I take. I don't know why it had to be him. I would never have chosen it to be this way. But it is. And I'm not sorry.

Carl, you have your wonderful, funny, sweet Sara. She's adored you since the two of you were in grade school, and I don't think you realize just how much she did. She waited for years for you to notice her. When we were in high school, she used to do the most amazing things to try to get your attention, like falling out of a tree when you drove past and dropping her books at your feet. Sara and I were studying together the night she found out you'd asked Jenny Stone to your senior prom. She cried that night. You hurt her terribly, and now I'm going to hurt all of you by going away with Zack. Sara loved you anyway. Please love me too after the hurt subsides. At least try.

Ted, you're going to be the angriest of all about what I've done and the last to forgive me, I think. You still haven't forgiven yourself for turning your back on your marriage, and you can't seem to forgive Katherine for her part in what happened. You can't forgive and you can't forget, so you're caught in a trap of your own making. And the funny thing is, of all of us, it is you and I who love so blindly and completely that it rules our minds. You love me that much. I know you do. You said you'd walk through hell for me, and now I'm going to put you through hell, and I hate that. But my only other choice is to do what you've done with Katherine—I could turn my back on Zack, who loves me and needs me, and then spend the rest of my life hating myself and blaming him because I was afraid to take another chance.

After I leave, all of you are going to hear more things about Zack, awful rumors and vicious conjecture from reporters and police and people who never even knew him. I wish so much you could have known him. Since that isn't possible, I'm leaving something for you, something from him that will show you a glimpse of the man he really is. It's a copy of a letter, a very personal letter, from him to me. A small part of the letter will be blocked out, not because there was something there that would have changed your opinion, but because it refers to someone else and a very special favor that person did for us both. When you read Zack's letter, I think you'll know that the man who wrote it will love and protect me in every way he can. We'll be married as soon as we're together.

That was the last of what Julie had written so far, and it didn't seem like enough. She picked up her pen, her ears attuned an announcement of a news update and began to write again:

Carl, I'd like you and Sara to have all my household things that you can use for your new place. Think of me sometimes when you're watering my plants.

Ted, there's a ring in the top drawer of my dresser that belongs to you. You'll recognize it. It's the wedding band you threw away when you and Katherine split up. It belongs on your finger, my beloved, foolish brother. Try it on for size . . . just for old times sake. Okay, for my sake. No other ring will ever fit you as perfectly as that one does, and you <u>know</u> it! The two of you are going to hurt each other if you get together again, but you won't suffer nearly as much as you've been doing without each other. And—"

Julie's head snapped up as the announcer on television said, "*We're interrupting our special on the China situation to bring you a late-breaking development in the Zachary Benedict manhunt. According to police in Orange County, California, Benedict, who escaped from Amarillo State Penitentiary, where he was serving a forty-five-year sentence for the murder of his wife, has been spotted in Los Angeles by a former acquaintance. The acquaintance, whose identity is not being released at this time, said there is no doubt the man was Benedict. The search for Benedict has been intensified by that news and the discovery that he reportedly made phone calls today to several members of the cast and crew of the movie Destiny who were present on or around the scene of his wife's death, threatening to kill them. Orange County police are warning anyone who was on the set of Destiny to exercise extreme caution, since Benedict is known to be armed and dangerous.*"

The pen Julie had been holding slid to the floor along with her letter as she lurched to her feet, staring at the television. Fighting for control, she raked her hair off her forehead and picked up the letter and pen. It was a hoax, she told herself. It had to be a hoax! Some maniac was pretending to be Zack just to scare people and make news.

Of course, a hoax, she decided as she turned off the television and went to bed.

But when she finally slept, her dreams were filled with faceless specters who hid in shadows, calling out warnings and screaming threats.

The sun was rising when she finally tore free of the nightmare. Afraid to close her eyes again, Julie got up and went into the kitchen to pour herself a glass of orange juice. She drank it without tasting it, then she braced her hands on the Formica counter and her head fell forward. "Oh, Zack," she whispered, "what are you doing? Call me and tell me everyone is lying about you. Please . . . don't let them torture me like this."

She decided to go to church, then spend the day at school, catching up on paperwork there, just in case Zack heard what was happening in Los Angeles and wanted to call her to explain. He couldn't call her at home. He'd try her at the school. Surely he'd realize she'd go there to wait, even on a Sunday, if something important like this happened.

57

"JULIE, ARE YOU ALL RIGHT, HONEY?" FLOSSIE ELDRIDGE tapped on the car's windshield as she spoke. "You've been sitting out here in the dark for almost a half hour with the engine running."

Julie's gaze jerked to her plump, concerned face, and she groped for her car keys, turning off the ignition and hastily getting out. "I'm fine, Miss Flossie, really—I was thinking about something—a problem at school and I forgot where I was."

Shivering in the frosty night, Flossie pulled her coat around her. "You'll catch your death of cold, sitting out here."

Mortified at having lost track of where she was, Julie pulled her briefcase out of the back seat and tried to smile at her elderly neighbor. "I had the heater on in the car," she said, although she wasn't completely certain now that she had.

"No, you didn't," Flossie said. "Your windshield has frost on it—look. You're working awfully late tonight, and on a Sunday, too!" she said, noticing Julie's briefcase.

"There's always a lot of work to do," Julie said. "Here, let me walk you back to your house," she added, putting her hand beneath Miss Flossie's elbow and walking her slowly across the lawn that separated their houses. "It's hard to see with no moon, and I don't want you to stumble in the grass."

"Julie," Miss Flossie said hesitantly when she'd stepped into the circle of yellow light spilling from the porch, "are you all right? You look peaked. You can tell me the truth. I won't tell Ada. Are you pining away for Zachary Benedict?"

The state of lethargic distraction that had plagued Julie all day gave way to alarmed awareness in the second it took Flossie to pronounce Zack's name. "Why on earth would you think a thing like that?" she said with a laugh that sounded choked and forced to her own ears.

"Because," Flossie said as if the answer should be obvious, "you were sitting in your car in your own driveway and staring into space. When I was a girl and I was pining away for Her—for someone, I recollect doing just that."

"You mean," Julie tried to tease, "you drove into your driveway and sat there for a half hour?"

"No, of course not," Flossie said with a girlish giggle that crinkled her eyes. "You know I never learned to drive. I meant, I stared off into space, just like you were doing tonight."

Trying to avoid lying or answering, Julie evaded the question by saying brightly, "I don't believe in pining away for something, Miss Flossie. If I can't have it and I know that, then I face it and try to put it out of my mind forever and I go on as best I can."

Instead of accepting that or returning to her original question, which Julie half-expected her to do, Miss Flossie put her hand on Julie's arm and said, "What would you do if there was something you've always wanted, and you could have had it—maybe you still could—but you're afraid that everyone will laugh at you. And you're afraid if you get it, you might be sorry?"

Julie's laugh was more genuine than her last one, and she shook her head. "That's a tough one," she admitted. "If I wasn't happy without it, I guess I'd want to take a chance on being happy with it."

"It's a him, not an it," Miss Flossie confided.

Julie had figured that at the outset of the conversation. "Who is it?" she asked in case Miss Flossie wanted to confide. "I mean, who is he?"

"Oh, that's a secret."

No, it's not, Julie thought sadly, and then because she had nothing to lose and Flossie had everything to gain, she said, "I think that what Herman Henkleman needs is a good woman to believe in him and stand by him and give him a reason to be proud. Of course," she added to the mortified Flossie, "Herman will never take the risk of asking the woman he used to love to take a chance on him, not after the mess he's made of his life so far. The woman will have to make the first move, and that takes a lot of courage."

Impulsively, Julie leaned down and pressed a kiss on her parchment cheek. "Good night," she said. *Good-bye,* she thought. Six of the eight days Zack had allotted her were up.

On her own front porch, she fumbled for her keys in her purse, inserted the right one in the lock, went inside, and closed the door behind her. She was reaching for the light switch when a male voice said, "Don't turn on the light." The scream of terror caught in her throat when he added, "It's okay, I'm a friend of Zack's."

"Why should I believe you?" she said, her voice shaking as hard as her hand.

"Because," Dominick Sandini said with a smile in his voice, "I came to have a look around and make sure you're clear to take a little trip if you should suddenly decide to."

"Damn it, you scared the hell out of me!" Julie exploded half in anger and half in laughter as she collapsed against the door.

"Sorry."

"How did you get in here?" she said, feeling a little absurd talking to an invisible man in the black dark.

"I came in the back after having a look around. You've got a tail on you, ma'am."

"A—a what?"

Julie was so disoriented she actually started to reach for the back of her skirt to check for a tail before he clarified, "You're being watched. A blue van parked down the street covers the house and a black pickup truck follows you wherever you go. It's gotta be FBI—they use cars that ain't worth stealin', but they're better at surveillance than the local yokels. Cars," he added proudly, "are a specialty of mine. Take yours, for example, you got a 1.5-liter engine, probably a factory radio, no telephone, so it's worth mebbe $250 stripped for parts."

"You—you're a used car salesman?" Julie said, temporarily ignoring the problem of the FBI because she was so absurdly glad to have someone near her who called himself Zack's friend.

"You could say that," he added with a chuckle. "But when I sold 'em, they didn't have titles if you get my meaning."

"You . . . you . . . *stole* cars?" Julie added uneasily.

"Yeah, but not any more," he explained with another smile in his voice. "I'm reformed now."

"Good!" she said gustily. It was not nearly as reassuring to have Zack's friend be a car thief. Realizing that her faceless visitor might be able to banish her other fears, Julie said quickly, "Zack isn't in Los Angeles is he? He's not threatening those people?"

"I don't know where he is or what he's doing, and that's the truth."

"But you must! I mean, you've obviously spoken to him—"

"Nope, not me. Zack would have a shi—a fit," he corrected hastily, "if he knew I came here myself and got involved. This was supposed to be handled purely by outsiders, but I figured this would be my only chance to meet his Julie. You must love him one helluva lot."

He fell silent, and Julie said quietly, "I do. He must mean a lot to you, too, for you to risk coming here like this."

"Hell—heck, it's no risk," he said in a cocky voice. "I'm not doing anything illegal. All I'm doing is stopping by to visit a friend of a friend, and there ain't no law against that nor in coming in the back door and waiting for her in the dark. In fact, I even fixed the lock on your back door while I was waiting. That thing wouldn't have kept a kid out of this house if they wanted inside. Is that being a law-abiding citizen or what?" he joked.

He'd said he had come here to make sure she was "clear" to take her trip, and Julie was about to ask him what he meant by that when he provided the answer in the same jovial, unconcerned voice. "Anyway, the reason I'm here is 'cause Zack wanted you to have a new car—you know, if you should suddenly decide to go for a long drive in a couple days—so I volunteered to deliver it. And here I am."

Julie assumed instantly she was probably to use this car, not her own, to throw off her followers when she made her escape from Keaton in two days. "Tell me it isn't stolen," she said in a dire tone that made him laugh.

"It's not. Like I told you, I'm retired. Zack paid for it, and I decided to deliver his gift, that's all. There ain't no specific law against an escaped con buyin' a car for a lady with his own hard-earned, honest money. Now, how she chooses to use that car ain't none of my business."

"I didn't see any car in front of the house tonight."

"Of course not!" he said in exaggerated horror. "I didn't think I should break some city ordinance or something by cluttering up your nice street. So I delivered it to the parking lot behind a place in town called Kelton's Dry Goods."

"Why?" Julie said, feeling stupid.

"That's an interesting question. I'm not sure just why I got a crazy impulse like that," he joked, suddenly reminding Julie of the incorrigible, irrepressible, eight-year-old boys she taught. "I guess I figured that if you was to park your own car on the street in front of that store one morning, you might want to go inside, look around, and then go out the back door and take your new car for a little test drive. Of course, that might annoy the guys who are tailing you. I mean, it'd be awful hard for them to figure out which way you went, what you're drivin,' and what you're wearin'—assuming you was also to get a sudden desire to change into a different sweater or somethin' that you happened to have in your briefcase. If you get my meanin'."

Julie nodded in the dark, shivering at the clandestine overtones of everything he'd said. "I get your meaning," she said with a tight, nervous laugh.

The rocking chair creaked as he stood up. "It's been nice talkin' to you," he said, as his hand briefly touched her arm. "Good-bye, Zack's Julie. I hope you know what the hell you're doin'."

Julie hoped so, too.

"Don't turn the lights on in the back of the house until I'm gone."

She listened to his slow footsteps and had the feeling he moved with a slight limp.

58

TONY AUSTIN HEARD A NOISE BEHIND HIM AND HE REACHED for the lamp on the table beside him at the same moment he saw the curtains stir beside the sliding glass doors. "Don't turn on the light!" the voice commanded as a shadow moved away from the curtains. "I can see you fine from right here."

"I don't need light to recognize your voice! Why the hell didn't you come to the front door?" Austin said, jerking his hand away and masking his surprise behind contempt. "I left it open for you."

"Do you have any idea how much I've wanted to kill you?"

"You blew your chance five years ago. Where's the money?"

"You're like a vampire, you bleed people dry."

"Shut up and hand over the money."

The shadow at the curtains raised its hand and Tony saw the gun. "Don't be a fool! If you kill me now, they'll figure out it was you in twenty-four hours."

"No! They won't. Zack Benedict is on the loose, he's on a rampage, haven't you heard?" The laugh was chillingly shrill. "He's making threatening phone calls. People think I got one, too. I made sure they do. They'll think he killed you. I waited such a *long* time for this moment—" The gun lifted, aimed, adjusted . . .

"Don't be crazy! If you kill me, they'll tr—"

The explosion from the barrel of the gun blew a small hole in Tony Austin's chest near his collar bone, but the fact that the hollow point shell had missed his heart didn't matter. On impact, it fragmented throughout his entire chest cavity, killing him instantly.

59

"IT'S WONDERFUL OF YOU TO HAVE ALL OF US OVER FOR DINNER like this," Mrs. Mathison told Julie as she stood up to help her clear the table. "We shouldn't wait for special occasions, the way we often do," she added.

Julie picked up four glasses and smiled at her mother. It was a very special occasion—the last night she would ever spend with them, because she was leaving to join Zack in the morning.

"Are you sure you don't want Carl and me to stay and help put the dining room back to order?" Sara asked as Carl helped her into her coat. "Carl needs to work up a bid for the recreation center, but that could wait for another half hour."

"No, it can't," Julie said, walking quickly into the living room and giving Sara and then Carl a hug. She held them both longer than necessary, and she added a kiss to their cheeks. Because this was good-bye. "Take care of each other," she whispered to them both.

"We only live a mile and a half from here," Carl pointed out drily. Julie watched them walk down the sidewalk, memorizing the moment, then she closed the door. Ted and her father had settled down in the living room to watch the news and Katherine was helping clear the table.

"Sara is such a sweet girl," Mrs. Mathison said when she was alone with Julie in the kitchen. "She and Carl are so good together, so happy." Glancing over her shoulder into the dining room where Katherine was gathering plates, she whispered, "I think Ted and Katherine have found each other again, don't you? Katherine was so young before, but she's settled down and matured, and Ted loved her so much. He never got over her."

Julie smiled somberly as she stacked the dinner plates Katherine was carrying from the dining room into the dishwasher. "Don't get your hopes up too far. I invited Katherine tonight, Ted didn't. He's still seeing Grace Halvers—fighting whatever he feels for Katherine probably."

"Julie, is something wrong? You seem strange tonight. Preoccupied."

Picking up the dishcloth, Julie fixed a bright, attentive look on her face and began wiping off the sink. "Why do you say that?"

"For one thing, the water is still running, the dishes aren't done, and you're trying to wipe the counters. You were always a neat girl, Julie," she teased as Julie hastily tossed the dishcloth aside and returned to her earlier task, "but that's carrying things a little too far. You're still thinking about Zachary Benedict, aren't you?"

It was a golden opportunity to prepare her mother for what she was going to read in Julie's letter and she decided to take advantage of it. "What would you say if I told you I fell in love with him in Colorado?"

"I'd say that's a very pointless, painful, foolish thing for you to believe."

"And what if I can't help it?"

"I recommend tincture of time, honey. That cures everything. You only knew him for a week, after all. Why don't you fall in love with Paul Richardson instead," she said half-seriously. "He has a good job, and he's crazy about you—even your father noticed."

Realizing the conversation about Paul and the mundane chore of doing dishes were both wastes of what precious time was left with her family, Julie tossed down her dishcloth. "Let's go into the living room," she said, hustling her mother out of the kitchen. "I'll finish the dishes later." Raising her voice, she called, "Does anyone want anything from the kitchen?"

"Yes," Ted called in answer. "Coffee."

Katherine, who had just come in to help at the sink, reached for cups and saucers, but Julie shook her head. "Go and spend some time with Ted. I'll come back for the coffee when it's ready."

Julie was partway into the living room, carrying a tray of cups, when she heard her father hiss, "Ted, turn the television set off, Julie doesn't need to hear that!"

"I don't need to hear what?" Julie asked, stopping in cold dread as Ted dived for the television set. "Leave it on, Ted," she warned sharply, knowing instinctively it was something about Zack. "They've got Zack, don't they," she said, shaking so violently the cups on her tray rattled. "Answer me," she cried, looking at four appalled faces.

"They didn't get him," Ted fired sarcastically, "he's gotten himself another victim!" As he spoke, the television commercial ended and Julie saw a stretcher being taken out of a house, the body covered in a white sheet, while the newscaster's voice seemed to loom in the room: *"Repeating the news of the hour, Tony Austin, who starred with Zachary Benedict and Rachel Evans in* Destiny, *was found dead in his Los Angeles house today from a fatal gunshot wound in the chest. Preliminary reports indicate that the bullet was a hollow point shell, similar to the one that killed Zachary Benedict's wife, Rachel Evans. The coroner has tentatively fixed the time of death at approximately ten o'clock last night. Orange County police officials have confirmed that Austin reportedly received a threatening phone call last night from Zachary Benedict and that Benedict was allegedly seen in the area earlier last evening. Other members of* Destiny's *cast and crew who also received threatening calls from Benedict have been warned to exercise extreme caution—"*

The rest of his words were drowned out by the crash of breaking china as Julie dropped the tray and covered her face with her hands, trying to blot out the memory of the white-shrouded body being put into an ambulance and the recollection of Zack's cold voice:

"Leave Austin to me. There are other ways to handle him."

"Julie!" Voices rushed at her and hands reached for her, but she stepped back, staring blindly from her mother and Katherine who were bending to pick up the broken china to her father and Ted, who were standing near her now, watching her in alarmed consternation. "Please!" she choked. "I need to be alone now. Dad," she said, reining in her hysteria so tightly that her voice was constricted, "please take Mother home. She shouldn't get upset over me. It's not good for her blood pressure."

She turned and walked into her bedroom, closed the door behind her, and sat down in the dark. Somewhere in the house she heard the telephone begin to ring, but it was Mrs. Stanhope's voice that was screaming in her mind:

"Zachary killed his own brother, and he killed his wife. In his movies, he played men who murdered needlessly and then escaped the consequences because they were 'heroes.' . . . He can no longer separate reality from fantasy. . . . Zachary is insane."

"If he had gotten help, Rachel Evans would not be lying in her grave. . . .For your own sake, turn him in. Otherwise, there will be another

victim someday, and you will live the rest of your life carrying the same burden of guilt that I must bear. . . .

Tony Austin's famous, charismatic face swam before Julie's eyes, his smile endearing and sexy. He wouldn't smile again. Like Rachel Evans and Justin Stanhope, he was dead. Murdered.

She heard Matt Farrell's warning, "*We also discovered evidence that points to Diana Copeland . . . Emily McDaniels . . . Tommy Newton.*"

Reaching into the nightstand drawer, Julie took Zack's letter out and clutched it to her, but she didn't need to read it; she'd memorized every word. Wrapping her arms around her stomach, she bent forward, rocking back and forth in a tearless agony, pressing the letter to her heart, silently keening his name in the dark.

Muted voices came from the living room, slowly dragging her from the abyss where nothing existed for her except the torment of the moment, voices that forced her slowly to her feet. Voices of people who need to know . . . to help . . . to tell her . . .

60

HER FATHER BROKE OFF HIS CONVERSATION WITH TED AND Katherine as Julie walked into the living room, her body stiff as wood, the letter she'd intended to leave for them clutched in her hand.

"I sent Mother home," her father said.

Julie nodded stiffly and cleared her throat. "That's good." For a moment, she twisted the letter she'd written to them in her hands, then she thrust it at him. When he took it and opened it, holding it out so Ted could read it, too, she added, "I was . . . was leaving to join him tomorrow."

Ted's eyes snapped to hers, narrowing in furious disapproval.

"It's true," she said before he could speak.

Julie watched him move toward her, but she jerked away when he reached for her arm. "Don't touch me!" she warned hysterically, clutching the back of a chair. "Don't touch me." Switching her gaze to her father's grim, hurt face, she watched him finish the letter, drop it on the table, and stand up. "Help me," she told him brokenly. "Please help me. You always know what's right. I have to do what's right. Somebody help me," she cried to Katherine, who was blinking back tears, and then to Ted.

Suddenly she was pulled into her father's arms and clutched tightly to him, his hand soothing her back as he'd done when she was a little girl crying over a minor hurt. "You already know what you have to do," he said gruffly. "The man has to be caught and stopped. Ted," he said sounding shaken, but taking over, "you're the lawyer. What's the best way to handle this without further incriminating Julie?"

After a moment of silence, Ted said, "Paul Richardson is our best bet. I could call him and try to make a deal with him. Julie turns Benedict in and he holds her blameless. No questions asked."

The word *questions* jerked Julie out of her tortured stupor. Her voice vibrating with wild alarm, she warned, "Tell Paul I won't answer any questions about how I know where Zack is going to be!" She thought of Matt and Meredith Farrell and the laughing young man who'd brought her a car to drive—all of them loyal to a man who'd betrayed their trust because he was sick. Because he couldn't help himself. "If you call him," she repeated, trying to keep her voice steady, "he has to agree that I won't be expected to tell him anything except where Zack is going to be tomorrow night. I won't involve anyone else in this, I mean it!"

"You're up to your neck in illegal intrigue and you're worried about protecting somebody else!" Ted bit out. "Do you realize what Richardson could do to you? He could haul you out of here in leg irons tonight!"

Julie started to answer, but the restraint she'd been exerting was collapsing, and she turned on her heel instead. Walking into the kitchen, she sank down into a chair at the table, because that was as far as she could possibly get from the phone call that was going to betray her lover. Her shoulders shaking with silent sobs, she covered her face with her hands, and the tears she'd been fighting streamed in hot torrents down her cheeks. "I'm sorry, darling," she wept brokenly, "I'm so sorry . . ."

Katherine pressed a handkerchief into her hand a few minutes later, then sat down across from her, lending silent support.

By the time Ted walked into the kitchen, Julie had managed to get herself under a semblance of control.

"Richardson will take the deal," he said. "He'll be here in three hours." He turned as the telephone rang on the kitchen wall and yanked the receiver out of the cradle. "Yes," he said, "she's here, but she's not taking calls—" He frowned and paused, then he covered the mouthpiece and said to Julie, "This is someone named Margaret Stanhope. She says it's urgent."

Julie nodded, swallowed, and reached her hand out for the phone. "Have you called to gloat, Mrs. Stanhope?" she asked bitterly.

"No," Zack's grandmother replied. "I have called to ask you, to plead with you, to turn him in if you know where he is before another innocent human is murdered."

"His name is Zack!" Julie choked fiercely. "Stop calling your own grandson 'him'!"

The other woman drew in a sharp breath and when she spoke again, she sounded almost as tormented as Julie felt. "If you know where *Zack* is," she pleaded, "if you know where *my grandson* is," she added, "please, for the love of God, stop him."

Julie's animosity dissolved when she heard the anguish in that proud voice. "I will," she whispered.

61

"ON BEHALF OF THE CREW OF FLIGHT 614, THANK YOU FOR flying Aero-Mexico," the flight attendant said. "Remember," she added cheerfully, "we're the airline that got you to your destination twenty minutes ahead of schedule." Her voice becoming businesslike, she continued, "Please remain in your seats with your seat belt securely fastened until the aircraft has come to a full stop at the gate."

Seated near the back row of the crowded plane between Ted and Paul Richardson, Julie clutched her brother's hand in a death grip, her stomach churning as the plane lurched to a stop and the jetway swung out to meet it from the terminal. Her heart was beginning to scream that this was wrong, her conscience shouted it was right and she was trapped helplessly in the crossfire. Beside her, Paul Richardson noticed her chest beginning to rise and fall in fast shallow breaths, and he took her other hand in his. "Take it easy, honey," he said in a low, reassuring voice. "It's almost over. The airport is secured at every exit."

Julie jerked her gaze from the passengers who were beginning to stand up and gather their belongings from the overhead racks. "I can't do it. I can't. I'm going to be sick!"

He tightened his grip on her clammy fingers. "You're hyperventilating. Take slow deep breaths."

Julie made herself obey. "Don't let anyone hurt him!" she warned in a fierce whisper. "You promised you wouldn't let anyone hurt him."

Paul stood up along with the passengers in front of them, and with his hand on her arm, gently urged Julie to stand, too. She yanked her arm away. "Promise me again that you won't let anyone hurt him!"

"No one wants to hurt him, Julie," he said as if he was speaking to a terrified child. "That's why you came along. You wanted to be sure no one would hurt him, and I told you there'd be less chance of violence if Benedict sees you and believes you'll get caught in the middle. Remember?"

When she nodded jerkily, he began moving forward with his hand beneath her elbow. "Okay, this is it." he said. "Ted and I will stay just a few paces behind you from now on. Don't be afraid. My people are spread all over the terminal and outside it, and your safety is their first priority. If Benedict starts shooting, they'll put their lives on the line to protect you."

"Zack wouldn't hurt me!" she said scornfully.

"He's not sane. You don't know what he'll do if he realizes you tricked him. That's why, no matter what happens, you're going to pretend to be on his side until he's safely in custody. Remember, we talked about all this before?" He drew back as they were about to reach the attractive brunette flight attendant standing at the front door of the plane. "Do you have it all clear?"

Julie wanted to start screaming that nothing was clear, but she dug her fingernails into her palms and somehow made herself nod.

"Okay, you're on your own now," he said, stopping in the doorway and carefully taking her coat off her shoulders and draping it over her arm. "In five minutes, this will all be over. Keep thinking of that—just five more minutes. And remember, don't look for him, let him find you."

He stopped, watching as she walked slowly ahead of them down the jetway, letting her gain several yards on him, then he stepped forward with Ted at his side. The moment they were out of hearing of the flight crew, Ted said in a low, furious whisper, "You had no right to put her through this. You said yourself the whole airport is swarming with FBI and Mexican police. You don't need her here to draw him out!"

Paul unbuttoned his jacket and loosened his tie—a casually dressed business-man coming to Mexico City with a friend for a few days' business and pleasure. Shoving his hands in his pockets, he said with a tight smile, "She insisted on coming to make certain Benedict isn't hurt, and you know it. I had the pilot radio ahead for a doctor; he'll be on hand to give her a sedative as soon as this is over."

"If you were half as clever as you think you are, your people would already have him in custody, and they don't, do they? You found that out when you went up into the cockpit to use the radio, didn't you?"

Paul's smile widened, but his words were ominous. "Right. He's slipped past them somehow, or else he didn't come. The FBI has no jurisdiction in Mexico. Until we get Benedict across the border we can only 'assist' the Mexican police in this operation, and they aren't very good with this sort of thing."

Shaking from the tips of her feet to the ends of her fingers, Julie walked unsteadily into the noisy gate area, where passengers were being met by family and friends, her gaze searching wildly for a tall, dark-haired man loitering at the edge of some cheerful group, and when she didn't see him, she took a few steps beyond the gate into the terminal and faltered, paralyzed with a conflicting mixture of relief and panic.

"Pardon, senorita!" a Mexican called, jostling past her, running for his flight with a boy in one hand and a suitcase in the other.

"Pardon!" another man said, shoving her rudely—he was very tall and dark, and his face was turned away. "Zack!" she whispered in terror, whirling around, watching in confusion as he ran toward a gate where passengers were swarming off their plane. Three Mexicans leaning against a post stared at her, then at the man, then at her, and she noticed them at the same time she saw the dark man's face. Not Zack's face.

The public address system seemed to blare in her ears: *"Flight 620 from Los Angeles is now arriving at Gate A-64. Flight 1152 from Phoenix is arriving at Gate A-23. Flight 134 . . ."*

Shaking harder, Julie reached a trembling hand up, shoved her hair off her forehead and began walking swiftly and blindly down the terminal, wanting it to happen without her seeing it now. Four more minutes. If she walked fast, she thought, if she didn't look right or left, Zack would move out from behind a post or a pillar, materialize in a doorway, and they'd take him and it would be over.

Please, God, let it happen quickly, she prayed in a chant that matched her long, quick strides after she passed unchallenged through customs. *Don't let them hurt him. Let it happen quickly. Don't let them hurt him. Let it happen quickly.*

Walking swiftly, she shoved past the passengers emerging from the crowded security check gate, and without breaking stride, she glanced at the overhead sign with an arrow pointing to the terminal exit, turned in that direction, and kept right on going. *Don't let them hurt him . . . Don't let them hurt him . . . Don't let him be here,* she chanted hysterically as she walked. Two more minutes. Ahead were the doors leading out to the brightly lit area where taxis and cars were waiting with their headlights on. *Don't let him be here. Don't let him be here. Don't let him be here. Don't let him be—here.*

He wasn't here.

Julie stopped dead, oblivious to the fact that she was being shoved and jostled by streams of laughing, talking people trying to get around her to leave the terminal. Slowly she turned, her gaze drifting past Paul Richardson, who'd halted and seemed to be chatting with Ted . . . past the group of laughing Mexicans rushing toward her . . . past the tall, stooped, elderly man with graying hair, who was carrying a suitcase, his head bent . . . past the mother with— The old man! Julie's gaze shot back to him just as he slowly lifted his head and raised his eyes to her . . . his warm, smiling, golden eyes.

Screaming a silent warning to him, Julie stepped forward once, twice, and started running, shoving through the crowd, trying to throw herself between him and danger at the same time a male voice boomed, "HOLD IT RIGHT THERE, BENEDICT!"

Zack froze, men grabbed him, throwing him against the wall, but his eyes stayed riveted on Julie, warning her fiercely to stay away. Pandemonium erupted with the shouts of passengers scrambling to get out of the way of Mexican Federales, who were running forward drawing guns, and Julie heard herself screaming at all of them, "Don't hurt him! Don't hurt him!"

Paul Richardson grabbed her, jerking her back.

"They're hurting him!" she cried, struggling in his grip to see around the bodies of the men crowded around him. "They're *hurting* him!"

"It's all over!" Paul shouted in her ear, trying to restrain and calm her. "It's all right! It's over!"

The words finally registered and Julie froze. Unable to pull free or look away, she watched in paralyzed anguish as Zack was surrounded and searched under the supervision of a short, impeccably dressed man with thinning hair who suddenly seemed to be in charge. He was smiling as he watched Zack being frisked by the Mexican Federales, and she heard him say, "We're going home, Benedict, and we're going to be together for a long, long time—" He broke off as one of the Federales pulled something out of Zack's pocket, and he held out his hand. "What's that?" he snapped.

The Federale dropped the object into his palm and Julie felt her body go cold at the evil in his smile as he looked from the object in his hand to Zack's expressionless profile. "How sweet!" he sneered, then he turned suddenly toward Julie, striding forward.

"I'm Warden Hadley," he said, holding out his hand. "I'll bet this was meant for you."

Julie didn't react, she couldn't move, because Zack was looking at her now, and the expression in his eyes made her want to die. He was silently telling her he loved her. Telling her he was sorry. Telling her good-bye.

Because he still thought she'd led them to him by accident.

"Take it!" Hadley snapped in an awful voice.

Jolted by his tone, Julie automatically reached out her hand.

The object he dropped into it was a slender diamond wedding band.

"Oh, no—" she moaned, squeezing it to her chest as tears raced down her cheeks. "No, no, no—"

Ignoring her, Hadley turned to the Mexican police. "Get him out of here," he ordered, jerking his head toward the doors where dozens of squad cars with whirling lights had silently appeared. But as the Federales shoved Zack forward, Hadley seemed to think something was wrong. "Wait a minute," he snapped, then he turned to Julie as Zack was yanked to a stop beside her, and he said with an oily, malicious smile. "Miss Mathison, I've been very rude. I haven't thanked you yet for your cooperation. If you hadn't helped us set this whole scheme up, Benedict might never have been caught."

Zack's head jerked up, his gaze raking Julie's guilt-stricken face, and she watched in agony as his eyes registered first disbelief. And then hatred. A hatred so deep that all the muscles in his face tightened into a mask of rage. In a burst of fury, he twisted against his captors and lunged toward the door.

"Hold the sonofabitch!" Hadley shouted, and the alarm in his voice made the panicked Federales lash out with billy clubs.

Julie heard the crack of wood on bone and sinew, she saw Zack hit the floor on his knees, and she went wild when they raised their clubs to hit him again. Tearing free of Paul's grip, she launched herself at Hadley. Whimpering with maddened pain for the man on the floor, she clawed the side of Hadley's face and kicked at him in a mindless frenzy while Paul was trying to restrain her. Hadley doubled up his fist to strike her but halted at Paul's enraged warning:

"You sadistic bastard, touch her and I'll tear your larynx out!" Lifting his head, he shouted to one of his men, "Get the goddamned doctor over here!" Then he jerked his head toward Hadley and added, "And get him out of here!"

But he needn't have worried about breaking up another uneven fight . . . Julie was slowly sliding down in his arms in a dead faint.

62

DR. DELORIK WALKED OUT OF JULIE'S BEDROOM CARRYING HIS black bag and smiled reassuringly at Julie's worried family and Katherine who were gathered in the living room, waiting for his prognosis. "She's a sturdy thing. She'll be fine physically in twenty-four hours," he promised. "You can go in and tell her good night if you like. She's sedated so she won't know it's actually morning, not night, and she may not respond or even remember you were here, but it may help her rest easier anyway. It'll be a couple of days before she feels like going back to work."

"I'll call her principal and explain," Mrs. Mathison said quickly, standing up, her anxious gaze on the open door to Julie's room.

"You won't have to explain much to him or anyone else," Dr. Delorik said flatly. "In case you haven't had a television set on yet, you may as well know that what happened in Mexico last night is all over every news program on the air this morning, complete with videotapes of the whole thing provided by vacationers who had minicams with them in the airport. The good news is that, despite the beating Benedict got from the Mexican police on those videotapes, the press is making Julie sound like a heroine who collaborated in a clever scheme to trap a murderer."

Six faces looked at him without a trace of pleasure in his "good news," so he continued as he shrugged into his coat, "Someone should stay with her for the next twenty-four hours—just to keep an eye on her and to be sure someone is here when she wakes up."

"We'll stay," James Mathison said, putting his arm around his wife.

"You'll both go home and get some sleep if you want some free medical advice," Dr. Delorik said firmly. "You look exhausted. Mary, I don't want to have to admit you to the hospital with your heart kicking up over all this stress."

"He's right," Ted said with absolute finality. "You two go home and get some rest. Carl, you and Sara go to work and come by tonight if you want to. I'm off for the next two days anyway, so I'll stay here."

"No way!" Carl argued. "You haven't slept since the day before yesterday, and besides, you sleep like the dead. If you're sleeping, you won't hear Julie if she needs you."

Ted opened his mouth to try to dispute that, then came up with a better solution. "Katherine," he said, turning to her, "will you stay here with me? Otherwise, Carl and Sara will lose a half day of work arguing with me. Or do you have something else you have to do?"

"I want to stay," Katherine said simply.

"That's settled then," Reverend Mathison said, and the family proceeded down the hall to Julie's bedroom, while Katherine went into the kitchen to make Ted a light breakfast.

"Julie, honey, it's me, Dad. Mother's here with me."

In her drugged dream, Julie felt something touch her forehead, and her father's voice whispering from very, very far away, "We love you. Everything's going to be just fine. Sleep tight." Then her mother's voice was there, tearful and soft. "You're so brave, darling. You've always been so brave. Sleep well." Something bristly brushed her cheek and made her wince and turn her head away, and Carl's gruff laugh touched her ear. "That's no way to treat your favorite brother, just because I haven't shaved yet . . . Love you, honey." Then there was Ted telling her in his teasing voice, "Carl's full of it! *I'm* your favorite brother. Katherine and I are right here. If you wake up, just call us, and we'll wait on you hand and foot." Sara's gentle voice whispered, "I love you, too, Julie. Sleep well."

And then the voices receded, sinking into the darkness to mingle with all the other strange sounds and disturbing images of people running and shouting and shoving, guns and swirling lights and icy eyes like golden daggers stabbing her, and airplane engines roaring and roaring and roaring.

Katherine heard the front door close as she put toast, jam, and a glass of orange juice on a tray. As he'd promised to do yesterday, Ted had called her as soon as he got Julie home, this morning, but when Katherine arrived, the family had already gathered, so all she really knew about what had happened in Mexico City was the brief, undoubtedly diluted, version that Ted had provided to his worried parents.

Carrying the tray, she headed into the living room, then stopped at the sight of Ted, sitting on the sofa, hunched forward, with his elbows on his knees and his head in his hands. It was a posture of such unparalleled despair that she realized instantly it came from much more than weariness.

"It was bad in Mexico City, wasn't it?" she asked quietly.

"Worse than bad," he said, rubbing his hands over his face as she put the tray on the coffee table and sat down at the opposite end of the sofa. Propping his arms on his legs, he turned his head to her and said harshly, "It was a nightmare. The only tiny blessing was that Julie was so hysterical, so overwrought, before it even began that I know she didn't register half of what was going on. Also, Paul Richardson managed to keep her where part of her view was blocked by the chaos, so she couldn't see well. I, however," he said grimly, "had a ringside seat with a clear view, and I was not hysterical. Jesus, it was worse than anything I imagined . . ."

When he didn't seem to know how to begin to explain, Katherine said, "Do you mean Benedict was violent? Did he try to get at her and hurt her?"

"Violent?" he repeated in an embittered voice. "Hurt her? I almost wish to God he'd tried! It would have been so much better, so much easier on her."

"I don't understand."

With a harsh sigh, he slumped back against the sofa, staring up at the ceiling, and gave a grim laugh. "No, he didn't get violent. The instant he knew what was going down, he froze, he didn't try to move or duck or run, he just stood there without struggling and stared at Julie and shook his head, warning her to stay away and hide. He didn't flinch or say a word, not even when they slapped the cuffs on him and threw him against the wall to frisk him. The Federales—the Mexican police—don't have any compunction about using what we call 'undue force,' and they roughed him up but good under the pretext of frisking him. One of them clubbed him in the kidneys, another one nailed him behind the knees, and he never ever struggled or fought them or made a sound. God, I've never seen a man act like that when he was busted in my life, not when things get violent. It was as if he was so desperate to keep things calm that he didn't care what they did to him. Julie couldn't even see most of what they were doing to him, and she was still screaming at them not to hurt him."

"Drink this, before you tell me more," Katherine said, handing him a glass of orange juice. He straightened and took it with a brief, grateful smile, as if he'd wanted it all along, but didn't have the strength to reach for it. "Was that the end of it?" she asked when he'd finished most of the orange juice.

He shook his head and resumed his former posture, arms on his knees, shoulders hunched forward, and rolled the glass between his hands, staring into it. "No," he said caustically, "that was just the *good* part."

"What was the bad part?" Katherine asked, her voice filled with dread.

"That came a few minutes later when they were dragging Benedict out. Hadley, the warden from Amarillo State Penitentiary, who also happens to be a sadistic son of a bitch, stopped to congratulate Julie right in front of Benedict."

"Why does that make him sadistic?"

"You had to see the smile on his face to understand. With Benedict standing there, Hadley deliberately made it sound like Julie had conceived the entire plot to join him in Mexico just so she could trap him and turn him in."

Katherine's hand went to her throat and Ted nodded agreement at her unconsciously defensive gesture. "You've got the picture, and Benedict got it, too. Jesus, you should have seen the look on his face. He looked . . . murderous, that's the only word I can think of, and that doesn't even describe it. He tried to get at her or maybe to turn away, I'm not sure, but either way, the Federales used it as an excuse to start beating the shit out of him right in front of her. That's when Julie went crazy and attacked Hadley. Then she fainted, thank God."

"Why didn't Paul Richardson do something to stop all that from happening in the first place?"

Ted frowned into his glass, then he put it down. "Paul's hands were tied. So long as we were on the other side of the Mexican border, he had to work within their system. The only reason the FBI was involved in the first place was because they had a federal warrant out against Benedict for kidnapping. The Mexican government honored that warrant and agreed to cooperate with surprising speed in the deal at the airport, but the Federales have complete jurisdiction over Benedict until they hand him over at the American border."

"How long will that take?"

"No time at all in this case. Instead of driving him to the border, which is what they'd normally do, Paul talked them into flying him to our border in a small private plane. His plane took off about the same time ours did. Before we left the airport, the Federales developed a belated social conscience," he added sarcastically. "They went around, confiscating all the film they could get their hands on from whomever had cameras. Paul got ahold of a couple videotapes they overlooked, not because he cared about the Federales, but because he was trying to protect Julie from being seen here in the films. I saw one of the tapes they obviously missed on a newscast in the airport, but the camera was on Benedict nearly the entire time. That's one small blessing, at least."

"For some reason, I assumed Paul would come back here with her."

Shaking his head, Ted said, "He had to be at the Texas border to take Benedict into custody from the Federales, then he'll hand him over to Hadley."

Katherine studied his face for a moment. "Is that everything that happened?"

"Not quite," he said tautly, "there was one more detail, one more death blow to her that I left out."

"What was it?"

"This," Ted said, reaching into his shirt pocket. "Benedict had this on him, and Hadley presented it to her with great enjoyment." Opening his fist, he dropped the ring unceremoniously into an unsuspecting Katherine's outstretched hand, watching her eyes widen with shock and then fill with tears.

"Oh, my God," she whispered, staring at the diamond circlet sparkling in her palm, "he obviously wanted her to have something very special. This is exquisite."

"Don't go all sentimental," Ted warned, but his own voice was gruff. "The man's a maniac, a murderer."

She swallowed audibly and nodded. "I know."

He glanced from the ring in her right palm to the enormous rock on her left finger. "It's tiny compared to that boulder you're wearing."

She laughed chokingly. "Size isn't everything, and besides, he couldn't have let her wear a ring like this, because it would have drawn attention to them wherever they went. So he got her one like this instead," she speculated softly.

"It's just an ordinary diamond wedding band."

Katherine shook her head in denial. "There's nothing ordinary about this ring. The band is platinum, not gold, and the diamonds go all the way around it."

"So what, they aren't very big," Ted said bluntly, but he was as relieved as she obviously was to digress for a moment from their former subject.

"Size isn't everything," she said again, turning the ring in her fingers. "These stones are exceptionally fine, and they're a very expensive cut."

"They're square."

"Oblong. The way they're cut is called 'radiant.'" In a suffocated voice she added, "He has . . . beautiful taste."

"He's insane and he's a killer."

"You're right," she said, laying the ring on the table, then she looked up at him and Ted gazed at a beautiful face that used to mesmerize him and numb his mind. She was different now . . . older, softer, sweeter . . . concerned, instead of self-absorbed. And five times as desirable. "Don't start blaming yourself for Julie getting hurt," she said gently. "You saved her from a life of hell or worse. Julie knows that."

"Thank you," he said quietly, then he stretched his arm across the back of the sofa, leaned his head back, and closed his eyes. "I'm so damned tired, Kathy." As if his body was reenacting a memory without the approval of his exhausted mind, his hand curved around her shoulder and he drew her close. Not until her cheek came to rest against his chest and her hand splayed over his arm, did he realize what he'd done, but even then it seemed harmless enough.

"We were so lucky, you and I," she whispered. "We saw each other, we loved each other, we got married. And then we threw it all away."

"I know." The aching regret he heard in his own voice made his eyes snap open in annoyed surprise, and he tipped his chin down, staring at her. She wanted him to kiss her, it was written all over her somber face.

"No," he said tautly, closing his eyes.

She rubbed her cheek against his chest, and he felt his resistance begin to crumble. "Stop it!" he warned, "or I'll get up and go to bed in the other room." She stopped instantly, but she didn't pull back in anger or lash out at him, and he held his breath, wishing she would. A minute ago he'd been limp with exhaustion; now his mind was numb but his body was stirring to life and his voice seemed to have a will of its own. "Either get up," he warned without opening his eyes, "or else take off that ring you're wearing."

"Why?" she whispered.

"Because I'll be damned if I'll make love to you while you're wearing another man's ring—"

A billion-year-old diamond, appraised at a quarter of a million dollars, bounced unceremoniously onto the coffee table. His voice came out in a half-laugh/half-groan. "Kathy, you're the only woman in the world who would do that to such a diamond."

"I'm the only woman in the world for you."

Ted leaned his head back and closed his eyes again, trying to ignore the truth of that, but his hand was already curving around her nape, his fingers sliding into her hair, tilting her face up. Opening his eyes, he gazed down at her, remembering the months of hell that had been their life together . . . and the cold emptiness that had been his life without her and he saw the tear trembling at the corner of her eyelid. "I know you are," he whispered, and bending his head, he touched his tongue to the salty tear.

"If you'll give me another chance, I'll prove it," she promised fiercely.

"I know you will," he whispered, kissing the second tear away.

"Will you give me another chance?"

He tipped her chin up and gazed into her eyes, and he was lost. "Yes."

63

STILL A LITTLE DISORIENTED FROM THE DRUGS SHE'D BEEN given twenty-four hours ago, Julie held her hand to her aching head and walked unsteadily from her bedroom into the kitchen, then she stopped short, blinking at the unbelievable sight that greeted her: Ted and Katherine were standing near the sink, locked in an embrace that looked definitely passionate. Her mind was a comfortable, fuzzy blur at the moment, and she smiled at the cozy, domestic picture. "The water is running," she said, startling all three of them with her dry, croaking voice.

Ted lifted his head and grinned at her, but Katherine jumped as if she'd been caught in the act of doing something wrong and pulled out of his arms. "Julie, I'm sorry!" she blurted.

"For what?" Julie asked, walking over to the cabinet and taking down a glass that she filled with water. She drank it all, trying to quench the strange thirst she felt.

"For letting you see us like that."

"Why?" Julie asked, holding the small glass under the faucet to refill it, but her head was already beginning to clear and the memories were trying to crowd in.

"Because," Katherine babbled awkwardly, "we shouldn't be doing this in front of you, not when we're supposed to be helping you deal with what happened in Mexico—" she broke off in horror as the glass slid from Julie's hand and crashed to the floor.

"Don't!" Julie burst out, bracing her hands on the counter, trying to shut out the sudden memory of Zack's enraged face just before the Mexican police started hitting him and the sound of his body thudding to the floor at her feet. She shuddered again and again, clenching her eyes closed against the vision, then after a minute, she managed to straighten and turn. "Don't talk about it ever again," she said. "I'm all right," she added with more determination than accuracy. "It's over. I'll be all right if you don't talk about it. I have to make a phone call," she added, glancing at the clock on the wall above the sink, and without realizing she was doing the opposite of what she'd just asked them to do, Julie picked up the telephone, called Paul Richardson's office, and gave the secretary her name.

The last explosion of emotion left her feeling drained and afraid. She was strained to the breaking point she realized, looking at her trembling hands, and it had to stop right now. Life was hard for a lot of people, she reminded herself, and she had to stop reeling from every blow. Right now. Immediately. She could either get a prescription for tranquilizers and turn herself into a zombie, or she could deal with the future in a calm, rational way. Tincture of time would cure the rest. No more tears, she vowed. No more outbursts. No more pain. People depended on her—all her regular students and the women she taught to read at night. They especially looked up to her and she had to show them how *she* dealt with adversity.

She had classes to teach and football and softball teams to coach. She'd have to get busy and stay busy. She *must not* fall apart.

"Paul," she said with only a slight tremor when he finally took her call, "I have to see him, I have to explain—"

His voice was sympathetic, kind, and final. "That won't be possible right away. He can't have visitors at Amarillo for awhile."

"Amarillo? You promised me he'd go to a mental hospital for evaluation and treatment!"

"I said I'd try to accomplish that, and I will, but these things take time, and—"

"Don't talk to me about 'needing' time," she warned, but she held onto her composure. "That warden's a monster. He's sadistic, you could see he was in Mexico. He'll have Zack beaten until—"

"Hadley isn't going to lay a hand on him," Paul interrupted gently, "that much I can promise you."

"How can you be sure? I have to be sure!"

"I'm sure because I told him we were going to want to question Benedict in connection with kidnapping charges and that we'd expect him to be in perfect condition when we do. Hadley knows I don't like him and he knows I mean business. He won't screw around with me or the FBI, especially not when he's already under investigation by the prison authorities as a result of that prison uprising last month. His job and his skin are both too precious to him."

"I will not," Julie reminded him forcefully, "be a party to charging Zack with kidnapping."

"I know that," Paul said soothingly. "It was just a means to keep Hadley under control, not that I think it's really necessary. As I said, he knows the prison authorities are investigating his conduct and watching him closely."

Julie's breath came out in a rush of relief, and he said, "You sound a little better today. Get some rest. I'm going to come see you this weekend."

"I don't think that's a good—"

"Whether you want to see me or not," he interrupted firmly. "You can worry about Benedict, but it's you I'm worried about. He's a killer and you did what you had to do, for his sake and everyone else's. Don't ever let yourself think anything else."

Julie nodded, telling herself firmly that he was right. "I'll be fine," she said. "Really I will."

When she hung up, she looked at Katherine and Ted. "I will," she promised them both. "You'll see. It's nice to know," she said with a tremulous smile, "that something good came from this nightmare—the two of you."

She ate the breakfast they forced on her, then she got up to make a second phone call.

With the firm intention of urging Matt Farrell to use his considerable influence to get Zack into a hospital, Julie dialed his private number in Chicago. His secretary put her call through, but when Matt Farrell picked up the phone, his reaction to her call was beyond Julie's worst imaginings: "You vicious, scheming bitch," he said, his voice hissing with rage. "You should have been an actress! I can't believe I was stupid enough to swallow that act you put on and let you use me to trap Zack!" He hung up on her. Julie stared at the dead phone in her hand while the realization slowly hit her that Zack's friend obviously hadn't thought Tony Austin's death was Zack's doing: The need to accomplish her goal and also exonerate herself became a compulsion. She called Chicago, got the telephone number for Bancroft & Company's main department store, and asked to speak to Meredith Bancroft. When Meredith's secretary insisted on knowing Julie's name before she'd put the call through, Julie fully expected Meredith to refuse her call.

A few minutes later, however, Meredith's voice came across the distance— cool and reserved, but at least she was willing to talk. "What can you possibly want to discuss with me, Julie?" she said.

Unable to keep the pleading from her voice, Julie said, "Please just listen to me. I called your husband a few minutes ago to ask if he has any influence to get Zack transferred to a mental hospital, and he hung up on me before I could ask him."

"I'm not surprised. He hates you thoroughly."

"And you?" Julie said, swallowing to steady herself. "Do you believe what he does—that the night you were here I concocted a scheme to trap Zack and turn him in and that I used both of you to do it."

"Didn't you?" Meredith asked, but Julie sensed a hesitancy in her voice, and she grabbed at it.

Her words spilling out in a desperate jumble, she said, "You can't believe that. Please, please don't. I went to see his grandmother after you were here and she told me the truth about how Zack's brother died. Meredith, Zack *shot* him! Three people who made him angry are dead! I couldn't let him hurt more people, you have to understand that and believe me . . ."

Hundreds of miles away, Meredith leaned back in her chair and rubbed her temples, remembering the laughter and love in Julie's dining room. "I—I do believe you," she said finally. "The night Matt and I were at your house, that just couldn't have been an act. You loved him very much, and trapping him was the furthest thing from your mind."

"Thank you," she whispered simply. "Good-bye."

"Are you going to be all right?" Meredith asked.

"I don't remember how 'all right' feels," Julie said with a broken laugh, then she shook off her self-pity and said politely, "I'll be fine. I'll cope."

64

IN THE WEEKS THAT FOLLOWED, JULIE COPED IN THE ONLY WAY she knew how: Shunning the television set and radio completely, she immersed herself in work and a dozen civic and church activities, and she kept herself going until she dropped into bed at night, exhausted. She took on tutoring assignments, volunteered to head the church fund drive, and accepted the chairmanship of Keaton's Bicentennial Celebration, which was scheduled to take place during the last week of May with festivities that ranged from fireworks and a dance in the park to a carnival. No one in Keaton had any doubt about the cause of Julie's endless round of feverish activities, but as day faded into day, their surreptitious, pitying glances came less often, and they were never foolish enough, or heartless enough, to congratulate her on her bravery for turning in the man she had obviously loved.

Days merged into weeks that passed in a blur of frantic activity, but slowly, very slowly, Julie began to find her balance again. There were days when she actually went for four or five hours without thinking of Zack, nights when she didn't reread his only letter before she fell asleep, and dawns when she didn't lie awake staring dry-eyed at the ceiling, remembering things like their silly snowball fight or his wonderful snow monster or the husky sound of his whispered endearments when he made love to her.

Paul spent every weekend in Keaton, staying first at the local motel and then, at her parents' invitation, at their house, and the entire town gossiped that the FBI agent who'd come to Keaton to arrest Julie Mathison had fallen in love with her instead. But Julie refused to consider that possibility. She refused because facing it would have forced her to tell him he was wasting his time, when she wanted to keep seeing him. She had to keep seeing him, because Paul could make her laugh. And because he reminded her of Zack. And so they went out as a foursome with Ted and Katherine, and he took her home afterward and kissed her good night with slowly increasing ardor. It was during his sixth weekend in Keaton that his patience and restraint began to fray. They'd gone to a local movie with Ted and Katherine, and Julie had invited all three of them to her house for coffee. After Ted and Katherine left, Paul had caught her hands and pulled her to her feet.

"I had a wonderful weekend," he said and teasingly added, "even if you did make me play football with a bunch of handicapped kids who ran me ragged."

She smiled at that and his face softened. "I love it when you smile at me," he whispered. "And just to make sure you smile whenever you think of me, I bought you something." Reaching into his pocket, he extracted a flat, velvet box, and put it into her hands, watching as Julie opened the box. In it was a small gold clown with tiny sapphire eyes that was suspended from a long, beautiful chain. When Julie carefully removed the chain, she noticed the clown's arms and legs jiggled, and she laughed. "He's beautiful," she said, "and funny."

"Good. Let's take this chain off and try him on," he said, noticing the slender chain beneath her collar. Julie clutched involuntarily at it, but it was too late. Paul had already pulled it out and seen the wedding band Zack had in his pocket in Mexico.

Swearing under his breath, he caught her shoulders. "Why?" he demanded, making a visible effort not to shake her. "Why are you torturing yourself by wearing this? You did the right thing when you turned him in!"

"I know," Julie said.

"Then let him go, damnit! He's in prison and he'll be there for the rest of his life. You have your life—a life that should be filled with a husband and children. What you need," he said, his voice softening as his hands slid down her arms, "is a man who'll take you to bed and make you forget that you ever went to bed with him. I know you did, Julie," he said when her eyes snapped to his. "And it doesn't matter."

She put up her chin and said with quiet dignity, "When it stops mattering to me, then I'll be ready for someone else. Not before."

Caught between frustration and amusement, Paul touched his thumb to her chin. "God, you're stubborn. What would you do," he said half-seriously, "if I went back to Dallas and never came back?"

"I'd miss you a lot."

"I suppose you think I'll settle for that for now," he said irritably because it was true.

In answer she gave him a plucky smile and nodded, "You're crazy about my mother's cooking."

Chuckling, he drew her into his arms. "I'm crazy about *you*. I'll see you next weekend."

65

"THERE MUST BE SOME MISTAKE," EMILY SAID AS SHE LOOKED from her husband to his accountant. "My father would never buy stock or invest money in anything Tony Austin touched, not if he knew Tony was involved."

"The facts prove otherwise, Miss McDaniels," Edwin Fairchild said mildly. "Over the last five years, he's invested over $4 million of your trust fund in TA Productions, which was owned by Mr. Austin. It was all quite aboveboard, I assure you, although it certainly was unprofitable and ill-advised on your father's part, since Austin apparently used the money exclusively to pay his living expenses. I'm not implying there was any wrongdoing on your father's part," he assured her when she continued to frown at him. "Your father purchased stock for you in TA Productions, and the stock is in your name. My only reason for bringing this up at this time is that as your new financial advisor, I think it's time to sell the stock back to Austin's heirs if they'll buy it or else give it to them for a penny a share, so that we can take a loss on your next joint tax return."

Emily struggled to put her thoughts into coherent order. "What did my father say about all these bad investments in TA Productions?"

"It's not my place to discuss it with him or question his judgment. He's handled your trust fund since you were a child, I understand, and how he chose to invest the money for you has been exclusively his province. All that is rightfully between you and him. The only reason I'm involved now is that I've handled your husband's financial matters for years and since you're now married, there are questions of joint income tax returns and so forth."

"My father couldn't possibly have realized that Tony Austin was TA Productions," Emily stated firmly.

Fairchild's white eyebrows rose at what he clearly thought was incorrect. "If that is what you prefer to believe."

"It's not a question of what I prefer to believe," she said with a ragged laugh, "it's just that my father being tricked into buying stock in Tony's company is utterly . . . Machiavellian. He despised the man."

"I can't see how he would have been tricked," her husband told her in a carefully neutral voice, knowing how sensitive she was about her father. "Edwin and I discussed this earlier on the phone today, and it's clear your father had to have purchased the stock directly from Austin."

"What makes you say that?"

"Because TA isn't traded on the stock exchange. As Edwin mentioned a few minutes ago, it's a privately held company, and the only way to buy stock would have been from Austin or his representative."

Emily looked from her husband to his accountant. "Did he have any representatives?"

Edwin Fairchild shook his head and put on his glasses, perusing a photocopy of some document. "He certainly never paid anyone to represent him or work for him in any capacity. According to TA's corporate charter, which is a matter of public record in Sacramento, Austin was the only officer, director, and shareholder. I checked some sources of mine, and he was also the only employee." Removing his glasses, he glanced at the heavy gold Rolex on his wrist and said, "I see it's already after six o'clock. I didn't mean to keep you so late, but we've gone over everything that needed to be discussed. If you intend to try to sell the TA stock back to Austin's heirs, the sooner you approach them the better, otherwise they'll very likely be all wrapped up in probate court proceedings. As soon as you let me know whether you intend to keep or sell the stock, I'll be able to finish your tax liability projection for the next year."

Dick nodded and Fairchild turned to Emily, his tone conciliatory. "Don't look so upset, Miss McDaniels. Even though your father lost $4 million of your money in Austin's company, we'll be able to take that as a tax loss against profits from your other investments. The tax benefits from doing that will reduce your loss to less than $3 million."

"I don't understand finances or taxes," Emily told them both. "My father's always handled all that for me."

"Then you ought to discuss the TA stock with him. He made almost twenty separate purchases over the last five years, and he must have had some profit motive in mind that we don't know about. Perhaps he'll be able to give you some reason why it would be wise to hold the stock a little longer."

Reaching out, Emily shook his hand. "Thank you, Mr. Fairchild, I'll do that."

"Before you go," Fairchild said as Emily tucked her hand in her husband's arm, "I want to make it clear that in every other respect, your father's trusteeship over your funds has been above reproach. He's invested your money wisely and accounted for every penny that was spent for the last fifteen years, including the money invested in TA Productions."

Emily's face stiffened. "I don't need you or anyone else to tell me that my father has acted in my best interests. He *always* has."

In the car, Emily watched her husband maneuver the shiny BMW through rush hour traffic. "I was rude to him, wasn't I?" she asked.

Dick shot her a wry look as they stopped for a red light. "You were defensive, not rude. But then you're always a little defensive where your father's concerned."

"I know," she sighed, "but there's a reason."

"You love him and he devoted his life to you," Dick recited.

Emily lifted her gaze from his hand on the gear shift. "There's another reason, too. It's been a well-known scandal that, in the old days, a lot of the parents of child stars squandered, and even stole, every dime the child earned. My father was just the opposite. Even though there are laws to prevent all parents from doing that now, a lot of people have still treated my father as if he lives off of me and very grandly."

"Obviously, they haven't seen his condo, or they'd know better," Dick said, shifting from second into third gear as traffic began to move again. "He hasn't painted a wall in ten years, and he needs new furniture. The neighborhood is on the downslide, and in a few years it's not going to be safe to live there."

"I know all that, but he hates to spend money." Reverting to the earlier topic, she continued, "You can't imagine how humiliating it's been for him at times to be my father. I can still remember when he went to buy a car five years ago. The salesman was happy to sell him a Chevrolet until I got there to help Dad pick out a color. As soon as the guy realized who I was, ergo who Daddy was, he said in this nauseating, presumptuous voice, 'This changes everything, Mr. McDaniels! I'm sure your daughter would rather you have that sharp Seville you liked, wouldn't you, honey?'"

"If what people thought of him bothered your father," Dick said, forgetting for the moment to hide his distaste for the man, "he could have gotten a nice, respectable job doing something besides looking out for his little Emily. Then maybe he'd have something to do besides get drunk and wallow in self-pity because little Emily grew up and got married." From the corner of his eye, he watched her face fall and he stretched his arm across the seat, curving his hand around her stiff shoulder. "I'm sorry," he said. "I am obviously a jealous jerk who gets bent out of shape over my wife's unusually close relationship with her father. Forgive me?"

Nodding, she rubbed her cheek against the back of his hand, but her pretty face remained pensive and he saw it.

"No, you haven't," he said, trying to tease her out of her unusually somber mood. "An apology wasn't enough. I deserve a kick in the ass. I deserve"—he hesitated, thinking—"to have to take you to Anthony's tonight and buy you the most expensive dinner in Los Angeles and sit there while everybody gapes at my wife!"

She smiled at him, her famous dimples peeking out, and he touched his hand to the side of her face and said quietly. "I love you, Emily." Jokingly, he added, "Even though you've got those funny dents in your face, I love you anyway. Not every guy would be able to overlook a manufacturing defect like that, but I can."

Her laughter bubbled out and he grinned at her, but his grin faded as she challenged, "Do you love me enough to take me by my father's place before we go to dinner?"

"Why?" he said irritably.

"Because I have to talk to him about the money he invested with Tony. I can't figure it out, and it's driving me crazy."

"I guess," Dick said, flipping on his turn indicators and changing lanes so he could make the turn toward her father's neighborhood, "I even love you that much."

Emily pressed the buzzer beside the door of her father's condominium, and after a lengthy pause he opened it, a glass of whiskey in his hand. "Emily, baby?"

he slurred, looking at her with bloodshot eyes in an unshaven face bearing a three-day growth of beard. "I didn't know you were coming by tonight." Completely ignoring the presence of her husband, he looped his arm around her shoulders and drew her inside.

He was drunk, Emily realized with a pang of frustration and sorrow as she looked around at the gloomy interior of his place, not dead drunk but stumbling drunk. Once, he'd been a virtual teetotaler, but during the past several years, his bouts of drunkenness had been occurring with increasing frequency. "Why don't you turn on some lights," she suggested gently, reaching out and turning a single lamp on in the living room.

"I like the dark," he said, reaching behind her and turning the lamp off. "It's safe and sweet."

"I prefer a little light so Emily doesn't fall over something and kill herself," Dick said firmly, reaching out and switching the lamp back on.

"What made you decide to come by?" he asked Emily as if Dick hadn't spoken. "You never come to see me anymore," he complained.

"I was here twice last week," Emily reminded him. "But to answer your question, I came to talk about business if you're up to it. Dick's accountant has some questions he needs answered before he can prepare tax estimates or something."

"Sure, sure. No problem, honey. Come on into my study where I keep all your files."

"I have several phone calls to make," Dick told Emily. "You talk to your father and I'll use the phone in the—" He looked around for a phone and couldn't see one in the living room.

"In the kitchen," she explained, and he nodded, already heading off in that direction.

Emily followed her father upstairs into the bedroom he'd converted to an office years ago, and he sat down behind his desk, which was the only clear surface in the house, if one discounted the coating of dust. The credenza and file cabinets that lined the wall behind him were covered with dozens and dozens of framed photographs of Emily—Emily as an infant, a toddler, a child of four; Emily in her ballet tutu, in her Halloween costume, in the costume she wore for her first starring role; Emily at thirteen with her hair in a pony tail, at fifteen with her first corsage from a boy. Now, as Emily looked at the photographs, she realized for the first time that he was with her in nearly all of them. And then she noticed something else—the light from the lamp on his dusty desk was shining brightly on the glass inserts in all the picture frames as if they'd been recently cleaned.

"Whadyou want t'know about, honey?" he asked, taking a swallow of his drink.

Emily considered mentioning his need for some sort of treatment for what had clearly become an alcohol addiction, but the last two times she'd brought that up, his reaction had been first crushed and then enraged. Summoning her courage, she plunged tactfully into the matter at hand. "Dad, you know how grateful I am for the way you've put all my money into a trust fund and managed it for me all these years. You do know that?" she prompted when he crossed his arms and seemed to stare through her.

"Sure, I do. I've socked away every cent you made and guarded it with my life. I never took anything for myself but an hourly wage of twenty dollars and only when you insisted I had to do it. You were so cute that day," he said wistfully. "Sixteen years old and confronting your old dad like a mature woman, telling me that if I didn't draw a larger salary, you were going to fire me."

"That's right," Emily said absently. "So I don't want you to think for a moment I have any doubts about your integrity when I ask you the next question. I'm only trying to understand your reasoning. I'm not complaining about the money I lost."

"Money you lost?" he said angrily. "What the hell do you mean?"

"I mean the $4 million you invested in Tony Austin Productions over the past five years. The stock is worthless. Why did you do it, Dad? You know I hated him, and I always had the feeling you despised him even more."

For a moment he didn't move, then he slowly raised his head, his eyes like sunken, burning coals, and Emily unknowingly pressed back into her chair. "Austin . . ." he said softly, his smile turning first malicious, then soothing. "You don't have to worry about him anymore, honey. I took care of him. We won't have to buy any more of his phoney stock. We'll keep it all our little secret."

"Why did we have to buy his phoney stock in the first place?" Emily said, unaccountably nervous about his expression, his voice, and the gloom of the poorly lit room.

"He made me do it. I didn't want to. Now, he's dead, and I don't have to."

"How could he possibly make you invest $4 million of my money in his company if you didn't want to?" she demanded more sharply than she intended.

"Don't you use that tone on me, Missy!" he snapped in a sudden rage. "I'll show you the back of my hand."

Emily was so startled by this unprecedented threat from a man who'd never raised a hand to her in her life that she stood up. "We'll discuss this some other time when you're rational!"

"Wait!" With surprising speed, he reached across the desk and grabbed her

PERFECT

arm. "Don't leave me, honey. I'm scared. That's all. I haven't slept in days because I'm so scared. I'd never hurt you. You know that."

He looked suddenly and truly terrified, and Emily was shaken by that. Patting his hand, feeling like the parent, not the child, she said gently, "I won't go, Daddy. Don't be scared. Tell me what's wrong. I'll understand."

"You'll keep it a secret? Cross your heart?"

She nodded, wincing at the childlike plea.

"Austin made me buy that stock. He—he was blackmailing us. For five long years, that bastard has been bleeding us for money."

"Us?" she blurted with a mixture of disbelief and impatience.

"You and I are a team. What happens to one, happens to the other, doesn't it?"

"I—I guess so," she said warily, trying to keep her inner shaking from affecting her voice. "Why was Tony blackmailing . . . us?"

"Because," her father said, dropping his voice to a conspiratorial whisper, "he knew we killed Rachel."

Emily lurched out of her chair and stood stock still, gaping at him. "That's crazy! You—you must be so drunk you're hallucinating! What possible reason could you have had for killing Zack's wife?"

"None."

Emily braced her flattened hands on his desk. "Why are you talking like this? It's crazy."

"Don't ever say that to me! That's what he said, and it's a lie! I'm not crazy. I'm scared, why can't you understand that?" he said, his voice switching to a whine.

"Who said you're crazy, Dad? And why are you afraid?" she asked patiently, as if she were addressing a confused, befuddled octogenarian.

"Austin said I was crazy the night I killed him."

"Zachary Benedict killed Tony Austin," she said firmly. "Everyone thinks so."

His eyes turned wild with fear and he tossed down the rest of his drink. "Everyone doesn't think so!" he cried, slamming his glass on the desk. "Men—private investigators—have come to talk to me twice since that night. They want me to account for where I was when it happened. They're working for somebody, they have to be, but they won't tell me who it is. Someone suspects me, honey, don't you see? They've figured out Austin was blackmailing me, and pretty soon they'll figure out why he was, and then they'll know I killed Rachel and Austin."

Trying to sound skeptical when every fiber of her body was vibrating with wild alarm, Emily said, "Why would you kill Rachel?"

He raked his hands through his hair. "Don't be dense—I meant to kill Austin!

I wanted to kill him. I wanted him to die, but that stupid Benedict changed his mind about who should fire the first shot—Austin or Rachel."

Emily dragged air through her constricted lungs. "Why did you want to kill Tony?"

"You know why!" he said, collapsing in his chair with tears beginning to drip from his eyes. "He gave my baby girl drugs and he got her pregnant. You thought I didn't know, but I did," he grated, closing his eyes. "You'd been getting sick in the mornings, and I called that doctor's office in Dallas to find out what was wrong, and the nurse told me. She thought I was your husband when she heard my name." Rubbing his hand over his eyes, he said on a sob, "You were only sixteen years old, and he got you pregnant and let you go all by yourself to have an abortion. And all the while, he was carrying on with that slut—Rachel—and they were laughing behind your back. Ever since you got married, Austin's been threatening to tell your husband that he got you pregnant . . . and about what you did."

Emily lifted her hands from the arms of her chair and her damp palms left twin imprints on the leather. She had to clear her throat twice before she could speak, and the words she said had nothing to do with the raging furor in her mind. "Dick knows what happened to me all those years ago. A few weeks ago, I even told him it was Tony. I kept it a secret from you all those years ago because I didn't want to hurt you or make you ashamed of me."

"Somebody knows what I've done," he said, putting his head in his hands, his shoulders shaking with sobs. "I'll kill him when I find out who it is—" he said, lifting his head, then his eyes riveted on the doorway and his hand slid to his desk drawer.

"Then you'd better start with me," her husband said from the doorway, walking into the room and pulling a quaking Emily out of her chair, "because I know, too."

Instead of reacting with terror, George McDaniels looked at his daughter and said in a conspiratorial whisper, "He's right, Emily. I'm afraid we're going to have to kill your husband." He stood up and Emily saw the lamplight gleaming on the gun in his hand.

"No!" she screamed, trying to shield her husband with her body while he tried to move her aside.

"Move away, honey," her father ordered. "This won't hurt him. He won't feel a thing. He'll be dead before he hits the floor."

"Daddy!" she cried, shoving Dick backward toward the door, her arms outstretched, "you'll have to shoot through me to hit him. You—you don't want to do that, do you?"

Dick's voice was strangely calm, even though his fingers were biting into her arms, forcing her to safety. "Put the gun down, George. If you kill me, you'll have to kill Emily to stop her from telling the police, and I know you could never harm her. You've only been trying to protect her."

The man with the gun faltered, and Dick continued gently. "Put the gun down. We'll help you explain to people that you were only trying to protect her."

"I'm tired of being scared," he whined as Emily slipped out the doorway and raced into his bedroom, grabbing the phone and dialing 911. "I can't sleep."

Walking slowly forward, his hand outstretched, Dick said. "You won't have to be scared any more. Doctors will give you pills to help you sleep."

"You're trying to trick me, you bastard!" McDaniels shouted, and Dick lunged for the gun just as McDaniels leveled it at his chest.

In the bedroom, Emily heard the muted explosion of a gunshot, the heavy thud of something hitting the floor, and she dropped the phone, whirled, and collided with her husband's chest as she ran from the room. "Don't go in there!" he warned, dragging her into his arms and back into the bedroom, reaching for the phone.

"Daddy!" she screamed.

"He'll be all right!" Dick said, trying to control her and order an ambulance at the same time. "He hit his head on the desk when he fell and he's bleeding like a stuck pig!"

66

THREE LAWYERS STOOD UP FROM THE CONFERENCE TABLE. THE one closest to Emily reached out, taking her clammy hand in his own, squeezing it. "I know how hard this has been for you, Miss McDaniels, and I can't tell you how much I appreciate the trouble you went to this morning in order to find out that we're representing Zack Benedict and to come to us without delay.

"It was no trouble," she said, her voice taut with stress and anguish. "I remembered what law firm used to represent him, and when I called them this morning, they referred me to you."

"When Mr. Benedict was charged with murdering Tony Austin, a close friend of Mr. Benedict's decided he would be better represented this time around by us."

Pulling her hand free of his grasp, Emily squeezed her palms together. "Can you get him out of prison today?"

"I'm afraid not. However, if you're willing to accompany me to the police department this morning and give them the same statement you just gave us, that will go a long way toward hastening his release."

Emily nodded, but her tormented mind was on the old films she'd seen of Zack being taken away from his trial in handcuffs and the new one she'd seen repeatedly during the last few weeks of him being beaten in Mexico . . . all for a crime he'd never committed . . . a crime she was indirectly responsible for. "I don't see why they can't let him out of jail today," she said, fighting to keep herself from crying out with guilt and shame. "We'll wait in the reception room."

When she left with her husband, John Seiling looked around at his grinning law partners and reached for the telephone. "Susan," he said to his secretary, "Get Captain Jorgen on the phone, then put a call in to Matthew Farrell in Chicago and tell his secretary it's an emergency. After that, get ahold of William Wesley in the prosecuting attorney's office in Amarillo, Texas. Next, get all three of us reservations on a flight to Amarillo in the morning."

Five minutes later, his secretary buzzed the conference room. "Captain Jorgen is on line 1."

"Thank you," he said, then he pressed the button for line 1. "Captain Jorgen," he said jovially, "how would you like to clinch your chances to become our next police commissioner and at the same time become a hero in the media?" He listened, his smile widening. "All I need is someone there who can take a statement regarding the death of Tony Austin and Rachel Evans and keep their mouth shut about what they hear until I give you the word in a day or two." He listened again and said, "I thought you'd be able to handle that. We'll be there in forty-five minutes."

Two more lights were already lit on the telephone when he hung up, and his secretary's voice came over the intercom. "Mr. Farrell is on line 2, and William Wesley, the prosecutor in Amarillo, is on line 3."

Seiling took the call on line 2, and when he spoke, his voice lost its impersonal note. "Mr. Farrell," he said in a respectful voice, "you asked us to keep you informed of any progress, and I'm calling you to report we've had an unexpected breakthrough in Zack Benedict's case this morning."

In his Chicago office, Matt turned his back on the meeting of Intercorp's executive committee taking place around his desk and said, "What sort of breakthrough?"

"Emily McDaniels. Last night, her father admitted killing Rachel Evans and Tony Austin. He's in a local hospital right now, undergoing a mental evaluation, but he's confessing to everything. Emily herself has given us a statement as well as the murder weapon used on Austin."

"You can give me the details later. How soon can you get Zack released?"

"We'll go to the prosecutor in Texas tomorrow, show him Emily McDaniels's statement, and hand him a writ of habeas corpus, which we will then convince him to take before a trial judge without delay. With luck, the judge will agree to sign it, then it will go to the state capital in Austin to be signed by an Appeals Court judge, and Mr. Benedict should then be released on bail."

"Bail," Matt repeated in a low, scathing voice, "for what?"

Seiling flinched at the tone of voice that had reportedly reduced Farrell's business adversaries to a state of sweating incoherence. "Whether he was innocent or not, when he escaped from prison, he broke Texas escape laws. Technically, he committed an offense against society. Unless we're very lucky and very persuasive, the county prosecutor in Amarillo can, and probably will, want to take some time to decide what to do about that problem. We'll point out that the well-publicized physical beating he took in Mexico City was more than punishment for that. Depending upon the prosecutor's mood, he can either agree and recommend the trial judge forego bail and dismiss the whole thing, or else he can dig in his heels."

"Then put him in a good mood or bring a shovel," Matt warned implacably.

"Right," Seiling said.

"If we don't get instant cooperation from the authorities, I want the media notified of everything. *They'll* get action."

"I agree. My partners and I are leaving for Amarillo tomorrow morning."

"Tonight, not tomorrow," Matt said. "I'll meet you there." He hung up before Seiling could list his objections and pressed the button on his intercom. "Eleanor," he said to his secretary, "cancel all my appointments for tomorrow and the next day."

In Los Angeles, the lawyer dropped the phone in the cradle. Raising his brows, he told the other two men, "If you've ever wondered what Benedict and Farrell have in common, I just found it out—they are two cold customers."

"But they pay big retainers," one of the attorneys joked.

Seiling nodded, turning brisk. "Let's start earning ours, gentlemen," he said and pressed the button for line 3. "Mr. Wesley," he said, modulating his voice so that it was both firm and pleasant. "I realize your predecessor, Alton Peterson, prosecuted the Zachary Benedict case five years ago, and I understand none of this is your fault, however, there seems to have been a vast miscarriage of justice. I need your help to rectify it as quickly as possible. In return, I will be certain the media understands you yourself acted swiftly to right a wrong. Regardless of what you do, Zack Benedict is going to come out of this as a martyr and hero. The media's going to want someone's blood for the injustice done to him, and I'd hate to see it be your blood." He paused, listening. "What the hell am I talking about? Why don't we discuss that over dinner at seven o'clock tonight?"

67

KATHERINE SLAMMED ON HER BRAKES AND BROUGHT HER CAR to a screeching stop in front of Julie's house, cursing when she saw a bicycle in the front yard, which meant Julie was tutoring. Leaving her purse in the car, she ran up the sidewalk, opened the front door without knocking, and walked into the dining room where Julie was seated at the table with three little boys. "Julie, I have to talk to you," she said breathlessly, "in the living room."

Laying her reading primer aside, Julie smiled at her students and said, "Willie, keep reading aloud. I'll be right back." Sensing that something exciting was going on, Willie Jenkins read until she was out of hearing, then he grinned at his two companions. "Something's up," he told them lowering his gravelly voice to a whisper, leaning sideways in his chair for a better view of the living room.

Johnny Everett looked over his shoulder as he turned his wheelchair sideways, peering in the same direction. Tim Wimple, whose right leg had been amputated at the knee, swiveled his own wheelchair into place and nodded. "Somethin' big, I'll bet."

Appointing himself as moderator and spy, Willie tiptoed to the doorway.

"Miss Cahill's turning on the television set . . ." he told them over his shoulder, then he turned back to the living room.

"Katherine?" Julie said shakily, sensing that her friend's tense face and the way she was frantically searching for a particular television channel both had something to do with Zack. "Don't do this to me! Tell me what's happened! It's Zack, isn't it? Is it bad?"

Shaking her head, Katherine stepped back from the set. "It's all over the newscasts. They're interrupting the regular programs to announce it. NBC said they'd have a videotape of it to show at four-thirty." She glanced at her watch. "That's right now."

"What is it!" Julie burst out.

"It's good news," Katherine said with an anguished laugh. "Or it's bad, depending on how you take it. Julie, he's—" She broke off and pointed to the set as the announcer said they were interrupting their regularly scheduled programming for a special news bulletin. Tom Brokaw's face appeared on the screen. "*Good afternoon, ladies and gentlemen,*" he said. "*One hour ago, in Amarillo, Texas, Zachary Benedict was released from Amarillo State Penitentiary, where he was serving a forty-five-year sentence for the murder of his wife, actress Rachel Evans. Benedict's lawyers obtained his release as a result of a formal statement provided by Emily McDaniels, who costarred with Benedict, Evans, and Tony Austin in* Destiny."

Without realizing it, Julie reached for Katherine's hand, squeezing it in a death grip as Brokaw continued, "*NBC has learned that Miss McDaniels's statement apparently contained sworn testimony that two days ago, her father, George McDaniels, confessed to her that he had murdered Rachel Evans and actor Tony Austin, who was found dead in his Los Angeles home last month.*"

A moan of pleasure, of torment, and of crushing guilt, tore from Julie's chest. She grabbed at the back of a chair with both hands to hold her upright as the screen switched to the gates of Amarillo State Penitentiary and she saw Zack walking out, clad in a dark suit and tie, escorted through the rain to a waiting limousine, while Brokaw said, "*Benedict left prison a free man, accompanied by his California attorneys. Waiting for him in the limousine was his long-time friend, industrialist Matthew Farrell, whose unswerving faith in Benedict's innocence has been no secret from the media or the authorities. Also standing on the sidelines was a young woman with a familiar face, though her famous dimples weren't in evidence at this moment. From the looks of this videotape, it's clear that she didn't expect to be seen but had come to assure herself of Benedict's safe release.*" Julie watched as Matt walked swiftly toward the limo then stopped, looking off to his left, where Emily McDaniels was standing beneath an umbrella with her husband, her face a mask of sorrow. For a moment Zack stood there, looking at her, then he slowly walked over to her.

Tears raced down Julie's cheeks as she watched Zack pull Emily McDaniels into his arms. He let her go, handing her over to her husband, then he vanished into the limousine, which sped away while Brokaw added, *"Amarillo reporters who'd discovered Benedict's release raced to Amarillo's airport terminal in hopes of getting a statement. However, he left with Farrell aboard the latter's private jet. NBC has learned that the flight plan filed by Farrell's pilot lists their destination as Los Angeles, where Farrell owns a home, although it is currently leased to movie star Paul Resterman and his wife."*

Choking on her tears, Julie looked at Katherine and said hoarsely, "Matt Farrell never stopped believing in him. At least Zack had *one* loyal friend."

"Don't start torturing yourself," Katherine warned, but her own voice was strained with emotion and Julie wasn't listening anyway. She was staring at the screen and listening as Brokaw said, *"Amarillo Prosecuting Attorney William Wesley is about to make a statement from the courthouse there—"*

The picture switched to the steps of the courthouse, where a dark-haired man in his thirties was walking out the doors and addressing a mob of reporters waving microphones and shouting questions at him. *"Hold your questions,"* he warned them, putting on a pair of glasses, *"until I've made my statement, and then I'll answer what I can."* When the furor died down, he raised the paper he'd been holding in his hand and began to read: *"Yesterday, Zachary Benedict's California attorneys requested a special meeting with my office here in Amarillo. During that meeting we were provided with a sworn statement from Miss Emily McDaniels testifying to the fact that her father, George Anderson McDaniels, had admitted to the murders of Rachel Evans and Anthony Austin. Miss McDaniels, who dictated her statement before Police Captain John Jorgen in Orange County, California, also provided a .45-calibre automatic weapon belonging to her father. Preliminary ballistic tests performed this morning, indicate that the bullets that killed Mr. Austin were fired from that weapon. Immediately following our meeting with Mr. Benedict's attorneys, they filed a writ of habeas corpus here in Amarillo, demanding the release of their client from Amarillo State Prison. The writ was signed, with no objection from my office, by Judge Wolcott and then forwarded to the state capitol in Austin for signature by an Appeals Court judge. That signature was granted this morning, and Zachary Benedict has been duly released. There are still some legal formalities to be dealt with regarding his escape from Amarillo State Penitentiary two months ago, which technically violates Texas law. However, it is the opinion of this office that Mr. Benedict has already paid a high price for his brief illegal freedom at the hands of the Mexican police, as well as five years imprisonment for a crime he appears not to have committed. Any questions?"* he asked, looking up at the reporters. There were dozens of them, but the one that came across the loudest was the one he answered: *"What about Zack Benedict's kidnapping of Julie Mathison? Will he have to stand trial for that?"*

"That will depend upon whether or not Miss Mathison wishes to press charges against him in criminal or civil court. Our office has nothing to do with that, however."

In the doorway, Willie dragged his gaze from his teacher's agonized face and returned to his companions at the dining room table, who hadn't been able to hear or see the television program. "It's that jerk Benedict again," he whispered furiously. "He's out of jail, and she's cryin' over him." Picking up his books, he began shoving them into his gym bag. "We might as well pack up and get out of here. Miss Mathison ain't gonna want us to see her cryin' over him, and from the way she's bawlin', she ain't gonna be able to stop for a long time."

The other boys hastily obeyed their leader's command, but Johnny Everett lifted his worried, freckled face to Willie's. "Why does seein' Benedict on television make her cry, Willie?"

Grabbing his gym bag, Willie automatically gave Tim a hand with his wheelchair. "My mom says he broke her heart, that's why. My mom says the whole town knows it, too."

"He's a jerk," Tim said.

"A *big* jerk," Johnny agreed, backing his wheelchair away from the table and heading it toward the kitchen where a specially constructed ramp led from the back door to the driveway.

On the sidewalk in front of the house, the three boys paused, looking through the open curtains at their teacher, who was blowing her nose while Miss Cahill patted her shoulder. She glanced up and saw them standing there and she smiled reassuringly, waved, and nodded that they were right to leave.

In helpless consternation, they started down the street. "I hate Zachary Benedict," Johnny announced.

"Me, too," Tim said.

"Yeah, me, too," Willie said, pushing his bike. With a combination of protectiveness and practicality, he added, "Johnny, you and me will get to school early in the morning. We'll warn the kids in our class to take it easy on Miss Mathison for a while. No spit balls. No cutting up. No stuff like that. Tim, you don't gotta worry about your class, 'cause Miss Mathison doesn't teach it. Your job is to spread the word to the kids on the teams she coaches. Tell everybody to go real easy on her."

"They're gonna ask me why," Tim said, expertly maneuvering his chair around a dead branch lying partially across the sidewalk.

"Tell 'em Benedict broke her heart again and made her cry. It ain't no secret if all the grown-ups in town already know it."

68

"WELCOME BACK, MR. BENEDICT!" THE MANAGER OF THE Beverly Hills Hotel rushed forward when he saw Zack registering at the lobby desk the afternoon of his release from prison. "I've put you in our best cottage, and the entire staff is at your disposal. Mr. Farrell," he said politely as Matt signed in at the desk beside Zack, "your secretary told me you'll only be with us for tonight. Please let me know if I or my staff may be of service to you."

Behind them, a lobby full of people were turning to stare, and Zack heard his name being whispered like wind rustling through the trees. "Send a magnum of champagne to my cottage," he instructed the obsequious desk clerk, shoving the registration form forward. "Then send dinner for two at eight o'clock. If any calls come in through the switchboard for me, tell the callers I'm not registered here."

"Yes, Mr. Benedict."

With a curt nod, Zack turned around and almost collided with a beautiful blonde and a stunning brunette who were holding out cocktail napkins and pens to him. "Mr. Benedict," the blonde said with a dazzling smile, "may we have your autograph?"

With a brief smile that didn't reach his eyes, Zack obliged, but when the brunette handed him her napkin to sign, he saw a room number written on the corner of it, and he felt the unmistakable impression of a key being pressed into his palm beneath it. He scribbled his name on the napkin and handed it back to her.

From the corner of his eyes, Matt watched the familiar tableau occur just as it had hundreds of times in their past. "I take it," he said dryly as they followed the manager out of the lobby toward the cottages that surrounded the hotel, "that I'm on my own for dinner tonight?"

In answer, Zack glanced at the key in his palm, flipped it into the shrubbery, and looked at his watch. "It's four o'clock. Give me two hours to make some phone calls, then we'll continue celebrating my release."

Two hours later when Matt walked into Zack's cottage, Zack was changing into a new shirt and pair of slacks that his old tailor had hastily delivered to him only moments before. The tailor had departed with tears in his faded eyes and Zack's order in his pocket for two dozen new suits, shirts, slacks, and sport coats. The local Rolls Royce dealer had been similarly overjoyed at Zack's return and had promised to deliver three automobiles for his inspection to the hotel in the morning. "I don't suppose," Matt said at seven o'clock, when Zack finally hung up from a long phone call during which he convinced his tenants to accept a large payment in return for vacating his Pacific Palisades home, "I have a prayer in hell of convincing you to check into a hospital for a few days for a complete physical? My wife is adamant that you should do that."

"You're right," Zack said drily as he headed over to the bar to fix them both a drink, "you don't have a prayer of convincing me to do that." Glancing toward the array of bottles on the bar, he grinned and added, "Champagne or something stronger?"

"Something stronger."

Nodding agreement, Zack dropped ice into two crystal glasses and added Scotch with a splash of water, then he handed one of the glasses to Matt. For the first time since he'd been released from prison, Zack let himself begin to relax. He studied his friend in silence, luxuriating in the reality of his freedom and the inexpressible gratitude he felt toward Matt. "Tell me something," he said solemnly.

"What do you want to know?"

Hiding his poignant sentimentality behind a joke, Zack said, "Since there's no way I can possibly repay you for your loyalty and friendship, what can I give you for a belated wedding present?"

The two men looked at each other, both of them aware of how profoundly meaningful the moment was, but they were men and too much sentimentality was unthinkable. Matt took a swallow of his drink and quirked a thoughtful brow, as if giving the matter his full attention. "Considering the extent of the trouble you put me through, I think a nice island in the Aegean would be a suitable token of your gratitude."

"You already own an island in the Aegean," Zack reminded him.

"You're right. In that case, let me talk it over with Meredith when I get back home."

Zack watched his eyes soften when he mentioned his wife's name and the subtle trace of pleasure that threaded his voice when he said *home*. As if Matt knew what he was thinking, he looked into his glass and took another swallow of his drink. "She's anxious to meet you."

"I'm anxious as hell to meet her, too." Humor threaded his voice as he continued, "When I was in prison I kept up with all the . . . er . . . dramatic publicity surrounding your renewed courtship of your own wife." Sobering a little, Zack added, "I was surprised that you'd never even told me that you'd been married to her fifteen years ago."

"I'll tell you the real story behind that—the part the newspapers weren't able to dredge up—some other time. When you're settled in, I'll bring Meredith and Marissa out here, and we'll spend some time together."

"How about in six weeks? That will give me plenty of time to get everything rolling and back to normal. I'll give a party, in fact." He thought for a minute. "On May twenty-second, if that works with your schedule."

"Six weeks? What can you possibly accomplish in six short weeks?"

Zack tipped his head toward the table beside the telephone and said dryly, "Those are all 'urgent' messages that the switchboard operators felt I should know about even though they told the callers I wasn't registered here. Take a look at them."

Picking up the messages, Matt leafed through them. Among the messages in the stack were ones from the heads of the four major studios, several independent producers, and two from Zack's former agent. Tossing them aside, Matt said with an amused grin, "They all say the same thing—'Welcome home, we knew you were innocent, and now we have an offer you won't be able to resist.' "

"Fickle bastards, aren't they?" Zack said, his voice devoid of rancor. "Funny, they never sent me love notes like that in prison. Now they're calling every hotel in town where they think I might be staying, leaving messages."

Matt chuckled, then he sobered, bringing up a worry that had been plaguing him since Zack's release. "What do you intend to do about Julie Mathison? If she charges you with—"

Zack's smile vanished, his eyes turning into shards of ice. "Don't ever mention her name to me again," he bit out. "Ever."

Matt's brows pulled together at his tone, but he let it pass. Later that night, in his own cottage, he called Meredith to tell her he was flying home in the morning and to bring her up to date on Zack's activities. "He's got blanket film offers coming in by telephone from every studio in Hollywood already. And he wants to give a party in six weeks, on the twenty-second, if we can be there."

In Chicago, Meredith twisted the phone cord around her finger and cautiously brought up the name of someone who Matt completely despised. "What about Julie Mathison?"

"She's not invited," Matt said sarcastically. Softening his voice, he said, "If you think I'm irrational about her, you can't believe Zack's reaction to the mere mention of her name."

Stubbornly, Meredith said, "Has anybody stopped to consider how she must be feeling right now, knowing that he's innocent of those murders?"

"She undoubtedly feels disappointed that her public image as a heroine just went to hell."

"Matt, despite what you think, she loved him! I know she did. I could tell."

"We've had this debate already, darling, and it's a moot subject in any case. Zack hates her, and it's not a temporary state of affairs. I'll be home in the morning. How's Marissa?"

"She misses you."

His voice deepened with tenderness. "How's Marissa's mommy?"

Meredith smiled. "She misses you even more."

69

"MR. BENEDICT, COULD WE HAVE A PICTURE WITH YOU AND Miss Copeland?" The *Los Angeles Daily News* reporter shouted, raising her voice to be heard above the music and raucous clamor of the five hundred guests attending a lavish weekend party at Zack's home. When he didn't hear her, she turned to the other reporters with a laughing shrug. "What a bash!" she said, motioning to one of the fifty tuxedo-clad waiters moving around the crowd offering trays of hors d'oeuvres and drinks to those guests who didn't want to bother wandering over to the huge white canopy where the caterers were providing lobster, caviar, and a host of delectable food. Behind them, the enormous swimming pool with its Roman columns was filled with more guests, some of them fully dressed, drinking and shouting. "He's only been out for six weeks and look at this!" she continued happily, helping herself to a glass of Dom Perignon champagne from the waiter's tray. "He's back on top of the world, hotter than ever. The kingpins of the industry are all here at his beck and call, overjoyed with the honor to be included in his 'homecoming party.'" She took a sip of champagne and, for the sake of conversation, confided something most of them already knew. "His agent said that Paramount, Universal, and Fox have all offered him any script he wants, and the bidding for his next film is up to $20 million. He's holding out for twenty-five and a bigger piece of the gross."

"Not bad for a guy who's been away from the business for five years," the CBS reporter said with a chuckle, and like the *Daily News* reporter, he scrupulously avoided the use of the word *prison,* not because he was particularly tactful, but for a more practical reason: Zack's publicist had made it clear to all the reporters who were lucky enough to be admitted to this party that there were three subjects that, if brought up, would get them ejected and also permanently eliminate their chances for any future interviews with him. Those permanently banned subjects were his imprisonment, his dead wife, and Julie Mathison.

The NBC reporter looked at his watch, then he looked around for his cameraman and saw him standing by the swimming pool, trying to flirt with a starlet clad in a micromini spandex dress with a plunging neckline. "His publicist said he'd give us all a two-minute interview and pose for some pictures if we stayed out of his hair during the party. If he doesn't do it soon, I'm not going to be able to get this tape on the ten o'clock news."

As if finally realizing their dilemma, Sally Morrison, who'd handled all of Zack's dealings with the media for years, motioned to them to gather into a group, then she wended her way through the crowd to where Zack was listening to three producers who were vying for his attention while Diana Copeland kept her hand through his right arm. As they watched, Sally spoke to him, he nodded, looked over at the reporters, and excused himself from the group surrounding him, walking toward them with Diana at his side.

70

"WHAT A FUN EVENING THIS HAS BEEN," KATHERINE SAID enthusiastically as she slid into the restaurant booth occupied by her husband, Julie, and Paul Richardson. Going to the movies on Saturday night, then stopping at Mandillos afterward for dinner had become a ritual during the six weeks since Julie had decided to throw herself into life with a vengeance that had them all more alarmed than reassured. "Isn't this fun?" she said, looking around at their bright, smiling faces.

"Terrific," Ted said.

"Great," Paul averred.

He put his arm around Julie's shoulders. "What do you think?" he teased. "Would you say the four of us getting together every weekend is fun, terrific, or great?"

"It's wonderful," Julie decreed instantly. "And did you notice how balmy it is tonight? May has always been my favorite month." In the six weeks since Zack had been released from prison, more than just the weather had changed. Last month, Ted and Katherine had quietly remarried in the living room of the Cahills' home with Reverend Mathison officiating.

Paul Richardson had come to Keaton from Dallas for the wedding, and their weekends had become a ritual. Julie's father, however, was now hinting that he'd be pleased to perform another wedding whenever Paul and she were ready. Paul was ready. Julie was not. Despite her outward gaiety and animation, she had achieved a state of blissful emotional anesthesia toward any sort of deep feeling, and it was a state of being that she enjoyed. She clung to it and nurtured it with fastidious care. She could laugh and smile and work and play and feel . . . very nice. No better than that. And definitely no worse. So strong was her carefully acquired emotional balance, that she had not shed a single sentimental tear during Ted and Katherine's wedding, although she had been very,

very happy. She had cried all of her tears over Zack, and now she had found a peaceful insulation that could not be broken or pierced by anyone or anything.

The waitress wended her way through the tables filled with Keaton residents and pulled out her pad. "The usual, you guys?" she asked. "Four New York strip steaks, medium rare, and baked potatoes?"

"Sounds great, Millie," Ted said.

Julie added a question about her husband. "How's Phil doing with his new job at Oakdale's Garage?"

"Great, Julie. Thanks for putting in a good word for him there. Phil says you practically cinched the job for him."

"He's a terrific mechanic," Julie replied. "He's kept my car running all these years. I did Oakdale's the favor, not Phil."

Mandillos had a juke box with a small dance floor in one corner, tables for diners across the center of the room, and, at the opposite end, a lounge with a bar and big-screen television set, which was especially popular during the football season. "I have some quarters," Paul said, digging into his pocket. "How about helping me pick out songs on the juke box?"

Julie nodded and smiled, sliding out of the booth beside him. In a restaurant filled with people she knew, it took ten minutes to get past the tables, where she stopped repeatedly to talk to friends, and only two minutes to pick out the songs.

"The juke box is turned off because the television set is on," Paul said, as they slid back into their U-shaped booth. "I'll ask Millie to turn the television off," he said, looking around for their waitress.

"Wait about two minutes," Ted said. "The news is on and I'd like to know how the game ended."

As he spoke, all four people glanced up at the television set, idly watching the news.

"*Before we switch to sports,*" the announcer said, "*we have a special report from Amanda Blakesly, who's attending a fabulous weekend shindig in Pacific Palisades at the palatial estate of Zachary Benedict . . .*"

The mention of Zack's name shut down conversations all over the restaurant as people glanced with nervous sympathy at Julie's booth, then began talking with renewed force in a futile effort to block out the volume of the set. When Ted, Katherine, and Paul also launched into a diversionary babble of conversation, Julie dismissed their efforts with a wave of her long fingers. "It doesn't bother me in the least," she told them, and to prove it, she perched her chin on her hand and sat there watching and listening, a faint, interested smile fixed on her lips. Her eyes wide and unblinking, she watched Zack talking affably to a throng of reporters while camera flashes exploded and Diana Copeland beamed at him, looking incredibly gorgeous. He was holding a glass of champagne in his hand . . . the same hand that had once caressed and intimately explored every inch of her body, and his lazy white smile was as devastatingly attractive as it had been in Colorado—more so because he was tanned now. "He certainly looks nice in a tuxedo," Julie remarked in an impartial voice to her uneasy group. "Don't you think so?"

"Not particularly," Paul said, watching her face lose what little color it had.

"Every man looks nice in a tuxedo," Katherine quickly pointed out. "Just look at the other men at the party. They all look nice. Even Jack Nicholson looks great in a tuxedo."

Julie muffled a laugh at Katherine's needless attempt to disparage Zack, but she didn't stop watching as the camera slowly panned the crowds of dancing, laughing, talking people, many of them with famous faces. She watched and she felt nothing, not even when someone called out to Diana, "*How about a welcome home kiss for him, Diana?*"

Unflinching, she watched Zack grin and oblige, sliding his arm around Diana's waist as she gave him a long, hot kiss that made the guests start to laugh and clap. Julie endured that without reaction, but when he bent his head and whispered something to Diana . . . or nipped her ear . . . the teasing, affectionate gesture gouged a hole in Julie's emotional barricade. *Bastard,* she thought with a flash of unjust angry pain that she squelched instantly. Firmly, she reminded herself that she had no reason to be angry with him just because he was happy and she was . . . dead inside. She liked not feeling anything, it was her choice, after all, and a very comforting choice.

Zack left with Diana, ending the brief interview, but the reporter wasn't finished. As the camera came in for a close-up, she told the audience with a conspiratorial smile, "*There are rumors circulating around here tonight that a marriage between Zachary Benedict and long-time friend Diana Copeland might be imminent.*"

"How nice for him," Julie said brightly, looking around at everyone. "Oh, here's our dinner."

A half hour later, Paul watched Julie and Katherine heading to the ladies room, Julie's smile bright again, her conversation animated as they wended their way past the tables, pausing to talk to friends. Pulling his worried gaze from her back, he looked at Ted. "How much weight would you guess she's lost?"

"Too much. She laughs a lot, though," he added with pointed irony.

"She's got a strong will."

"Yep. She's working and playing with a vengeance."

"That's a good sign, isn't it?"

Ted sighed angrily. "It doesn't mean a damn thing, except she's trying to hide from her memories."

"What makes you so sure."

"Among other obvious signs, when Julie is under stress, she organizes and tidies things up. In the last six weeks, in addition to teaching her classes, coaching her handicapped kids, giving private tutoring lessons, working on every civic and church committee in town, and taking charge of the Bicentennial Celebration, she has also wallpapered every room in her house; rearranged every closet, drawer, and cabinet she has; and repainted her garage. Twice. She has now descended to filing her groceries in alphabetical order in the kitchen cabinets."

Paul choked on a laugh. "She's what?"

"You heard me," Ted said, but he wasn't smiling. "And it's not funny. She's stressed to the max, and she's ready to break. Now I have a question for you," he added, leaning forward. "You got her into this nightmare and so did I. We worked on her, convincing her Benedict was guilty until she believed it. You made her go to Mexico City, like a lamb to the slaughter, and I went along with it. I accept my share of the blame. Do you dispute yours?"

Paul shoved his dessert plate aside and shook his head. "No."

Leaning forward, Ted said tersely, "Then suppose you and I come up with something to get her out of this mess!"

Paul nodded. "Let's talk about this tonight, after I take Julie home."

71

SINCE PAUL COULDN'T SPEND THE NIGHT AT JULIE'S HOUSE, even platonically, without causing a storm of local gossip on top of the gossip about her aborted relationship with Benedict, he'd started staying at Ted and Katherine's new apartment at their insistence when he came to Keaton.

The front door was unlocked when he got there after taking Julie home, and Ted was sitting in the living room, obviously waiting to talk to him. "This thing between Julie and Benedict has to be brought to a head," Ted said as soon as Paul sat down across from him. "Personally, I wish he'd drop off the face of the earth, but Katherine thinks that until Julie makes some sort of peace with him, she's not ever going to find peace with herself. Or with you, if that's what you're hoping for. Is it?"

Surprised and momentarily irritated by Ted's prying, Paul hesitated, then nodded curtly. "I'm in love with her."

"Katherine said as much. She also said that Julie's conscience is tearing her to pieces, though if anyone deserves to feel guilty it's that bastard, Benedict. All Julie did was offer him a ride because she thought he'd fixed her tire. As a result, there are 200 million people in this country who've seen that film of him being beaten in Mexico City, and now they blame her for it. The same people who applauded her courage for turning him in now think of her as some sort of scheming witch who brought an innocent man down on his knees. At least the people around here don't feel that way, and that's something. Not much, but something. The press still hounds her, trying to get her to talk, and their questions are vicious."

Katherine walked out of the bedroom in a robe and slippers, obviously determined to join the discussion, and sat on the arm of Ted's chair. Disregarding the subject of public opinion, which she felt was a trivial problem, she brought up the main issue. "Julie wrote letters to him when he was in prison, and he returned them unopened. Since he got out, she's written to him in care of his attorneys—simple, polite letters, this time asking him how to return the car he gave her. He won't answer those either. Until he does—until she or someone else can make him understand that Julie did not lie about wanting to join him in Mexico so that she could spring your trap, she's not going to let herself care for you or anyone else. Nor will she let any man care for her. Among other things, she's punishing herself."

Paul stared at her in frowning surprise. "That's all that's stopping her from going on with me . . . with her life? She needs absolution from Benedict?"

"As far as I know for certain," Katherine hedged.

"Fine," he said curtly after a moment. "If that's what it takes, I can get it for her, and she won't have to wait another six weeks or even six days." He stood up looking like a man with a mission. "I'll get it for her within forty-eight hours. Tell Julie something came up and I had to cut our weekend short."

Twisting around, Katherine watched him walk toward the guest bedroom. "But, he won't even talk to her, Paul."

"He'll talk to me!" Paul said over his shoulder.

"What makes you think he'll talk to you?" Ted said when Paul emerged from the guest bedroom a few minutes later carrying his overnight bag.

"This," Paul said, flipping his identification badge into Ted's lap and getting his suit coat from the closet.

"That may get you into his house, but it's not going to make him believe you."

"The son of a bitch doesn't have to believe me. Who has the letter that Julie was going to leave for you when she ran away with him?"

"I do," Katherine said getting up to look for it, "but that's not going to convince him either. You can't prove to him she didn't write this yesterday," she added when she returned from the bedroom with the letter and gave it to him. "Remember, he's rich and famous now; he'll be doubly suspicious of anything that looks like an attempted reconciliation on Julie's part."

"Maybe so. But I have something in my office in Dallas that he'll *have* to believe!"

"What?"

"Videotapes," he said shortly, holding out his hand to Ted for his ID badge. "A videotape of that press conference she gave when she was trying to sway the world to his side."

"That won't do it either. He'll presume it was all part of her grand scheme to trap him for you."

"And," Paul added, shoving his tie into his coat pocket and picking up his overnight bag, "a confiscated videotape of what really took place in Mexico City—the part showing Julie's reactions when Benedict was being taken into custody. Any man who can watch her in that film without feeling torn up has a stronger stomach than I do. In case you haven't already figured it out," he added wryly, reaching for the door, "I'm driving to Dallas to pick up what I need, then I'll fly to L.A. in the morning. We'll have his California address somewhere in our files."

Ted grinned sardonically. "Surely you aren't going to crash his party?"

"Screw his party. He's fouled up my life and Julie's for months, and I'm fed up with it. And if this fails," he added to Ted, "if he still won't listen to me or look at the evidence I give him, then I suggest you file a civil suit against him for kidnapping Julie and for the mental torment she's been under as a result of that. If Benedict won't listen to me, he can listen to you in court and pay up with a nice, fat check!"

"Thank you, Paul," Katherine said, kissing him after he shook hands with Ted. "Good-bye," she added with a catch in her voice, "Call us after you've seen him." She watched him walk down the sidewalk for a moment, then she closed the door and found Ted watching her with an odd, speculative look. "You sounded very sad when you said good-bye—like you were telling him good-bye forever. Why?"

"Because," she said with a guilty look, "I am a truly terrible person who does not deserve to be loved by a man as wonderful as you."

"Translation?" he asked with a wary smile.

"There's something I didn't mention to you or Paul," she admitted. "You see, Julie may think all she wants is Zack's forgiveness, but what she really wants is the man. She always did. Even when he was a hunted fugitive. If Paul accomplishes his goal, Julie will get more than peace. She'll get Zack Benedict."

"The guy's a hotshot movie star again. You saw him on television tonight with women hanging all over him. You saw the mansion he lives in. He doesn't have to settle for little Julie Mathison."

"I read the letter he wrote her," Katherine said with absolute conviction as she blandly studied her manicure. "That was love, the real thing. At least I think it was." Looking up, she added with a smile, "And if he did love her, then he'd better hope 'little Julie Mathison' is still willing to settle for *him* after what he's put her through. She's angry, Ted. Deep down inside, she is furious, really *furious* at the injustice done her. She blames herself for losing faith in Zack, but she blames him for everything he's deliberately put her through, starting with taking her captive and lying to her about how his brother died and refusing to read her letters or see her when she went to talk to him in prison."

"She laughs all the time and most of it's real," Ted argued, because it worried him to think otherwise. "She had us in stitches tonight, telling us that story about accidently dumping glue down the principal's suit."

"She's angry," Katherine insisted, "and she has every right to be. In fact, I rather hope I'm around when she gives him what he deserves. It'll be a test of his merit if he can take it and overcome it."

"And if he can't or doesn't want to bother?"

"Then she'll have gotten it out of her system, made her peace with him, and she can still have Paul."

Standing up and turning out the lamp, he asked, "Who are you rooting for, Richardson or Benedict?"

"Julie."

72

SEATED IN THE SUNNY SOLARIUM, ZACK WORKED HIS WAY carefully through the sheafs of data that Matt had provided to bring him up to date on his financial holdings. Outside, beyond the glass walls that were tinted to prevent anyone from being able to see into the solarium, someone called his name, and he looked up, not to answer, but simply to luxuriate in being home again and to pleasure himself with the familiar view. On the other side of the glass, a lush expanse of green lawn sloped down to an enormous curving swimming pool with graceful Roman columns and marble statues. At the edge of the yard were guest pavilions in the same Roman architecture as the main house—all of them filled with people now. Zack's tenants had kept his gardener on during his absence, and the results of the aging man's painstaking care were evident in the colorful flowers that bloomed ecstatically beneath carefully pruned shrubbery and shade trees.

The thick glass surrounding the solarium muffled the sounds of the party in full swing a few feet beyond, where a hundred people were cavorting in his pool, using his tennis courts, or sunbathing. The remaining three hundred guests would return tonight for the second night of festivities, and the caterers were already setting up beneath a white tent on the east edge of the lawn.

"Where is Zack Benedict?" a woman in a green string bikini called to her friends, without realizing Zack could see and hear her. "I've been here all day and I still haven't laid eyes on him. I'm starting to think he's a legend who doesn't exist." It wasn't surprising she hadn't seen him, since this wing of the house was off limits to all but Matt and Meredith Farrell. They were Zack's only actual houseguests, the only people he permitted into his inner sanctum. For that reason, he scowled when he heard another woman's voice calling from the hallway just beyond the solarium, "Hey, has anyone in here seen Zack?" He was going to have to put in an appearance out there, he realized, or that chant, which had been escalating for the last hour, would continue unabated until someone came to find him.

Behind him, Meredith Farrell's soft, cultured voice laughingly said, "Have you seen Zack Benedict?"

"No, I'm afraid not," Zack joked, politely coming to his feet.

"Everyone seems to be looking for him," she teased, putting her hand in his outstretched palm.

Zack leaned down and kissed her cheek, slightly startled by the instantaneous affection he'd felt for Matt's wife. Until he actually met her two days ago, Zack had been inclined to dismiss most of Matt's praise of his wife as uncharacteristic infatuation, but having met her, he was completely impressed. Meredith Bancroft Farrell had the poise and beauty that the society columns always credited her with, but none of the cool hauteur Zack had expected. Instead, she had a gentleness, a gentility, and an unaffected warmth that both disarmed and touched him. "I hear," he confided, "that Benedict is an antisocial sort who doesn't particularly like big, sprawling parties very much, at least not this one."

She sobered, her eyes searching his. "Really? Why do you suppose that is?"

He smiled and shrugged. "I guess I'm not in the mood right now."

Meredith considered bringing up Julie Mathison, as she'd considered often during the last two days, but Matt had not only asked, he had instructed her not to mention Julie's name. "Am I interrupting your work?" she said instead, glancing at the thick folders on the table beside his chair.

"Not at all, I'd enjoy the company." Zack looked around her for the Farrell's enchanting two-year-old daughter, who he rather hoped would come flying into the room with her usual demand for a hug from him. "Where's Marissa?"

"She's having a tea party with Joe before her nap."

"The little flirt," he said, glancing toward the antique Sevres china tea set he'd had his housekeeper put on the coffee table a while ago, "she promised to have a tea party with me!"

"Do not even consider," Meredith warned, "letting Marissa touch those exquisite cups. Lately she seems to think you drop teacups on the floor when you're finished."

Matt strolled in on the end of that conversation looking rested, relaxed, and amused. "She obviously does that because I told her she's a princess. Which she is. Where's Joe?" he added. "I need to send him—"

As if the mention of the good-natured chauffeur's name had conjured up the man, Joe O'Hara strode purposefully into the solarium, but he wasn't smiling. "Zack," he said, "your housekeeper just stopped me in the hall. It seems you've got yourself a visitor who flashed his badge at her and put her in a tizzy. He's FBI. Name's Paul Richardson. She put him in the library."

Swearing under his breath at the thought of having to talk to an FBI agent, Zack started out of the room.

"Zack?" Matt called behind him. When he turned, Matt asked, "Alone? Or with witnesses?"

Zack hesitated. "Witnesses, if you don't mind."

"Are you up to this, whatever 'this' is?" Matt asked Meredith.

She nodded and they both caught up with Zack, walking alongside him down the long hall and into the mahogany-paneled library.

Rudely ignoring the tall, dark man who'd been looking at the books on the shelves, Zack waited until Matt and Meredith were seated, then he sat down behind his desk and snapped, "Let's see your identification." The FBI agent, who Zack had already recognized from Mexico City, removed a leather case from his inside jacket pocket and held it out. Zack glanced at it and then at him. "It's a lousy picture, but it looks like you."

"Let's skip the games," Paul countered with equal discourtesy, testing for the best way to deal with his adversary. "You knew damned well who I was the minute you saw me just now. You recognized me from Mexico City."

Benedict dismissed that with a shrug. "Either way, I have no intention of speaking to you or anyone else from the FBI without the presence of my attorneys."

"This isn't an official visit, it's a personal one. Furthermore, you don't have to say a word. I'll do all the talking."

Instead of inviting him to sit down, Benedict inclined his head slightly toward a chair in front of his desk. Squelching his annoyance at the tone the meeting had already taken, Paul sat down, put his briefcase on the floor beside him, and opened the locks. "Actually, I'd prefer to discuss this in private . . ." he said, glancing over his shoulder at the man and woman watching him from the sofa, identifying them at a glance, ". . . without Mr. and Mrs. Farrell present."

"What you would 'prefer' is of absolutely no interest to me," Benedict said. Leaning back in his leather chair, he picked up the gold pen lying beside a tablet on his desk, rolling it between his fingers. "Let's hear what you have to say."

Hiding his mounting temper behind a coolly polite facade, Paul said, "I will begin by reminding you that you are in an extremely vulnerable position regarding the kidnapping of Julie Mathison. Should she decide to press charges against you, there's an excellent chance she could put you behind bars for what you did to her. For purely personal reasons," he added pleasantly, "I would thoroughly enjoy prosecuting that case."

He watched Benedict's expressionless face, and when he saw no reaction at all to his jibe, Paul tested out a tone of genuine courtesy. "Look, in return for my personal guarantee that she will not press charges against you, all I ask is that you give me five minutes and agree to listen to what I have to say ."

"Was that actually a polite request I just heard from you?"

Paul squelched the urge to smash his face. "Yes."

Benedict glanced at his watch. "In that case, you have four minutes and fifty seconds left."

"I have your word to let me finish?"

"So long as you can do it in four minutes and forty seconds." The gold pen began to tap on the pad in a clear indication of impatience, and Paul said curtly, "So that you don't doubt my credibility or the validity of my information, I want you to understand that I was in charge of your case. I was in Keaton while she was in Colorado with you, I was there when she returned, and I am the one who had her put under constant surveillance when we left Keaton because I had a hunch she would try to get to you or you to her. I am also the one she called on the night before she was to join you in Mexico City. Now," Paul said, his voice gaining emphasis as he came to the point he needed to make, "despite what you think and how the media has made it sound, I also know beyond all doubt that Julie did *not* agree to join you in Mexico so that she could entrap you and hand you over to us. The truth is that my office did not know anything about her plan to join you until the night before she was supposed to do it. She finally panicked and called me for two reasons: Three days before she was to leave, she went to visit your grandmother, Margaret Stanhope, out of some hair-brained notion of healing old family hostilities for your sake. Instead of accomplishing her goal, she was shown proof that you'd confessed to the accidental killing of your brother, and she was further informed by your grandmother that she herself believed you'd deliberately murdered the boy and later your wife."

Paul expected those verbal bombs to get a reaction, but except for a muscle that began to twitch in Benedict's jaw at the mention of his relative, there was none, and he continued doggedly. "Julie returned from Ridgemont, and that night, she learned that the cast and crew of *Destiny* were receiving threatening calls, allegedly from you, and she *still* did not turn you in to us. Not until the night before she was supposed to leave, when Tony Austin wound up dead, did she finally notify us of your intention to meet her in Mexico City." He waited again and when Benedict continued to sit there, staring at him with contempt,

Paul lost his temper. "Did you hear me, damn you? It was not a trap from the beginning! Is that clear to you?"

Benedict's face tightened, but his voice was ominously soft. "Use that tone of voice just one more time, and I will personally throw you out on your ass, regardless of my promise to hear you out." Sarcastically he added, "Is that clear to *you?*"

Forcibly reminding himself of the need to succeed here for Julie's sake, Paul said tersely, "Let's knock off the adolescent sparring. We don't like each other, so let's drop it. The point is, I did not come here to antagonize you, I came here to give you proof that Julie did not originally set a trap for you in Mexico City. The truth is that what she saw happen to you there combined with your refusal to let her explain or answer her letters have hurt her more than you can possibly know or imagine. Her family is worried about her, and so am I."

"You are?" he repeated with insolent amusement. "And why is that, I wonder?"

"Because unlike you, I feel a responsibility for the part I played in Mexico City and the damage it did to her." Reaching into his briefcase, Paul withdrew a large envelope, then he closed his case and stood up. Tossing the envelope distastefully onto his adversary's desk, he said, "And because I'm in love with her."

Benedict didn't reach for it or glance at it. "Now why is it," he mocked, "that announcement doesn't surprise me?"

"Maybe you're clairvoyant," Paul snapped. "Either way, the evidence is in there—two videotapes and a letter. Don't take my word for anything, Benedict, see for yourself. And then if you have even a trace of a decency left, do something to alleviate her suffering."

"How much do you think it will take," he asked with scathing sarcasm, "to 'alleviate her suffering'? One million dollars? Two million? Twice as much, because you plan to share the bounty with her?"

Planting his hands flat on Benedict's desk, Paul leaned forward and said savagely, "I should have let the Federales beat the shit out of you all the way to the Texas border!"

"Really? Why didn't you?"

Straightening, Paul raked him with a scornful look. "Because Julie made me promise before she turned you in that I wouldn't let anyone hurt you. The only thing she lied to you about was being pregnant. She did it so that you'd let her join you. She must have been insane to think she was in love with you, you heartless, arrogant bastard."

At that, Benedict got out of his chair and started around his desk. "Try it,"

Paul invited holding his arms out to his sides. "Please try it, movie star. Just throw the first punch, so I can finish it for you."

"Enough!" Matt Farrell thundered, grabbing Zack's arm. "Richardson, you've had your five minutes. O'Hara!" he shouted. "Show Mr. Richardson to the door."

Joe O'Hara instantly materialized in the room from the doorway where he'd been eavesdropping. "Nuts, it was just starting to get good," he said. Eyeing Paul Richardson with a modicum of respect, he gestured grandly to the door and said, "I've never met a lawman before who wears a suit and is willin' to step out from behind his badge and put up his fists. Allow me to show you to your car."

His humor did nothing to diffuse the tension that stretched taut in the room when he left.

"I think we should go," Matt said.

"And I think," Meredith argued, drawing a startled look from both men, "we should wait while Zack looks at the evidence inside that envelope." She turned to him. "I also think it's time I tell you that I believe beyond all doubt that Julie loved you very much. I also believe that everything Richardson said is true."

"If that's what you think," Zack retorted with biting sarcasm, "then I suggest you take the 'evidence' with you and look at it yourself, Meredith. Then you can burn it."

Matt's face went white with fury, "I'll give you five seconds to apologize to my wife."

"I'll only need two," Zack said curtly, and Meredith smiled before Matt did because she was listening to his words, not his tone. Reaching his hand out for hers, Zack smiled grimly. "I apologize for my tone. I was inexcusably rude."

"Not inexcusably," she said, studying his eyes as if searching for something. "I'll take you up on your offer, though, and take that envelope with me, if you don't mind."

"Since your husband is still debating about whether or not to throw a punch at me, and since I've already earned it," Zack said dryly, "I don't think I ought to press my luck by turning you down now."

"I think that's very wise of you," she said, transferring her laughing gaze to her husband. Picking up the envelope from the desk, she tucked her hand into Matt's arm. "There was a time when the mere mention of my name could drive you to similar fury," she reminded him gently, making a clear effort to diffuse the remaining tension between the two men.

His scowl softened to a reluctant smile. "Was I really as big a jackass as Zack is?"

She laughed. "Now there's a question guaranteed to get *me* into a fight with one of you."

Matt affectionately rumpled her hair and drew her tightly to his side.

"We'll see you at the party after we've changed," she called over her shoulder as they walked out.

"Fine," Zack said, watching them go, marveling at the closeness they shared, at the way it had changed Matt. Once, not long ago, Zack had imagined that Julie and he—Furious that she'd even entered his mind, he walked over to the windows and opened the drapes. He wasn't certain what he despised more— her treachery or his gullibility. At thirty-five she'd reduced him to pouring out his heart in sappy love letters and gazing at her picture for hours, not to mention risking his neck to buy her just the right wedding ring at one of the most exclusive jewelers in South America. The shame and self-disgust he felt about things like that almost outweighed his humiliation at being beaten on his knees in front of half the world. She was responsible for that, too. And everyone with a television set knew it—they knew he'd been so blindly, insanely besotted with a small-town schoolteacher that he'd risked his life to get to her.

Firmly dismissing her from his mind, Zack looked out at the increasing crowd gathering for the afternoon festivities. Glenn Close was talking to Julia Roberts. She looked up, saw him standing at the window, and waved.

Zack lifted his hand to her in a salute. On his lawn, most of them available to him at the crook of a finger, were some of the most beautiful women in the world. Bracing his hand high against the window frame, Zack studied them, searching for one who especially stood out and appealed to him—one with particularly fine eyes, a romantic mouth, and piles of sexy, healthy hair . . . someone with warmth and wit and goals and ideals . . . someone who'd thaw the ice inside of him. He shoved away from the window and headed into the master suite to change clothes. There wasn't a big enough blow torch in the world to thaw him out and make him feel the way he had in Colorado, and even if it were possible, he'd never let it happen to him again. Behaving like a lovestruck ass was *not* his style. He must have been insane in Colorado. No doubt it had been a combination of the time and place. Under normal circumstances, he'd never have felt that way about any woman alive.

He was going to be more attentive to his guests than he'd been so far today, he vowed. He didn't know why, after only six weeks, some of his delight in his renewed career was already beginning to fade. He was exhausted, he decided, unbuttoning his shirt. In six short weeks, in addition to meeting with six producers, five studio heads, and countless other business associates, he'd also read dozens of scripts, managed to bargain the tenants out of both his houses, hire new staffs, rehire part of his old staff, buy two cars, and order a plane. He needed to relax and enjoy the taste of success now that it was his again, he decided, tossing his shirt onto the bed. Behind him the door opened, and he turned, his hands on his belt.

"I've been looking everywhere for you, Zack," the redhead said with an inviting smile as she walked purposefully forward, her breasts swelling invitingly from her halter top, hips swaying in their long silk pants, jewels sparkling on her wrists and fingers. "And I've found you just as you're getting undressed. Isn't that an amazing coincidence."

"Amazing," he lied, trying to remember who the hell she was. "But then that's what bedrooms are for, isn't it?"

"That's not all they're for," she whispered, sliding her hands up his chest.

Gently, he took her hands between his. "Later," he said, turning her around heading her firmly toward the door. "I need a shower, and then I have to get out there and play host."

73

"GREAT PARTY, ZACK," AN UNMISTAKABLE VOICE WHISPERED teasingly in his ear, "but where'd you find so many monkeys willing to wear fancy clothes?" Grinning, Zack turned away from the group talking to him beside the pool and looped his arm around her shoulders, pulling her close to his side. "I was hoping you'd come."

"Why, to relieve your monotony?" she said, surveying the party that was getting into full swing at one o'clock in the afternoon.

When she started to move away, he tightened his grip. "Don't abandon me," he joked. "Irwin Levine is bearing down on us and he's going to pounce on me about a film Empire wants me to do. Stay by my side for the rest of the day."

"Coward, I'll show you how to handle this." Ignoring his warning squeeze, she held out her long fingers with their lacquered nails. "Irwin, darling," she purred, kissing his cheek, "Zack wants you to go away and let him enjoy his party in peace."

"Bitchy as always, aren't you, Barbra," he snapped.

"Nice work," Zack said dryly, watching the other man stamp away in affront after a minute. "My agent has that same effect on a lot of people these days when he starts talking about money."

"Never mind your agent. Why didn't you answer my letters, you jerk? I don't send care packages to prisons for just anyone, you know."

"Because I was ashamed and I didn't want charity. Now shut up and hum something pretty to me while we circulate."

Laughing, she looped her arm around his waist and began softly singing, "'People—people who need people are the luckiest people' . . ."

74

"THAT DOES IT!" MEREDITH JUMPED UP FROM THE SOFA IN THE living room where she and Matt and Joe O'Hara had watched the videotapes that the FBI agent had handed over. Brushing the tears from the corners of her eyes, she shoved all the 'evidence' into its envelope. "I'll make Zachary Benedict look at these if I have to tie him up first!"

"Meredith," Matt said gently, grabbing her wrist. "You were right about Julie, I can see that, but I know Zack. You can't make him watch those until and unless he's ready to do it."

She hesitated, thinking, then a resolute smile dawned across her face. "Yes I can—and I know how!"

He stood up. "If you're determined to try, I'll go with you and hold him down while you tie him up."

"That won't work," she said. "You'll lose your temper, but if you aren't there, I can use you very effectively to shame him into doing it."

"I doubt it."

"Let me try," she said, leaning over and kissing his forehead. "If I need your help, I'll come and get you."

Before he could object, which he looked to be on the verge of doing, Meredith slid open the patio doors and headed across the back lawn. Spotting Zack standing by the pool surrounded by a group of movie stars and studio heads, she lifted her chin and struck off in that direction, her Italian sandals slapping softly against her bare heels as she wended her way purposefully around white-coated waiters passing trays and throngs of guests gossiping about each other.

Zack was laughing at a joke when he caught sight of Meredith walking across the yard with a large brown envelope in her hand and his smile abruptly faded. "Excuse me a minute," he said to Barbra, his eyes narrowing on that envelope.

"I wondered where you and Matt were," he said with his most deliberately disarming smile as he carefully avoided the sight of the envelope in her hand. "You haven't changed clothes yet."

"We were in the living room, watching something on the television set," she said, and Zack realized her eyes looked as if she'd been crying. "May I speak to you alone?"

"There's a party going on," he pointed out evasively. "Come with me and I'll introduce you to Kevin Costner. He asked to meet you last night."

"Later," she persisted stubbornly. "This really can't wait."

With no choice left, Zack nodded and followed her into the house and down the hall to the library. "What's on your mind?" he said curtly, perching on the edge of his desk and turning on a lamp as she drew the curtains over the windows, throwing the room into almost total darkness.

Turning from the windows, she walked over and stood in front of him. "The contents of that envelope are on my mind."

"I asked you to destroy what was in it."

"Yes, you did," she retorted, facing him like a cool blond spitfire. "And now I have something to ask *you*."

"What is it?"

"Do you feel any obligation to my husband for the things he did for you while you were in prison?"

Zack nodded warily.

"Good. Matt will not impose on your friendship to ask a favor of you in return."

"But you will," he concluded shortly.

"You're right. In return for his years of loyalty and assistance, I am asking a favor in his behalf. We want you to sit in here and watch those videotapes and read the letter that's in the envelope."

Zack's jaw tightened, but he nodded and started to stand. "I'll do it later."

"No, now."

He glared down at her from his vastly superior height, but without any success. "It's little enough to ask of you," she pointed out irrefutably. "A half hour of your time."

"Fine," he snapped. "Will you allow me to do it alone, or do you want to watch me to make sure I keep my word?"

Having won, she conceded with disarming sweetness, "I'll accept your word. Thank you." She walked over, slid the first videotape into the player, turned on the set, and handed him the remote controller. "The first tape is of a news conference that Julie gave a day or two after she left you in Colorado. Have you seen it already?"

"No," he clipped.

"Good, then you're in for a triple shock. The second tape was filmed by an obvious amateur while you were being taken into custody in Mexico City. Keep your eyes on Julie when you're watching that."

When she left, Zack punched the start button on the remote controller, but he got up and walked over to the bar. The mere mention of Julie Mathison, the reminder of his stupid gullibility, made him want to drown himself in liquor. The realization that he was going to have to watch her in this room, in his house, made him swear long and eloquently as he threw ice cubes into a glass and filled it with whatever liquor was in the nearest decanter. Behind his back on the television, the mayor of the jerkwater town she lived in was announcing that she was going to give a press conference and everyone should treat her with respect.

With a contemptuous smirk, Zack walked back to his desk, perched his hip on the edge of it, and crossed his arms over his chest. Despite the fact that he was braced for the sight and sound of her, he flinched when her unforgettable face looked back at him, her dark hair caught at the nape in a bow. When she began to speak, his first reaction was mild surprise that she was so poised in front of what looked to be at least two hundred reporters.

A few minutes later, Zack slowly put his glass down, frowning with disbelief at what he was hearing. Despite the fact that he had sent her away from Colorado with every intention of crushing any feeling she had for him, she was looking at the camera, trying very successfully to make her captivity sound like a lark and Zack himself like a quick-witted hero who had amusingly thwarted her attempt to escape at a rest stop and then risked his life in an effort to rescue her from the creek during her second attempt.

At the end of her statement, when questions were being shouted at her from everywhere, she maintained her smiling poise while scrupulously avoiding incriminating Zack by giving explanations that Zack knew were honest although incomplete. When a reporter asked if he'd threatened her at gunpoint, which Zack knew he had, she'd evaded with a joke: *I knew he had a gun because I saw it, and that was enough to convince me—at least in the beginning—that I shouldn't pick a fight with him or criticize his old movies."*

Biting back a reluctant smile at her wit, Zack sternly reminded himself that she'd probably said all this because she thought he might see her interview and be lured more quickly out of hiding. A minute later, however, when she was asked if she intended to press kidnapping charges against him, he watched her give a sunny smile and deflect the subject of what had been a federal crime with another clever joke: *"I don't think I could get a conviction. I mean, if there were women on the jury, they'd acquit him in a minute, as soon as they heard he did half the cooking and cleaning up."*

Zack reached for his drink, but a moment later her answer to a question made him set it down again, his brows drawing together in a frown of disbelief: *"Miss Mathison, do you want to see Zachary Benedict captured?"*

"How could anyone possibly want to see a man who was unjustly imprisoned sent back to prison? I don't know how a jury ever convicted him of murder, but I do know that he's no more capable of that than I am. If he were capable of it, I would not be standing here now, because as I explained to all of you a few minutes ago, I repeatedly tried to jeopardize his escape. I'd also like you to remember that when he thought we'd been found by a helicopter, his first concern was for my safety, not his own. What I'd like to see happen is for this manhunt to be stopped while someone reviews his case."

Zack picked up the remote controller, intending to rewind the film and listen to her last answer over again, watching her face for a sign of slyness or deceit, but the next question froze his finger on the button. *"Miss Mathison, are you in love with Zachary Benedict?"*

He watched her hesitate, then she lifted her eyes to the camera and said with a soft smile, *"At one time or another, most of the female population of this country has probably imagined themselves in love with Zachary Benedict. Now that I've known him, I think they showed* excellent *judgment. He—"*she faltered, then said with a catch in her voice, *"he is a very easy man for any woman to love."*

Zack hit the rewind button and played her last two answers again, watching the screen, studying her face and vocal intonations, searching for a hint of the underlying deceit he knew was there somewhere. He couldn't find it. What he saw and heard was courage and poise and all the things he had loved about her in Colorado.

Telling himself he was overlooking something, some scheme, some hidden reason for her to behave like that in front of millions of people, he took the other videocassette out of its cardboard case, got up, and shoved it into the VCR. This time, he walked behind his desk and sat down, bracing himself to watch a scene he could never forget; a scene that had put him on his knees, humbled before the world, and all because he'd lost his mind over a scheming little liar . . .

Who'd admitted to the world that she loved him.

Even though he'd kidnapped her.

And sent her away from Colorado after telling her she didn't know the difference between sex and love.

Zack was so lost in his thoughts that it took a moment before he recognized what was happening on the television set, and his jaw tightened as he saw himself being shoved into the wall and handcuffed by the Federales. Everybody was screaming and shouting, and whoever was taking the film kept swinging the camera around, trying to follow the voice of a woman who was screaming about someone being hurt.

Then he leaned forward, watching in disbelief as Julie tried to get past the police, screaming, *"Don't hurt him!"* He saw Richardson catch her arms, yanking her back, and he saw that she was crying, watching whatever they were doing to Zack.

The camera's view switched back to Zack and Hadley, and after several seconds, Zack realized Hadley had just taken possession of the wedding ring he'd had in his pocket. The camera tracked Hadley, following him to Julie, who held her hand out in response to whatever Hadley said to her, and when she looked down at her hand, she started crying hysterically, clutching the ring to her chest.

Zack half-rose out of his chair at the sight of her tormented features, then he forced himself to sit back down and watch what he knew was coming next. It happened just as he remembered it . . . the Federales shoving him forward, then Hadley making them stop when he was almost beside Julie. Whoever took the film had grown bolder and moved in for a closer shot because even the sound was clearer. Not that Zack needed to hear it. What Hadley said next was permanently branded into Zack's brain. *"Miss Mathison, I have been very rude. I haven't thanked you yet for your cooperation. If you hadn't helped us set this whole scheme up, Benedict might never have been caught."*

Zack remembered the cold shock that had roared through him, and he saw himself on film, looking at her in an agony of fury, before he jerked his arms, trying to force them to take him out of there . . .

And then all hell broke loose on the film, just as it had in that airport. Suddenly he was on his knees, being clubbed . . . Except there was another uproar going on—Zack saw it just to the right edge of the film, and he got up, walking closer to the television set to see it clearly: Julie had evidently gone wild when they started beating him, and she was attacking Hadley, sobbing and clawing at his face, beating on his chest, and when Richardson pulled her off, she landed two ferocious kicks in Hadley's groin. She fainted then, and Richardson started shouting for a doctor while they dragged Zack out of the airport.

His heart beginning to hammer in deep, aching beats, Zack rewound the film, only this time he didn't take his eyes off her face, and what he saw made his stomach clench. His hand shook as he took the letter from the envelope and unfolded it.

Dear Mom and Dad, and dear Carl and Ted,

By the time you read this letter, you'll know that I've left to join Zack. I don't expect you to condone what I'm doing or to forgive me, but I want to explain it to you so that maybe you'll at least be able to understand someday.

I love him.

I want so much to give you more and better reasons that just that one, and I've tried to think of them, but there don't seem to be any. Maybe it's because that's all that really matters. . . .

After I leave, all of you are going to hear more things about Zack, awful rumors and vicious conjecture from reporters and police and people who never even knew him. I wish so much you could have known him. Since that isn't possible, I'm leaving something for you, something from him that will show you a glimpse of the man he really is. It's a copy of a letter, a very personal letter, from him to me. A small part of the letter will be blocked out, not because there was something there that would have changed your opinion, but because it refers to someone else and a very special favor that person did for us both. When you read Zack's letter, I think you'll know that the man who wrote it will love and protect me in every way he can. We'll be married as soon as we're together. . . .

Zack leaned back and closed his eyes, caught between torment and tenderness over what he had seen and read. He saw her agonized face when he was being put into chains and he heard her soft voice during their only phone call: *"I love you so much. . . . I can't stop loving you. . . . Save your prayers for later, darling. You're going to wear your knees out when I get there as it is, . . . praying I let you get some sleep at night, praying I stop giving you babies . . ."* He had figured out weeks ago that she'd lied about being pregnant, but he'd thought it was to force him into her trap.

Everything else had been the truth . . .

Julie in Colorado, tripping him in the snow . . . lying in his arms at night, giving herself to him with an unselfish ardor that had driven him crazy with desire and the need to please her as she pleased him . . . Julie with her glowing eyes, musical laughter, her prim vocabulary, and jaunty smile.

He could still feel her lying in his arms that last night, her fingers spreading over his heart when she told him she loved him . . . still see her eyes darken with sympathy when he told her that stupid story about a teacher refusing to dance with him . . . *"I would never have turned you down, Zack."* . . . He remembered the way her entire face had lit up when she talked about watching grown women learn to read . . . *"Oh, Zack . . . It's like holding a miracle in your hand!"*

If she hadn't conceived that insane idea of visiting his treacherous grandmother, Zack realized she probably wouldn't have broken under the pressure of Tony Austin's death. Richardson had said she'd handled the first blow without losing her resolve. She'd broken under the second one.

She had been real. And she had been his. She had loved him when he had nothing to offer her except a life in hiding with a fugitive. She had clutched that wedding ring to her chest and wept as if her heart was breaking . . .

She had done and been all those things. It hit him suddenly that Richardson had not said Julie was still in love with him, but only that she was guilt-stricken now over Mexico City. Other things began to occur to him, too: Richardson had apparently spent enough time with her in the past three months to fall in love with her. She had only known Zack for a week, and he, on the other hand, had turned her life into a living hell. Paralyzed with a mixture of urgency and fear, Zack slowly stood up.

75

MATT AND MEREDITH EXCHANGED SMILES OF PROFOUND pleasure as Zack strode into the living room carrying a suitcase. Leaning back against the sofa, Matt stretched his legs out and studied the blue suit Zack was wearing with a knowing grin. "No one wears a suit to a California party, Zack. It just isn't done."

"I forgot about the damned party," he said glowering out the window at his own guests. "Stand in for me, will you? Tell them something urgent came up. Can I borrow your pilot?" he added, absently putting his suitcase down and tying his tie.

"Just my pilot?" Matt said, glancing up at Meredith, who'd perched on the arm of the sofa and laid her hand on his shoulder. "Not my plane?"

Zack turned aside as his housekeeper rushed in to give him two briefcases she'd packed at his instructions. "Your plane *and* your pilot," he said impatiently.

"That depends on where you plan to go."

Satisfied that he had everything he needed for the next few days, Zack finally turned his full attention on his friend. "Where the hell do you think I'm going?"

"How should I know. If it's Keaton, Texas, don't you think you should call Julie first?"

"No, I don't know how she'll react. I don't want her taking off somewhere to avoid me. If I fly commercial, it will take me hours longer to get there."

"What's the rush? You've let her wait for six weeks already while Richardson's been there holding her hand, no doubt, giving her his broad shoulder to cry on. Furthermore, private planes are expensive toys—"

"I don't have time for this b—" Zack cut off the curse word on Meredith's behalf, started forward to kiss her good-bye, then he stopped as Joe O'Hara said from the doorway behind him. "I've got the car out in front, ready to go, Matt.

And I talked to Steve on the car phone. He says the plane's fueled and ready to fly. Zack, when are you going to be ready to leave?"

"I think," Matt joked dryly, "he's ready now."

Giving Matt a disgusted look, Zack pulled Meredith into his arms. "Thank you," he said with quiet sincerity.

"You're welcome," she replied, beaming at him. "Give Julie my love."

"Give her my sincerest apology," Matt said, standing up and sobering as he held out his hand to shake Zack's. "Good luck."

They watched him stride swiftly out the door, then Meredith looked up at Matt and her smile wobbled as she said, "That man loves her so much that he doesn't care that many people will think he's a fool for wanting her after what she did to him in Mexico City. All that matters to him is that she loves him."

"I know," Matt replied somberly gazing into her misty eyes, "I recognize the feeling."

76

"HEY, HERMAN, CAN YOU PICK UP SOME GUY WHO'S LANDIN' AT the airstrip in twenty minutes?" The squawk of the walkie-talkie was scarcely noticed in the noisy high school gymnasium where 175 Keaton citizens were gathered for the dress rehearsal of the bicentennial celebration pageant that was to take place tomorrow after the parade. Shoving the saber that hung from the waist of his general's uniform aside, Herman Henkleman groped for the walkie-talkie beneath it and held it to his mouth. "Sure thing, Billy. Julie Mathison just said I've already got my part down great."

Feeling very grand in his uniform, Herman looked around for Julie, who was in charge of the entire pageant, and spotted her standing off to the sidelines beside her brother and sister-in-law, watching the rehearsal taking place on stage. "Howdy, Ted—Katherine," he said as he wended his way through the crowd to her side. "'Scuse me, Julie," he added, and when she looked up and smiled at him, he explained, "Billy Bradson has started lettin' me drive the taxi on weekends to earn some extra money. I gotta go make a pickup for him at the airstrip. Some guy's landin' in a plane out there in a few minutes."

"Go right ahead," Julie said, oblivious to the swift, questioning look that Katherine gave Ted. "We're almost finished here, and besides, you don't need any more rehearsal."

"I know," he said proudly. "I got that part about 'Charge, here come's the enemy' down great.'"

She laughed. "Yes, you certainly do!"

He hesitated, glancing across the room at Flossie Eldridge, then he leaned lower. "If Flossie asks where I am, you could probably tell her I had something real important to do."

Julie had deliberately given him a part in the pageant that required him to be close to the elderly twin, who still blushed like a schoolgirl whenever he spoke to her. "Why don't you tell her yourself," she whispered. "She's looking right at you."

Herman gathered up his courage, and as he headed for the auditorium doors, he stopped in front of Flossie and Ada Eldridge, who were dressed in matching ball gowns, their hair styled into identical masses of ringlets. "I gotta make a run to the airstrip for Billy Bradson," he told Flossie. "I'm helpin' him out on weekends, now, besides doing my electrical work."

"Be careful, Herman," she said shyly.

"Don't blow up his car," Ada said scornfully.

Herman felt his collar turn hot. He stepped away, then stepped back, glowering. "Ada," he said, confronting the woman for the first time in decades. "You are a mean-hearted, spiteful, bloodless woman, and you always have been! I told you that years ago, and it's still true."

"And you," she retorted, turning red, "are a useless good-for-nothing."

He slapped his general's hat on his head and put his hands on his hips, his expression ominous. "That's not what you used to think when you were a girl, chasin' after me, tryin' to turn my head from Flossie!" He walked out, leaving Flossie gaping at her angry twin with a look of hurt and dawning understanding.

Katherine waited until Julie walked up onto the stage to round up the children for their own rehearsal, then she squeezed Ted's hand tightly, her face a mask of hope and tension. "Ted, do you think it's Benedict landing at the airstrip?"

He shook his head. "Not a chance. They said on the news last night that he's giving a weekend party at his house, remember?"

Her face fell and he patted her hand. "It's probably Larraby coming in from Dallas to make his monthly inspection of that factory he's building over in Lynchville."

* * *

"Buckle up, hold on, and say your prayers," the pilot joked over the intercom as the Lear began its swift descent through the encroaching dusk, diving toward the concrete ribbon below. "If this airstrip was six inches shorter, we couldn't set her down here, and if it was any darker, we'd have to land at DFW. Evidently, they don't light this sidewalk up at night. By the way, your taxi's waiting down there."

Without taking his gaze from the videotapes of Julie he'd brought with him to watch on the plane, Zack buckled his seat belt. A few minutes later, however, he looked up with a startled frown as the pilot slammed on the brakes at the moment of touchdown and the sleek plane bucked down the runway, brakes screaming, finally coming to a teeth-jarring stop only a few feet from the end of it.

"Mr. Farrell's going to need new brakes after two landings on this strip," the pilot said, sounding a little shaken and very relieved. "What's the plan for tonight, Mr. Benedict? Should I check into a motel for the night or head back to the West Coast?"

Zack reached over to the intercom button on the console between the two sofas, then he hesitated and faced what he had tried to ignore all the way here: He did not have the slightest idea whether Julie now hated him more than she'd loved him. He didn't know what sort of reception he was going to get from her or how much time it was going to take to convince her to come back to California with him or if he could ever convince her to do that. Pressing the button, he said belatedly, "Check into a motel for the night, Steve. I'll send the cab back here for you."

The pilot was still shutting down the engines when Zack walked swiftly down the steps. The taxi driver was standing at attention beside the open door of his cab wearing the most ludicrously unauthentic Civil War uniform Zack had ever seen, assuming that's what it was supposed to be. "Do you know where Julie Mathison lives?" he asked him as he slid into the back seat and put his briefcase down. "If not, I need to find a phone book. I forgot to bring her address."

"Of course I know where she lives," the driver said, his eyes narrowing on Zack's face, his expression turning ferocious as he recognized it. He got into the front seat and slammed the door with unnecessary force. "Your name Benedict?" he demanded several minutes later as they drove past the elementary school and into a quaint downtown district set around a courthouse, with shops and restaurants surrounding the square.

Zack was busy looking around at the town where Julie had grown up. "Yes."

A half mile from the downtown district, the cab pulled to a stop in front of a neat one-story house with an immaculate lawn and big shade trees, and Zack felt his heart began to beat in nervous anticipation as he dug in his pocket for money. "How much do I owe you?"

"Fifty bucks."

"You're kidding."

"For anyone else, the ride costs five bucks. For a skunk like you, it costs fifty bucks. Now, if you want me to take you to where Julie really is, instead of leaving you here, where she ain't, it'll cost you seventy-five."

Torn between anger, surprise, and tension, Zack ignored the aspersion cast on his character and sat back. "Where is she?"

"At the high school where she's handlin' the rehearsal for the pageant."

Zack remembered passing the high school with its crowded parking lot. He hesitated, desperate to see her, to set things straight, to hold her in his arms if she'd let him. His voice tinged with sarcasm, he said, "Do you also happen to know how long she'll be there?"

"It could go on all night," Herman lied out of sheer spite.

"In that case, take me there."

The driver jerked his head in a nod and pulled away from the curb. "I don't see why you're in such a hurry to see her, now," he said, glaring at Zack in the rearview mirror. "You left her here all this time to face the reporters and the cops all by herself after you snatched her and took her to Colorado. When you got out of prison, you didn't come to see her either. You've been too busy with your fancy women and your parties to bother with a sweet girl like Julie, who's never hurt anybody in her whole life! You've shamed her in front of the whole world, in front of this whole town! People outside of Keaton hate her because she did the right thing in Mexico, only it turned out to be the wrong thing. I hope," he finished vengefully as they pulled up in front of the doors to the high school, "she pokes you in the eye when she sees you! If I were her daddy, I'd get out my shotgun and come lookin' for you, soon as I heard you're in town! I hope he does."

"You'll probably get both your wishes," Zack said quietly, pulling a hundred-dollar bill out of his pocket and handing it to him. "Go back to the airport and get my pilot. He's not a skunk, so another twenty-five dollars should cover your trip."

Something in his voice made Herman hesitate and turn around in his seat. "Are you plannin' to finally make it up with her? Is that why you're here?"

"I'm going to try."

The hostility on his face died. "Your pilot's gonna have to wait a few minutes. This, I want to see. Besides, you may need a friend in that crowd."

Zack didn't hear him, he was already striding into the school, following the direction of the noise coming from behind the double doors at the end of the corridor to his right.

77

HE SPOTTED JULIE IN THE CROWD BEFORE THE GYMNASIUM doors swung closed behind him. She was conducting a chorus of children dressed in various costumes, some of whom were in wheelchairs, while a pianist accompanied them up on the stage.

Mesmerized, he stood there, listening to the sweet sound of her voice, watching her incredible smile, and the shattering tenderness he felt made his chest ache. Clad in jeans and a school sweatshirt, with her hair pulled into a ponytail and tied with a scarf, she looked adorable . . . and thin. Her cheekbones and eyes were more prominent now than before, and Zack swallowed over the knot of guilt in his throat when he realized how much weight she'd lost. Because of him. The cab driver said Zack had shamed her in front of the town; he was going to undo some of that now if he could. Ignoring the startled glances and exchanged whispers beginning to circulate around the room as people in the bleachers and on the floor noted his presence and recognized his face, he started forward.

"Okay, you guys, what's the problem?" Julie said, when several of the older children stopped singing and began to whisper and point. Behind her, she was distantly aware of the hush falling over the cavernous room and the echo of a man's footsteps on the wooden floor, but she was preoccupied with the increasing lateness of the hour and her students' flagging attention. "Willie, if you finally want your chance to sing, then pay attention," she warned, but he was pointing to something behind her and whispering furiously to Johnny Everett and Tim Wimple. "Miss Timmons," she said, looking up at the pianist who was also gaping open-mouthed at something behind her. "Miss Timmons—let's run through it again." But when Julie looked back down, part of the children's chorus was breaking up and moving forward in a small group being led by Willie Jenkins. "Where do you think you're going?" Julie burst out as they passed her. She spun around. And froze.

Zack was standing fifteen feet away from her, his hands at his sides. He'd finally read her last letter, she thought wildly, and he'd come at last to get his car. She stood there, afraid to speak, afraid to move, gazing at the sternly handsome face that had haunted her dreams and tormented her days.

Willie Jenkins stepped forward, his gravelly voice loud and belligerent. "You Zack Benedict?" he demanded.

Zack nodded silently, and suddenly several other boys moved forward, fanning out in front of Julie, three of them in wheelchairs—all of them ready to defend her against the monster in their midst, Zack realized.

"Then you better just turn around and get outa here," the one with the bullfrog's voice warned, thrusting out his chin. "You made Miss Mathison cry."

Zack's solemn gaze stayed on Julie's pale face. "She made me cry, too."

"Guys don't cry," he scoffed.

"Sometimes they do—if someone they love hurts them very much."

Willie glanced up at his beloved teacher's face and saw tears sliding slowly from her eyes. "Look at that! You're making her cry again!" he warned with a ferocious glower. "Is that why you came here?"

"I came here," Zack said, "because I can't live without her."

Everyone in the auditorium gaped at the famous tough-guy movie hero who was humbling himself by making these astonishing admissions in front of them, but Julie didn't notice their stares. She was rushing forward through the children, walking fast, then running . . . running into the arms that were opening wide to her.

They closed around her with stunning force, his hand cradling her tear-streaked face against his chest, shielding her from their audience as he bent his head and whispered hoarsely, "I love you." Her shoulders shaking with sobs, she slid her hands around his neck, her face buried against his chest, holding him fiercely to her.

At the far end of the auditorium, Ted put his arm around Katherine and drew her close. "How did you get so damned smart?" he whispered.

Herman Henkleman was of a more practical, albeit equally romantic, mind. Winking at Flossie, he shouted, "Rehearsal's over folks!" Then he slapped the light switches off, plunging the room into total darkness, and trotted off to get his taxi.

By the time someone found the light switch, Zack and Julie were gone.

"Hop in," Herman said with a grand gesture of his general's hat as they raced out the school doors, hand in hand. "Always wanted to drive a getaway car," he added, shoving the accelerator to the floor and sending the cab jolting away from the building. "Where to?"

Julie was past all rational thought for the moment.

"Your house?" Zack asked.

"Not if you want to do any smoochin'," Herman said. "Whole town'll be comin' by and callin'."

"Where's the closest hotel or motel?"

Julie looked at him uneasily, but Herman was more blunt: "You tryin' to tear her reputation up or fix it?"

Zack looked down at her face and felt speechless and helpless and desperate to be alone with her. Her eyes told him she felt the same.

"My house," she said. "We'll take the phone off the hook and disconnect the doorbell if we have to."

A minute later, Herman pulled the cab up in front of the house, and Zack reached into his pocket for more money. "How much do I owe you this time," he asked dryly.

The man turned in his seat and with a look of wounded dignity handed Zack's hundred-dollar bill back to him. "Five dollars, round trip, including picking up your pilot. That's a special rate," he added with a startling boyish smile, "for the man who wasn't afraid to admit he loves Julie in front of the whole town."

Oddly touched, Zack handed him a twenty-dollar bill and said, "I left a suitcase and another briefcase on the plane. Would you bring them back here after you take my pilot to his motel?"

"Sure thing. I'll leave them at Julie's back door so you don't have to answer the doorbell."

78

JULIE WALKED INTO THE LIVING ROOM AND TURNED ON A lamp, but when Zack reached out for her hand, she came wordlessly into his arms, kissing him with a silent desperation that matched his own, holding him to her, crushing her soft mouth to his, her hands rushing over him. Zack clutched her tighter to him, his lips ravaging hers, his hands hungrily memorizing her beloved form.

The shrill ring of the telephone right beside them made them both jump, and she reached out a shaky hand to answer it.

Zack watched her as she lifted it to her ear, and he smiled to himself at the way she self-consciously lowered her eyes when he began to take off his jacket.

"Yes, it's true, Mrs. Addelson," she said, "he's really here." She listened a minute and then said, "I don't know. I'll ask him." Covering the phone with her hand she gave him a helpless look and said, "Mayor and Mrs. Addelson would like to know if you—we—are free to have dinner with them tonight."

Zack stripped off his tie and began unbuttoning his shirt and slowly, emphatically shook his head no, watching a gorgeous blush climb her cheeks as she caught his unmistakable meaning.

"I'm afraid we can't. No, I'm not certain what his immediate plans are or his future plans either. Yes, I'll ask him and let you know."

Julie hung up the phone, then hastily picked it up, shoved the receiver under a sofa pillow, straightened, and nervously rubbed her palms against her thighs. Dozens of questions raced through her mind as she stood there looking at him, doubts and uncertainties and hopes, but over it all was a feeling of joyous unreality that he was actually standing there, in her living room, his eyes gentle, amused, sexy. "I can't believe you're here," she whispered aloud. "A few hours ago, everything seemed so—"

"Empty?" he provided in the deep, compelling voice she'd longed to hear again. "And meaningless?" he added, walking toward her.

She nodded. "And hopeless. Zack, I—I have so much to explain if you'll let me. But I—" Her voice broke as he pulled her into his arms and she touched his face, her fingers trembling. "Oh, God, I've missed you so much!"

Zack answered her with his mouth, parting her lips with his; pulled the scarf out of her hair; and shoved his fingers into the luxuriant mass, and she crushed herself against him, answering his passion with the same wild, exquisitely provocative ardor that had haunted his dreams in South America and awakened him in a sweat in prison. He dragged his mouth from hers. "Show me your house," he said in a thickened voice he hardly recognized. He really meant, show me your bedroom.

She nodded, knowing exactly what he meant, and she led him straight where he wanted to go, but when he stepped through the doorway and saw the white wicker furniture, the lush green potted trees, and the froth of white ruffles on the bedspread, canopy, and dressing table, the room was so identical to his imaginings that he stopped short. As if she understood the direction of his thoughts, she said hesitantly, "How did I do?"

"It looks exactly as I imagined it when—"

Julie watched the tension on his face and ended his unfinished sentence for him, her voice somber: "When you were lying in bed on your boat, you mean, imagining me here in this room because I asked you to do that on the phone. When," she continued with brutal honesty, "you still believed I was going to be there with you . . . when you never believed I would trick you into coming for me and betray you to the FBI and get you beaten and sent back to prison."

He looked at her, a grim smile touching his mouth and eyes. "When all that was true."

She sank down onto the bed, her face turned up to his, eyes honest and searching. "Could we lie here for a little while and talk first?"

Zack hesitated. On the one hand, he longed to put the past behind them and spend the present making love with her on that frilly, virginal white canopied bed, which seemed absurdly exciting when she was sitting on it. On the other hand, she was clearly upset and they couldn't very well begin again until the past was dealt with. "For a little while," he agreed.

She propped up a pile of pillows against the headboard for both of them and he stretched his arm out, curving it around her shoulders as soon as she moved next to him. When she cuddled close, her hand resting atop his chest, he remembered the mornings they'd spent in bed in Colorado, sitting exactly like this, and he smiled. "I forgot how perfectly you fit me."

"You're thinking about the mornings in Colorado, aren't you?"

It was a statement, not a question, and he tipped his head down and smiled. "I also forgot how perceptive you are."

"Not perceptive, really. I was thinking about the same thing." She smiled, and then made a hesitant attempt to open the dangerous discussion of their most recent past. "I don't know where to begin," she said, "And I'm . . . I'm almost *afraid* to begin. I don't even know what finally brought you back here today."

Zack's brows drew together in surprise. "What brought me back here today was Richardson. Didn't you know he was going to come to see me?" When she gaped at him in shocked silence, he added, "He appeared at my house in California this morning, all decked out in his Brooks Brothers suit, Armani tie, and genuine, authentic FBI badge."

"Paul came to see you?" she said, stunned. "Paul Richardson? You can't mean my Paul."

Zack stiffened. "Evidently, I do mean 'your Paul.'" It hit Zack then that although he'd told her he loved her, she had said only that she'd missed him. In a carefully expressionless voice, he added, "Somewhere I got the idea that you would want me to come here for more reasons than just to make peace with you. Now that I think about it, that was purely a conclusion I drew from what I saw on those videotapes. I think," he said tightly, making a move to withdraw his arm, "this discussion might be better held in the living room. Or maybe tomorrow, in the lobby of my hotel, wherever that is."

"Zack," she said shakily, tightening her hand on his arm, "don't you dare leave this bed! If you ever shut me out again without giving me a chance to explain, I'll never forgive you. Paul is my friend. He was here for me when I was desperately unhappy and lonely."

His head fell back against the pillow and he wrapped his arms tightly around her, his voice heavy with irony and relief. "What is it about you that demolishes my mind. In Colorado, you made me feel like an emotional yo-yo, and it's happening again."

Reverting to their original topic, he said, "I came here today because Richardson barged into my house this morning, flashing his badge and slapping a large envelope on my desk containing two videotapes and a letter." His lingering jealousy over Richardson's friendship with Julie and his own guilt made him continue in a sarcastic tone, "In between expressing doubts about my legitimacy and trying to get into a fistfight with me, he also managed to tell me that, contrary to what Hadley wanted me to believe in Mexico City, you had *not* come up with the idea of joining me there as a way to entrap me. He also explained that it was a visit to Margaret Stanhope combined with Austin's death that finally drove you to turn me in."

"What was in the videotapes and the letter?"

"One videotape was the news conference you gave when you got back from Colorado. The letter was the one you wrote to your parents when you were planning to join me. The other videotape was from the FBI files—it was of both of us in the airport in Mexico City, showing everything that happened."

Julie shuddered in his arms at the mention of the airport. "I'm sorry," she whispered brokenly, turning her face into his chest. "I'm so sorry. I don't know how either of us is ever going to forget that." Zack registered her reaction and made a decision, but he withheld that for a few minutes. Instead, he tipped her chin up and said, "What in God's name ever possessed you to go to see Margaret Stanhope?"

The doorbell rang and they both ignored it.

With a sigh, Julie explained, "You said in your letter that you wished you'd reconciled with her long ago. You even suggested that I give her our baby to raise. And on the phone you said you felt like we were inviting a curse by leaving so much unhappiness behind us. So I decided to go to her and explain to her that you loved her and regretted the estrangement."

"And she laughed in your face."

"Worse. Somehow, the subject of Justin came up, and the next thing I knew she was telling me that you murdered him after a fight over a girl and handing me a file full of news clippings where you admitted shooting him. And I—" She drew a shaking breath, hating to accuse him. "I realized you'd lied to me, Zack. I tried to tell myself you lied to her, not me, but when Tony Austin was murdered, that was three people whom you'd quarreled with, and all of them had died at your hands, or so it looked. I thought . . . I started to believe, as your grandmother believed, that you were insane. I betrayed you. I thought it was for your own good."

"I did not lie to you about Justin, Julie," Zack said with a harsh sigh. "I lied to the police in Ridgemont."

"But why?"

"Because my grandfather asked me to, because a suicide brings down an investigation as to possible causes, and my grandfather and I wanted to protect that vicious old woman from having to face Justin's homosexuality when the cops discovered it. I shouldn't have bothered," he added tightly. "I should have let her wallow in what she would have felt was disgrace. Justin couldn't have been hurt by it."

"Knowing how she felt about you," Julie said, "how could you possibly have thought she'd care for our baby?"

He raised his brows in amused challenge. "What baby, Julie?"

The infectious smile that had brightened his life in Colorado dawned across her face with a touch of beguiling guilt to add to its appeal. "The baby I invented so you'd let me come to you."

"Oh, that baby."

She opened another button on his shirt and pressed a kiss against his throat. "Answer my question."

"Keep doing that and you stand a better chance of getting a real baby than an answer to your question."

With a laugh, she leaned her forearms against his chest, but her eyes were slumberous. "I'm terribly greedy, Zack. I want both."

Tenderly, Zack cupped her face between his hands, his thumbs rubbing over her cheeks. "Do you, darling? Want my baby?"

"Desperately."

"We'll work on that tonight if you're up to it."

She bit her lip, her shoulders shaking with laughter. "Going strictly from fading memory, you understand, I think it's a matter of whether you are."

"Up to it?" he provided, enjoying the sexual banter and the exhilaration of the unique combination of laughter and love she'd always made him feel.

She nodded.

"Actually, I've been 'up to it' most of the time since I read your letter this morning. The proof is within your reach."

The doorbell rang again, and they ignored it again, but it made Julie guiltily jerk her hand away from what he'd hoped was going to be her search for 'proof.' "Are you going to finish answering my question?" she asked.

"Yes," he sighed. "If you'll think back to the letter I wrote you, you'll remember I specifically said I'd write to her before I sent you there with our baby. Actually, I'd have written to Foster first, not to her."

"Foster? You mean the old butler?"

Zack nodded. "My grandfather and I swore him to secrecy, but he knows what happened. He was in the hall when the shot came from Justin's room, and he saw me run from my room down to Justin's. I would have released Foster from his promise and told him to speak to his employer and tell her the truth."

"She's your grandmother, Zack. Stop avoiding calling her that. I think she loved you more than you imagine. If you saw her now, talked to her, you'd realize how much of a toll all this—"

"She is dead to me, Julie," he interrupted with a bite in his voice. "After tonight, I never want to hear the woman's name or have you refer to her."

Julie opened her mouth to argue, then made a different decision, but she withheld it for the time being. With a smile in her voice, she said, "No one gets a second chance from you, right?"

"Right," he said implacably.

"Except me."

He brushed his knuckles over her smooth cheek. "Except you," he agreed. "How many chances do I get?"

"How many do you need?"

"A lot of them, I'm afraid," she said with such a gusty sigh that Zack burst out laughing and snatched her into his arms. When he let her go, he noticed the small silver chain peeking out from between the side of her collar and her throat. "What's that?" he asked.

She put her chin against her chest. "What's what?"

"This," he said, looping his finger under the chain.

Afraid that the sight of the ring would remind him of the ugliness of Mexico City, Julie hastily put her hand against her chest, trapping the ring. "Leave it alone. Please!"

Zack's eyes narrowed at her anxiety, and he felt again the unfamiliar stirrings of suspicion. "What is it?" he asked, careful to keep his voice reasonable. "A gift from an old boyfriend?"

"Something like that. I'll stop wearing it."

"Let's see it," Zack said.

"No."

"A man has a right to know something about the taste of his predecessors."

"He had wonderful taste! You'd approve. Leave it alone."

"Julie," he warned, "you are a rotten liar. What's attached to that chain?" Without giving her a chance to stop him, he brushed her hands aside and pulled out the chain.

A platinum wedding band gleamed in his hand, diamonds sparkling in the light.

Tenderness washed through him, and he pulled her onto his chest. "Why were you afraid for me to see that?"

"I'm afraid of anything that might remind you of Mexico City. I don't think I'll ever be able to forget the way you looked at me before you realized I hadn't led them to you by accident . . ." Her voice shook, "Or the change in your face when you realized it was deliberate. I know I won't. Not ever. I'll always be afraid to see that look."

Zack regretfully postponed making love to her and moved her off his chest, sitting up. "Let's get it over with."

"What?" she said, panicking already. "Where are you going?"

"Do you have a VCR?"

Her fear turned to puzzlement. "In the living room."

79

"WHAT ARE YOU DOING?" SHE ASKED AS ZACK SAT DOWN BESIDE her and the videotape he'd taken out of his briefcase began to run. Nervously, she teased, "I hope it's *Dirty Dancing* and not a sexy scene from one of your movies."

He put his arm around her and quietly said, "It's the tape I've watched several times today, the one the FBI confiscated of us in Mex—"

She shook her head wildly, trying to grab the remote controller. "I don't want to see that. Not tonight! Not ever again!"

"We're going to watch it together, Julie. You and I. After that, it won't be able to come between us or hurt us, and you won't have to be afraid."

"Don't make me watch this!" she said, shaking as the voices began to explode in the airport. "I can't stand it!"

"Look at the screen," he said implacably. "We were there together, but I never knew until today what you were doing while they were taking me into custody, and I have a feeling you don't have a clear recollection of it either."

"Oh, yes, I do! I remember *exactly* what they were doing to you! I remember that it was my fault!"

He turned her face to the screen. "Watch you, not me. Watch and you'll see what I did—a woman who was suffering more than I was." Julie dragged her gaze to the television set, staring blindly at a scene she only wanted to forget. She saw herself screaming at everyone not to hurt him, saw Paul yanking her back, shouting at her that it was "all over," saw Hadley walking up to her with a malicious grin and dropping the ring into her hand. She saw herself clutching the ring and weeping.

Zack's voice was aching and tender, "Julie," he whispered, pulling her tight, "look at you, darling, and see what I see. It was just a ring, a piece of metal and stones. But look at how much it meant to you."

"It was the *wedding ring* you picked out for me!" she said fiercely. "That's why I was crying."

"Really?" he teased softly. "I thought you were crying because the diamonds were so small."

Her mouth dropped open, and an hysterical giggle slid out even while she blinked back the tears from her wondrous eyes.

"Now watch this," he added with a grin, pulling her tighter. "This is my favorite part. Don't watch what they're doing to me," he said quickly when she started to jerk her gaze away from the Federales' raised clubs. "Watch what you're doing to Hadley on the right of the screen. That," he added admiringly, "is one hell of a right hook you have, lady."

Julie forced herself to watch and was slightly surprised and shamefully pleased to see herself attacking that particular human being. "I don't actually remember much of that," she whispered.

"No, but I'll bet Hadley remembered what comes next. When Richardson dragged you off and you couldn't get at Hadley with your nails or hands, you—"

"Kicked him!" Julie narrated, watching in shock.

"Right in the groin," Zack said proudly with a laugh as Hadley doubled over, clutching himself. "Do you have any idea how many men there are in this world who've longed to do that?"

Julie shook her head in silence, watching the end of the film as a doctor rammed a hypodermic into her arm and Paul held her. Zack let the VCR keep running and sobered as he looked at her. "I'm going to tear Hadley to pieces legally before I'm done. I have a meeting scheduled with the Texas Board of Criminal Justice week after next. When I'm finished with him, he'll be occupying one of his own cells."

"He's a devil!"

"And you," Zack said somberly, tipping her chin up, "are an angel. Do you have any idea how I've felt every time I watched you on that film?"

She shook her head, and he said, "I felt loved. Incredibly, completely, unconditionally loved. Even when you thought I was a deranged murderer, you were still fighting and crying for me." Lowering his mouth to hers, he whispered, "I have never known a woman who has as much courage as you . . ." He kissed the corner of her eye, dragging his lips across her cheek to the corner of her mouth, "Or as much love to give." His hands slid under her sweatshirt and down the waistband of her jeans. "Give it to me, darling," he whispered, "all of it . . . now." He opened her mouth with his, deepening the kiss, his hands moving over her soft bare skin, his tongue searching her mouth, driving slowly into it, and when she unbuttoned his shirt with shaking fingers and spread it open and touched him, the moan he heard was his. But the ringing in his ears

PERFECT

came from the doorbell, and the pounding in his brain he slowly realized was a fist hammering on the door. Swearing, Zack sat up, intending to take her into the bedroom, and held out his hand.

"Julie!" Ted's voice accompanied the second round of hammering on the door.

"It's my brother!" she said.

"Can't you suggest he go away and come back tomorrow?"

She was about to nod, when Ted's laughing voice called, "Answer this door for your own good. I know you're in there," and she shook her head instead, hastily tugging her shirt back down and trying to restore order to her hair. "I'd better see what he wants."

"I'll wait in the kitchen," Zack said, raking his hands through his hair.

"But I want him to meet you since he's here."

"You want him to meet me now?" He glanced down meaningfully and then at her in amusement. "Like this?"

"On second thought," she said, blushing gorgeously, "you'd better wait in the kitchen," then she headed for the door while he walked in the opposite direction.

Julie pulled it open just as Ted raised his hand to knock again, and his gaze swept over her in a knowing, laughing scrutiny. "Sorry to interrupt. Where's Benedict?"

"In the kitchen."

"I'll bet," he laughed.

"What do you want," she said, exasperated, embarrassed, and beaming at him because she belatedly realized that he had to have given her letter to Paul.

"I might as well tell both of you at the same time," he said, sauntering down the hall, pausing to look in the bedroom, obviously and irrationally enjoying himself hugely.

Zack was drinking a glass of water at the sink when Julie said behind him, "Zack, this is my brother Ted."

Startled by their silent arrival, Zack turned, his eyes riveting on another familiar face.

Ted nodded. "You're right, I was in Mexico City with Julie."

Recovering from his surprise, Zack extended his hand, and said, "I'm happy to meet you under better circumstances."

"But not at this particular moment," Ted joked, shaking his hand, and Zack felt a surprising and instant liking for the younger man. "If I were you," Ted continued to Zack with a grin, "I'd fix myself something stronger to drink than water." Glancing at a puzzled Julie, he explained, "Dad wants to see both of you at the house. *Immediately*," he emphasized in a comically dire tone. "Katherine

• 461 •

is over there now with Mother, helping to convince Dad that it will be so much nicer if he waits there calmly instead of coming over here, which was what he was determined to do when he couldn't reach you on the phone."

"Why is he so anxious to see us?" Julie asked.

Slouching against the wall, Ted shoved his hands in his pockets, lifted his brows, and looked at Zack. "Can you guess why Julie's father might be a little, shall we say, . . . determined . . . to have a word with you upon your unexpected arrival in town?"

Zack swallowed the rest of the water and filled the glass again. "I think I can guess."

"Julie," Ted ordered with a chuckle, "go and comb your hair and try not to look so . . . ah . . . delightfully rumpled. I'll call Dad and tell him we'll be there shortly."

She turned on her heel and fled toward her room, calling over her shoulder that the phone was off the hook in the living room.

When Ted came back into the kitchen after making his phone call, Zack was in the bathroom, shaving. He emerged a few minutes later wearing a fresh shirt, his hair combed, and walked into the kitchen. Ted paused in the act of searching through all the cabinets and said over his shoulder, "I don't suppose you know where Julie put the vodka this time?"

"This time?" Zack said, shifting his thoughts from his forthcoming meeting with his future father-in-law.

"Julie has a peculiar little habit," Ted explained, bending down and looking under the sink. "When something is bothering her, she rearranges things . . . puts them into order, you could say."

A tender smile quirked at Zack's mouth when he remembered seeing her do that in Colorado. "I know."

"Then you won't be surprised," Ted continued, opening the refrigerator in his fruitless search for the liquor, "to learn that since you were released from prison, she has rearranged every closet, drawer, and cabinet she has and repainted her garage. Twice. Take a look at this refrigerator," he said pointing to the shelves on the doors. "You will note that the bottles and jars are all arranged in descending order by size, tallest on the left. Now, on the next shelf, she has reversed that for artistic purposes, so that the tallest items are on the right. Last week, everything was arranged by color. It was something to see."

Torn between amusement at what he was hearing and regret for the heartache that had caused her to do it, Zack said, "I'll bet it was."

"That's nothing," Ted continued dryly. "Take a look at this," he said, and opening a cabinet, he pointed at the cans and boxes on the shelves. "She's filed her groceries in alphabetical order."

Zack choked on a laugh. "She's what?"

"Look for yourself."

Zack peered around the other man's shoulder. All the cans, bottles, and boxes were mixed together but standing at military attention in precise rows across the front. "Applesauce, asparagus, beets," he murmured in amused disbelief, "cauliflower, Cheerios, flour, Jello, beans . . ." He looked at Ted. "She misfiled the beans."

"No, I didn't," Julie said, walking into the kitchen and trying to look perfectly nonchalant when both men turned to her in laughing amazement. "They're under *L*."

"*L*?" Zack said, trying unsuccessfully to keep his face straight.

She dropped her embarrassed gaze to an invisible speck of lint she was flicking off her sweater. "*L*—for legumes," she informed him. Zack choked on his laughter and pulled her into his arms, burying his face in her hair, basking in the joy of her. "Where's the vodka?" he whispered in her ear. "Ted wants it."

She tipped her head back, her eyes filled with laughter. "It's behind the legumes."

"What the hell is it doing there?" Ted asked, shoving the cans of beans aside and seizing it.

His shoulders shaking with suppressed mirth, Zack managed to say blandly and correctly, "It's under *L*—for liquor. Naturally."

"Naturally," Julie confirmed with a giggle.

"Too bad there's no time to drink it," Ted said.

"I didn't want any," Zack replied.

"You'll be sorry."

Ted's squad car was waiting at the curb, and he held the back door open for them. Zack reluctantly slid into the back seat behind Julie, his expression turning tense.

"What's wrong?" she asked, so vibrantly attuned to his presence that she instantly sensed the slightest change in his voice or expression.

"This isn't my favorite mode of transportation, that's all."

Zack saw her eyes darken with sorrow, but she rallied almost instantly and deliberately made a joke he knew was designed to lift his spirits. "Ted," she said, keeping her smiling eyes on Zack, "you should have brought Carl's Blazer. Zack thinks it's much more . . . attractive."

It made both men laugh.

80

FIFTEEN MINUTES LATER, ZACK WASN'T LAUGHING; HE WAS seated across from Julie's father in his small study, getting his ass chewed out by Reverend Mathison, who was pacing angrily in front of him. Zack had expected the ass-chewing, he even accepted it as his due, but he had expected Julie's minister-father to be a small, meek man who would deliver a monotone lecture on whatever commandments he felt Zack had broken. He had *not* expected Jim Mathison to be a tall, robust man, capable of delivering a scathingly descriptive, eloquently worded tirade that would have put George C. Scott's monologue at the opening of *Patton* to shame.

"I cannot excuse or condone anything you did! Not one thing!" Jim Mathison finished at last, flinging himself into the worn leather chair behind his desk. "If I were a violent man, I'd take a horsewhip to you. I'm tempted to do it anyway! Because of you, my daughter was subjected to terror, to public censure, to heartbreak! You seduced her in Colorado, I know damned well you did! Do you deny it?"

It was insane, but at that moment, Zack admired everything about the man; he was the sort of father Zack would have wanted—and wanted to be someday—a deeply concerned parent with strong principles about what was acceptable and what was not—a man of integrity and honesty who expected the same behavior from those around him. He intended for Zack to feel ashamed. He was succeeding.

"Do you deny you seduced my daughter?" he repeated angrily.

"No," Zack admitted.

"And then you sent her back here to confront the media and defend you to the world! Of all the cowardly, irresponsible—how can you face yourself or me or her, after that?"

"Actually, sending her back here was the only decent thing I did," Zack said, defending himself for the first time since the tongue-lashing had begun.

"Go on, I'm waiting to hear how you figure that."

"I knew Julie was in love with me. I refused to take her to South America and sent her back here instead for her sake, not mine."

"Your sense of decency was certainly short-lived, wasn't it! A few weeks later, you were scheming to have her join you."

He waited again, demanding an answer with his silence, and Zack reluctantly complied. "I thought she was pregnant, and I didn't want her to have an abortion or endure the humiliation of unwed motherhood in a small town."

Zack sensed a subtle reduction in the other man's hostility, but it wasn't evident in his next acid comment. "If you'd exercised any decency, any restraint over your *lust* in Colorado, you wouldn't have had to worry about her being pregnant, would you?"

Torn between anger, embarrassment, and amusement at Mathison's scornful, biblical use of the term *lust,* Zack lifted his brows and looked at him.

"I'll thank you for the courtesy of an answer, young man."

"The answer is perfectly obvious."

"And now," he said angrily, leaning back in his chair. "Now you come breezing back to town in your private plane to make her into a public spectacle again, and for what? So you can break her heart! I've heard and read and seen enough about you before you went to prison and after you got out to know what sort of life you lead in California, to know what sort of licentious, superficial, amoral life it has been—wild parties, naked women, drunkenness, dirty movies. How do you answer to that?"

"I have never made a dirty movie in my life," Zack replied, tacitly admitting to the other charges.

Jim Mathison almost smiled. "At least you aren't a liar. Are you aware that Paul Richardson is in love with her? He wants to marry her. He's asked for my blessing. He's a fine, decent man with principles. He wants a wife for life, not just until the next buxom blond movie star comes along and turns his head. He wants children. He's willing to make sacrifices for her—even to the extent of going to California to see you. He comes from a close, loving family like Julie does. They could have a wonderful life together. Well, what do you say to that?"

In the midst of a blaze of jealousy, Zack suddenly realized that Jim Mathison was merely using Richardson as a means to force Zack to face his shortcomings as Julie's potential husband, and he was also skillfully and deliberately maneuvering Zack into a position where he could either declare himself and lay his cards on the table or back off and go away. Despite the personal discomfort Mathison had deliberately subjected him to, Zack's admiration for the man doubled and he leaned back in his chair. "What I have to say is this," he began, responding to the list of Richardson's qualities in the order Mathison had given them: "Richardson may be a plaster saint, and he may be in love with her, but so am I. Furthermore, Julie loves me. I am not interested in buxom blondes or redheads or any woman except Julie. Forever. I, too, want children, just as soon as Julie is willing. I will make whatever sacrifices for her are necessary. I cannot change the way I lived my life before now, I can only change the way I live it from this point on. I cannot help the fact that my family was not close, I can only let her teach me how a family is supposed to be. If I can't have your blessing, I'd at least like your reluctant acceptance."

Mathison crossed his arms over his chest, his gaze direct. "I haven't heard the word *marriage* from you."

Zack smiled. "I thought it was a foregone conclusion."

"In whose mind? Has Julie actually agreed to marry you, I mean since you've come back?"

"There hasn't been time to ask her."

His brows shot up. "Not even during the hour that her phone was off the hook tonight? Or were you too busy trying to convince her to start that family you say you want?"

Zack had the appalling feeling that he was going to blush like a schoolboy.

"It seems to me," Mathison continued curtly, "that you have a distorted view of what is proper and decent. In your world, couples have sex, then babies, and *then* when they get around to it, they get married. That is not an acceptable order of things in Julie's world or God's world or mine!"

Restraining the urge to squirm in his chair, Zack said shortly, "I intended to ask her to marry me tonight. In fact I thought we could stop in Lake Tahoe on the way to California tomorrow and get married there."

Mathison lurched forward in his chair. "You what! You two have known each other for seven days, you've already slept together, and now you intend for her to drop everything and go away with you and then get married in some sleazy civil ceremony. She has a job, a family, and other people to consider. What do you think she is, some brainless pet you can snap a leash on and lead off to Disneyland? Where's your sense of justice and priorities! I expected better of you after the speech you made me a few minutes ago."

Zack walked straight into the trap. "I don't think I understand. What is it you expect me to do?"

Mathison sprung it. "I expect you to behave like a gentleman, to make a few sacrifices. In short, I would expect Julie's future husband to spend time here getting to know her, to treat her with *reverence* and *respect,* as God intended for us to treat our women, and then to ask her to marry him. Assuming she agrees, you will be engaged for a suitable time, and then you will be married. The honeymoon," he finished implacably, "takes place *after* the wedding. If you are willing to make all of these sacrifices, then, and only then, would I be willing to give my blessing or perform the ceremony, which, by the way, I feel certain is the only way Julie would feel truly and happily married. Am I making myself clear?"

Zack frowned. "Very."

Jim Mathison saw the frown and pounced. "If those few sacrifices of personal convenience and your physical satisfaction are already too much for you to make, then—"

"I didn't say they were too much," Zack interrupted, his thoughts hopelessly tangled up in the heretofore unconsidered realization that Julie would naturally want her father to perform the wedding ceremony.

"Fine, Zack," he said, using Zack's name for the first time. With a smile that was suddenly warm and even paternal, he said, "Then everything's settled."

Surfacing from his private thoughts, Zack caught the other man's pleased smile, realized he had been coerced into almost agreeing to something that was absolutely out of the question, and said shortly, "Not everything. I'm willing to stay in town as much as I can, but there is no reason for Julie and I to 'get to know each other' before I ask her to marry me, nor am I willing to wait for months for the wedding. I'll ask her to marry me right away. Once she agrees, as far as I'm concerned, we're engaged."

"You're engaged when you slide a ring on her finger. Formality and tradition exist for a reason, young man. Like celibacy before the wedding, they give a special and lasting meaning to the event itself."

"Fine," Zack said a little testily.

Mathison smiled, "When do you want to be married?"

"As soon as possible. A couple weeks from now at the most. I'll talk to Julie."

"You sure you don't want any help, Mom?" Julie called, watching her mother put out a tray of cookies on the dining room table.

"No dear. You children stay in the living room and have a nice talk. It's so good to see all three of you so happy."

Julie was almost more nervous than she was happy. Glancing at the closed door of her father's study, she looked at Ted and Katherine who were seated together on the sofa, teasing her warmly about Zack's speech in the gymnasium. "What on earth is going on in there?" she asked.

Ted grinned and glanced at his watch. "You know what's going on. Dad's giving one of his famous premarital lectures to the prospective groom."

"Zack hasn't actually asked me to marry him again."

Katherine looked at her in disbelief. "After the beautiful things he said to you in front of half the town tonight, do you have any doubt he wants to?"

"No, not really. But Dad's taking too long in there for one of his normal lectures."

"This one's taking longer," Ted said with unhidden enjoyment, "because Dad felt a paternal need to tear a strip off Zack first for kidnapping you and all that."

"Zack has already suffered more than enough for anything he did to me," Julie said feelingly.

Katherine swallowed a giggle and her Coke. "He's going to suffer a whole lot more if he takes the bait and agrees to the usual bargain."

"What bargain?" Julie asked.

"You know, the 'tradition-means-everything, no-sex-before-the-wedding, long-engagements-are-best' bargain Dad tries to extract from every prospective bridegroom."

Julie laughed. "Oh that. Zack will never agree to that. He's older, wiser, and more sophisticated than most of the men Dad deals with."

"He'll agree," Ted said with a laugh. "What choice does he have? Dad is not only clever or merely the minister who'll perform the wedding ceremony, he also happens to be your father. Zack knows he already has three strikes against him in Dad's book. He'll agree for your sake and for the sake of familial harmony."

"You mean you *hope* he does," Katherine teased, "because you did."

Ted leaned over and playfully nipped her ear. "Stop it, you're embarrassing Julie."

"Julie is laughing. You're the one who's blushing."

"I'm blushing, my talkative wife, because I'm remembering what was the longest, most painful month of my life and at the memory of what our wedding night was like as a result of one month's abstinence."

Katherine looked at him, Julie's presence momentarily forgotten. "It was beautiful," she argued. "Special—like the very first time for both of us. I think that's your father's whole purpose in asking people to agree to wait until the wedding night to make love, even if they've already been doing it."

"Does anyone care that I'm listening to this," Julie joked shakily.

The door to the study opened, and they all turned. Reverend Mathison looked pleased, Zack looked dazed and annoyed, and Ted's shoulders began to shake with laughter. "He went for it!" he choked. "He has that stunned, angry look they all have. My movie hero," he said, shaking his head. "All those posters of him that I used to have in my room, and he turned out to be a mere mortal after all, another piece of unsuspecting putty in Dad's hands. Prison couldn't break him, but Dad did."

Zack threw a speculative glance at the mirthful group in the living room as he walked forward, but Mrs. Mathison delayed him with an invitation to come into the dining room for cookies and he turned. "No, thank you, Mrs. Mathison," he said, glancing at his watch. "It's late. I need to find a hotel and check in."

She tossed a questioning glance at her husband, who smiled and nodded slowly, then she said, "We'd like very much for you to stay with us."

Zack considered the number of phone calls he would receive and make while he stayed in Keaton and the disruption he was likely to cause to their household, and he shook his head. "Thank you, but I think it would be better if I stayed in a hotel. I brought work with me, and I'll have more sent down here and probably some business meetings too," he threw in when she looked genuinely disappointed. "I think a suite in a hotel would be better."

He missed the odd, uneasy look Julie gave him at the mention of a suite, but he was anxious to leave, to order champagne sent up from room service, and then to take her in his arms and ask her to marry him with appropriate ceremony and atmosphere. "Would you mind taking me to the hotel?" he asked her.

81

"THIS IS IT," JULIE SAID A HALF HOUR LATER WHEN THEY pulled up before Keaton's only motel. "Keaton's best motel." Ted and Katherine had dropped them off at her house and they'd gotten Zack's suitcase and briefcases and Julie's car.

Zack looked in disbelief at the long ramshackle building with black doors at twelve-foot intervals that somehow reminded him of rotted teeth, and the empty swimming pool that practically sat on the shoulder of the highway, then he raised his gaze to the flashing neon sign above it and read it aloud: "The Rest Your Bones Motel," he repeated in disbelief. "There has to be another motel around here."

"I wish there was," she said on a suffocated laugh.

An old man with a Stetson and a cheek full of chewing tobacco was sitting in front of the office on a metal chair, enjoying the balmy evening when they pulled up to register. He stood up as Zack got out of the car. "Howdy, Julie," he called, identifying her with a brief glance through the windshield.

Zack abandoned all hope of a nice, anonymous trysting place and stalked into the office, his mood going from fair to poor.

"Mind if I keep this for a souvenir?" the manager asked when Zack scribbled his name on the registration form and shoved it across the desk.

"No."

"Zack Benedict," the manager uttered reverently, picking up the form and studying the signature. "Zack Benedict, right here, stayin' at my motel. Who would've guessed it could happen?"

"Not me," Zack said flatly. "I don't suppose you have a suite?"

"We got a bridal suite."

"You're kidding," Zack said, glancing over his shoulder at the uninviting building, and then he saw Julie leaning against the office door, her feet crossed at the ankles, her face aglow with mischievous laughter, and his spirits lifted crazily.

"The bridal suite's got a kitchenette," the manager added.

"How romantic. I'll take it," Zack said, and he heard the magic of Julie's muffled laughter. It made him smile.

"Let's go," he said, escorting her out of the office and toward his room while the manager followed them out and stood beneath the overhang. "Am I imagining it," he asked dryly as he opened the door to the bridal suite and stepped aside for her to proceed him, "or is that guy watching to see if you go in here."

"He's watching to see whether I go in here, whether or not we close the door, and how long I stay. By tomorrow, the whole town will know the answers to all three of these questions."

Zack turned on the wall switch, took one look at the suite, and quickly turned the lights back off. "How much time can we spend at your house without causing a lot of gossip?"

Julie hesitated, wishing he'd tell her he loved her again and what he wanted to do about it. "That depends on your intentions."

"I have very honorable intentions but they'll have to wait until tomorrow. I refuse to discuss them in a room with a red velvet heart-shaped bed and purple chairs."

Julie's relief came out in an explosion of musical mirth and Zack dragged her into his arms. Groping in the dark for her face, he cradled it between his hands, laughing while he kissed her, and then slowly, the laughter faded as she held him to her and kissed him back. "I love you," he whispered. "You make me so damned happy. You made hiding out in Colorado seem like fun. You make this suite from hell feel like a bridal bower. Even in prison, when I hated you, I'd dream of the way you dragged me home, half-frozen, and the way you danced with me and made love to me, and I'd wake up wanting you."

She brushed her fingertips over his lips and rubbed her cheek against his chest. "Someday soon, would you take me to South America, so we can stay on your boat? I dreamed of being there with you."

"It wasn't much of a boat. I used to have a large yacht. I'll buy another one for you and we'll take a cruise on it."

She shook her head. "I'd like to stay with you on the boat in South America, just the way we planned, even if it's only for a week."

"We'll do both."

Reluctantly, he let her go and steered her out the open door. "It's two hours earlier in California, and I have some phone calls and arrangements to make. When can I see you again?"

"Tomorrow?"

"Naturally," he said dryly. "How early?"

"As early as you'd like. It's a county holiday. There's a big parade, a carnival, picnic, the works, for the bicentennial celebration. It will go on all week."

"That sounds like fun," he said and was surprised because he rather meant it. "Pick me up at nine, and I'll buy you breakfast."

"I know just the place—best food in town."

"Really, where?"

"McDonald's," she teased, laughing at his appalled look, then she pressed a kiss to his cheek and left.

Still grinning, Zack closed the door and turned on the lights, then he walked over to the bed and reluctantly put his briefcase on it. Taking out his cellular phone, he made his first call to the Farrells, who he knew would be anxious to discover the outcome of his trip. He held on while Joe O'Hara went outside to get Matt and Meredith from among the party guests.

"Well?" Matt Farrell's voice was filled with expectation, "Meredith is here, and you're on the speaker phone. How's Julie?"

"Julie's wonderful."

"Are you married yet?"

"No," Zack said, thinking irritably of the agreement Julie's father foisted on him, "we're going steady."

"You're what?" Meredith sputtered. "I mean, we thought you'd be in Tahoe by now."

"I'm still in Keaton."

"Oh."

"At the Rest Your Bones Motel."

He heard Meredith's muffled laughter.

"In the bridal suite."

She laughed harder.

"It has a kitchenette."

She shrieked with mirth.

"Your pilot must be stuck here, too, poor devil. I should invite him over for poker."

"Watch out if you do," Matt warned dryly. "He'll walk away with most of your money."

"He won't even be able to see his cards in here. He'll be blinded by the red velvet heart-shaped bed and purple lounge chairs. How's the party?"

"I made a polite announcement that you were called away on urgent business. Meredith stepped in to oversee the staff and play hostess. Everything's fine."

Zack hesitated, thinking of the engagement ring he needed and of the superb jewels Bancroft & Company was famous for carrying in their exclusive stores. "Meredith, could I ask a favor?"

"Anything," she said with quiet sincerity.

"I need an engagement ring right away—tomorrow morning if possible. I know what I want, but I won't find it here, and if I show my face in Dallas, I'll be recognized. I don't want the press following me and descending on this town until the last possible minute."

She understood at once. "Tell me what you have in mind. Tomorrow morning, when our Dallas store opens, I'll phone the head of the Fine Jewelry Department and have her select several rings. Steve can pick them up by ten-fifteen and bring them to you."

"You're an angel. Here's what I want—"

82

THE CELEBRATION OF A BICENTENNIAL IN A SMALL TEXAS town, Zack realized the next day, was an elaborate affair, with a kickoff speech from the mayor and a week-long schedule of events that included parades down the main street, sports events, livestock shows, and a variety of entertainments.

"That's Mayor Addleson," Julie told him as they arrived at the park in the middle of town and stopped at the edge where they'd be seen by the fewest people. She nodded toward the tall man in his late forties who was walking briskly onto the pavilion, which was appropriately decked out in red, white, and blue bunting. "And that's his wife, Marian, in the yellow linen dress," she added, indicating a pretty woman in a chic dress and hat who was sitting among the honored guests on a specially erected grandstand at the side of the pavilion, watching her husband prepare to begin. "Mayor Addleson was widowed a long time ago," Julie provided informatively. "Marian was an interior designer in Dallas when he met her there two years ago. He brought her back here, and Daddy married them. They have a wonderful ranch outside of town and they're building a new house up on the hill. They're very nice."

Zack slid his arm around her from behind, pulling her trim buttocks against him, and smiled into her hair. "You *feel* very nice."

She leaned lightly against him, and he felt his body surge and harden. "So do you."

Swallowing, Zack diverted himself by concentrating on Mayor Addleson. Addleson's thick hair was the strange grayish yellow blond that seemed more common in Texas than anywhere Zack had ever been, but the mayor obviously shared every politician's love of pomp and speech making, because he talked for almost a half hour about the grand battle once fought on Keaton's soil and about the history of the town, beginning with its founders. Zack was mentally comparing the individual merits, or lack thereof, of the movie scripts he'd read last week, when he realized the mayor's speech was over and he was talking about Zack:

"Before we sound the cannon and open up the celebration, I'd like to spend just a minute talking about the special visitor we have in town. It's no secret from any of you that Zack Benedict is here right now or that he's visiting Julie Mathison. It's also no secret that the great state of Texas hasn't been very friendly or lucky for him in the past. I know how much y'all are hopin' to meet him and how eager we all are to change his impression of Texans, but folks, the best way to do that is to give him some space and let him get to know us in his own way. You all know what he's been through, and you've all seen the way people mob movie stars and pester them for autographs. Zack probably has nowhere in the world where he can relax and be treated like ordinary folks like to be treated. Except here. Let's show him what it's like to have a hometown like Julie's, where people care about each other and look after each other!"

That invocation was greeted with a loud burst of applause, a drum roll from the bandstand, and friendly grins and waves from hundreds of people aimed at Zack, which he politely returned.

To Zack's surprised pleasure, the townspeople adhered to the mayor's suggestion, and Zack had the best and most relaxing day in a public place that he could ever remember having in fifteen years. Nor was he immune to the mood of celebration and the uniquely Americana flavor of what was going on around him. As day drifted into evening, he had an amazingly enjoyable time doing foolishly simple things like visiting booths where homemade items from cakes to crocheted linens were on sale, devouring hot dogs slathered with mustard, and joking with Ted and Katherine about whether or not all the games in the booths were fixed or just the ones they'd tried to win. But then, he was with Julie, and as he'd already discovered in Colorado, she had a gift for making even the mundane seem like an adventure.

She was also a great favorite of the townspeople, and their affection for her seemed to tentatively include him, too—now that his words at the gymnasium last night gave them every reason to expect he'd come here "to do right by her." Zack was dying to prove it to them and to the world by sliding the engagement ring he'd chosen that morning onto her finger, but he was waiting for the right moment. After the calamity of their last attempt to exchange rings, he was adamantly determined that this attempt would make up for the grimness of the other, that it would be joyous, memorable, and lighthearted.

Now, as he walked with her through the noisy, brightly lit carnival grounds at sunset, he was well aware of the ten-carat radiant-cut diamond in his pocket as well as the smiling, curious glances of the hundreds of Keaton citizens who were enjoying the carnival rides and booths and all of whom were undoubtedly wondering if and when he was actually going to declare himself. Occasionally, he noticed people taking pictures of them, but they were discreet about it.

"Want to ride the ferris wheel?" Zack asked her, when Julie paused to look up at it.

"Only if you promise you won't make the seat rock," she said, pulling off a piece of her pink cotton candy and feeding it to him.

"I wouldn't dream of it," Zack lied, chewing it. "Julie, that stuff tastes terrible. How can you eat it? Give me another bite."

She laughed and pulled off another sticky pink glob and they both smiled at the couples who passed them with a friendly nod. "I meant what I said about rocking the seat," she warned when he dug in his pocket for money. "I'm . . . well . . . a little edgy about ferris wheels."

"You?" he said in disbelief. "The woman who nearly got us killed a few minutes ago in that flying rocket capsule thing when you made it spin."

"That was different. We were enclosed in a cage. Ferris wheels," she said as she tipped her head back looking at the very high ferris wheel, "are open and a little scary."

Zack was about to walk up to the ticket booth when a barker called out behind him, "Step right up and win a gen-u-ine gold-filled ring set with simulated jewels! Shoot five ducks and win your girl a ring, shoot ten, and win a giant teddy bear for her to cuddle."

Zack turned, glanced at the mechanical ducks moving in an endless row, at the fake shotguns propped in the booth, and the tray of rings with huge glittering fake "jewels" in every color from egg-yolk yellow to ruby red. And inspiration struck.

"I thought you wanted to ride the ferris wheel," Julie said, as he took her arm and turned her firmly around.

"First," he announced, "I want to win you a gen-u-ine gold-filled ring with a simulated jewel."

"How many chances do you . . . want?" the man in the booth said, his voice trailing off as he stared at Zack's face. "You sure look familiar, buddy." He took Zack's money and handed him the gun without taking his eyes off his face, then he turned to Julie. "Your boyfriend looks just like—you know—whathisname —the actor. You know—" he prompted her when Zack ignored him and raised the gun, testing the sight. "You know who I mean, don't you?"

Julie met Zack's sideways smile with a provocative one from beneath her lashes. "The good-looking guy?" she clarified, talking to the barker. "Rugged? Handsome? Dark hair?"

"Yeah, him!"

"Steven Seagal!" she joked, and Zack missed his shot.

Lowering the gun, he gave her an indignant look and raised it again.

"Nah, not him," said the man. "This guy's taller, a little older, better looking." Zack gave her a smug smile.

"Warren Beatty!" Julie cried, and he missed his second shot.

"Julie," he warned out of the side of his mouth, his shoulders shaking with laughter, "do you want a ring or not?"

"Not," she said smugly. "I want a teddy bear."

"Then stop drooling over my competition and let me shoot these damned ducks before we draw a bigger crowd."

She glanced around and saw that despite their obvious desire to adhere to the mayor's suggestion and leave Zack alone, a large group of townspeople had stopped to watch, drawn to the amazing spectacle of the real-life Zack Benedict reenacting a shoot-out scene, like something from one of his movies, except the targets were metal ducks, not Mafia hit men, spies, or bad guys.

Zack hit eight out of eight ducks and someone clapped, then hastily stopped. "Turn around, honey," Zack said. "You're making me nervous."

When she complied, Zack reached into his pocket, winked at the man behind the booth and quickly put the diamond engagement ring in the tray with the glass ones, then he fired twice more and deliberately missed. "Okay," he told Julie, picking up the tray, "turn around and pick out a ring."

Julie turned around. "What? No teddy bear?" she asked, oblivious to the gaping carnival barker who was staring open-mouthed at the ring tray.

"Sorry, I missed the last two shots. Which ring do you like?"

Julie glanced down at the rainbow of large yellow, pink, red, and dark blue stones glittering atop cheap gold settings. And she saw the diamond. Larger by far than all the glass stones, it sparkled and glowed, reflecting the revolving lights on the ferris wheel. She recognized the cut because it matched the diamonds in her wedding band, and when she looked up at Zack, she recognized the somber, tender look in his eyes. "Do you like it?" he asked.

The people who had watched him shoot sensed that something was happening, or perhaps it was the gaping stare of the man in the booth that drew them forward to get a closer look.

"I like it," Julie said softly, shakily.

"Shall we take it with us and find a place to put it on?"

She nodded wordlessly, he took the ring out, and when they turned, the small crowd of onlookers saw the grin on his face and began to smile. "Up there," Zack said, pulling her toward the ticket booth at the ferris wheel. "Quick," he said, laughing as the man in the booth called to the crowd in a loud, stunned voice. "That guy—the one who looks like Warren Beatty—just took the biggest damned diamond ring you've ever seen out of his pocket and gave it to her!"

Reverend and Mrs. Mathison were talking to the mayor and his wife and Katherine's parents, who'd flown in for the festivities. They were standing near the Tilt-a-Whirl when Katherine and Ted came running up followed by a group of their own friends. "It's official," Ted said, laughing. "Julie and Zack just got engaged." In a deliberate and successful effort to discomfit his father, he added, "With a ring Zack won in one of the booths."

"That doesn't sound very official to me," Reverend Mathison said, frowning.

"I was kidding, Dad. It's a real ring."

Everyone turned in delighted surprise, looking around for the engaged couple to congratulate them. "Where are they?" Mrs. Mathison said, beaming.

Katherine pointed to the ferris wheel, which was stopped now, with a crowd cheering uproariously at the base of it. "They're up there," Katherine said, smiling at the uppermost chair, "on top of the world."

By the time they reached the ferris wheel to offer congratulations, the crowd was chanting, "Kiss her, Zack! Kiss her!" and the photographer from the *Keaton Crier* was aiming his camera at the couple in the topmost chair and lending his voice to the effort.

With his arm around her, Zack tipped Julie's chin up with his free hand. "They aren't going to let us down until they see us kiss."

She bit her lip, her cheeks flushed with color, her eyes bright with love, her palm protectively covering the diamond ring he'd slipped on her finger. "I can't believe you did this here—in front of everyone. You hate publicity."

Zack tightened his arm, pulling her forward. "Not this publicity, I don't. The whole damned world," he whispered, lowering his head, "has witnessed our misery. Let them see what happens when a hardened escaped convict meets up with an angel who believed in him. Kiss me, Julie."

In the midst of the cheer that went up down below at the sight of the couple locked in an embrace, Mayor Addleson grinned at his wife and looked around at Ted. "Did your father get him to promise?"

Ted's shoulders shook with laughter. "Yep."

"Poor devil," Addleson said, looking up at the long, thorough kiss that Zack was giving his new fiancée. "He's not going to be able to stand much of that then."

"Nope."

"When's the wedding?"

"Zack said something about wanting it to happen in two weeks."

"Not soon enough," John Grayson, one of Ted's friends, put in with a knowing grin. He looked at his wife. "It'll seem like two years. Remember, Susan?"

She nodded, peeking at Katherine. "Your father-in-law is a truly treacherous man."

"And a very wise one," Mayor Addleson added, sobering.

"That's not," Marian Addleson reminded him, "the way you felt before our wedding, dear."

"No, but it was how I felt on our wedding night."

Grayson considered the kissing couple for a moment, then added, "I suppose he knows about the cold-shower trick."

83

JULIE, DON'T, DARLING. I CAN'T STAND MUCH MORE OF THIS," Zack muttered several nights, later, reluctantly pulling her arms from around his neck and sitting up on the sofa in her living room. After two days in the Rest Your Bones Motel, Zack had realized Julie's parents were genuinely hurt that he wasn't staying with them, and he'd gratefully checked out of the motel and accepted their invitation. The accommodations were much better and the food was wonderful, but he was sleeping in Julie's old bedroom, surrounded with reminders of her. During the day, while she was at school, teaching her classes, he worked at her house, going over scripts, talking to his staff in California, and discussing potential deals with producers on the telephone, and he was able to think about something besides his increasing sexual frustration. But when Julie came home, he took one look at her and desire inevitably led to foreplay, which invariably led to frustration, and it started all over again.

So fragile was his remaining hold on his self-control that, instead of staying home with her in the evenings, he'd begun preferring to spend them with Julie and her friends at the local dinner and entertainment spots. Two nights ago, he'd actually ended up necking with her in the back row of the local movie theater, where he knew things couldn't go too far, and the night before, he'd suggested they go bowling, where he knew things couldn't go anywhere at all.

Swearing under his breath, Zack set Julie firmly away from him and got up from the sofa. "I should never have let your father talk me into this ridiculous notion of premarital celibacy. It's archaic, it's pointless, and it's juvenile! He did it to get even with me for kidnapping you. The man is clever and he's sadistic! The only time I felt right about this promise was in church on Sunday."

Julie bit back a helpless smile and said with an attempt at gravity, "Why do you suppose that happened?"

"I know why it happened! The hour in church was the only time in the past week I haven't had an erection."

This was not the first time Zack had mentioned the bargain he'd made with her father, but he was so sensitive about it that Julie was almost afraid to tell him that he was not an isolated victim. He had a great deal of pride, and he was essentially a very private person. Because of that, she wasn't certain how he'd react to the discovery that every male in town who'd been married by her father knew exactly what was going on. She looked up as he began to pace in front of her.

"I am thirty-five years old," he informed her bitterly. "I am a reasonably sophisticated man with an above-average IQ, and I not only feel like a sex-starved, randy eighteen-year-old, I'm behaving like one! I've taken so many cold showers, your mother must think I have a cleanliness obsession. I am becoming irritable."

Julie shoved her hair off her forehead, stood up, and looked at him with exasperated amusement. "I would never have noticed."

With an irritated sigh, he stacked the scripts he'd been reading on the table and said, "What do you think we should do tonight?"

"Have you considered the sedative benefits of reorganizing the kitchen cabinets?" she teased, her shoulders lurching. "That always worked for me. We could do it together."

Zack opened his mouth to snap a retort, but the phone rang, so he jerked it up and took his frustration out on whoever was on the other end of the line. "What the hell do you want?"

Sally Morrison, his publicist in California said dryly, "Good evening, Zack. So nice to talk to you. I'm calling to talk to Julie. She needs to tell me now whether you want the wedding invitations delivered by limousine tomorrow morning or by courier. I've already phoned the lucky fifty people who are going to receive a coveted invitation, so they'll have time to make arrangements to be in Texas bright and early Saturday morning. No one declined. Betty and I," she added referring to his secretary, "have arranged for limos to meet them at DFW and get them to Keaton, and I've reserved blocks of suites for them on Saturday night in the Dallas hotels that met your approval."

Some of Zack's former annoyance faded. He waited until Julie walked into the dining room, then he lowered his voice and said, "Does she have any idea who's going to be here?"

"No, boss. In accordance with your instructions to surprise her, I told her to count on having fifty of your most boring business associates in attendance. Fifty-one, including me."

"What about the press?" Zack asked. "How are you keeping them out of our hair? They know I'm here, and they know I'm getting married Saturday. It's all over the network newscasts. I've only seen a couple reporters hanging around and they keep their distance. I figured they'd be swarming over us like locusts by now."

Sally hesitated for a pregnant moment. "Didn't Julie tell you how she decided to handle the press?"

"No."

"Then you'd better ask her. If you don't approve, I'm going to have a hell of a time trying to back out of our deal with them."

"What deal?" Zack demanded.

"Ask Julie after we hang up. Can I talk to her now?"

Zack held the phone out and looked over his shoulder. "Julie, Sally needs to talk to you."

"Be right there," she said. She walked in carrying the ever-present tablet she used to keep track of whatever details seemed to occupy women when a wedding was imminent, and he watched her pull off her right earring and tuck the phone between her shoulder and chin. "Hi, Sally," she said with a pleasant softness that made Zack feel like an irascible, belligerent, selfish jerk who couldn't control his own sexual urges and manage to behave like a gentleman. "What's up?" She listened for a minute and then said, "I'll ask Zack."

She smiled at him, which made Zack feel worse, and said, "Sally still wants to know whether to have your invitations delivered to the California people by limousine tomorrow or whether to use a messenger service." She consulted her tablet. "Using limousines will cost four times as much."

"Limousines," Zack said.

"Limousines," Julie repeated into the phone.

When she hung up, Zack looked at her and all of his impatience turned to admiration. Despite the incredible pressure Julie was under, getting ready for their wedding at the end of the week, she never lost her cool. Rachel had spent months of time on their wedding and a quarter million dollars of Zack's money to create a three-ring media circus that required the efforts of two publicists and an army of servants, consultants, and assistants to pull off, and Rachel had been used to dealing with the pressures of public life. Even so, by the day of the wedding, Rachel had been behaving like a frantic virago for weeks and popping tranquilizers like M&Ms.

Julie had spent a week on their wedding with only the help of Katherine and the long-distance aid of Zack's competent California staff. At the same time, she had continued with her regular job and arranged to sublease her house, and she had neither lost her temper nor slighted Zack. Because the entire citizenry of Keaton had gone so far out of their way to make Zack feel comfortable and welcome and because Julie was so much a part of their town, the decision had been made to limit the guests at the afternoon wedding ceremony to family and close friends, but to invite all of the Mathison's vast circle of friends and acquaintances to the evening reception, which was scheduled to take place in the park. The decision to invite 650 people instead of having a small, intimate reception had been made at Zack's urging. In the days that he had been here, he'd enjoyed more honest companionship with decent, down-to-earth people than he'd ever known in his entire life. Despite his complaints, he'd thoroughly enjoyed the simple things they'd done together while he was here. He'd liked dancing with her in a restaurant where friends of theirs joined them without ever intruding; he'd loved going to the movie in town with her, eating stale popcorn, necking in the back row, and then walking her home, holding her hand in the balmy night air. Last night, he'd played pool at the senior Cahills' house with Ted and his friends, while Julie, Katherine, and the other wives brought in food and cheered their men on, and then he'd watched in amazement as Julie took on the winner—and beat him.

Somehow she'd managed to do all that as well as make arrangements with a dozen local women to handle the catering for the reception, hire musicians, go over the music selections, order flowers from the local florist, and arrange for white canopies to be sent down from Dallas to be used in the park by the caterers. Zack, who'd listened to the arrangements periodically, had the amused hope that this second wedding reception of his would make up for the decorum and beauty it was probably going to lack with warmth and a festive atmosphere. If not, it had all the earmarks of becoming a ludicrously corny disaster. In which case, he devoutly hoped it would rain.

The only thing that had given Julie momentary pause was the question of a wedding gown and gowns for Katherine, Sara, and Meredith, who she'd decided should be her only three attendants. Meredith had volunteered the solution to that problem when Julie called to invite her to be in their wedding: She'd had pictures of all the wedding gowns and attendants gowns available from Bancroft & Company's exclusive bridal salon sent down by overnight mail for Julie to peruse. Julie had settled on three possibilities, which were picked up the next day in Chicago by the Farrells' pilot and flown to Keaton. Rachel had deliberated for weeks over the selection of a wedding gown; Julie, Katherine and Sara deliberated for two hours, made their selection, and brought their gowns to the Eldridge twins to be altered to fit. Meredith, who was back in Chicago with Matt, was being fitted for hers there.

During all that time, the only disagreement Zack and Julie had took place the night of their engagement, and it was about Zack's adamant insistence on paying for the wedding. He'd finally settled it in private with Julie's father, who, thankfully, had absolutely no conception of the cost of a wedding gown from Bancroft & Company or jet fuel, which Zack was going to compensate Matt for, or much of anything else. Zack had "graciously relented" enough to let Reverend Mathison contribute $2,000 toward the cost of the wedding, then he volunteered—with equal graciousness and less honesty—to have his accountant in California handle the tedious business of paying all the bills and to refund Reverend Mathison any excess.

Now, as Zack looked at Julie who was making notes on her tablet, he thought of all the pressure she was under and how gracefully she coped with everything. In comparison, his own days had been wonderfully peaceful and filled with accomplishment. Free from the constant interruptions he'd have had in California, he'd been able to read scripts, which was his most pressing current task, and consider what he wanted to do as his first film project. The studio heads and producers and bankers he needed to meet with would all wait until he got back home. His dramatic escape from prison, his recapture, his subsequent release, and now his marriage to the young teacher who'd been his hostage had combined to make him into an even bigger "legend" than he'd been before he went to prison. He didn't need to read *Variety* to know he was now the hottest property in the film business. Beyond attending to his work, the only other problem he'd needed to handle personally in the last week had been the issue of Julie's public image. Originally, when the tapes of his arrest in Mexico City had been shown, Julie had been regarded by the world as a heroine who'd trapped a deranged mass murderer. A few weeks later, when Zack had been proved innocent and released from prison, those same tapes had made him into a heroic martyr to police brutality and Julie into a treacherous bitch who'd betrayed him. Rather than let her continue to suffer from the taint of that, Zack had quietly sent a copy of the tape he'd gotten from Richardson to a friend at CNN without first consulting with Julie. Within twenty-four hours of the first broadcast of it, the world had reacted to Julie's hysterical suffering just as Zack had done when he saw the tape.

Now, as he remembered all that had transpired in her life in the last week, Zack felt guilty and ashamed for his irascibility over what was, after all, only two weeks of enforced celibacy in the presence of a woman he desired more than he'd have imagined possible. Walking over to her, he took the tablet out of her hands, kissed her forehead, and said softly, "You are an amazing woman, sweetheart. Unfortunately, you're marrying an oversexed, bad-tempered jerk who happens to want you desperately."

She leaned forward and kissed him with enough ardor to make him groan and move her away again. "All you have to do," she reminded him, "is either break your word or tell my father his deal with you is off."

"I'm not going to break my damned word."

She chuckled and shook her head, picked up the tablet again, and pulled the pencil out of her shiny hair as if she'd already forgotten the kiss that still had his blood running hot. "I know. I'd be disappointed if you did."

"It might help," Zack said, irrationally irked by the same patience that he'd admired only moments before, "if I thought this sexless arrangement was driving you just half as crazy as it's driving me."

Julie tossed the tablet aside and stood up, and he realized for the first time that either she wasn't nearly as serene about the wedding plans and their enforced celibacy as he'd thought or else his own disposition was wearing her down. Or all three. "We're supposed to be on the baseball field tonight, remember?" she said testily. "This is a very special game between the Little League team I've helped to coach all year and our rivals in Perseville. You agreed to umpire, and everybody's all excited about that. Let's not argue. Or if we're going to disagree, then save it for the game."

Zack did, and they did.

Three hours later, with two stunned Little League teams looking on and the bleachers filled with amazed parents, Zack Benedict reaped the unpleasant rewards of a week of unjust impatience he'd inflicted on his overstressed fiancée.

Crouched behind home plate during the end of the seventh inning, with the bases loaded and the score tied, Zack watched from behind his obligatory umpire's mask as Julie's second star runner slid toward home base. "Out!" he called, throwing up his arm in the ritualistic symbol. As he'd already discovered during the past seven innings, Texans took their sons' Little League baseball games seriously, and not even a famous movie star who'd they'd all begun to like was immune from the indignant outrage aimed at any umpire who made an unpopular, if accurate, call. The crowd from Keaton booed and yelled their disapproval at him.

To Julie, who was seated on the coach's bench on the sidelines, Zack's call against her team was not only unpopular, it looked as wrong and unjust as his last two calls had seemed. This time she didn't merely grind her teeth, she shot off the bench and marched onto the field to confront him. "Are you crazy!" she burst out to Zack's amazed disbelief. "He was safe!"

"He was out!" Zack said.

She plunked her hands on her hips, oblivious to the shouts and laughter beginning to come from the crowd who was watching the argument, and said furiously, "You're taking out your ridiculous frustration with me on my team and I won't stand for it!"

Zack looked up at her from his crouching position, his own temper beginning to ignite at this unjust—and embarrassing—public assault on his judgment and sportsmanship. "He was out! Now, sit down on that bench where you belong," he said, pointing to it. Too late, he realized that the laughter that followed Julie as she angrily obeyed and marched back to the bench was going to scrape her strained temper to the breaking point.

Her third batter made two strikes, wound up, and stepped away from a pitch that missed being a bad one by a hair. "Strike 3!" Zack called, and because it had been such a close call, even from his vantage point, he wasn't at all surprised when the crowd roared with outraged disapproval. He was, however, very surprised when Julie shot off the bench, shouting at her dejected team to stay on the field and marched over to him like a bristling virago. "You need glasses!" she exploded, shaking with anger. "That was a ball, not a strike, and you know it!"

"He's out!"

"He is not! You're so busy trying to prove to everyone how unbiased you are that you're cheating my team!"

"He's out and you're going to be out, too, if you keep this up."

"You wouldn't dare throw me out of this game!"

Zack slowly stood up. "You are making a scene," he bit out. "Sit down!"

"That wasn't a scene!" she flung back and to his disbelief, she kicked dirt on home plate so he'd have to brush it off and then on his shoes. "*This* is a scene!" she said furiously.

"You're out of the game!" Zack blasted back, throwing his arm up in the unmistakable gesture of an umpire ejecting a coach, and the balmy night exploded with boos and cheers and roars and applause as Julie marched off the field. "Play ball!" Zack yelled, gesturing the other team off the field, and returning to his crouch behind home plate. From the corner of his eye, he watched the stiff set of Julie's shoulders, the gentle sway of her hips, and the breeze tumbling her hair around her shoulders as she walked over to the bench and grabbed her sweater. He was going to regret his action, Zack realized. She was going to make sure he did.

Young Willie Jenkins was of a similar opinion. As Willie walked off the field past Zack, he warned in his gravelly carrying voice, "You're in deep shit, Zack."

Julie's team lost 4 to 3. When the losers and the losers' parents gathered at a local restaurant for the meal and drinks that Zack had understood were a ritual after every game, Julie was there waiting for them. She had words of consolation and approval for all her boys and nothing whatsoever to say to Zack when he tried to hand her something to drink. The other adults seemed willing to forget that his call had cost their team the game, and several of them offered to buy him a beer, but Julie deliberately turned her back to him and continued talking to Katherine and Sara Mathison and some other friends of hers.

Left with no choice except to either try in public to sooth her ruffled feathers, which he sure as hell wasn't going to do, or else retreat to the bar where he saw Ted, Carl, John Grayson, and Mayor Addelson having pizza after the game, Zack decided on the latter. Ted saw him heading toward them and turned fully around, leaning his elbows on the bar behind him. "That was a bad move you made during the game, Zack," he said with a grin.

"Very bad," Carl agreed.

"Really bad," Mayor Addelson seconded, chuckling and tossing a handful of peanuts into his mouth.

"It was a good call," Zack said flatly.

"Might've been a good call," Addleson said, "but it was a bad move."

"The hell with it," Zack said, angrier than he would have believed possible because she was still ignoring him. "If she can't take the heat, she shouldn't get near the fire!"

For some reason, that simple, trite platitude caused all four men to guffaw with laughter.

Zack ignored them, his anger building steadily at the sudden realization of the absurd, undignified, unjust situation she'd stuck him in. He was thirty-five years old, he was worth over $100 million, and except for five years in prison, he'd spent his life eating in the finest restaurants, staying in the best hotels, and fraternizing with brilliant, talented, famous people like himself. Instead of that, he was now relegated to eating pizza while standing up in a crass restaurant in the thriving metropolis of Snake Naval, Texas, while being ignored by someone who should feel honored that he wanted to marry her! He had a good mind to march her out of the restaurant, lay down the law to her, and then take her straight to bed like any adult male deserved to be able to do with the woman he intended to marry. That wasn't a bargain he'd made with her father, it was malicious, petty revenge on the part of some Bible-thumping, arrogant, manipulative asshole . . .

Zack shoved away from the bar.

Mayor Addelson's hand landed heavily on his shoulder, and he said in a paternal voice, "Take some advice from a man who's already been where you are: Don't do it."

"What?" Zack snapped.

Ted leaned around the mayor and grinned at Zack. "Have yourself something cold to drink, eat a hamburger, then go home and take another cold shower and sit tight for another week. Someday, you'll look back on this and laugh."

"I don't know what the hell you're talking about."

"We're talking about what is generally known around town as the Mathison Method of Premarital Misery," Ted said mildly. "It is my father's well-intentioned way of restoring the element of suspense and anticipation to the wedding night in an age where he feels couples are deprived of the magic because they grab it prematurely."

Zack's jaw tightened with fury in the mistaken belief that Julie's father had actually gone around town, telling everyone about the ridiculous bargain he'd foisted on Zack in retaliation for kidnapping his daughter. "What did you say?" he demanded.

John Grayson heard his question and leaned around Ted. "He's going deaf already." With an attempt at lewd levity, he added, "You know what they say that comes from doing?"

Ted took a swallow of his drink. "No, you go blind, not deaf, from doing that."

"What the fuck are you talking about?"

"We're talking about you, my friend," Ted said. "It is not Julie who can't take the 'heat,' it's you. Just like it was us. Half the men in this town got talked into the same bargain you made, and most of us—the ones who stuck with it—ended up picking roaring fights over nothing with our wives-to-be."

The fury and frustration Zack had been feeling evaporated in a flash of stunned disbelief mixed with mindless hilarity at the absurdity of what he was hearing.

"Tell him, Mayor," Ted invited.

"It's hell. I've got ten years on you, son, and I couldn't believe how bad I wanted something partly because I agreed not to have it. It takes its toll on the women, too, only I am of the opinion their discomfort is lessened by their suppressed enjoyment of seeing the male of the species reduced to a state of desperate need of them. That last part about women," he added with a grin, "isn't my theory, it was a generalization that came from a professor of sociology I had during my second year at A&M. Where did you go to college, by the way? You've got the look of a Yankee, but the accent's a little off."

Still torn between annoyance and disbelief over the Mathison Method, Zack hesitated, knowing Addelson was trying to diffuse the situation, then he looked at Julie's pretty profile and considered the amusing fact that his sexual frustration was known by, and understood by, most of the other males in the restaurant, and he capitulated with an irritated sigh. "USC."

"What was your major?"

"Finance and film."

"Dual major?"

Zack nodded, his eyes on Julie, still unwilling to make a second public attempt to soothe her unjust anger at him.

At the far end of the bar, Ed Sandell hooked his scuffed boot over the rung of his stool and wiped the back of his sunburned neck with his handkerchief, then he looked at the other two ranch hands with him. "My sister, Holly, met Benedict at church on Sunday," he said, nodding toward Zack, who was standing at the juke box. "She said he's nice."

"He's a pansy," Jake Barton said, shoving his hat back on his head. "All those Hollywood types are."

"No way," Martin Laughlin disagreed. "I mean, the guy spent five years in the pen doing hard time."

"Big deal. He's still a pansy. Look at those jeans he's wearin'. Right off some de-sign-er rack."

"C'mon, Jake," Laughlin argued. "He not only spent five years in prison, but he had enough guts to escape."

"He got caught, too. He's a pansy," Jake said flatly.

Ed Sandell signaled to the waitress and said idly, "He umpired the game with Perseville tonight. Julie Mathison hassled him over a call he made, and he threw her out of the game."

Jake Barton looked up. "No shit?"

"Nope."

His expression filled with a dawning respect, Jake looked round at Zack Benedict, then he glanced at the waitress with a grin. "Tracy," he said, "bring Mr. Benedict a drink, and put it on my tab."

Across the room, Julie stole a glance at Zack. He caught her, his gaze leveling on hers, his expression impassive. Waiting. The last remnants of her anger died. She loved him so much, and they'd been through so much. She'd been wrong tonight, and she knew it. She wished she'd let him make amends earlier when they first got here, so that she didn't have to swallow her pride and go to him now, when everyone was sure to be watching. On the other hand, she decided, excusing herself to the people standing and talking to her, it was insane to waste another minute of their lives in this ridiculous standoff. When she reached Zack, she nodded to the mayor, her brothers, and John Grayson, then she shoved her hands into the pockets of her shorts, hesitating.

"Well?" Zack said mildly, trying not to notice the way her T-shirt stretched delightfully across her breasts.

"I'd like to order something to eat," she said.

Disappointed that she wasn't going to give him the courtesy of an apology, Zack looked up and nodded to the waitress, who hurried to their side.

"What's it gonna be, folks?" Tracy asked, hiding her unease over their widely known quarrel on the baseball field by staring at the pad and pencil in her hand.

"I can't decide," Julie said. Shifting her gaze from the waitress to her fiancé, she solemnly asked, "Should I order crow, Zack? Or humble pie?"

Zack's lips twitched with laughter. "What do you think?"

Julie looked at the waitress, who was trying unsuccessfully to keep her face straight. "An order of each, please, Tracy."

"With extra cheese and pepperoni," Zack added, switching their order to a pizza and grinning as he looped his arm around Julie's shoulders, pulling her tightly against his side. Waiting until Tracy stepped away, Julie called out, "Oh, and bifocals for the umpire, too, Tracy."

A silent sigh of relief swept around the restaurant, and the laughter and noise escalated dramatically.

They walked home in the balmy spring night, holding hands. "I like it here," Zack told her as they turned up her sidewalk. "I didn't realize how badly I needed some normalcy. I hadn't stopped to relax since the day I walked out of prison."

When she opened the front door and started to go inside, he shook his head and stayed on the porch. "Don't tempt me again," he teased, pulling her close for what he intended to be a brief kiss. His lips brushed hers, and he started to let her go, but she tightened her arms around his neck, kissing him back with all the love and apology in her heart. Zack lost the battle, and his mouth opened hungrily on hers, his hands shifting restlessly over the sides of her breasts, then cupping her buttocks and holding her tightly against his aroused body while he kissed her until they were both on fire.

When he finally pulled his mouth from hers, she kept her arms around his neck and rubbed her cheek against his chest, a kitten with the claws she'd shown him earlier sheathed now. Her body was still pressed tightly to his and Zack was debating about the wisdom of torturing himself with another kiss when she tipped her head back, smiling invitingly into his eyes. He felt his entire body tighten and surge in response to that provocative look, and he reluctantly shook his head. "No more, my beautiful little jock. I'm already so turned on that I can hardly stand here. And besides," he belatedly added, trying to look stern, "I still haven't forgiven you for not telling me your father inflicts his miserable bargain on every male who asks him to perform the wedding ceremony."

In the moonlight, he watched her eyes light with an embarrassed smile. "I was afraid it would make you more uncomfortable if you knew everyone else knew what you were going through."

"Julie," he said, pulling her hips tighter against his arousal to illustrate his next words, "I could not possibly be more uncomfortable than I am now."

"Me either!" she said so forcefully that he burst out laughing and kissed her again, then he gently moved her away. "You make me very happy," he said with a tender grin. "I've had more fun with you than I've had in my entire life."

84

SEATED AT MR. MATHISON'S DESK TWO DAYS BEFORE THE wedding, Zack looked up from the script he was reading and smiled absently at Mary Mathison. "Zack, dear," she said, looking a little distressed as she put a plate of freshly baked cookies on the desk, "could I ask you for a special favor?"

"Absolutely," he said, reaching toward the plate.

"Don't spoil your appetite with too many cookies," she warned.

"I won't," he promised with a boyish grin. In the nearly two weeks he'd stayed in their home, Zack had developed a deep, genuine affection for his future in-laws. They were like the parents he'd never had, and their home was filled with all the laughter and love that his had lacked. Jim Mathison was intelligent and kind. He stayed up late, getting to know Zack, beating him at chess, and telling him wonderful stories about Julie and Ted's childhood. He treated Zack as if he were his adopted son, warned him about saving money and being thrifty, and sternly advised him not to make any R-rated movies. Mary Mathison mothered Zack, scolded him about working too hard, and then sent him to town to do errands for her as if he were her own son. To Zack who had never been sent to a butcher shop or a dry cleaners in his adult life, it had been both touching and disconcerting to be handed a list of errands and sent on his way. It had also been strangely pleasant to have shop owners smile at him and ask after his new family. "How's Mary holding up with all the wedding plans under way?" the butcher asked, handing Zack a package of chicken wrapped in white paper. "She's looking after her blood pressure, isn't she?"

The owner of the dry cleaners handed Zack an armful of table linens that he'd cleaned. "No charge," he said. "We're all doing our part for the wedding, and we're happy to do it. You're marrying into a great family, Mr. Benedict."

"The best," Zack said and he felt that way.

Now, he hid a concerned frown when he saw the worry that Mary Mathison was trying to conceal as she smoothed her apron and looked at him. "What favor did you want?" he prodded. Teasingly, he added, "If it's peeling more onions like yesterday, it'll cost you an extra batch of cookies."

She perched on the edge of a chair. "It's nothing like that. I need some advice—well, reassurance actually."

"About what?" Zack asked, prepared to reassure her about anything at all.

"About something Julie did and that I encouraged her to do. I need to ask you a hypothetical question—as a man."

Zack leaned back in the chair, giving her his undivided attention. "Go ahead."

"Let's say that a man—my husband, for example," she said guiltily, and Zack instantly assumed the male under discussion was definitely Jim Mathison, "let's say that he had an elderly relative who he'd quarreled with a very long time ago, and I knew for a fact that this elderly relative very much wanted to make up with him before it was too late. If we—Julie and I—also knew that Julie's wedding might be the last—and best—opportunity for that, would we be wrong or right to invite that relative here without telling him?"

Zack suppressed the uncharitable and amusing thought that this was his opportunity to repay his father-in-law for his insufferable bargain. He did not, however, think Julie and Mrs. Mathison's scheme was a good one, and he was about to say that, when she added meekly, "The problem is, we've already done it."

"I see," Zack said, smiling a little. "In that case, there's nothing to do but hope for the best."

She nodded and stood up, retying her apron. "That's what we thought. The important thing to remember," she added in a meaningful voice as she started to leave, "is that it's wrong to carry grudges. The Bible warns us to forgive those who trespass against us. The Lord made that very, *very* clear."

Zack looked suitably grave as he replied, "Yes, ma'am, that's what I've heard."

"Call me Mom," she corrected him, then she walked forward and put her arm around his shoulder for a hug of maternal approval that made him feel very young. And very special. "You're a fine man, Zack. A very fine man. Jim and I are proud to have you join our family."

An hour later, he looked up again as Julie returned from her classes and peered over his shoulder. "What's that?" she asked kissing his cheek, her hands on his shoulders.

"The script for a film I think I'd like to do. It's called *Last Interlude,* but it has some major problems that need a lot of work."

He told her a little about the story and the problems and she listened attentively. When they'd exhausted the subject, she said hesitantly. "I'd like to ask you for an important favor. Tomorrow isn't just my last day of teaching regular classes, it's also my last night with the women I've been teaching to read. It would mean a great deal if they thought you made a special effort just to meet them. I'd especially like you to meet Debby Sue Cassidy. She's so smart, and she's so down on herself because she thinks the fact she can't read like a college grad after a few months proves she's hopeless. She's very well read—from books on tape," Julie clarified when he looked blank, "and she has a wonderful way of saying things very simply and yet making you *feel* what she's saying. She wants to write a book someday."

"Doesn't everyone?" he teased.

She gave him an odd, guilty look, then she nodded. "Probably. But don't discount her. With a little encouragement from someone she particularly admires—"

"Like me?"

Julie laughed and kissed his forehead. "How'd you guess?"

"What time do you want me to appear tomorrow?"

"Around seven. That will still give us plenty of time to be at the rehearsal."

"It's a date. By the way, one of the twin ladies stopped me when I was in town and made me come into her shop to see their needlework. I'm no expert, but it looked really good."

"You city fellers are all alike," she teased. "You think talent only flourishes in big cities. Our local florist gets selected by the Florists Association to head up a team that decorates the White House for the Inaugural Ball! Just wait until you see how your wedding reception turns out. All the women who are working on it are also going to be guests, too, so they're doubly eager to make it wonderful for us."

"As long as you're there and we're married, it will be wonderful," Zack said, cautiously refraining from venturing an opinion on the competence of the ladies working on the reception.

Without warning, she turned somber and a little anxious. "I'll be there. Right now, the important thing is that you love me enough to forgive me if I were to do something that might seem foolish or even very wrong to you."

"This doesn't involve another man does it?"

"Of course not!"

"In that case," Zack said magnanimously, "you'll find me the most forgiving of men. Where you and other men are concerned, however, I seem to have a streak of possessive jealousy a foot wide," he added, thinking of Richardson. "Now, what have you done that's either foolish or wrong?"

"Oh, I didn't say I'd actually done anything like that," she evaded. "It was just a rhetorical question. I have to help Mother with dinner," she added beating a sudden retreat.

"Are you certain nothing's wrong?"

"There's nothing wrong yet," she said unanswerably and vanished.

Despite Julie's assurance, Zack had the feeling all through dinner that something was definitely bothering Julie and her parents. As soon as the dishes were cleared away, Reverend and Mrs. Mathison announced their intention to visit friends and took themselves off with an abrupt haste that added to Zack's growing sense that something was odd, then Julie declined his offer to help in the kitchen, which was also unusual, so he returned to the study, pondering their strange behavior. He was looking over some legal documents his lawyer had sent him when she reappeared in the doorway a half hour later.

"Zack," she said, her smile a little too bright, "there's someone here to see you."

Zack got up, walked into the living room, and stopped dead, his gaze riveting on the elderly woman who was standing in the center of the room, a cane in her hand. Her voice sounded exactly as he remembered it—forceful, cool, and arrogant. With a regal nod of her head, she said, "It's been a long time, Zachary."

"Not long enough," he snapped. Turning the freezing blast of his gaze on Julie, he demanded, "What the hell is the idea?"

"The idea," Julie said calmly, "is for you to listen to what your grandmother needs to tell you." Zack started to turn his back and walk out, but Julie put her hand on his sleeve. "Please, darling. For my sake. Make it my wedding present. I'll go into the kitchen and make some tea."

Zack yanked his gaze from her face and passed a contemptuous glance over the old woman. "Say whatever it is you came to say and then get the hell out of my life and stay out!"

Instead of slashing at him verbally, she nodded and said in a halting voice, "I came to tell you how . . . how grievously sorry I am for the things I have done to you."

"Fine," Zack said sarcastically. "Now get out."

"I also came to ask you to forgive me."

"Don't be ridiculous."

"And to tell you that I—I . . ." Her voice trailed off and she looked helplessly to Julie for assistance, but Julie had already gone to the kitchen. Holding out her hand in a gesture of appeal, she whispered, "Zachary, please."

Zack looked down at the aristocratic hand held out to him; it was older now and too thin, her gold wedding band the only adornment on it. When he refused to take it, she dropped her hand to her side and said with a proud lift of her chin, "I will not beg you." Turning toward the windows, she straightened her shoulders and, looking out at the quiet street, said, "However, I came to explain things to you, and I shall do it." She was quiet for a moment, and when she spoke, there was an uncertainty in her voice that Zack had never heard before. "Shortly before Justin died, I had gone upstairs to put a vase of fresh flowers on the table near the landing. I heard the two of you quarreling in his room. You were quarreling about who should take Amy Price to the dance at the country club . . ." She drew a shaky breath and then said, "A few minutes later there was a gunshot, and Justin was dead."

Glancing over her shoulder, she said bitterly, "I knew you were lying when you told the police you'd fired the gun accidently, I could see it in your eyes. Only I—I thought you were lying about killing him accidently."

Zack looked at the bleak sorrow on her face and steeled himself not to react, but he was amazed that she'd heard him quarreling with Justin and belatedly aware of how damning that must have seemed to her. He'd actually quarreled with Justin for trying to back out of taking Amy Price to the dance and insisting he was doing it for Zack's sake.

"Please," she said hoarsely, "say something!"

Standing off to the side, Julie gently interceded when Zack would not. "Mrs. Stanhope, why didn't you tell the police about Zack's quarrel with Justin?"

Margaret Stanhope looked down at her folded hands atop the cane as if ashamed of her weakness. "I couldn't," she said. "I couldn't bear the sight of Zachary, but neither could I bear the thought of his being sent to prison. And so," she finished, raising her gaze to Zack's impassive face, "I sent you away, out of my sight. Away from your home and your brother and sister. I knew you would survive very well," she added, her voice gruff with emotion. "You see . . . I knew you were the strongest of my grandchildren, Zachary." She drew another harsh breath and continued, "And the smartest. And the proudest." When Zack still didn't react, she said, "Your grandfather made you and Foster promise never to tell me that Justin killed himself or why he did. Foster broke that promise the day you were let out of prison. He felt too many injustices had already been done you, and he couldn't bear the burden of his promise anymore. Now it is I who must bear the burden for all the wrongs I've done you. It was I who robbed you of your brother and sister, I who cast you out of your rightful home, I who made Julie believe you were truly capable of murder. And it was I who frightened her into betraying you to the authorities."

Finished, she waited for him to say something, and when he didn't, she looked helplessly to Julie. "I told you he would not forgive. He is too much like me to accept a mere apology for the unforgivable." She turned and stepped toward the door, then stopped and looked at Zack with an anguished laugh. "How pathetic I must seem to you now. And how blind! I've wasted my whole life steeling myself against loving your grandfather and then you. And now Julie tells me that you both loved me more than I ever imagined. Now, I shall spend the rest of my life regretting all my wasted years and my stupidity, cruelty, and blindness. A fitting penance for me, don't you agree, Zachary?"

"No," Julie burst out, sensing Zack's internal struggle as she watched his jaw clench and relax. "It is not a fitting penance at all, and he doesn't think it is!" Reaching out, she touched his rigid jaw, refusing to back down from the chill in his eyes. "Zack," she said softly, "don't let this happen. You can end it now. I know you loved your grandmother, I know you did! I could hear it in your voice when you talked about her in Colorado. She heard you quarreling with Justin right before he died, did you know that before tonight?"

"No," he clipped.

Tightening her hand on his arm, Julie pleaded desperately, "You've forgiven me for much worse."

Mrs. Stanhope turned to leave, then she stopped and reached into her purse for a small velvet box. "I brought this to give to you," she said, holding it out to him. When Zack refused to reach for it, she handed it to Julie and said to him, "It was your grandfather's watch." Straightening her shoulders she nodded at Julie and said with a wan smile, "Thank you for what you tried to do today. You are a remarkable, warm, courageous young woman—a fitting wife for my grandson." Her voice broke on the last word and she reached for the doorknob.

Behind her, Zack said curtly, "Julie made tea. She would probably like you to stay for it." It was the closest thing to a declaration of a truce he was able to make, but both women knew exactly what it meant. Mrs. Stanhope looked at the tall, proud, handsome man who had survived and triumphed in the face of enormous odds and then at the courageous young woman he loved. "Your sister and brother are waiting in the car," she told him in a husky voice. "They would like to see you if you're willing."

Julie held her breath while Zack hesitated, then he walked slowly out onto the front porch. He stopped there, looking at the limousine pulled up at the curb, his hands shoved into his pockets. He would not go to the car, Julie realized, or even meet them halfway, but he was giving them an opening.

They took it.

The back door of the limo was flung open and a young boy wearing a dark suit and tie sprinted out, followed more slowly by his mother and his uncle who walked up the sidewalk. He bolted up the steps of the porch and stopped in front of Zack, his head tipped back, studying the man's face. "Are you really my Uncle Zack?" he demanded.

Zack looked down at the dark-haired child and smiled reluctantly at the realization that the Stanhope features had bred true once again; the little boy looked so much like Zack at that age that it was almost uncanny. "Yes," he said, answering the boy's question. "Who are you?"

The little boy grinned. "I'm Jamison Zachary Arthur Stanhope. You can call me Jamie, everybody does. My mommy named me Zachary after you. It made Grandmother very angry," he confided.

Zack bent down and scooped the child into his arms. "I'll bet it did," he said dryly.

In the doorway, Julie watched the tableau unfold. She heard Zack quietly say, "Hello, Elizabeth," and she watched with a teary smile as his sister ran up the steps and flung her arms around him. Zack's brother held out his hand, his face uncertain, "I won't blame you if you don't want to shake my hand, Zack," he said. "If positions were reversed, I wouldn't."

Zack transferred his nephew and his weeping sister to his left arm and extended his right hand to his brother. Alex looked at it, took it in his, and then enfolded his brother in a bear hug, clapping Zack on the shoulder.

Jamie looked at his mother, his great-grandmother, and then at Julie. "Why are they all cryin'?" he demanded of Zack.

"Allergies," Zack lied with a reassuring smile. "How old are you?"

* * *

Seated on the steps of Julie's front porch later that night, they watched the stars twinkling in the black velvet sky while they listened to the chorus of crickets serenading them. "I'm going to miss this place," Julie said quietly, leaning back against his chest.

"I know you are," Zack replied. "So am I." During the last two weeks, he'd made two business trips to California, and both times he'd looked forward to returning to Keaton and to Julie with an almost boyish eagerness. Tomorrow, he had to fly to Austin for a morning meeting with the Texas Board of Criminal Justice, who were considering appropriate disciplinary action against Wayne Hadley. The day after that, he was getting married.

"I wish you didn't have to go to Austin tomorrow."

He kissed the top of her head and slid his arm around her waist, "So do I."

"Don't forget to come back as early as you can tomorrow."

"Why?" he teased. "Are you planning to spring any more estranged relatives on me?" She tipped her face up. "Do you have any more?"

"No!" he said forcefully. He saw her try to smile and tipped her chin up. "Now, what's wrong?"

"I don't like you going near anything that has to do with prisons."

Zack smiled reassuringly, but his tone was implacable. "It's something I have to do, but there's nothing to worry about." Jokingly, he added, "If they try to lock me up, I know I can count on you to bust me out in time for the wedding."

"You're right!" she said, and so ferociously that Zack laughed.

"I'll be at your school at seven o'clock tomorrow night," he promised.

85

THE NOSTALGIC SMELL OF FINGER PAINTS AND PASTE ASSAILED Zack's nostrils as he walked slowly down the empty hallway to the only classroom with lights on at the end of the corridor. He could hear women's laughter as he neared the doorway, and he paused just inside the classroom, unnoticed for the moment, looking around at the downsized desks occupied by seven women at the front of the room.

Julie was leaning against her desk, surrounded by chalkboards with children's drawings hanging above them and the letters of the alphabet displayed around the room in giant size. She was already dressed for the dinner that would follow the wedding rehearsal tonight, her hair caught up in a soft chignon that made her look startlingly sophisticated. He was admiring the way she looked in her clingy peach summer dress when she looked up and saw him standing there. "You're right on time," she said to him, straightening from her position and smiling at him. "We've finished our lesson for the night and we've been reminiscing and having a private little going-away party." As she said that, she tipped her head to the small cake and paper cups on her desk and held out her hand to him. Drawing him forward and linking her fingers through his, she explained to the women, "Zack came here tonight because he was very anxious to meet you before we leave tomorrow night." Seven faces studied him with every reaction from outright unease to total awe. "Pauline," Julie began, "I'd like you to meet my fiancée. Zack, this is Pauline Perkins—"

By the second introduction, Zack realized that Julie was carefully making it seem as if the honor of the introduction was his, not theirs. She did that simply by telling him something special about each, and Zack watched their tension dissipate and smiles begin to burst out.

Impressed by her tact, he straightened after shaking the last woman's hand and stood beside Julie at her desk. The moment of awkward silence was broken suddenly by a young woman in her midtwenties with a small baby in a carrier on the desk beside her, who Julie had introduced as Rosalie Silmet. "Would you . . . like some cake," she burst out awkwardly but with determination.

"I never turn down cake," Zack lied with a smile to put her at ease, then he turned to the desk and sliced himself a piece.

"I made it myself," she volunteered hesitantly.

He was turning back with a piece of chocolate cake in his hand when he saw Julie silently mouth one word to her: "How?"

"I—" her thin shoulders straightened. "I *read* the recipe!" she declared with such pride that Zack felt a funny clutch in his chest. "And Peggy drove us here," she added, tipping her head to the woman named Peggy Listrom. "Peggy read all the street signs we passed on the way out loud."

"He doesn't care about that!" Peggy Listrom said, blushing furiously. "Anybody can read street signs."

"Not anybody," Zack heard himself say, because at that moment as he looked at the women with their eager–hopeful expressions, he would have done *anything* to make certain they left that classroom feeling special. "Julie told me she couldn't read for a long time."

"She *told* you that?" one of them said, dumbfounded that Julie would have confessed it.

He nodded. "I admired her tremendously for having the courage to change it." Switching his gaze to Peggy Listrom, he added with a grin, "Now when you learn how to read maps, will you let me know the trick of it? I get lost the minute someone unfolds a map."

Someone giggled, and he added, "Who brought the punch?"

A hand went up. "I did."

"Did you read the recipe?"

She shook her head with so much pride that Zack was mystified until she added, "It's from a can. I read the label. In the grocery store. It cost one dollar and sixty-nine cents. I read that, too."

"May I have some?"

She nodded, and Zack felt that same funny clutch as he poured some of the red liquid into a small paper cup. He was so preoccupied that he spilled some of it on his shirt cuff, and Rosalie Silmet shot to her feet. "I'll show you where the bathroom is, so you can put cold water on it."

"Thanks," he said, afraid to hurt any tender feelings by declining. "I must be nervous tonight about meeting Julie's students," he joked. "I'm afraid she'll call the wedding off if you don't like me," he added as he started out of the room on Rosalie Silmet's heels, and he felt like he'd accomplished something wonderful when the room exploded with laughter.

When he returned, the party was winding down, and everyone was worried that Julie would be late for their wedding rehearsal. "There's still enough time," she told them as Zack stood on the sidelines, sipping his punch. He noticed Rosalie Silmet lean over and whisper urgently to Debby Sue Cassidy, who shook her head. So far, Julie's protégé—a young woman with straight brown hair tucked behind her ears and held in place at the crown with a barette—hadn't spoken much, Zack realized, and he wondered what could possibly impress Julie so much about her. The others were so completely appealing.

"Julie," Rosalie said, "Debby Sue wrote a good-bye poem for you, but now she won't read it to you."

Realizing immediately that he was the reason, Zack started to appeal to her, but Julie's voice interjected, soothing and encouraging. "Please read it for me, Debby."

"It's not very good," Debby said desperately.

"Please."

Her hands shook as she reluctantly picked up a piece of paper on her desk. "It doesn't rhyme."

"Poems don't have to rhyme. Some of the most wonderful poetry on earth doesn't rhyme. No one has ever written a poem just for me," Julie added. "I'm honored."

Debby seemed to gain courage from that, and her shoulders squared. Casting a last apprehensive glance at Zack, she said, "I called it 'Thanks to Julie.'" When she began to read, her voice gained more strength and emotion with each word:

> I used to be ashamed
> And now I am proud.
>
> The world once was black
> And now it is bright.
>
> I used to walk head bent
> And now I stand up tall.
>
> I used to have dreams.
> But now I have *hope*.
>
> Thanks to Julie.

Zack stared at her, the simple, expressive words reeling through his mind, the punch forgotten halfway to his mouth. He watched Julie smile and ask to keep the poem and he saw her hold it to her chest much as she'd held his wedding ring in Mexico City. The party broke up, and he said all the appropriate things and watched them troop out of the classroom.

While Julie cleared out her desk, he sauntered over to the bulletin board on the side wall, but his mind wasn't on the children's drawings of spring flowers in front of his eyes. He kept remembering that poem he'd just heard, the one that said exactly what he felt about Julie, and he kept thinking of her in Colorado, holding out her hand to him, her face filled with wonder and awe as she tried to make him understand: "*Oh, Zack, . . . watching them discover they can read is like holding a miracle in your own hand.*"

A rubber band missed his ear by a fraction of an inch and bounced softly off the bulletin board, and he glanced up thinking something had fallen from above his head. The second one whizzed by his temple, even closer than the first one had been, and he turned around, smiling and trying to shake off the poignant feelings he had. Julie was leaning against her desk, a rubber band cocked on her fingers as she drew a bead on him. "Nice shooting, Wyatt," he tried to joke.

"I've been taught by experts," Julie returned with a slight smile, but she wasn't the least bit deceived by his attempt at humor. "What's on your mind, Mr. Benedict?" she enquired softly as she dropped her arm and effortlessly switched her target to a book on the back desk. And hit it.

Her briefcase was packed and closed and Zack walked toward her, uncertain how to answer her question.

She obviously knew what was on his mind, because she tipped her head to the side, crossed her arms over her chest, and asked innocently, "How did you like my ladies?"

"I—your Debby Sue Cassidy is something else. They're all—not what I expected, is the best I can say."

"A few months ago, you couldn't have made any of them say a word if you were here."

"They seem pretty confident now."

"You think so?" she asked with a funny, dubious sound in her voice. "If they'd known you were coming tonight, I wouldn't have been able to drag them here. The butcher's wife is coming to our wedding reception, the parents of all my students are coming to our reception, the *church janitor's* wife is coming to our reception. But I could not make one of those women believe that I wanted them to be my guests, and I've spent more time with them than most of the others. That's how much self-esteem they have. After I came back from Colorado with the money I'd raised in Amarillo, I ordered specialized tests designed to gauge their abilities."

"How do you test someone who can't read?"

"One on one. Verbally. With the right materials it's simple. And you don't call it 'testing' because they're so insecure they fall apart at the mention of the word. Do you know what I found out?"

He shook his head, mesmerized by her zeal and humbled by her caring. "I found out that Debby could already read at the third-grade level and two of the others have moderate learning disabilities, and that's why they can't read. And do you know what they need as much as they need to be taught that?" When he shook his head again, she said achingly, "They need *me*. One person who cares. God, they—they *bloom* when another woman believes in them and spends a little time with them. It doesn't have to be a teacher— just another woman. The future of that baby of Rosalie's depends completely on whether or not Katherine, who's taking over from me, can keep Rosalie believing in herself and learning. If she can't, that child will grow up on welfare and the fringes of poverty, just as her mother has done. There are a few groups starting up around the country, some of them funded by corporations, and one of them called "Literacy. Pass It On." has a national program that is devoted exclusively to women. I didn't know about it until a couple of days ago."

Listening to her, watching her, Zack didn't know whether to offer to write a check or teach a class.

"I know Rachel decided she couldn't give up her career as soon as you were married, and I—I have to tell you now I want to keep teaching in California, Zack. Adult women, not children. I want to get involved in that program," she said a little desperately.

"And that's why you wanted me to come here tonight," he said dryly, thinking how absurd the comparison was between Rachel's unbridled, self-centered ambition and Julie's desire to help her own sex.

Completely misjudging the reason for his tone, she lifted her eyes to his and said pleadingly, "I have gifts to give, Zack. I *have* to do this."

Zack snatched her into his arms and crushed her to him. "You're the gift," he whispered fiercely. "You have more sides than that diamond you're wearing, and I'm so damned crazy about all of them . . ."

When he lifted his head and relaxed his grip a little, she rubbed her finger over his patterned silk tie and gave him a hesitant look. "Debby's out of a job because the family she's worked for since she was a teenager is moving away. She isn't ready to do much yet except housekeeping . . ."

Zack tipped her chin up and gave in without a struggle. "I have a very big house."

86

"ARE YOU SURE EVERYTHING IS READY AT THE CHURCH?" ZACK demanded of Matt Farrell as he quickly shoved the tiny studs into the front of his tuxedo shirt.

"Everything is ready, but you," Matt said with a chuckle.

Because he'd had to be at the rehearsal dinner last night and couldn't make a phone call from the Mathisons' house without the risk of being overheard, he'd had to rely on Matt and Meredith, who'd flown in yesterday and spent the night at Julie's house, to relay last-minute information and instructions between Sally Morrison and himself.

"Is everyone here from California?"

"They're at the church."

"Did you warn Meredith to keep Julie from looking into the church before she starts down the aisle?" Zack continued, staring in the mirror and fastening his black tie. "I don't want her to know who's there. I want it to be a surprise."

"Meredith and Katherine Cahill have Julie firmly in hand. She won't be able to draw a breath without one of them seeing her do it. By now she probably feels as if they're glued to her side and she's wondering why."

Zack shrugged into his black tuxedo jacket. "Are you certain that Barbra is here?"

"She's here, with her accompanist in tow. I talked to her in Dallas at her hotel last night. By now, she's standing in the choir loft, waiting for things to get under way."

Zack ran a hand over his jaw to ascertain that his shave was close enough. "What time is it?"

"Ten minutes to four. You have ten minutes to get to the church. Ted Mathison is already there. On the way, I'll go over the part you were supposed to have learned during rehearsal last night."

"I've already had a full-dress rehearsal," Zack said dryly. "I've been through this once before, remember?"

"There are a few major differences," Matt pointed out with a grin.

"Really, what?"

"You weren't this happy, but you were calm last time."

There was another major difference between his last wedding and this one, and despite his offhand remark, Zack knew it. He knew it even before he stepped out in front of a smiling crowd and stood before his future father-in-law in a church aglow with candlelight and perfumed with lavish bouquets of white roses tied with white satin ribbons. There was a reverence in him this time, a sense of quiet joy, as he waited for Julie at the altar. He watched Meredith walk down the aisle toward him wrapped in apple green silk, followed by Katherine and Sara in identical gowns, all of them beautiful and smiling and serene, as if they, like Zack, sensed the absolute rightness of what was about to happen.

The organ music swelled to a crescendo, and Zack felt as if his heart would burst at the sight that greeted him.

Starting toward him in a drifting swirl of white appliquéd silk with a cloud of veil trailing behind her was the woman he had kidnapped and laughed with and loved. She moved through the candlelight, her face glowing, and in her eyes he saw all the love in the world, the promise of his unborn children, a lifetime filled with all the joy she had to give. He saw all that, and then he saw her eyes widen when Barbra Streisand's voice rose from the choir loft, and the song was the one Zack had asked her to sing when Julie came down the aisle.

> *Long ago and far away, I dreamed a dream one day—*
> *And now that dream is here before me.*
> *Long the skies were overcast,*
> *but now the clouds are passed—*
> *You're here at last.*
>
> *Chills run up and down my spine.*
> *Aladdin's lamp is mine.*
> *The dream I dreamed was not denied me.*
> *Just one look and then I knew—*
> *That all I longed for long ago was you.*

Zack reached for Julie's hand and took it firmly in his, then they turned to the front.

Reverend Mathison smiled and raised the book he was holding in his hands. "Dear friends, we are gathered here together, in the sight of God . . ."

At the front of the church, Matthew Farrell gazed steadily into his wife's eyes; Ted and Katherine Mathison smiled softly at each other.

Near the back of the church, Herman Henkleman shifted his hand and reached for Flossie's, lacing his fingers tightly in hers.

In the row directly behind them, young Willie Jenkins observed the elderly couple's exchanged looks and clasped hands, then he nudged the little girl beside him and in a loud stage whisper laughingly announced, "I'll betcha Herman Henkleman won't go along with Reverend Mathison's bargain. He's too old to wait . . ."

To which the little girl primly replied, "Shut up, Willie, I don't know what you're talking about."

Undaunted, Willie said, "My older brother told me the bargain is for no kissin' until the wedding night."

"Yuk," said the little girl with a shudder, leaning as far away from him as she could get. "Kissing!"

87

THE RECEPTION IN THE PARK THAT ZACK HAD HALF-EXPECTED to be rather plain turned out to be a lavishly festive affair with twinkling lights in the trees and linen-covered tables groaning under an array of beautifully prepared food that equaled in taste anything Zack's caterers had ever provided.

Standing off to the side with Matt Farrell, he watched Patrick Swayze cut in on Harrison Ford, who'd been dancing with Julie, and he smiled to himself at the memory of her shocked face in the receiving line when Zack began introducing her to nearly all the men she'd mentioned being her favorite movie stars. After her initial amazement, however, she had recovered and handled her famous guests with an unaffected graciousness that had filled Zack with pride.

"Great wedding, Zack," Warren Beatty said, holding his wife's hand and juggling a plate of hors d'oeuvres in the other. "The food is fantastic. What is this stuff anyway?"

Zack looked at the plate. "Bar-be-qued ribs," he said dryly, "Texan style."

When they left, Zack glanced at his watch, then he looked around for Julie and saw her dancing with Swayze again, laughing at whatever he was saying to her.

"She's captivated all of them," Matt said with an approving grin.

"Especially Swayze," Zack observed, noting how well she danced with Swayze and trying not to note how closely he was holding her.

Matt nudged him a few minutes later and nodded toward Meredith. "Look what I have to endure—that's Costner's third dance with her. Meredith," he added, "is a great admirer of his."

"And vice versa, it would seem. Luckily, Swayze and Costner are both married," Zack observed with a lazy grin. Putting his champagne glass down on the table beside him, he said, "I think it's late enough to claim the last dance and then leave."

"In a hurry to start your honeymoon?"

"You wouldn't believe the kind of hurry I'm in," Zack joked. Reaching out, he shook Matt's hand, but he didn't thank him for the years of unflagging friendship or his many favors. His gratitude was too deep for that, and they both understood it.

Pausing to ask the orchestra leader to play a particular song, Zack went to retrieve his wife. She abandoned Patrick Swayze with gratifying speed, coming into Zack's arms and smiling into his eyes. "It's about time you came to get me," she told him softly.

"Ready to leave?" he asked her as the orchestra's song came to an end.

Julie was dying to leave, to go away with him and be alone together. She nodded and started to move away, but he shook his head and said in a husky, meaningful voice, "After the next song."

"What song?" she asked in the silence, but he only smiled, and then the song Zack had asked the orchestra to play began its hot, steady rhythm.

"This one," he said, meaningfully as the seductive words to Feliciano's song began to pound in the night.

"Light my fire, Julie," he ordered huskily, beginning to move with her to the beat of the music.

Julie fell under the spell of his heavy-lidded eyes and inviting smile within seconds. Oblivious to the crowd who was turning to watch them, she moved closer to him, her body matching the subtle movement of his. He slid his hands around her waist, holding her closer. "More."

88

CURLED UP ON THE SOFA IN THE PLANE'S LUXURIOUS CABIN, Julie peered into the inky darkness beyond the windows. Far below she could see an occasional light, but otherwise they seemed to be descending into a black wilderness. Zack was sitting across from her, his feet propped up on the coffee table, his tuxedo jacket open—the picture of contented patience. He'd rushed her on board Matt Farrell's waiting plane as soon as they left the reception, refusing to let her change into traveling clothes, but now that they were on their way to a destination he refused to name, he seemed perfectly willing to wait until they got there to consummate their marriage. "I'm going to feel awfully silly walking into a hotel lobby in this gown," she said.

"Are you, darling?" he asked softly, smiling.

Julie nodded, wishing he'd let her change into one of the new outfits in her suitcases. "I could change into something else in a matter of minutes."

He shook his head. "I'd like for both of us to be dressed exactly as we are when we get there."

"But why?"

"You'll see," he said, holding out his arm to her.

She moved over to sit beside him. "Sometimes," she said wryly, "I don't understand you at all."

But she did understand. She understood perfectly the moment she stepped off the plane onto a small runway where a car was waiting, and she looked around at the looming shadows of mountains. "Colorado!" she breathed, hugging herself against the chilly night air. "We're in Colorado, aren't we!"

Driving up the private road to the mountain hideaway they had shared during that tumultuous week was an unbearably poignant experience for Julie. So was walking into the house with Zack and seeing the beautiful, familiar rooms where she had fought with him and danced with him and then fallen in love with him.

While he brought in their suitcases and built a fire in the fireplace, she walked over to the windows and looked out at the place where he had once built his "snow monster."

Zack came up behind her and slid his arm around her waist, drawing her back against him, and in the window was their own reflection . . . a tall groom holding his bride in his arms. They looked at their reflection and Zack saw the tears shimmering in her eyes. "Why are you crying?" he asked softly, bending his head to nuzzle her neck.

Julie swallowed and tipped her head back. "Because," she whispered achingly, thinking of the sentimentality that showed in everything he did for her "You are so perfect."

Zack tightened his arms protectively around her. "We're perfect together," he whispered.

"I'll make you happy," she said, her voice shaking with emotion. "I swear I will."

Her husband turned her in his arms, and there was a smile in his voice as he lifted his hand to smooth her hair back. "You've made me happy from the first night we spent here together, when you sat on that sofa and blithely pointed out the absurdity of football rules which allow a tight end, but no *loose end*."

She smiled a little at that, but she saw the firelight glinting on the wedding ring he now wore on his left hand, and she pressed his palm to her cheek while her lips touched the ring. "I love you, Zack," she whispered. "I love the sound of your voice and the touch of your hand and the way you smile. I want to give you babies . . . and a life filled with laughter . . . and I want to give you me."

Desire began to beat fiercely in his veins, fueled by weeks of abstinence, and Zack pulled her close, his mouth opening over hers with sudden urgency. "Come to bed with your husband, wife."

Husband. Wife. The words revolved slowly in Julie's mind, soft and sweet and profound, as she walked with him into the bedroom they'd shared. They swelled in her heart as he took her in his arms in bed and turned to her in love and need. She responded to both with an exquisite eagerness that made Zack's hands tremble as they rushed over her, caressing her skin and pulling her hips tightly to his. She met his passion with her own, encouraged him with stirring kisses and when he finally slid deep into her, she wrapped her arms tightly around his shoulders and whispered, "Welcome home, Zack."

The sweet words tore a low groan from his chest and he began to move within her. His wife moved with him, bathing his senses in extravagant pleasure until the wild beauty of what they were doing to each other drove them both to a shattering climax.

Wrapped in each others arms, sated and spent, they floated slowly back to reality in the same bed where once they had not dared to think of the future. His hand drifting slowly over her back, Zack thought of the years that lay ahead with the woman who had loved and trusted him and taught him to forgive. *Welcome home,* she'd said.

For the first time in his life, he finally knew how it felt to have a home and a family. Julie was his home, his family.

Epilogue

SURROUNDED BY LAVISH BOUQUETS OF LONG-STEMMED ROSES IN every color of the rainbow, Julie cuddled her newborn son to her breast in her private room at Cedars–Sinai Medical Center, but for the first time since the birth of their son two days ago, her attention was not on the tiny, perfect infant that she and Zack had created.

Until a few minutes ago, the nurses had been crowded into her room to watch the Academy Awards with her, but they'd left to carry babies around to mothers, and Julie was secretly relieved to be alone. The award for Best Actor in a Leading Role was coming up pretty soon, and although she was quite certain Zack was going to win it, she really didn't want an audience when the winner was announced.

"Look, Nicky!" she whispered, turning him slightly so he could see the television set, "There's your future godfather and godmother, Mr. and Mrs. Farrell. And your daddy's right beside them, even though the camera didn't show him this time."

Nicholas Alexander Benedict, who'd stopped nursing a few minutes before, took immediate exception to being deprived of his mother's breast, so Julie settled him back into place and helped him find what he was searching for, then she returned all her attention to the television set.

Zack's first movie after their marriage had not only broken box office records, *Last Interlude* had also garnered Academy Award nominations in a number of categories for the people who participated in it, and tonight it was cleaning up. Zack had won for Best Director, Sam Hudgins had won for Best Cinematography, and so had people involved in everything from visual effects to musical score.

Zack had wanted to stay here and watch the awards ceremony with her, and when Julie couldn't talk him out of it in any other way, she'd argued implacably that he should be there for the sake of the other people who'd worked on *Interlude,* including the supporting cast who were also up for Oscars.

In reality, Julie felt this was his night to shine, and she was adamantly determined that neither she nor the baby nor an act of God would interfere with that. This morning, the advance copy of the book that Zack had agreed to let her write to help raise support for women's literacy programs had finally arrived at the house. Although she was nervously eager to show it to him and get his opinion, she'd asked Sally to send it over, then made her promise not to show it to Zack or tell him it had arrived.

The nominees for Best Screenwriter were being announced, and Julie anxiously bit her lip, then she laughed softly as Peter Listerman's name was called out and he strode swiftly up to the stage to accept it for his work on *Interlude.* "Nicky, look," she whispered happily, "there's Pete and he won! You should be very grateful to Pete," she teased. "Thanks to him you have the only high chair on earth that looks like a director's chair with your name across the back."

Pete was one of Julie's favorites. Part of it was because the studious-looking man had spent so much time at the house working with Zack on *Interlude* that she'd gotten to know him well, and part of it was because he seemed to be developing some sort of love–hate relationship with Debby Sue Cassidy, who'd quietly mentioned to Zack and him, while they were trying to figure out a better ending for the screenplay one day, that *she'd* thought of one. Pete's bland looks masked a fiery artistic temperament, and the only thing that had saved poor Debby Sue from his ire at her interference was that Zack instantly liked her idea. Really liked it. He made Pete work on it with Debby's input, and it was *Interlude*'s new, touching climax that had helped make the film such a hit.

Pete's acceptance speech went along the usual route until the very end, when he looked up at the camera and added, ". . . And I'd also like to thank Miss Debby Cassidy, whose contribution to my work was invaluable."

"Pete, you darling!" Julie cried, hugging Nicky tightly to her. Debby's unquenchable desire to learn coupled with her tireless efforts and Pete's reluctant admiration and demanding tutelage were working miracles.

A few minutes later, Julie felt her heartbeat quicken and her entire body tense as Robert Duval and Meryl Streep walked out on stage and began to read the nominees for Best Actor in a Leading Role. "Cross your fingers, sweetheart," Julie said. She kissed his tiny fist, then she wrapped it around her finger and laid her forefinger over it for good luck.

"And the nominees are"—Meryl Streep looked up at the camera—"Kevin Costner, for *End of the Rainbow.*"

"Kurt Russell, for *Shot in the Night*," Duval added.

"Zachary Benedict, for *Last Interlude*," Streep put in.

"Jack Nicholson, for *The Peacemaker*," Duval finished.

He stretched his hand out for the envelope and Julie felt a strange, inexplicable prickling begin at the back of her neck.

"And the Oscar goes to"—he looked at the slip in the envelope and broke into a broad grin—"Zachary Benedict! For *Last Interlude!*"

Applause exploded and rose to a thundering crescendo as some of the attendees rose to their feet in a standing ovation; the camera aimed at a tall, dark man in a tuxedo striding swiftly down the aisle toward the stage, and Duval leaned forward, and added, "Accepting the award for Zack is Matthew Farrell . . ."

And Julie suddenly knew the reason for the strange prickling at the back of her neck . . .

Leaning against the pillows with a helpless smile, she said without looking toward the doorway, "You're here, aren't you?"

"How'd you guess," Zack's voice teased.

Turning her head, she watched him stroll forward with his tuxedo jacket slung negligently over his shoulder and hooked on his thumb, the gleaming gold Oscar he'd won for Best Director dangling from his left hand.

"You're supposed to be there, accepting your award," Julie reminded him, but she wrapped her free arm tightly around his broad shoulders as he sat down beside her hip. "Congratulations, darling."

Careful not to squash his sleeping son, Zack kissed his wife's mouth and then her cheek, "I'm exactly where I wanted to be at this moment," he whispered tenderly as he nuzzled her neck. "The only place I wanted to be."

She brushed her fingertips against his cheek. "Nicky and I are awfully proud of you," she said softly, and Zack felt the unaccustomed sting of tears behind his eyes as he looked at her shining face and his son cuddled at her breast, his tiny fist resting on a satin fold of her dressing gown. "He's falling asleep," he said, his voice husky with emotion. "Shall I put him in his crib?"

"You can try," Julie said, carefully handing the sleeping baby over to him.

After putting his son down, Zack kicked off his shiny tuxedo shoes and stretched out beside her on the bed, pulling her tightly to his side. "Thank you for my son," he whispered, and because his emotions seemed perilously close to the surface tonight, he looked around for something to distract him. His gaze fell on the book lying face down on the table beside the bed, and he seized on that. "What book are you reading?"

Not once during the writing of Julie's book or its steps through production had she been willing to discuss it with him. Zack was an exacting professional, and she'd been afraid that any criticism from him would either crush or panic her. The time of reckoning was here, however, and she drew a nervous breath. "It's my book—an early copy, fresh off the press. Sally sent it over to me this morning."

"Why on earth didn't you tell me!" he said, reaching for it. "This is very exciting."

"Because this was Academy Awards day and I didn't want the book or anything else to detract from it, even for a minute."

Touched by her needless concern, Zack picked the book up, turning it over, and Julie watched with a mixture of anxiety and eagerness for his first reaction to the cover. "It's beautiful," he said decisively, holding it out and studying the colorful roses in full bloom that were heavily embossed on a dusty pink marbled background.

"What do you think of the title?".

He smiled and said it aloud: "You named it **Perfect**."

She nodded.

"I like it," he said with a grin. "How did you happen to come up with the title?"

"That was the easiest part," she whispered, lifting her eyes to his. "It's our story, but the book is really all about you."

Zack's smile faded and tenderness burst inside him. He yanked her into his arms, burying his face in her hair and holding her. She had stood by him when the world branded him evil, wanted him when he had nothing to offer her, and taught him about forgiveness. She cheered for his triumphs, supported him when he was right, and stubbornly opposed him when he was wrong. She reinvented his life for him and filled it with purpose and meaning and laughter and love. And then she gave him his son.

He remembered the words of the poem Debby Sue Cassidy had written for her:

I used to be ashamed
And now I am proud.

The world once was black
And now it is bright.

I used to have dreams
But now I have hope.

Thanks to Julie.

"Don't cry, darling," Julie whispered, amazed by the dampness on the hard cheek that was pressed to hers. Curving her hand around his nape to hold him closer she teased shakily, "You haven't read my book yet. I may be a better writer than you think."

In the midst of one of the most achingly poignant moments of his life, Zack burst out laughing.

A Letter from the Author

Dear Readers,

Matt and Meredith Farrell, the main characters from my novel *Paradise,* appear here as the result of a deluge of mail from readers who simply did not want to say good-bye to two characters they obviously loved.

Like Matt and Meredith, Julie Mathison and Zack Benedict are fictional characters. However, the existence of the "Literacy. Pass It On." program that Julie Mathison refers to in this novel is very real. It is as real as the plight of Julie Mathison's adult students, who represent the twenty percent of women in America who are functionally illiterate.

Since readers are usually interested in what goes on "behind the scenes" of a book, I think you'll particularly enjoy knowing how *Perfect* actually became the novel you've just read. Last year, I was approached by representatives of the "Literacy. Pass It On." campaign, which is sponsored by Coors Brewing Company. It is the only national literacy effort with programs geared specifically to women.

Coors acquainted me with some staggering information that I'd like to share with you now. While it's obvious that illiteracy is devastating for both men and women, it has particularly harsh consequences for women. Not only are women already burdened with social and economic inequities, they are often solely responsible for raising children—children whose success in school, and in their future lives, depends heavily upon their mothers' literacy.

The women's program of "Literacy. Pass It On." asked me to write a book to highlight the problem of women's illiteracy, and parts of the novel you have just read are the result of that. Moreover, I have already made a financial contribution to the program, and that contribution will be automatically increased, based on the number of copies of this book that are actually sold.

Each and every one of us has an opportunity to make an enormous difference in another woman's life—to become a heroine like Julie Mathison—simply by volunteering at a local literacy center to teach another woman to read, or by making a contribution, no matter how small. Be sure to complete the card inserted in this book, too, because Coors will contribute up to an additional $25,000 to women's literacy programs based on the number of cards they receive.

Join me, I urge you— Take an interest and make a difference.

If you have any comments to make, or if you would like to receive a free semiannual newsletter about my forthcoming books, please write to me at the address below.

Judith McNaught

Judith McNaught
P.O. Box 1547
Friendswood, TX 77546